Four Fires

By the Same Author

The Power of One

Jessica

The Potato Factory

Tommo and Hawk

Solomon's Song

BRYCE COURTENAY

Four Fires

MICHAEL JOSEPH
an imprint of
PENGUIN BOOKS

MICHAEL JOSEPH

Published by the Penguin Group
Penguin Books Ltd, 80 Strand, London WC2R 0RL, England
Penguin Putnam Inc., 375 Hudson Street, New York, New York 10014, USA
Penguin Books Australia Ltd, 250 Camberwell Road,
Camberwell, Victoria 3124, Australia
Penguin Books Canada Ltd, 10 Alcorn Avenue, Toronto, Ontario, Canada M4V 3B2
Penguin Books India (P) Ltd, 11 Community Centre,
Panchsheel Park, New Delhi - 110 017, India
Penguin Books (NZ) Ltd, Cnr Rosedale and Airborne Roads,
Albany, Auckland, New Zealand
Penguin Books (South Africa) (Pty) Ltd, 24 Sturdee Avenue,
Rosebank 2196, South Africa

Penguin Books Ltd, Registered Offices: 80 Strand, London WC2R 0RL, England

www.penguin.com
www.brycecourtenay.com

First published by Penguin Australia 2001
Published in Great Britain by Michael Joseph 2002
1

Cover images by Garry Moore and Australian Picture Library
Author photograph by Graham McCarter
Maps on pp 778-9 based on maps by Don Wall and information from Lynette Ramsey Silver

Set in Fairfield
Printed in Great Britain by Clays Ltd, St Ives plc

A CIP catalogue record for this book is available from the British Library

ISBN 0-718-14587-9

This book is dedicated to all the soldiers of the 8th Australian Division, especially those who were sent to Borneo and did not come home

There are four fires of our dreaming.
The bushfire of our land's renewal.
The war fire of good men killing.
The soul fire of a different God.
The fires of a consuming love.
They are the bitter/sweet
chalice from which we
all drink and which,
in turn, make us
what we are.
These
fires
of
the
white fella's dreaming.

BOOK ONE

1955–1956

Chapter One

When we were kids, my dad never talked about the war, not even on Anzac Day, when, like every other bloke he wore his medals and marched behind the high-school band to the rotunda at the top of King Street on which the names of the dead had been inscribed.

If Tommy happened to be in gaol on the big day, the governor let him out and he'd say nothing when our mum brought him back legless in the garbage truck that night. She had saved up a few quid for him to blow on grog and two-up and you could count on him coming back penniless and pissed.

Most of the other kids at school knew a bit about what their dad did in the war, but we five Maloney kids only knew stuff everyone knew, like the fall of Singapore and we Australians being taken prisoners of war by the Japanese. Tommy, which was what we called our father among ourselves, taught us this poem. He was a bit of a bush poet in his day although he never claimed it was his own.

Singapore

A mighty island fortress
The guardian of the East
Impregnable as Gibraltar
A thousand planes at least
Simply can't be taken

Will stand a siege for years
We'll hold the place forever
And show our foes no fears
Our men are there in thousands
With defences quite unique
The Japanese didn't believe us
And took it in a week.

The other thing Tommy told us before he clammed up permanently was different, but couldn't be used for fear of being mocked. He once told us that in Borneo, if you dug a hole in the ground miles from a river or a creek and it filled with rainwater, because it rains in the tropics every day, in three days you'd have fish six inches long. Another thing he told us was that in the jungle the sudden rainstorms came down so fierce that lightning smashed down tall trees. That was okay but he told us about this one Pommie prisoner of war who was having a piss in the middle of the rainstorm and the lightning aimed for his piss-stream and ran up it like a welding arc and electrocuted him on the spot, flames shooting out of his body like a Guy Fawkes Night bonfire.

Fish that came from nowhere, out of thin air, now that had to be bullshit. You couldn't skite about something like that when your commonsense said you'd get howls of derision from your mates at school. The lightning also, electrocuted through your piss-stream, why didn't the lightning just strike him dead? I mean, c'mon? Tommy must think us kids are idjits!

You couldn't even insist that your dad told you, like use his authority to confirm the truth. If your dad was on the council or the publican or someone important and you said he'd told you, well, your mates might have to think twice about doing a mock. But Tommy Maloney carried no authority whatsoever (except when the bushfires threatened), and was known by one and all to be a thoroughly unreliable witness.

Us Maloneys had a bad reputation in Yankalillee, which wasn't entirely fair, but then things in small towns seldom are. Sergeant Donovan once told Nancy, our mum, that never you mind, there were a lot worse than us around.

Maloney is an Irish name and we were Catholics but we didn't go to St Stephen's, the Catholic school, which meant we weren't just Micks but dirt poor as well and couldn't afford the fees. Nancy said she probably could have talked to them but she was buggered if she was going to go cap in hand to anyone, even to His Holiness the Pope or his local representative, Father Crosby. Later I came to understand it was because of the nuns. Nancy was afraid that because she'd had four of us out of wedlock, the nuns would have a go at us and make things miserable. This act of independence and protection in the face of hardship made us one of only a few Catholic families at the local state school, which was not a good situation to find yourself in, but probably not as bad as the nuns being against you.

I didn't see it at the time, kids don't, but now when I look back I can see why being Church of England was somehow many notches up from being a Catholic. Nineteen fifty-five was just about the last gasp of the old colonial system where Catholic and Protestant were separated by what Nancy called 'the great divide', which had begun long before the first convicts of either religion reached Australia.

Ireland has always been the racial malignancy in the English bloodstream and it continued to manifest itself in country towns in Australia where, after five generations, the Pope and the Queen were still at loggerheads.

But around this time the great influx of poor European migrants started to arrive and small country towns such as Yankalillee found themselves having to deal with people whose names ended in 'ic', 'vitch', 'zak', 'zov' and 'ski', strange folk who stumbled and tripped over perfectly ordinary words in our mother tongue. They were called 'reffos' and people said they'd been through a hard time and were willing to do anything to get on.

One girl in my class, her name was Anna Dombrowski, but we called her 'Anna Dumb-cow-ski' because she talked sort of slow and her English words were pronounced funny, she once stood up in class and told us her family had been in a concentration camp in Pooland.

I remember Crocodile Brown, our teacher, shook his head slowly, then said how terrible it was and how her family had suffered enough and he hoped Australia would be different for them now they were safe. 'Them' was only her and her mum because her dad was dead.

That afternoon Bozo and me were building a billycart from four pram wheels we'd collected. 'What's a concentration camp?' I asked him.

He considered for a moment, 'It's where they send you to learn to concentrate,' he said at last.

'It's in Pooland,' I said.

'Yeah? Pooland?' You could see he'd never heard of the place, but then he decided he had the answer, 'Yeah, well, what do you expect, it's like us, we get into the poo in class when we're not concentrating.' Normally he would have said 'shit', 'we get into the shit', and he seemed pretty pleased with the answer he'd invented. You could never tell with Bozo, sometimes he came up with things you didn't think he ought to have known, maybe this was one such occasion.

'But a whole camp. They got sent to a camp in Pooland for punishment! Imagine that, eh. We only get sent to stand in the corner and don't even get the strap for not concentrating.'

'Yeah, well, they must have been *really* bad,' he said, in an offhand sort of way. I could see he'd lost interest.

'Yeah, they suffered terribly, but Crocodile Brown said he hoped Australia would be different for them now they were safe.'

'Course it will, stands to reason. We're different see, we don't have to concentrate that much.'

Maybe I should have asked Sarah or Mike. Bozo didn't even know where Pooland was on the dented tin ball that had a map of the world printed over it, which we'd found in somebody's garbage.

With migrants settling in the town, we had a reason to feel racially superior for the first time, that is if you don't count the Abos, who didn't really count because my great-grandpa and his mates had chased them all off, got rid of most of them.

Catholic Australians were automatically bumped up a notch in the social pecking order and the migrants assumed the all too familiar bottom rung on the ladder. The Bonegilla Migrant Camp was only twenty-five miles down the road and we had a fair few migrants choose Yankalillee. Only it turned out they didn't choose us, they were just sent by the government, told that's where they had to go. The government said we had to call them 'New Australians' but most people called them 'reffos' or 'dagoes', or if a woman was in polite company she'd call them 'people from away'. Anyway, they were fresh victims to exploit and an opportunity for even the Micks to participate in. We heard stories of how some of them were doctors and professors in their own country and were now forced to work on the Snowy Mountains Scheme because their qualifications weren't recognised in Australia.

We concluded that if people who were doctors and professors elsewhere became council workers here, some even ditch-diggers, then our Australian standards had to be vastly superior to anywhere else in the world. We all felt a bit smarter as a consequence.

It was Bozo who first came up with this theory of how clever we were and, while I liked the idea a lot, I was forced to challenge it. If you were going to use a fact like that at school you had to be able to back it up. After all, if Tommy wasn't a burglar he'd be about your average ditch-digger standard and he couldn't have been a professor or doctor by any stretch of imagination.

'Prove it, who've we got?' I demanded.

'Don Bradman!' Bozo said, quick as a flash.

I was convinced.

There must have been something to the theory, because even Irish-Catholic Australians with almost no standards to speak of were getting jobs in the lower echelons of the bureaucracy.

If those were hopeful times, with a lot of traditional attitudes changing after the war, reconciliation comes slowly in the bush and, I dare say, if you scratch the irritation, you'll still find pockets of the old malignancy that exist to this day. The ancient quarrel between Protestant and Catholic is a scabious wound-in-waiting, still capable of producing pus and pain long after those ditch-digging migrants and the clever children they gave us became proper Australians and doctors and professors once more.

Though I have to say, all this social upheaval and toing-and-froing of people didn't seem to affect the Maloney family's status in Yankalillee. Our family had one foot planted firmly in the dirt at the base of the social ladder while the other was still poised in the air above the first rung. We were Micks who lived in Bell Street and we didn't have a government job, although Tommy spent a good deal of his life within the confines of a government institution.

The warders at the gaol were almost to a man, Catholics. So were the nurses and workers at the mental hospital, who were pretty thick, the men mostly drunks and the women pill addicts. Nancy said that the things that went on there you wouldn't read about.

The nurses at the Old People's Home were Catholics though the main doctor there, Dr Hughes, was an Anglican but he was also a town doctor who only visited the home if some old person was sick or dying.

The bush-nursing hospital was different though. It was perfectly okay to be a Protestant and a nurse. Pure nursing, or a nurse's aide, was sort of at the lower end of the top and not the top end of the bottom, not like a psychiatric nurse in the mental asylum where all the loonies lived. The matron, Sister Baldwin, was also a Protestant and all-powerful. The two town doctors, old Dr Hughes and young Dr Wallis, were both Protestant and sort of above any particular ranking because all doctors were automatically important and above suspicion. There was a consistent rumour that old Dr Hughes was giving the whisky bottle a bit of a nudge and had given up evening surgery, but most people didn't want to believe this, even if it was true. Doctors sort of got taken off the gossip list.

The fact that the largely Catholic institution workers were also government employees with guaranteed employment and regular salaries that made a huge contribution to the prosperity of the town, seemed to make little difference to the Yankalillee interdenominational pecking order.

The respectable jobs, with few exceptions, were owned by the Protestants, mostly the Anglicans and the Presbyterians. There were seven pubs along King Street which isn't all that long, six of them owned by Protestants and one by a real Irishman, Mickey O'Hearn from County Cork. Nancy said a drunk could be thrown out of one, dust himself off, and, just by standing up, find himself miraculously at the bar in the next pub with a beer already poured and waiting for him. Everyone was drinking themselves to death in this sanctimonious little bush town.

The shire president, Councillor Evans, was Church of England

and all the elected shire councillors as well, except for Mickey O'Hearn, a good Catholic, who was supposed to represent the common people like us, but who was outvoted on every issue he ever proposed. The shire councillors were the important people in the town and surrounding district; what they wanted was what we got and no more questions asked thank you very much.

There was always a Yerberry, Yankalillee's first family. Their grandfather, Joseph Yerberry, founded the soft-drink bottling plant. Mrs Yerberry wore a fur stole, a hat with a colourful feather from a partridge tail sticking out of it, and white gloves to every occasion, summer or winter, while Harry Yerberry drove the latest Packard, always the same shit-brown colour.

Then came the grazier families, the real big hats in the district, foremost among them the Barrington-Stones, who had a Piper Cub and once entered a horse in the Melbourne Cup that came last. Still, it was a great honour to make the cut. There were always one or two grazier families who, in the high-handed manner of aristocrats, guarded over their own self-interests and took turns to be on the council.

Next came the orchardists at Stanley, the Andersons (cherries) and the McNuttys (apples). Then the small land-holders (sheep or cattle) who were mostly soldier settlers and only sometimes managed a representative. They were resented by the other farmers because they only paid three-quarters of one per cent on their government loans, which meant they just scraped onto the bottom end of the acceptable list whether they were Protestants or not.

Most of these leading citizens undoubtedly belonged to the Masonic Lodge, a single-storey red-brick building next door to the Mechanics Institute hall. The window panes of the lodge were painted in white, and had bars across them, while the double doors were always chained and locked. What went on in there was a mystery, but if you were a Catholic you couldn't belong because, Nancy told us, whatever it was they did, it was the devil's work. They also had a secret handshake nobody knew except themselves and they used to scratch each other's back, she said.

In the town proper Philip Templeton (note one 'l' in Philip), the Holden dealer, then either Tim McRobertson or James Hayley from

McRobertson–Hayley Solicitors and Conveyancing, and Hamish Middleton, the town's jeweller, 'where everyone buys their wedding gifts', were also members of the council. The town chemist, Bluey Porter, was once a member and although he was a Protestant and even sometimes played organ in church, he was an inebriate, because only Catholics were drunks, so the rest of the council eventually put the kybosh on him being a member.

The owner of the local rag didn't make it either. *The Owens & Murray Gazette* was owned by Toby Forbes who, Nancy said, was rough as guts. 'After him, Tommy's almost a gentleman,' she'd say, while scoffing at something he'd written in the *Gazette*. There must have been something that went on between the two of them once, because there were lots that were worse than Toby Forbes in town and he didn't seem such a bad bloke. Sometimes, when he had a special edition coming out, he'd pass by the house and see if we wanted to do a paper run with the garbage in the morning, and he always paid cash on the knocker.

Vera Forbes, Toby's wife, had social pretensions and wrote a weekly column in her husband's paper called 'Yacking On', which was a feeble enough play on the town's name. She also acted as a reporter and was able and willing to dish the dirt on everyone who wasn't on the Anglican Women's Guild. She was often referred to by those of us at the bottom end of town as 'Big Mouth Saggy Tits'. She'd wear these dresses in the summer without a brassiere and you could see her tits through the material, they hung nearly to her waist without sticking out much either. Mike called them razor strops.

Then there was Stipendiary Magistrate Oliver Withers, known to one and all as 'Oliver Twist'. This nickname came about because a magistrate can only impose sentences for petty theft, which is a maximum of two years. Oliver Withers, who hated this restriction on his power, would as often as not ask for a 'second helping', in other words, additional time for the prisoner, by referring a case to the district court judge.

Naturally, he was our family's mortal enemy and was also a lay preacher in the Congregational Church and, although high up in the law, was nevertheless a government worker. Nancy calls him a jumped-up clerk. Because of his government job and his holy-roller religion, he'd never have made the shire council in a month of fire-and-brimstone Sundays.

But, to be totally fair, our side held a couple of much-needed aces as well. The sergeant of police, Big Jack Donovan, and the governor of the prison, Mr John Sullivan, both belonged to the Catholics. The shire council would rather have disbanded than have those two come on board. Nevertheless, they were men with power hard-earned and they knew their way around town and who was up whom.

In our particular family's case we had more to contend with than simple religious prejudice. Tommy spent as much time inside the prison on the hill as on the outside. More probably. We also had twin aunties, Dot and Gwen, both in the loony bin a little further up the incline, referred to as 'up top'. All of which didn't help the Maloney public image a whole heap.

Auntie Gwen, thin as a cinnamon stick, once escaped in the nuddy and went wandering off into the town proper, walking down the main drag, King Street, rosary beads in hand, shouting out her Hail Mary. *'Hail Mary full of Grace, the Lord is with thee. Blessed art thou amongst women, and blessed is the fruit of thy womb, Jesus. Holy Mary, mother of God, pray for us sinners now and at the hour of our death. Amen.'*

Someone got a hold of Mum, who went to fetch my auntie in the Diamond T and delivered her back to the asylum. Nobody ever forgot that – Mum bringing her mad sister back in a garbage truck. The town tongues were wagging overtime for weeks.

Then of course there was politics, Protestants voted Country Party and Catholics were being asked by Father Crosby to vote for the brand-new DLP (the Democratic Labor Party). He said it was our duty and an order from the Bishop. There were a few fanatics who voted Labor. They passed out leaflets at elections, smoked pipes and never answered a question first off, pretending to think while sucking on their pipe stems. They held poorly attended meetings in local pubs, and said anyone in the Country Party was as stupid as Brown's cows.

Then there was the final Maloney putdown. To make things worse for our family, we were the town garbage collectors. 'Maloney & Sons –

Garbage' was what Tommy had painted on the side of the Diamond T and that just about summed it up for the folk from Yankalillee. Mike wanted to paint out the sign but Nancy said that Tommy always fancied himself as a bit of a signwriter and had done it himself and was dead proud of the paint job. We'd just have to live with it, sticks and stones etc.

Tommy had won the contract from the shire council when he returned from the war and all went well for a while until his war wounds started him drinking. He had a crook shoulder and only one good eye and a caved-in cheekbone, his shoulder had been smashed with the butt of a Japanese rifle and he was left with only fifty per cent mobility and his eye was done in at the same time. There were those who said he shouldn't have got the garbage contract, him being what he was, but he could drive a truck and, despite his shoulder, he could work as hard as anyone lifting garbage cans. He had this amazing technique, he'd sling a can up over his right shoulder and jump up on the running board at the back of the Diamond T and sort of bend and empty the can into the back of the truck all in one movement. He was getting a part disability pension but didn't qualify for the full TPI when he came out of the repatriation hospital. Probably a good thing, as most of what he got from War Veterans went on grog. Then he started getting into trouble with the law. His first visit to His Majesty's boarding house up the hill was for petty larceny when he got six months and Nancy was forced to take over the business.

When the contract came up for renewal, Tommy was still in the clink so the shire council put it up for tender. Nancy put in for it, and since nobody else did, the council let her have it. I think it was mostly because the town clerk was a Catholic and the final decision was left to him. Nancy probably became the only woman garbage collector in business in the whole of Australia. That is, if you could call emptying people's garbage cans a business. She would laugh and say, 'Well, equal pay for women has to start somewhere, I guess.' But I don't think the job paid very well because there never seemed to be quite enough to get us through the month and Nancy had to do her layette work to make ends meet.

Naturally us kids were not that chuffed at being called 'dirty garbo!' Nancy said it could have been worse, we could have been the nightsoil collectors and that when the previous operator, Fred Bellows, had died tragically on the job and the contract was up for grabs Tommy had put in an unsuccessful bid for that job as well. His crook shoulder and one eye probably ruled against him this time around.

'Don't know how the silly bugger thought we'd manage both,' Nancy remarked. 'He was full of grand schemes when he first came back from the war. "Waste disposal, it's the coming thing, the average person creates fifty pounds of waste a year and that's only human waste, shit and piss! Then there's all the stuff they throw out. "It's a business that's never gunna run out," he'd say, "like being an undertaker only you don't have to handle stiffs."

'"Yeah, only turds," I said.

'"That's just it, Nance, that's my very point! In Borneo, the villagers use human waste to grow their vegies, nothing to stop us doing the same, dry it into briquettes and sell it to farmers, make a fortune, eh?"'

Tommy, of course hadn't taken the advent of the flush toilet into consideration. A sewage works had been started before the war but it hadn't progressed very far and the shire council was yet to restart it. But sooner or later it would be completed and that would be the end of Tommy's dream of briquettes of dried shit for the local farmers.

Some people though did have septic tanks. The Templetons and the Yerberrys and Oliver Twist were supposed to have flush toilets inside the house but nobody we knew had ever seen them. The dunny was still out the back and an indoor toilet was a real status symbol. In fact, we had never been into anyone's house that had one. Our dunny, like almost everyone else's, was out in the yard with a little lane leading to the back of it from the street. It had a small door that opened up in the rear so the nightsoil collector could place the can under the toilet seat.

A lot of people in Bell Street and elsewhere used torn-up squares of newspaper in their dunny but Nancy said we had to draw the line somewhere and the line was our bums. Somehow we always had shop-bought toilet rolls. Mind you, they had one distinct disadvantage, the paper was shiny on one side and soft on the other and, if you forgot, the shiny side would slip over your bum without getting a good grip, which would often result in a bit of you-know-what ending up on your fingers. It was not until much later that I discovered there were toilet rolls with nice soft paper. Ours was the same as we got in the school dunny so I suppose it was the very cheapest possible but still not newspaper.

Fred Bellows, the dead nightsoil collector, had always been a bit of a loner, a huge bloke who could cart nightsoil all night but didn't have much to say for himself and liked to work on his own, using a huge Percheron, a large grey draughthorse, to pull the wagon that carried the night cans.

Nancy explained that Fred wore this oilskin headgear that fishermen use in storms and you see in pictures on sardine cans. It fits over your head and covers your neck and shoulders. Over this he wore a flat-top tin hat so he could carry the full nightsoil cans on his head. The replacement cans came with a lid, which was removed and placed on the full can so there would be no spillage if Fred happened to stumble in the dark. The lid screwed round the rim and locked firmly into a groove to become watertight.

Well, one night, Fred Bellows removed a night can that must have been pretty damn full and, as usual, he locked the lid into place before he swung it up onto his head. The bottom of the can was rusted and his head, tin hat and all, went straight through it, with the container jamming down onto his shoulders. The oil-cloth headgear prevented much of the contents from leaking out but the rust hole refused to widen and, with the additional aid of the oilcloth, it gripped vice-like around Fred's neck. Strong as he was, Fred couldn't pull the can up off his shoulders without ripping his head off as well.

He must have tried to unlock the lid so he could bend over and empty the can in order to breathe, but he couldn't get the right purchase on the lid. He couldn't shout out neither, because his head was immersed in you-know-what. According to the coroner's report, Fred Bellows died of asphyxiation or, put less politely, he drowned in the town's shit and so, in a manner of speaking, became a pretty good metaphor for what was happening to our family.

After Nancy told us that story, we agreed being the town garbage collectors wasn't the worst thing that could happen to a Maloney under Tommy's parental guidance. Fortunately for us there wasn't a lot of him around, and our mum, Nancy, together with Sarah, was responsible for dragging us up on a day-to-day basis.

Nancy wasn't all that superstitious for someone whose ancestors had been Irish. Although we always seemed to be drowning in economic effluent, she didn't blame fate and believed that people made their own luck. 'A lot of Australian Irish in our situation think the hand of God is turned against them,' she'd say. 'It isn't the hand of the Almighty that's against them but the one that brings the bottle too frequently to their lips!'

Nancy didn't believe in feeling sorry for yourself. 'Shit happens,' she would say, 'can't help that, but there's one thing we can all do, eh?' She rose from where she was sitting and said, 'Follow me.' We traipsed into the kitchen after her, whereupon Nancy took a large spoon out of the drawer and placed it in the sink directly under the tap. 'Righto, everyone gather around.' Then she turned on the tap hard and the jet from the tap hit the curved spoon and we were all splashed in the face and over our clothes. 'It's a lesson for life, what's called a metaphor,' she then said. 'Maybe we can't always plan things perfectly, but what we can do is to make sure we take the spoon out of the sink before we turn on the tap.'

This saying became our Maloney motto: *Always take the spoon out of the sink before you turn on the tap*. If one of us was planning something that could have been a bit dicey, someone in the family would always ask 'Taken the spoon out?' You know, looked at every possible angle, anticipated every possible problem before going ahead with the project. Of course this couldn't have registered with Tommy, because, if it had, I dare say he'd have spent a lot less time contemplating his navel up on the hill.

Like Tommy, we called Mum 'Nancy' when she wasn't looking and 'Mum' when she was. It wasn't a sign of disrespect, she was our mum and we loved her, it was just something that happened between us kids. Mostly because when your father is in gaol a lot of the time, it's hard to think of him, well, you know, as your dad. You have to abstract him somehow so it doesn't look as bad as it is. Sarah started it when she said if we were going to call our father 'Tommy' whenever we talked among ourselves, then it was only fair to call Mum 'Nancy'. Mike wanted to know why that made sense. After all, Mum wasn't a crim.

Sarah said that was precisely the point. Because if Tommy was singled out, it was sort of an insult by us kids to our father, like a denial or something, but if we did the same to Mum then it was okay. Nancy also called him 'Tommy' in everyday conversation and seldom referred to him as 'your father' when talking to us except when she was sad or serious.

Nancy Maloney drove the garbage truck, a big, clapped-out old army-surplus Diamond T Tommy had bought at a US Army Disposal Depot. The Yank sergeant in military transport told him it had a donk like a Texas mule, slow and stubborn, but would go anywhere and never fail to arrive at a destination, that it would virtually last forever. He probably didn't think we'd take his words literally. The only thing was that the Diamond T ate up tyres and, while we drove them right down to the canvas, the tyre piggy bank, a Milo tin kept on the kitchen shelf, never seemed to contain enough when we needed a new set. When that happened, we all knew it was offal week! Kidneys, tripe in white sauce, ox bollocks, lamb's brains done in breadcrumbs, pressed sheep's or ox tongue, and lamb's fry for the next week or month and nothing much to eat you could buy in a grocery shop.

Sarah, our oldest sister, stayed at home first thing in the morning and got things ready for when we returned from our rounds. I was christened Peter but everyone called me 'Mole', because as a baby I'd burrow down under the blankets, even covering my head. I still do.

Me and my two brothers, Mike and Bozo, both older than me, went out in the Diamond T from Monday to Friday with Nancy to collect the town's garbage.

Nancy was no lightweight and would have gained the respect of any sumo wrestler. Each of her arms could have won prize ham at the Wangaratta Show and her legs were like old-man Yarra trunks. She sat behind the wheel of that big, old garbage truck practically filling the entire cabin with warm, pink flesh. Because it was US disposal, it had a left-hand drive, so the driver's side was on the wrong side of the road, which caused no end of confusion to other drivers. Especially the local yahoos in their old man's ute yelling out abuse as they passed us pissed after a bender. They'd be on their way home or out for an early-morning burn and they'd stick their heads out the ute window, only to see no driver where a driver was supposed to be. Sometimes they'd skid to a halt and reverse fifty yards to take a gander and get an earful for their trouble from Nancy.

The three of us used to have to push Nancy up into the driver's seat, our hands placed flat on her bum with room to spare, our legs propped, straining, our heads down, pushing upwards with all our might. Then, from her position behind the wheel, she proceeded to direct operations.

Mike, Bozo, his five dogs and me would run behind the Diamond T, us boys emptying everyone's garbage into the truck. 'Put the bloody lids back on quietly!' Mum would yell at us, making more noise with her shouting than the clanking bins and the neighbourhood dogs that came out to bark at us.

Bozo's dogs never joined in the noise. Bozo wouldn't allow it. They all answered to the same name, 'Bitzer', which was what they were, mongrels of every description, except large. Nancy wouldn't let Bozo have a big dog and her objection had nothing to do with how much it ate. 'It tells people things about you, you don't want them to think,' she said.

Bozo's dogs all came from the pound in Wang, which is short for Wangaratta, and were more like dogettes than what you'd call a proper dog. Except for the little Fox Terrier–Maltese cross, where you could see a bit of light under its tummy, all of their chassis were pretty low to the ground. They were piebald, smooth-haired, long-haired, furry, curly, pop-eyed, eyes you couldn't see behind an awning of hair, sprig-eared and floppy, stump-nosed or long-snouted. Several of every combination of small-breed dogs seemed to be represented in each of them. None could, by any stretch of imagination, be called a good-looking mutt. But I tell you what, they were bloody smart doggies for all that.

There were Bitzers One, Two, Three, Four and Five. When Bozo shouted 'Bitzer!', just the single name, they all came. 'Bitzer, sit!', they all sat. 'Roll over!' 'Jump!' 'Play dead!' They did everything in unison like it was a circus act. But if he called out 'Bitzer Three!', the little mutt, who was mainly Fox Terrier and Maltese Terrier with just a hint of sausage dog added to the blend, would come running and sit in front of

Bozo, tail thumping the dirt, waiting for instructions. They all knew their own number. Those dogs loved my brother to death and would do anything he said. Also, they wouldn't eat anything without first hearing the password, which was 'Bog in!' That way they couldn't be fed a poison bait, which was common enough if someone didn't like your dogs.

If one of the neighbourhood dogs thought to have a go at one of us, Bitzers One to Five would immediately surround him and the errant dog would soon enough show his neck to Bitzer One, a fearless little bloke mostly Dandie Dinmont and Pekinese and a few other things you couldn't even hazard a guess at. He was the enforcer of the pack. Bozo said when a dog lifts its chin and shows its neck to another dog, in dog language that's putting up your hands and saying 'Okay, fellas, I'm outta here!' Bitzer One, with the others doing the growl chorus, could intimidate a full-grown Doberman.

In those days the garbage cans were made of tin and we clattered from house to house like an off-key brass band, brakes squeaking as we slowed, pistons rattling like the clappers of hell, the exhaust pipe vibrating, madly spewing out dark exhaust fumes, which polluted the bright, clean morning air as the clapped-out engine, badly in need of a de-coke, over-revved every time we pulled away.

We would start the run at three o'clock in the morning. The route would be different each day because it took a week to do the whole town. But on a Monday we'd begin at number 50 Hill Street, at the home of Oliver Withers, the stipendiary magistrate. Mondays we'd do all the other bigwigs that lived up on the higher part of the hill looking down their nose at the town in the valley below. The magistrate's house was at the far end of the street, which ended on the edge of a small cliff. We'd go to the end of the street first and turn the empty truck around. The reason for this was so that we didn't have to make a difficult turn with the old Diamond T full of rubbish in case the brakes failed and the weight took it over the cliff. This meant that Oliver Twist's rubbish was the first to be emptied and always well before dawn.

By the time Friday came we'd do the workers' cottages, which included our own street, Bell Street. Nancy said this was our way of sticking it up the rest of the town. By Friday the nobs on the hill would have full garbage bins and still have the weekend to go, but the Bell Street mob would have nice empty garbage tins for the weekend. I could never quite see what the point was, but it was Nancy logic and you couldn't argue with that.

Our street was called Bell Street because, to add insult to injury, the Anglican Church was at one end, its bell tower casting what Nancy called 'its long, dark, treacherous shadow' over the first half-dozen houses in the street. All the cottages in Bell Street belonged to Catholics and Nancy saw this as a deliberate act of provocation by the Church of England, another example of what she constantly referred to as 'the bitter divide'.

It would be seven-fifteen when we finally got back to Bell Street. Most of the workers who lived in the street would already be up, or if they weren't they'd use our arrival as their alarm clock. In the cottages, all of which were identical and had the kitchen facing the street, you'd see their men sitting in their singlets and braces, already having a first ciggie and cuppa tea in the kitchen, the wives fussing with breakfast at the stove. We'd usually cop a thank-you wave as we emptied their bins with barely a clank.

Sometimes one of the men would stroll out and hand Nancy a leg of mutton or half a sack of spuds, or a couple of cabbages or a bag of carrots from their vegie garden. 'Good on ya, Nance,' they'd say, hoisting the stuff up into the cab for her to grab a hold of. Nancy would smile and quietly thank them, no big display. But you knew that if one of them had a baby, they'd be getting a christening robe with the full rosebuds and forget-me-nots, wrapped in brown paper. It would be left in their emptied garbage bin with the person's name in Nancy's neat-as-a-pin handwriting so that they'd know it wasn't garbage left behind. Nancy didn't like to make too much fuss.

'We don't take charity,' she'd say. 'It's not the Maloney way. But we're not up ourselves neither. Someone is kind to us, you remember it, you wait long enough, the opportunity will surely come when you can return the favour.'

Getting up at three in the morning in the summer wasn't too bad. With a hot day ahead, at that time in the morning there was usually a bit of a breeze coming up the valley. Winter was a different matter entirely. Every minute out there on the run was bloody awful and us kids had chilblains and runny noses all winter long. For chilblains we had to soak our feet in a bucket of boiling salt water for hours until they turned red as a lobster.

Mike, ever the questioning one, once pointed out to Mum that it would be far more logical to start work in Bell Street on a Monday. It took a good fifteen minutes of wasted time in an empty truck to make the slow climb to Oliver Twist's house on Hill Road. 'Fifteen minutes saved on the entire morning's run meant we could hose out the back of the truck and be back home by seven instead of a quarter past,' he explained to Nancy. Bozo and me immediately agreed, nodding our heads. In terms of getting ready, if we were late to school on a Monday morning we got detention as well as a caning. A quarter of an hour saved on a Monday was valuable.

'Well, darlin', you're probably right,' Nancy replied, leaning down from the cabin and putting her big hand on Mike's shoulder. 'But there's a principle involved, what I call "Maloney payback".'

'Huh? What's that when it's at home?' Bozo asked.

'Well, it's like this see, every time that pompous, self-righteous old bugger Oliver Twist places his scrawny elbows on the bench and removes his glasses and sets about wiping them with his clean linen handkerchief and at the same time proceeds to give Tommy another one of his half-arsed twopenny lectures before sentencing him and then adds a second helping, another six months, I say to myself, "Right, Your Honour, that's every Monday you're going to start the week having had a bad night's sleep!"' She hesitates and looks at each of us in turn, 'Just because Tommy's done a bit of time on the hill in the past doesn't mean he can treat us like dirt.'

'But we are dirt!' Bozo says, grinning. 'We collect the garbage.'

Nancy doesn't laugh. I guess she doesn't like what we're doing for a crust any more than we do. 'It's honest work, Bozo, which is more than can be said for a lot of the locals. Right then, where was I before I was so rudely interrupted by my own child?'

'Maloney payback,' Mike reminds her with a bit of a sigh.

'Yes, righto. Well, us getting Oliver Twist's two German Shepherds barking their heads off and you three banging the bins and me yelling out at you at the top of my voice to keep the noise down so as to make absolutely certain the miserable bugger is good and awake, that, my dears, is Maloney payback.'

I have to admit, we had the routine down pat. Bozo would line Bitzers One to Five up in a row directly in front of the magistrate's gate, right up close. 'Okay, sit!' he'd command, then 'Silence!' he'd order next, bringing his forefinger up to his lips as if they were humans. You see, Oliver Twist kept these great big ferocious German Shepherds running loose in his high-fenced, quarter-acre property because he was paranoid that someone he'd sentenced might some day come after him. He probably thought that someone would be Tommy, who was one of his more frequent victims.

The two dogs would come hurtling down the side of the house, skidding, their nails scrabbling on the cement path as they tried to gain traction around the corner to the front, both barking fit to kill.

Bozo's Bitzers would be waiting, their snouts just out of reach beyond the wrought-iron gate. The German Shepherds would push their noses through one of the fancy iron grilles, slavering at the mouth, fangs flashing at the sight of Bozo's mutts, who would sit there staring at the two killer dogs, like they were dirt or something. Which goes to show how well they were trained, you try stopping a small dog barking at a big one. I swear Bozo had taught them how to do a bored sort of a yawn in sequence.

It never failed to work, we'd hear Oliver Twist cursing and trying to get his upstairs bedroom window up to abuse us, whereupon Bozo would give this little whistle and his dogs would leave the gate and hurry to the blind side of the truck so that their intimidation act couldn't be seen by the furious beak.

The window would eventually go up, but before the furious magistrate could ever get the first word in, Nancy, her head already stuck out the truck window, would shout up at him, 'Better call those brutes off, one day they're going to get out and bite one of my boys!' Her tone of voice always suggested that such an event would be more trouble than even Oliver Twist could handle on his own.

The magistrate in his red-striped pyjamas would open his mouth to say something and Nancy would quickly add, 'They're a menace to society!' Which was what Oliver Twist had once said about Tommy. Lost for a reply, he'd try to call his dogs off and we'd be away with a clank and a roar, sending a perfumed cloud of carbon monoxide up through his bedroom window. Nancy would yell out over the noise of the engine, 'Half-past three and all's well!' like the night watchman in that movie *Great Expectations*, or was it *The Hunchback of Notre Dame*?

Oliver Twist really pissed Nancy off. Tommy never took personal property, like jewellery and stuff, or broke into someone's house. He only did warehouses or commercial premises where the insurance would cover the loss. He mostly worked in Albury–Wodonga or the industrial areas in the western suburbs of Melbourne and only occasionally in Wangaratta. Nancy reckoned that Tommy didn't deserve more than one stretch at a time for being such an honourable crook.

Shortly after six-thirty we'd be at the tip a mile out of town for the last time that day, having been out twice already. Unfortunately the Diamond T wasn't a tip-truck and so each trip out the three of us would pull on our broken old gumboots, grab a blunt shovel and shovel the shit that came out of people's bins onto the tip.

Then on the way home we'd stop at the abattoir and hose the back of the truck clean while Mum went in and fetched us a bit of meat for that night and Bozo got half a sack of bones and scrag ends for the dogs. Fridays we'd eat fish, mostly smoked cod in white sauce which us kids hated. Once Bozo caught a fish in the Sawell Dam and it tasted of mud. We all had about a teaspoon each of that fish to comply with God's wish and then filled up on bread and jam. It was the first fresh fish we'd ever eaten and we vowed it would be the last if we had any say in the matter.

Bozo and Nancy had the selfsame thing going for them, they had mates everywhere and the abattoir workers never saw us short, although Nancy would always pay, even if sometimes she'd have to put stuff on tick. Maloneys didn't take charity. 'Nothin' worse than someone feeling very sorry for you,' Nancy would say.

We'd be back at Bell Street by seven-fifteen, just in time for a cold shower out the back shed, winter or summer. The smell of garbage clings on, gets up your nostrils and into the pores of your skin, in your hair, everywhere. So we'd need to scrub real hard, using Velvet soap on our arms, legs, stomach, up the bum crack, between our toes, back of the ears, places you wouldn't normally care much about. Each spot had to be rubbed practically raw with the scrubbing brush. Last of all, you'd get Mike or Bozo to do your back.

Sometimes, in the winter, it would be below freezing. We'd come home from riding in the back of the truck, breathing frost smoke, and freezing our balls off. Sarah would've put our school clothes in the shed with the towels and straight off we'd have to go into the shower or we'd be late for school and cop the strap.

Often times in the winter we'd have to first knock the ice from the shower rose. We'd dance about on the cement floor, sucking in our breath, the shower sending deadly ice needles raining down on us, piercing us to the very bone. But we still scrubbed till it hurt. We took as much time as we could stand without freezing to death to get rid of the smell of garbage and the shame Sarah said it would bring if people smelt it on us kids.

You'd be standing under the shower, gasping, trying to rinse off your all-over-body soaping with frantic hands, Mike and Bozo waiting, eyes closed from the soap dripping down from their hair, both still furiously scrubbing, slapping themselves, yelling out to me to bloody hurry up. Bozo's balls would disappear somewhere up between his legs and they'd only drop down when he was warm again. 'Sometimes,' he said, 'they only came good during the second period at school.'

Sarah said we had our pride and even if we were the town garbos and Tommy was in gaol, so what? Nobody was going to say a Maloney wasn't a clean person. She'd have ironed our school clothes with the creases in our shorts sharp as a knife. Then when we came in from out the back, all dressed for school, there'd be these big enamel plates filled with steaming oatmeal porridge with a ring of melted brown sugar on the top, hot milk, thick wedges of white toast and plum jam as well as tin mugs of hot, sweet tea waiting for us on the kitchen table. After that we'd wash our mouths and clean our teeth at the sink, grab our jam sandwiches for school lunch, kiss and hug little Colleen and call 'Cheerio!' to Nancy out the back verandah.

'You four stick together, you hear? You tell me if any teacher gives you trouble!' She'd shout the same thing every morning from where she'd settled down in the old cane couch, and she'd already be halfway through a large bottle of milk stout. Her latest layette order, together with her embroidery stuff and the old Singer sewing machine, would be on the work table beside her.

We'd be out the front gate and off to school in a great tearing hurry, Sarah walking along with us, the three of us boys scrubbed properly to her satisfaction. She'd be neat as a pin in her box-pleated tunic and blazer with her prefect's stripe sewn on just below the school badge. If you looked at Sarah, who had this shining red hair, Nancy called it 'titian', and just a sprinkle of speckle freckles around her nose, it would make us proud that at least one Maloney had turned out okay.

Sarah, Mike and Bozo, together with Bozo's dogs, would peel off to the high school and I'd make my way alone to the primary school down the road a bit. I know I'm carrying on a bit about Bozo's dogs but you've got to understand they were truly amazing. They'd wait at the school gates minding their own business, never giving any trouble, until school came out. They did the same when Bozo and me were in primary school, going crazy with joy when they saw us at the end of the day, you'd think we'd been away on holidays. Which never happened of course. In fact, it was Bozo's dogs waiting at the school gates that was the real reason for him becoming a boxer.

It happened like this. We were in the playground and this kid, Brent Middleton, bigger than Bozo by a good head and surrounded by nine of his mates, comes up to us and says, 'Hey, Bozo, is it true your auntie escaped from the loony bin and went starkers down King Street?' He's got this half-smile on his face and the others with him are all grinning their gobs off.

Bozo's got no option, has he? So he smacks the bastard, only it's with his fist and the perpetrator drops like a stone. Well, he knocks him down anyway. Brent Middleton is one grade above Bozo and the school bully and the leader of a gang and, before you know it, there's four or five of them having a go at my brother.

I get stuck in, but at the time I'm too little to do much damage, but they've got Bozo down and they're kicking the daylights out of him. He manages somehow to get up and he clocks a couple of them in the mouth and eye. Old Bozo's going at them like a threshing machine but now there's nine of them and only the two of us. He's taking a hiding and I'm getting an unwelcome slap or two as well.

And that's when the cavalry arrive. Bitzers One to Five get stuck in and suddenly there's mayhem, kids scattering every which way, dogs yapping and snapping at ankles, jumping up and grabbing a hold of the hems of khaki shorts, biting at bums, everyone's yelling, teachers come running and there's blood and torn uniforms everywhere you look.

Bozo gets up off the deck, calls the dogs to heel and makes them sit at his feet. You can see they're not too happy neither, wanting to finish off what they've started, but they do as they're told. My brother's nose is bleeding and he's missing a tooth and has a split lip and a torn left ear. I'm okay, having just been pushed aside with a couple of stiff belts to the ear, and only copped a thick lip. Bozo's the worst wounded of all by far, but he still has the presence of mind to send the dogs home, knowing they're going to be in deep shit caninewise.

Because of the dog attack, the teachers all blame Bozo for what's happened and he's hauled off to the headmaster's office while the rest of us, Brent Middleton and his cohorts and me, are herded into the spare classroom next door.

Brent Middleton has been bit good and proper and has a black eye and a bloody nose where my brother's punched him first and second time around. Several of the others have something to show for their trouble, Bitzer bites, and a bloody nose or thick lip as well, compliments of Bozo's whirring fists.

Mr Flint, the headmaster, doesn't even listen to Bozo's side of the story before he phones Hamish Middleton, who has the jewellery shop in Fitzroy Street, 'Jonah Middleton & Sons, Est. 1872', and tells Mr Middleton what's happened and asks him to come over to the school.

Nancy later says that Flint's a real crawler and it's obvious he was more interested in damage control than whether or not Bozo was hurt. Anyway, the headmaster calls several of the other parents to come over. Then he phones Dr Wallis at his surgery and arranges for him to come to the school to give all those who've been Bitzer-bit a tetanus shot. Last of all, he phones Sergeant Donovan and Nancy. He turns to Bozo. 'Maloney, you'll probably be expelled for this, what you've done cannot be overlooked, I'll deal with you later. Now get next door with the others!'

The long and the short of it is that Nancy goes in to bat for me, Bozo and the dogs. But the various parents who've made it to the school want the dogs put down and Bozo severely punished. I guess I'm too little for them to bother about. Hamish Middleton assumes the leadership and mumbles out loud that he'll gladly do the job on the dogs himself and, looking directly at Nancy, he barks, 'That boy of yours is way out of line and should be sent to the boys' home!'

'What did you say, Mr Middleton?' Nancy says, real slow and soft, her blue eyes narrowed down to chips of ice. What Bozo's done to his son, Brent, ain't nothing to what's coming to him if he decides to repeat what he's just said. Nancy's dressed in one of her floral dresses that's big as a circus tent which she's made herself, all of them the exact same pattern and design – white daisies on a yellow background. With her great ham arms sticking out the sides larger than Hamish Middleton's thighs, the poor bastard is no match in the intimidation stakes and the look from Nancy sends the town jeweller and council member two paces backwards.

'Your lad has to be punished, Mrs Maloney,' Middleton senior repeats, though this time his voice is way downwind.

'He'll be punished if it's his fault, but that hasn't been clearly established yet,' Nancy says coldly. She's a dab hand at court procedure and adds, 'Would you mind if we waited until all the evidence has come in, Mr Middleton? Or is this going to be some sort of kangaroo court? Parents of Yankalillee Primary School versus Maloney?'

Vera Forbes from the *Gazette*, who's already sniffed out the story and has come running, has a second go at Nancy. 'Well,' she says all hoity-toity, 'those vicious brutes will have to be put down before they attack and kill someone!'

'Are you referring to the boys who attacked my son, or the dogs?' Nancy says, quick as a flash.

'That's enough from all of you!' Sergeant Donovan says, trying to conceal his smile at Nancy's crack back at Big Mouth Saggy Tits. 'Why don't we start at the beginning and try to get to the bottom of this mess, hey? Maybe the headmaster here can get someone to make you all a cup of tea and I'll go next door and see if the doctor's completed the tetanus injections and then I'll question the boys involved in the fracas.'

Big Jack Donovan is a country cop from his boots to the point of his cap, well over six feet with a barrel chest and stomach to match, an untidy-looking sort of chap who will dominate any room he steps into. In his heyday he was a famous ruckman for South Melbourne and played at the MCG in the Grand Final against Richmond. He's known to be even-handed and doesn't take any crap from anyone. Because he wasn't allowed to join up, being classified as Essential Services, he's been in Yankalillee more than twenty years. Him, not Oliver Twist, is the real voice of the law in this town. Not everyone loves him, though, he's got his fair share of enemies in high places. Nancy says he's in the know on just about everyone in town and the word, even among the bigwigs, has long been out that it doesn't pay to mess around with Big Jack Donovan. But all the lags know he'll give a battler a break if there's family and hardship involved and if some misdemeanour they've perpetrated can be patched up without too much fuss. Now he nods his head and smiles again, backing away towards the door. 'Righto then, excuse me, ladies . . . gentlemen, be back soon enough.'

'Shouldn't we be with you, Sergeant?' Hamish Middleton calls out. He's plainly miffed at the way things are turning out, with him not playing an important role in the proceedings and what with Nancy getting the better of him and Vera Saggy Tits Forbes. 'After all, they're our children!' he protests. Two of the parents nod their heads, agreeing.

'No, I don't think so, Mr Middleton.' Big Jack is firm. 'You know how it is with young fellas? I'd best see them on my own.' Then he turns and goes out and comes into the classroom next door where the doctor is just finishing up sticking a needle in the bums of those who got bit, and the young nurse's aide he's brought with him from the local bush-nursing hospital is busy patching us up with Mercurochrome and long strips of sticking plaster she's tearing off a big roll with her teeth because she forgot to bring the scissors.

Sergeant Donovan stoops as he enters the classroom and takes off his cap and puts it on the teacher's desk. 'Afternoon, Doctor, Nurse. Afternoon, boys!' he says cheerfully.

We all chorus 'afternoon' back at him, though ours doesn't sound that cheerful. There's twelve of us in the classroom, ten from Brent Middleton's mob and Bozo and me.

'Right then, I'll just make myself comfortable while the doctor and the nurse finish up dressing your wounds. How's it goin', Doc?' Big Jack Donovan asks as he pulls the teacher's chair way back and sits down and puts his big policeman's boots up on the desk and starts to look at each of us in turn. When he reaches me, I try to look back but it's impossible and, like everyone else, I look down at the desk. Suddenly I'm guilty as sin and I don't even know why.

'Won't be much longer, Sergeant,' Dr Wallis says, then he points to Bozo, whose nose and lip have stopped bleeding but who is holding a wad of cotton wool to his left ear. 'Lad here needs a couple of stitches to his ear, that's about it. You can send them all home after you're through with them.' You can see the blood that's soaked the cotton-wool pad peeping through Bozo's three fingers. 'I'll send my report on to you later,' Dr Wallis adds.

'Good on ya, Doc,' Sergeant Donovan replies.

Doctors in those days were really somebody and even though I'm shitting myself at Sergeant Donovan's presence in the classroom, I'm still pretty impressed at the easy way he handles Dr Wallis. Nancy's always said Sergeant Donovan was a good bloke and a good Catholic, if we ever got into trouble, to tell him 'The truth and nothing but the truth so help me God'. It was years before we found out where she'd got that expression from.

The doctor finishes off with Bozo, who only does a couple of tiny winces when the stitches go in, and then the doctor and the nurse take their leave.

We've all been standing and now the sergeant says, 'Sit, boys, take the weight off your legs.' He indicates the ink-stained school desks stretched out in front of him. There's the usual scuffle as we go to sit down, Bozo and me to the one side and Brent Middleton and his mates to the other. Some of the blokes have bites on the bum and you can hear them wincing, probably exaggerating, as they slide themselves into a desk.

Then there's silence. Nothing. Sergeant Donovan looks up at the ceiling, then out the window and slowly he fixes his eyes on all of us. I'm gone, shit-scared and ready to confess to anything he wants. I look at Bozo, but his broken face gives nothing away, although his eyes flicker briefly as he looks at me before he looks to the front.

'Hmm . . .' the policeman says. Then nothing again.

We all look down at the desk in front of us, not willing to meet his eye. The nothing continues.

Then suddenly, so we all get a start, 'Tell me, Mister Middleton, is Mister Maloney here a mate of yours?'

'No, no, sir,' Brent Middleton stammers, looking up, surprised at being so formally addressed.

Now Sergeant Donovan turns to the other blokes on Brent Middleton's side of the classroom. 'And, you lot, are you friends of Mister Maloney?'

'No, sir,' they all mumble, not looking at the policeman.

'Why is that?'

'Dunno, sir,' they mumble.

'Is it because he's a Catholic?'

'No, sir,' they chorus anxiously.

'Just don't like each other, hey? Well, that happens sometimes. Just don't like the cut of a man's jib?'

The classroom remains quiet as a mouse.

'Mister Middleton, would you stand up please and come up here, you too, Mister Maloney.' Bozo gets up out of the desk and so does Brent Middleton. 'Up here on the platform, please.' They both step up onto the teacher's platform. 'Now stand back to back, if you'll oblige me please, gentlemen.' Bozo turns and he and Brent Middleton touch backs. The pocket of Bozo's khaki shirt has been torn and hangs in a flap, he's got blood down the front of it and two buttons missing as well, Sarah's not going to be too happy when we get home. Sergeant Donovan turns back at us. 'Right, now who would you say was the tallest and the heaviest, Mister Middleton or Mister Maloney?'

'Middleton, sir,' several of us mumble.

'By a good head, I'd say and by what . . . say, one and a half stone in weight?'

Silence from us all.

'Eight inches and twenty pounds, that'd be about right, don't you think, gentlemen?' We don't say anything. Brent Middleton is the biggest bloke in the school and he knows it, that's what makes him the school bully and head of a gang, everyone's been shit-scared of him until Bozo today.

'Righto, you two can separate, but stay up here if you will, please.' Bozo goes to stand with his back to the blackboard. Brent Middleton stays where he is but turns front on, looking down at us. 'Now, tell me, who threw the first punch?'

'He did, sir,' Brent Middleton says quickly, wanting to gain the advantage.

'Oh, I see, the little bloke attacked the big bloke, is that it?'

'Yes, sir, he king-hit me and knocked me down.'

He points to Brent Middleton's left eye, 'Looks like you've got a bit of a stinker coming on, Mister Middleton. Good punch, was it?'

'Dunno, sir. Suppose so, sir.'

'Dunno? You said a king-hit, didn't you? Hit you when you weren't looking, took you by surprise?'

'No, sir, yes, sir.'

'Just walked up and whacked you?'

'We was talking, sir.'

'Just talking, then he up and hit you?'

'Yes, sir.'

'And, Mister Middleton, what precisely were you talking about? Was it something you may have said to Mister Maloney? You see, in my experience, little blokes don't go around hitting big blokes unless they're very stupid or drunk.' He turns to Bozo. 'Were you drunk, Mister Maloney?'

The blokes all giggle, our laughter breaking a bit of the tension. 'No, sir,' Bozo says, trying not to grin through his split lip.

'Stupid then? You don't look stupid to me.'

Bozo blushes, but doesn't reply.

'Some of us got hit by him as well,' Brent Middleton now offers, side-stepping Sergeant Donovan's original question. There follows a mumble of approval from his side of the classroom.

Big Jack Donovan stops and thinks, then says, 'Us? Oh, I see! It wasn't just you and Mister Maloney fighting, Mister Middleton, the big bloke and the little bloke, there were others involved?'

'My friends, sir, they came to help me.'

'And what did they do to help you, Mister Middleton?'

Brent Middleton looks at Bozo, 'Tried to pull him away, sir. He'd gone off his scone, sir.'

'Little bloke hits big bloke, big bloke's friends, all bigger than little bloke, come to his rescue and get hit in turn by little bloke who has turned into an unstoppable, raging bull. Doesn't seem to make a lot of sense, does it now?'

'Then the dogs come, sir,' Middleton bursts out, again not responding to the sergeant's question.

'Dogs? What dogs? Is that what happened to Mister Maloney? I see he has a split lip and stitches in his ear and it looks like he's had a nose bleed, and, judging from his eyes, he's going to have a couple of stinkers.' He pauses, then adds, 'That nasty bruise above his knee, I could have sworn was a kick from a boot. Do you mean to say the dogs did all that to him?'

'No, sir, they were *his* dogs, he set them onto us,' Brent Middleton explains.

'Hmm . . . how did the dogs come? I mean, did Mister Maloney stop beating you all up and turn and, you know, whistle for them?'

'Dunno, sir, maybe, sir.'

'But no one heard him whistle or call out?'

'There was a lot of noise, sir. Whistle, I suppose.'

'With his lip split open and his nose bleeding and nine blokes trying to pull him away from you and all that noise and . . . amidst all this confusion he had time to whistle for the dogs? By the way, where were these dogs? Were they standing around waiting for instructions, a whistle from their master, permission to attack?'

'I dunno, sir, they just come at us from nowhere.'

'Come now, Mister Middleton, nowhere? They must have come from somewhere?'

'The school gates I suppose, they's always there.'

'How far would you say the school gates were from where the fight took place?'

'Dunno, sir.'

'Would you say ten, twenty, fifty, a hundred yards?'

'About fifty yards, sir.'

Sergeant Donovan looks out of the window for a long time. He takes his feet off the table and pulls the chair up, so he's sitting with his elbows leaning on the teacher's desk, his hands cupped under his chin. 'Well, well, well, if they were Mister Maloney's dogs, I've seen them myself on numerous occasions and there isn't one of them that stands much taller than ten inches off the ground. As I recall, they're well trained to obedience and I've never had any complaints about them being vicious. So there must have been a good reason for them to come at you lot, wouldn't you say, Mister Middleton?'

There is a mumble of 'No, sir, no reason, sir' from their side of the classroom.

'Your point is well taken, Mister Middleton, some sort of signal must have passed. May I put it to you that any dog worth its salt will come to his master's rescue if they see him attacked? I put it to you, the signal wasn't a whistle from Mister Maloney, but simply the unprovoked and cowardly attack on him and his brother by you and your friends. That, I suggest, is what got the dogs going.'

'No, sir, he hit me first!' Brent Middleton protests again.

'Then I suggest there must have been some sort of provocation on your part, Mister Middleton? I asked you previously what you'd said to Mister Maloney and, on that occasion, you refrained from answering. Perhaps this time you'll tell me what it is you said to Mister Maloney?'

'It was a joke, sir. We was only teasing him.'

'A joke? What sort of a joke? It must have been a very strange joke to make a little bloke like Mister Maloney go berserk and run amok? What was this joke?' His voice grows suddenly stern, 'Come on, boy, let me hear it and no more bullshit!'

'It was about his auntie, sir,' Brent Middleton's voice shakes, he is suddenly dead-scared.

Sergeant Donovan jerks up straight and bangs the desk with his fist. 'What about his auntie? What did you say about his auntie?'

Brent Middleton begins to sniff and now he's looking down at his shoes. 'About her escaping from the asylum without clothes and walking down King Street, sir. We was only mucking about, sir, teasing him, sir.'

'Why you little shit!' Sergeant Donovan yells out, kicking back his chair and drawing to his full height so that his huge body seems to fill the whole room and spill out the door.

Brent Middleton begins to shake and then to blubber and back away, 'I'm sorry, sir, I'm sorry, sir.' Some of the others also start to cry and there's a good deal of blubbering going on all around.

'Right, all of you except for the two Maloney boys are under arrest. I'm arresting you for causing grievous bodily harm and for defamation!' He reaches down for his cap and jams it on his head. 'Follow me!' He turns to Bozo, then me, 'You two may as well come along as witnesses, see that justice is done.'

Of course, we had no idea he was bluffing about arresting Middleton's mob and one of them, a boy named Bluey Taylor, wets his pants on the spot, piss running down his leg onto the floorboards. Sergeant Donovan takes three giant strides to the door and we shuffle after him as he makes a right turn into the headmaster's office where all the parents are waiting.

It is a pretty crowded gathering but we all somehow fit in, the twelve of us, six parents, Mr Flint the headmaster, and the police sergeant. Most of the Middleton gang are now sniffing and getting themselves generally het up, thinking they're going to be thrown into the clink with the key thrown away.

Sergeant Donovan looks around until he spots Hamish Middleton. 'Sir, your boy will now tell us all what happened to provoke this fight, which I must say was just a tad one-sided, with your bully-boy son and nine of his gutless mates against the two Maloney boys.' He turns to Brent Middleton, 'Step up, son, tell your father and the other parents here exactly what you said to Bozo Maloney.'

Brent Middleton bawls and chokes and gulps and by the time he's finished telling the truth of what happened there's two snot runs under his nose, his eyes are all puffed up and red, and his shoulders are shaking like he's having some sort of a fit.

The decision is finally taken that each parent should punish his own child. Bozo and me, though, are let off scot-free, with Sergeant Donovan saying to one and all that we showed a lot of character and true guts. The headmaster didn't say anything, you know apologise for threatening to expel Bozo. Nancy called him right the first time, he'd rather stay thick as thieves with the right people in town than be seen apologising to a garbage collector.

Nancy now tucks us, one on either side, under her arms and we walk out the school gates where she's got the Diamond T parked right in front of the school. We have to push her into the driver's seat, which must have looked pretty damn funny, though those parents following us didn't laugh. It was a rare victory for the Maloney family against the forces of evil.

Chapter Two

Nothing more was said about the dogs and it was suggested that Vera Forbes keep the incident out of the *Gazette*. It probably wouldn't have stopped her talking her head off around town anyway and the verbal version would have turned Bozo and me into villains.

But the long and the short of it is that Sergeant Donovan comes to see Nancy and says that there's a prisoner doing a brick (ten years) on the hill who was a handy boxer in his day. He once fought for the Victorian professional welterweight crown but lost on a knockout in the first round. Still and all, that's pretty big time for Yankalillee. He explains that he's talked to the prison governor, Mr Sullivan, about starting something up for the town's kids, who've got nothing to do and always seem to end up getting into trouble with the police. He's thinking of a boxing club under the auspices of the police and with the help of the prisoner, namely Bobby Devlin, who he hopes will be the coach. He'll call it the Police Boys Boxing Club and he wants Bozo and me to join, Mike also if he'd like to.

Nancy says it's up to us to decide but that she doesn't object in principle. She points out to Big Jack Donovan that we don't have much time and we could only attend training afternoons after school and no weekday evenings except Fridays because of the garbage collecting next morning. Saturday nights would also be okay because we could sleep in Sunday mornings. She's throwing what's left of our lives away willy-nilly but she puts the kybosh on Mike joining up, although she doesn't tell Sergeant Donovan it's because she needs him to help her with the layettes in the afternoons. Mike tells us he wouldn't have joined anyway and Sarah says that at least one of us has some brains.

Bozo loved it from the first go and couldn't get enough of boxing. Though it turns out to be a big ask for me and, although I stick at it for a while, to tell you the truth I'm not that good and I'm that bloody exhausted after getting up at three in the morning, I can hardly stay awake waiting for my turn to spar. Sometimes I'd fall asleep leaning against the big red punching bag. The mornings at school are bad enough, let alone spending the afternoons learning to get my head knocked off.

Most mornings I'd snooze at the back of the class during the first period of the day and often enough take the strap coming to me from our teacher, Mr Brown. He was English and known to one and all as 'Crocodile Brown' because he had these big yellow teeth from smoking little black cigars and his eyes had these heavy lids so they'd never open properly and, when he smiled, you knew you were in deep shit.

'Peter Maloney, are you asleep again?' he'd shout from the front of the class.

I'd wake up with a start. 'No, sir, only thinking.'

'Thinking? Hmmm . . . that would make a nice change in a Maloney,' Crocodile Brown says all sarcastic like. 'And what were you thinking about, laddie?'

'The lesson, sir?'

'The lesson? Well, well, then perhaps you'll be so kind as to enlighten us a little, eh? What was the last thing I said?'

'Missed that, sir, too deep in thought.'

Laughter from the class.

'Don't be cheeky, lad. We don't like clowns in our classroom, do we now?'

'No, sir, sorry, sir.'

'Sorry isn't good enough, Maloney. You're not paid to think, laddie, you're paid to listen!'

'I didn't know we were being paid, sir.'

More laughter.

'Right, that's just about enough from you, Maloney! Up you come.'

Whack, whack, whack, three of the best, the deadly strap whistling through the air, the new welts on my bum freshening up the ones the bastard gave last time round.

A lot of the teachers in country schools were bloody sadists, and Mike and Bozo copped the same as me until they got to high school. Anyway, Crocodile Brown had it in for us Maloneys. He was the choirmaster at the Anglican church and when Mike was ten he heard him singing at the school assembly and came to see Mum.

Nancy offered him a glass of milk stout, but he said no thanks. Sarah made him a cup of tea and Mike brought a wicker chair out to the back verandah.

'Mrs Maloney,' Crocodile Brown leaned forward in the rickety old chair and looked serious, 'I'm here to tell you, your son Michael is a boy soprano with perfect pitch.' He leaned back again, pleased with himself, glancing at Mike and then smiling his yellow smile at Nancy, 'I say, you really ought to be proud with such a lark in your midst.'

'Thank you,' Nancy said, not giving too much away, but then she added, 'I'm surprised he has any voice at all with all the carbon monoxide he swallows of a morning.' Crocodile Brown misses her reference entirely and takes a sip from his cup to cover his confusion. Though we never tell her anything about what happens in school, something about him must have leaked out somewhere, because Mike says he could see Nancy wasn't that keen on him and wasn't going to give Crocodile Brown too much rope.

Crocodile Brown brings his cup down to the saucer balanced on his lap, 'Well, we'd like to have him in the Anglican church choir, train his voice properly, eh?'

Nancy took her time, which was always a bit of a warning. She put her head to one side and looked at Crocodile Brown and slowly put down the layette she was working on, her eyes never once leaving the schoolmaster. 'And what do you think Father Crosby would say to that notion, Mr Brown?'

'Well, er . . . I must say . . . I hadn't really given that much thought,' Crocodile Brown stammered. It wasn't at all the reaction he'd expected. 'Your boy isn't at St Stephen's so . . . er, naturally, I assumed . . .' His voice trailed off then came on again. 'But . . . but the Roman Catholics haven't got a boys' choir, Mrs Maloney.'

'Ah, yes, but they have got my boy's immortal soul in their safekeeping and we'll not be giving *that* to the Church of England,' she paused then added, 'And, by the way, Mr Brown, we're Catholics not Roman Catholics.' Nancy hated to be called a Roman Catholic. In fact, Mike's soul was out of Catholic circulation as Nancy had declared us all collapsed Catholics, or that's what we thought she said and we only found out years later that she'd meant 'lapsed Catholics'.

Nancy's refusal to hand over his immortal soul to the Anglicans, Mike reckoned, started it all with Crocodile Brown and us. He said to take the hidings like a man, no use telling the sadist bastard that we'd been up since three in the morning, shovelling the shit out of his garbage can. He knew anyway and he'd done the exact same to him and Bozo. Instead, Mike said we'd have Bozo's Bitzers catch a couple of live rats on the tip and leave them in his garbage bin. Maloney payback.

'He'll know it's us and he'll report me to Mr Flint,' I say fearfully.

'No way!' Mike says. 'We'll leave the lid off so he can't positively prove the rats didn't get in on their own.'

'Rats'll jump out a bin,' Bozo points out.

'Not if we grease the bottom and inside,' Mike replies.

We did just that, left Crocodile Brown a couple of live-rat letters of warning not to mess with a Maloney. The next time we emptied his bin it had eight holes in the bottom where he'd blasted the rodents with a .22 rifle.

One of the kids who lived in his street said Mrs Crocodile Brown had gone out on the footpath to fetch the garbage bin and nearly dropped dead on the spot from a heart attack. She was last seen running screaming back into the house, pulling at her hair. Crocodile Brown must've buried the dead rats to stop them smelling because only the eight holes were there when we tipped his bin up next time around. But he must have got the message. While the thrashings didn't stop completely, they didn't happen as often and not for about a month afterwards, which gave my bum a bit of a rest.

I can safely say we were bloody weary most of the time, but it wasn't true about us being stupid. Sarah was dux of the school and had to refuse being made head prefect. That's because of what she had to do at home. She washed and ironed and cooked and cleaned and looked after Colleen, which left her no time to do the school job properly, because the head prefect had to have meetings and do other extra-curricular duties after school. It was her own decision to turn it down.

They made her vice-prefect anyway because she was better and more popular than Murray Templeton, whose father was the Holden dealer in town and so was only made head prefect by Sarah-default.

I admit Bozo's reports weren't always up to scratch but that didn't mean he was stupid. Nobody could call Bozo stupid, he just wasn't that interested in school work. Even as a thirteen-year-old he wasn't big, but he was wiry and bloody strong and could lift two garbage bins at once into the back of the truck if we were running late of a morning. He was also a self-taught mechanic and kept the Diamond T going after it should have long since conked out. He could fix anything mechanical and when the family was on the bones of our arses, Bozo could always be relied on to sell something he'd repaired.

We'd collect stuff people had thrown away, bits of bicycles, old hand-pushed lawnmowers, hot-water jugs, electric kettles, hedge clippers with the blades rusted, kids' scooters, prams with wheels missing, old deck chairs, primus stoves, hurricane lamps, Vacola Bottling Systems, anything that could be re-wired or scraped back, cleaned, repaired or painted. Bozo would do the fixing and I'd do the scraping and painting and we'd go halves when we sold it. Sometimes I'd have money jingling in my pocket, enough to toss my jam sandwiches in the bin and buy a Herbert Adams pie one day and a Four 'n' Twenty the next for school lunch for a whole week. I never could decide which tasted the best. Or I'd pay for the family to go to the pictures, though we generally ended up giving our profits to Nancy when a cash crisis hit, which was just about all the time.

Bozo even built two complete bicycles from scratch from parts collected over three years. All we needed was tyres, tubes and valves and half a dozen new spokes. Miraculously Tommy came good with one of his very rare wins with the local SP bookmaker and gave us the money. It was magic. Me and Bozo had our own bikes. But then shortly after, Tommy went up the hill again and the SP bookie came around to see Nancy. It turned out that the money Tommy had given us wasn't won on the horses after all, that he owed the SP ten quid, and where was it?

I suppose we could have argued that we weren't responsible for Tommy's gambling debts and the bookmaker would just have to wait until he came out of gaol. But that wasn't Nancy's way. 'When you do that, all you do is accumulate shame. Soon enough you're drowning in it and people don't trust your word any more. Better to do without, pay our way and keep our noses clean.'

'Yeah, yeah,' Mike would say afterwards, mimicking Nancy, 'it's not your father's fault, it's something that happened to him in the war.'

So after only three weeks of the luxury of riding to school and parking our bikes with the other kids in the shelter behind the boys' toilet, they were sold for eight pounds and Nancy found the other two quid somewhere and we paid the SP bookie in full.

The thing I couldn't understand was, except for the bike tyres that cost three quid, we never seemed to benefit from Tommy's life as a burglar. The Shamrock did, the SP bookie certainly did, but our family fortunes remained permanently at low tide. I mean, he couldn't have got nabbed *every* time he did a heist, could he? There must have been times when he'd fenced stuff and was suddenly flush with dough and we should've benefited, but I don't remember it ever happening in my time.

Mike and me never once failed a class and Mike always came top in art and music while I generally came in the top half, sometimes even close to the top of the class, and in biology and science I was never beat.

Considering we were half asleep all the time, it wasn't too bad really. Mike didn't play much sport, only when it was compulsory, but Bozo and me were good at footy and cricket and Sarah was captain of the girls' hockey and basketball teams and played for the state in the Australian Inter-Schools Hockey Tournament.

As we grew a bit older, our sporting endeavours saved us a lot of abuse. Nobody would pick on Bozo who was already the state amateur champion in his weight division and was going to represent Country Victoria in the National Police Boys Club Championships in Sydney later in the year. Big Jack said that his coach, Bobby 'Rock Fist' Devlin, the ex-Victorian welterweight contender, thought Bozo was a certainty for a gold medal. That he might even make it to the Olympic Games next year. But Nancy said not to count your chickens. It was kind of strange with Bozo being, like, Big Jack Donovan's favourite boy boxer and him being the son of a crim who, more often than not, was arrested by Sergeant Donovan and charged and placed under remand. But then life is strange, I suppose.

I'd better line us Maloneys up, because if you work it out, given his years as a prisoner of war in Borneo, Tommy Maloney couldn't be the daddy of all of us. Sarah was the eldest and was seventeen in 1955, born a year before the war was declared. Tommy, wanting to get away from the farm, decided to join the permanent army and was doing his training at Broadmeadows in Melbourne. She was shotgun number one, the result of a weekend leave pass. Nancy, who was doing her nurse's training at the time, said Sarah was definitely Tommy's daughter, because he was her first and it happened after the Women's Auxiliary Dance when Tommy offered to walk her back to Mrs Frost's boarding house. She laughs when she tells how they never got any further than the concealment of the bulrushes beside Lake Sambell.

Nancy's dad reckoned that with a bun in the oven growing bigger by the day her nursing career was over anyway, so he took Nancy back to their dairy farm at Allan's Flat to hide the family shame and to keep a sharper eye on his daughter in future. As it turned out, he proved to be a pretty lousy watchdog.

When Tommy was confronted with the prospect of fatherhood, he pointed out that he needed the permission of his company commander to marry and several weeks later reported that the big brass had put the kybosh on a young soldier marrying because he'd got some girl up the duff. Tommy even showed Nancy's old man his application for permission to marry with a rubber stamp over it that read 'Permission Refused'. The old bloke was too ignorant to know that these application forms with rubber stamp intact could be purchased for two bob on the sly in any military training establishment. But when war was declared in 1939 Tommy must have had a sudden softening of the heart, thinking that perhaps he might be killed without offspring, the Maloney name in Yankalillee extinguished forever (not necessarily a bad thing). He'd come to see Nancy on her parents' farm, begging her to give Sarah his name and promising that should he return from the war he would marry her. 'Wait for me, Nancy, our little daughter will be well looked after when I return.' It was about as close as he ever got to saying anything that might vaguely be taken as romantic.

However, Nancy wasn't very good at waiting. She thinks Mike, who is fourteen, was begat by an Italian who worked on her old man's dairy farm and who later, when Italy declared war on us, became a prisoner of war. The government said he could continue to work on the farm, only now he was an enemy alien. So Nancy couldn't be said to have been consorting with the enemy because Mike happened before his father was the enemy. Although, she's not absolutely dead certain about the Italian. 'There were dances and things,' she explains offhand, but then she'll add, 'It must have been the Eyetalian, Mike's the musical and artistic one with the dark hair, isn't he?'

Bozo's next, who at thirteen doesn't quite make the correct Tommy chronology either. Mum's certain he is the result of a red-hot fling with a Yank marine that lasted only four days but one she never forgot. She was in Sydney because of the death of her Auntie Molly. Her father had come down bad with rheumatic fever and her mum had to take care of him on the dairy farm as well as run the place and take care of Sarah and Mike, who was just eighteen months old, so Nancy was sent to Sydney by train to attend the funeral and pack up her auntie's stuff and put her cottage on the market.

This was in 1941 before the Americans were in the war, but it just so happened that the American cruiser *Portland* from the US Asiatic Fleet was in Circular Quay on a diplomatic visit and Nancy, along with just about every young girl in town, went down to the dockside to visit the ship. She must have been a pretty good-looking sort because the sailors and the marines on board could have picked anyone they wanted, but this marine sergeant in his full dress uniform took one look at Nancy and said, 'Hi ya, good lookin', what's cookin'?' and that was that.

Nancy took him by the arm and straight home to her dead auntie's cottage though they didn't do a lot of cooking but made love instead. He returned every day for the four days the cruiser was in town to do the same. His name was Sergeant Bozonik, although she is never quite sure of the exact spelling, possibly because the cruiser sailed away early on the fifth morning without leaving a forwarding address and without him saying goodbye. The only thing she knew about Sergeant Bozonik was that he'd been the welterweight champion of the US Asiatic Fleet and came from Idaho. But Nancy must have liked him a fair bit because she named Bozo after him even though he'd done the dirty on her.

But Nancy's not quite through yet. Although I'm a true Maloney, I'm not Tommy's son. It seems in 1943 Tommy's cousin visits from Darwin where he's been in the military hospital. Earlier, he's fought in New Guinea and was wounded and repatriated to Darwin where he spends four months in hospital and then is given home leave before rejoining his regiment. He visits his folk in Gippsland and maybe he gets bored or something because he decides to visit Mr Baloney. Well, he hears all about Tommy's daughter from them and decides to have a look for himself, see how Tommy's little girl is getting on, and finds Mike has mysteriously joined the Maloney clan and that Nancy's a pretty good sort and not married to Tommy.

Nancy explains it like this, 'Well, he was quite a decent sort of a bloke and he took me dancing and I suppose, having seen little Mike about, he reckoned he might be in with a bit of a chance.' Nancy laughs, 'It was all over with the Eyetalian, I couldn't fraternise with the enemy now, could I? With Tommy's cousin, Sean, I reckoned it was sort of, you know, keepin' things in the family and doing me bit for the war effort at the same time. Poor sod, wounded for King and country and in need of a bit of a cuddle and me alone again. So next thing it's Maloney number two on the way, same rotten blood, different bloke.'

I'm born in December 1943. So I'm the only boy in the family who's a true-blue Maloney, which is a bit of a disappointment really as Nancy says, Mike and Bozo have probably got the better blood. My real dad, Tommy's cousin, went back to his regiment and was killed in New Guinea in 1944 so there's no knowing how he would have turned out.

But Nancy says he was a Maloney and you wouldn't want to take any bets, there'd never been a good one yet, so why now.

Then, of course, little Colleen is born, she's six years younger than me and the reason there's this big gap is because the first three years Tommy came back from the war he was that crook nothing happened. Then he gets three years for robbery with possession of a firearm.

Him and Lenny Smith, a crim he'd met, were caught doing a warehouse which was storing those new electric jugs. They were all the rage at the time and everyone wanted one. Tommy, as I said before, never did houses, only industrial sites. 'You don't shit in yer own backyard,' he'd say. But I think that the real reason was Nancy, who would have beaten the crap out of him if he'd robbed someone whose garbage we collected.

But on this occasion with Lenny Smith, the police had been tipped off. With the cops closing in, Tommy's so-called real-good mate planted an old army service revolver he'd been carrying under his leather jacket in Tommy's burglar bag. Tommy said later that he didn't even know Lenny Smith was armed and the bloody thing turned out not even to be loaded. Himself, he never carried anything but a pinch bar and a few tools, glass-cutters, drills, hammer, hacksaw, all that sort of respectable and harmless burglar gear.

There was a night watchman present on the property, even though he was pissed and snoring his head off at the time and was later dismissed for incompetence, Tommy was charged with armed robbery. Oliver Twist gave him a year for breaking and entering and then added a second helping, two years extra for possession of a firearm. He served two years and three months and got nine months off for good behaviour because of a bushfire he'd played a big part in diverting. He came home and did the job on Nancy that got us little Colleen exactly nine months later, so she is the only legitimate Maloney in the entire collection of kids.

One thing I'll say for Nancy, she was quite open about us all, including Tommy. When people who didn't know, which wasn't very many, asked about her husband, she'd simply say, 'My husband's in prison for burglary.' If they expressed their sympathy, she'd reply, 'He's better off up on the hill than in the bloody pub,' and leave whoever asked with egg on their face.

'There's nothing to hide,' she'd say. 'Better the truth than always having to live with a lie. God Himself knows that the first four of you were born out of wedlock, it's His and my business and nobody else's.' She'd grin suddenly. 'Anyway, I reckon when I knock on the pearly gates He'll look the other way when He sees how good you lot all turned out. I only took Tommy in holy matrimony after he'd got fattened up a bit in the repat hospital in Heidelberg. I was broody at the time and we definitely did the deed right after he came back looking like a drover's dog, all prick and ribs.' She chuckled, suddenly remembering, 'It was like banging a bag of Bozo's dog bones, bloody good thing I'd developed a bit of upholstery in the meantime. Mole was still small when we were finally married by Father Dunstan seven years after Sarah was born. We christened Mole the selfsame day, killing two birds with one stone.' She gave Sarah one of her tender looks, 'I must say, darling, you made a lovely flower girl and I made you the prettiest pink dress.'

I remember we were all gathered around the old cane couch with its sagging cushions, Sarah was sitting on the one arm and Mike on the other, with Nancy filling up the remainder of the couch except for little Colleen who was squeezed in at the very end, her legs sticking out in front of her. The rest of us were sitting on the cement floor at Nancy's feet.

Sarah was working on a broderie anglaise coverlet and Mike was doing a garland of forget-me-nots on a christening robe, using bullion stitch, detached chain stitch and French knot. Mike was a champion embroiderer, much better than Nancy or Sarah, he could do rosebuds perfectly and rose leaves so you could see the little veins in the leaves. Under Nancy and Sarah's names he'd win the blue ribbon every year at the Wangaratta, Albury and Wodonga Shows. At the Royal Melbourne Show the previous year he'd entered a design for a Quaker-style baby's bonnet, bib, booties and a summer blanket which Nancy had made in natural-coloured linen and Mike had embroidered. Nancy called it 'Bush Blossoms for Bonnet, Bib, Booties and Blanket', with all the 'b's lined up like that. Clever, eh?

We'd gone out and collected all these little wildflowers and Mike created this garland which was scattered over the whole ensemble. It took a long time and he used just about all the stitches available. We Maloney kids knew the twelve embroidery stitches off by heart, even little Colleen. It was a rhyme Nancy taught us, you had to say it very fast without becoming tongue-tied. Nancy said her mother taught it to her and her mother before her until way back time out of mind.

Wicked witches wear pretty britches
Made from silk with fancy stitches
Bullion, back stitch, crafty fishbone
Scattered from the knee to hipbone
With knots colonial all tight tied
Enough to send you glassy-eyed
Back stitch, hem stitch, lazy daisy
Stitches meant to send you crazy
Stem stitch, straight, fluffy feather
All those stitches worked together
Cretan, pistil, chain for hitches
Stitches for wicked witches' britches.

It was sort of our own 'If Peter Piper picked a peck of pickled peppers', you know the one? If you work it out, there's all twelve common embroidery stitches in the rhyme. Anyway, Mike used them all and then some.

Nancy said his design probably wouldn't get anything because it wasn't traditional. You know, rosebuds and forget-me-nots in fairy gardens or Beatrix Potter bunnies in Farmer Brown's vegie patch and all that dumb shit. She said it was *the* Royal Melbourne Show after all, and the Queen, who was English, might get all snotty if we did something Australian for a change. But she did add that this was the first woman in charge of the throne since Queen Victoria and she probably knew a bit more about embroidery.

So, for insurance, Mike and Sarah did an 'England's Cottage Garden' summer bonnet in Egyptian cotton. Mike did the bullion-stitch roses, forget-me-nots and detached chain-stitch daisies and other cottage-garden flowers, all of which covered the top of the crown and stretched across the edge of the brim, and Sarah filled any remaining spaces with colonial knots and then she did the broderie anglaise that made up the remainder of the bonnet.

The Queen must have been in a good mood that year because Nancy was dead wrong. Mike got the blue ribbon in his section and also Best of Show for his 'Bush Blossoms for Bonnet, Bib, Booties and Blanket'. 'England's Cottage Garden' also won the baby-bonnet section.

Nancy said it was probably because the Queen was a young woman of twenty-seven when she'd come to Australia last year and she'd probably seen some of our beautiful bush flowers. Nancy didn't care much for the English, but she said they'd got it right this time, Queen Elizabeth was very popular in Australia and seemed like a nice person despite her religion. From the way she said it, I was convinced the Queen had given us the prize herself. Anyway, Nancy said it was the biggest thing that would happen in our lives and we were jolly well going to the presentation!

I can tell you, getting ready for the big day was quite a to do, we washed the Diamond T with disinfectant and polished it to within an inch of its life. Except it was never meant to be shiny because it was military paint, sort of green-brown with spots where the paint had worn off. It also had a fair few scratches, but it had never looked better since way back when Tommy first brought it home. We took blankets and cushions and put a mattress in the back for Nancy to sleep on at the showground. Bozo took his toolkit because the Diamond T hadn't travelled that far before, nor, for that matter, had us kids, except for Sarah, when she'd played hockey for Country Victoria Schools.

Anyway, we set out early, all high and hopeful, for Melbourne, Nancy driving with Sarah and Colleen in the front all squashed up and us on the mattress, comfortable as you can get, with Bozo's mutts, all of which had been dusted up with flea powder. I tell you what, we were that excited and proud. Nancy said it was a pity Tommy was on the hill and couldn't come with us. But I know we didn't agree with her, though of course we wouldn't have said so.

The Diamond T wasn't all that used to getting out of second gear and the hundred and thirty miles to Melbourne was going to take all day. About halfway, near Seymour, it started to rain and soon it was pissing down and the mattress got soaked through. We pushed the blankets and cushions under it and they only got a bit wet then dried out in the wind later. 'There goes Nancy's sleep,' Mike says. 'We didn't take the spoon out the sink.'

'What do you mean?' I protest. 'We couldn't help that it rained!'

'Canvas, we should have wrapped it in the back-verandah canvas, Nancy's going to be cranky as hell.'

'At least the rain will wipe the squashed grasshoppers from the windshield,' Bozo says. 'The radiator's probably half blocked with the blighters.' After it stopped raining, he banged on the roof and Nancy drew to a halt and Bozo was dead right, the radiator was almost clogged with dead grasshoppers. That's what I mean about Bozo, maybe we didn't get it right with the mattress but the Diamond T was his personal responsibility and he'd taken the spoon out of the sink. The Diamond T could easily have overheated and then God knows when we'd have gotten to Melbourne, if ever.

The Diamond T held up after that and we came into Melbourne just as the lights were coming on. We couldn't believe it, stretching as far as the eye could see were lights dancing like a million fireflies in the dark. We'd dried out a bit in the meantime and fortunately the big old army duffle bag we'd packed our posh clothes into for the presentation had kept them dry. Bozo wasn't all that happy about the duffle bag being used for our clothes. He'd filled it with river sand and it hung from the back verandah as his punching bag. We had to empty all the sand out so we could use it for the trip.

'What if the Queen gives us the prize, wants to hand it to Nancy personally?' I say, as we're coming in to the showground.

'Better not, if Nancy has to curtsy she'll fall on her arse,' Mike laughs.

Bozo shakes his head, 'Don't think she'd do it.'

'Do what?' I ask.

'Bow and scrape to the Queen,' Bozo replies.

'More than that, she's also head of the Church of England,' Mike says. 'We've got the Pope and they've got the Queen.'

'Nancy has to, it's the law,' I protest. 'She's the Queen of England *and* Australia, they told us in school, she's higher up even than Bob Menzies.'

'Still and all, I don't like her chances, Nancy's pretty stubborn,' Bozo counters.

Mike cuts the argument short, 'Queen's not even in the country, so I wouldn't worry too much, maybe she'll come year after next for the Olympic Games and stay over for the show.'

'What do you mean, not here? Nancy said the Queen likes bush blossoms because of what she'd seen before?'

'That's just Nancy, because it's called The Royal Melbourne Show,' Mike replies. He seemed to be thinking. 'Still an' all, it would've been nice to get the prize from the Queen. Her handing it to Nancy.'

We couldn't believe our ears. Bozo was the first to recover. 'Jesus, what do you mean? The Queen's a Protestant *and* she's English and head of their church, you said!'

'Yeah, I know, it's not that, it's all the hoity-toity people in Yankalillee, they'd eat their livers.' He spread his hands, like he was reading a newspaper, 'I can see the *Gazette*, in these big black letters on the front page, there it would be for all to see: MRS NANCY MALONEY MEETS THE QUEEN! They'd puke with envy. Imagine Mrs Yerberry in her fox stole hearing the news, she'd have a conniption, maybe drop dead on the spot!'

'Conniption' was a Nancy word and it meant something like 'they'd almost shat their pants they'd be so angry', only it's in polite language. We laughed at the image Mike had portrayed. It sure would be nice to bring all the town's snooty-nosed bastards to heel for once, make them see they weren't the only ones who could do things around the place.

Mike wasn't like the other blokes his age and he could make you laugh about things you never thought about before. Nancy said it was because 'he was of a sensitive nature'. Stuck on the wall beside his bunk he had these pictures he'd torn out of magazines like *The Women's Weekly*. They were of dresses. Not like, you know, horny pictures, just dresses. Sometimes, if he didn't like a hat, he'd cut the heads off. Often he would have drawn over some of them with a pencil, like he'd make the skirt narrower or change the neck or collar, or put a belt on the waist or take up the hem. 'It's a fashion statement,' he'd say if you asked.

When I asked Bozo what he thought of them, he said he'd already had a close look. 'Isn't one worth wanking over,' he declared, dismissing the lot.

'One day Mike will be famous,' Sarah said. After we came back from the trip, Mike designed the dress Sarah wore at the end-of-year school social which was held a few weeks later, at the end of the month. Although Sarah was in the fifth form, she had already been told she would be head prefect for her matriculation year and had turned it down.

Nancy had got the material sent from Myers in Melbourne and it was silk shantung and 'cost a fortune'. It was a sort of shiny, smoky peacock-blue but when she moved in it, there was this green colour like a budgie's breast, not shiny like a mirror, a sort of a soft, rich shine Nancy called 'subtle'. Sarah looked very beautiful even though she didn't have a date.

Mike said it was because she was a Catholic and all the blokes were Protestant and their parents would drop dead at the thought of their precious son going to the school social with a Mick.

But Sarah said it was because they were all creeps and she wouldn't be seen dead with any of them, not even Murray Templeton, who was going to be head prefect, and was already the captain of the footy team and a bit of a hero all round, even to me.

This was also the year Sarah should have gone to the debutante ball but she told Nancy she didn't want to go, even though Nancy said we'd find the money somehow. So the posh dress was sort of Nancy's way and Mike's way to make up for her not being a debutante, which secretly we knew she'd have liked to have been.

Nancy burst into tears when Sarah came out of the bedroom on the night of the school social. The skirt of Mike's dress was splayed out like an inverted tulip and ended just above her knees. A broad belt, made of the same shantung material, like a solid band, clipped at the back with press-studs, clasped her tiny waist and then the top of the dress was off her shoulders so that her long neck and smooth shoulders sort of grew out of the dress. '*Très èlègant*!' Mike said, clapping his hands together. He sometimes said weird things like that.

Sarah had on these white shoes she'd been saving up for, with high heels. She was wearing lipstick and her hair fell down past her shoulders and shone so you almost had to squint to see it properly. I have to say, even though I probably wasn't much of an authority on girls' looks at ten, nearly eleven, Sarah looked beautiful to me. Bozo, who had recently turned twelve, said the same.

Nancy saw us to the front gate, still wiping her eyes and smiling her big smile at the same time. We boys then walked with Sarah to the Town Hall. It was funny seeing Sarah walk in her new shoes. She was wobbling a bit, teetering, like she was about to fall over any second.

After about a hundred yards, she sighed and took her shoes off and only put them on again when we'd practically reached the Town Hall. All the way Mike kept pulling at the dress and doing stuff to it, until Sarah told him to stop fussing, that someone might be looking. He stopped then, but you could see he was pleased with what he'd done, and no wonder. We left our sister outside the Town Hall and you could hear her dress rustle when she climbed the steps and turned to wave goodbye to us. Then she said to Mike, 'Thank you for my lovely dress,' but not so loud that anyone could hear and Mike was so proud he nearly burst wide open. '*Enchanté*!' he said.

But then a nice thing happened at the dance. Murray Templeton, who could have had any girl in the school because they were all falling over him, didn't come with a partner either. So everything was all right in the end, head prefect and vice-prefect for the next year sort of being together but not being together so tongues could wag, if you know what I mean?

As it was a Saturday with a sleep-in Sunday, we all stayed up to see Sarah come home. She wouldn't allow us to go and fetch her and said she was quite capable of walking home on her own. Sarah didn't want us hanging around the Town Hall steps at midnight so that people would think she needed to be protected or anything.

Anyway, then came the big surprise. Sarah arrived home in a brand-new yellow Holden, it was a colour Murray's dad had specially sprayed for his dealership so it would be different from the other Holdens around. Nancy started to bawl again. 'The Princess has arrived home in a pumpkin carriage,' she sobbed.

The Yerberrys' shit-coloured Packard was the best car in town but the Templetons' Holden was the one most of us noticed because of its bright pumpkin colour. Murray, the football captain and all-time hero, had brought Sarah home. He was eighteen so already had his driver's licence. They didn't kiss or anything, he came around to her door and opened it and then said goodbye and she said goodbye to him, shaking his hand and holding her new shoes in her left hand. After he drove off, we came rushing out of the house to welcome her home. Sarah looked happy and the lipstick was off her mouth.

That was a big month for us Maloneys with the Melbourne Show also in September. I guess these days everyone's been to the show so knows what it's like. But we'd never seen anything like it. We were country kids so we knew about animals and stuff and that part wasn't all that different to the agricultural show at Wang, only more of the same. They had about a thousand types of chicken in the poultry section, some even had feathers sticking out their legs and these plumes from their heads. Weird-looking buggers. Did you know chickens came from China?

Nancy must have saved real hard, because she bought us each a show bag and we spent money like water, going on the Big Dipper and Bozo won a pink kewpie doll with a ballerina skirt for Colleen by knocking down three sets of skittles with three balls. Later we went into the boxing tent, that is, Mike, Sarah, Bozo and me.

There is this skinny-looking Aboriginal guy who challenges all comers within twenty pounds of his own weight. Bozo says he'll have a go and Mike says not to and Sarah gets mad and says she'll tell Nancy and then she leaves the tent. But Bozo is pretty stubborn and he steps up to the scales and is three pounds heavier than the Abo. The promoter asks him how old he is and Bozo fibs and says sixteen.

Some of the old blokes in the tent, who are full of hops, are shouting encouragement, saying, 'Give the kid a go, yer mug!' and things like that, waving one-pound notes. 'A quid on the kid, what odds?' and everyone laughs except Bozo and me and the bloke in charge. So with all the pressure, the bloke in charge, who had this thin pencil moustache and greasy curly hair like some wog, finally says to Bozo, 'Are you sure you're sixteen?'

'Ask my brother,' Bozo says, turning to me.

The bloke doesn't ask me, but I nod, so it is only half a lie. 'Righto, put the gloves on,' the promoter says. 'Three rounds or a k.o.! I have the right to stop the fight at any time, referee's decision is final!'

'Yeah,' someone yells, 'if the Abo's gettin' beat and you're the ref, the other bloke goes t.k.o.?'

But the wog, who isn't a wog because he speaks proper Australian, ignores him and holds up a five-pound note and winks at the Aboriginal boxer. 'Winner takes all!' he shouts.

Well, I suppose it was a good example of not taking the spoon out of the sink and Bozo lasts one round and is no match for the black guy. After the first round Bozo's nose is bleeding, though only a trickle, and you could see the Aboriginal boxer is toying with him and could have hit Bozo any time he wanted to.

When the bell for the second round comes, the Abo guy stands up, waving his gloves to show the fight is over. Then he walks over and raises Bozo's hand and declares him the winner. The greasy bloke with the moustache doesn't look too happy about it, but the crowd is on our side and so he has to give Bozo the five quid and we are suddenly rich. All the onlookers cheer and throw coins into the ring, so I reckon they must have nearly got their money back.

Later, when we were feeding our faces on these hot dogs on sticks, Bozo says to me, 'After the first round I knew I was gunna get a thumping, Mole.' Then he looks at me, and there is tomato sauce all over his mouth. 'I'm never going to say nothing bad about the Abos again.'

Bozo's fight worked out for Nancy as well, though at first I thought we were in the shit. We were in the back of the Diamond T later that night, trying to sleep with the mattress taken out and leaned against the side of the truck to dry. Colleen and Sarah were in the back with us boys, and little Colleen was sleeping on the pillows. We'd spread the blankets on the deck of the truck because it wasn't really cold. Nancy was up front trying to kip sitting upright in the cabin when this bloke comes up and talks to her and we hear him say, 'Saw the young bloke having a go in the boxing tent.'

'Shit, we're in for it,' I whisper to Bozo. I know Mike or Sarah wouldn't have dobbed us in to Nancy.

'Boxing tent? What's this?' Nancy says.

'Oh, sorry,' says the bloke, realising he'd made a mistake. 'It's nothing, madam.'

'Bozo, come here!' Nancy commands, sticking her head out the cabin window.

'What?' says Bozo, sounding all innocent, but knowing he is in trouble.

'What's this about the boxing tent?'

'We was in it,' Bozo mumbles.

'And?'

'Look, madam, I'm sorry,' the bloke says, all apologetic. Then, 'The kid's got guts.'

Nancy ignores him, 'I'm waiting, Bozo?'

'I had a go, Mum,' Bozo says, real soft.

'It's my fault, madam. I've gone and dobbed the lad in.' He turns to look at Bozo. 'I'm sorry, son.' Then he has this good idea. 'You sleeping rough, I see. None of my business but . . .'

'No, it ain't!' Nancy says, cutting him off.

But the bloke keeps on, 'Look, there's the hay room back of the stables,' he says quickly. Then he looks up at the sky. 'Rain's forecast, I've got the key, how about you all bed down there? Let you have a bit of canvas to put over the hay so it don't prickle.'

He says it so nicely that Nancy knows he's a good bloke and means no harm. You can see he's from the bush like us.

Nancy turns back to Bozo. 'You'll keep,' she says, then thanks the bloke and sticks her hand out the window.

'Adams, Johnny Adams, Merrindale Stud, Gilgandra.'

'Nancy Maloney, Yankalillee, pleased t'meetcha, Mr Adams.'

'Johnny,' he corrects, smiling, 'no point being formal then, is there? We'd invite you to share our trailer, but we've got a new baby, see, gets the colic bad, could keep you awake all night.'

Bingo! Somebody's going to get a christening robe.

So we spend the night in the hay shed, comfy as you like, with the hay for a mattress. Johnny Adams was right, it did rain that night, came down in buckets, we'd have been pretty miserable, but for him.

Next morning Sarah and Mike persuade Nancy that Bozo

shouldn't be punished as his boxing had got us out of the rain and all he'd suffered was a bit of a nose bleed.

'I don't know what's to become of that boy,' Nancy says, tut-tutting, before agreeing reluctantly to let Bozo off the hook. But we know she doesn't mean it. Bozo is loved by her just the same as all of us and she was dead proud whenever Big Jack Donovan stopped by to tell her Bozo was going great at boxing.

Then Bozo hands Nancy three pounds and ten shillings, which is what's left of his winnings, and says he's sorry and all is forgiven.

We take the morning looking around and spending Bozo's money. Then that arvo we've got the presentation, it's not the Queen, only the Lady Mayoress of Melbourne. Still and all, we have on our best clothes and Sarah wore this dress Mike tie-dyed and remade from an old one. Nancy had the usual daisies-on-a-yellow-background but she wore a big hat and these white gloves Sarah had crocheted and Mike had embroidered with a sprig of bush blossom to keep the theme going. So they both looked great standing up there on the stage with the flash bulbs going off *pop, pop, pop* and people clapping.

Nancy and Sarah got their names in the women's section of *The Weekly Times* with a black and white picture of the two blue ribbons arranged over 'Bush Blossoms'. The Melbourne *Sun* also gave them a mention and the *Border Mail* had a black and white picture, but they got it wrong and showed Sarah and Mike's 'England's Cottage Garden' by mistake. Toby Forbes gave the win a big spread in *The Owens & Murray Gazette*.

BUSH BLOSSOMS
BELTS ALL BONNETS,
BIBS, BOOTIES & BLANKETS
BEST OF THE BEST!
ROYAL MELBOURNE SHOW

Nancy said Toby Forbes was being a smart-arse and, anyway, why wasn't our name in the headline. But it seemed pretty damned good to me, our big win in black letters that took up half of the front page of the *Gazette*. I tore it out and sticky-taped it to the wall next to my bunk.

Some of the teachers at school came up to me in the playground the week after and said we should be really proud. For about five minutes the Maloneys were famous in Yankalillee and I reckon we stuck it up a few people even without the Queen. Showed them they weren't the only ones who could do good things.

Mike was a boy wonder at embroidery but couldn't ever share in the glory. We had all his blue ribbons pinned onto the picture rail in the front room. Of course, he'd probably have killed us if we'd told anyone at school. But we knew it was just something he did to help Nancy and because he was the artistic one in the family. Sarah said we must never speak about it, that it was a Maloney thing to help each other and that people wouldn't understand.

Nancy could do all of this stuff real well herself, of course. It was her who taught Mike and Sarah in the first place. Because they were so good, they'd do the special pieces and Nancy would concentrate on the smocking. Altogether it was a pretty good team and I doubt if there was anyone in our part of Victoria who could take us on at embroidering.

It was one of those days when Nancy was in a mood to talk and so she continued with the saga of our family.

'After we were married I stayed faithful, no more hanky-panky. I took the vows before God and there's been no one else since, except for Tommy.' She looked at us and gave a small shrug as if to apologise for her error in judgement, 'I couldn't leave the poor miserable bugger after all he'd been through in the war. Besides, his heart's in the right place, there's not too many blokes who would have gone away on a promise to make his pregnant sweetheart respectable when he returned and then found that, in his absence, his obligations had increased to four. You've got to hand it to Tommy, he done the right thing.' She laughed, a big open sort of guffaw, 'Mind you, I must say he hasn't taken his subsequent obligations too seriously. But it must have come as a bit of a shock to the system coming home near dead from three years of starvation as a prisoner of war to find out I'd popped out three babies he hadn't had a hand in and didn't even know about.'

She smiled again, this time real sweet. 'Come here, all of you. Give your old mum a hug then. You're all mine from the selfsame womb and I wouldn't want it any different. A wog, a Septic Tank and three fifth-generation Aussies whose ancestors came here from Ireland as convicts and whose father seems determined to keep up the family tradition.'

We took turns giving her a hug and then Nancy patted her great belly. 'All of them blokes were needed to make you lot, the mighty Maloneys, and I thank God he gave you to me because if it had been left to Father Crosby, Lord knows where you would have been.'

'Why's that?' Bozo asks.

'It's why we are collapsed Catholics,' Nancy said. 'With each of you, soon as it was known I was pregnant, Father Crosby came around. "Now Nancy," he'd say, "you'll be wanting those taken care of, we've a nice place you can go to have your baby where the nuns will take good care of you and, then, when the wee mite is born, we'll have it adopted by a good Catholic family. There's plenty of good deserving couples the Lord has not seen fit to bless who'll take a healthy child. It's the best thing to do all round, my girl."' Nancy's got his voice down pat, only her voice is a bit deeper than Father Crosby's.

'My God!' Mike says, slapping his palm against his forehead. 'I could have been adopted into a rich family and slept in every morning of my life!'

We all laugh, Mike's a real card when he wants to be.

'I was having none of that,' Nancy said. 'I wanted each one of you, but the Church wouldn't leave me alone. They put pressure on my parents and said I could even have been excommunicated if I didn't do it their way. But I knew that was crap. I decided then and there the Church, not my faith, that's different, but the Church had no room for me and my children. "Where does it say in the Bible that Adam and Eve were married?" I asked Father Crosby.'

'"To be sure, Nancy O'Shane, Eve was made from Adam's rib, there was no hanky-panky going on there now." Then he said, "A rib isn't fornication outside of wedlock."

'"A rib, is that what they called a man's percy in those days, Father?" I said to him.

'"That's blasphemy, and you'll be punished for that, Nancy O'Shane, God is not mocked!" and he sweeps up the edge of his soutane and storms off. "You'd better come to confession," he shouts out.'

'Weren't you frightened, Mum?' Sarah asks.

'Scared out of my wits, but I wasn't going to give you up, darling. Then, after you were born and I wasn't struck by lightning nor got leprosy, it was easier to resist the pressure when your brothers came into the world under similar circumstances.'

'Is that why you didn't send us to the convent?' Sarah asks.

'It was well known that you were all born out of wedlock and I didn't want the nuns to get at you. They would have, to be sure, and they can be cruel as witches.' Nancy smiles, 'What a lovely bunch of Maloneys you all turned out to be.'

'But technically we're not all Maloneys,' Mike points out. 'Bozo and me, we're not.'

'Might as well all be called Maloney, eh?' Nancy says. 'It's a damn sight better than Vincentio Tomasetti or Audry Bozonik, even if the present and rightful owner of the Maloney name isn't this town's most upstanding citizen. Though we mustn't forget he fought and suffered for his country.'

So there we were back to Tommy's mysterious war. We'd heard Nancy say he'd come back like a drover's dog all prick and ribs and words like 'after all he'd been through' and 'near dead after three years of starvation' but we still knew nothing except that he'd been a prisoner of war under the Japanese in Borneo.

When on occasions we tried to push her further on the subject, she'd say, 'It's not all his fault. Your father's the way he is because of what happened to him in the war,' and then she'd say no more. Sometimes you'd see her eyes close as if she was about to weep or was trying to understand herself what had happened to the nice young bloke who'd gone laughing off to Singapore, promising to return and take care of her and whatever the bun in the oven turned out to be. Then she'd sniff and say quietly, 'It's not something he can talk about.' It was as if there was some other man, a sweet ghost lurking in the background somewhere, who had been replaced by Tommy Maloney, small-time crook, alcoholic, chronically unlucky punter, loner, loser, bushman and a grand fighter of bushfires.

It was in this last couple of respects that Tommy seemed the greatest contradiction, he loved the bush and when he was out of gaol he'd spend days away from home simply wandering about in the eucalyptus trees that covered the deep valleys and the surface of the hills leading up to the Snowy Mountains. It must have been sheer hell for him to be locked up at night in a prison cell up the hill.

We'd come home from school and know almost immediately that things were different, the air was lighter somehow, or something weird like that. 'Tommy's gone bush,' Nancy would announce, then she'd give this sad little smile. 'Good thing, too, get him out of the pub for a spell, eh?'

Having Tommy around the place when he came down from the hill, which was the expression used when he came out of gaol, wasn't easy. It meant Sarah and Colleen had to move out of Nancy's bedroom into ours and we boys had to move onto the back verandah.

In the summer this was okay, even quite good, there'd be a bit of a breeze blowing on hot nights. But it was shit in the winter when we'd rig a piece of canvas from the roofline that dropped to the cement floor and which we held down with bricks to make a sort of outside wall to keep out the wind.

It was colder than charity out there on the back verandah with the wind buffeting the canvas wall and wailing along the roofline. Once there were drifts of snow piled up against the outside of the canvas. It may seem a bit far-fetched in these affluent times, but there were never enough blankets, so Mike and Bozo slept with two of the dogs each and I had the woolliest one, Bitzer Four, a mainly Scottish Terrier–Cocker Spaniel combination. I reckon a dog in the bed is worth three blankets any time.

But then we'd wake up one morning or, as I said, come home from school, and Tommy would be gone. Halle-bloody-lu-yah! We'd move back and things would be normal again!

'Your father has to have the bush. It's for his nerves,' Nancy would say, forgiving him for the utter bastard he'd been the couple of weeks before he'd gone AWL, coming home drunk most days and behaving badly.

Not that coming home drunk was a sin. In Bell Street it was an everyday occurrence and every family accepted it as normal. Half an hour after the six o'clock swill when the men would stumble home from the pub, the trouble would start in our street. Not just Bell Street, you'd see kids in school with stinkers or split lips and bruises over their bodies. Like the kids in our street, they were too ashamed to talk about it. If a teacher asked them about it, they would say what their mothers told them to say, that they'd walked into a doorknob. There were doorknobs in Yankalillee to fit every-sized child in the school.

Though I've got to say this for Tommy, he wasn't violent like some of the fathers in our street. There was one case when I was six when a bloke in our street came home drunk and twisted his wife's neck right around so that their kids found her in the morning seated at the kitchen table, staring out the window, a bowl of peas she'd been shelling still on the table in front of her, only she was dead with her head turned the wrong way around. The police went into the bedroom to arrest her old man and found him lying across the bed, fully dressed, one shoe missing and his big toe sticking out of a hole in his sock, snoring his head off. When Big Jack Donovan questioned him he had no recollection of what he'd done. He got ten years for manslaughter. Nancy said they should've locked him up and thrown away the key. But most people thought it was a fair whack, seeing he was drunk and all and not responsible for his actions.

A man has the right to drink, nobody's disputing that, but he doesn't have the right to beat the living daylights out of his wife and kids when he gets home, that's not on. But unfortunately it was what happened in Bell Street far too often and the next day their wives, wearing a black eye or a split lip or broken nose, would make the standard excuse, 'He's a good bloke really, it's only that he can't handle his grog.'

When we were little and Tommy came home with a skinful, he'd hit out at us. I don't mean he beat us up deliberately, Tommy wasn't like that. But when he was drunk, he'd lash out if he got annoyed with one of us and you'd fair cop a backhand that would sometimes land you on your arse.

When this happened and Nancy heard us bawling, she'd come steaming in. 'Bugger off, you bastard, get out!' she'd scream. 'You touch one of my kids again and I'll kill you, you hear?' Tommy would try and say something back, but the words would come out wet and slurred, his lips all sloppy and not able to grab a hold of the words, which seemed to slide over his bottom lip to the floor.

There was never any question of Tommy beating up his wife. Nancy would've slaughtered him with one arm tied behind her back. But when he'd had a go at one of us kids, later she'd be the one to apologise to us on his behalf, 'Your father isn't really like that, it's what happened in the war that's done this to him.'

'Yeah, fucking war's been over ten years,' Mike would say when we were away from Nancy's presence.

But at the time I'm talking about we were big enough to fend for ourselves. That is, with the exception of Colleen and, even drunk, Tommy wouldn't have been game to put a hand on her. Mike wasn't much of a fighter but Bozo, the Boy Boxer, would see that Tommy stayed in line. As well, Sarah would have flattened him, no risk. If she had her dander up, watch out, mate!

It was like Tommy had this thing in him that would build and build. Nancy called it 'his demons'. He'd yell at us for nothing, his mouth spit-flecked and his blue eyes bulging. Sometimes, not even drunk, he'd smash his fist into the wall and once he rammed his head right through the screen door of the kitchen. Afterwards we laughed about it because it looked very funny.

'Good thing it was only the screen door and not a bucket of shit his head was stuck in,' Bozo said, reminding us of poor Fred Bellows.

'His head's already drowning in shit,' Mike quipped back.

But mostly it was no laughing matter. This would go on for a few days and little Colleen would cry a lot. Then Tommy would have to get away, disappear, go bush, sometimes for a month at a time, thank goodness.

Tommy would come back from the bush scratched about and looking a bit of a wreck, even more so than usual. But the funny thing was, some of the trouble would be gone out of his eyes, they'd be clear and his skin brown as a gumnut. In the wintertime he must have done it tough. Though his clothes were usually torn, he was never dirty and they would always have been washed before he fronted home again. He'd have grown a beard, ginger speckled with grey, which he shaved off first thing and he wouldn't touch the grog sometimes for a fortnight.

To be completely fair, there was a definite up-side as well as a down-side to having Tommy home. The big advantage was that we boys could go on a roster. With him doing garbage duty, Monday to Friday, each of us got to have a sleep-in three out of every nine working days. We called it working a three-in-nine and, I tell you what, it made a heap of difference. We happily copped a fair amount of crap from him just for that luxury alone. Hail or shine, hungover or still half-pissed, Tommy never shirked garbage duty and he did more than his fair share on the job too. Nancy said, 'Deep down his character is still there.'

'How deep have you got to dig?' Mike mumbled under his breath. Nancy could say anything about Tommy, but we had to be careful in front of her.

So there it was again, Tommy's war with no answers. It had obviously screwed him up real bad but there was no getting at the details. There was one other bloke in town who'd been a prisoner under the Japs building the Burma Railway. Allan Gee, who had a soldier's settlement farm about three miles out of town at Wooragee where our grandpa used to live. Mr Gee was on Legacy. Legacy was for kids whose dads had died in the war or later on from war wounds. I can't say whether he had 'the demons' like Tommy. He was a pretty popular sort of bloke and seldom drank and was half-blind from starving as a prisoner. Usually if a bloke didn't drink, he'd earn the scorn of just about everyone and be called a 'bloody wowser' or a 'sheila', but it didn't happen in his case. Most of the battlers knew he was a good bloke and respected him for what he'd been through.

His son, Bruce, who was in Bozo's class at school, knew a whole heap about what had happened to him. There was even a movie made later, I think it was in 1957, *The Bridge Over The River Kwai* starring Alec Guinness, which we all went to see at the pictures, expecting to see someone playing the part of Allan Gee. Which was a bit stupid, I suppose.

We thought maybe what had happened to Allan Gee was the same as what had happened to Tommy and if, like him, it could all be discussed in the open, our father might come good and be different in future.

But when we talked this theory over with Nancy, she said maybe we were right but 'Your father wasn't with Allan Gee, who was a sailor and on the HMAS *Perth* when it sank in 1942. Tommy was infantry defending Singapore and then when the Japs took it he was put in Changi and from there he was,' she paused a fraction of a second, 'taken somewhere else.' The way she said that '*taken somewhere else*' and then clammed up again, somehow made things worse. Like there was something more to be ashamed of in the Maloney family, which she didn't want us kids to know about.

The only thing we could take pride in with Tommy was bushfires. Like our grandfather and his father before him, he could read a bushfire better than most people could read a book. My great-grandfather was the first to be known as 'The Maloney Factor', meaning that his presence on the scene of a bushfire could make a big difference to its outcome. By the next generation this expression had simply become a way to describe a bushfire fighter who was the best in the fire brigade and had been modified to 'the real maloney'. He's the real maloney, people would say, not even using it as a surname any more and even forgetting where the expression originally came from. Tommy was the real maloney for the Owens Valley Bushfire Brigade.

Nancy said it was our only real family tradition, except, of course, for Maloneys always trotting off to every war on offer, but lots of families did that. I must say, if you were looking around for something to be proud about, bushfires wasn't exactly a big deal. Though, I suppose it was something to be a little bit proud of.

There must have been a time when the first Maloney came out as a convict from a lush-green, rain-sodden Ireland and knew nothing about the Australian bush or the highly combustible nature of eucalyptus trees. But for at least four generations our family has had the gift of calling a fire to a halt.

The first week of December 1955 when Sarah sat for most of her examinations was also the month of my twelfth birthday. Then in the same week Sarah did her matriculation, Tommy was released from gaol.

Sarah worked every moment she could and we had high hopes for her. She was going to apply for a place in Medicine at Melbourne

University and had also put in for a Commonwealth Scholarship. The Education Department said that if she got the same marks as she got in her matriculation trials she'd definitely get one.

Tommy said Sarah wanting to be a doctor was bloody ridiculous. He pointed out that most of his mates' children had left school when they'd turned fourteen. 'Kids have to go out and earn money and help the family,' he said. 'No bloody use feeding them to go to university!'

Nancy got really cranky with him, 'You've been saying that since she was a nipper! She's always wanted to be a doctor. It's bloody high time things changed in the bush and, besides, maybe she'll practise in Sydney or Melbourne, where being a woman doctor isn't thought of as a crime against humanity!'

'She won't bloody get in, they'll naturally give all the places to blokes.' Tommy didn't usually get involved but he seemed pretty het up about Sarah wanting to go to university, let alone be a doctor.

'Then I'll become a journalist,' Sarah shouted from where she was studying at the kitchen table. 'The *Age* has cadetships and I'm applying for that as well!'

Tommy even had something to say about that. 'Yeah, writing up tea parties about the Toorak matrons. Journalist, huh? That's just about as bad as a woman doctor, only less pay.'

'That's enough, Tommy!' Nancy warned, 'You've had your say, now leave the girl alone.'

'That girl's getting much too big for her boots, I hear she's going out with Phil Templeton's boy, who does she think she is?'

It was true, after the social, Murray Templeton started walking Sarah home from school every day and they'd hang around the gate for an hour talking. 'That boy's beginning to hang around like a bad smell,' Nancy said after a while. 'You've got things to do and then there's your study. I don't want him walking you home, you hear? He seems a nice boy, that I'll admit, but the Templetons are not for the likes of us and it won't work.'

Sarah got pretty upset and she and Nancy didn't talk for three days and the both of them were in a real shitty mood. With all of us walking on eggshells, Mike tried to work out a deal with Nancy.

'Mum, you were only seventeen when you had Sarah and you were going out with a soldier,' Mike reminded her.

'Times were different then, most girls were married by the time they were sixteen.'

But Mike kept at her. He could talk Nancy into just about anything. When we'd ask Nancy if we could do something and she'd refuse, I'd complain, 'But you always let Mike do what he wants!'

'That's because he has a good head on his shoulders,' Nancy would reply.

'So what's so wrong with my head?' I'd ask.

'It lacks maturity, still soft.'

'And Bozo?'

She'd laugh, 'Him, too.'

So Mike's good head negotiated Sarah's plight. In return for Murray Templeton not walking Sarah back from school, they could go out to the pictures, which finished Saturday night at half-past ten. Sarah had to be home by a quarter to eleven so there could be no driving out to the lake after. It was Saturday night out with her boyfriend, or if he was playing in a footy game, she could go to it with him. One or the other, not both on the same day. It was this either–or scheme that finally won Nancy over. Mike said later that it allowed her to back down gracefully and still seem to have some control, because deep down she knew Sarah was tougher and more stubborn than her.

Of course, I knew Murray Templeton was a Proddy but I'd gained a fair bit of kudos at school because he was taking Sarah out. Kids would say they saw him and Sarah at the flicks Saturday night or in the Holden, or they'd seen them together at the footy. Philip Templeton, his dad, would use a car off his used-car lot if he was going out of a Saturday night and give his son Nancy's pumpkin carriage. That's how much he trusted him.

The summer was the hottest it had been for several years and the bushfire danger was way up past the high-alert stage. When the north winds blew, gusting up through the valley, people would say, 'Very bad for fires', looking up at the burning sky.

The eucalyptus underbrush was bone-dry and heaped high after three years of good rains and then a drought the following year. People in the pub, looking over the frothy top of a schooner, would say darkly, 'Bloody shire council's not done near enough clearing or burning off.

Firebreaks up near the gorge have all but disappeared, gorn, mate, grown over. It's a bloody disgrace.' But you could bet London to a brick not one of those lazy bastards would volunteer to get off his arse, borrow a tractor and make up a work gang to clear firebreaks or maybe do a bit of back-burning to help the CFA. 'Too bloody hot, mate, whose shout?' The conditions in mid-December 1955, taken along with the town's in-born lassitude, had all the ingredients for a major disaster.

Anyway, with Tommy just back, Nancy as usual tried to keep him off the grog, hoping he'd stay on the straight and narrow at least until Christmas. To her delight, he was still sober when my birthday arrived.

We didn't go in much for birthday presents in our family, except for Nancy and Colleen, when we all put in for a combined gift. Usually a box of Cadbury's Roses chocolates and a nice card for Mum and a bright ribbon and socks for little Colleen. Ah, yes, and once a pair of tiny, shiny red shoes with silver buckles. You should have seen the little kid, she went half-crazy with excitement.

I remember my birthday fell on a Saturday, a sleep-in day. Hooray! A grand sleep-in on top of the fact that, what with Tommy home, we were working a three-in-nine. That was birthday present enough for Mole Maloney, thank you very much, put down your glasses.

It was still dark when I was rudely shaken awake in my bunk. 'Hey, Mole, wake up!' It was Tommy's voice.

I sat up fast, but then realised I couldn't smell any drink on his breath, so relaxed again, falling back into the bare mattress.

'Wha . . . what's the time?' I mumbled, rubbing my eyes.

'Never mind, mate, it's not that early, get your gear on, you and me is goin' bush.'

'Bush?' I sat up again, fast.

'It's your twelfth birthday, Mole. I promised your grandfather. It's time you learned the gift.'

'Learned? Gift? What?'

'Fire! Lessons start today.'

I wanted to cry out, object. Tell him it wasn't fair. But I knew I couldn't humiliate myself in front of the little bastard. So I put on my clothes and followed him, going through the kitchen, because with him returned, we were sleeping back on the verandah. There was a block of light the colour of ice coming through the kitchen window. Then I saw Sarah. She was bent over the kitchen sink, throwing up. The light from the window glowing like the light from embers on her hair.

'What's wrong?' I asked her, 'You all right?'

She sort of spat into the sink and then turned on the tap and looked toward me, half-hunched over. She wiped her mouth on the back of her hand, 'I just feel a bit sick, that's all. It must have been the fish last night,' she smiled weakly.

'C'mon, Mole,' Tommy called impatiently, 'we've got to scram.'

'Sarah's sick,' I said, 'I should wake Mum.'

'No, don't wake her, Mole. I'm all right, really,' Sarah called.

'You heard her, ferchrissakes, it was something she ate. She'll be right! C'mon, let's kick the dust, mate.'

'You go, Mole, I'll be okay,' Sarah said, bringing her free hand up to her tummy.

We were going through the front door when she called out, 'Happy birthday, Mole!'

Yeah, yeah, I thought, 'It's okay for you, all you've got is a sore tummy. How about me? It's my twelfth birthday and my whole life's been ruined forever.'

Chapter Three

In Yankalillee the locals used to refer to my grandfather William D'Arcy Maloney as 'Mr Baloney'. This was not because he talked nonsense or was a fool, though admittedly, in the Maloney tradition, he was undistinguished in most things. Baloney was simply a conjunction of his name, Bill, combined with his surname, which, in the parlance of Australians, inevitably became Baloney.

The 'Mister' was added for four reasons. The traditional gesture of respect for an old-timer, the second reason was because he fought in the Boer War, Australia's first real away-from-home war, the third because of his reputation as the best fighter of fires in the Snowy Mountains district and the last, but by no means least, because he drank like a fish but could hold his grog and be relied on to be good company in the pub. All of this served to give him a respectability independent of his reprobate son.

Mr Baloney lived on a run-down small farm at Wooragee, a dot on the map which served as postbox number for the locals, many of whom had come to farming via the Soldier Settlement Scheme. During the gold rushes, Wooragee had been a Cobb & Co. stop when it had boasted a stone store, a tin pub and half a dozen wattle and daub shacks. In the twenties a primary school was built to dish out a fundamental education to the farm children thereabouts. It boasted a solitary teacher, responsible for all six classes. Today only the school remains, the rest has long since gone, eroded by the wind or plundered for building material. The school served as the postal address and letters were marked R.M.B. Wooragee, VIC. The teacher sorted out the mail into family names and had the kids bring it home or drop it in for their neighbours.

Mr Baloney was seventy-four when I was seven years old, the year he passed away. At the age of twenty-five and already married with two sons, he'd fought in the Boer War with the Colonial Detachment and received a bullet in the knee from a Boer Mauser at Potchefstroom in the Western Transvaal and ever after walked with a slight limp.

The second son, James, died at Gallipoli in 1915 and Francis, the oldest, at Pozières in France in 1918. Their mother Caroline was one of the twelve thousand Australians who died in the great flu epidemic in 1919 thought to have been brought back from Europe by the troops returning in 1918. My grandpa would say he'd lost two sons and a wife in the Great War and that, after five generations in Australia, the Maloneys still hadn't escaped the scourge of the bloody English.

Tommy was born in 1920, the youngest of his three sons and the only child to Mr Baloney's second marriage to Charlotte McKinley, a spinster who was over forty herself. She was said to possess a small inheritance, which proved to be correct. For once a Maloney had lucked in. But, as usual, there was a price to pay. His wife would spend the remainder of her years bemoaning her marriage to him and telling anyone who would listen that it was her money that kept them alive during the Great Depression. She'd add that, while other men searched desperately for ways to put food on the table for their suffering families, her husband's entire Boer War veteran's pension was poured down his useless Maloney throat and, what's more, if she hadn't kept a good grip on her dowry that's where it would have gone as well.

'Nursing me sorrows for marrying you, m'dear,' my grandpa would say if he happened to be present at one of these perpetual whinges.

As a seven-year-old I was often enough farmed out to my grandparents. Tommy was probably on the hill at the time and Nancy, who was expecting Colleen, was too busy making ends meet to take care of me. Sarah would have had her hands full with Mike and Bozo and was too young to assume the responsibility for me while still going to school each day.

My grandma was always referred to in our family in the over-formal English manner as 'Grandmother Charlotte'. This was because, although Australian-born, she came from 'decent British stock', a distinction she felt compelled to make if, in a conversation, she was connected in any way with a Maloney.

She was an English Catholic, which seemed to mean that she was at the less bitter end of the bitter divide, English Catholics being mysteriously superior to all other Catholics, in particular those originally from Ireland.

Unlike us, who were collapsed Catholics, Grandmother Charlotte was devout. She'd walk the three miles into town and back twice a week, Thursday nights to do the Stations of the Cross, then waking up at dawn, winter and summer, to get to Sunday Mass at seven o'clock. She could easily have slept in because there was a Mass at half-past nine. She'd snort with derision at this suggestion, the first Mass of the day was what an English Catholic attended, the later one was for the bone-idle Irish.

I recall very little about her, except that she appeared to permanently regret having married William D'Arcy Maloney. I remember that she invariably spoke to my grandpa in a raised and irritated voice, while her manner towards me was brusque and lacked the indulgent tones usually associated with grandmothers. Nancy told us it was because she was from English stock.

My grandpa dropped dead of a heart attack in the Shamrock on the day of the cattle sales when the joint was packed with some of the local farmers and the blokes from down the saleyards and the abattoir, and any other serious drinkers who could dredge up an Irish surname somewhere in their family's past. To the eternal admiration of this roistering send-off committee, he carked it with half a pot of beer, in the very act of raising it to his lips.

After all the years of long-suffering martyrdom and putting up with my grandpa, his death seemed like a good opportunity for Grandmother Charlotte to sell the property at Wooragee and check into a retirement home. Not one like the Owens & Murray Old Age

Home, which was seen as God's waiting room, but something for decent folk. She'd spent almost half her life with a man she actively disliked and had spawned a son by him whom she loathed with a great intensity. Now her turn to put up her feet, free of a male encumbrance, had arrived at last. She would constantly refer to a place called Sunnyside on the Mornington Peninsula, a retirement home often advertised in *The Stock and Land*. 'It is as far as I can possibly get from the taint of a Maloney,' she'd say. In her mind it had become a Shangri-la, her haven of peace and the stairway to heaven itself.

However, as commonly happened in the bush in those days, when the will was read, the property went to the oldest-surviving son, who was Tommy of course. While the will allowed for her to live in the house until she died, Grandmother Charlotte was penniless, left pushing shit uphill with a broken stick. Maloney payback.

William D'Arcy Maloney, who had stolen her inheritance in the first place, had robbed her of the few days she had left in her troubled and unsatisfactory life. The retirement she had anticipated, lazy days spent lounging in a deck chair with the tide lapping at her feet and a soft breeze blowing in from the ocean, was over before it had begun.

After that, Grandmother Charlotte quickly faded away and lost the will to live. Less than three months later she followed her husband to the grave. When the end was nigh, she summoned Father Crosby so she could say her final confession and have him administer the last rites. Two days later, with her English-Catholic conscience clear before God and a final unconfessed curse on her lips for the two Maloneys who had denied her the comforts of old age, she skipped purgatory and went straight to heaven.

Alas, death has no conscience and even less shame and she was buried without fuss in the same burial plot as her errant husband. 'So them two can still go at it hammer and tongs,' Nancy chortled.

Following so closely on her deceased husband's heels caused people everywhere to say that, despite everything, they must have been devoted to each other and that Grandmother Charlotte must surely have died of a broken heart.

'Broken heart, my arse!' Nancy snorted. 'After your grandpa died, the old witch had nobody to nag. More like she died swallowing her own venom!' Then, thinking perhaps that speaking of the dead in this manner might bring us bad luck, she added reluctantly, 'I'll say this for the old tartar, she made a bloody good Christmas pudding.'

It takes two to tango, I guess. In retrospect I now realise how hard it must have been for the old girl. Indeed, how difficult it was for any woman at the time. If anything went wrong it was the woman's fault and, as Nancy did at Grandmother Charlotte's funeral, even women often took the man's side. Women seemed to do it automatically, turning on their own kind. They still do. God knows, Mr Baloney, by anyone's reckoning, was a drunk and a layabout and my grandmother put up with him for thirty years. Like most of her generation, she deserved a lot better in life.

But at that time I didn't understand this cruel imbalance of the sexes, particularly in the bush. When Grandmother Charlotte died and Tommy came into his inheritance, it seemed to us, like for once, a bit of good fortune had come into our lives.

Though he loved the bush itself, Tommy had no desire to be a farmer. Mr Baloney, more interested in the pub than the paddock, had neglected the property something terrible. His land was covered in a seasonal calendar of noxious weeds: red sorrel, St John's wort, thistle, castor-oil plant and, to top off these floral catastrophes, the most prevalent of all, the dreaded Paterson's curse that could turn a paddock purple and useless quick as look at you.

Foxes happily crawled through gaping holes in an ancient chookhouse and stole his chickens. Rabbits chewed away at what clumps of grazing grass survived. If anything remained worth eating, you could bet your boots there'd be a locust plague to turn the paddocks to dust in a few days. Even the old apple tree in the backyard seemed always to drop its fruit before ever it ripened. Tommy, casting sentiment aside, decided to sell up and we Maloneys eagerly contemplated the meaning of being stinking rich with a thousand pounds in the bank.

We should've known better. It turned out the property was hocked up to the eyeballs to the State Savings Bank of Victoria. In the end we only had enough, after paying off the debt to the bank, to do a major overhaul on the Diamond T and equip it with a brand new set of Dunlop tyres.

With a bit of money to be used at his own discretion, Tommy took on a mantle of self-importance we'd not seen in him before. In a fit of sentimentality he paid for an expensive marble tombstone for Mr Baloney that featured two pure-white marble angels on top of a polished granite slab. Nancy said it was pure extortion and they'd seen him coming. In vain she pointed out to him that the money could have been better spent elsewhere and that one angel would have been sufficient to remind everyone that Mr Baloney was no bloody angel.

Nancy was driven to despair by his arrogance, 'I know it's your money, Tommy, but I'd like the kids to have a proper education. Sarah says she wants to go to the university, be a doctor, won't you let me put some of it away?'

'A doctor, my arse, she's a girl!'

'What about Mike then? You've spent more on Mr Baloney's headstone than what an education for one of them would cost.' She couldn't shout at him like she normally would, because it was his money. 'Be nice if one of them was the first Maloney to go to a university.'

'So? What are you saying? There's never been a Maloney that's finished high school, isn't that enough for you? There's never been a Maloney had a decent headstone neither. That's another bloody first. At least we'll get a bit of respect in the cemetery from now on. How much respect yer reckon a bloody sheila quack would get in Yankalillee?'

In all this extravagance of Catholic-burial ritual, where the dead drunken male is instantly sanctified, Grandmother Charlotte very nearly got the bum's rush. Even though she was buried in the selfsame plot as Mr Baloney, her presence there remained incognito, silent as the grave, and that's how Tommy intended leaving it.

'She can kiss my bum, she ain't getting nothing,' he said.

'She'd have a fair bit of trouble doing that, now she's dead!' Nancy said, 'But what you're doing is burying her in an unmarked grave. That's not fair, she's not a murderer! If Father Crosby finds out, you'll be in trouble, mate.'

'That old poofter! If he's the best the Pope can do, His Holiness should have saved himself the trouble. Wouldn't surprise me if he was fondling one of the altar boys. Irish priests! Jesus Christ, why should I take any notice o' one of them.'

Nancy ignored this outburst, sticking to the subject. 'Tommy, *she was your mother* after all, you came from her womb.' While she may have disliked Grandmother Charlotte, as far as Nancy was concerned, and despite the fact that she herself had jumped into it a little prematurely, motherhood was a sacred duty and credit should be given where credit was due.

'My mother! Jesus, I'd a been a damn sight better off being born an orphan,' Tommy shouted. 'I should a been took away the moment they cut the birth cord.'

'She prayed constantly for your safety during the war, Tommy,' Nancy reminded him. 'I know that's true, she spent hours on her knees in front of the altar at St Stephen's. "If the power of prayer can do it, then Tommy's coming back to make you a respectable woman," Father Crosby would tell me often enough.' Nancy paused, 'And you bloody did come back, though, I admit, a bit worse for wear. So give her a bit of credit, will ya!'

Tommy wasn't having any of it. 'Yeah, and look where all her praying got me, dysentery, beri-beri, three years and five months under the fuckin' Nips!'

'That wasn't her fault!' Nancy protested.

'Oh yeah? Don't be so sure. I wouldn't have put it past the old cow to write to General Tojo in Tokyo, give him my identity-tag number and tell him, if ever he comes across me, to kick the shit outta yours truly!'

And so it went, back and forth, for nearly two weeks the two of them arguing. Eventually Nancy prevailed and Tommy allowed the stonemason to chisel Grandmother Charlotte's name into the granite slab, though right at the bottom as an afterthought, and he absolutely refused to have it picked out in gold paint like Mr Baloney's.

What was left of the money allowed Tommy to shout all his friends at the Shamrock and stay drunk for a month as well as lose a few quid on the horses at Flemington with a clear conscience.

Then, I remember, we invested the last fifty quid on Tatts tickets. For the second time we speculated on how we were going to spend the fortune we stood to win. True to form, the Maloney luck held firm and we got bugger-all back. So, there you go, the water from the tap had hit the spoon in the sink as usual. Life on Bell Street continued as before.

My grandpa's funeral was a big affair with Tooley's funeral wagon draped in black crepe and more flowers than the combined floats at the Golden Hills Festival. It was followed by a wake at the Shamrock with several of the town's leading Protestants present. The entire district bushfire brigade attended, some coming from as far as Yarrawonga. Of course, all the town's Catholics were there. Anything for a free piss-up.

At the wake they'd rigged up this tape recorder to a loudspeaker and played a bush ballad which Mr Baloney used to sing when he'd had a skinful. The recording was in his own voice. A bloke at the ABC, visiting the town from Melbourne a couple of years earlier looking for stuff for the wireless, had recorded it in the pub one night. It's called 'The Ballad of Billy Brink' and goes like this:

There once was a shearer by the name of Bill Brink,
A devil for work and a devil for drink,
He'd shear his two hundred a day without fear,
And he'd drink without stopping two gallons of beer.
Chorus from the people in the pub
And he'd drink without stopping two gallons of beer.

When the pub opened up he was very first in,
Roaring for whiskey and howling for gin,
Saying, 'Jimmy, my boy, I'm dying of thirst,
Whatever you've got here just give it me first.'
Chorus from the people in the pub
Whatever you've got here just give it me first.'

Now Jimmy the barman who served him the rum,
Hated the sight of old Billy the bum;
He came up too late, he came up too soon,
At morning, at evening, at night and at noon.
Chorus from the people in the pub
At morning, at evening, at night and at noon.

Now Jimmy the barman was cleaning the bar,
With sulphuric acid locked up in a jar.
He poured him a measure into a small glass,
Saying, 'After this drink you will surely say "Pass".'
Chorus from the people in the pub
Saying, 'After this drink you will surely say "Pass".'

'Well,' says Billy to Jimmy, 'the stuff it tastes fine,
She's a new kind of liquor or whiskey or wine?'
'Yes, that's the stuff, Jimmy, I'm strong as a Turk –
I'll break all the records today at my work.'
Chorus from the people in the pub
'I'll break all the records today at my work.'

Well, all that day long there was Jim at the bar,
Too eager to argue, too anxious to fight,
Roaring and trembling with a terrible fear,
For he pictured the corpse of old Bill in his sight.
Chorus from the people in the pub
For he pictured the corpse of old Bill in his sight.

But early next morn there was Bill as before,
Roaring and bawling, and howling for more,
His eyeballs were singed and his whiskers deranged,
He had holes in his hide like a dog with the mange.
Chorus from the people in the pub
He had holes in his hide like a dog with the mange.

Said Billy to Jimmy, 'She sure was fine stuff.
It made me feel well but I ain't had enough.
It started me coughing, you know I'm no liar,
And every damn cough set my whiskers on fire.'
Chorus from the people in the pub
'And every damn cough set my whiskers on fiiiiiiiiiiiire!'

'Was it, you know, weird hearing the old man's voice after he was already dead?' I asked Tommy when he told me about the song and the funeral one day when we were in the bush together.

'Nah, they loved it. Brought the old bugger fresh back into the pub like he was attending his own wake.'

Mickey O'Hearn generously donated two eighteens for the wake and the bushfire mob had added a niner and Tommy had somehow scratched up the shekels for another nine-gallon keg. So the joint was awash with grog and, once the collective tongues were sufficiently oiled, just about every man and his dog made a speech or had a yarn to tell concerning the dearly departed, who had grown a dozen inches in stature since he'd hit the deck with a clunk.

There was plenty to tell. Except for the Boer War and once to attend a bushfire conference in Melbourne in 1937, Mr Baloney had never left the valley and almost its whole history was encompassed in his life. Of the Boer War he'd say, 'We should have lost. Them Boers were better than us, ride all day at a half-gallop, shoot the eye out of a potato at five hundred yards, in the end we outnumbered them twenty to one!' Of his only visit to the big smoke: 'Couldn't get 'ome quick enough. Ratbags the lot of 'em, talked about bombing bushfires with water from the air!'

Mickey O'Hearn, who'd made his particular oration fairly late in the day when the crowd sentiment was full to overflowing, mentioned how the dearly departed had sent half a pot of Victoria Bitter crashing to the floor moments before he'd been whisked up to the great pub in the sky.

'Now, such a waste may be thought by some to bring shame to a drinking man of Mr Baloney's reputation,' Mickey intoned. 'But I assure you I am not among his critics. No, sir! As an Irishman and as a publican of twenty years' standing, I regard myself as an expert in these matters. I'll be after tellin' you now, ladies and gentlemen [there were no ladies present at the wake], the unconsumed ale is a very clear sign if ever I saw one.' He paused to make sure everyone was paying attention. 'It means, Mr Baloney will be back for the other half, don't you bother yourself about that now!'

This sentiment was rewarded with clapping and whistles and banging on the tables. Then, quite possibly carried away by the occasion and no doubt also from the effect caused by having imbibed too much of his own amber liquid in an effort to regain somewhat from his generosity, Mickey made this grand announcement. 'Henceforth, a pot of beer will be left on the main bar of the Shamrock every night to await the dear man's return or until the Second Coming of our Lord, whichever occurs the sooner. God bless you all.'

It was a fine gesture which brought tears to the eyes of several hardened drunks and was loudly applauded by all. Mr Baloney's half-finished beer was instantly dubbed 'The Beer of the Second Coming'.

Except that, after two weeks either Jesus had come and nobody in Yankalillee had noticed (which was not entirely impossible) or Mickey O'Hearn had reneged on his promise. No pot of beer now rested on the polished-cedar bar counter where Mr Baloney had customarily perched.

Tommy waited a week or two to make sure this wasn't an oversight, then he confronted Mickey O'Hearn, 'How come me old man's beer ain't on the bar like you promised, mate?'

Mickey O'Hearn looked surprised. 'Come now, Tommy Maloney, that's funeral talk, that's all that is, Irish blarney. I put the beer out the first two weeks, fourteen beers. To be sure now, that's not a gesture to be taken lightly.'

'Twelve, pub don't open Sundays.'

'Twelve then.'

'Yeah, and you filled the glass from the slops tray, thought we wouldn't notice, eh?'

Michael O'Hearn, the representative of the town's poor and downtrodden, was clearly taken aback and became somewhat agitated. Jabbing his forefinger into Tommy's chest, he said, 'Do you expect me to pull three hundred and sixty-five fresh beers a year minus fifty-two Sundays and let them go to waste! Jaysus, you wouldn't be serious now, would you, Tommy Maloney? I'm not the bloody Aga Khan!'

Tommy shook his head slowly, his eyes directed at the floor. Like most recidivists he was a convincing actor. 'I dunno, mate, seems a real shame. Like you said at me old man's funeral, tradition and all that. What with him lingering in purgatory, a cold beer might go down real good after a day on the hot coals.' Tommy looked up at the Irishman, his one good eye registering a deep and profound sadness at this insult to the memory of his departed father. Mickey O'Hearn didn't need to be reminded, though Tommy now lost no time reminding him, 'Me old man spent almost his entire Boer War invalid's pension every month at the Shamrock, Mickey. It's just not right what you done, mate.'

Like all his kind, at heart Mickey O'Hearn was a sentimental bloke and, as well, not a stupid one. Most of the lags drank at the Shamrock when they weren't safely tucked away up the hill, and Mickey could ill afford to have Tommy badmouth him among the criminal community. With seven pubs in the town, loyalty could be a fickle business and, besides, your average crim and ex-con is well known to have a very large thirst.

'Tell you what, Tommy, I'll meet you halfway,' Mickey said, adopting a reconciliatory tone. 'A pint costs two bob, right? You put down a deaner for the first pint you drink every day and I'll take care of the remainder. That's a silver shilling in your own pocket and you get to drink the pot Mr Baloney left behind when he so sadly departed this mortal coil.' Mickey smiled, 'Can't be fairer than that now, can I, Tommy?'

Tommy's sense of tradition evaporated into the nicotine-fumed air above his head. He grinned at the Irishman, 'Fair enough, mate. Thanks, Mickey, you've got me.'

'Just the one, mind!' Mickey warned, pointing his finger at Tommy. 'The first of the day.'

You think there's not a lot you remember about your early childhood, but pictures, words, incidents are constantly coming back to me, scenes reappear in my mind's eye. What returns is always the memory of the two of us, Grandpa and me, enjoying each other's company.

In my fifty-fifth year I seem to be living both in the past and in the present, you must forgive me if at times my voice lapses into childhood, it is an evocation that comes complete with its own small-town grammar so that I see and inwardly hear myself speaking as a child. They say this sometimes happens to older people, yet I am not old enough to be included in this category. Perhaps age is more about experience than it is about the passing of the years. We are where we've been. There is some comfort to me in the fact that I can return to times past that remind me of who I am and help explain why I have become the way I am. The voice of Mole, the little shit-kicker, often becomes as real to me as that of the adult Peter Maloney and so I hope you will go along with me in this.

Mr Baloney and I would go for what seemed to me at the time long walks in the bush, where he'd point out things to me. The names of flowers and, in particular, the various types of eucalyptus. 'A good burner, dangerous bugger,' he'd say of one, while of another he'd remark, 'Fire resistant, loves the flame, burns off all the stringy bark, leaving the trunk green and clean as a whistle.'

He'd show me insects lurking underneath leaves, stick insects so cleverly disguised you'd have to be inches away before you realised they weren't a knotted twig, or emerald-coloured praying mantis, their front legs delicately touching their long feelers. Codling moths cocooned in nests made of their homespun cotton wool in the old apple tree behind the house and fat white witchetty grubs lurked under bark that curled into a tight smooth circle at a touch. Mr Baloney would tell me the feeding ways of the bright green grasshoppers. He knew the name of every type of cicada and he told me that the high-pitched noise that filled every corner of the bush and sent the air vibrating was made with their back legs. We'd find spider webs and nests of the dangerous redbacks and the safe huntsmen and the less safe trapdoor spiders, and he'd pull me to safety away from nests of bull ants. He'd call out the names of the butterflies as they bobbed about in the sunlight or settled on wildflowers, their wings opening and shutting in slow motion.

Mr Baloney could imitate the song of most of the birds and spot a possum's den in a hollow tree trunk where there'd sometimes be baby possums looking back at you, eyes dark as creek water over black pebbles. Occasionally we'd come across a snake sunning itself. 'Red-bellied black snake,' Grandpa would say softly, 'don't want nothing to do with that bugger, son, nasty bite.'

We'd come across a stand of blackberries, 'Nasty stuff this, takes a hold of the bush and won't let go, kills everything. Shouldn't be here at all. It's the bloody rabbit of the plant kingdom, this and Paterson's curse. Both brought in by the English. Fancy being homesick for a blackberry bush! Only a Pommie, eh? Took off like smoke, though, loved the place and now neither God nor man can get rid of the mongrel.' He'd reach carefully into the bush for a blackberry and pop it into my mouth, his fingers smelling of tobacco. 'Too much scratch to the bite,' he'd say dismissively, pointing to the thorny stalks. 'Mind you, the blue wrens love it. Small bird, see, prey for the bigger ones out in the open, blackberry gives them a source of food and hides and protects them. Nasty bloody stuff all the same.'

I guess Mr Baloney told me a whole heap more, because when four years later Tommy started to do the same, a lot of what he said seemed vaguely familiar. Sometimes I'd come across something in the bush, perhaps a small flowering plant tucked away in the undergrowth. 'That's a greenhood orchid,' I'd say, its name simply popping into my head as a gift from Grandpa past. 'Where'd you learn that?' Tommy would say, surprised, 'The old man tell ya?'

There is something else I remember about Mr Baloney. He was a champion farter, though I don't suppose this fact was well known among the general population nor do I believe it was mentioned at his funeral. But as his more or less constant partner on rambles, I was privileged to hear his complete repertoire, from basso profundo to rapid machine-gun fire.

We'd be walking, my hand buried in his big, calloused fist, him shuffling with his bit of a limp and me hopping and skipping, the wind rustling high and fierce in the big old gum trees above us, making a sound like waves lapping on some distant seashore, when, without warning, my grandpa would let go a rip-snorter! A real tearing sound that could last five seconds with a stuttering cluster of encores to follow.

'Oh, my gawd, the hippobottomus* is following us again!' he'd exclaim, turning to glance backwards and then waving his one hand furiously in front of his nose, 'Bugger's gorn again, but you can smell where he's been!' He'd point at the ground below his bum, 'He was right there before he escaped, did you see him, Mole?'

* first-known Maloney word

I'd shake my head. 'What's a hippo-bottom-us look like, Grandpa?' I'd ask, the game begun for the hundredth time.

'Smelly creature, big round bum like your grandmother's,' he'd confide, 'Don't want to meet him face to face, could blow a little fellow like you right off the mountain.'

Sometimes he'd let one go at the table during tea. 'You disgusting old bugger!' Grandmother Charlotte would yell out, taken by surprise by the burst of thunder down under and completely forgetting her airs and graces. She'd push back her chair, often knocking it over in the process, backing away, almost stumbling, to stand in the kitchen doorway, her hand fanning the air furiously in front of her nose. 'Bog Irish!' she'd scream, 'Don't know any better, filthy creatures the lot of you. You're disgusting!'

My grandpa would wink at me. 'Just expressing my opinion of the English, my dear,' he'd say to a fuming Grandmother Charlotte.

'In front of the child too!' she'd continue, then stop to catch her breath and in the process she'd remember she was an English Catholic and from good stock. Drawing herself up to her full height and crossing her arms over her ample breasts, Grandmother Charlotte would arch her eyebrow and regain her snooty voice. Looking imperiously down at the both of us, she'd announce, 'But then he is a Maloney, isn't he? You can't make a silk purse out of a sow's ear. Poor stock doesn't breed out.' She would turn on her heel and storm into the kitchen to make a cup of tea and sulk in front of the stove.

Boy! That hippobottomus could sure get her into a state, knock her right off the mountain.

I can't say I was all that chuffed at Tommy's rude awakening on my twelfth birthday. As I mentioned, nobody made too much of a fuss over birthdays, but at least you got to sleep in, which was always your birthday treat. Besides, it was going to be one of those really stinking-hot days in December and it was a good five miles onto the hilly, tree-covered slopes he and I were headed for.

Tommy was now pretty fit from no grog while in gaol and nearly a month at running behind the truck carrying a full garbage bin so we set off at a fair pace. We seemed to be taking nothing with us except for a small hand axe and a pocket knife he always carried on his belt in a small leather pouch. I was feeling sorry for myself. It was my bloody birthday and I wouldn't even get breakfast or dinner.

'What are we going to eat?' I asked him.

'Bush tucker, mate. If we're lucky. Depends what we find. Ever tasted a witchetty grub?'

'Yuk!'

'Delicious, mate, there's other things too, but it's not easy. You've got to work to get a feed in the bush. Might find a possum's den with babies, ever eaten baby possum?'

I didn't say anything. If he was trying to be funny I didn't want to join in. Who did he think he was? Instead I watched his back as we started to climb. Already there was a damp patch of sweat showing between his shoulders and the sun hadn't come up yet. He was like a mountain goat, jumping from rock to rock, nimble on his feet.

Tommy always was a skinny, wiry sort of bloke despite the beer he drank. 'A potbelly on a slender frame' was how Nancy described him. The pot would flatten when he was a guest of Her Majesty up on the hill and he certainly didn't carry any excess baggage now. Nevertheless he was far from being like he'd be after he came back from a long stay in the bush when he was all skin and bone. While I wasn't exactly fat myself, what Tommy looked like was not how I wanted to end up in life. If we were going to depend on him for a feed in the bush, I didn't much like my chances. What's more, if he'd been eating baby possums they hadn't put any flesh on his bones, that's for sure. I could see it was going to be a long hungry day and we'd be bloody lucky to get home in time for tea. Sarah always had our tea ready at six o'clock and I couldn't remember her ever waiting back until later.

And then there was the other thing, just being with Tommy alone all day. Even when he were home, we kids didn't mix much with him. He hadn't played a big part in our lives. We were sort of permanently at arm's length. If he sat on the back verandah we'd avoid it, if he was in the front room we wouldn't go in. At the table the conversation circled around but he was seldom included or seemed inclined to want to be a part of it. If he decided to talk, we'd all fall silent. It wasn't deliberate, it was just how it was. When we were out of a morning collecting the garbage, we were too busy to talk much and so that worked out okay.

Tommy wasn't what you'd call a father figure and he knew it. We were polite to him and all that, but I'd be lying if I said we respected him. He must have known this, because he didn't try to win us over or fit in when he was sober. When he was on a binge, he only came home to sleep and then not always. Nancy would try to include him in conversations but I guess all the years he'd spent in gaol locked up in a cell didn't exactly turn him into a good conversationalist. What do you say to a bunch of kids you haven't seen growing up?

Now here I was alone with him in the bush, a boy on his birthday with a dad he didn't like or trust. It was pretty scary.

We walked for about an hour before the sun came up, him in front and me following ten paces behind. Each step you could feel the tension building up between us. Then we stopped and rested beside a dry creek bed among the trees.

'Bad year,' Tommy said, 'you can usually find drinking water in this creek.' He looked about him and then pointed to a gum tree that didn't look that different from the others around. It had a smooth dark and light-grey bark, I'd seen hundreds like it. 'Know what that one's named?'

'It's a gum tree, eucalyptus,' I said, giving the correct name to show him I wasn't stupid.

He stared at me, 'I know it's a fuckin' eucalyptus, what's it bloody called?'

His sharp tone of voice took me by surprise. I'd answered best I could and he'd roused on me. I was suddenly shaking inside. But Maloneys don't cry, don't show they're scared. Nancy said that even when you're shaking in your boots, you look people in the eye. It was dumb advice. If you looked a teacher in the eye, he thought you were giving cheek or being defiant and you got the strap. I shrugged, looking down at my feet, not answering.

'Yellow Box! It's a Bloody Yellow Box! Common as dirt!' Tommy shouted it out.

This time I looked up at him, trying to look defiant. How was I supposed to know it was called Yellow Box? 'I don't give a fuck,' I said, swallowing hard.

I waited for him to hit me, get it over with. If I'd used that word in front of Nancy, she would have made me wash my mouth out with Velvet soap. But I didn't care. I'd have a go if he hit me, even if he ended up beating the daylights out of me. He only had one good arm and I'd work on his blind-eye side and I reckon I could've taken him. Instead, Tommy started to laugh.

'Righto, that's a good place to start. You don't give a fuck and I don't give a shit what you feel. What do you say to that, hey, boy?'

'Let's go home then.'

Tommy shook his head. 'It's not that easy, Mole. You see, I promised Mr Baloney I'd teach you and I'm going to keep that promise. If you won't be bloody taught,' he paused and looked around, 'well, son, that's up to you, we're going out bush every Saturday anyway.'

'You can't make me,' I said defiantly.

'No, that's true, but your mother can and she's agreed.'

'Nancy! Mum?' I suddenly felt terribly betrayed. Nancy had shopped me. I couldn't believe my ears.

'You're lying, she wouldn't do that.'

'It's true, Mole. Do you think I could haul you out of bed at sparrow fart without her knowing, her saying it was ridgy-didge?'

'I don't suppose you both could have asked me?'

He grinned, 'Nah, what good would that have done, eh?'

'Tom . . . er . . .' I stopped, I'd never called him Tommy face to face.

'Tommy will do fine,' he said. 'No point calling me "Dad" if I ain't earned it. And I ain't. Like me calling you "son", when you don't feel like you're my boy. I tried it on a moment back, didn't work, did it? So let's not pretend, eh, Mole? Tommy 'n' Mole will do until we both decide otherwise, what say you?'

Confused, I forgot what I was going to say in the first place. So I just shrugged, 'Okay by me.'

'Good! That's settled then.' He seemed to think for a while then said, 'Can I tell you something, Mole?'

'Suppose,' I said, still not trusting the bugger one inch, thinking any minute he's going to go off half-cocked again like with the Yellow Box. How was I suppose to know, anyway?

'When you were knee high to a grasshopper and you used to go walkabout with your grandpa, he was *that* proud of you. He used to say he liked the lot of yiz kids, but you were special, you had the gift of calling a fire.'

'How would he know! I was only seven. I don't remember putting out any fires.'

Tommy chose to ignore my sarcasm. 'He said you had a feel for the bush, knew where to look. Naturally curious and remembered everything he told you.'

'All small kids do that. Colleen does it. Small kids' heads are still empty, plenty of room for them to remember stuff you tell them.' I looked directly at him and shrugged. 'I don't remember nothing now, so my grandpa was wrong, wasn't he?'

'Maybe. But let's find out, eh?'

His change of tone was confusing me. I didn't want to be friends with him. This was a different Tommy, not even the one we knew when he was sober. But also, deep down, I wanted him to be my dad. It was very confusing. I guess he had to learn how to treat me as well as me him. 'What if it doesn't work? If I've forgot everything, which I have. What then?' I said.

'Yeah, okay.' He seemed to be thinking. 'Gimme every Saturday up till Christmas and then half the Christmas holidays, then you can decide.'

'Ha! Come Christmas, you'll be on the grog again!' I couldn't help it, it just slipped out without my thinking.

He was sitting on a rock directly opposite me with a small twig in his hand, using it to dig in the sand at his feet. Now he looked up slowly and our eyes locked. Looking into his one good eye, I held his gaze defiantly and he held his. It went on and on until my head began to spin and I could see nothing but a blur in front of me. Then, at last, Tommy looked away. 'You could be right, Mole,' he said softly. 'But if you'll give it a go, I'll give it a go. What do you say, mate?'

I was trapped, the bastard had trapped me fair and square. What could I say? 'Okay,' I mumbled.

'Let's begin with Yellow Box then,' he said, this time his tone was like easygoing.

I looked up at the tree, 'Why is it called Yellow Box? I don't see any yellow.'

'It's the bark, sort of yellow colour.' He rose from the rock and walked over to the tree and broke a small piece of bark from the stem. He brought it over and handed it to me. The bark was a sort of brown-yellow. 'More brown,' I said, 'wouldn't call that yellow.'

'There you go then, botanists have strange ways of classification. Good tree though, good for firewood, excellent burner which is a problem come bushfire time. It's called *Eucalyptus melliodora* which means 'honey-scented'. Makes the best honey, bees love it because it flowers right through summer, always plenty of tucker for them. Nice tree, yellow blossoms, maybe that's why it's called Yellow Box, eh?'

I didn't answer, though I could have said lots of gums have yellow blossoms. Even I knew that much.

'Eucalyptus is a hardwood,' he went on, ignoring my truculence. 'There's two types of wood, see, softwood and hardwood, Australia's got the tallest hardwood trees in the world.'

'No, it hasn't!' I shot back.

'Beg yours?'

'Redwood in California, we learned about it in class, they're the tallest trees in the world.'

'You're right and then again you're wrong,' Tommy said, his voice still even.

'What's that mean?'

'Californian Redwood is the tallest tree in the world, but it's a softwood.'

'Oh,' I said, looking at Tommy to make sure he wasn't making it up.

'Redwood, *Sequoia sempervirens*, grows to three hundred and thirty feet.'

'Shit, hey?' I was dumbstruck, Tommy knew a Latin name for a tree twice. It was all I could think to say.

Tommy laughed, 'Wouldn't be too impressed if I were you, mate. I got it from this woodwork book in the carpentry shop up on the hill.'

He'd returned to sit on the rock and commenced to dig again. I could see the sand was starting to come up wet. I wasn't completely ignorant, I knew you could dig for water, but the sand on top was dry as a powder keg and looked anything but promising. 'Should get a drink out of this soon enough,' Tommy said, without looking up.

For want of something to say, I said, 'How tall can our trees grow, the hardwood?'

'Three hundred feet, just a few feet short of them giant redwoods, there's a tree in Tasmania that's even a bit taller. It's that old, Captain Cook would have seen it sticking out of the forest canopy when he sailed by.'

'Captain Cook never sailed by Tasmania.' Crocodile Brown was suddenly coming in very useful for once in his life.

'Yes, he bloody did, he bloody discovered Australia,' Tommy said, certain he was right.

'But he never saw Tasmania.'

'How come?'

'Didn't cross Bass Strait. Abel Tasman was the first to see Tasmania. He was a Dutch sea captain. He could've seen that tree, he sailed past Tasmania even before Captain Cook discovered Australia and he named it after the Governor-General of the Dutch East Indies, Van Diemen. He even named Australia first up, called it New Holland.'

The certainty in my voice made Tommy hesitate. 'This Demon bloke, he do something wrong, how come it's now Tasmania?'

'Nah, we called it that later, it was called Van Diemen's Land first up.'

'So why didn't the Dutch claim Australia, when they called it New Holland, you know, for themselves. Stands to reason they would, wouldn't they?'

'Dunno, they didn't want it I suppose. They were looking for something else and weren't all that interested.' I was impressed by my own erudition.

'You're a pretty smart young fella, ain't ya?' Tommy said. 'Maybe you could learn something about eucalyptus trees, heh?'

'It's a native of Australia,' I said, getting carried away again.

'Yeah, and what else?'

'What do you mean?'

'Well, f'instance, how many varieties are there?'

He had me, I should've known I'd come a cropper sooner or later, I'd probably been having a snooze when we were told that in class. I took a stab at it, 'One hundred and ten,' I guessed.

'Not even close, mate!' It was his turn to be smug.

'How many then?'

'Just over six hundred! That's how many.'

'Know them all, do you?' It was an attempt to regain my former position as the authority on Australian history.

Tommy chuckled, 'No way! Lucky if I know seventy, just the varieties around here and Mount Buffalo, maybe some like Snow Gum and Buffalo Sallee up high on the Snowy Mountains.'

'That's a lot,' I said, deciding to come off my high horse. History wasn't my best subject anyway. Besides, Tommy could have said, yes he knew the lot and I'd never have known any better. I mean, I was aware there was more than one kind of gum tree, you could see that just by looking, but seventy was a whole heap. I found that, despite myself, I was becoming interested. Even if I only learned about twenty names from Tommy, with a couple of them Latin ones thrown in, Crocodile Brown might have to take me seriously for a change.

'Have you ever seen a really big one?' I think he could tell from my voice that I wasn't as snotty as before.

'There's a big old man Alpine Ash, *Eucalyptus delegatensis*, in a deep ravine I know about. Not many people know of its existence.'

'Where's that? Can we go and see it?'

Tommy laughed, 'That's your prize if you pass.'

'Saturdays and after Christmas?'

'No, if you learn something in the process. I doubt there's five people in the world know of its existence. Maybe just me. Trunk is more than ten feet across and damn near two or three hundred feet tall, been there at least three hundred and fifty years, maybe more.'

He waited for my response. 'And you'll show it to me, take me there if I learn stuff?' He must have heard it in my voice, I was suddenly dead keen.

'We'll see,' he said. 'Play your cards right, it could just happen.'

'Did you find it yourself? Discover it, like?'

'Nah, Mr Baloney showed it to me when I was about your age, and his father told him before that. It's been known to our family probably eighty years.'

I was impressed. I was maybe going to learn a secret nobody knew except a Maloney. 'You sure it's *only* you knows about the tree?' I asked.

'Can't be sure about nothing in this world, mate. Pretty certain there's not too many who know about the Alpine Ash, bloody hard to get to that ravine, wouldn't know it was there unless you flew over it or stumbled upon it by mistake. It's hard-yakka country, everywhere else the timber-getters have long since cut down the big ones. Be another six generations before we see anything like it again in this region.' He leaned back, 'There you go then.' He pointed to the hole in the sand which had now filled with fresh, clear water, 'Take a drink, never know where the next one's coming from, eh? Time for a gasper and then we're off, plenty to do before sunset.' It was the longest statement I'd ever heard Tommy make.

He took out the makings and rolled a cigarette. Licking the glue edge of the fag paper, he handed it to me. 'No thanks, not now,' I said, trying to sound casual, like as if I smoked but didn't feel like one at the moment.

'You don't use 'em then?' he asked. 'I did at your age.'

No use lying. 'Nah, tried it, didn't like it much.'

'Good thing,' he said. 'Wait until you're a bit older, hey.' He lit his fag which was rolled thin as a lemonade straw, you can tell if a bloke's been in prison by the way he rolls his cigarettes. Tobacco's precious inside so a fag is rolled as thin as possible so the makings will last longer. Tommy inhaled deeply then exhaled and pointed at the water with his cigarette. 'Go for your life, Mole.'

I got up from where I was seated and went down on my knees and scooped water into my mouth. It tasted clean and fresh like a precious gift we'd discovered and, like the secret old man Alpine Ash, something that nobody else but us Maloneys had found.

I forget much of what happened that day. Tommy was over-anxious and rambled on much too fast, firing information at me until I was bleary-eyed and weak-brained. Firebreaks and the nature of undergrowth, bark varieties and their potential for combustion, the names of trees, wind directions, curvature of a hill and how it affects fire, you'd have had to be a genius to remember it all. Tommy, not accustomed to teaching anybody let alone a kid of twelve, was firing with both barrels and he'd blown my mind to little bits long before the day ended.

We got home about seven o'clock, an hour after Sarah normally gave us our tea. I hadn't eaten anything all day except a few blackberries as I had flat refused to eat the fat white grubs Tommy'd found under the bark of a dead eucalyptus tree. I think its name was Mountain Swamp Gum, but I can't be sure, I was that tired.

To my joy and with me starving to death, Sarah had waited for us to return. 'It's your birthday, couldn't start without you, could we?' Then, when nobody was taking notice, she drew me aside. 'You won't tell anyone about this morning, will you, Mole?'

I'd had so much happen to me since then I'd forgotten about her being sick that morning. Besides, Maloneys never snitched on each other. 'No, of course not,' I replied.

'Good,' she said, 'it must have been the fish.' I was with her on that one, the fish with white sauce was worse than offal.

'Yeah, I know what you mean,' I said. 'That's a dumb rule God came up with for Fridays.'

'Are you hungry?' she asked. 'We've got a special treat for your birthday.'

'I haven't eaten all day except for some blackberries,' I said, feeling sorry for myself.'

'Great, then you'll have a good appetite. How was your day with Tommy?'

'Shithouse!' It came out, just the one word, like an explosion.

I was not yet ready to admit that there'd been some stuff that I'd quite liked. Anyway, it was true, mostly I hated it and hadn't really warmed much to Tommy neither. There was too much he'd done to us for him to win me over just by naming a few trees in Latin and pretending everything was all right. It bloody wasn't and I knew sooner or later, sooner probably, he'd go off half-cocked again or go on a bender. Leopards don't change their spots.

'Talk to Nancy,' Sarah said, 'tell her.'

'Wha' for? It was her betrayed me.'

'It's important knowing about fires,' Sarah offered. 'Like, it's our family tradition.'

'Yeah, why pick on me? Why not Bozo or Mike? All that fire stuff, it's all bullshit!'

She smiled and tilted her head, 'Poor Mole, you're tired.'

'Yeah, sick and tired of this whole bloody family pickin' on me.'

'Afraid it's the only one we've got. We've got to stick together through thick and thin, Mole.'

'So I'm the poor bastard that has to go out with the thin bloke. It's not bloody fair!'

Sarah laughed. 'Thick and thin, big and small, Nancy and Tommy! Hey, that's very funny, Mole.'

'Yeah, hysterical,' I grunted. But I secretly thought it was quite clever myself. I mean, considering how buggered I was.

Just then Nancy came into the kitchen and said she'd make the gravy and for me to go wash my hands and face, that I looked like a ragamuffin. She didn't even ask about my day. Bloody traitor.

We had steak that night, Nancy must have got it at the abattoir yesterday. A huge juicy steak and roast potatoes and gravy and pumpkin and peas and orange cordial. I didn't have to eat the pumpkin.

When we'd all finished, there was stewed fruit and custard for sweets. Sarah said to wait on. As soon as she returned from the kitchen she shouted, 'Close your eyes, Mole!' Then, moments later, 'Okay, you can open them.'

There in front of me was a cake with twelve lighted candles round the rim. It was made with this pink icing and, across the middle in blue icing in running writing, was '*Mole Maloney 12*'.

'Blow! Make a wish!' everyone shouted at once and then when I'd blown all the candles out in one go, they sang 'Happy Birthday' and 'For He's a Jolly Good Fellow'! We'd done the same for little Colleen on her birthday, but never for us other kids. But I have to admit, it was very nice.

The wish I made when I blew out the candles should have been to be released from my Tommy sentence, but I must have been brain-damaged from all the stuff he'd been going on about all day and, instead, I wished I'd soon be shown the big old-man Alpine Ash. Only I wished it was somebody else showed me, like my grandpa come to life again, not Tommy.

Then Nancy cut the cake and we were all having a slice when Tommy, with this mouth full of cake, says to Sarah, 'How you feeling, girl?'

It was completely unexpected, like. Usually him and Sarah didn't say much to each other.

'Fine,' Sarah replied, surprised. She must have forgotten that Tommy was with me in the kitchen that morning.

'You seemed pretty crook this morning, vomiting in the sink.' Normally Tommy didn't give a bugger about us family. Besides, he'd done a fair bit of vomiting in his time and probably wouldn't have taken it seriously anyway. Maybe what had happened between him and me during the day had given him some encouragement and he was, like, you know, practising fatherhood or something?

Sarah went a beetroot-red colour, she could blush like a sunset. 'I'm better now,' she said in a small, tight voice.

'You didn't tell me you were sick?' Nancy said suspiciously.

'It was nothing,' Sarah said, 'I think it was the fish last night.'

'Fish? It was smoked haddock. Nobody else was sick.' She looked around the table, 'Anyone else sick?' she asked. We knew something was coming and none of us said anything. Tommy coughed twice. Even little Colleen sensed something was up and stopped chewing cake. 'Vomiting, were you? First thing in the morning?' She seemed to be thinking for a moment, 'Hmm, I see.' Nancy's lips were pulled tight, 'You're not pregnant are you, Sarah?'

Sarah began to sob. She sat with both her hands in her lap and her head bowed and sobbed.

Mike and Bozo and me stayed silent, Tommy too. You could hear Sarah breathing, taking in great gulps of air. There was nothing we could do for her, us kids who had to stick together through thick and thin were helpless when we were needed. Then Mike sort of cleared his throat and said, 'Yeah, me too. I was a bit nauseous this morning.'

'Bullshit!' Nancy snapped.

And then there was just Sarah sobbing.

Chapter Four

With Sarah pregnant, things were not the same with us. Sarah still carried on, but she wasn't her old self. In so many ways she ran things around the place that Nancy couldn't have taken over if she'd wanted to, but you could see Sarah didn't have her heart in it.

Nancy still wore the pants, of course, but Sarah ran our lives and made us feel worthwhile. Now she was up the duff and none of us felt good any longer. There'd always been laughter around the place and now there wasn't. Nancy took to adding another bottle of milk stout to her morning ritual which didn't do her temper any good and she picked on Sarah all the time until she got her crying. It was the worst thing that could happen to a Maloney and especially to Sarah, who'd always had a lot of pride. 'Dignity,' Mike called it. 'Sarah has dignity.' Mike said that Nancy's smocking was ratshit and he and Sarah had to do it all over again when she wasn't looking.

Then there was the fear grabbing hold of all of us. The dread of what people were going to say, the deep-down fear of the Protestants. 'Bloody Catholics, what do you expect? Those Maloneys, always been the lowest of the low.' When a convent girl got pregnant they'd usually say things like 'They're like a dog off a chain once they leave the convent, they'll go with any Tom, Dick or Harry.'

That was one good thing, at least they couldn't say that about Sarah, who never went to the convent in the first place. Other things you'd hear people say were, 'That girl's nothing but a harlot, those slacks are so tight around her backside you'd have to peel them off with a paint scraper, she wants locking up before she gets knocked up.' But that wasn't Sarah neither. Sarah was the vice-prefect, dux of the school, and polite to everyone she met. People liked Sarah right off, you could see it in their eyes.

Our eldest sister did everything for us, she even cut our hair and she never had time to hang out at the Greek's, the Parthenon cafe, to meet boys, like some of the other girls did. It doesn't matter much what Sarah wasn't. They'd soon enough forget all that, there's nothing like present trouble to wipe out past glory.

Mike said, 'Take a look at us, will ya? We've got Tommy, we're the garbage collectors and we're Micks to boot, we don't have a snowball's hope in hell!' Then he turned to Bozo and me, his teeth clenched and eyes closed tight, 'One day I'm going to come back to this bloody shit-heap of a town and show them they were wrong about us!'

It just wasn't fair! Sarah was the one who always made sure we were proud of ourselves and now this had happened to her. We were lucky that she'd finished her exams so she really didn't have to go back to school if she didn't want to. Although, as vice-prefect, she still had things to do, like go through the routine with next year's head prefect and give a short speech at the final-year assembly. But that was something Murray Templeton, the head prefect, would have to do alone this year.

After three days the headmaster called Mike into his office and asked him if there was anything wrong with Sarah, she was supposed to come in and see him earlier in the week. Mike said she wasn't well. 'What's the matter with her?' Frank Morris asked, 'She hasn't taken a day off from school in three years.' Mike said he didn't know exactly, a cold or something, better call Nancy.

Nancy told him Sarah was worn out from the exams and needed a rest. He didn't seem too pleased with this answer and said, 'We've all been under a strain, Mrs Maloney. The school expects its vice-prefect to see out the year.' Nancy stayed firm, knowing he couldn't make Sarah come in now she'd done her exams. Later she called him a 'pompous old bugger!' and added that she couldn't care less what Frank

Morris thought, Sarah wasn't going back to that place. 'Next thing the teachers will be saying she's looking a bit puffy round the ankles and then won't the tongues start wagging.'

It was only a matter of time, though. Nancy knew it, we all knew it, you couldn't keep anything secret for long in Yankalillee. The town's stickybeaks could sniff trouble a mile off and they'd soon be landing like crows on a dead cow. Hmm, what have we got here? And, soon enough, another reputation bites the dust.

Not that Nancy was doing all that well with her own attempts at damage control. She'd gone ape-shit the first night when Tommy dobbed Sarah in. It wasn't the mum we knew, an entirely new Nancy came out and there's still a fair bit of this new person hanging around the place.

I mean, fair enough, you could understand her being pissed off at what had happened. But it was a bit hypocritical when you think about it. What had Sarah done that Nancy hadn't done herself? Who was she to blame Sarah? All of us, except Colleen, had been born out of wedlock. She and Sarah were almost the same age when she was up the duff the first time. It was a clear case of the pot calling the kettle black. But that didn't stop Nancy going spare.

That night around the table with all of us munching away on birthday cake and Sarah admitting the deed by bursting into tears, Nancy came wading in, a great dreadnought with all guns blazing. 'You've ruined your life, girl!' she screamed at Sarah. 'You've destroyed your chances and you've destroyed us! For once in our lives we looked like we might crawl out from under the miserable rock the Maloneys have been hiding under for-bloody-ever! All our dreams! All our hard work, and you open your legs to the first Protestant boy who touches you on the tits! How could you do this to us?'

'Hey, wait on, Mum,' Mike says. 'That's not fair!'

Nancy turns furiously to Mike. 'You! Shut the fuck up!' she screams. 'You should talk, God only knows where you'll end up!'

Mike is shocked and humiliated and looks down at the uneaten piece of cake on his plate. Nancy's never spoken like that before, not even ever used that word before in our presence, turning on both her kids like they're dirt. It's as if she's someone else who's gone right off her scone.

But Nancy doesn't care. 'Just once!' she yells and then looks up at the ceiling appealing to God, 'just for once things seemed to be going right and now this! What is it?' she says to God. 'What is it that I've done! Didn't go to bloody Mass! The Eucharist, is that it? Eat yer body and drink yer blood! Can't you leave us alone? Pick on someone else for a change!' Boy, did she give God a big serve, I expected lightning to come down and fry us all on the spot.

She looks around and her eyes are strange, wild, popping out her head, like she doesn't even see us and is in some sort of blind panic. All of a sudden she brings her hands up to cover her face and she starts to wail. She's wailing and Sarah's sobbing. Little Colleen's watching all this going on around her, not understanding, her green eyes big as saucers and on the verge of tears, her bottom lip trembling. Then she too starts to cry. Colleen's crying, Nancy's wailing and Sarah's sobbing. You've never seen so much misery in the one room at the same time.

Mike looks at Bozo and me and goes over and puts his arm around Sarah and nods, indicating we must do the same to Nancy and Colleen. Tommy's looking down at the oilcloth that's stretched tight over the table and drawing-pinned to the underside. He's taken out a drawing-pin and is using it to pick the dirt out of his nails, not looking up even once.

Bozo goes to Colleen and picks her up and sits down in her chair. Putting her on his lap, he pulls her head into his chest, stroking her soft blonde hair. I go behind Nancy's chair and put both my arms around her neck. Her whole body is shaking, like she's got the trembles, then her shoulders start to heave like an earthquake's about to happen. She goes silent and you can't hear any sound coming out, just the trembling and heaving, then it comes out again, rushing up like a volcano, angry and unstoppable. Nancy starts to roar this time, making an angry sound we've never heard come out of her before, like a wild animal that's been wounded and is dying and is going to have one last shot at getting to its tormentor.

'Mum! Mum!' I shout out as I hug her tight. But her great arm flings back and catches me to the side of the neck and I'm sent flying, *splat* into the wall behind. Now she turns on Sarah again. 'You little bitch! You randy little bitch! You filthy harlot!' she screams and her hand comes up and with a fresh roar of anger she starts to rise, she's going to hit Sarah, she'll kill her, but before she's properly out of her chair she seems to freeze in midair, then drops like a stone, crashing to the floor.

'Christ, she's had a heart attack,' Tommy shouts out. He hasn't done nothing until now, just sat there like a stunned mullet cleaning his nails. Him who started everything in the first place.

Nancy is lying like a great hippo spread-eagled on the floor, not moving. Her yellow-daisy dress has pulled right up around her navel and the elastic of her pink crepe de chine bloomers is cutting into her tree-trunk thighs just above her knees and again across her enormous stomach. Tommy rushes over and jumps astride her and starts right off giving her mouth-to-mouth resuscitation.

Suddenly Nancy opens one eye. 'Get off a me, you great pillock!' she yells out and her arm sweeps across and it's Tommy's turn to go flying under the table. Then she wipes her mouth with the back of her hand like she's just ate something really nasty.

It must have been her blood pressure. When she got up too suddenly from the chair, she must have momentarily blacked out. We all rush over, even Sarah, who pulls Nancy's dress back down over her knees. Then we start to pull her to her feet, which ain't easy, her lying flat like that on her back. Getting her into the Diamond T is a piece of cake compared to this effort.

Tommy's bleeding above the eyebrow where he's caught it against the edge of the table leg and he doesn't look too happy. Eventually we get Nancy back into her chair, she's huffing and puffing, her huge breasts rising and falling like a blacksmith's bellows. She's red in the face and sweating like a pig. I think that now maybe she *really* is going to have a heart attack, because she's gulping for air and wheezing something terrible. Mike has grabbed Friday's *Gazette* and he's fanning it furiously in front of her face and Bozo's rushed into the kitchen to get her a drink of water and a Bex.

Nobody notices as Sarah leaves the room. Later, when things have calmed down around Nancy a bit, we realise she's gone. Sarah's not to be found in the house and we go outside looking for her, then down Bell Street, but she's nowhere to be seen.

There's a place I know near the lake she likes to go sometimes, so that's where I head off on my own.

I find her sitting looking out into the lake. 'Sarah,' I say, 'that you?' Of course I know it's her, but I'm not sure I'm welcome.

'Hello, Mole,' she calls softly.

'You all right?' It's another silly question.

'Yeah.' She gives a bitter little laugh, 'Good as can be expected.'

'You want to be alone?'

'No, come sit with me.'

I sit next to her and we don't say anything, her and me looking out into the lake, which isn't a real lake but open-cut diggings made during the gold rushes with the local creek diverted into it later to make the lake. It's a near full moon with just a bit of the side missing so it's easy to see things. A couple of ducks glide past and go *quack, quack*. You can also see some of the lights from the houses up on the hill reflected in the water and there's the sound of the wind through the bulrushes. The frogs are croaking away, going at it hell for leather in a frog chorus before suddenly stopping for no reason, then it's on again for one and all. Frogs do that and nobody knows why. Maybe they're singing a song, only we don't know it because our ears think it's all the same tune. But it isn't and they're taking a smoko before they start the next number.

We're sitting on almost the exact spot where Bozo caught the redfin that tasted of mud, when we swore we'd never eat fresh fish again and we haven't. Maybe if Bozo had caught another fish that tasted like that last one, Sarah might have got away with her excuse because we all wanted to vomit after eating that first one.

Sarah's arm comes around my shoulders and she pulls me close in and ruffles my hair, 'I've really fucked up, haven't I, Mole?'

I can't tell her, that's the truth and then some. 'They say he's been signed up to play for Richmond, is it true?' It's all I can think to say.

'They've made an approach, but he's going to Duntroon.'

'Duntroon, what's that when it's wearing baby booties?' (Maloney expression.)

'The Royal Military College in Canberra. Murray wants to be a cadet officer and then go into the permanent army.'

'What?' I can't believe my ears. A chance to play for Richmond and he gives it up to be a soldier. I'm beginning to think Murray Templeton must be a bit of a dead-head.

'His grandfather was a lieutenant general in the first world war, he wants to follow in his footsteps, it's a family tradition.' Sarah pauses a moment, then gives a bitter little laugh, 'Like me following in Nancy's footsteps, that seems to be *our* family tradition.'

It doesn't seem appropriate to mention that bushfires are our tradition as well. 'Are you going to have a baby, Sarah?' I'm full of dumb questions. Of course she is, but I can't think of another way to put it.

'Looks like it, unless I have a miscarriage.'

'Miscarriage?' It's not a word I've heard before.

'Lose it, something goes wrong and you lose your baby,' Sarah explains. 'But with the Maloney luck that's not going to happen to me.' She turns and looks at me, her mouth pulled down at one corner and sort of wobbling, like she's trying not to cry again. 'Forgot to take the spoon out of the sink, Mole.'

I'm twelve years old that very day and I know she must mean she didn't use a franger. Or Murray Templeton didn't. Perhaps she meant that she shouldn't have done it in the first place. Which we all know is true, but too late thinking about that now.

I'd never seen a franger, but Bozo has. He said that this guy brought one to boxing, pinched it from the barber shop where they sell them. He was having his hair cut and Billy Tucker the barber went to answer the phone out the back and there was this drawer half open and he could see these red packets in it. He thought it was chewing gum and so he pinched one. Then he found out later it was a franger.

Bozo said they all got fats on in the shower out back of the police station and took turns to try it on. 'It's that strong, but it fits real smooth and tight,' he told me. Then later they filled it with water and he said it took more than a gallon of water and didn't break. You could also blow it up like a balloon. Bozo said how he'd heard of these bank robbers in America using them. Only they call them frenchies over there, we do sometimes too. I tried to imagine Tommy with one pulled over his head, but I couldn't. If it fits so tight, like Bozo said, how come they could breathe? So that bit about the bank robbers was probably bullshit. Bozo said, 'Its real name is Ansell Contraceptive, because on the outside of the pack it said "Ansell Contraceptives – for your *unconcerned* pleasure"!'

So, you see, I knew what a franger was all right. It was just that I couldn't imagine Sarah doing 'it' with one. You know, like a parent would. Matter of fact, before tonight I couldn't have imagined her doing it anyway. Now my commonsense told me that if she was going to use a franger, like she meant when she said she didn't take the spoon out the sink, that would mean she was doing it all the time with Murray Templeton. I'm positive now that's not true. What's happened to give her a baby was a definite one-off mistake. Them two not using a franger when they did it is positive proof it only happened the once. Stands to reason, don't it? Think about it. Bozo said this bloke at boxing said you had to be asked. The barber would say while he was cutting a grown-up's hair, 'Do you need any home supplies, sir?' which is the secret code for a packet of frangers. Murray Templeton couldn't just walk into Billy Tucker's barber shop and say, 'Hello, Mr Tucker, packet of frangers,' right out in the open, him being a schoolboy and all. So it was a spur of the moment thing for sure. They probably didn't even know that every time you don't use a franger you get a baby.

I also wondered a bit how you could lose a baby when it's inside you. I'd heard of people losing one before. Nancy would say of some women she knew 'She's lost her baby, poor thing.' Until now I hadn't really thought about it, other than that it was something women occasionally did, lost babies. What's more, I also never thought it was something that was lucky when it happened, that is, until now with Sarah saying, with our Maloney luck, meaning bad luck, she wouldn't lose hers.

There was a long silence then between Sarah and me. Silence can build up and after a while the air around gets tighter so you think any moment it's going to tear, rip apart, right above your head. Then goodness knows what would happen. That's when you have to say something to stop it happening. 'What are you going to do?' I say to Sarah.

Like all my questions to her tonight, it's the wrong one again, because she drops her head and starts to sniff. But then she looks up over the lake and takes her hanky that's already sopping wet from all her tears and nose-snuffling and blows her nose. 'I don't know, Mole,' she says in a real small voice.

We're silent for a long time again and I'm throwing these pebbles in the lake, *plop, plop, plop*, when she says, 'I could go to the nuns' hospital in Melbourne and have it. You're allowed to hold it the once and then they take it away for adoption.' I can see she can't yet call it a baby. What's in her stomach is still an 'it'.

We're both thinking the same thing, her with a big tummy and what people will say if Sarah stays in Yankalillee. 'Them Maloneys, been here since Ned Kelly was a lad, but they're still Bog Irish!' Or they'll say, 'Not young Templeton's fault, boys will be boys, she's a real little cock-teaser that one. Makes out she's so ladylike but you can bet she was planning to get her hooks into him all along.'

We can't send Sarah away neither, there's nowhere to go, no relatives or anyone that we've kept up with. Who'd want one of Tommy's kids anyway?

'Will you marry him?' I now say, because that's the next question needs to be asked.

Sarah turns and puts her arm around me again and pulls me into her and gives this little whimper, 'Oh, Mole, I love him so much. They're High Church of England and we're Catholics and Murray's going to Duntroon, his parents will never allow it!'

I can see right off we Maloneys are up shit creek without a paddle. But I already knew that. And it was me who thought she only had a sore tummy this morning and I was the one who was having his whole life ruined! Me feeling sorry for myself when it's really her who's in the shit! Sarah's now sobbing quietly, but it's nice with my head against her chest.

I must have fallen asleep because next thing I know she's saying to me, 'Wake up, Mole, it's time to go home and face the music again. It's been a long day for you, you're on your last legs, mate.' She gives me a kiss on the forehead, which normally I wouldn't allow. 'You poor old sausage, it hasn't been much of a birthday, has it?'

Well, matters go from bad to worse in our family. Monday morning, after we've done the garbage rounds, Tommy's off to wait for the pub to open. Monday, come six-thirty, he staggers home and collapses at the front door and has to be dragged in and put to bed. He's back on the grog in a big way. Tuesday morning at three I go to wake him, he gets up and comes out, but he's still so pissed from the night before he's about as useless as a one-legged man in an arse-kicking contest. He's falling over bins and tripping and calling out and swearing and we're getting behind on the job cleaning up the mess he's making. He's got this half-jack of brandy and he's taking swigs from it and falling on his arse. Funny how they never seem to break the bottle. Tommy is normally a McWilliams sweet-sherry man, which is bad enough, but now it's Tolleys brandy and that's a real bad sign. We try to put him in the Diamond T cabin with Nancy but he won't have a bar of it and in her present mood she's not that keen to accommodate him neither.

So we have to leave him by the side of the road to sober up, which is real bad for our image. We know what will happen, he'll go wandering off, shouting and swearing and staggering all over the place until half the bloody town will have looked out their windows and seen him before breakfast.

But then, as we're trying to figure out what to do, he takes out his donger and starts to piss in someone's empty garbage bin. His trousers fall down below his knees and he's waving the half-jack above his head, trying to keep his balance. Then he commits a mortal sin and takes a kick at Bitzer Four and sends the little mutt flying and himself on his arse, with the piss-stream spraying every which way.

'Right, that's bloody it!' Bozo shouts.

'Mary, Mother of God!' Mike says, spitting to one side in disgust.

So we gag Tommy and tie his hands and ankles with a bit of rope and toss him on top of the garbage. In about two minutes he's fast asleep.

'Never seen him looking more at home,' Mike grunts. Nancy doesn't even look through the back window of the Diamond T while all this is going on.

We know Tommy's pattern of old. Once he starts on the grog he's on a bender that could last a week or all the way to Christmas. One good thing though, no bush-whacking of a Saturday for old Mole. Fuck the Yellow Box and the bees making honey, fuck all the other eucalyptus trees as well, I'm a free man.

Nancy's not herself neither, instead of shouting out and calling directions she hardly speaks at all. Though, all is not lost, she still makes sure we get Oliver Twist shouting down at us from his bedroom window, but she doesn't laugh or shout 'Half-past three and all's well,' as usual as we drive away.

It's three nights later when Nancy asks Sarah if she's told Murray Templeton she's pregnant. You'd think it would have been one of the first questions asked, which goes to show how bad things were, how we've lost all our commonsense.

Sarah says she has.

'When?' Nancy wants to know.

'When I first started getting sick in the morning,' Sarah answers.

'When was that?'

'A week ago, three days before Mole saw me in the kitchen.'

'And?'

'He said he'd speak to his parents.'

'And that was a week ago and he hasn't been back?'

'He hasn't been to school either,' Mike interjects. 'I heard someone say he was supposed to play in the parents and teachers versus the school's first eleven cricket match but didn't turn up.'

'I see. Seen him since then, Sarah?'

Sarah bows her head, she's ashamed. 'No,' she says.

'You sure?' Nancy is suspicious.

'No, Mum!' Sarah looks her straight in the eye. You can tell she's telling the truth. More than any of us, she's the one who never tells a lie.

'Why the rotten little shit!' Nancy shouts out. And we all know immediately that the old Nancy is back. Someone's done something to one of us kids and they're going to have to pay. 'We'll soon see about that!' she says, scraping back her chair.

One thing that hasn't changed with us since the bad news is that we're still all included in what's happening. Maloneys do things together. Except for little Colleen, who's gone off to bed and is too young to be a part of it. And Tommy, who hasn't come home and is probably sitting down by the lake with the other town no-hopers getting himself paralytic on sweet sherry. We're sitting at the table after dinner where this conversation is taking place. Nancy now gets up and goes to the phone and dials the exchange.

'Mum, don't do that!' Mike yells out. 'They listen in, you know that!'

But Nancy takes no notice. 'Philip Templeton,' she snaps to the girl at the telephone exchange. We all groan and bring our hands up to our faces, just the tone of her voice is sufficient to put the exchange on red alert. 'Mr Templeton?' a slight pause then, 'This is Nancy Maloney, Sarah's mother. We're coming over right now!' Murray Templeton's father must have said something like it wasn't convenient, because Nancy snaps, 'That's just too bad, you've had a week to contact us, you can expect us in fifteen minutes!' She slams down the phone. 'Right then, everyone into the Diamond T.'

'Oh, Mum!' Sarah howls.

'You shut up!' Nancy says. 'I've had enough. Who do they think they are?'

'What about Colleen?' Bozo says.

'Wrap her in a blanket and bring her along, they might as well see how the other half lives.'

We're in our clothes for around the house and barefoot, even Sarah.

'We'll need to change,' Mike says.

'No time for that, now,' Nancy snaps, 'We'll go as we are, they can jolly well take us as they find us.'

Sarah's already run into her and Nancy's bedroom, her eyes full of panic. Because of the heat, she's wearing an old pair of shorts and a sort of bra thing that's the top from her bathers. It's going to be tough on her having to face the parents.

It seems like only moments later when she emerges. She's carrying Colleen who is still asleep and wrapped in a blanket. Sarah's done a lightning change and she's wearing pedal pushers and tennis shoes with a clean white T-shirt. From where I am, I can see her from the back, her waist is slim as ever and, from looking every time I see her, I know there still isn't any bulge in front to show what's happened. She's even had time to put a brush through her hair. Sarah looks about fourteen years old.

We heave-ho Nancy up into the Diamond T. Sarah and Colleen climb in after her and the rest of us stay in the back, including Bozo's mutts. Bozo doesn't go anywhere without Bitzers One to Five. 'They're our family too,' he always says. 'They guard the Diamond T.'

'Who's going to be stupid enough to steal it?' Mike wanted to know.

It doesn't take long to get to the Templetons' house which is up the side of the hill a bit further along the same street from Oliver Twist. His and their house are the only ones in Yankalillee that are double storey. Once I remarked on how lucky they were to have a big house and everything. Nancy said not to, that being envious of someone else, wanting to be like them, was to be a second-best person and not the first-best person you can be by yourself. There's also something we know about the Templetons, us being the town garbage collectors but Nancy says we don't talk about what's in people's garbage because it humiliates us more than them. Now after what they've done I don't care, so I'll tell it. There's always two or three Gilbey's gin bottles in their garbage, which tells something about Mrs Dora Templeton she wouldn't want anybody to know.

You'd think they'd bury the bottles in the backyard or something, though, being them, they'd probably explain it away by saying they have a lot of visitors. Not so easy to do if you think about it for a moment. Men don't drink gin and all them white-glove set mostly drink dry sherry or sometimes brandy and dry, but often it's only lemon squash. Two bottles of gin for entertainment purposes would last a year under those conditions. If you ask me, the Gilbey's gin bottles are a dead give away. After all, we know pissedness (a Maloney word) when we see it. If I'm not mistaken, Dora Templeton drinks like a fish.

We're all pretty nervous going up to the front door, though Nancy is in front and we're all sort of protected by her massive body. She's still wearing a pair of worn green-felt slippers and, of course, her yellow-daisy dress. She raps on the door. They've got this brass lion's head with a ring through its mouth and Nancy goes *rap, rap, rap* against the door hard as she can, then *rap, rap, rap* again and when there's no response, mainly because she doesn't wait long enough for anyone to have time to come, she shouts out, 'Open up!' and goes *rap, rap, rap* again, so you know she's nervous as hell.

We know the Templetons must be home because the garage door is open and the pumpkin-carriage Holden is parked inside. Sarah's beside me holding Colleen and she's that mortified she's got her head buried in Colleen's blanket. The door opens and it's Mr Templeton.

He doesn't say anything, just nods his head in the direction of the interior. You can see from his tight-lipped expression that he's not that thrilled at our appearance at his front door. He leads us into the lounge room, a big room, nearly as big as our cottage, with windows that look out over the lake. There's no Dora Templeton in sight. Probably upstairs pissed.

Philip Templeton indicates the sofa and various armchairs, which look brand new almost and which are enough to accommodate us all and then some. He still hasn't said a word. When we're seated, he nods at Sarah. 'Sarah, Mrs Maloney,' he says, the rest of us he ignores.

'You know why we're here,' Nancy says.

'Yes, I think so,' Philip Templeton replies.

'Where's your boy? He ought to be here,' Nancy's tone is not real polite.

'I'm afraid he's gone away, he's with his uncle and aunt in Manildra in New South Wales.'

'How very convenient,' Nancy says, then she kind of sneers, 'Your missus? She gone to Manilda too?'

'Manildra,' he corrects her. Then adds, 'I'd prefer to sort this mess out on my own. Dora is upstairs with a migraine.'

'Hmmph! That what they call it nowadays?' Nancy quips.

'I resent that, Mrs Maloney,' Philip Templeton says, lifting his voice.

'Righto, then. Now there's something for you to resent. I have a resentment as well, Mr Templeton. Sarah tells me she told your boy a week ago about her pregnancy and you haven't seen fit to get in touch with us.'

'Well, ah . . . we had to see what our legal position was.'

'Legal position?' Nancy looks genuinely confused. 'How about your *moral* position, Mr Templeton? Or don't that come into it? Let's not beat about the bush, your boy knocked up our Sarah, what are you going to do about it? He going to marry her or what?'

Philip Templeton actually laughs, 'Whoa, steady on, not so fast, Mrs Maloney. It's not quite that easy.'

'And why is that?'

'Well, for instance, we may need to explore other avenues, don't you think?'

'No, I don't, Mr Templeton! What other avenues have you got in mind?'

'Well, I'd rather not say, I mean with all your children here, it's not something I'd like to discuss in front of them.'

'We're a family, Mr Templeton, a poor one and, you may think, not a very important one, but nevertheless a very loving one. We're talking about Sarah. What are you saying, she shouldn't be here?'

'Well, yes, as a matter of fact, I don't think she should be here.'

'With us it's one in, all in, we've got nothing to hide from the world nor from each other. You already know my husband is a drunk and a crim.' Nancy now stabs a finger at him, 'So go on then, what other avenues?'

Nancy's got on her courtroom manner, like she'd done the time me and Bozo got beat up at school by Brent Middleton and his gang and she had a go at Brent's dad, Hamish, and Vera Saggy Tits Forbes.

'Well, adoption, for instance? We thought, that is Mrs Templeton and I, we . . .'

'Don't go any further! You expect my daughter to be traipsing around town for the next seven months with swollen ankles and her belly sticking out for all to see and, then, give away her baby when it comes and, after, simply get on with her life like nothing happened? Is that what you're proposing?'

'Well, it is a solution. I'm sorry but the female is the one who carries the baby, not much I can do about that, Mrs Maloney.'

'I see, and what does the male who made it happen propose?'

'What do you mean by that?'

'Well, it seems he's told my daughter often enough that he loves her,' Nancy says, then repeats, 'So, what does he propose?'

'He's set his mind on going to Duntroon.'

'Duntroon? What's that?'

'It's a military college in Canberra, he is to become an officer cadet.'

'You mean the bloody little coward ran away, couldn't face up to his responsibilities, is that it?'

'No, that isn't it! It's been our plan for a long time. I'm not going to have him ruining his life because this has happened.'

'It's okay to ruin Sarah's life, is it?'

'I have no opinion on that. All I know is they don't allow married cadets at Duntroon.'

'As far as I know, there are no unmarried and pregnant students allowed in Medicine neither.'

'What do you mean by that?'

'My daughter has applied for Medicine. She wants to be a doctor.'

'A doctor?' Philip Templeton seems genuinely puzzled, 'But she's a girl, you mean a nurse?'

'No, a doctor! I'll grant you she's a girl and a very pretty one too, glad you noticed. What's more she's very bright, which is not what I hear about your son.'

'I don't know where all this is leading, Mrs Maloney.'

'That should be perfectly obvious to you, Mr Templeton. If my daughter remains unmarried, *her* life is ruined. She can't take up her scholarship, she's permanently shamed as an unmarried mother even if she gives up the child for adoption. She says she loves your son and he has repeatedly told her that he loves her. And now she's carrying his child. Doesn't that mean anything to you?'

'Love my son? They're school children for God's sake! They're still wet behind the ears. What do they know about love, eh? Infatuation, yes, I can understand that. I'm told Murray is quite a catch. It's a high-school romance, Mrs Maloney! Puppy love! Whether your girl says she loves him is neither here nor there. I'm not going to ruin my boy's life because she saw her opportunity to compromise him and grabbed it with both hands.'

Nancy's been pretty good so far, but she has her limits. 'I beg your pardon!' she shouts at Philip Templeton and starts to rise. 'Say that again, you arsehole!'

Oh shit, Nancy's going to slaughter him. He's a big bloke but his gut spills over his belt and hangs halfway to his knees, he's what Bozo would call 'gone soft', and Mike calls 'solar perplexus'. Put

Nancy's great ham fist into that stomach and he'd take off out the picture window and across the lake at a thousand miles an hour like a balloon with the air escaping.

It is at this very moment that Dora Templeton walks into the room. She takes two faltering steps, steadying herself on the banister of the stairs, and already you can see she's pissed. She's got a fag sticking out the corner of her mouth in a very unladylike manner, one side of her hair is flat, sort of like she's slept on it. Her skirt is unbuttoned and has slipped halfway down past her waist.

One time in the garbage we found this sort of stretched pink-rubber thing and Nancy said it's called a step-in or a girdle and that women wear it around their bums and tummy to pretend they are not as fat as they are. It sort of squashes the fat bits in behind the rubber, like giant strips of Elastoplast wrapped round them. Well, she's wearing one of them things and it's sticking up out of where her skirt has slipped down but the fat's escaped over the top of it so she's got this spare bicycle tube of white flesh around her waist. Anyway, she looks pretty well rearranged, her lipstick is sort of smudged in one corner of her mouth and she's squinting, one eye closed because the cigarette smoke is getting into it.

'What's going on, Philip?' she calls out. 'Who are these people? You didn't tell me there were people coming.' Then her eyes widen, 'Oh, hello, Sarah!' And then she catches on about what's happening, 'Brought your little family, have you?'

'Hello, Mrs Templeton,' Sarah says, all meek and mild with her eyes turned downwards, not looking.

Nancy, who is halfway up on her way to punch Philip Templeton, falls back onto the lounge.

'Go back upstairs, Dora,' Mr Templeton orders.

'No,' Dora Templeton says firmly, 'No, I don't think so, Philip.' The cigarette is wagging up and down at the corner of her mouth, her eyes still squinting from the smoke. 'No, I don't want to. I know what this is about. It's about Murray, isn't it? I told you we should have sent him to Geelong Grammar. Wouldn't have happened then, would it?'

'Dora, will you please go back upstairs!'

Dora Templeton folds her arms and looks at her husband. 'No,' she says, then after a moment she uncouples her arms and takes the ciggie from her mouth. She gives her husband this little half-smile. 'No, Philip, Murray is my son too, I have every right.'

'Dora, I'd rather do this my way. Now please!' You can see he's cranky as hell but doesn't want to show it.

He walks across to his wife and takes her by the elbow. But she pulls away, 'No!' she exclaims.

'Dora, I have to insist, my dear. You're not well.'

'I'm purrfect-ly well!' She staggers backwards and grabs a hold of the banister. Philip Templeton is quick for a big bloke and he grabs her by the back of the shoulders and tries to push her up the stairs. But she's not having it and puts her foot against the second stair so he can't budge her. He's embarrassed, she's making a fool of him, but he's still trying to keep his temper.

'Dora, I won't ask you again,' and gives her a shove. She loses her balance and goes down, clutching on to the third stair. She drops her cigarette and it hits the edge of the stairway and falls to the carpet below. 'Let go of me!' she screams. Her hair is hanging down over her eyes. He steps back, you can see he's pretty angry and he's gone red in the face and his jowls are shaking.

'I've got something to say and I'm going to say it!' she shouts up at him and then gets to her feet. She's swaying a bit and her eyes are trying to focus. She looks up at Sarah again, who has Colleen still asleep in her lap and raises her arm and points. 'Get rid of it! We don't want your Catholic bastard, you hear! Get an abortion, you little slut!'

'Dora!' Philip Templeton roars, 'Shut up!' He tries to grab her arm but she's too quick for him and pulls away.

'Well, that's what we decided, wasn't it? We'll pay to get rid of it!' Turning back to us, she shouts, 'We'll pay for the abortion! Thought you could trap us, did ya? Thought you'd marry my son, did ya? Well, you can't, see. We don't want your Catholic filth in our family!' Then she starts to laugh hysterically.

That's when Phil Templeton hits her. It's a slap, but it comes from a fair way back and lands across her mouth. Dora Templeton drops back to the carpet onto her knees, cupping both her hands across her mouth. 'Now shut up, will you? Shut up, woman!' Templeton yells out.

Dora Templeton's hands come away from her mouth and I see that there's a trickle of blood running out one corner. He's slapped her pretty hard but it don't shut her up, she starts up again, pointing at Sarah once more. 'You Catholic bitch, you thought he'd be a good catch, didn't ya? Well, I'm his mother and he's mine, not yours! Go away, get out of my house!'

Philip Templeton pulls her to her feet and he's leading her up the stairs and, this time, she's not resisting him. 'I need a drink, a little drinky-poo!' she shouts, laughing. 'Where's my glass?'

Halfway up the stairs, Philip Templeton looks down at us. 'I don't want to see you here when I come back down. Come and see me in my office, we'll sort something out.'

'It's not that easy, Mr Templeton,' says Nancy, her voice now calm. Like what we've just seen happen has taken away her nerves.

'If you're still here when I get back, I'll call the police,' Mr Templeton says, 'You're trespassing in my house.'

'Mr Templeton,' Mike says suddenly, 'you're trespassing into my sister's life.'

Templeton ignores Mike and then Nancy says, 'You go ahead, Philip Templeton, call the police. We'll be waiting down here for Sergeant Donovan to arrive.'

Templeton continues up the stairs, pushing his wife ahead of him. We wait until we think they must be upstairs, maybe in the bedroom, then Bozo says, 'Crikey, that Dora, she'd make a Maloney look respectable.'

He gets up and walks to where Mrs Templeton has dropped her cigarette at the foot of the stairs. There's smoke coming up out of the thick floral pile and he goes to stamp it out, but hesitates because he's barefoot. He walks over to this big vase with pink gladioli in it and takes the flowers out and pours water onto the burning cigarette and jams the flowers back in the vase.

'You should've left it to burn, Bozo,' Mike says, 'Burn the bloody place down.'

Sarah, who is crying softly, pleads, 'Let's go, Mum. Please can we go home!'

Nancy turns to look at her, 'No, darling, we only get one go at this.

He'll have a lawyer and witnesses in his office. Now is the time to get at this bastard. We're going to wait and, with a bit of luck, he'll call Big Jack Donovan.'

'Mum, then everyone will know!' Sarah wails.

'Maybe. But at least one of them will know the truth and Jack's no fool.'

A short time later Philip Templeton comes down the stairs again. Putting his wife to bed or whatever he's done has calmed him down, given him time to gather his wits. 'I'm sorry about that,' he apologises to Nancy. 'Dora's very highly strung.'

'Dora's very pissed!' Nancy says. She's not going to let the bastard have an inch. 'But that doesn't change what she said, Mr Templeton. We're Catholics and what you've suggested we do is a mortal sin. Besides, it's illegal. When is Big Jack Donovan coming? Perhaps you or your wife would like to repeat your offer to pay for an abortion for Sarah when he gets here, eh?'

Philip Templeton shakes his head. 'I didn't call him. You're right, Dora is drunk. Understandably, she's been under a strain. There's been no suggestion about an abor–'

'Don't insult our intelligence, Mr Templeton!' Nancy interjects.

'Can't we sit down and discuss this like sane people?' Templeton asks. 'What's happened is terribly unfortunate, we'd be happy to pay for Sarah to go away and have the baby away from prying eyes.'

'Mr Templeton, I love Murray and he loves me, he told me so! Can't I just talk to him, even on the phone?' Sarah pleads.

Philip Templeton's lips draw tight. 'I'm afraid that's not possible, Sarah.'

'But I know he loves me, he does, he's told me lots of times! Isn't it his decision also? Hasn't he got a right as well?'

'Murray's only eighteen, when he turns twenty-one he can make up his own mind. Besides, he's set his heart on joining the army, going to Duntroon. Mrs Templeton and I have discussed it at length with him and he's in full agreement. He doesn't want to marry you, Sarah.'

'I'd like him to tell me face to face,' Sarah sobs, 'I don't believe you.'

'I believe he's writing you a letter,' Philip Templeton says, 'explaining his position.'

'Starting off his military career as a coward should make him a great officer,' Mike says.

'You've got a big mouth, son!' Templeton suddenly roars. 'You'll keep!' He turns back to Nancy, trying to stay calm, but Mike's remark has thrown him. You can see he suddenly decides he's had enough. 'You've heard my offer, Mrs Maloney, and it's not going to change. If you want your daughter out of harm's way, we'll pay for her to go away. A boarding house, we know of a good one in Melbourne, St Kilda. Think about it and let me know your decision.'

'A boarding house? Away from her family?' You can see Nancy is shocked out of her tree. 'You've got a bloody nerve, Mr Templeton.'

'Well, it's up to you, we're not made of money, you know. Your daughter would be comfortable enough, full board and lodging and it's a sixpenny tram ride into the city.'

'And on her own at her age and away from us. No! I won't have a bar of it. We want to talk to the boy, you have no right to keep him from us. After all, it's him who's knocked her up.'

'That's it, that's bloody it!' Philip Templeton roars. 'Oh, yes, I bloody have! Legally, we're in the clear. We're his legal guardians until he's twenty-one. What's more, my son didn't exactly rape your daughter. It was mutual consent, they carry equal blame in the eyes of the law.' He takes a breath, 'Mrs Templeton and I have made you a generous offer. May I remind you we don't have to do anything.'

'Oh, yes, you do! You have to make my daughter respectable. She has to marry your son! She's far too good for him, but she's carrying his child.'

Templeton gives a little smile, 'I don't think you heard me, Mrs Maloney. My son is not going to marry your daughter. Now, just what do you propose you can do to make him, Mrs Maloney?'

'You'll see soon enough,' Nancy shoots back.

But now he's finally lost all patience. 'Look at you!' he yells, 'you're on the bones of your arse, you're nobody and, if you're not bloody careful, you'll be less than nobody with the garbage contract taken away from you. And don't think I won't do it, lady, it would give me a great deal of pleasure after tonight!' Philip Templeton has got his dander up, he's decided to go for the jugular and he's going at a thousand revs a minute. 'You bloody tykes are all the same, always shitting on your own doorstep and expecting somebody else to clean up after you. Well, I don't pick up other people's shit like you do. This time it isn't going to work. The boy isn't going to marry the girl, you understand? It's not going to happen. There's been a Templeton here for four generations and there's been Maloneys just as long and, may I remind you, madam, your lot has never been anything but drunks and layabouts. Useless bastards.'

'There must have been one of you, but I've never heard of a Templeton that turned up to fight a bushfire,' Nancy shoots back.

'I've got better things to do with my time than go out on the bloody fire truck in a pair of overalls!' Templeton shouts. 'Your miserable lot wouldn't know a day's work if you stumbled into it!' He stabs a finger at Nancy, 'I remember you, Nancy Maloney, high heels and skirt hoicked up to your arse, not exactly the Virgin Mary either, were you? First a wog and then half the bloody US Army!'

'And I remember *you*, Philip Templeton! You were around like a bad smell when all the other men were at the war,' Nancy snaps.

'I had flat feet.'

'Funny how most yellow bellies end up with flat feet!'

Templeton ignores the insult. 'Do you really think this town is going to take your side against us? Because if you do, think again. You're the dirt collectors. I've been shire president three times. Did you imagine for one moment we'd fall into your trap, sending your pretty little daughter to seduce my son? I dare say you put her up to it, didn't ya? "Good catch, go for it, get a bun in the oven, then he'll *have* to marry you." That's what happened, wasn't it?' Templeton sweeps the back of his hand in the direction of the front door, 'G'arn, scram, vamoose, take your ugly kids and get out of my house, you stupid, fat bitch!'

Nancy rises slowly, her eyes locked onto Philip Templeton's. He stands his ground as she advances towards him, you can see he's not backing away from a sheila. Bozo starts to push past me to go to Nancy's aid. Philip Templeton is a big bloke. Not as big as her admittedly, but big enough. There's his great gut sticking out, heaving up and down, not knowing quite what to expect. That's where she'll go, biff him in the bread basket, take the wind right out of the bastard's sails.

I don't know where Nancy learned it, but she feints to the right and Philip Templeton brings both his arms up to ward off the blow. You can see the shock on his face as Nancy throws a left that catches him under the jaw and lifts him clean off his feet. His top false teeth loop in the air and land yards away as he crashes to the ground like a wall of demolition bricks. Philip Templeton is sprawled on the carpet knocked out stone cold.

'Jesus, Mum, where'd you learn that?' Bozo yells out in admiration.

'Sergeant Bozonik, welterweight champion of the US Marines,' Nancy says. Then, cool as a cucumber, she leans down and grabs Philip Templeton by his shirt front and pulls him up onto his knees and holds him so he's looking up at her. He's just coming around and she waits until his eyes are clear. 'Two words you should never forget, Mr Templeton, "Maloney payback".' She drops him back to the carpet. 'C'mon, you lot, let's leave this shithole. Sarah, stop crying at once! That little shit who screwed you isn't worth a single Maloney tear.'

But, I must say, I don't like our chances. Mr Templeton's right, they're the ones got the power and we're the shit-kickers. That's how this town works, Templetons on top, Maloneys at the bottom. Maloney payback is one thing, real life is another. You can't get to mongrels like Philip Templeton, they've always got their arses covered.

But, as it turned out, I should have known better than to underestimate Nancy Maloney, who doesn't make threats lightly nor take too kindly to anyone having a go at her kids.

Chapter Five

I need to say something about the Bonegilla Migrant Camp reffos, because a lot is about to happen to us that's got to do with them. We didn't think that this bunch of strangers down the road a bit were having much influence on us, but they were.

For a start, they were taking the jobs nobody else wanted, which made everyone who was here already feel better about themselves. Their women started working, not just at fruit-picking time like us, but doing office-cleaning jobs and lots of things women weren't supposed to do now the war was over. For instance, working in small factories and the fruit cannery and meat-packing plants in Albury and Wangaratta. Our women had done some of those jobs in the war but we'd pulled them out and back into the kitchen quick-smart when peace arrived.

The migrant women wanted a new life and were prepared to work for it although they didn't always get the life they wanted. It turned out things weren't easy for them, many of their men were brought out to work on the Snowy Mountains Scheme, Greeks, Italians, Yugoslavs and other nations, they weren't educated and didn't want to change things from how they'd been where they came from. They thought of their wives as being their slaves, and their daughters as well. The men ruled the roost and it wasn't like us where the wife has a say in how things are done. The women couldn't speak English, had to do all the dirty work and then give all their money to the men. They had no personal freedom, so you really had to feel sorry for them. Although, of course, not all the reffos were like that, some of them were educated and treated their wives better than we treated ours. Not that our men were to be held up as shining examples, Nancy said.

Sarah had read all this stuff about reffo women in some magazine and told us about it and said thank God she was Australian and she'd never let a man persecute her. I could have pointed out to her that she and Nancy did the bossing around and us boys were the persecuted ones, but you can't win that sort of argument with them two.

Then the very next day Sarah came home from school furious, banging pots around and being generally huffy. At tea she sat down and ate her food in silence.

'Cat got your tongue?' Nancy eventually asks.

'Bloody men!' Sarah says and goes on eating.

'You have a fight with that Templeton boy?'

'Nah, the careers counsellor came to school today. He said, I quote: "Sarah, one day you'll make a beautiful wife and mother and until you get married to some lucky boy, I would advise you to be a florist or a hairdresser."'

Then Sarah tells us how the careers counsellor has been to their classroom and all the Sixth Form students have been given an interview.

'He looked at my term marks and said they were very good. He had all my exam results from Form Three on in front of him.'

'That's nice, dear,' Nancy says.

'Yeah, but then he says, "Look at this!" He's really excited, turning back to one of my old reports. "Domestic Science! These marks are excellent, Sarah."

"Yes, sir, thank you, sir, but you're looking at my Fourth Form marks, I gave up Domestic Science two years ago!" I say to him.' Sarah looks around the table, 'As I've been cooking, baking and doing needlework around here since I was practically a baby, it's hardly surprising that I've topped Fourth Form in Domestic Science. Then right off he says that's not important, they're not skills I will have lost in two years, but my marks show I've got a solid background in Domestic

Science, that I should become a hairdresser or a florist until I get married.'

'You sure he wasn't joking?' Nancy questions. 'You know, taking the mickey?'

'Mum, he was deadly serious! "You're artistic and good with your hands, either of these vocations will be ideal for you, Sarah." That's what he bloody said.'

'Christ on a crutch!' Nancy protests.

'So I told him, "But I want to be a doctor, sir."

'He looks at me as if I'm mad. "A doctor? Are you sure? It's a profession and . . ." he spread his hands, "not really suitable for a girl. You'd need to get a matriculation with first-class honours in Science and Maths, in fact in most subjects."

'So I lean over and turned the page in front of him and put my finger first on my October exams, my trial-matric Maths mark and then on the Biology and Chemistry. All are over ninety-five per cent.'

'Good on ya,' I say to Sarah.

'He looks down at where I'm pointing and then up at me and he's gone all huffy, "Yes . . . that's all very well, but I'm not convinced." He rubs his chin, "There's a lot more to becoming a doctor than good marks. Medicine is a science, you know, and women are not good at the sciences."

'Christ, Mum, I've just shown him I got ninety-five per cent in Science!'

Nancy shakes her head and Bozo says this bloke must be a real fuckwit.

Sarah continues. '"There's also the temperament," he says, "A medical career is better suited to the male temperament. I'm not at all sure women are suited to the profession. What happens when you marry, eh? You have to give it all up. Then, of course, there's the question of money. Are your parents well off, Sarah? A medical degree costs a lot of money, you know."

'"If I get a university pass in my Matriculation Certificate, I can get a Commonwealth Scholarship, sir."

'"A scholarship?" he says. I can see he's astonished. "Well, I never!" Suddenly he's lost for words and after a while takes a deep breath. "Of course I can't stop you, Sarah, but you must understand, scholarships to university go to the brightest of the bright, the crème de la crème." He chuckles, "The migrant boys seem to be winning them all these days, hah, hah. Some people are not too happy about that, can't say I disagree, we pay to bring them out and then they get all the perks." You can see what he's trying to tell me is that I'm a country kid and a girl and there's no way I'm going to get one!

'"Sir, all I need is a good university entrance pass to get a Commonwealth Scholarship," I tell him again.

'"That's all very well, Sarah, but how will you compete? Only the best students are accepted for Medicine."'

'The gall of the man!' Nancy shouts.

'Then he removes his glasses and rubs the bridge of his nose, "I don't want to discourage you, Sarah, but I want you to understand, in all my twenty years' experience as Victorian Country Schools Careers Officer, I've heard of several young country girls winning scholarships but never of one who went on to study Medicine. Don't you think you may have ideas above your station?"'

'You should've belted him, Sarah,' Bozo says, 'Bastard has no right.'

Sarah's well into her stride by now and can't stop, her voice has grown shrill she's that angry. 'Then he tells me, "You could always be a nurse? I can see you're bright enough. Why, you might even end up as a double-certificate sister or even the matron of a small hospital."'

Sarah looks around at us, wanting to see our reaction to this statement. But we're all just as gobsmacked as she is. 'Then, Mum, get this, he says to me, "Take my advice, Sarah, in my opinion that would be a terrible waste for a girl like you." He smiles and flicks the page back to my Domestic Science report, "Look at this, it's positively outstanding!" He reads Mrs Evans's comment at the bottom of the page, *Sarah's sponge cake is the envy of the school. You'll make someone a wonderful wife one day and be a beautiful little mother when the time comes.*"'

We all gasp and Nancy says, 'I'm going to call the headmaster! What a bloody cheek! Careers counsellor, my bum! Did he touch you, put his hand on you? Sounds like a pervert to me!' She gets up and goes into the kitchen to fetch a Bex.

That just about sums things up for Yankalillee and I dare say lots of other country towns. A woman's life was seen as a dutiful servitude to a husband who usually drank too much but remained the boss even if he was a total no-hoper.

There was only one criterion, a wife and mother was what good girls should aspire to. They could also be a kindergarten teacher or even a teacher, but once the babies started to arrive that was that. This bloke at the school was no different to Tommy, the idea of a woman being a doctor was unthinkable.

In fact, the idea of a woman challenging a man in anything was seen as both unladylike and somewhat ridiculous. It wasn't that a woman was less than a man, she simply wasn't one, and that was enough, no further questions asked.

A woman's role in life was to bring up boys who followed in their fathers' footsteps, a path that usually led directly into the pub. On the other hand, everyone knew that girls followed in their mothers' footsteps and the first thing to be instilled in a daughter was the mortal fear that if she wasn't married in her late teens or early twenties, she'd end up on the shelf as an old maid, shorthand for 'a total disgrace and burden to the family'.

Many of the town's daughters complied with their mothers' wishes by getting up the duff while still at school or shortly after leaving at the age of fourteen. A shotgun marriage was fairly hastily arranged, so that Yankalillee was famous for the number of premature births among its population. In the eyes of the town the problem had been rectified and respectability restored. After all, life goes on.

This rather hasty nuptial binding, between a girl only barely past the giggling stage and a boy whose major interest in life was tuning his Holden or Ford or Austin and getting pissed of a Saturday night and then going for a burn with his mates, was almost inevitably the beginning of a disaster. Unless his folk had a few quid or were on the land, he had few if any prospects and was totally unprepared for the responsibilities of fatherhood. Increasingly he escaped to the pub to drown his sorrows. This invariably meant he would return home and take his frustration out on his teenage missus who was nursing the baby that had ruined both of their lives by arriving about five years too early.

Marriage was everything, because respectability was the only thing that counted. Much better having a drunk who beat you than being an old maid, which was considered a fate worse than death except for one other thing, the ultimate disgrace Sarah now faced. If she kept the baby she would be an unmarried mother. For this last sin there was no forgiveness. You were a slut when you did it and you remained one for the remainder of your life.

The correct procedure towards marriage for a young woman in Yankalillee went like this. You worked as a typist in the front office of the soft-drink factory or as a waitress in the Parthenon cafe, a hairdresser in Kells Beaute Parlour or learned the florist trade with Florence's Fabulous Flowers or worked as a secretary for the Forestry Commission. During this period you assembled your glory box. In your early twenties, if not before, you became engaged, had a party, which consisted mainly of *oohs* and *aahs* and exclamations at the largeness of your very small diamond ring by all your girlfriends. This was followed by your kitchen tea, whereupon you resigned your job and got a set of double-bed sheets or a nice tablecloth from the management and staff, and finally the marriage took place, the full extravaganza in vestal gown and veil to the pealing of church bells and your picture in the local rag.

From this moment on, your husband was the breadwinner and you were his wife, more an animated and useful possession than an equal partner. If he turned out to be a poor provider with an unquenchable thirst and a tendency towards violence, well, that was sad, but not a reason for splitting up. You were no better or worse off than most. Your husband wasn't a bad bloke really, he got drunk on a Friday and again on the Saturday night after which he demanded a legover without precautions. If you were Catholic or unlucky with the diaphragm, or stupid, the kids just kept on coming until brewer's droop finally killed your husband's potency and snoring took over from grunt, push and burp. In the meantime you'd put on weight, lost your looks and were trapped with nowhere to go. What you endured was the female role found in many a typical bush-town marriage.

Mr Baloney and Grandmother Charlotte were the classic pattern in unequal partnership set long before their own misbegotten marriage and this was a tragedy to be repeated in the bush unto the next generation and the one after. Had it not been for the advent of television in 1956 and the new perceptions it brought into Australia, this state of male/female disparity and constant disharmony in marriage might well have continued until today. In some places it's still like that, though I'm sure Australia isn't alone in this.

However, Australia was a backwater at that time and the small towns within it were stagnant pools of disaffection between husband and wife. I suppose there must have been lots of good marriages and happy couples but it would be wrong to say that females had a fair go in the bush.

Nancy, for instance, had never considered divorcing Tommy, not only because she was a Catholic but also because she was a country girl. Her reputation was permanently sullied from having had four children out of wedlock but the one thing that redeemed her slightly in the eyes of Yankalillee was that she'd eventually married a local boy who had fought in the war and, despite his unfortunate ability with a glass-cutter and a pinch bar, she had kept her marriage to him intact.

It was not only the migrant women but also their men who changed the established work patterns in our small town. The reffos, who mostly couldn't speak English, put in a hard day's yakka and seldom complained, even when they got ripped off and were paid too little for their non-unionised skills.

The difference between them and us was this. Most of our blokes spent all their spare time in the pub and quite a lot of what shouldn't have been spare time there as well. A beer at lunchtime would often enough spill over into the afternoon and then on to six o'clock closing.

Blokes would get a few beers under their belts and in this temporary state of euphoria they'd volunteer to be in anything going that was good for the community. Go out and burn firebreaks. Volunteer to work a weekend on the extension to the bush-nursing hospital. Re-timber the seats on the football stand. Repair the stone fence running alongside the Anglican church. Or simply man a sausage sizzle at the local fete. If such a request was made on any given afternoon in any of the town's seven pubs, the response would be immediate, 'Name the time and the date, mate, we'll be there, no worries.' You'd be all set, thinking you'd got it set up, only you'd forgotten you were talking to a bunch of drunks who'd wake up the next day and would either not remember what they'd promised or decide that the commitment was just too bloody hard, so when the big day came around, nobody would turn up.

Almost nothing you could call civic duty really got going in Yankalillee. If it required a donation of time and effort from your average male citizen, it wouldn't happen. In fact, the two characteristics you could absolutely rely on from them was an insatiable thirst and the fecklessness that comes from a perpetual hangover.

Women did all the charity work in town, this usually involved church bazaars, fetes, street stalls, debutante balls, school socials, B & S dances and the like. If it wasn't something that required baking cakes and scones, selling raffle tickets, bottling preserves, doing a bit of jam-making or needlework, it just didn't happen.

The only events men seemed to organise were the Anzac Day March, the 'Men's Day' at the golf club and the footy finals. This required a minimum of fuss. Every male golfer attended as a matter of course and with the footy final, every man in town considered his attendance compulsory, especially if his team was going to win.

Anzac Day, for instance, mainly involved turning up with your medals pinned more or less in a straight line on your left breast. George Fisch, who probably fought for the other side, knew to assemble the town brass band at the top of King Street and to make sure Bluey Porter, the chemist, and a regimental bugler during the war, didn't get too pissed the night before so that he could render the last post, generally these days off-key.

Red Turnbull, the Anglican minister, who flew with the RAF in the Battle of Britain, knew his part off by heart and so did Father Crosby, who did the benediction at the end of the two minutes' silence.

The remaining effort required from the generally out-of-step males marching was to fall out at the rotunda and disperse to any one of the town's seven pubs to play two-up and lose more than they could afford and, in the process, get thoroughly pissed meanwhile bullshitting their mates about their deeds in the army, telling waries, how they personally won the war. As the sun set over those Anzacs who were still alive, their wives arrived and picked them up off the pub floor or the footpath and drove them home legless to snore all night on the couch in the living room with their medals still bravely pinned to their chests.

On the other hand, the migrants worked all hours of the day and night, gobbling up any overtime available as a result of the lassitude of the general population. Although they were not great civil-duty volunteers themselves, this was mostly because nobody thought to ask them. The Catholics, or more specifically Father Crosby, could always rely on the Italians to do a bit of concreting or brickwork to the glory of God and Il Papa in Rome. If you didn't watch the Italians carefully, they'd throw a bit of red or green concrete dye into the cement just where you didn't want it. Later, when they had their own houses, they'd cement the front yard with green concrete, better than mowing the lawn or having bindies in the grass I suppose. The Balts and the Maltese would manage a bit of voluntary carpentry for the church as well.

The town wouldn't think to ask a migrant for voluntary help, on the basis that they weren't one of us. This inferred a state of acceptance that couldn't be bought and could only be earned after completing a couple of generations in the town or immediate district. We Maloneys may have been at the bottom of the heap but our rights as citizens of Yankalillee were solid as a drilled and bolted rock face.

Although most migrants applied for and were granted Australian citizenship at a naturalisation ceremony after their five-year migrant status had expired, this in no way helped at the local level. In the eyes of the locals they remained strangers and foreigners for as long as they lived.

George Fisch, a German migrant who took over as volunteer bandmaster when old Willie Perkins attempted a high note on the trumpet during a rendition by the band of 'Colonel Bogey' and suffered a heart attack, was only elected to the position because there wasn't anyone else with a local background who could do the job. Before the war he had studied at the Conservatory of Music in Vienna and George was Yankalillee's best-trained musician by a country mile. Furthermore, the brass band was a tradition unbroken since it was formed by melodiously inclined miners during the gold rushes for the purpose of Sunday-afternoon entertainment and for drumming up membership to the miners' union. After a great deal of discussion by the shire councillors, it was reluctantly agreed that George should take charge of the band.

During his twenty years as bandmaster, Yankalillee's brass band, hitherto unknown and unsung, became nationally respected and was a source of constant pride to the town and district. Yet, in all that time, George Fisch was never invited into the home of a single important citizen. To the very end he remained an outsider and when the band won the National Brass Band Championships in Melbourne in 1968, it was Harry Yerberry, the shire president at the time, not George Fisch, who stepped up to the rostrum to claim the coveted award. George paid his own share of the train fare that took the band to Melbourne and sat in the audience with the band members to watch the awards ceremony and listen to Harry Yerberry's 'From Gold Rush to Gold Medal' thank-you speech in which his name wasn't once mentioned.

The Bonegilla Migrant Camp was about half an hour down the road and Sundays we'd go and have a squiz at these strange creatures we were allowing to share in the future of our glorious nation. To us locals they were the Sunday-afternoon sideshow. You know, like you'd go and look at the site of a motor-car accident where somebody had got killed or at a house that had burnt down with two young children asleep upstairs, or some other such vicarious happening.

Here's how it happened in our family. Bozo would work on the Diamond T Sunday mornings, getting the old girl ready for the week ahead, cleaning the points, flushing out the carburettor, filling the battery, checking the radiator and the hose and doing anything else that needed doing, which was usually something fairly nasty. Then, after dinner when he'd finished, we'd all go for a Sunday-arvo drive. If Tommy wasn't on a bender he'd drive us and let Nancy stay home to read a book. She always liked to read a book she'd taken out of the library of a Sunday afternoon. 'I never had any education but books,' she'd say. That's why sometimes she had these big words to use on us even if she didn't always talk proper like Sarah. Even when she drove, she'd take a book and we'd stop somewhere for an hour or so and she'd read while we mucked about or went for a walk in the bush.

Sarah would come along, though mostly to give little Colleen an outing. She would sit with Tommy in the front, or if Nancy drove she'd be in the back with Bozo and me and little Colleen, who loved to feel the wind in her face. Mike almost never came. A couple of miles or even further from Bonegilla you'd come across the first lot of reffos, people from the camp going for a Sunday walk. They didn't have cars or any way of getting away except on foot so they'd walk along the road. They'd often wear their national costumes and whole families or groups would be walking, holding hands, sometimes even singing folk songs with one of them playing a squeeze box or piano accordion.

Sometimes you'd come across the reffos having a picnic under a clump of gum trees and they'd have weird things to eat. 'Garlic Munchers' we'd call them. They'd eat things you wouldn't touch with a barge pole. Pickled cucumbers and dried-up tomatoes, pickled cabbage, and soup they'd made out of beetroot. Can you imagine something as terrible as beetroot soup! They'd have these big sausages that stank to high heaven, but you could almost understand those because they were a bit like a saveloy, only bigger and much stinkier. There was also pigs' feet, stuff we wouldn't eat even on an offal week.

They had this bread that wasn't white like proper bread, but dark-brown, like a chocolate colour. I'm not kidding. It looked stale and we thought the poor buggers had to eat it because they couldn't afford not to. But it wasn't, it was baked like that, the colour of dark chocolate. We once tried a slice that was given to us, it had pickled cucumber on it in thin slices, which looked like your proper cucumber only smaller and lighter green so you could nearly see through it and it rested on this soft white stuff Sarah said was some sort of cheese, although it didn't look like cheese and it didn't taste like any cheese I've ever et. I must have made a face because the husband and wife who gave it to us laughed. I wanted to spit it out but couldn't, because, even though they were reffos, I didn't want to hurt their feelings. Anybody eating stuff like that must be very poor, and not very civilised, is all I can say. I reckon they got to Australia just in time.

The migrants had no money and had to hope they could get out of Bonegilla as soon as possible and get jobs in the town or the district. The big hope was to get a job on the Snowy Mountains Hydro-Electric

Scheme. But the problem with that was that if they did they usually had to leave their families behind. Only the engineers and people like them, the big nobs, got houses in the Snowy and the rest of the workers lived in the men's single quarters, dormitories or barracks.

The wages were good, much higher than in the towns, and they could save a bit and, Sarah said, make a fresh start in a new country. They claimed the Snowy Mountains Scheme was the biggest construction works going on in the world at that time and that Sir William Hudson, who was in charge of it, was an absolute genius who was showing the world how these things should be done. Also, they lost a man for every mile of tunnel they dug, which was very good considering how many people other nations lost doing the same thing.

If you were a little bloke you stood a better chance of dying. The reason was this. When they cemented the walls of the tunnels, they'd pour concrete through a hole in the top of these huge steel-cylinder moulds and when it was half full, some little guy had to climb in through the hole with a shovel and see that there were no air pockets. If he found some, he had to tamp the cement down. Sometimes the concrete would collapse and he'd be buried in it and when that happened there was no way of getting him out. So when you go through one of those tunnels, there's skeletons from just about every nation in the world buried in the walls somewhere. But, you'll be glad to know, less than if someone else except Sir William Hudson had been in charge. 'Bill Hudson is the best large-project manager in the world,' people would say and we'd all be proud.

Once we saw this documentary at the flicks and it showed how Mussolini, the Eyetalian dictator, built these tunnels through the Eyetalian Alps and they said it was a masterpiece of engineering. 'Ha!' I thought, 'I'll bet there's hundreds of dead workers' skeletons concreted over, mile after mile of bones of little Eyetalians buried in the cement.' I mean, they wouldn't tell you the truth, would they?

It was lots of fun seeing the migrants jabbering away in their lingo or singing in funny languages, all dressed up in their Sunday best and sweating like pigs. They'd be carrying a small stem of gum leaf to whisk the flies off them and you'd see family groups who would stand for hours looking at a paddock of sheep or cattle. Bozo and me used to laugh at them and feel very superior until Sarah said we shouldn't, and it wasn't their fault that they weren't born in Australia, where cows and sheep weren't a curiosity.

The reffos seemed to like the Diamond T and crowded around it when we stopped. Some of them explained that they remembered it when the Americans arrived to liberate them from Adolf Hitler and they'd come in these big old Diamond Ts among their army trucks. So we were a sort of all-round good memory for them.

After a while Tommy started taking the kids for a ride down the road a bit, piling about fifty little kids in the back and off he'd go, so that we were soon very popular and everyone would practise their English on us. Sarah would teach them new words and help them with their pronunciation. They sometimes gave us food to eat and we'd say thank you and explain that we'd eat it later and then we'd throw it out the window on the way home.

Anyway, one Sunday we meet this couple. Well, we didn't exactly meet them. The Diamond T has a flat tyre on account of we're down to the canvas again. Tommy leaves us to fix it and goes for a walk in the bush. Bozo and me have removed the tyre and taken out the inner tube, pumped it up and are trying to find the puncture spot. The tube already has about fifty patches so that finding the leak is anyone's guess. Usually you'd push the tube into a tub of water to see where the bubbles rise from the air escaping from the puncture. Only there's no water around to immerse the tube. Bozo's running his hand over the tyre, hoping to feel the air escaping from the puncture spot, when this little bloke comes walking up. He stands there with his hands clasped behind his back, watching us and clucking 'titch-titch'. Every once in a while he'd shake his head and soon he's about as welcome around us as a bad smell.

Eventually he says, 'Excuse please, sir?'

We look up at him, though we're not that friendly. He's only about my size but he's got this heavy black-wool overcoat on that comes down to his ankles and is buttoned all the way up to show only his collar and tie and a bit of white shirt. The collar is shiny and made of celluloid and his tie is black wool and very old and frayed. You can see the gold collar-stud above the knot and just below his Adam's apple. On his head he wears a sort of round fur cap. It's the middle of bloody summer and it must be hot as hades inside his heavy coat. We're both on our haunches crouched over the inner tube. 'Gidday, 'ow yer goin'?' Bozo grunts, squinting up at him.

'Sand, no?'

'What's he saying?' Bozo asks me. I can see, like me, he's getting jack of the little bloke just standing and looking down on us, shaking his head and going 'titch-titch', like we're imbeciles or something.

'Sand!' he repeats. We are right next to a dry creek bed and now he goes over and takes up a handful of river sand and with his other hand points to the inner tube, 'Sand funeral.' And then he lets the sand run out of his hand.

'Sand?' I ask, not knowing what he's talking about.

'I think he said "funeral",' Bozo adds. 'What the fuck's a sand funeral?'

'Funeral za wheel!' The little bloke is getting quite excited by this time. He turns suddenly, goes over to the creek, gets down on his knees and starts to dig a big shallow hole in the fine sand. 'Funeral!' he says, pointing to the tube. 'Find *pffftt*!'

'Eh? Bloke's mad, should be up top with the twin aunties,' Bozo whispers and I can't help giggling. Dot and Gwen, Nancy's twin sisters in the loony bin, we always just call them 'the twin aunties' when we're talking about them.

'Funeral! Sand funeral, *pffft*!' the little bloke keeps saying, furiously digging like one of Bozo's Bitzers burying a bone.

'Crikey, I think he means "bury",' I exclaim. 'He wants us to bury the tube in the sand.'

'Whaffor?' Bozo asks, scratching his forehead.

The little bloke has now dug this big wide hole about the circumference of the inner tube, about ten inches deep. He stands up and walks over to Bozo, dusting sand from his coat with both hands. 'Funeral!' he says again and indicates that Bozo must give him the tyre at once. He's only a little bloke, but he's got a lot of authority about him that makes you want to do what he says.

Bozo shrugs, 'Why does he want to bury it, Mole?'

'Buggered if I know,' I say, but Bozo lets him have the tube anyway.

Poor bugger is in a lather of sweat, it's running down his neck and his starched collar and, where his shirt shows on either side of his tie, it's sopping wet and you can see the hair on his chest through it.

Well, this reffo bloke walks over to the hole he's made and we follow him and squat down on our haunches to watch. He places the blown-up inner tube in the hole and starts to cover it in dry sand. Just a very light dressing. But nothing happens. Bozo looks at me and shakes his head. I know what he means, we've got ourselves a real loony. The reffo does another 'titch-titch' and removes the inner tube and turns it about-face. Then he covers it again with a second dusting of sand. And suddenly there it is, the air escaping from the leak is blowing the sand away from the surface of the inner tube. He's discovered the location of the puncture.

'Jesus!' Bozo says, 'Why didn't I think of that? Bloody clever, eh?' He gets up and shakes the little bloke's hand. And I do the same. And we all laugh.

'Bozo Maloney,' Bozo says, 'Pleased ta meetcha, sir.'

'Mole Maloney,' I say, grinning.

'Moshe Zukfizzleski,' the little bloke says, laughing and mighty pleased with himself. He points to the inner tube, 'Okey-dokey, very goet, no?'

Sarah is standing with his wife a few yards back and they both clap, like he's a hero or something. Suddenly everyone's laughing and his wife is hugging little Colleen.

Well, it turns out this little bloke's a professor. Only, like I said before, he can't be one here in Australia because he's not good enough.

'Where you from then?' Bozo asks, as we set about repairing the puncture.

'From?'

'You know, what place in Europe?' I say.

'Ah, Europe.' He taps his chest, 'Poland me.'

'Pooland?' I say. 'Where they've got concentration camps?' Just like Anna Dumb-cow-ski told us.

'Ja!' he says, surprised, 'Poland, Auschwitz.'

That must be the name of the town he comes from, I think.

'It's not Pooland, Mole, it's Poland,' Sarah corrects.

'No, Pooland!' I protest, looking to Bozo for confirmation.

'Professor Zukfizzleski comes from Poland and he's Jewish,' Sarah says and the little bloke nods his head, smiling, like he's telling her she's got it right. So much for Bozo's theory about Anna Dumb-cow-ski's family being in the *poo* in *Poo*land. But it doesn't clear up the bit about them not concentrating and being sent to a camp. I should have known better than to trust Bozo. But he's busy with the tyre iron, feeding the tyre back into the rim, and he pretends he isn't listening. 'Looks like offal month coming up,' he says, running his hand along the canvas strips on the tyre. It's him trying to change the subject.

Professor Zukwhatzizname has unbuttoned his overcoat and I see he's got another heavy suit on underneath, poor bugger must be practically melting. I forgot to say he has this great big moustache that has sharp points sticking out at the end which curl up nearly to touch his ears. Then he takes off his fur cap and he's bald except for these two tufts of hair in front, like an extra set of very large eyebrows only higher up. All I can think of is that he looks exactly like a picture I once saw of an African wart-hog.

The professor's wife's name is Zofia and she seems to be quite a lot younger than him. She speaks English a lot better too, which wouldn't be hard, and she and Sarah are soon getting on like a house on fire. You can see she loves little Colleen to bits, she can't stop hugging and kissing her and once or twice Zofia wipes tears from her eyes with the back of her hand. 'I am very heppy to know you,' she keeps saying.

They ask us if we'll stay for a cuppa and that's when we get the black sandwich with see-through cucumber and mushy white sour cheese on it. Zofia makes a bit of a fire from twigs and boils this little pot and makes black tea and puts a lot of sugar in it, like four heaped tablespoons. They've only got two tin mugs because I suppose they weren't expecting us. But Bozo and me and Sarah say no thanks to the tea. We can't come at the black tea. The heavy sour black bread with weird stuff on it was bad enough but tea without milk is definitely a no-goer. Though I don't suppose they could help it, not being civilised like us.

After the bread and tea, Tommy comes back and we introduce him and then we take them back to Bonegilla and drop them off at the camp gate. Zofia's crying and hugging little Colleen and Sarah and the professor is bowing and taking off his fur cap and showing his extra eyebrows and grinning. It's not hard to tell they've had a good time. It's like we're royalty and not Maloneys and you can see they really like us and want us to be their friends. It's quite nice knowing there's people lower than you that you can be nice to because you know what it feels like to be a nobody yourself. Even Tommy says the professor is a good bloke, he's sat in the front of the Diamond T and they must have had some sort of a conversation, though I can't think what they could've said to each other.

'Jewish? What's that when it's got booties on?' I ask Sarah later when we're going home in the truck. Colleen's tired and doesn't want to go in the back and so we're all squashed in the front of the Diamond T.

Sarah sort of shrugs her shoulders and I can tell from the sound of her voice, she doesn't really know. 'He's . . . you know . . . ah . . . a Jew.' She thinks for a moment, 'Like Jesus in the Bible.'

'Oh,' I say, though I'm none the wiser. I always thought Jesus was a Catholic.

Then Sarah tells us more about the professor and Zofia. She's had a proper chinwag with his wife, the way women have of getting all the latest goss even if they've only met for the first time. She tells Bozo and me how they've had a terrible time. He's been in Auschwitz and she's been in another concentration camp and then three years in a refugee camp in Germany before Moshe became the medical officer of a refugee agency in Germany and at the same time worked as a doctor in a hospital for the survivors of the concentration camps.

I'm still not sure what a concentration camp is, but I sense that it's not what we thought with Anna-dumb-cow-ski, that it's something much, much worse.

Sarah then says that Moshe and Zofia spent almost seven years in Germany after the war, but still they could not get used to the faces. Zofia said that the fear never left her, she would look into the face of a railway guard or a doorman and the cap he wore would turn into an SS officer's cap with the death's head badge and she would start to tremble, even sometimes to wet her pants. 'Za faces, zey are in mine brain, I can't forget it,' she tells Sarah. So, when Moshe felt he had done as much as he could to make up for what he was forced as a doctor to do in the concentration camps, they decided to get away from Germany. 'Away from za faces!' Zophia said, 'In my sleep also, I see za Nazi faces.'

Sarah explains how Hitler hated the Jews, of whom there were a whole lot in Europe, mostly in Germany and Poland, but also other places. I mean a *whole lot* like millions and he decides to exterminate them.

'All of them?' I ask Sarah.

'Six million!' Sarah says.

'Six million! We're only eight million in Australia! What for?' Bozo asks. 'They must have done something *really* bad?'

'It was their religion, Jewish is a religion and Hitler hated the religion and he didn't want them mixing their blood with Germans.'

'Like Catholics and Protestants?' I say.

'Yes, but he wanted to kill *all* the Jews, not just hate them. He decided to kill every single one.'

'Shit, hey? How'd he do that? I mean, there's six million of them!' Bozo exclaims.

'That's it, he took them from everywhere and put them in cattle trains and sent them to these extermination camps called concentration camps. There were lots of them scattered around Germany and Poland mostly.'

I shoot an accusing glance at Bozo now that the concentration-camp question has finally been cleared up.

Sarah continues. 'Those he didn't want to work to death first before he killed them, like for instance the old people and children and pregnant mothers and small babies, he told them they were going to have a nice shower. They were dirty and bedraggled from the days in the cattle trains and this was the first nice thing that happened to them. They were instructed to take off their clothes and go into these big sheds. They were even given a bar of soap among six of them. Women, babies and girls were told to go into one shower shed, old men and young boys in another. Only, it turned out, they weren't showers at all, they were gas chambers. Instead of water coming out of the showers, Zyklon-B came out and they all died a horrible, terrible, suffering death.'

'What about the others he didn't send to the showers?' I ask her.

'Those who had skills or could be made into slave labourers in Hitler's factories, he worked and starved to death. He didn't care, there were plenty more where they came from. Cattle trains crammed with Jews, and some of them dying before they arrived, were coming from every direction in Europe. And them having to shit and urinate right there, jammed into the trucks closer than sardines in a tin and given no water or food.

'When the concentration camps became so full and Hitler couldn't bury the ones he'd killed fast enough because there were so many, he built these giant ovens and shoved them in there and you could smell the burning flesh for miles around. The smoke darkened the sky.'

This was a picture I would keep in my head for the remainder of my life. Long grey endless tin sheds and hundreds of ovens with tall red-brick chimneys coming from them. The sky, as far as you could see, was a cumulus of dark smoke rolling and billowing upwards, blocking out the sun itself, and everywhere the silent scream of death clawing its way up to heaven where God sat too stunned to weep.

Sarah went on. 'Before he put them in the ovens or buried them, Hitler cut off their hair and used it to make blankets and the linings for his army coats. Then he took the gold out of the corpses' teeth and melted it down and kept it for himself. There were millions of pounds worth of gold, and also mountains of shoes and eyeglasses and practically a mountain range of clothes. Nothing was wasted. Sometimes Hitler even made lampshades out of human skin!'

Sarah didn't tell us all this that day going home. I'm telling it all together as if she told us in one go, but it came out over a long period of time as we got to know the professor and Zofia when their English had improved.

It turned out the professor was the Professor of Surgery at the University of Kraków before the war and when he was sent to the concentration camp he was useful as a doctor so he survived in Auschwitz.

Zofia, who wasn't married to him then, went to another camp called Buchenwald and she worked as a servant in the home of the Kommandant and managed to stay out of the showers and the ovens.

But both of them still starved and had lice in their hair and you could see their bones sticking out under their skin and their toes nearly rotted off and they looked like walking corpses when they were finally released. When the Americans liberated the camps they used DDT to get rid of the lice and the bugs and the fleas, because, it seems, no matter what happens vermin stay alive. I've seen a flea, but I've never seen a louse or a bedbug. The concentration camp was also where the professor went completely bald, keeping only those two high-up 'eyebrow' bits.

Well, that was the effect the migrant camp at Bonegilla had on the Maloney family.

What's more, for people who weren't supposed to be as clever as us Australians, I tell you what, the professor and Zofia learned English amazingly quickly. The professor got a job as a lab assistant up top at the mental asylum with the twin aunties and Zofia worked in the soft-drink bottling plant stacking the filled bottles into wooden crates. After work most days they'd visit us, and Sarah and sometimes Mike, or even Nancy, would give them English lessons. Zofia turned out to be very useful at smocking and broderie anglaise and she'd work with Mike, Nancy and Sarah as she absorbed her lessons. I think it made them feel that they were paying their way and not sponging on us.

Eventually Zofia and the professor found this small corrugated-iron shed behind the Golden Fleece petrol station and they moved into town. They were soon spelling and writing and reading everything they could lay their hands on in English. You weren't surprised that Moshe had become a professor in Poland because he was really brainy and you only had to tell him something once and he never forgot it.

One afternoon, after the professor had read the whole front page of the *Gazette* out loud without making a mistake, he turns to Sarah. 'Zofia and me also, we want we should have English name, English surname for us and first name also.' Then he hands Sarah a slip of paper, 'Wot you sink, Sarah?'

Sarah looks down at the scrap of paper, 'Sophie? That's nice.' She smiles up at Zofia. 'Though I don't see too much wrong with Zofia, it's a very pretty name.'

'You like!' The professor claps his hands together and turns to

Zofia, 'Now, my dear, you are a Sophie okey-dokey, very nice, zank you very much!' Then he hands Sarah a second bit of paper and when she reads it she starts to giggle and brings her hand over her mouth to stop herself laughing, but she can't.

'You don't like?' the little bloke asks, concern written over his face.

'Professor Zukfizzleski, you *can't* call yourself Suckfizzle!'

'Is not goet, Suckfizzle?'

'Well, it's . . . ah,' Sarah bursts into laughter again and now we all break up.

'This is joke, no?' The professor, clearly puzzled, asks again.

'Well, people won't forget it in a hurry, that's for sure,' Nancy chortles.

Sarah explains, 'They're two action words, to *suck* and to *fizzle*, and they end up being funny when you join them together in English, Professor.'

'Two action words?' He thinks for a moment. 'Ja, this I like, to suck and to fizzle, very nice, my dear.'

'People will laugh at your name, Professor,' Mike warns, laughing himself.

'Tch! Better to laugh and remember, zen Zukfizzleski and always to forget. Now they will remember my English name. "Two action words, to suck and to fizzle," I say to them ven zey ask, "suck and fizzle, now you remember, madam, okey-dokey?"' He holds his hand above his head, forefinger pointed to the roof. 'Zukfizzleski no more! Suckfizzle, yes! One more! I am not Moshe. Moshe is now finish. I am Morrie. Morrie now begins!' He stands to attention, sticking his chest out. 'Mr Morrie Suckfizzle and Mrs Sophie Suckfizzle, congratulations, she'll be right, mate! No worries! Just a moment I go to kitchen.' He's said it all in one breath and now turns sharply and marches from where we are on the back verandah towards the kitchen. He stops and turns at the door. 'You wait, please.'

'What's all that about?' Nancy asks and Zofia, who is now Sophie, giggles but says nothing.

In a couple of minutes the professor returns, but he's walking backwards toward us.

'What the –?' Bozo says.

Then the little bloke turns around, 'Surpriseski!' he shouts. 'Now I am English, Morrie Suckfizzle, Australian gentlemans!'

We all gasp. Morrie's shaved off his moustache.

He's prancing around us with delight, then he rushes over to Sarah and, grabbing her hands in both his own, he proceeds to shake them vigorously. 'Sarah Maloney, I am Morrie Suckfizzle, please ta meet choo, zis is Sophie, my wife, gidday, mate.' He introduces himself in perfect Australian, only his pronunciation is a bit crook. Then he repeats the exact same words to each of us, except of course for our individual names. You can see he's pleased as punch with his new self-appropriated, two-action-words surname, but it's hard to look at him without his big curled-at-the-corners-up-to-his-ears moustache. It's like seeing this chicken that's been around all year suddenly plucked and on a roasting dish ready to go into the oven for your Christmas dinner.

We'd known the professor and Sophie for some time when Sarah became pregnant and they both knew of her wanting to be a doctor, of course, which more than delighted Morrie Suckfizzle. The two of them would have long discussions about medicine and what it meant to be a good doctor. By this time both he and Sophie spoke very good English with a slight Polish accent. I reckon if I had to learn Polish I'd never get that good so quick.

So, when Sarah got pregnant we didn't know quite what to do and we decided to say nothing for a while, not even to Morrie and Sophie Suckfizzle. Nancy said it was Maloney business and whatever happened we'd handle it ourselves. As it turned out, this was a big mistake.

It wasn't that hard to keep our secret from them as we weren't seeing a lot of Morrie and Sophie just then. I mean they were terrific friends, the best we'd ever had. In fact, they were the only grown-ups who ever came to the house for a proper visit and not just to pick up a christening robe or a baby's layette. It was just that both of them now had their day jobs and, as well, at night Sophie worked as a cleaner at The Pines for the Forestry Commission and Morrie as a travelling door-to-door salesman for Rawleigh's products, so they never had any time for visiting except for one Sunday every month when we'd go with them to the Bonegilla Migrant Camp.

Morrie bought this little clapped-out Austin 7 from the mechanic at the Golden Fleece petrol station for twenty quid and, with Bozo's help, they'd got it going pretty well. Bozo built a roof rack to carry Morrie's boxes of household-cleaning products. He'd do the town and nearby places like Silver Creek, Wooragee, Chiltern and Stanley on weekday evenings, and places like Yackandandah, Allans Flat, Bright and Myrtleford and the farms and properties surrounding them on the weekends.

I don't think Morrie was a very good salesman at first, but after a while he became terrific. It happened like this.

One weekend Morrie visits an outlying farm where the farmer is busy dehorning several Herefords he's just bought. Sitting there on the race, he's covered in blood from the horns he's been cutting, and the posts of the cattle race are the same. Somehow the farmer's slipped and gone head-first into the race, and the uncut horn of the Hereford has hooked into his groin, ripping it open and slicing through the femoral artery and generally making a huge wound. The blood is pumping out of the artery and the poor bugger is bleeding to death right in front of the family's eyes. His wife can't drive and it's going to take an hour or more for the ambulance to come from Wangaratta because it's the weekend and it's at the footy match.

Just then, old Morrie comes up the dirt road in the little Austin 7, bumping and jumping at every rut and suddenly it's all happening. He hops in and gets to work, gives this bloke a couple of stiff shots of brandy, ties the artery and eventually stems the blood flow. Then he cleans the massive wound and, using a sharp kitchen knife which he first sterilises in boiling water, he cuts away the lacerated bits of flesh, I think it's called tissue. He uses the farmer's Mercurochrome to stop short-term infection, then he sends the wife out to get several hairs from the tail of the kid's pony and, after he's sterilised them, he uses a darning needle and the horsehair to sew up the big gaping wound.

The ambulance arrives three hours later but the farmer doesn't want to go to hospital because he reckons he's all right. Morrie says he must, to get antibiotics and have the wound properly dressed and sutured and he probably needs a blood transfusion.

At the hospital the doctors can't believe it, not because it's a botched job, just the opposite. Morrie's done everything perfectly and they've never seen horsehair stitches before. The doctors say afterwards that they were perfect and very neat and that the whole job had obviously been done by a very skilled surgeon.

They give the farmer a blood transfusion and then open him up, dress his wounds again and stitch him with proper hospital stitches, but forever afterwards the farmer, whose name is Harry Trumble, would claim that it was all totally unnecessary, that Morrie Suckfizzle had done the job perfect in the first place and they should've left it alone.

After this incident Morrie became a sort of local hero in the district and whenever he went out to sell his cleaning stuff, if there was a sick kid in the house or if someone else in the family was crook, people would ask him to take a look.

They got to like Morrie a lot because he wasn't like your normal doctor who you had to treat like a little tin god or something and who never told you anything anyway. He'd always listen very carefully first. 'Listen to your patient, Sarah, they will tell you what's wrong with them. To be a clever listener is to be a good physician,' he'd often say to her. Then when he'd heard it all and asked a few questions of his own and if he thought it required treatment from a doctor, Morrie would write down what they had to say to their doctor. If it was something that could be treated by stuff you could buy at the chemist, he'd write the medicine down for them to get. But he'd always say that he wasn't qualified to treat them in Australia and if they were worried they should go to the doctor. If he recommended they see a local doctor, they had to do as he said or he wouldn't be able to help them again if something went wrong.

But country folk know when things work and when they don't and a lot of them came to swear by him. Morrie always carried his doctor's bag with him and other things like bandages and plaster of Paris and a few basic medicines. This didn't make the two local doctors, old Dr Hughes and young Dr Wallis, too happy even though they benefited from the patients Morrie sent them. The two doctors tried to stop Morrie helping people but as he wasn't practising medicine for profit and never charged for his services or prescribed drugs that weren't readily available at the chemist, there wasn't anything they could do except have sour grapes. Morrie would often come across a broken finger or stitch a cut on a kid's leg, or someone would break an arm and he'd set the bone and do the plaster of Paris and nobody could find fault with the job he'd done.

So even if Morrie wasn't a good salesman, in the end he was, because people always bought heaps of his Rawleigh's products, just in case they might be sick the one time he called around. He could easily have opened up a surgery in town with a brass plate outside which said:

PROF. MORRIE SUCKFIZZLE
NOT QUALIFIED TO PRACTISE IN AUSTRALIA.

Sarah said people would still have come to him anyway, because he was much better than the two town quacks, although, as Mike said, 'The old Sarah's just a tad biased, wouldn't you think?' But of course it would be against the law because he couldn't take any money from his patients.

Morrie Suckfizzle was probably the only migrant who broke through the migrant-prejudice barrier. But only for some people, the small farmers and the working-class people in the town. The bigwigs, nobs, graziers, and the would-bes-if-they-could-bes would simply have shooed him from their front door, because they wouldn't have wanted people to think that they bought Rawleigh's cleaning products in the first place. But the working-class people didn't call Morrie a 'wog' or a 'dago', even behind his back. They had this special name for him, 'the bush doctor', and welcomed him into their homes.

Morrie also did another good thing. Once a month he'd come over on a Sunday morning and Bozo would help him to service the Austin 7. Then they'd follow us to Bonegilla with Colleen hugged all the way and squeezed in on Sophie's lap.

The migrants would bring their sick kids, and the adults who were crook would also turn up and he'd question, then examine them and write down in English what they had to ask the camp doctor. He'd also treat minor wounds and abscesses and tell them things to ask the camp doctor. Unlike the town doctors, the doctors who came to the camp were too busy to mind him interfering. It turned out Morrie could talk five languages, Polish, Russian, German, Hungarian and Yiddish, in addition to English, and he made things a lot easier for them, so they decided that Morrie was a good bloke to have around.

He and Sophie were saving every penny they made so that they could move to Melbourne where Morrie could study for his medical degree at the university. He'd have been okay if he'd come from England or a Commonwealth country where they teach you to be a doctor in English, but not if you came from Poland or any other place that speaks a different language. If Morrie wanted to be a doctor in Australia, he had to sit an examination, which if he passed, he was permitted to skip the first year at medical school and do only five years instead of six to qualify.

Morrie and Sarah would talk about doing their degree together and laugh about it a lot. They'd say how they'd hold hands when they graduated and then they'd open a practice together, the old bull and the young heifer. That was their wonderful dream which all the Maloneys shared, the thing that was going to get us out from under that rock Nancy was always going on about. That's the big joke now, the old bull and the young heifer, a heifer is a young cow that has never had a calf. Now Nancy didn't want us even to tell our family's best friends about the Maloneys' latest tragedy. I guess she was that ashamed she couldn't face them.

Chapter Six

Bozo came home from boxing one night a day or so after we'd been to see the Templetons and called Mike and Sarah and me together into the washhouse out the back. Nancy was having her afternoon kip and so was Colleen, who always goes with her, the lump and the morsel, so we were safe enough.

Bozo's expression is real serious and he even makes Bitzers One to Five wait outside before he blurts out, 'There's this bloke at boxing whose sister got a bun in the oven and she went to see this old lady who lives in a bark hut at Silver Creek, she's Indian or something like that, and she gave her some medicine and it got rid of her baby.'

'What sort of medicine?' Sarah asks.

'Just stuff to drink,' Bozo says. 'She had to make up this concoction and drink it about five times a day.'

'And it worked? She got rid of it?' Mike asks.

'That's what this bloke said.'

'And his sister, is she okay?' Sarah says.

'Yeah, right as rain. He said she was a bit crook for two days, that's all.'

Sarah gets on her stern face. 'Bozo, what's this boy's sister's name?'

'I'm not allowed to say,' Bozo pleads. 'I promised him. We all took the boxer's oath.'

'Promised this bloke?' Mike reaches forward and grabs Bozo by the shirt front, pulling him towards him. 'You mean you told him about Sarah?'

'Christ no!' Bozo exclaims.

'Well then, what's her name?' Sarah demands.

Bozo looks around, he's got the trapped look Sarah can get you to have when she wants to know something. 'Please, Sarah,' he now begs. 'Nobody knows his sister was up the duff and, if it gets out, the family will be in disgrace. He only told us after we'd all taken the boxer's oath.'

'What's that when it's got booties on?' Mike asks.

'It's when there's a secret only we know. You know, us Police Boys boxers.'

'That's bullshit, Bozo,' Sarah says. 'What's her name?'

'It's an emergency and family comes first,' Mike reminds him.

Bozo can take the long way or the short way, but he knows he's going to lose. When Sarah wants to find something out nothing can stop her. She'll ask you all these little innocent questions and you'll answer them and then discover that she's got you trapped, that there's no way to go except to tell her.

'Is this bloke a Catholic?' Sarah begins.

See what I mean? Already she's started. No harm in answering that, is there? Well, that's the beginning of the trap and Bozo knows sooner or later she'll nail down the truth.

'No, he's a Proddy.'

'Ah, so he goes to our school, then so must his sister.'

Bozo sighs. It's only a matter of time so he reluctantly decides to go the short way. 'Her name is Angela Morrison.' Bozo's not too happy, he's good at secrets and now he's gone and broken his boxer's oath.

'Ah-ha, Angela Morrison, eh? Well, well, who'd have thought that, she never says boo to a mouse,' Sarah exclaims.

The next day when I get back from school, Sarah calls me into the kitchen, 'Mole, I want you to come with me to Silver Creek.'

'What about Mike and Bozo, they coming?' I ask.

'No, just you.' She doesn't explain why it's me she wants to go with her. She only says she's been to see Angela Morrison and we're going to see this old lady at Silver Creek.

'When?' I ask.

'Now,' she says. She hands me a jam sandwich she's made. 'You can eat this on the way.'

Silver Creek is only about two miles out of town so we can walk it easily enough. Sarah doesn't say much on the way out, only that she'd been lucky enough to find Angela Morrison alone at home so she could talk to her frankly, with none of her oldies in the way.

'What did she say? I mean she must have wanted to know, you know, how you knew about her?' I ask.

'She was pretty shitty when I told her why I'd come,' Sarah said. 'At first she said she didn't know what I was talking about. Then I told her I was a Catholic. "I know that," she said.'

'What did you say, then?'

'"Well," I said, "if you're afraid I'll tell someone about you, imagine what would happen if you told someone about me." "What do you mean?" she asks. "If you're a Catholic, getting rid of a baby is a mortal sin, the Church will excommunicate me and my mother will never speak to me again in her whole life!"'

'Is that true? I mean about Nancy?' I say, shocked. I knew it was a mortal sin against the Church, but being collapsed Catholics I wasn't too worried about it. Nancy said God would understand about us being born out of wedlock and I reckoned when the time came, He'd sort of throw this in as well. But Nancy not ever speaking to Sarah again, that would be unbearable.

'Nah, she'll be real shitty for a while, but in the end she'd forgive me.'

I'm terrifically relieved to hear this, I must say. 'What did this Angela girl say when you told her that?'

'She said she was glad she wasn't a Catholic, but knowing how bad it would be for me if she talked, she knew I'd never talk about her and if I didn't start it she wouldn't retaliate.'

'Good one! Did she tell you who put her up the duff?'

'Mole!' Sarah gasps.

'Well, did she?'

'Mole, haven't you been listening? I said I'd never talk about her, and I won't. You better not either, you hear?'

'Course I won't!'

'Swear it! C'mon, swear it on a stack of Bibles!'

'I swear on a stack of Bibles I'll never tell, cross my heart and hope to die,' I say, adding the extra bit for good measure.

'Swear it on the Virgin Mary's heart!'

I've never heard that one before, but I say it anyway. 'I swear on the Virgin Mary's heart.'

'So help me God!'

'So help me God,' I repeat.

Sarah seems satisfied. 'Good boy, Mole.'

'You'll have to do the same with Mike and Bozo, they also know her name.'

'You're right. Good thinking, Mole.'

'Did she say how much it would cost?' I now ask.

'I asked, but she wouldn't tell me, she said the old lady told her not to.'

We get to Silver Creek, which is nothing but a few old houses on small-acre ridges where nobody lives and a hayshed that's half fallen down with an old rusted tractor in it. There's nobody about and there's no bark hut to be seen for love nor money.

'She said it was in back of the house in the gum trees a bit further on,' Sarah says.

So we set off into the eucalyptus, mostly ironbark, and blunder around for a while looking for a track. We're getting nowhere fast and we're making a helluva racket in the undergrowth when suddenly this voice calls out, 'Looking for me, dearies?'

Standing about fifteen feet from us is this old woman who's a dead ringer for a witch. Her hair is white and hangs down over her face, which is dark, like very sunburned. She's wearing an old brown dress that goes right down to her ankles and is torn and ragged at the hem and she's sort of stooped over and leaning on a long stick. 'Looking for me, are you?' she repeats. She's got a strong voice that rings out, not a cackle like you'd expect from a witch.

Sarah says, 'Good afternoon, Angela Morrison sent us.'

'Who?'

'Angela . . . Angela Morrison?'

'Never heard of her in my life!' the old woman says firmly. Then she crooks her finger. 'Come, come, we're not having all day to waste.'

'Are you the Indian lady?' Sarah asks.

'Yes, yes, come now.' She walks into the bush and Sarah and me follow her.

After about five minutes we come to this hut in a clearing. It's made of bark like Bozo's boxing mate said, with a lean-to that's for cooking. There's a big black kettle on an iron tripod over some glowing ashes and a wisp of steam is coming out of the spout of the kettle. The yard is very neat with the ground swept all around and a little creek running past what looks like a well-tended vegie garden, green and growing. There's also a big sunflower about six feet high growing in its centre, the flower on the stalk is bigger than a soup plate. She sees me looking. 'For the birdies, they pick at the sunflower seeds,' she says. 'You like the birdies?'

To tell the truth I'm not that interested in birds, though later with Tommy I will become so, but at that stage in my life a bird is a bird, a thing that flies and goes *chirp-chirp* except if it's an emu or something like that. But she doesn't wait for my answer and goes into the hut. Sarah and me are unsure whether to follow her or stand outside. So we stay put.

Then after a moment or so the old lady sticks her head out of the door again, 'Always waiting and waiting, come along, come along, children.'

We go inside and it's neat as a pin. The first thing we notice is this big soft carpet that nearly covers the whole area of the hut. It's got millions of colours in it with a sort of mixed-up design which Sarah will tell me later is a mosaic. There is an army cot against the far wall with a shiny peacock-blue bed cover and along the wall directly facing the door is a bench built in with silk cushions in lots of bright colours arranged on it. There's also a small table with a single chair drawn up to it and a beautiful white-linen broderie anglaise tablecloth covering it. On the wall opposite the bed is a counter with a mortar and pestle and a wooden cutting block and spoons and a small scale and some glass bowls. Also on the counter is, like, this little enamel dish of lots of colours like the carpet. Sticking out of it is a thin rod that looks like a little black stick, but dead straight and about six inches long. A tiny wisp of smoke is coming from it. There's also this strange smell about the place. I mean it's not a truly bad smell, like poo, just different, like it's foreign and you wouldn't choose to have it around the place. I've never smelled anything like it before and I can only think it must be coming from the stick. There's enough smells around in the bush and not all of them the best, so why would you go and make one yourself that was a bit on the nose?

Under the counter made from cut-out four-gallon kerosene cans joined together on their sides are storage drawers and the woman's painted each of the drawers a different colour, pink and blue and violet and yellow and white and red.

All the furniture has been built with bush carpentry but it's very tidy. Above the counter are shelves to the ceiling with mostly Fowler's Vacola preserving jars and a few old books on them. There's stuff in the jars but it isn't preserves; sticks and dried leaves and bits of bark and seeds and a few things floating. Not snakes, lizards or toads, just sort of vegetable and root things in green-looking liquid that could be dirty water. We can see all this because behind the long bench is a window that is open and throws light into the whole place which isn't a bit spooky. On the wall next to the window is a large oval framed photograph of Queen Elizabeth. If you didn't know it was a bark hut, you'd think you were in a beautiful room, which you were I suppose.

'This is lovely broderie anglaise,' Sarah says, going over to the table and touching the freshly starched tablecloth.

'Goodness gracious me, you knowing broderie anglaise?' the old lady says in a surprised voice.

'Oh, I do it all the time, did you do this yourself?'

The old girl shrugs, 'I am having something to do with my time, my dear. Titch, it is nothing.'

'It's beautiful work,' Sarah says, and you can hear from her voice that she means it.

'My mother taught me in Calcutta when I was a little girl. She was British, my father was a Bengali, but also a gentleman. Later when my mother died and we are going to live in Fiji, they are thinking him a very pukka sahib, everyone who is knowing him is saying so. Now, sit down and we are talking the gossip.'

She points to the long bench. Sarah and me sit down and she sits on the chair at the table. She smiles at us and her teeth are a yellow colour like Crocodile Brown's except that almost every one has a gold filling or the whole tooth is gold. I think it's a good thing Adolf Hitler didn't get hold of her because she'd be a goner for sure. She also has what looks like a diamond through one side of her nose. He'd have took that quick smart as well.

'First we are introducing each other and then I am making and we are drinking some Darjeeling and then we are talking the polite gossip small talk, after this you will tell me how long you have been pregnant, my dear.'

Both of us gulp. She's picked it right off without being told. I wonder what this Darjeeling is we have to drink, but if it's going to help Sarah I decide I'll drink anything except tea with no milk like Morrie and Sophie drank before they became Australian. Maybe it's one of her secret concoctions like Bozo's mate said she mixed, but of course not the one that got rid of it for his sister, I mean, it stands to reason she wouldn't give *that* to a boy. Christ, I hope not.

I've never seen an Indian before, the only black person I've ever seen face to face is the boxer who gave Bozo a thumping at the Royal Melbourne Show. Anyway, this lady isn't like, you know, *really* black; it's like she has a lot of sunburn and you wouldn't think twice if you passed her in the street. Well, maybe twice, but it wouldn't be a big deal.

'I am Mrs Karpurika Raychaudhuri,' she laughs. 'You are not pronouncing it, so you will call me "Mrs Rika Ray", last and first syllables of my first and surname.'

'Thank you, Mrs Karpurika Raychaudhuri,' Sarah says, getting it right straight off, 'Karpurika is a lovely-sounding name. I am Sarah Maloney and this is my brother, Mole Maloney.' Sarah is sounding a lot more confident than I think she is inside.

'Mole? That is a strange name for a boy. Mole, like the little rodent animal with the long snout that lives under the ground or the one that grows on the skin?'

'The one that burrows, it's like a nickname,' Sarah offers. 'He's had it since a baby because he'd burrow under his blankets.'

I don't say anything but I think Karpurika Raychaudhuri is a pretty bloody strange name if you ask me. I've been called Mole so long I've forgotten it's my nickname, even the teachers at school have taken over calling me Mole. How'd you go at school being called Karpurika Raychaudhuri?

'Time for Darjeeling,' Mrs Rika Ray announces. She goes out of the hut and comes back with the old black kettle I'd seen hanging on the tripod over the fire. She reaches for a teapot and, from one of the kero drawers under the counter, she takes three little china cups and saucers. Then she puts four teaspoons of some stuff that looks just like tea-leaves to me into the teapot and pours hot water over them. She lets it draw a bit and finally swirls the teapot slowly several times to strengthen the brew, just like you always do with tea. She lets it rest a few moments and then pours this Darjeeling out. First she hands me this delicate little cup, then Sarah, and finally herself. 'Well, my dears, it is a happy conclusion we are looking for. Bottoms up!'

I look at Sarah and see that she's brought the cup up to her lips and has taken a tiny sip. Her expression doesn't change and she doesn't drop dead on the spot. So I take a sip, because the old lady has also done so. I can't believe it. It's tea without milk. Shit! Just plain ordinary tea without milk. Yuk! I'm traperated again. (Maloney word.)

'Ah, nothing like a good cuppa,' the old lady says, she's got her eyes closed like she's in heaven. (Boy, some people have a lot to learn.) 'The English have never learned the secret of tea. They take this pure ambrosia, this nectar from the Gods grown on a gentle hillside estate so the bushes will be nourished by the early-morning mist, and then they are pouring fat and sugar into it. If I didn't know any better, I'd think they were savages. Though, I do believe the Queen is also drinking her tea Darjeeling-style and without the fat and sugar. A very, very beautiful lady.'

There's no place to put the tea and maybe when she's not looking I can throw it out the window, but she's sitting right opposite us and if I take a chance and she sees me throwing away this stuff from the Gods that's not proper tea, maybe she won't help Sarah. When we get out, I'm going to tell Sarah she owes me a roast dinner.

The old lady glances over to Sarah, 'Now, my dear, it is not usual to be discussing these womanly matters with a young boy present.'

Sarah blushes, she goes red all over and she can't hide it, I can see she's nervous. 'Mrs Karpurika Raychaudhuri, Mole knows all about everything. We discuss everything together in my family.' She hesitates, like she's looking for the right words. 'Ah . . . er . . . it's just I'd feel better if he was here.'

Mrs Rika Ray smiles, 'It's all right, my dear. I'm not a witch, you know. I'm a healer, an Ayurvedic doctor. Ours is a very, very old medical tradition that is going back for many, many thousands of years. It is all right for your brother to stay if you say so. Now I must ask you some questions. You have to be telling me the absolute truth, you understand?' Sarah nods. 'When did you fall pregnant?'

Sarah looks confused, 'You mean, when did he, the boy, do it to me?'

'That will do nicely.'

'We've been going out a year almost. I started going out with him after the school social last September and we've been seeing each other ever since. Then the fifteenth of August it was my boyfriend's birthday and, well, I just couldn't say no again.'

'I see, it only happened once after all that time, you are a good girl, Sarah. It is not easy when the male person is always jolly well going on and on about it, wanting, wanting, all the time wanting. Tell me now, when was your period due and how soon after?'

'Yes, ah . . . my period? It was due a week later.' Sarah's voice is very small and she starts to blush again.

'That is very unfortunate. Why didn't you come to me before this? Over three months is very difficult.'

'We only heard about you yesterday. Please, Mrs Raychaudhuri, can you help me?'

'My dear, I can see you are a very nice young lady and also very unlucky. But I must tell you the honest truth, I don't know if I can help.'

'But what about Angela Morrison, you helped her?'

'We don't use names here. After you have left, I will not recall your name, it is better like that. But the girl you mention has missed her periods two weeks only, that is very, very different matter.'

'Angela wouldn't tell me how much it will cost,' Sarah says, coming close to tears.

'Cost? No, my dear, I am not an abortionist. I am a natural healer. For gallstones, kidney infection, lung congestion, urinary-tract blockage, haemorrhoids, blood cleansing, rheumatics and a hundred other afflictions there is a definite charge. For *this*, I do not take money.' She looks at Sarah, she has these dark eyes with dark rings around them, her eyes are like shining pieces of coal and they have grown soft and polished. 'Why always the woman must do the suffering? You have come very late, herbs work best in the first month, you are already four months.'

'Oh, please, please can't we just try,' Sarah begs.

'Yes, Sarah, we can try, that is all I can promise. It will not be very nice and I don't think it will work.'

'Thank you, thank you!' Sarah cries, 'I don't care how awful it is.'

The old lady gets up and walks over and selects five of the jars from the shelf and puts them down next to the black kettle.

'Can you build up the fire, Master Mole?' she asks me. I nod and she points to the black kettle, then takes a tin mug from a hook under one of the shelves and puts it beside the kettle. 'Fill it from the creek, the water is sweet, then boil me the kettle and bring it in.'

I go over to get the kettle and the mug. The jars are right next to it, I'm quite good at remembering names of things and I see the labels on three of the jars, the other two are turned the wrong way around, but it's no good because the names are written in some strange language with lots of curves and squiggles and dots. It must be Indian, I suppose.

'When you are bringing back the kettle boiling, then also bring me the second smallest pot that's hanging there by the fire,' the old lady instructs.

I take the big old kettle out and fill it from the creek using the tin mug. It isn't too difficult getting the fire going and I soon have a good flame licking up. I sit on an old log which you can see is used as a seat because the bark is stripped and the wood is polished from the old lady's bum.

There's lots of things going through my head and I'm feeling very confused. Nobody's told me anything about babies and I can't even imagine what's inside Sarah's tummy. I think maybe it's like the kewpie doll Bozo won at the Melbourne Show, only smaller. So how's it going to come out of Sarah just because she drinks something? What's a period? Why must it be due? The old lady has also said we've waited too long and maybe it won't work. What will happen then? If it is a small kewpie doll, is it alive? The more I think about it the more I worry because there's nobody to ask. I could ask Morrie Suckfizzle but we've been banned. He'd know because he's a doctor. I'm only twelve years old but I sense that everything is changing for us, that things will never be the same again and that Sarah may be in some sort of danger and there's nothing I can do to protect her.

The kettle boils and I take it and the pot back into the hut and the old lady starts to work. She puts two tablespoons of something from one of the jars into the pot and pours about a quart of water from the kettle onto it. 'Here, take,' she says, handing me the pot, 'put it again on the fire and bring it to a boil for a few minutes, Master Mole.'

I do as she says, the liquid in the pot is a sort of bluish colour but also brownish and I wait for it to boil for about three minutes before I take it back. She's put the herbs in the other four jars into an empty Vacola jar. She takes the pot from me, pours the stuff I've boiled over the other herbs then seals the jar with the rubber ring and clip and lets it stand for a while. During the time we're waiting, she tells us how part of her family came to Fiji to work in the sugar plantations as indentured labour and eventually prospered and became merchants and, two generations later, her part of the family, herself and her father, followed to help with a shipping business the family had become interested in. She told us how she'd married an Australian sea captain who turned out to be 'an all-round rotten rascal'. He brought her back to Australia, where he used to get drunk and beat her so she left him and went back to her own name again 'because blood's thicker than water'. Her husband's name was Porter and you'd think she'd have stuck with it because Australians can remember a name like Porter but they'll never remember Karpurika Raychaudhuri.

After the stuff in the jar has stood a while, she strains it through this sieve back into the pot and reheats it. This time she goes to the fire herself because she says she doesn't want it to boil. Then she pours this dark liquid it's become into the Vacola jar again, seals it and turns to Sarah.

'Every four hours you must be taking a steaming cupful during the day for five days, but also you must add one tablespoon brewer's yeast I am giving you. Now, my dear, I am warning you, there is blue cohosh root and it is toxic so we must be careful. If you are getting headaches or wanting to do the vomit, you are calling the doctor or you are sending Master Mole to get me, no ifs or buts, we must be very, very careful.'

She turns to me, 'Master Mole, you must come here every day for five days to get another jar. I am making fresh every day for Sarah.' Now she puts her hand on Sarah's shoulder, 'Don't be hoping for too much, my dear. It is very late that you are coming and I cannot promise the making of miracles.'

Sarah thanks Mrs Raychaudhuri and then bursts into tears.

'Now, now, my dear, we can only be hoping for the best,' the old lady says.

On the way back with me carrying the jar in a brown paper bag and her carrying the yeast, I ask her about the little burning stick.

'I think it's called incense,' Sarah says, 'I read about it once.'

'Why would you smell up the place like that when you didn't have to?' I ask.

'It must be an Indian thing, different people like different smells and dislike others we might like quite a lot.'

'Morrie and Sophie don't have different smells,' I point out.

'Yes they do. Sophie can't stand the smell of boiled mutton. That's what they got every day in Bonegilla and people from Europe don't know about mutton, but we like the smell of roast lamb, don't we?'

'Everyone knows about mutton!' I exclaim, 'There's more sheep in New Zealand than people.'

'New Zealand's not in Europe!' Sarah says.

'I know that! I just told you a fact I knew,' I say defensively.

I think Sarah's heard enough about mutton because she stops and puts her hand on my shoulder, 'Mole, you're not to tell anyone about our visit to the old lady today.'

'Not even Mike and Bozo?' I don't like that, we share everything and now Sarah wants me to keep a secret on my own.

'They'll only worry. Mike will be silent and Bozo will be walking around the place with a big frown and a long face so Nancy will cotton on there's something wrong. Best keep it to ourselves, eh, Mole.' I don't like it, though I reluctantly agree because she's right, that's exactly what will happen.

'What if something happens to you?' I say, though I'm not sure what that something might be.

'We better hope it does, then Nancy will think it's a miscarriage,' Sarah says and I can see she's very upset and there's tears running down. 'Mole, let's not talk about it any more.' She starts to cry as we walk along and I don't know what to do to comfort her. At least I know what a miscarriage is.

'It will be all right,' I say, but it's just words and she knows it and I know it and we know we don't know what's going to happen and that talk is cheap.

For the first three days nothing happens except I can see Sarah doesn't feel well and is very pale but she carries on. However, she doesn't eat at tea and tells Nancy she's feeling unwell but ate something earlier at dinner. Nancy thinks it's just the baby and tells Sarah it's still morning sickness, which you can get at night sometimes, that she did with little Colleen, and to take two aspirin and have a lie down.

Then on the fourth afternoon when I get back from school to drop my books in before setting out to get Sarah's jar of medicine from the old lady, I can't find Sarah. The Diamond T isn't out the front so Nancy's out. Little Colleen isn't home, so Nancy must have taken her with her and, I think, Sarah must be with them. But the old lady said she mustn't leave the house because the medicine might work at any time if it's going to work at all. Mike will be back soon but Bozo will go straight from school to boxing.

Anyway, I have to take my school clothes off and change into my old clothes and then take my school things up to the copper in the washhouse so they can be put in like we have to do every day. I walk into the washhouse and there is Sarah on the floor and I think she's dead. There's vomit all around her and she's lying sprawled with her cheek against the cement floor with her eyes closed. Her tummy and shoulders start to heave and she dry retches and I know she's alive.

'Sarah, Sarah! What's the matter?' I shout.

Sarah tries to lift her head but she can't. 'Mole,' she whispers and falls back.

I can't think what to do. Then she retches again and this green stuff comes out her mouth. 'I'm going to call Morrie!' I scream.

Sarah manages to lift her head, 'No, Mole, don't.' But there's no strength in her voice and she retches again and falls back, her eyes closed.

I don't wait a second longer, Sarah's dying is all I can think and I'm off up the hill. Even running, it takes me half an hour to get to the Mental Asylum where Morrie works in the lab. I know where it is right at the back of the grounds, a little army Nissen hut they've erected. I burst in, almost collapsing, unable to talk. Thank God, Morrie is there. I'm gulping for air and all I can say is 'Sarah, you've-got-to-come . . . Quick!' I've got my hands on my knees, bending over trying to get some air, my words gasping out.

Morrie doesn't waste time asking questions and in a few moments we're in the Austin 7 which he had to crank start, and we're off. He drives like a maniac and someone yells 'Mug lair!' out at us. I tell him how I've found Sarah and about the vomiting.

'Poison maybe. You eat the tinned fish last night?' He's hunched over the Austin steering wheel like a racing-car driver, trying to get the maximum out of it. '*Cholera yasna!*' he keeps shouting at the car, like he's trying to push it into going faster, shaking the steering wheel and banging it with his fist and swearing in Polish. But when he talks to me his voice is calm, because now that I've got my breath back, I'm crying.

'No, it's not Friday,' I choke. 'It's only fish on Friday.'

'Never mind, Mole, we get there soon.'

We brake outside the house and I jump out and Morrie comes after me carrying his doctor's Gladstone bag.

We take Sarah down to the verandah and lie her on Nancy's wicker couch. Morrie sends me to fetch a glass of water and a damp kitchen cloth and he cleans up Sarah, who is whimpering. Then he goes into the kitchen and looks around the cupboards and finds some Mylanta which Nancy has to have when she's got her indigestion. He gives Sarah a tablespoon full and then says, 'I think she must go to the hospital.'

Sarah is weak from all the vomiting, but she manages to get her head up. 'No! No!' she says, but she isn't retching any more and a bit of colour has crept back into her cheeks.

Morrie turns to me, 'Mole, please you go into kitchen, I call you again ven I need you, I must talk also to Sarah.'

It's quite a long time before he calls me because I think he's forgotten. Sarah's crying and he's holding her against his chest and she's been talking in between the crying and I think she's told him about her being up the duff and going to the old lady. Morrie is nodding his head and stroking her hair like a proper father and Sarah is gulping a bit but now she's stopped crying. Morrie makes her sit up so she's facing him, he has a hand on each shoulder to steady her and he looks directly into her eyes. 'Sarah, do you have some of the mixture this woman gave you?' Morrie asks.

'No, I had the last lot after dinner and then washed the jar so Mole could take it back,' she stammers.

'Do you know what maybe is these herbs she gives you?' Morrie asks again.

'One of them's blue cohosh root, that's what she said,' I answer right off, 'but I couldn't read what the others were.'

'Such a clever boy!' Morrie exclaims, clapping his hands together. 'Abortifacient! She's given you an emmenagogue combination. He shakes his head and turns to Sarah, 'For your kidneys and your liver this is not goet, but it is not such poison you will die.'

'She said maybe it wouldn't work,' I now say.

'She is right,' Morrie says, 'Sarah is in her second trimester, it is too late for herbs.' He turns to Sarah, 'You must have a regular examination, my dear. In Poland herbal abortifacients is very common, it can cause the placenta to implant very low.'

'Please, Morrie, can't you do it? Can't you examine me? You're a doctor!' Sarah cries.

Morrie feels her pulse, 'I listen to your chest and your stomach then we will see if you go to the hospital.' He's got his stethoscope around his neck and he instructs me to turn my back. 'You are very strong and healthy, Sarah. We will put you to bed and when Nancy comes we will talk. Now I go to the chemist to get some medicine for you to stop the nausea and headache and some other things also. You must drink a glass of water every fifteen minutes to wash your kidneys from the poison. Mole, you bring the water every fifteen minutes, tomorrow the same.' Then he turns and he's off at top speed and a few moments later I can hear the little Austin 7 backfire as he cranks the engine to life.

A short time later Mike walks in. 'What's Morrie Suckfizzle doing here? I saw him going down the road.' Then he looks at Sarah and sees her eyes are all red from crying. 'What's happened?' he says, dead concerned.

When Sarah and me tell him the story, he goes spare. 'Jesus! How could you do this!' he shouts and lets one go and catches me behind the head with the back of his hand and sits me on the seat of my pants. I jump up because I'm sure I can take on Mike. Sarah screams at both of us but we can't stand her screaming and calm down. 'You're going to have to tell Nancy,' Mike says. He's angry and concerned and a bit panicky, all of it together.

'Morrie said she has to lie down and have lots of water,' I say.

We both go to take an arm to get Sarah up. 'I'm not an invalid!' she protests, but she agrees to lie down in her and Nancy's bedroom and I follow her with a mug of water like Morrie said I must.

It's nearly five o'clock and Sarah is asleep when Morrie arrives back and, shortly after, Nancy and little Colleen. Bozo doesn't get back from boxing until tea time, which is half-past six.

Well, Nancy is none too pleased as you would expect but she can't make too much of a fuss because Morrie is there. Mike draws me aside and tells me he ought to give me a bloody good hiding for not telling him. 'Oh, yeah, you and whose army?' I say, still a bit cheesed off from the backhand he give me.

'We're a family, Mole, we have to stick together through thick and thin, you should've told me and Bozo.' It's no good telling him Sarah said not to, because he's right, I should've.

Nancy tells Morrie she'd prefer it if he examined Sarah, if that's a safe thing to do, but if he says she has to go to hospital, we'll take her to Wangaratta, she doesn't want her going to the bush-nursing hospital to be examined by old Dr Hughes, who's a secret drunk and that's why he doesn't do house calls at night. He's also a butcher who practically tore her open when little Colleen was born and she doesn't trust him as far as she can throw him, which would probably be quite a distance. But I think it's really her last attempt to keep the lid on Sarah's pregnancy as long as she can because she could just as easy go to young Dr Wallis.

Morrie comes out of the bedroom about half an hour later and says there's no bleeding and everything seems to be in the right place. But if she starts vomiting again or feels nauseous, he is to be called at once. 'Sarah is a very strong, healthy girl,' he says again. 'I come tomorrow night if you don't call me before. Water, Mole, lots of water!'

Well, I won't tell you what happens after Morrie leaves, but none of it is good and I'm in deep shit with all concerned. Yet after I've copped a right earful, Nancy says I did the right thing calling Morrie Suckfizzle, and Mike and Bozo agree. Nancy makes tea that night, which is tripe and onions, and by eight o'clock I'm that bushed I'm dead to the world.

Three o'clock the Wesclock's alarm goes and it's work as usual. Nancy says she isn't coming. Sarah's slept right through but Nancy wants to be there when she wakes up. So it's Bozo driving and Mike and me on the cans with Bozo hopping down to help. But we're half an hour late for school and Crocodile Brown gives me two hundred lines to do after school and it's a quarter to five before I get home.

Sarah's up and working away in the kitchen and I don't know what to expect. I've gone and let her down by calling Morrie and everything's a proper cock-up. But she gives me a kiss and a cup of tea and makes me a bacon and egg sandwich which is my favourite and I didn't even know we had any bacon, it being an offal week. 'Thank you, Mole,' is all she says. Though of course I want to ask her what's going to happen next. But I can see she doesn't want to talk. Poor Sarah, she's in more shit than the night Fred Bellows died with the nightsoil can stuck over his head.

There's a couple of backfires outside and it's Morrie and Sophie Suckfizzle. Sophie's lugging a big basket and it turns out she's got a bottle of milk stout for Nancy and a big bottle of creaming soda she'd bought from the soft-drink factory and these juicy steaks, each one as big as my two hands which must have cost a fortune, and potatoes and some onions. 'Tonight I am the cook!' she announces, 'We cook Australian food, steak and sheeps!'

If you're wondering what's happened to Tommy in all this, he's gone bush again. He came home drunk two nights ago and in the morning he was gone. He'd left a note for Sarah with only two words, 'Gone bush'. It was enough to make us happy until, of course, later the same day when the Sarah-vomiting thing happened.

We sit down to tea and it's great. Sophie's cooked the steak just perfect and made these great chips and we have the creaming soda (my favourite) and Nancy has a glass of milk stout and does a burp and says '*Excuse moi*', which Mike taught her, and touches her two fingers to her lips. We all reckon Sophie's turned into a proper Australian, and Morrie says, 'Me also, I am proper Australian, 'ow yer goin', no worries, mate!'

But then after tea while we're sitting around the table, Morrie clears this throat. 'Nancy, we are friends. Goet friends. For Sophie and me you are our family in Australia.' We all grin because it's a nice compliment. 'Sophie and me also, we would like to tell you something what happened to us in the war. Is this okay?'

We've all gone quiet and then Nancy nods, 'Nothing you can't say in front of us, Morrie.'

'It is very difficult for us,' Morrie says, 'because we don't like to talk. It is over what happened in Europe. Australia, this is our new country. But now we find out about Sarah and Sophie says we must talk to you uzzerwise we are not your friends if we don't want to help you.'

We're all looking down at our cups of tea because we don't know what's coming next.

'Not a lot anyone can do,' Nancy says. ''Cept see it through, cop it sweet, the scandal and all.' I hear Sarah gasp and know that it's not all over yet between Nancy and her.

'I want to tell you a story,' Morrie says. 'Please, excuse, it takes maybe long time?'

'Go ahead, Morrie,' Nancy says, 'we ain't goin' nowhere.' You can see from her expression, her lips are pulled a bit tight, that she doesn't know what's coming and I can tell she's a bit nervous. Deep down, Morrie and Sophie are still foreigners who come from a world she doesn't understand. It's easier for us, I suppose, because we're younger.

Morrie begins, 'Before the war I am already a married man with a family, two girls and a boy, my wife is Zara and I am a professor and also a doctor in Kraków. Then come the Nazis and after a while we go in the cattle trains to Auschwitz.

'When we are coming to Auschwitz the loud speaker it is saying "*Doktor austreten!*" This means doctors must step out of za line. I don't know what to do. I want to be with my wife and my children but then I think if they are wanting doctors maybe it will be better for us all, so I am step out the line. Then,' Morrie looks up, 'I have told already this, my wife and children they are taken to have a shower, you know what means this. I don't see them again.' Morrie shrugs, 'It is not a new story and my tears are the same as others, to lose your wife and children is to lose your life.

'The SS they look at my papers and they see I am a doctor and a surgeon and they tell me I must be a hospital orderly in the camp, in Auschwitz. I am a lucky one, there is soup and bread, not much, but also much more than the others in the camp. Then there is coming in the camp SS Herr Doktor Josef Mengele. He is a younk man and always he is dressing very smart and wearing za iron cross and uzzer medal also. He is like movie star Rudolph Valentino, very handsome and everything perfect, how you say, not vun hair is not missing.'

'Not a hair out of place,' Sarah corrects.

'Ja, thank you, and also his fingernails is polished. One morning I am getting told I must go and see this doctor. I go to his office and he calls out "*Komme!*" I go to stand there by his desk. "You wanted me, Herr Doktor Mengele?" I say, but I am not looking at him because it is *verboten*, forbidden to look at an SS officer.

'He is looking at this paper. "Herr Doktor Zukfizzleski, I see here you were a noted surgeon and a professor of medicine before you came to us?" I don't speak, I don't say nutsing. "Well?" he say to me, "Is this true?"

'"Ja, Herr Doktor, it is true."

'"And you are an orderly here?"

'"Ja, Herr Doktor."

'He shakes his head, "That is not goet. To use a man of your qualifications to pick up swabs and clean the floor, that is a bad waste. You and me, we are men of science, we must work for the glory of scientific study. You will be my assistant in the operating theatre." Then he smiles, "We have many interesting experiments we must do to help the cause of science. I was wounded on the Russian front and now medical science will benefit, we cannot waste such an opportunity."'

Morrie stops and looks at us. 'At this time I do not know what will happen. Here is only a doctor, a young man, maybe in all this death will come some good. "I am a physician," I say to him, "I must help to save life." "Goet!" he replies. "That is *wunderbar*! You may go now." He smiles at me and with his hand he waves I should go. Then when I am going out the door he shouts out, "We will start with the children!"

'I turn around, "Children?" In the camp the small children are always first to be killed.

'"Twins, I am very interested in twins, Dr Zukfizzleski."

'"Those who are sick, Herr Doktor?" I ask him.

'"Sick!" he shout to me. He jumps up from the desk and bangs his fist down. "*Nein!* The healthy ones! The sick must go to the showers for racial hygiene!"'

Morrie stops and shrugs. 'What can I do? Maybe I should kill myself then, but to hold on to life is a very deep instinct. All around me is death, to die is nutsing, it is easy. I would be just one more.

'Always Mengele himself comes to the Auschwitz railhead. He is not a big man, but he stands straight with his chin up like so, his dark-green tunic is very clean and his SS cap with the death's head badge he wears a little to one side,' Morrie tilts his head, 'what you call it?'

'Rakish,' Mike says. It's a word I've never heard before.

Morrie sighs deeply, 'When he finds twins from the cattle trains there is excitement in Josef Mengele, he jumps from the one foot to the next and claps his hands, "A treasure, we have found another treasure!" In his pocket he has sweeties and always he gives to the twins, he has a tender touch in his hands as he touches them, then in his own car or in the Red Cross ambulance he takes them to the hospital. When we are coming to Auschwitz we are seeing za Red Cross ambulance and everyone they are thinking it's all right, za

Red Cross is in this place. But of course, it is not so, this is not za Red Cross it is . . .' he struggles for the word.

'Deception?' Sarah asks.

'Ja, a deception, so za people will not know what is happening, sometimes they use this ambulance to put people in who are very sick, then they are driving away and the Jews who have just come think they are going to za hospital, but inside the ambulance is a gas chamber.

'In two years with his cane Mengele is sending four hundred thousand people to the right, to the gas chambers. One time in the children's block we are going to select some children for experiments. So he draws a line on the wall, 156 centimetres.' Morrie stops and works it out for us, 'Is about five feet. Then the children come to stand against that wall. If their heads don't come to the line or maybe higher, they are sent to the gas chamber.'

Morrie stops and puts his head in his hands and his shoulders begin to shake.

'It's all right, Morrie, no more, love,' Nancy says.

Morrie looks up, I think for a moment he doesn't know where he is, his eyes have a sort of far-off look. I can see he can't cry, there are no tears left to use. Then he says, 'No, excuse please, Nancy, I must tell. It is not confession, Sophie and me, we have a goet purpose to tell you this story. Mengele he wants always I must assist him in the operation theatre, then one day is coming two Gypsy children, twins also, and we must sew them together and take the organs from one and connect to the other. I cannot do this and I go to the washroom behind the theatre and I cut so my wrists.'

Morrie now turns his arms inwards and we see the long white scars running down the centre of each wrist, one scar cutting through the number tattooed on his inner arm.

'But Mengele himself he find me on the floor, "Kill me now, Herr Doktor, please!" I beg him. But he laughs, "You are too valuable and I cannot kill a member of my own profession."

'When I am better he put me in his special pathology laboratory. "Now they are already dead, Doktor Zukfizzleski, your delicate Jewish conscience is clear." Here I must dissect the children he has killed and write up the notes he wants.

'One night he comes himself with fourteen pairs of Gypsy twins. He put them on the long dissecting table, the little nude bodies lying sides by sides, then he is injecting them in the heart with chloroform so they die instantly. All night he is dissecting them. In the morning he says to me, "A good night's work, you must clean up now, throw them in the ovens, Zukfizzleski, Gypsies love to be around a fire." There is all over the floor and the table the parts of twins, like a butcher shop in hell. The blood trays are full and spilling over on the floor with this innocent blood.'

'It is enough, Moshe,' Sophie says quietly. 'You see, I am also married with children, twins, Eva and Bernard. They took my babies away, maybe to send to Auschwitz or maybe to kill in that gas showers in Buchenwald.'

Nancy and Sarah are crying and I wish Sophie wouldn't go on, Morrie has said enough for a lifetime and then more.

Sophie turns to Sarah, 'Sarah, I am telling a lie about the Kommandant when I say to you I am working in his house as a servant girl. The truth, I am put in a brothel for German soldiers and I am coming pregnant. If you are pregnant, they kill you in that place. So I steal from the German woman who is superintendent of this brothel a knitting needle and I try to make finish what is inside me, how you say, make abortion, with that knitting needle.'

'She is making a uterine perforation with that needle and bacteria is coming in the peritoneal cavity,' Morrie explains. 'In that place she will die of peritonitis, she cannot be saved.'

'But only in two days is coming the Americans,' Sophie now continues. 'If I know this before I would wait of course! But I don't know. They put me in the hospital but also they give me hysterectomy.'

Sophie looks up and there is a long silence with Sarah crying softly. Then Sophie says quietly, 'Please, Sarah, more than my life I want the baby you are having inside you. Morris says it is four months, maybe more, it has hands and feet and everything is formed and the tiny heart is beating.' She starts to cry, 'There has been too much death, too many babies killed. Please, I beg you, let us have your baby!' And Sophie begins to sob uncontrollably, her head in her arms and her shoulders jerking and all of us crying as well.

Chapter Seven

Well, Christmas Day comes and as usual it is no big deal with us. Little Colleen gets some ribbons and Nancy a box of Yardley's face powder with its own powder puff inside and we have roast lamb and gravy, though Sarah makes mint sauce for Mike and Nancy, roast potatoes, which is real beaut, and baked pumpkin, which isn't. Then there's plum pudding with the cream old Alf Darby, who keeps a few cows on the edge of town, leaves for us twice a year at Christmas and Easter. But I must say, in the long run Christmas only means one thing in the Maloney family; there's almost twice as much garbage to collect on Boxing Day. And also, we have to go to Midnight Mass on Christmas Eve, though none of us can take communion because we haven't been to confession but there's also another reason Father Crosby gives us a filthy look and doesn't wish us a happy Christmas afterwards.

By this time Sarah is beginning to show and Nancy thinks it might be a good idea for her to stay at home, but Sarah won't.

'Mum, they all know already and the gossipmongers will talk all the more if I'm not there with you,' she protests. And so Nancy agrees and says that she wasn't ashamed when she carried us, so Sarah need not be. We all know it's not the same, that she never expected herself to amount to anything, but Sarah's different, all Nancy's hopes were pinned on her eldest daughter and she's pretty shattered but trying not to show it.

Father Crosby, who can sniff out a rumour faster than a ferret can shoot down a rabbit hole, has already been to see us. He came a few days before Christmas. We seen him coming down the road on his bicycle heading for the front gate and the five Bitzers go leaping out but don't bark because Bozo calls to them not to.

'Hello, here's trouble,' Mike says and yells out to Nancy that the priest is on his way.

Nancy's at the front door with her arms crossed and her chin stuck out by the time Father Crosby has taken off his bicycle clips and is lumbering up the front path with the Bitzers all sniffing and jumping around the hem of his soutane, tongues lolling, thinking he must be a good bloke because Bozo's banned a bark.

The town priest is very red in the face when he gets off his bicycle. He's got a bit of a stomach on him and his florid complexion may be due to the exertion on a hot day, though it's all downhill from St Stephen's and he's known to be bit fond of the altar wine or anything else in a bottle he can get his sainted hands on.

'You'll not be lookin' at me like that, Nancy Maloney!' he says, even before he gets to the front door. 'It's the same old story now, is it?'

'Don't know what you mean?' Nancy says, tight-lipped, knowing exactly what he means.

'Well, I'd have hoped for better, a lot better, that's a fine young daughter you had and all.' He shakes his head, 'Such a pity, such a terrible waste.'

'Sarah's still a fine young daughter and we don't need your pity,' Nancy says, real pugnacious.

'You're stubborn, Nancy Maloney, stubborn as a mule. You'll need to ask forgiveness from the Lord and we'll need to make arrangements.' The priest has come up to the door and is wiping his face with his linen handkerchief, the two of them are standing face to face, almost chin to chin.

'You'd better come in then,' Nancy says, not calling him 'Father' right off like she should. Turning her head in the direction of the kitchen, she calls out, 'Sarah, a cup of tea for the good priest.' She turns back to Father Crosby, 'I'm sorry we don't have anything stronger to celebrate the occasion of your visit, Father.'

Father Crosby knows this is a deliberate insult but he chooses to ignore it. 'It's strong words that will be needed and a cup of tea will be fine then, two sugars,' he replies. Him and Nancy are old opponents and he knows his turn will come.

Nancy leads him out to the back verandah and, as they go through the kitchen, Father Crosby stops, 'We've not seen you at Mass, Sarah. I'd like to see you there, that is after you've been to confession, where I don't believe you've been in some time, is that right then, my girl?'

'Yes, Father,' Sarah says, suddenly scarlet in the face. She's turned and done a little curtsy.

So, there it is, Crosby payback. Like I said, it don't take too long.

Well, it doesn't take Father Crosby too long to come to the point either. 'Nancy Maloney, this time you *must* listen to me. Times have changed, my dear. You have a daughter who they tell me is the dux of the school, even though she has not had the benefit of a good Catholic education.'

'Hmph! The convent? You call that an education, with the nuns chattering on like a cage of budgies about the children being born out of wedlock. No thank you very much,' Nancy says, clearly annoyed at the way Father Crosby has taken advantage of Sarah.

'There's none better, my girl, and perhaps if she'd attended St Stephen's she may have been safe from the clutches of the Protestants, from the Templeton boy.'

So Father Crosby knows everything. We should have known. There's not a lot you can keep from a priest in a small town. He's been waiting for Nancy to come around to the church and confess all to him. When she hasn't, he's come to see her himself.

'And what may I ask are these arrangements you've come to make, Father?'

'Well, as you well enough know, Nancy Maloney, we've got good Catholic couples the Lord has not blessed with offspring, barren couples who will give a child born out of wedlock their name, love, security and all the privileges of a family life with none of the shame and the stigma.'

'If the Lord has not blessed them with offspring, then perhaps He doesn't want them to have children?' Nancy says. You can tell she's panicking, it's not much of an argument and not up to her usual standard. You can see she knows it won't hold water for long. She's feeling pretty intimidated and the fight is going out of her. Deep down, the fear of the Holy Roman Church is still in her.

'On the contrary,' Father Crosby says, smiling. 'These are the couples God, in His infinite mercy, has set aside to repair the mistakes young, misguided Catholic girls make from time to time.'

Nancy's usual booming voice has been brought almost to silence as she says very quietly, 'Well, misguided or not, my answer is the same as last time when it was one of my own precious children in my womb, Father. Sarah is not giving her baby away to a stranger.'

Father Crosby suddenly loses his patience, 'Look at you! For God's sake, Nancy Maloney. Your husband, Tommy Maloney, is a thief and a drunkard and you and your family of ragamuffins collect the town garbage! You Maloneys have been a thorn in the side of the Church for five generations! You've never amounted to an ounce of good, the lot of yer!' Then he corrects himself, 'Except for the sainted Charlotte Maloney who, may I remind you, was not a Maloney by birth or blood!' He points a finger at Nancy, 'You've a fine daughter and now you're to ruin her life as well! You'll burn in Hell for this, Nancy Maloney!'

Nancy starts to weep, she's a strong woman but the Church inside her is even stronger, 'We've promised Sarah's baby to someone else, we've made other arrangements, Father.'

'Other arrangements? Without first consulting me?' Father Crosby can't believe his ears.

'Yes,' Nancy sniffs, her voice now barely above a whisper, 'Good arrangements. Like you said, a couple who God intends to bless.'

'A Catholic couple?'

'No, Father, they are Jews,' Nancy says, her voice almost down to nothing.

'Jews!' Father Crosby is truly flabbergasted. 'Don't talk blasphemy, girl! You've given God's child to the Christ-killers! How dare you take it upon yourself to decide! The Church, through the Holy Father in Rome, will decide for you. As His priest in Yankalillee, it is for me to decide! You hear? Me! I will decide what's best for your daughter! Giving her child to the Jews is sacrilege and I forbid it! Do you hear me, girl?'

Nancy looks up at him, Father Crosby has gone too far this time. Maybe the Church is stronger than she is, but Father Crosby isn't. Now it's his will against hers. By nominating himself as the decision-maker he's eliminated both God and the Pope from the contest, it's local priest against local Maloney and I don't like his chances one bit. She knuckles the tears from her eyes, which are suddenly blazing with indignation. 'Go to hell, Father, you're not getting Sarah's baby!'

Father Crosby's face has gone bright red! His jowls wobble like a turkey's wattle and I think he's going to have kittens on the spot. But Nancy is back in control. 'Sometimes God speaks directly to a person and this time I think He has, Father. I am sure, and so is Sarah, that we are doing the right thing and that God will forgive us when the time comes.'

Father Crosby is too dumbfounded to speak. But it isn't a comfortable silence, it's as if the air above his head is about to be torn to shreds at any minute. You can see he's cross with himself and knows he shouldn't have had that last outburst and threatened Nancy personally. He had the Church and the Pope as the seconds in his corner and had her on the ropes hanging on for dear life and now he's copped an uppercut and lost the fight on a t.k.o.

'Right,' he says after a while. 'If you refuse to obey the directions of the Church, I shall have to take this up with the Bishop.' He looks up at Nancy and, rising, points a finger at her. 'You've not heard the end of this by a long shot, Nancy Maloney!'

Nancy's chin is back sticking out. 'Ain't that the truth, Father. This godforsaken little town won't let us forget and no doubt you'll do your bit to add fuel to the fires as well.'

'It's the fires of Hell you should concern yourself about, Nancy Maloney! You have blasphemed and gone against the Church! You have delivered your offspring to the murderers of the Son of God!' He crosses himself, 'Only He can forgive you! I will pray to the Almighty for your redemption!'

It's all pretty scary stuff and you can see that he doesn't hold out too much hope for his personal prayers of intercession either. Sarah is quaking beside us, biting her nails, eyes downcast. We've all been in the kitchen listening to the goings on and now Father Crosby brushes past us with a grunt and is out the front door, his arms pumping and his priest's robes flapping every which way. Bozo's Bitzers meet him at the door and escort him to the front gate. I reckon we must be about the most collapsed Catholics in the world at that very moment. It's hard fighting the Church because there's just you, and they've got God and the power to turn you into a sinner any time they like and heaps of money. You can tell just by looking at the bicycle Father Crosby rides, it's a Malvern Star 5 Star and costs heaps.

We go to Nancy who, now the priest has gone, has lost all her bravado and has dissolved into tears and is wailing on the old wicker couch. 'It's all so hard,' she sobs. 'It's all so bloody hard! Oh, God! What am I to do?'

Then, as I said, Christmas comes and after Midnight Mass we are all a little surprised (a lot actually) when Father Crosby only gives us a dirty look and ignores us but doesn't kick us out of his church, like excommunicate us in front of everyone. There are even some who come up to Nancy and wish us happy Christmas and thank us for services rendered over the year and say there'll be a bottle of milk stout next to the garbage can next time we come down their street. Nancy can generally count on two months' supply of stout as a Christmas box. Sometimes there's shortbread baked for us as well.

Then, when we get home from church on Christmas Day, there's Tommy large as life. He's got presents for everyone. A big bottle of Lily of the Valley perfume for Nancy and a manicure set in this pink leather case for Sarah, a doll with long blonde hair that shuts its eyes and makes a baby noise when you turn it upside down for little Colleen, a pocket knife in a leather pouch that fits onto your belt for me, a pair of Stamina boxing gloves for Bozo, and a set of pencils, a sketchpad and a box of Windsor & Newton watercolours and brushes for Mike so he can do his fashion designs. It's the biggest nice surprise we've had since winning at the Melbourne Show and we don't ask him where he's found the money. Nancy says later that we should let sleeping dogs lie and that he's probably left his fingerprints all over the scene of the crime and you can be sure Sergeant Donovan will be round sooner or later. What's more, Tommy is stone-cold sober and it's Christmas Day with the whole town pissed!

I'm a bit suspicious about the pocket knife though, it's like the one he's got on his own belt and I can see the words 'going bush' invisibly written all over it.

Well, I wasn't wrong. First Saturday after Christmas he's standing shaking me awake in my bunk at dawn. 'Mum, I'm sick!' I mumble, thinking it's Sarah come to wake us up for garbage. It's what I say every morning and Nancy takes no notice because you've got to be dying or have one leg chopped off for her to let you stay home. Then, remembering it's Saturday, I groan 'Whassamatta?', opening my eyes for the first time and there's Tommy. 'Shit!' I say, sitting up.

'There's a scrub fire up near Silver Creek, let's get going, Mole.'

'Whajamean?' I'm still half asleep, 'I ain't in the brigade?'

'Gotta start sometime, now's good as ever.'

'What about Bozo and Mike?' I protest, now fully awake.

'You're the chosen one, Mole.'

'That's not fair, you didn't keep our deal, I'm off the hook, like we agreed.'

'That was going bush, this is fighting fire, that's different. C'mon, hurry, there's people outside waiting.'

'Kids don't fight fires,' I say, 'I'm only twelve!'

Tommy laughs, 'This Maloney kid does. I've got permission from the CFA. Put on a long-sleeved cotton shirt.'

I get dressed and, I can tell you, I'm not that happy. 'You got a woollen jumper?' Tommy then asks.

'Whaffor, it's summer?'

'Bring the jumper and your beanie,' he says, not explaining. I have trouble finding my beanie, which I only wear in winter. Tommy's wearing a pair of overalls and an old felt hat I've seen when he's gone out before, but he's got a knitted jumper under his arm. Like mine, it's old with holes in the elbows, only his is blue and mine is red. 'Good colour,' he notes, 'See your whereabouts in that. Where's your gumboots?'

'Gumboots? I've only got the garbage ones and they're ripped open, one at the toe, the other the back of the heel.'

'Shoes, yer must have shoes?'

'Only for school.'

'Put them on.'

'No way! Mum'll kill me, they're only for school.'

'Put them on, Mole! You can't fight a bloody bushfire barefoot!'

'Will you tell her then, when they're messed up?'

'Yeah, yeah, okay. Now hurry! Can't keep a bushfire waiting.'

What I can't understand is why Bozo and Mike don't wake up during all this talk, which isn't exactly whispering. Then I realise that they probably are awake, but they're playing possum, buggers not wanting to get involved. Lying in of a Saturday is the best thing that happens all week and I'm missing out again.

Outside there are two blokes in blue overalls in a ute with the engine running. I recognise the driver, it's John Crowe, Tommy's best friend, maybe his only friend, they've been together since kids and were only separated by the war. He's a good bloke and often brings Tommy home when he's been on a bender. He shouts gidday to us. 'Jump in the back, Mole,' Tommy says, hopping into the back himself. There's shovels and rake-hoes and a pile of wet hessian wheat bags, two army blankets folded, two knapsack stirrup pumps and a hand axe in there already. We stand up, hands flat on the roof. Tommy bangs on the top of the ute with his good arm and we're off.

It's just coming up light but you can smell the smoke before we see the fire. It's only then that I think of the old Indian lady in her bark hut.

'Where'd you say the fire was?' I shout at Tommy.

'Silver Creek!' He points ahead and I can just see a spiral of smoke rising in the early-morning light.

'There's an old lady lives there!' I shout against the wind.

'Nah,' Tommy shakes his head, 'Nobody, the old houses on the ridge are abandoned!'

'No, in a bark hut, in the bush about two hundred yards in back of that old tractor shed, next to the creek.'

Tommy grips the top of the driver's side window frame and leans over and shouts down to John Crowe, his words carried away in the wind, but suddenly the ute picks up speed and he straightens up and nods at me. 'Do you know exactly?' he shouts.

I nod, but don't answer. I've been there four times to get Sarah's medicine.

We get to the fire and there's three other utes already there but the Furphy tank towed behind someone's ute hasn't arrived yet, probably still filling up with water. About eight men are working with wet sacks to prevent the fire jumping the road, which would take it in the direction of Yankalillee. Then I see that one of the old houses and a barn are alight and the fire appears to be in a wide arc and there's a lot of smoke. It's still a grass and scrub fire and doesn't appear to have reached the stand of ironbark where Mrs Rika Ray has her hut in a clearing among the trees. Though, in all the smoke, you can't really gauge the distance. Anyway the tops of the ironbark are not yet ablaze but everywhere you look it's smoke and flames with embers and ash dancing up into the sky.

I point the whereabouts of the hut out to Tommy. 'It's next to the creek,' I say.

Tommy nods, 'Righto, we'll get to its nearest point and follow the creek around, hope we can get there in time.' He points to the back of the truck. 'Grab two sacks, Mole.' Then he turns to John Crowe and the other bloke in the ute and talks to them. They nod and one takes a rake, the other a shovel and they grab two sacks each.

I take two of the sacks from the back, which are pretty heavy because they've been soaked in water. Tommy takes one of them and, with his pocket knife, rips the seam on one side and also the bottom of the sack open. He shows me how to put it over my head like a monk's hood, so it covers my shoulders and back, but first he makes me put the sweater on. 'Wool's near fireproof,' he says. He points to the other wheat sack. 'That one's for beating out the fire.' He puts both his hands on my shoulders and looks directly into my eyes, his expression dead serious. 'Follow me, Mole, do exactly what I do and never get ahead of me, you understand? You walk where I walk, jump where I jump.'

I nod, but he still grabs a hold of me, 'Even if you think I'm doing wrong and your instinct tells you to do otherwise!' He gives my shoulders a little shake, 'You understand?'

I nod and then we're off, heading towards the fire. I notice that John Crowe and the other man, who Tommy hasn't introduced me to, so I don't even know his name, are also following Tommy, who is clearly the boss. It's pretty weird because I've never seen Tommy in charge of anything or anybody and for a moment I'm a bit proud of him. Then I'm not so sure. We're headed straight into the fire, into the flames, and we're running sort of zigzag.

I'm a dead man! I think to myself and I'm only twelve years old. There's flames either side of us and we run through this corridor and it's hot on the leather soles of my school shoes. Then we're out the other side and onto an unburnt patch of ground, but there's flames everywhere around us, leaping up, embers licking at the edges of this unburnt island we're standing on. Tommy darts off again, back into the flames it seems to me, but again we're through, we dodge and zigzag and Tommy seems to anticipate the changing of the breeze, so one moment there's flames and the next there's not and we've got past somewhere you couldn't have a moment before. The sack on my back is getting warm and there's steam rising from it and my whole body is so hot I can't believe I'm not going up in a puff of smoke and a sizzle of flame.

We hit the stream and it's only about ten inches deep but running fairly fast and we drop into it, getting wet all over. But only for a moment. It feels like heaven, I'm still alive and it's a miracle! Then it's on again, following the stream which goes in a wide arc and is not the quickest way to where the hut is, but it's wide enough to keep us clear of the flames on either side.

We come around a small bend in the creek and there's the hut, or more exactly there's the conflagration that was the bark hut, the flames roaring and rising up, the lean-to collapsing in an explosion of sparks just as we arrive. It's still not even half-past five in the morning and the old lady would have been asleep when the fire hit. Tommy looks back at me and shrugs. 'There's nobody coming out of that alive!' he shouts back.

Then I see the carpet, it's in the creek ahead of us, water all around it and just a big bump in the middle sticking up above the surface. The flames are roaring and the canopy of the ironbark is beginning to catch, orange licks of flame cutting through the branches to the sky. I point to the carpet and start to move towards it. The water at this point has formed into a pool about three feet deep which the old lady must have once made for herself. When we get to the edge of the carpet, which is underwater, we all start to pull it up. But a heavy woollen carpet that's soaked weighs a ton and it needs all our combined strength.

Now we see what's happened, the sticking-up part is because there's a pole holding it up, a stout green eucalyptus tree used like a tent pole. There's a hole cut near the apex of the tented carpet. We manage to pull the carpet back over the pole and under it crouches a terrified Mrs Karpurika Raychaudhuri, with only her mouth and the top of her head sticking out of the surface of the water, her grey hair floating every which way around her and her dark eyes large as bottle tops. Also floating or sunk to the bottom in the pool are all her various bottles and cushions and bits 'n' pieces and I can see air pockets of her damask tablecloth with the broderie anglaise suddenly rising up above the waterline.

I must have been the first person she saw because her mouth falls open, 'My goodness, it is the Mole boy himself! I am seeing a ghost maybe?' It's like she's already decided she's dead and better make the most of it and now she's alive again. Hooray! Then she looks around and sees the others. 'You are coming to the rescuing and I am very, very grateful.' She's shaking all over, but her voice is calm enough.

Tommy laughs, 'Nah, you've rescued yourself, lady. You could've sat under that there carpet all day and come to no harm. It's wool, see, and soaked through, practically fireproof. The creek would have had to dry up or started to boil before yiz would have been in trouble, though the heat's always a bit of a worry. Bloody good thinking cutting that hole in the carpet, though, let the air in, eh? If yiz hadn't a done that you might have suffocated to death.' He looks over to where her hut was. ''Fraid yer house has gorn up in smoke, no saving that.'

It's a different Tommy who's talking, his voice has got this authority, like a teacher or someone.

'We are thanking God for small mercies, for the fiery furnace I am not yet getting ready and the carpet I am soon mending like new,' the old lady says cheerfully.

'Well, we'd better all stay put until the last of the fire passes over, wind's blowing away from us. Let's hope it don't change.' He grins, 'We'll probably all be heroes for this, though we've done bugger-all.'

'You are talking the modest poppycock!' Mrs Karpurika

Raychaudhuri exclaims. 'You came to rescuing an old Indian lady and that is exactly what I am telling everyone. "They have walked through the flames like Vishnu himself," I am saying. You are heroes the one and all, also you, Master Mole, you are saving my life and I am very, very grateful.'

'Yeah, right enough!' Tommy grins, 'It was him who told us about you.'

'Master Mole is a very excellent and very, very intelligent boy with the head screwed on right as rain,' the old lady says.

John Crowe is usually a pretty talkative bloke but he hasn't said a word, I reckon them two have never come across someone like Mrs Karpurika Raychaudhuri before. They're just standing there in the pool grinning and looking at me with the water up to their knees and the fire raging on either side of the creek. Then John Crowe says, 'In Hepburn Springs they've got this hot crick, water's bloody near boilin', smells of sulphur, folk go there to get rid of their rheumatiz.'

'Yeah?' the other one says. 'Heard o' that. Couldn't do it meself, though. Couldn't stand the smell. Flamin' sulphur smells like rotten eggs.'

'Best sit, fellows, it's getting a bit hot, oxygen supply is better at the waterline,' Tommy instructs. They both crouch down in the water and I do as well so that I'm up to my neck in the creek. My head's copping the heat and the three blokes' faces are black so I suppose mine must be as well. My eyes smart and we're all doing a bit of coughing from the smoke.

So there's the five of us sitting in the pool, the four of us blokes in a sort of a circle with the old lady in the middle with all her things and her skirt floating up so you can see her thin legs sticking out of her bloomers. There's this thing sticking into my bum so I put my hand below the surface and feel the spout of her old black kettle. Mrs Rika Ray's forgotten nothing.

'Master Mole, you are not minding your manners,' the old lady now says, 'you are not introducing me to your very, very nice friends who are helping you to making the rescuing!'

I bring my hand out from under the water and point to Tommy, 'This is my dad, Tommy Maloney.' I've never introduced Tommy to anyone before, least of all as my dad, and it feels strange but also quite nice. The old lady brings her hand out of the water and so does Tommy and they shake hands. 'And this is Mr John Crowe, me dad's mate and . . . er . . .'

Tommy jumps in, 'Ian McTavish, Ian and John and I'm Tommy.'

'How do,' Ian says, grinning.

'Gidday,' John says, doing the same.

'And you are . . . ?' Tommy asks.

'Oh, I'm sorry,' I say, because I've forgotten to say it, 'This is Mrs Karpurika Raychaudhuri.'

'Beg yours?' Tommy says, not sure he's heard it right in the crackle and roar of the bushfire.

'Mrs Rika Ray,' she says quickly. 'That Master Mole I am telling him only once and he is never forgetting my very, very difficult name, his sister too, you have a very clever family, Mr Maloney.'

'Yeah, right,' Tommy replies, not too sure how to take the compliment, seeing he's never thought about being a father to us and, as well, his being against Sarah studying to be a doctor.

After that there's silence. I'm the kid so there's not much I can say and the others are country blokes who probably don't have too much to say to an old Indian lady they wouldn't have known from a bar of soap until today.

I look to where the vegie garden is. I found out on the second visit to get Sarah's stuff that although it had quite a lot of vegies in it, carrots and potatoes, stuff like that, it was also a herb garden, where the old lady grew the herbs for her potions. Now it's simply a black-charred patch but amazingly the sunflower is still standing upright. Its stem is black and the yellow petals have been singed off so there's just the great soup-plate head that is smoking a bit now the fire has passed it by, but the seeds are still in it, roasted I suppose. I wonder to myself whether birds will eat roasted sunflower seeds.

Then Tommy speaks up. It's not like him to volunteer small talk but he does. 'What are you going to do about a home, missus?' I can see he's already forgotten even the short version of her name.

The old lady tries to smile, 'It's going to be jolly well all right, Tommy. When the sun is shining, I am drying out all my things and then I am sleeping under the stars tonight.'

'Tell you what,' John Crowe says, 'I've got a tent, army disposal, what say we let you have that for a bit, eh?'

The old lady looks at him amazed. 'I am thanking you from my heart's bottom, Mr Crowe.'

'No problems, missus. Just call me John, like Tommy said. Easier that way, Rika.' He points to the now smoking ruin of the bark hut, 'Shouldn't be too much trouble to knock yiz up one o' them humpy homes, few slabs o' bark and a bit o' bush carpentry, no problems.'

'Yeah,' Tommy says, 'termorra I'll go up the river a bit, cut a few bark slabs, some corner posts, roof beams, shouldn't be too hard.' He looks over at John. 'Bring your tent over today, will yiz? Using the ute termorra, mate?'

'Nah, I'll come with yiz, Tommy,' John says, 'take a sickie, be good to have a day doing a bit o' choppin' and cuttin', bloody sight better than stripping down a Dodge engine at the workshops!'

John Crowe works for the shire council as a mechanic.

'Yeah, I'll be in that,' Ian now volunteers, 'could do with a day off meself, not much going on at the abattoir.'

I'm sitting there feeling dead proud of Tommy and his two mates. They can see the old lady has a 'touch of the tar', but they've done the right thing by her anyway. She's a human being in distress and they've come good.

Lots of people I know would have thought she was just some old roadside Abo gin who could make a humpy herself and wasn't worth bothering about. Tommy doesn't know the story about Sarah's medicine, because he'd gone bush at the time. But in a funny way it's us should be grateful to her. It's not her fault the stuff she gave Sarah didn't work, because she said right off she didn't think it would. Although Sarah's copping a fair amount of shit from the town gossips, the best thing is that, because the medicine made Sarah sick, now Sophie and Morrie are going to have a new family and everything's turned out happily ever after. Well sort of, Sarah's still got to have the baby, which isn't an 'it' any more. The only person who's unhappy is Father Crosby and maybe God, but we don't know about Him yet.

The fire passes over and the three men climb out of the creek and, using the shovel and rake-hoe, they clear a bit of ground so the old lady can put her stuff out somewhere. We all help to get it out of the water and onto this clear patch so the carpet and the silk cushions and sheets and the tablecloth can dry. The old lady says, 'I am never-minding that the silk cushions are ruined, it's a pittance to pay.'

'Your jars are okay, that's one thing,' I say, trying to comfort her because the silk cushions were very beautiful and now they're stained. The Vacola jars are all watertight, so her herbs and medicines are okay inside, though I've had to recover a good few that floated down the creek a bit and some of the labels are missing, but I guess Mrs Rika Ray will know what's inside just by looking.

By the time we get back to the firefighters, they've already decided we were dead so there's lots of congratulations. The old lady has come with us to get something to eat, which is what Tommy insists she must do. That's something else I learned, it's just about breakfast time and there's this trestle table with five women there, two from Bell Street but the others I don't recognise. They've got sandwiches and some sausages going and hot tea from an urn and water to drink.

Mrs Karpurika Raychaudhuri tells everyone the story of the rescue and I've got to hand it to her, she's a bloody good storyteller because we come out like we are these heroes in a book. Tommy, Ian, John and me are shuffling our feet and kicking at the dust, saying it was nothing, pointing out how she's used her commonsense and protected herself real good with the carpet and the air hole. But I learn something that I'd not known about adults, that grown-ups, same as kids, like to believe in bravery and heroism, and the more the four of us protest the more the others believe her. If they gave out VCs for bushfires and they based it on the old lady's version of what happened, we'd all be awarded them for sure.

It's nearly lunchtime by the time we've got the whole fire under control and there's more women who have brought cold lamb and homemade chutney, bread and butter and more tea from the urn and all the cordial you can drink. It's like a party in the blackened bush and I find I'm a part of it. Old Mole Maloney is a fair-dinkum bushfire fighter, although all I've done is sit in a pool of water in the creek and beat at a few flames licking up beside the road. It's also the first time I've seen the people of Yankalillee come together and there's kindness in them I'd never known about.

And something else has happened also. I've seen a fire raging, been in among the flames and I know there's something in me that understands it, wants to learn more. Not just about fire, I want to know more about the bush, about how a fire behaves and the animals we've seen fleeing, little creatures you'd never normally see, going hell for leather and some not making it, burning up in a frizzle. I also have a new respect for my dad, Tommy Maloney, the little bloke with the slight limp and the crook arm and one eye.

On the way home in the back of the utility I say to Tommy, 'Dad, I'll come out with you into the bush any time you want.'

He looks at me surprised. 'What's changed yer mind then?'

'Well, it's only under one condition.'

'What's that?' he shouts above the wind. 'If I lay off the grog?'

'No,' I say, 'Mum says it's only you who can decide to go on the wagon.'

'What then?' he asks.

'If you promise to show me the Alpine Ash.'

'We'll have to see about that,' he says, 'I can't promise, yiz'll have to earn the right, son.'

Bloody hell! I think to myself, I thought I had him by the short and curlies, volunteering to go bush with him and all. Goes to show you can never guess how a parent is going to react.

'How are your shoes?' he asks.

I've forgotten about them but I look down and I see they're completely wrecked. The front of one has the sole coming off and a bit of the toecap is burned on the other, which must have happened before they got wet. They've dried out and all the polish has sort of come off and the leather uppers are crinkled real bad, no way the bootmaker can fix them.

'Shit, Mum will kill me!' I shout out.

'No, she won't, remember you're a bloody hero.'

'Oh yeah! If you think that will make any bloody difference, you're crazy.'

'I'll buy you a new pair next pension day,' he says, 'boots also, for the fires.'

What I think he's really saying is that he won't spend the money on grog and that's a pretty big promise so I decide not to hope for too much. If I have to go to school barefoot, it's not the worst can happen to a bloke and it's summer anyway. Funny, how suddenly when your attention is drawn to something, they start to hurt. I realise that my feet are swollen and I can't wait to get them into a bucket of water when we get home.

Well, weekends, mostly Saturday, I'm out with Tommy in the bush learning things, but because it's the bushfire season he concentrates on fire. I'd always thought that the danger in fire was the flames, but this turns out not to be the case. Of course, flames are pretty dangerous and you can't go taking them lightly.

'Radiant heat's the bastard, Mole,' Tommy tells me. Then he goes on. 'Three year ago, up near the Snowy, this old bloke is lookin' after his son's five kids on the farm. There's a bushfire heading their way and so he thinks, fair enough, take the kids to the dam, same as we did in the pool for that old Indian lady. Sit them in the dam, wait for the fire to pass over, everything will be ridgy-didge. Well, he sets off, plenty o' time, fire's still a mile and a half away. What he hasn't reckoned on is there's a wind blowing around twenty knots an hour and it's carrying these embers, which is what we call 'radiant heat'. It sucks all the oxygen out of the air, like the air burns up. They don't even make it halfway to the dam, which is only two hundred yards from the house. They've died of radiant heat.'

Then he tells me about embers. 'Watch out for embers, Mole. People think the fire has passed, just a few hot spots here and there, little flames you can stamp out with your boots. Don't, mate. Don't stamp at glowing embers. City bloke up from Melbourne come out with us. We tell him we don't think it's a good idea, but he's a big nob, a barrister and a friend of the Yerberrys, so there's not a lot we can do. He wants to skite, see, tell his mates back in the city that he's fought a bushfire. He's wearing all the right clobber, gumboots and long trousers and a wool jumper. It turns out later that his trousers are made of this new stuff called rayon. He doesn't know about not stamping embers and walks away from the group of us. He's having a fine old time stamping away when an ember flies up and drops down one of his gumboots. By the time we found him he was history. Died in the hospital three days later. Stupid bugger's gorn and took off his jumper because he's hot. The trousers are a firetrap and his legs are like burned mallee roots. He'd have been saved if he'd had his jumper on but with it off, the top half of him also goes up in flames and poor bastard had ninety per cent third-degree burns and wouldn't have been able to walk ten steps before he was a goner. Once a fire's down to embers, leave it be, unless you've got plenty of water to douse it and even that can spread sparks. It'll die out by itself once it's got no more fuel to feed it.'

There's lots of things I learn from Tommy and every once in a while I'll tell you something you probably didn't know. You never know when it might come in useful. For instance, did you know that a fire travels uphill faster than downhill? Well, it does. Fire travelling uphill doubles its speed for every ten per cent increase in the slope, up to thirty degrees. Up a twenty-degree slope, which isn't all that steep, a fire travels four times faster than on flat ground.

So, if you're fleeing a fire and there's a small hill or flat ground to choose from, don't go for the hill because you think it will give you protection. There's also something else to remember. Flames moving down a slope grow four times higher the moment they reach flat ground, but then if they start to travel uphill again the flames grow four times higher still.

Remember, if there's a slope with the fire behind you, run down the slope, it's better even than flat ground. But if there's a fire behind you and a hill ahead, don't run up the hill, run around it.

We're coming home one night from where Tommy and me have been to this bloke's farm to help him burn off and I'm pretty hot and tired from having the heat in my face all afternoon. We come to a bright-green patch where someone's grown some lucerne. Everywhere else you look the grass is brown and the late-summer landscape is dried out against a pale-blue sky without a single cloud.

'Wouldn't it be good if all of Australia looked like that?' I say to Tommy, pointing to the paddock that's got lucerne growing.

'Wouldn't be Australia then, would it?'

'What do you mean by that?' I ask.

'Australia is the driest land on earth, it's the continent that burns more than any other. We are a land that has adapted to fire, we've got to have it because many of our essential plants are pyrogenic.'

'What's that mean?' I ask. It's not like Tommy to use big words except when he's naming a eucalyptus tree with Latin names.

'It means certain plants can't propagate, renew themselves without fire. Most Australian native plants and even our animals and insects are fire-adaptive, they can survive a bushfire without too much trouble. Mate, we've gotta have fire, it's a good thing for us, fire isn't bad for the land, it's good. It's only bad when it threatens to burn our houses and towns, but that's mostly our own fault for not planning our townships properly. Remind me one day to tell you about Black Friday in 1939.'

And here I am thinking that fire's the worst thing can happen. The worst thing out. It just goes to show that when you start to learn things about stuff you can often be amazed at what's the real truth.

One Friday night in February, me and Tommy go to a lecture on firefighting at the CFA bushfire headquarters, which is in the Mechanics Institute next to the Masonic Lodge building and is shared with the Amateur Dramatic Society and the Ladies Auxiliary. It has a built-in stage and we have our meetings there. We also store all the fire-fighting gear and the Furphy tank in a tin shed behind the Institute.

We usually have firefighting lectures of a Sunday morning for an hour after all the churches have come out. But I don't suppose this bloke from the Melbourne Fire Brigade could make it then, since he is giving this lecture on a Friday so he can get back home for the weekend. He's rabbiting on and on in a monotonous voice. I've been up since sparrow's fart doing the garbage and I can't keep me eyes open. If I wasn't so tired maybe I'd have learned a bit more, but he's talking all this technical stuff about combustion in the pine woods in Canada and I don't think even Tommy's taking it all in. I must have fallen asleep because suddenly I hear my name called out and Tommy is digging me in the ribs. 'Wake up, mate!' he whispers, 'It's flamin' Templeton, the shire president wants you.'

Bloody hell, it's Mr Templeton who's calling out my name. The last time I seen him was when he was sprawling out cold on his own carpet from a Nancy haymaker.

'This young lad,' Philip Templeton is saying, 'showed intelligence, resourcefulness and great personal initiative as well as bravery when he took three firefighters to go to the rescue of Mrs . . .' He looks down at the paper he's holding, 'Mrs Kar . . . Ray . . . er . . . cha . . .' he looks up and then down at the paper again '. . . hadhuri.' Making a proper mess of the old lady's name. Good thing she's not here, I think.

'It is Mrs Karpu-rika Ray-chaud-huri!' A voice rings out at the back of the hall. The old lady must have come in after Tommy and me because I don't know she was there. 'You are calling me Mrs Rika Ray please, that will do nicely, sir! Rika Ray!' She pronounces it carefully again, then she says, 'Master Mole is learning it straight off, the whole naming catastrophe, Karpurika Raychaudhuri, he is a very, very intelligent boy!'

There's a laugh from the audience and everyone turns around to look at the old lady, who is wearing this beautiful yellow-silk dress down to the floor which is called a sari, though I didn't know the name of it until Mike told me later. Also the diamond in her nose is catching the light and she's pulled back her hair in a bun and has some bushflowers in it. She's painted this red spot in the middle of her forehead.

'Thank you, Mrs Rika Ray,' Philip Templeton laughs, trying to cover his embarrassment. 'Anyway, as I was saying, Peter Maloney, at great risk to himself, led three rescuers to the home of Mrs Rika Ray and effected her rescue. It is now my proud duty to present young Peter with a certificate of appreciation from the president and the members of the Owens and Murray Shire Council.'

'Bloody hell!' Tommy whispers. 'They didn't say nothing about this! Bugger must a wanted to keep yer mum away!'

'Peter Maloney, will you step up to the platform, please,' Philip Templeton shouts out.

I don't know what to do, because he's our mortal enemy and maybe I shouldn't go up.

'Better go, mate,' Tommy whispers, 'I'll explain to yer mum couldn't be helped.'

I get up and walk towards the platform, I'm pretty nervous and I don't trust Tommy to get it right when he's explaining it to Nancy, who is going to go right off her scone when she hears I've took this certificate from our family's mortal enemy.

There's all this clapping from everyone as I go up the steps to the platform. Philip Templeton shakes my hand and gives me the certificate and Toby Forbes from the *Gazette* has got this fancy flash camera which must be new because he didn't have it when he took pictures of Nancy and Sarah after Mike won at the Melbourne Show. He makes me and Mr Templeton shake hands again and with my other hand hold up the certificate. The flashbulb goes off and everyone claps and a few people shout, 'Good on ya, Mole!'

I'm about to leave the platform when Mrs Karpurika Raychaudhuri comes storming in like a steam train and charges her way up the steps to the stage. She stands facing Philip Templeton with her back to the audience. 'It is medals they must be giving this boy! Medals, not bits of paper for wiping your bottoms on!' Then she turns to face the stage and puts her hand on my shoulder and Toby Forbes's flash goes off again. As the din dies down, Mrs Karpurika Raychaudhuri has another go. 'This is a very, very brave boy and I am writing to the Queen and I am telling her the story of Master Mole who is fighting fires in Yankalillee and Silver Creek and rescuing old ladies from death and destruction and is only getting a piece of bottoms-wiping paper!'

Everyone's laughing and some are clapping and Mr Templeton doesn't look too pleased and has put up his hand and is trying to make everyone be quiet again.

I'm pretty embarrassed standing there next to the old lady with her hand on my shoulder. She has that same smell her house had when we first went in and that little stick was burning. When I went back the next day to fetch Sarah's medicine, I asked her if Sarah was right and it was called incense?

'Incense, yes, you are calling it correct. A very beautiful smell, this one is sandalwood, Master Mole,' she'd said at the time. But I can't say I agreed with her. It smelled like very old things burning. Now she smells a bit like that standing next to me.

The din eventually dies down and Mr Templeton calls out, 'Let's have three cheers for the brave little chap, eh!'

He says the hip-hips and the hoorays follow. But I hardly notice. I'm in deep shit. What do I do now? I'm sandwiched between a family enemy and an Indian lady who gave my sister Sarah stuff that didn't luckily get rid of her baby, which Morrie and Sophie want badly. Nancy's going to kill me!

But now everyone's clapping again after the cheering. Toby Forbes's new camera is going *pop-pop-flash* right in our faces and Philip Templeton puts his hand on my other shoulder. When everyone's quietened down, he looks down at me, his huge gut sticking out, then he sort of smiles and asks, 'Would you like to say something to us, Peter?'

Kids don't say things in front of grown-ups. He knows that. Everyone knows that. I'm embarrassed enough and wish there was a hole in the floor I could disappear down into. All I can think is that Philip Templeton is having his revenge on us Maloneys in front of everyone by asking me to say something.

The old lady has made a fool of him and a bit of me too, but I know she doesn't mean to. But he thinks it's those Maloneys having a go at him again. Most of the people, if not all, know about Murray Templeton and Sarah. It's popular gossip and the town's tongue-waggers haven't stopped working overtime and he knows that some of the firefighters would be on our side even though Murray Templeton was captain of the school footy team.

I shake my head and look down at the new shoes that Tommy's bought me and I can feel my face and the back of my neck is burning hot. There's no way I can say anything and my mouth is dry like my tongue is stuck to the roof.

When I get home I'll have to answer to Nancy who's going to question me about every detail of what's happened tonight. If I tell her I didn't say nothing, she's going to be disappointed. Like, she won't say anything herself, because she knows kids don't talk in public, but she'll think I've let us Maloneys down in front of Mr Templeton by not saying at least thank you for the certificate. Our manners are important and she's strict on them and she probably hasn't had her tongue stick to the roof of her mouth like mine is now. Now Mr Templeton's gone and pointed out to the rest of the town how Maloneys are real stupid and not able to say anything when they're asked and don't have nice manners like civilised people.

I somehow manage to get my tongue unstuck and I work up some spit so my mouth isn't all dried out. 'It wasn't me done nothing, sir. My dad, Tommy Maloney and Mr Crowe and Mr McTavish, they done everything except what Mrs Karpurika Raychaudhuri done herself with the tent pole and cutting a hole in the carpet to let the air come in so she didn't smother. All I done was sit in the creek.'

There's a lot of laughter, like I've said something funny, which I ain't. I've only told the exact truth. I'm so nervous my hands are sweating and I've gone and scrunched the certificate Mr Templeton gave me into a little damp ball in my fist.

But all I can think is that I've called Tommy 'my dad' in front of everyone and it feels real good and Mr Templeton can get stuffed for all I care.

Chapter Eight

What I want to know is this: if your name is Maloney, why trouble seems to follow you wherever you go. I didn't do anything brave to get that certificate and I wasn't a hero like they said I was, but that didn't stop Toby Forbes putting a big picture of me and Mrs Karpurika Raychaudhuri on the front page of the *Gazette* and writing under it in huge letters:

Silver Creek Fire
Local Boy
Peter Maloney
saves mysterious
Indian woman's life

What he's gone and done is cut Mr Templeton's picture out of the group, but if you look carefully you can see the toecap of his left shoe in the corner of the photo. The old lady has her hand on my shoulder and it looks to all the world like she's thanking me for saving her life. Then it goes on to say a whole heap of bull about the flames leaping and roaring around her house which was totally destroyed and, but for my quick thinking, Mrs Rika Ray, an elderly woman of Indian descent who has appeared mysteriously in our town, would have gone up in the 'conflagration'. There's almost nothing about Tommy and Mr Crowe and Mr McTavish and what they done, which is the true story as everybody who was there well knows.

Nancy says it's typical of Toby Forbes and his gutter journalism and then she goes spare because now the whole town will want to find out why we know this Indian lady and how come I knew that she lived in her humpy tucked away in the bush.

It's the word 'mysterious' in the headline that's the big problem. Why is she mysterious? Everyone wants to know. Admittedly, probably no one in town has seen too many Indian ladies walking around the place, but Mrs Karpurika Raychaudhuri has been in town shopping plenty of times before the fire and has been around quite a while. It's just that nobody's talked to her, because she's from 'over there'. So now she's all of a sudden mysterious? Being a herbalist doesn't help either. People don't know what to think. Maybe, like I admit I did that first time, they think she's a witch or something.

Tommy's also in the shit with Nancy for letting me go up on the stage at the Mechanics Institute but she says she'll deal with him later. 'Mole, you never took the spoon out of the sink!' she yells at me. 'Look what's going to happen now, everyone will want to know who this Mrs Rika Ray is and what we're doing associating with someone from away, who is a herbalist and some sort of witch doctor! Won't take them long to put two and two together neither. Then there'll be more damn silly rumours about Sarah to keep their tongues wagging.'

'The Indian lady said if anyone asked her a girl's name who'd come to see her, like Sarah did, she'd not remember any such name or person. It's true, Mum, I'll swear it on a stack of Bibles, you can ask Sarah, that's what she said to us. She hasn't talked about Sarah in the *Gazette*. She didn't the other night at the Mechanics Institute neither.'

Then, of course, I remember she mentioned Sarah to Tommy, John Crowe and Ian McTavish when she told Tommy we were both clever. I don't know if they're gossips or would even remember because it was when we were sitting in the pool. I decide it's best not to come clean on that one to Nancy, it would only cause more trouble for me and I'm in enough shit as it is.

'Let's hope so, Mole,' Nancy says, becoming a bit more

understanding. 'In the meantime, if anyone asks, you were just mucking around in the bush when you met her.'

'Mum, that's dumb! People know I don't muck about in the bush, there's joe blakes can get yer. I only go with Tommy of a weekend because he knows about snakes.

'Mole, I'm giving you permission to tell a lie. Sometimes you have to for the greater good. You were out bird-nesting or something. Right, there you go, that will do as good as anything, boys sometimes do that, bird-nesting, don't they? You were out bird-nesting and you come across the humpy and met this old woman.'

'Bird-nesting? They only do that in English comics like *Beano* and *Dandy*! I don't know nothing about birds, except crows and ducks and Mr Dorf's racing pigeons down the street and, yes, kookaburras, because they eat snakes and make a racket in the early morning and the evening. Ferreting maybe, to get rabbits, only we ain't got a ferret.'

'No, not ferreting, Mole! I don't want people to think you go ferreting! Ferrets smell to high heaven, garbage collecting and ferreting ain't a good combination. Get Tommy to teach you a few bird names, he knows them all,' Nancy says, like it's that easy. But I think she quite likes the old lady, though they haven't yet met. When I told her about the bottoms-wiping certificate she couldn't stop laughing for five minutes. 'She sounds like a woman after my own heart!' she cried. So she hasn't banned me from seeing Mrs Rika Ray.

To my surprise when I told her about Philip Templeton, Nancy didn't go ape-shit. She just said Sarah was lucky he wasn't going to be her father-in-law and that Dora Templeton was in love with 'Doctor Bottle' and the both of them weren't worth a pinch of 'you know what'. She also said that Tommy shouldn't have told me to go up and get the piece of paper which you couldn't call a proper certificate because it was written out on a typewriter with a worn ribbon and was typical of Philip bloody Templeton. Sarah tried to iron the certificate straight again but it was too far gone. Mike said, 'What can you expect from that shire mob? They're that cheapskate they wouldn't even put it in a frame with a bit of glass around it.'

But I didn't really mind because I didn't deserve the bottoms-wiping certificate anyway and it would only have reminded us that we'd got into even more trouble because of it.

Nancy is right. Everyone wants to know who Mrs Rika Ray is. She's not Mrs Karpurika Raychaudhuri any more, she's Mrs Rika Ray, because that's what Toby Forbes has called her in the *Gazette*. 'The mysterious Mrs Rika Ray from India' is how people refer to her now.

Even Crocodile Brown fronts me in the classroom, 'Mole Maloney, we saw your picture in the *Gazette* and we all congratulate you.' He turns to the class, 'A big clap for Mole Maloney, who makes us all very proud to be Yankalillians.'

Everyone in the class claps but I don't think they're that proud of me or of being Yankalillians neither. It's because of our garbage collecting. Even if what I done was true, a bit of spare bravery isn't going to help change the Maloney reputation overnight. So then Crocodile Brown says, 'Perhaps you'd like to tell us how you met the mysterious Mrs Rika Ray from India and led her to safety from the raging inferno?'

'No, sir, it was a lot of bull what they said in the *Gazette* about me saving her life. I didn't do nothing, sir. It was Tommy, I mean my dad, and the others, Mr Crowe and Mr McTavish, I just showed them where she lived, but she'd already saved her own life when we got there.'

I can tell you, I was getting bloody tired of explaining about the tent pole and the carpet with the hole cut into it for air.

'Ah, such modesty in one so young!' he exclaims and I think he's being sarcastic. 'How did you know her whereabouts in the bush in the first place?' he goes on.

Uh-oh! Here comes Nancy's lie for the greater good, 'I was bird-nesting, sir. Then I come across her house.' I don't want to say too much because I haven't thought about how bird-nesting should go and nobody I've ever known has done it. But I've got a few bird names from Tommy, just in case I get questioned, like I am now.

'I didn't know you were a bird-nester, Mole!' Crocodile Brown says. He seems very pleased with this notion. 'I say, I used to go bird-nesting when I was a lad. We'd go rambling in the Fens in Norfolk during school holidays. Perhaps we should compare notes, eh!' He turns to the class, 'We'll make a nature-study lesson from this. Who can name a bird to be commonly found in north-eastern Victoria?'

Half the hands in our class go up and, I must say, I'm dead surprised.

'Right, you, Noel Johnson,' Crocodile Brown points to Pissy Johnson.

'Crow and canary, sir!' All the other hands go down except for Anna Dumb-cow-ski who shouldn't know a bird because she's from away and a reffo and comes from Poland.

'Canary? The canary is a caged bird, used as a pet in this part of the world and is not found flying free in the district, Johnson.'

'Well, crow then, sir?'

'Yes, all right, crow. What about all the parakeets? The crimson rosella, the galah, the green grass parrot, the sulphur-crested and the glossy black cockatoos?' Crocodile Brown reels them off just to show he's smarter than all of us and that Pissy Johnson is an idjit.

'Yes, sir, sorry, sir,' Pissy Johnson says.

Pissy would know about crows because he lives on a farm near Yackandandah. When an animal, a calf or lamb, goes down, the crows come in to land thick and fast and they'll peck the eyes out of any beast. A bunch of crows can easily kill a lamb or a newborn calf. I'm also surprised he hasn't said eagle. Tommy says farmers see them as flesh-eating predators and so they shoot them whenever they can. I've seen it myself, these wedge-tailed eagles with their wings stretched out nailed to fence posts by the farmers as a warning to other eagles I suppose. Tommy says if they go on killing them like they are, they'll soon enough be killed out.

Anna Dumb-cow-ski still has her hand up and Crocodile turns to her, 'Yes, Anna?'

'Magpie, sir.'

'Yes, that's a good one!' Crocodile Brown smiles. He likes Anna because of the concentration camp, so he doesn't dump on her like he's just done with Pissy Johnson. If anyone else had said magpie, he'd have gone crook on them, because it's also a bird everyone knows but forgets about and isn't any better than saying a crow.

'Anyone else?' Crocodile looks around.

Somebody says a duck and someone else a dove and Crocodile Brown says what kind of duck and what kind of dove and nobody knows and nobody remembers a kookaburra, which, like the magpie and a crow, is one you always know but can easily forget when you're asked. It turns out the whole class is the same as me, they know bugger-all about birds.

'Right, this is not a rich vein of avian knowledge we're mining here,' Crocodile says, 'So now let's ask the true bird-nester among us.' He turns to me, 'Mole Maloney, which nests belonging to our feathered friends have you plundered recently?'

That's the problem with parents, they don't know the kind of shit they can get their kids into. Now I've got to lie beyond myself and it's like Sarah's always told us, you tell a little lie and then it has to get bigger and bigger until it becomes a whopper. But I also guess what's behind all Crocodile Brown's questions is that he wants to know more about Mrs Rika Ray. Probably his wife has set him onto me because of those rats in their garbage can, which he could never prove was us but knows it was.

I try to remember exactly what Tommy's told me. So I clear my throat to get a bit more time to think. 'Sir, there's the red-browed finch, that's the most common species of finch around here. It's got red eyebrows, that's why it's called a red brow and then it's got grey underpants . . .' The class roars with laughter at the mention of the grey underpants. I did too when Tommy told me that's what it's called in bird language. Crocodile Brown holds up his hand for silence. 'And a golden splash on the side of the neck and then the rest is sort of brownish-gold with a red patch top o' a longish black tail, sir.'

'A very good description, I know the red-browed Finch very well, loves the grass seed at the edge of my road.' Crocodile Brown seems pleased with himself for knowing my first bird. 'The eggs, Mr Maloney, what do the eggs look like?'

Shit, how would I know that? Tommy hasn't told me about the eggs. Here we go again! Far as I'm concerned eggs are either white or brown, hen eggs that is, don't see why birds should be any different. 'White, sir,' I say, which is the most common colour with hens.

'Well, well, then, it becomes obvious you know something of bird-nesting, Mole Maloney.' He stops and looks at the rest of the class. 'Which is more than I can say for the rest of you lot who are downright ignorant when it comes to things ornithological.'

I write down the word he's just said though I'm not sure how to spell it. Sarah will tell me what it means or she'll make me look it up in the dictionary.

'That will do nicely, thank you, Mr Maloney, we shan't belabour the point. I can see you know what you're talking about.' Crocodile Brown says all this a tad sarcastic like because I've given him the info on the red-browed finch a bit parrot fashion, following Tommy's own words almost exact. 'I must say I'm surprised, there are depths to you I've never plumbed,' he says. 'So, as you said, you met this mysterious Indian lady out bird-nesting. Would you consider bringing your bird-egg collection in for the class to see?'

See what I mean? There's always a trap. Just when you think you've escaped you're back in the shit and have to tell another lie. 'Sorry, sir, 'fraid I can't, sir.'

'It would make an excellent nature-study lesson for us all, maybe this lot of ignoramuses will learn something,' Crocodile Brown says, pressing the point.

'My dad, he won't allow it, sir. He says we're losing too many birds because of the insecticides farmers and orchardists are spraying like Dieldrin and DDT, and then there's the feral cats who are destroying the bird life and the small rodents and reptiles. He says I can look but I mustn't take. The eggs *must* stay in the nest.'

It's true enough, it's what Tommy said when I asked him. I mean what he said about the DDT and how, if I really was a bird-nester, he'd tell me not to take the eggs. Tommy's also dead against feral cats, who, he says, do the most damage to bird and wildlife. 'They'll wipe out a whole species and nobody seems to care. Had my way I'd put a bounty on feral cats, wipe the lot off the face of the earth.'

The lie for the greater good is getting bigger. But not by so much it's become a real whopper yet.

'That's very commendable, Mole Maloney,' Crocodile says. But I can see he's disappointed. He thought he had me there and nearly did. I pray he doesn't go on much longer, it's easy to forget what you've heard when you're in a bit of a panic like I am at the moment. If he asked for more birds, I was going to give him the painted honeyeater and the superb blue wren, but after that I could have been in big trouble.

'Thank you, Mole, now perhaps we'd better get on with the history lesson meant for this period.'

So I've squeaked through the lie by a hair's breadth and I don't have to answer anything about the old lady.

Tommy's kept his word to Mrs Rika Ray. Him and the other two men took John Crowe's ute to cut bark and struts and stakes, and in three days they've built a new bark hut for the old lady that is much better than her old one. It even has a three-sided kitchen with a stone fireplace and chimney so when it rains she can still have a fire and cook.

John Crowe brings some corrugated iron which he says 'fell off the back of a truck' and he uses it to put on a proper roof with guttering that won't ever leak. Lucky, heh? About ten pieces fell off the truck and it must have made a helluva racket landing on the road. All I can say is the driver must have been deaf as a post.

The fireplace is double-sided, the inside and outside sharing the same chimney. The sides are separated by a steel boiler door taken from an ancient steam engine left in the bush from during the gold-rush days a hundred years before. The door shuts off one half of the fireplace, depending on which side the old lady is cooking. The idea is that if she lights a fire in winter she can cook inside the hut and the fire will also keep the hut nice and warm as well. They've also found an old tank for catching rainwater in case there is a drought and the creek runs dry.

'I am counting my blessings because I am meeting you, Master Mole,' the old lady says to me all the time. There I go again, getting the credit when the others are doing all the work, which is something Nancy says we must never do. But when I tell Tommy, he says it's okay. John and Ian are good blokes and they understand it's because I'm a kid and the old lady can't go telling them every ten minutes how grateful she is, because it would become downright embarrassing to blokes like them.

It turns out that John Crowe is the expert who can do anything with bush carpentry and he even makes her a bed from native timber using the springs from her old army cot which the fire hadn't damaged. Only the paint was scalded off. But she has to buy a new mattress because she couldn't throw the old one in the creek as it would have been just as ruined in water, so she left it to burn. The mattress kept smouldering for days after and smelled a bit like that incense.

By mid-February Mrs Rika Ray's herb garden is coming on real good and, because I asked her to, she's planted a sunflower seed where the other once stood and it's about eight inches high already.

I go and see her a bit when I have the time, because now that I'm interested in the bush she says there are lots of things I should know. She'll teach me about plants and their medicinal properties and although she is Indian and not Aboriginal, she's learned a bit about Australian plants and will teach me stuff I should know in case I get lost in the bush or fall down a cliff or something.

Well, by January Sarah is getting bigger and bigger. I mean, you see ladies who are pregnant but you daren't look properly because you're not supposed to stare. But now that it's in front of your very eyes all the time you can't believe that Sarah could swell up like that and become so sticky-out all of a sudden in only five months.

Nancy says, 'God forbid, maybe she's having twins! I hope not, is all I can think, the last time there were twins, my two aunties up top, it didn't turn out so good.' But, Nancy's only kidding, because she says twins would show up much earlier than five months. One thing I'll guarantee, whatever she's having, it's going to be the best-dressed baby in the universe. Nancy and Sarah and Mike are making sure of that every afternoon on the back verandah, embroidering and smocking, probably using every stitch in 'Wicked Witches'.

But the good thing is that whatever the town is saying about Sarah, it ain't coming from us doing anything wrong for a change. Not even the town doctor is involved. Morrie comes with Sophie every week to check Sarah out so not even old Mrs Turkington who works for Dr Hughes in his surgery can pass on any juicy gossip.

Crocodile Brown making me talk to the class about birds turned out to be a good thing as well. All the kids must have went home and told their parents what had happened and soon enough there's tongues wagging overtime to everyone in sight and, whether they liked it or not, the bird-nesting theory was the best reason they had for me knowing the mysterious Mrs Rika Ray.

John Crowe and Ian McTavish turn out not to be gossips. Either that, or they forgot that the old lady mentioned Sarah when we were all sitting in the creek. So the lie for the greater good has worked, though I wouldn't want to go through the experience too often.

But that's the funny thing, I've become genuinely interested in birds and Tommy includes them in my lessons when we go bush.

Then at the end of January 'the letter' arrives for Sarah. It's from Melbourne University. There's this crest on the envelope so even the postie, Jimmy Phipps, knows where it's from. Nancy says he's got a big mouth and you can be sure that the arrival of the long-awaited letter will spread around town like wildfire. It's been a big month. Earlier Sarah's matriculation results have come through and she's got a distinction in every subject and over ninety-five per cent for Biology, Maths and Latin.

Well, we're very excited and it's me who gets the letter from Jimmy Phipps, so I go rushing through, shouting, 'The letter! It's the letter! It's come!' When anyone says 'the letter' it only means one thing and every day for weeks we've stored a little joy or sorrow energy in our hearts because maybe this will be the day it comes.

I give it to Sarah who's in the kitchen at the time and she says she has to sit down, then uses the envelope like a fan in front of her face. We all go to the back verandah where Nancy is working with Mike. Sarah sits down slowly on the old wicker chair and her hands are shaking as she starts to open it. Then she stops and puts it on her lap, looks out sort of into the backyard and I think I'm going to piss my pants if she doesn't hurry up and open it.

We've got a plan worked out if she gets in. Everything hinges on what's in the letter. It takes about a hundred years for her to open it and unfold it and start reading. Everything is stopped. Even Bozo's Bitzers know something's up and they're lined up, tongues lolling. Then Sarah closes her eyes and brings the letter up against her chest and we don't know whether it's good or bad but we think it's good. Then she opens her eyes and smiles.

'Yippee!' we all shout and start to kiss and hug her. Nancy starts to cry and so does Sarah and even Mike's having a bit of a sniff and Bozo's dogs are doing somersaults and rolling over and barking to his exact instructions.

'Read it!' Bozo shouts. 'Read it out aloud!'

Sarah wipes her eyes with the side of her hand but still has to fight back the tears. Bozo stops the Bitzers and lines them up and she starts to read, her voice not yet completely under control.

Miss Sarah Maloney
2 Bell Street
Yankalillee
Victoria
25 January 1956

Dear Miss Maloney,

It is with great pleasure that I inform you that the Council has approved the recommendation of the selection committee for the Faculty of Medical Science in 1956 and that you have been granted a position in the Medical Faculty. The first semester will commence on 12th March 1956. You will meet at the School of Medicine at Block 22 on campus at 10 a.m. to enrol. The Writer and Professor Marcus Block will be in attendance.

Enclosed please find a list of the textbooks and stationery you will require. You will also need two white lab jackets. The lab jackets are also obtainable from the University bookshop or you may purchase them elsewhere. They should have plain bone buttons and the hemline should not fall beyond the knee.

May I offer you my sincerest congratulations,

I remain your humble servant,

M. Tompkins
Asst Registrar

P.S. It can get cold in Melbourne around this time and you are advised to bring warm clothing with you.

The P.S. isn't typed like the rest of the letter but is written in a neat almost copperplate handwriting which Nancy says is nice to see in a man.

Well, I can tell you, we're that excited even though we know things can go wrong with the Grand Plan. That evening Morrie and Sophie come over. Morrie also has his letter saying he can be a student and they're just as happy for us as we are for them. We're totally wrapped, much too happy to ask ourselves what will happen if the Grand Plan fails.

This is how it happened, the Grand Plan, that is. When I said trouble seems to follow our name perhaps I wasn't being fair. Good things happen too. Remember how I told you the people who were at the very top of the social heap in Yankalillee were the graziers and the topmost of their mob are the Barrington-Stones, who once had a horse in the Melbourne Cup that came last and they also fly a Piper Cub?

Well, Mrs Barrington-Stone's daughter Claudina, who is married to a barrister in Melbourne and lives in a place called Toorak, is having a baby, so Mrs Barrington-Stone orders the works from Nancy. She wants a complete layette as well as a very posh christening robe. The full catastrophe, no expense spared. It keeps everyone pretty busy for a month during November and part of December and Nancy says, thank God, because it will help pay the bills that come after Christmas and take her mind off Sarah's pregnancy.

All was finished on December the fifteenth and Mike and me were meant to take it out next morning but then Mrs Barrington-Stone phoned to say could she have two extra bibs. It doesn't sound like much, but Nancy and Mike worked on them until about three o'clock the next day and they had to get them to Mrs Barrington-Stone that night because the next morning early she was flying to Melbourne in her Piper Cub to do her Christmas shopping. Mike and me had to take the two big brown-paper parcels the stuff is wrapped in to the property about seven miles out of town and so it's a fair hike. Luckily it's a Friday and it's summer so it won't be dark before we get home and, with no garbage, we can sleep in tomorrow.

We walk and we walk and eventually we get to the front gate, which has got a curved iron sign straddling two big red brick pillars.

The arched sign would be high enough and the pillars wide enough apart for the Diamond T to go through and under if Bozo had driven us. Which normally he would have done, but couldn't because he's gone with Sergeant Donovan in the police car to Wangaratta to attend a training session with their Police Boys boxing team. There has been some talk that Bozo might be invited to the Olympic boxing trials in Melbourne. The sign above the gate in these big iron letters says 'Passing Cloud' and then arched under it in smaller letters, 'Prop. J.P. Barrington-Stone 1872'.

We start to walk down this private road, which is their driveway I suppose. It's flanked on either side by huge eucalyptus trees. Big old trees that must have been there seventy or eighty years and are about eighty feet high.

'River Red Gum, *Eucalyptus camaldulensis*,' I say casually to Mike. 'Bit high up for them mind, usually found along the bank o' the Murray River, but they look to be doing okay.' I'm talking like Tommy, and Mike just grunts, I think he knows I'm showing off a whole lot. The trees have a smooth white bark with patches of grey and Tommy says that among the eucalyptus the River Red Gum is thought to be a most graceful tree. It's not his kind of language so he must have read that bit in a book. Anyway, the driveway with the River Red Gum is so long it goes over the crest of a hill and you can't even see the Barrington-Stone house from the big gate or even when you're nearly there.

Then when we see it, we can't quite believe our eyes. It is bigger than any house in town, with tractor sheds and haysheds and stables, an open-sided hangar for their new Piper Cub and a second older Cub that's used as a crop-duster. There is also a small airstrip leading away from the house. People say Mrs Barrington-Stone flies the Piper Cub herself to Melbourne and all over Victoria when she's going to the Country Women's Association meetings. People call her the Amelia Earhart of the bush. Nancy says she's a real bigwig in the organisation and has just been elected national president, which makes a nice change from the old busybodies who've done the job before her.

There is also a big garden with lots of bushes, like camellia, azalea and plumbago as well as beds of summer plantings, zinnia, marigolds, shasta daisies and others I don't know about. I only know those because of our class garden at school. There's also a trellis covered in wisteria and a big splashing fountain in the centre of the lawn with a fat little stone boy peeing in a big arc into the water that's very funny. When we see the fountain close up, it has goldfish which Mrs Barrington-Stone later calls carp, same as they have in the Murray River, but of course not all the good colours of these ones in the pond.

Anyway, three kelpies come barking out at us but they're wagging their tails. You can see they're old with grey muzzles and one has a milky eye so we take no notice, probably lost all their teeth anyway. We go to the back door like Nancy said we must. There's a screen door and we look into a large kitchen with a big fan turning quite slowly from the ceiling. We see a lady who we think must be Mrs Barrington-Stone. She's quite fat and is making a racket with a meat mallet, banging at a piece of meat on a large butcher's block. There's no place you can knock properly on a screen door and, besides, the lady's making such a noise she wouldn't hear us anyway.

'Mrs Barrington-Stone!' Mike shouts out, polite but also loud enough so she'll hear.

The banging stops and this lady looks around and sees us and smiles. 'Hello, boys, wrong lady, I'm the cook.' Then she comes to the door and opens it and indicates we must enter. She sees me looking at the meat mallet she's holding. 'Oh, just tenderising a bit of mutton for the dogs, they're too old to chew it unless it's practically mince.' She puts the mallet down on the chopping block, 'Wait on here, boys, and I'll call madam.'

I can't believe my eyes. On the kitchen counter next to the chopping block is what looks like a dish of raw tripe. The Barrington-Stones are supposed to be worth a fortune and they're having to eat tripe for their tea!

'Crikey!' I whisper to Mike. 'They've got a flamin' cook, so how come they're on an offal week!'

'Probably for the dogs!' Mike says out of the corner of his mouth.

'Nah, she said they've got no teeth, tripe's bloody tough raw.'

'So, simple, she'll cook it,' he says.

I don't say anything, even Bozo's Bitzers don't like tripe all that much and who'd bother to cook tripe for a dog. I remain unconvinced by Mike's explanation. Maybe they need new tyres for the Piper Cub or something?

I can see why we would have mistaken the cook for Mrs Barrington-Stone because when she comes into the kitchen she's about the same size. But she's dressed in moleskin pants and brown boots and a blue open-neck shirt, same as any big hat at the Wangaratta Show. 'Good afternoon, boys, you've come from Nancy Maloney, have you?'

We nod, holding out the two big brown-paper parcels. 'Oh, you'd best bring those into the dining room. Mrs Jackson is tenderising and we don't want a lump of mince to land where it shouldn't, now do we?'

We follow her through and she takes us into a dining room that's twice as big even than Philip Templeton's lounge room and it's only the dining room. The lounge room stretches halfway across the countryside, which you can see through this huge glass window at the end. The dining room has a long table that must have twenty chairs around it. In the centre is this silver candlestick with about ten branches for candles.

'How very exciting!' she says, 'I can't wait!' Pointing at the polished surface of the table, she shows where to put the two parcels we're carrying, 'Do put them down, please. This *is* such a nice surprise.' She stops and looks curious, 'I didn't hear a car coming up the drive? Is there someone waiting for you outside?'

'We walked, madam,' Mike says all proper, calling her 'madam' just like the cook did.

'Walked? You walked the seven miles from town? My goodness! You must be exhausted. You must have some tea.'

'No, no, it's okay,' Mike protests, 'our tea will be waiting for us when we get home.' I'm glad Mike said that because we'd have to have tripe for their tea and it ain't an offal week at home. It's only half-past five, they must eat real early, even we don't have our tea until half-past six.

'No, I won't hear of it, my boy. It's a hot day and you shall have some refreshment. What say lemonade and biscuits, there might be a bit of chocolate cake left over?'

I look at Mike and hope to hell he don't say no, now you're talking lemonade, biscuits and cake. A far cry from tripe. He sort of grunts, 'Thank you.'

'Good! Then why don't we all go out on the verandah where there's usually a bit of a breeze at this time of the day. Walked? I do declare!' Mrs Barrington-Stone has got this posh accent like she could almost be from England but you know she isn't because you can see she's Australian.

We sit around a big low wicker table looking out onto the garden and directly down at the splashing fountain with the stone boy pissing. Each of us is in a large wicker chair that's big and not broken like ours at home and has soft green canvas cushions you sit on and from which air escapes when you lean back into them.

Mrs Jackson brings in a tray with two king-size bottles of lemonade from the soft drink factory, three bread 'n' butter plates, white with pink roses and a gold edge sort of scalloped on them, there's a big plate of Brockhoff's biscuits on a silver stand as well as two slices of chocolate cake. There's two glasses and, also, there's these two starched white damask serviettes. I know they're damask because the cot covers we sometimes have to embroider are often made of damask.

Mrs Jackson the cook then says, 'Madam, we have a nice bit of tripe or will I do a roast for dinner?'

'Tripe? Oh, lovely, that's Jim's favourite, he will be pleased. With white sauce and onions, is it?'

'Yes, madam,' the cook says, a trifle scornful, because even I know you always get white sauce and onions with tripe. Yuk! Mrs Jackson leaves and I bet she's disappointed about the tripe against roast beef because she probably has to eat it too.

I'm nervous and a bit confused about this tripe incident. There's something very wrong with someone who chooses tripe when they could just as easily have a roast dinner. But I must say, Mrs Barrington-Stone is not up herself and seems a pretty normal sort of a person all round. She speaks a bit loudly but then so does Nancy, so you can't hold that against her.

She now points to the bottles of lemonade, 'Bottoms up, boys, you can't leave until each of you has finished your very own bottle. Have a piece of cake. You can leave the biscuits if you wish but you simply must eat the cake, you can't refuse it or Mrs Jackson will be very upset. She doesn't always feel appreciated and, as you would know, one must never ever upset the cook, a homestead is run on its stomach and I simply wouldn't be able to cope without her.'

'Yes, I know,' says Mike, who doesn't know at all, because he's never even seen a cook except Nancy and Sarah and that's not the same thing, they don't get paid.

'Well then, go ahead, tuck in, boys, I'm sure you're starving after that awfully long walk. You'll excuse me not joining you, but I had a cuppa just a few minutes ago.'

She's not wrong, we're both real hungry and you never know when your next slice of chocolate cake is going to come along and so we reach over and get going on the cake and soon there's sticky chocolate icing over my fingers and I can sense it's around my mouth because Mike's got a chocolate moustache already.

Oh shit, I think to myself, I'm going to have to use one of them starched damask serviettes, which you only see in the movies, folded and standing up like a little white tower. There's going to be chocolate cake all over it, like skid marks on undies. In the movies, all people ever do with them is pout their lips and then touch them ever so lightly with the corner of the damask serviettes before they put them down again on their lap. When they get up from the table the serviettes are never there. I can't use the back of my hand neither, because I know that's bad manners and we can only do it at home if Sarah isn't looking.

But then Mike picks up his serviette and unfolds it and wipes his mouth casual as you like. I look up at Mrs Barrington-Stone to see if he's done wrong and she's looking directly at him and chuckles and, pointing to his nose, she says, 'There's a blob of chocolate on the very tip of your nose, Michael. Mrs Jackson will be so happy you're enjoying her chocolate cake. It's her pride and joy so you'd better tell her how much you've enjoyed it before you leave.' She doesn't seem to mind that Mike hasn't pouted his lips and that he's mucked up the serviette a treat. So I do the same and there's smears of chocolate all over the starched whiteness.

'Oh dear, you must please excuse me for just a minute,' Mrs Barrington-Stone says, rising from her chair. 'I simply can't contain myself any longer, I must see what you've brought me. I know I should be patient, but it's not every day one has a lovely surprise like a new baby in the family, is it?'

'You're bloody right there, madam,' I think to myself, but I'm not so sure about the lovely surprise.

'I'll be back with you both in a couple of minutes,' she says. 'In the meantime I expect most of those biscuits to be missing by the time I return.'

Mrs Barrington-Stone is a real nice lady and I think she might have left us just so we could bog in without being polite only eating one biscuit each. Not every day you can eat biscuits bought in a shop, maybe at Christmas if you're lucky. Past Christmases, Oliver Withers the magistrate has always left us a big packet of Brockhoff's Chocolate Creams. Except last year when we got there, all there was, was the packet with one biscuit left which his Alsatian dogs missed because it rolled to the other side of the gate. Being the last garbage before Christmas we hadn't lined up the Bitzers to mock his dogs and, I must say, they looked a bit smug when they came round the corner to bark at us. Nancy said she wouldn't be surprised if he hadn't done it deliberately, Oliver Twist being the mean bugger he is. But I don't think he would've, it was just bad luck.

Mrs Barrington-Stone comes back about ten minutes later when we've had a good few of the biscuits and she sits down and clasps her hands together in front of her chest like she's praying, only she's cracked a smile that's practically spilling off the edges of her cheeks. 'My enormous and sincere congratulations! The work is simply marvellous! Please tell your mother how very, very delighted I am. Oh, and your sister too, I believe they work together. Sarah, isn't it?'

'Yes, madam. Thank you, I'll tell Mum,' Mike says. He's getting saying 'madam' down pat. I know he'd love to get some credit for doing the embroidery, but he can't and it must hurt a helluva lot deep inside. Bozo, the Boy Boxer, is winning every fight he's in and is a bit of a hero with the yobbos who hang around the Parthenon cafe and even at school for a change. And I've just got a bottoms-wiping certificate and my name in the *Gazette*. It's not fair. Mike's won the biggest prize you could ever win in your whole life at the Royal Melbourne Show and he can't tell about it or get any of the glory that's coming to us. All those blue ribbons drawing-pinned to the picture rail in the front room, and he can only look at them but can never hear people tell him how clever he is.

'The embroidery, in particular, such fine delicate work,' Mrs Barrington-Stone says. Her eyes show she's excited, 'It's astonishing that your mother's eyes have kept up, it's quite the best work I've ever seen and hardly surprising that your mother and sister won Best of Show in Melbourne.'

'Mike done it!' I blurt out, not thinking, because I've just been thinking about Mike not getting any glory. It just come out. A silent thought that's come out said out loud when you didn't want it to. Shit! Shit! SHIT!

Mike has blushed. He's going to bloody kill me. Nancy will slaughter me when she hears! I'm scared to look at my brother, knowing how I've just gone and humiliated him.

'Well, I never! Why, that's simply marvellous, Michael, *you* did that exquisite embroidery? How wonderfully talented you are.'

Mike looks down at his shoes and I can see he doesn't know what to say. They are the words he's always wanted to hear but knew he couldn't ever and now she's said them.

'It's a secret. You mustn't tell anyone,' I quickly say to Mrs Barrington-Stone. 'He's a boy, see!' It's much too late an attempt to make up to Mike for what I've said and he gives me a look that's not real hopeful for my future welfare.

'You are a talented boy, Michael,' Mrs Barrington-Stone exclaims. 'Of course, I read about your mother and sister winning at the Royal Melbourne Show. I was very excited for them and said so at the Country Women's Association regional conference in Shepparton in November. I told them it was good for Yankalillee and good for country people to know that we still have some of the British Empire's great craftswomen living in the Australian bush. And now the sorcerer's apprentice has become the master himself!'

The truth is, that Mrs Barrington-Stone is so nice and doesn't seem to care a bit about Mike being a boy who does embroidery and soon there's talk tumbling out of us like we've been friends for years.

She fetches the christening robe and Mike explains the various bits to her and, without thinking, says, 'I've used all twelve wicked witches' britches stitches on it.'

'Wicked witches' britches stitches?' she claps her hands together and throws her head back and laughs. 'How jolly, but you'll have to explain.'

Mike explains that there's twelve major stitches in embroidery and that's what we call them.

'That's lovely, but why?' she asks again.

'So we can remember them all. It's an old rhyme we do,' I say.

'A rhyme, will you say it for me?' she asks.

So I do. Going real fast, which is showing off, but that's truly how you're supposed to do it.

'Wicked witches wear pretty britches
Made from silk with fancy stitches
Bullion, back stitch, crafty fishbone
Scattered from the knee to hipbone
With knots colonial all tight tied
Enough to send you glassy-eyed
Back stitch, hem stitch, lazy daisy
Stitches meant to send you crazy
Stem stitch, straight, fluffy feather
All those stitches worked together.
Cretan, pistil, chain for hitches
Stitches for wicked witches' britches.'

'Well done, Mole,' she says and claps her hands. 'If my very life depended on it I couldn't recite that. My, what fun. You really are a very clever family.'

'Only Sarah is and Mike with embroidery,' I say, which is the dead-set truth, because Tommy ain't except for eucalyptus trees and the bush and Nancy ain't 'cept for smocking and Bozo and me sure ain't going to turn out to be brainy by some fluke of nature.

Mrs Barrington-Stone appears to be thinking for a moment. Then she says, looking serious, 'Am I right in supposing that Sarah and Dora

Templeton's boy had a *contretemps*? And that he's been sent to Duntroon to get away from the mess?'

She says 'mess' instead of 'scandal' and she doesn't mention the word 'pregnant' but you know she knows Sarah is up the duff. Now everyone knows from the bottom to the very top of Yankalillee and there's not much use denying it. There is silence between Mike and me, because we don't know what to say to her.

Mrs Barrington-Stone sighs deeply, 'Well, it isn't the first time, and I dare say it won't be the last, where a more fortunate family has left a young lady in the lurch who comes from a family that is not in a position to fight back.' Then she asks straight out, 'What will Sarah do? You're Catholics, aren't you? I believe there's no question of a marriage with the Templeton boy. It's all so silly, but Dora Templeton wears being an Anglican like a badge of privilege. You see, her great-grandfather's brother was the Archdeacon of Salisbury Cathedral and she really is a terrible bigot and an awful snob. You'd think he'd been the Archbishop of Canterbury the way she carries on about it!'

'Father Crosby says we've go to put it up for adoption. Sarah's got to go to the nuns' hospital in Melbourne to have it and when it's born she can hold it once and then they give it away to somebody she'll never know. But Sarah won't do it,' I say.

Mike gives me a dirty look, as if to tell me to shut my trap, that already I've said much too much and that Mrs Barrington-Stone may be nice and friendly but she's still a Protestant. But I don't seem to be able to help myself, she's better than Sarah or Nancy at getting things out of you and I don't seem to be able to resist her questions. What's more, just telling stuff to someone who isn't a Maloney seems to take a big weight off my mind, like it did that first time when we went to see Mrs Rika Ray.

'A strong gal, who knows her own mind, good for her,' Mrs Barrington-Stone now says.

'My sister wanted to be a doctor, now she can't,' Mike says, hoping to change the subject away from the bloody Templetons and the Protestants.

'A doctor? She's going to do Medicine?'

'Was,' Mike corrects. Which isn't strictly true, because she hasn't been accepted, the letter hasn't arrived yet.

'A clever girl, is she?' Mrs Barrington-Stone asks, looking straight at Mike.

'She's dux of the school and got a ninety per cent average in all subjects in her matric trials,' Mike boasts on behalf of our sister. 'She also has a Commonwealth Scholarship to go to the university.' But then he adds, telling the exact truth, 'but we haven't yet heard if she can get into Medicine.' He looks at Mrs Barrington-Stone, 'Doesn't matter much now either way, because she's not going to give her child up to the nuns.' Mike shakes his head, 'No way she'll do that!'

I don't know why he's gone crook on me, giving me a filthy look and all. Mike's spilling the beans about Sarah wanting to be a doctor. I must say I'm surprised at him and me. Maloneys don't talk much about things to anyone outside the family. Leastways Mike, who's a real zip-lip. We may have once been Irish, but it's not our way to tell our troubles to strangers. It's true, we'll whinge and argue among ourselves, but we'll always keep our traps shut with others present. Morrie says it's family keeping *stumm* and if you're a Jew it's something you learn to do very early in life.

Now, all of a sudden, Mike and me are talking our heads off to someone we wouldn't know from a bar of soap and who's also a Protestant. What's more, we're telling her all our troubles. It's like we're old friends and Mrs Barrington-Stone is like if Morrie and Sophie have just dropped in for tea and Morrie is telling us what the staff get up to in the loony bin on the hill, pinching the happy pills for themselves and being pretty heavy-handed to the inmates. But what can you do? Mrs Barrington-Stone hasn't put a single air and grace on in front of us since we arrived and it seems perfectly natural for us to be chatting away to her.

'It's such a waste, such a tragic waste!' she sighs. 'But I don't suppose it's practical for Sarah to nurse and care for a new baby while she's attending lectures and studying at the university. Medicine is a very demanding discipline, even for a man.'

'Oh, that won't happen,' Mike says, 'Sophie Suckfizzle is going to get the baby, she'll look after it, share it with Sarah, be its other mum.'

'Sophie S–?'

'Suckfizzle,' I repeat, because when you say it the first time people are never sure they've heard it correctly just like we warned Morrie would happen.

So the next thing is we're telling Mrs Barrington-Stone all about Morrie and Sophie and how the original plans were for Sarah to live with them in Melbourne and for her and Morrie to study together while Sophie looked after the baby. And how now that's not going to happen, because Sarah will be seven months pregnant when her university course starts. How Sophie desperately wants Sarah's baby but now Sarah doesn't know how she'll feel without her baby and having to stay home in Yankalillee.

'Can't she wait a year, then go to university? Nurse the baby?' Mrs Barrington-Stone asks. 'I mean, now that she has someone, this Sophie Suckfizzle, who will care for her child, and in a year the child will be weaned and much easier to manage.'

Mrs Barrington-Stone appears to be thinking for some time before she looks up. 'Well, there's no point in jumping the gun, is there? If Sarah is accepted in Medicine, I'd like to know immediately.' Suddenly her voice is all business. 'If the university won't accept a brilliant young gal because she's seven months pregnant then there is something terribly wrong with the system. After all, the Templeton lad, whom I've always thought a rather dull boy, wasn't rejected by Duntroon because he made your sister pregnant, was he? It's iniquitous, but then he's a man, isn't he? It's high time women made a stand. I'm national president of the Country Women's Association *and* state president of the Anglican Women's Guild, and, I dare say, James and I know one or two people connected to the university as well, and Claudina's husband is from an old legal family. The Bush, the Church, the upper end of Collins Street and the Law should make a fairly formidable combination and I shouldn't be surprised if we were able to bring some influence to bear on the stuffiest academic committee or board or whatever. If we can't pull a few strings for Sarah then I don't deserve to be in the CWA job!'

Mike and me are a bit stunned by all of this. I mean, we're the Maloneys, the town's garbage collectors, and the Barrington-Stones are practically royalty.

'Come on then, you two, finish the biscuits and I'll drive you home. Can't be having you walking all that way back, now can we?'

We tell her it's okay and we don't mind walking, but she insists. 'It's getting late and, besides, I'd like to meet the brave young gal in question and say hello again to her mother. We women have to stick together, you men have had things your own way for far too long.'

She can see from my face that I'm not too sure about her coming home with us. Nancy and Sarah will know we've been gossiping. I glance over at Mike and I can tell he's thinking the same. They'll think we've brought an outsider into our personal Maloney business and, if she's anything like Mrs Rika Ray, it can only lead to a lot of trouble we don't need right now. Then it will be Mike's and my fault, with Mole the guilty party both times.

Mrs Barrington-Stone smiles, 'Besides I have to pay Nancy for your marvellous work, Michael. Don't worry, boys, I won't dob you in.' 'Dob' is not her kind of word, but she's used it exactly right, because she's read our thoughts. If she and Sarah ever get together, I can tell you now, I'd hate to go up against them two for a start!

Chapter Nine

I mentioned that Bozo may be going to the Olympic boxing trials, but Bobby Devlin, the ex-boxer who is allowed out of the prison to coach the young blokes in the Yankalillee Police Boys Boxing Club run by Big Jack Donovan, got it wrong as usual. Big Jack said the Amateur Boxing Union stipulated that any boxer allowed to attend the Olympic trials must be seventeen years of age so Bozo will have to wait for the Olympics after the one in Melbourne. I don't know how Bobby Devlin could think a boy of fourteen could box in the Games. Nancy says it goes to show what boxing does to a person's brains.

Bozo isn't too disappointed, he knows he's young but could be right for the next Olympics. Mike points out that he'll get a trip to Italy, where the next Games is being held. 'Bloody sight better than a trip to Melbourne,' he points out, 'you'll be going to Ancient Rome.'

There's just one thing worrying Bozo; he's the only really class boxer among the Yankalillee bunch and he is too good for any of his under-seventeen opponents in the featherweight division. So how is he going to get the kind of experienced coaching he's going to need if he's to try out for the Olympics after this one?

It's not that he thinks he's a certainty for the Olympics in Rome, Bozo isn't like that, it's just that Bobby Devlin can't teach him any more and Big Jack is no boxing coach. Bozo is smart enough to know he's got heaps to learn about the boxing game.

So it's terrific news when the boxing instructor of the Russell Street police gymnasium in Melbourne calls Big Jack and tells him that they're having a weekend of boxing in Melbourne to check out the Olympic training facilities. It seems the Russell Street police gymnasium is one of the five training venues to be used for the Olympic Games and it will be the first time Bozo will experience professional facilities and a bigtime atmosphere.

The idea is for the Victorian boxers who may be invited to the trials to be examined over this special weekend by experts under the direction of the Victorian branch of the Amateur Boxing Union of Australia. Sort of like an Olympic trial before the actual trials to sort out the good local boxers. The police sergeant in charge asks Jack if he has any youngsters whom he'd like to attend.

Big Jack tells him about Bozo but admits he's only fourteen but has beaten everyone he's met that's older than him, even sixteen-year-olds. The police sergeant is an old mate of Big Jack's and says Bozo should come along anyway and spar, that if he's that good the experts will probably want to take a look at him for the future. As it's not the official trials or anything, Big Jack thinks it will be ideal for Bozo.

The thing is, though he isn't that big, Bozo's pretty strong for his age. Picking up and emptying garbage bins has given him a set of shoulders and arms and strong legs most seventeen-year-olds would envy. Also, Bozo's got a pretty mature head on his shoulders. You'd think, talking to him, he was at least sixteen. Anyway, Big Jack gets this official invitation in a letter and he happens to see Tommy in the street the same morning so he tells him the news and gives him the letter to bring home.

Tommy can barely contain his excitement as he rushes home to break the good news, glad for once to be the bringer of happy tidings. 'Good on ya, Bozo, proud of you, son,' he says, slapping Bozo on the back. I think Tommy thinks that because it's like connected to the Olympic trials Bozo has practically been selected. For once he feels like a proper dad and what's more he's sober when he breaks the news to Bozo. Tommy's fallen off the wagon a few times but he's joined AA, which stands for Alcoholics Anonymous, and he's come along a treat considering it's him.

Bozo hasn't got the same confidence in Tommy as I've got since going bush with him. He warns him that he doesn't know how Nancy will cop the news.

'Leave it to me, son,' Tommy winks. 'She'll be right, mate.' He puts his hand on Bozo's shoulder. 'Let me have a quiet word to your mother.'

Nancy is ropeable when he tells her. 'No way! Bozo's too young, he's only just fourteen,' she reminds him, because he probably doesn't know how old any of us are.

'Yeah, well that's his age, but he's sensible, he's more than that in his head,' Tommy protests.

'Until someone knocks his brains out!' Nancy shouts. 'What would you know about sensible! The boy is too young and that's all there is to it.' Bozo comes out of the kitchen as they're talking and Nancy calls out, 'Bozo, you hear me now, you're not bloody going!'

'Jesus! I'm the boy's father, don't I have a say in this?' Tommy yells.

'No, you bloody don't! What have you done to deserve a say? Go on, tell me! What have you ever done that gives you the right to be a parent?'

'Well, he's my bloody son, my flesh and blood!' In his anger at Nancy's outburst, Tommy becomes a bit confused on this issue of parentage.

'No, he bloody ain't! That's another reason why your opinion isn't asked for.'

'I bought him them gloves for Christmas,' Tommy protests, trying to recover from this mistake.

'And nobody's asked you where you got the money for them and the rest of your Father Christmas act, have they? Dare say it wouldn't take a lot of cross-examination to find out. You stay out of Bozo's life, Tommy Maloney, and just for the record, let me remind you again, he is *my* son and I decide what happens to him!' Even for Nancy this is pretty rough and Tommy is practically pole-axed with humiliation.

Bozo is also pretty upset by her decision and it doesn't help when Sarah agrees with Nancy that he's too young to go. Sarah's his last hope, see, she's the only one who can change Nancy's mind. She'll go up against her if she has to and she's been known to win.

I'm on Bozo's side, of course. He may be young but when things are really bad for us and it's even worse than an offal week or even an offal month, it's Bozo fixing things and selling them that often bails us out. He may be fourteen but he pulls his weight around the place and then some and I reckon he deserves to be treated better and should be allowed to go. I tell them of course, Nancy and Sarah. Sarah ruffles my hair and grins and says she's glad I'm sticking up for my brother, it's what she'd expect from me. Nancy tells me my head's still soft, like she always does.

'Bozo's taken the spoon out of the sink,' I argue. 'He's fought everyone he can and beat them and hasn't been hurt, only fair he should be given a go at boxers who think they can beat him. Women don't know about these things,' I point out, 'only blokes. It shouldn't be women deciding!' But it's like talking to a brick wall, the two of them convinced they know better. Sometimes it's like having two mothers when one is already enough to have to put up with.

I try to enlist Mike's help, but he says he agrees with Sarah and Nancy and that boxing is a blood sport and they ought to ban it from the Olympic Games. I tell him Tommy's on side and he shrugs his shoulders, lifts one eyebrow and says, 'I rest my case, your honour.' Sometimes Mike can be a real pain in the arse.

The next thing we know, Big Jack Donovan comes calling around. But he does the right thing by us, he doesn't come in the police car so the people in Bell Street will think it's Tommy again. He walks from the police station and knocks on the door and it's me who goes out to see who it is. When I see it's him, I yell out to Nancy.

Nancy comes out from the back as I'm greeting Sergeant Donovan and inviting him inside and she stands at the door leading into the kitchen from the front room and she's got her arms crossed, just like she does for Father Crosby. 'Wouldn't even bother to open my gob if I were you, Sergeant,' she says. 'The answer is No!'

Big Jack Donovan takes off his cap and holds it in one hand and, with the other, pushes his fingers through his hair and you can see he's going a bit bald on top. He's a big bloke with a bit of a gut and he's sweating from the walk across town from the police station and there's these big dark scallops under his armpits on his policeman's blue shirt. 'Now, don't be like that, Nancy,' he says. 'All I've come round for is a quiet little chat.'

'Chat my arse!' Nancy says. 'You've come about Bozo and the answer is no!'

'Yeah, I can't deny he comes into it, but maybe there's one or two other things to talk about, eh?'

'Tommy's going straight, he's joined AA, and he's slept in my bed practically every night since Christmas. Well, don't just stand there, Sergeant, you're in now, may as well have a cuppa,' Nancy jerks her head towards the back verandah, 'Come out back, but the answer is still no.'

'Now, what makes you think it's about Tommy?' Big Jack says, following her.

'Well, it's not about me entering the beauty queen contest for the Golden Hills Festival, is it?' Nancy says, sarcastic again. They sit down and Big Jack Donovan puts his cap down on the cement floor beside the wicker chair and Nancy yells for Sarah to bring the tea.

'Well, as a matter of fact I was thinking about you Maloneys this morning, not just Tommy but about a coincidence involving you, just before coming here. I was signing the police report for the insurance claim made by Hamish Middleton, you know for the burglary to his jewellery shop a week before Christmas. Funny that one, nothing of real value taken, just stuff you could hock easily in any Melbourne pawnshop or even in a Wangaratta pub. I could only conclude that the intruder must have wanted a little extra dough for Christmas. Silly bugger left one or two fingerprints behind.' Sergeant Donovan looks Nancy straight in the eye, 'A bit smudged, though, couldn't be absolutely certain when we checked them against the known offenders file.' He pauses, 'If you know what I mean? Anyhow signing that insurance report reminded me of Bozo and Mole's fight with the Middleton boy and his gang. If it wasn't for that schoolyard scrap, Bozo might never have become a boxer.' Big Jack Donovan smiles and looks at Nancy again, 'You can't be totally against your lad boxing, now can you, Nancy? Bozo did get a set of those very expensive boxing gloves for Christmas.'

You don't have to be Einstein to work out that Big Jack is saying stuff underneath that he isn't saying on top, and that Nancy's getting the message loud and clear, and so's Tommy, who's sitting further back on the verandah pretending not to be listening. Big Jack knows the situation between Nancy and Tommy well enough, and just by looking over at Tommy sitting on a kitchen chair way back on the verandah with his arms folded, he can tell this is not the time to enlist his help in changing Nancy's mind.

Nancy smiles, well sort of half-smiles. 'We don't mind Bozo boxing, Sergeant, but he's still too young to go to Melbourne for them trials, he's still growing and this is no time to put him up against older boys.'

'There'll be other kids there, Bozo's been boxing sixteen-year-olds all year, he can cope, believe me.'

'Cope? No way! Much as I trust you, Sergeant, Bozo's too young.'

You can see underneath she really likes Big Jack Donovan. It's just that, as a crim's wife, you can't show you like the law. It's a matter of principle, like secretly admiring some other footy team that's better than your own.

She turns to see Sarah coming from the kitchen with the tea and sees I'm there stickybeaking as usual. 'Mole, go call Bozo, no point him not being around to hear what the sergeant has to say.'

Bozo's in the shed out back painting a kid's tricycle, one of those trikes for little kids with solid wheels. We found it in someone's garbage with one back wheel missing and it's took a couple of months to find another the right size. He's cleaned off all the rust and sanded it right back and put on an undercoat.

I tell him about Big Jack Donovan's visit and that Nancy wants him. He whistles up the Bitzers One to Five and hands me a paintbrush. 'Here, do the inside of the wheels red but don't get any paint on the tyres. You can't get paint off solid-rubber tyres.' That's Bozo for you, everything has to be perfect and I'm a bit surprised he's trusted me to do the wheels. He must be real nervous over Sergeant Donovan's visit, thinking he may be able to change Nancy's mind, though I don't like his chances. Once Nancy's made up her mind it's like trying to lever Ayers Rock out of the ground with a broken stick.

'What's her mood? Is she being nice to him? Think Big Jack can make her change her mind?' He rattles off all three questions without really thinking about what he's saying or waiting for an answer.

'Dunno, can't say, she's not being overpolite to him. Tommy being there, saying nothing, just sulking, ain't helping neither.'

'Shit! Tommy? Okay, thanks Mole.' He wipes his hands on an old rag and tears off down the back garden. The Bitzers are jumping over each other and following in a furious barking and wagging, all of them wanting to be the nearest one to Bozo. One of these days one of them's gunna get its head kicked in and we're gunna have a fatal accident on our hands.

What I hear later about the first part of the conversation is Bozo's version, with a bit of Nancy and Sarah thrown in, because Nancy has told Sarah to be there after she's poured the tea as she knows Sarah's on her side.

Mike's not there. He's off at the Owens Valley Amateur Dramatic Society rehearsals in the Mechanics Institute where they're doing Oscar Wilde's *The Importance of Being Earnest* as part of the Golden Hills Festival. He's supposed to be designing the costumes. Mrs Barrington-Stone has roped him in. Her niece, Marjorie Delahunty, is producing the play and I think Mike's enjoying going there a lot. He spends most of his free time doing sketches of big ladies' hats with ostrich feathers in them and funny-looking dresses where the ladies have waists you can put your fingers around and bosoms that stick right out. He says the corsets women wore in Edwardian times were sort of like a step-in and made of the bones of whales because they didn't have rubber and they'd make them so tight that young women would swoon, which is Edwardian language for fainting.

The part of the conversation between Nancy and Big Jack Donovan when I wasn't present, as far as I can gather, went something like this. Sergeant Donovan looks over at Bozo and says, 'I've been talking to your mother about the Victorian trials at the new Olympic practice gymnasium, I guess you've read the letter, eh?' He knows Bozo's read the letter and Nancy's knocked the invite back or why else would he be here? Still, he's pretending he doesn't know Bozo knows he can't go. Bozo nods but says nothing. Big Jack then turns to Nancy.

'We know Bozo's young, Nancy, but this isn't the Olympic trials, it's a weekend of boxing to see the depth of Victoria's talent. There'll be expert coaches and it will be a great opportunity for your son to be seen and remembered. There's an Olympic Games every four years, the one after Melbourne Bozo could be ready for.'

'That's different,' Nancy says, 'Bozo will be eighteen then.'

'I understand your concern,' Big Jack says soothingly, 'but this weekend isn't about Bozo going up against older and more skilled boxers, it's about the coaches seeing him, marking him down for the future. Maybe suggesting a good coach who can train him?'

Nancy's no fool. 'Don't insult my intelligence, Big Jack! How are they going to evaluate my son without putting him in the ring with someone?'

'Someone, yes, but probably a sixteen-year-old also being put through his paces for the future. Bozo can handle someone like that on his ear, like I said, he's beaten all the sixteen-year-olds in the Owens Valley and as far as Albury.'

'Oh yeah, a local sixteen-year-old maybe, but the sixteen-year-olds at the trials will be like Bozo, the best in their district and not easy beats. No, I've made up my mind, the answer's "No!"'

'Wait on, let me finish!' Big Jack Donovan is just a bit jack of her being so stubborn. He's a cop and doesn't take too kindly to being constantly interrupted. 'You see, Australia's never done much good at Olympic boxing and, to be perfectly honest, we probably won't do much better this time. Australia hasn't won an Olympic medal for boxing since 'Snowy' Baker brought home a silver from the 1908 Olympics.'

'So there's your answer, ain't it?' Nancy says, unimpressed with Big Jack's journey through Australian Olympic boxing history. 'We're not very good at it, so there's no point Bozo getting his teeth knocked out and his nose busted and his brains mashed by someone who's tougher than him but who is not going to win at this year's Olympics in Australia anyway.'

At about this point I've finished painting the wheels and Bozo didn't say nothing about what colour he wants the bodywork, so I drop the brush in a jam jar of turps and tell myself I'll go back and clean it later and sort of creep down to the verandah and sit to the one side and try to be invisible.

'Let me finish, Nancy, it's not for nothing,' Sergeant Donovan says.

'That's the whole point! Bozo's gone about as far as he can go here in Yankalillee, he needs additional coaching. We've got to find him the right coach!'

Sarah, who has said nothing, now interjects. 'He's got Bobby Devlin.'

'Bobby Devlin is a good coach, but he's a fighter at heart and has his limitations,' Big Jack replies. 'What Bozo needs is a *really* good trainer who'll take him up a notch or two. The boy learns very fast, one such weekend could make a heap of difference to his boxing and get him noticed at the same time.'

But with the mention of Bobby Devlin's name, Nancy is suddenly off in a different direction. 'If Bobby bloody Devlin is a good coach then I'm Sophia Loren!' she exclaims. 'Bobby Devlin is a petty thief and a pug with fifteen wins, all on points, two draws, thirty losses, twenty-seven by knockout!' she says, reeling off Bobby's statistics. 'He didn't win a fight in the last five years of his so-called career. He's a Joe Palooka, Sergeant Donovan!'

I'd clean forgotten that Bozo's father was the welterweight boxing champion of the American Marines and so Nancy knows something about boxing and that must have been about the time that Bobby was around. Nancy can sometimes surprise you about what she knows. How'd she know about his boxing record for instance? I mean, exact, all his fights, wins, draws and losses? It's fairly obvious there must have been something between them two but until now she's never said, even though he's been training Bozo, the Boy Boxer, all this time.

Big Jack shrugs, he must know Nancy knows about boxing because he doesn't try to bullshit her. 'Don't give me a hard time, Nancy,' he says, 'I agree with you, Bobby Devlin isn't exactly Joe Louis or Sugar Ray Robinson, but he's done a good job on the kid. Now Bozo needs someone who can bring out the natural talent we all know he's got. Bring out the finesse, eh?'

Nancy's got on the same rock-hard face she has for Father Crosby, 'Sergeant Donovan, I'm glad you think Bozo's got talent and a future as a boxer, but his head is still soft, I don't want my boy hurt.'

Big Jack sighs then says, 'Nancy, with the greatest respect, you don't understand. Now is the time he needs to learn his skills. Bozo's an instinctive fighter with a lot of courage and some real natural skill well beyond a lad of his age. All I'm asking is that he go to these unofficial trials so they can see him work out. See him spar. See if we can find someone interested in taking him further.'

Big Jack makes a last effort to talk sense into her. 'Bobby Devlin is the first to agree with me on this, Nancy! He knows he was never a classy boxer, never had the brains or the boxing skills to be anything but a Saturday-night club fighter, but he's taught Bozo all he knows, put a lot of time into the boy. It's as if Bozo were his own son, he loves the lad and only wants the best for him, he wouldn't send him out to be clobbered.'

'You're wrong, Sergeant, that's exactly what Bobby would do! What stopped Bobby getting to the top was absolutely no talent, solid bone from the eyebrows up, too much Saturday-night grog and Saturday-night women and a not very gifted set of very light Saturday-night fingers! He'd think Bozo getting smacked around a bit would be good for him.'

'Nancy, Bobby's not like that, he may be a crim, but he has the boy's welfare at heart.'

Nancy looks up at Sergeant Donovan, 'Don't tell me what Bobby Devlin's like, Sergeant. I bloody ought to know, he nicked me a gold bracelet once, right under the pawnbroker's nose!'

Nancy's got her 'here comes a story' look on her face. Big Jack Donovan doesn't know it, but he better settle back and drink his cup of tea because he's here for a while.

Nancy grins, 'Bobby's asked me to the fights and this particular night he's won a tenner on a very doubtful decision. So we're flush and having a quiet drink in the Acland Street RSL in St Kilda where they staged the fights. We'd both had a few and Bobby starts to talk engagement rings. Him and me have been out a few times, which I haven't took serious, but I must have been more sloshed than I thought because I think at the time it's a romantic idea. There's a pawnbroker just across the road that stays open until ten o'clock of a Saturday night. We go in and tell him we want to look at engagement rings and, when the old bloke's turned away to get the tray of rings a little way down the display counter, Mr Light Fingers has this gold bracelet popped into the pocket of his sports jacket quick as you can blink.

'The old bloke behind the counter glances up and says the

engagement rings we're looking at ain't any good, mostly garnets, to wait on, he's got a tray out the back in the safe that he'd like to show us. He walks past the counter and we hear a sort of zizzing sound that don't mean nothing, then he goes into a little office. Next thing we hear the little ding as he picks up the telephone. "We're out of here, sweetheart, he's callin' the cops," Bobby says and we make for the door, but it's like deadlocked, it won't bloody open. "Shit! What now?" Bobby says. Well, he's half-pissed and that panic-stricken he doesn't even notice when I dip into his jacket pocket and take the bracelet out and lift me skirt and drop it into the back of my knickers.'

'Mum!' Sarah calls out, shocked.

But Nancy takes no notice, she's on a roll and nothing can stop her until the end. 'The old bloke comes out, he's smiling like nothing's happened and has this tray of rings. "Here, I got special, I guarantee already this ring's quarter carat, Miss," he says, calm as you like.

'"Look, we've just remembered an appointment," I say, "We'll come back later."

'"Yeah, it's with the doctor," Bobby says.

'"It is already ten o'clock at night? This doctor, he works hard, I think," the pawnbroker says. See what I mean about Bobby? Dead stupid!' Nancy doesn't wait for Big Jack to reply, but goes on, '"Be so good then to return for me the bracelet before you goink to the doctor, younk man," the pawnbroker says and holds out his hand nice and polite.

'"Bracelet? What bracelet?" Bobby asks, all innocent-like.

'"The one you are taking, please, no jokes, younk man. You give me the bracelet, you can leave before the police they comink."

'"You saying I took something belonging to you?" Bobby yells, like he's angry and the old man is accusing him. The pawnbroker just nods his head and puts out his hand again and smiles, "You give the bracelet, no police." He's looking at both of us so I can't up me skirt and get his flamin' bracelet out of my knickers, can I? We're in a real pickle. Bobby doesn't know the bracelet isn't in his pocket and I can't tell him to give it back, which I would do if it were still in his pocket. I'm pretty sure the old bloke is fair dinkum about letting us go if we return the bloody thing and Bobby's too dumb and too drunk to figure this out.

'The cops must have been just up the street when the police radio call went out because suddenly they're hammering at the door. The old bloke doesn't take his eyes off us as he pushes a little buzzer under the counter and there's the little zizz again and the door unlocks and two cops walk in. It's Sergeant O'Callaghan, built like the proverbial. He's the law around St Kilda and is known not to stand for any shit. With him is a young constable with a pencil moustache, don't know why I remember the moustache, black.

'"Oh, gawd!" Bobby mutters, seeing who it is and thinking about the bracelet in his jacket pocket, knowing it won't take O'Callaghan two minutes to find it. I can see he's already accepting he's for a night in the slammer.

'"Been up to your old tricks, Bobby?" O'Callaghan says before anyone's even opened their mouth.

'The old man points to Bobby, "A bracelet he is stealink," he shouts, now that he's got the courage to be angry. He points to the place in the glass display box where the bracelet had been, "From zere he is takink."

'The sergeant tells Bobby to lift his hands above his head and proceeds to search him, going through his pockets. I can see the surprised look on Bobby's face when he doesn't find the bracelet.' Nancy laughs. 'Then O'Callaghan makes him take off his shoes, drop his daks and his underpants, then remove his jacket and shirt so he's standing bollocky in the pawnshop with his hands cupping the family jewels. The sergeant winks at me and nods towards Bobby, "Nothin' here you wouldn't have seen plenty of times before, love. Pathetic, ain't it, hiding with two hands what don't need more than one?" I guess anyone going out with Bobby Devlin is going to make a cop jump to conclusions whether they deserve it or not. The sergeant turns to the old bloke. "Well, it ain't here, Mr Jacobs, less he's swallowed it," he says, bending down and picking up Bobby's clobber and shaking the lot before dropping it back on the floor. Suddenly he reaches out and grabs my handbag out of my grasp and hands it to the young cop, "Empty it on the floor," he says.

'The young cop hesitates, not sure what O'Callaghan means. "Empty the flamin' handbag, upend the bloody thing, everything on the floor!" He turns suddenly and lunges at me, both his hands grabbing my boobs and he gives me a feel-up, thinking the bracelet may be in my brassiere. He flips the waistline of my skirt and does a quick fumble around my body, back and front. "Righto, drop your knickers, lady," he orders.

'I can tell you I'm a bit flabbergasted and took completely by surprise. But I lift me skirt so my hands are underneath but they can't see them. Even then I'm a pretty big lass so, making like I'm pulling down my knickers, I wedge the bracelet between me cheeks, so to speak.'

'Mum! That's going too far!' Sarah exclaims, and starts to leave. But me and Bozo are giggling and Tommy damn near falls off his chair, even Big Jack is rocking with laughter. Nancy loves an audience.

'You're disgusting!' Sarah shouts at us, though I'm not sure she includes Big Jack in her disgust.

'Ah, sit down, love, the worst is over,' Nancy says to Sarah. Then proceeds again, 'So I drop me knickers to me ankles. "Open your legs," O'Callaghan commands. Well, that's it, game's up, I think. I open my legs as wide as they'll go with my knickers stretched to the limit, expecting to hear the tinkle of a gold bracelet dropping to the floor. But no such thing happens, there's enough good old bacon fat there to keep it wedged in place.

'But the old cop isn't through yet. He points to the contents of my bag strewn on the floor. "Pick up your stuff, put it back in your bag, keep your legs apart," he orders.

'"Can't open them any further!" I protest, pointing to my knickers which are stretched as wide as they'll go already.

'"Step out of them," he commands.

'What can I do? So I do what he says.

'"Legs wide, lady!"

'Next thing he's going to make me squat down and then there's no clamping possible.'

'"She ain't took it!" Bobby shouts. Oh gawd, I think, he's going to confess to save me further embarrassment.

'But the old cop isn't listening to Bobby. "Shut your mouth, son, or I'll have to do it for you!" he bellows. O'Callaghan's overweight and even Bobby would have dropped him in a fair fight.

'"Look," Bobby protests, "she didn't . . ."

'O'Callaghan cracks Bobby over the head with the flat of his hand. "You heard me, son, now shut the eff up!"

'I use the altercation between them two to keep me legs straight while gripping the you-know-what. It's a real test of character I can tell you, good thing the nuns wouldn't let us go to the toilet during class, because somehow I'm managing the deed. I guess I must have been pretty supple from a lifetime of milking cows because I can bend down with my legs straight and quickly fill me handbag.

'By this time I've sort of got my second breath so I pull myself together and point to Bobby, who's still got his hands cupped over his privates. "If you're going to undress me like him, I'm going to make a formal complaint," I warn O'Callaghan. "I ain't got a police record, I ain't a whore and I didn't steal the old bloke's flaming bracelet!" Then I add for good measure, giving a little sniff like I'm about to cry, "We only come in to look at engagement rings!"

'"Congratulations, you deserve each other," the sergeant says sarcastic. "You can both get your gear back on or leave it off and continue the romance." He turns to the pawnbroker, "Bracelet's not on her neither, sir."

'The old pawnbroker opens his till and hands Sergeant O'Callaghan a quid, "Sorry to make trouble, Sergeant," he apologises. "I am now not so sure." He points to the display case and shakes his head, "I am seeing this bracelet when it is there," he shrugs, "but maybe not."

'"Oh, you can be sure these bludgers took your bracelet, Mr Jacobs, no risk." The cop pockets the quid. "Very generous, ta." He looks at the pawnbroker. "Take my advice, have a good look around in the mornin'." He fixes us with a beady eye. "They've dropped the evidence somewhere, probably flung it. It will turn up in the morning behind or under something, you mark my words."

'When we were outside, Bobby Devlin turns to me, "It's a bloody miracle, Nance. Flamin' bracelet just disappeared out me jacket pocket!"

'"God must've took it, or the Virgin Mary," I say.

'"Yeah? Do you think so?" he replies, dead serious, crossing himself.'

Nancy laughs, remembering, 'I'm no thief so I wait a week and then take the bracelet back to the old man. I walk into the pawnshop and put the bracelet down on the counter. "Here's your gold bracelet, Mr Jacobs," I say. "I'm sorry we done what we did, we were drunk." He looks at me then at the bracelet and back at me again. He picks up the bracelet and offers it to me. "Here, take. Please, younk lady."

'"Huh?"

'"Take, please."

'I can't believe my eyes, he's giving me the gold bracelet. Well, I thank him and he shrugs his shoulders. "Enjoy. It is nothink," he says, smiling. About two years later I find out what Mr Jacobs meant. I tried to hock the bracelet in Wangaratta. It turns out it isn't even gold-plated, it's solid nickel. George Chan, the Wang jeweller, gimme two bob for it.'

Nancy pauses and brings up the piece of smocking she's doing and bites off an end of cotton. Then she looks at Big Jack Donovan, 'Bobby bloody Devlin is one of Tommy's mob, Sergeant. He couldn't tell the diamond in the centre of the Queen's crown from a piece of cut glass off the town-hall chandelier, that is if you held both up to the light and made him choose.'

Big Jack Donovan laughs, 'I ought to arrest you for being an accessory to a crime, Nancy Maloney. I remember Bertie O'Callaghan well. Tough as teak, a law unto himself, he was always being hauled in front of the commissioner for being overzealous in his duty. They put him on the liquor squad, a big mistake, the free booze killed him in the end.'

Big Jack clears his throat and, like the policeman he is, returns to the original subject of Bozo. 'Nancy, what must I do to convince you, eh? Can't you see this is in Bozo's ultimate interest? It's amateur boxing, he wears protective headgear, a good boxer like Bozo would have to go to a fair amount of trouble to get himself hit much less hurt.' Big Jack Donovan leans back and spreads his big policeman's hands wide, 'If you want my opinion, Bozo shows every sign of quite soon becoming a contender for an Australian bantamweight title and, if he's coached properly, is a certainty for the next Olympics.'

'I didn't bring up my kid to be a contender,' Nancy snaps.

'I wouldn't say it in front of the lad if it wasn't true,' Big Jack says. 'Bozo Maloney could bring glory to this town.'

Nancy suddenly sits upright, 'Glory? Bozo bring glory to this town? Pig's arse! We're the Maloneys, remember? Tommy's old man brought "drunk and disorderly" to a new level in Yankalillee. Tommy followed in his old man's footsteps and, while keeping up the family tradition, added one or two other bad habits to the Maloney ledger. I'm the walking whore with five kids from four different daddies, all of them except little Colleen conceived outside Holy Matrimony. This town believes justice is perfectly served by making us the bloody garbage collectors! Now Sarah has every tongue in the district wagging. "What can you expect?" they're saying "Like mother, like daughter, the next generation of harlot!"' Nancy throws back her head. 'Ha! Bozo bring glory to this town? Don't talk shit, Sergeant!'

Big Jack Donovan isn't that easily ruffled, I guess he's seen and heard just about everything in his time and been insulted by better than Nancy. I don't think he thinks the Maloneys are all that bad. He likes Nancy and us kids and he'll give Tommy a break whenever he can. So he ignores Nancy's outburst altogether, carries on like he hasn't even heard it and takes one last stab on Bozo's behalf. You've got to admire his persistence, I'll say this for him, he don't give up easy.

'Nancy, fer chrissake! Bozo's a natural and, in my experience, when you find a young bloke who is exceptional at something, I guess you try to help him develop his full potential.' Big Jack looks over at Sarah. 'I hear Sarah's been accepted to study Medicine at Melbourne University, now that makes us all proud, because she's using *her* full potential.'

To my certain knowledge we haven't told a single person except Morrie and Sophie and, of course, Mrs Barrington-Stone about 'the letter' and nobody except us knows the Grand Plan. Yet Big Jack already knows she's been accepted.

'Well, it's not all sweetness and light, Sergeant. You may have noticed Sarah's pregnant.'

Sergeant Donovan doesn't beat about the bush, but comes straight out and says, 'Yes, you already said so, but I knew anyway and I'm sorry it happened the way it did.' He turns to Sarah, 'I'm glad you're going through with it, girl. I want you to know we're on your side all the way. Not only the Micks, most of the town, most of the fair-minded people and there are a good few despite the evidence your mother has just given to the contrary. She's partially right, of course, this town can be pretty mean-spirited when it wants to be, but it can also make up its own mind about things. I want you to know most of us think that a certain someone's family, no names, no pack drill, has done the dirty on you, hasn't done the right thing. Is it true you're not giving your baby up to the nuns?'

Well, well, well! It ain't too hard to work out who's been spreading the gossip now, is it? Father bloody Crosby! He's the only one who knows Sarah's not going to let the nuns take her baby. We haven't told anyone except Mrs Barrington-Stone about the arrangement with Morrie and Sophie. It couldn't be Mrs Barrington-Stone who's told, because she specifically said when she talked to Nancy and Sarah the night she drove us home that it was best to say nothing to anyone about anything. 'Let them keep guessing, what they don't know can't harm us,' she said. 'Forewarned is forearmed, many a slip between the cup and the lip, best to stay mum, my dears.' She didn't put all them expressions together like that but she used them all when she was here so you could tell she was serious. It can only have been Father Crosby. I suppose he thinks if something ain't said in the confessional it can be public knowledge. He was *that* mad when he left here he was blowing steam through his nostrils, probably blurted it out to the first person he met in Bell Street.

'I don't want to give my baby away, Sergeant,' Sarah says quietly, and her voice is quite steady. It's the Sarah answering who's unbreakable and the one we know when butter won't melt in her mouth and, if she wants to, the Sarah who can make Nancy change her mind.

'Good on ya, Sarah,' Big Jack says quietly. 'Don't know how I can help, but you can count on me any time if I'm needed. You may think you're disgraced, but you're not. This town had a lot of respect for you before it happened and they still have. But let me tell you something, girl, they've lost a fair amount of respect for certain people who live in a big house up the hill. A real man doesn't run away from his obligations.

You stayed and faced the music. Take my word for it, this time it's not about religion, their sympathy is for you, your reputation as an outstanding young woman remains intact.'

'It's still bloody no!' Nancy says, but you can see she admires the big cop.

Now Sarah, copping all them compliments, does go red, because what she's just heard is not expected and it's not hard to tell Big Jack Donovan is speaking from the heart and means every word he's said. He looks over at Bozo and shakes his hand, 'Sorry, mate. I did me best. See yer in the ring tomorrow, lad.'

Bozo says nothing. He's biting his bottom lip and trying not to cry. Of the lot of us Maloneys, deep down Bozo is the most emotional, but he's never going to admit it and he always tries to act tough, Bozo, the Boy Boxer, the one all the hoons admire down at the Parthenon cafe.

'Okay, Sergeant Donovan, thanks for comin',' he mumbles then turns away and starts to walk back up the yard. The Bitzers know there's something wrong because there's not a tail wagging among the lot of them and they follow Bozo with their heads down, as if he's leading a funeral procession.

'Bozo!' Nancy calls after him.

Bozo stops, the Bitzers stop, but neither he, nor them, turn around.

'I love you, son, but you're too young to have a broken nose and no teeth.'

Bozo half turns, 'I'm good, Mum. I could do it, I wouldn't get hurt.'

'Wait until you're a little older, hey? Next Olympics will be somewhere overseas. You'll be eighteen then and you'll get to travel and see the world, eh? Be the first Maloney to go overseas without a rifle in his hand.'

Bozo doesn't say nothing but turns and goes on walking and I reckon I can see from his shoulders he's having a quiet blub. I decide I'll go and clean the brush a little later when he's had a bit of a sniff, Bozo wouldn't want me to see him crying.

Nancy turns to me, 'Mole, be so good as to see Sergeant Donovan to the door.' She looks up at the policeman. 'It was nice of you to call around, Sergeant. Don't think I don't appreciate what you've done for

Bozo, because I do, he's a good lad and you've helped to make him that.'

Then completely out of the blue, she says, 'My little brother Joe once asked me to write a letter to the army recruitment pretending to be our mother and faking his age. He wasn't much older than Bozo, and I told them he was eighteen because he was big enough to look eighteen. He never come back from Malaya. Never had a chance to grow up. Maybe you think this isn't the same, just a weekend of boxing, but fourteen is not old enough to fight with grown men or for glory.'

Big Jack Donovan thinks for a moment and shakes his head. 'I hear what you say, Nancy Maloney, but I'd be lying if I didn't say I'm disappointed. Perhaps you'll think about it, eh?' He reaches down and picks up his cap from the floor and turns to follow me. I see he hasn't touched his cup of tea.

When we're out of earshot I say to him, 'Mum's pretty stubborn once she's made up her mind, Sergeant.' I try to comfort him, because I know he has high hopes for Bozo, the Boy Boxer.

He grins down at me. 'All I hope is I never have to face your mother in court when she's a hostile witness, son.'

I'm on my way back to the verandah when Tommy comes towards me, he's also heading for the front door. Like I said, he's been there the whole time, back of the verandah sitting on a kitchen chair, leaned back in the chair with his arms folded so that the chair is mostly balanced on its two back legs. Nancy hasn't spoken to him even once, though Big Jack acknowledged him with a nod when he left and Sarah brought him a cup of tea with the others. Now he walks with his head down and I know exactly what he's about to do.

'Where you going, Dad?' I ask.

Tommy doesn't answer, brushes past me and keeps walking out the front door and down the steps and out the gate. I catch up with him and put my hand on his shoulder, it's his crook shoulder and you can feel all the lumps and bumps under his shirt. I ain't big but he's only a couple of inches bigger than me. 'Please, Dad,' I beg him, 'don't go to the Shamrock.'

He shrugs off my hand and faces me, 'Mole, what's the fuckin' use? The police sergeant comes to see yer mum about me boy and I sit there like a fuckin' sheila. I'm that proud of Bozo, the Boy Boxer, but I'm shittin' meself, not able to say nothing to help him. I can't even help a fuckin' cop when he's on my fuckin' side for a fuckin' change! Tell yer what, Mole, I'm not worth a pinch o' dog shit!'

'Dad, that's not true! *Please* don't go. *Please*, Dad, I'll call your help buddy at the AA!'

But he just walks away from me. Then he turns and shouts back, 'I done that heist on Middleton's, them's my fingerprints Donovan found.' He turns back and shouts at Sergeant Donovan who is about a hundred yards up the street. 'I don't need your fuckin' charity, you hear me, you bastard!' Sergeant Donovan seems to pause just a fraction before he walks on like he's not heard. Then Tommy starts to walk on down the road towards King Street and the Shamrock.

I stand there in the middle of Bell Street and he's so little with a bit of a limp and his crook shoulder is lower than the good one. With his one eye he can probably only see half the road. Tommy's wearing shorts and these steel-capped workman's boots with no socks so that they look like Mickey Mouse shoes at the end of his skinny brown legs. You can see these big deep-purple scars on his legs that you could disappear your whole thumb into, they're from tropical ulcers he got in Borneo when he was a POW. All I can think is he knows all those Latin names for eucalyptus trees and tonight he'll be lying with the rest of the town drunks down by the lake pissing in his own pants.

We have to jump forward a bit because the next big thing that happens to us is the Sunday morning in late February when Sarah, Morrie and Sophie leave for Melbourne in the Austin 7 to begin the Grand Plan.

Bozo's made a trailer using two bicycle wheels and several old pine packing cases. Between Bozo's trailer and the roof rack, which takes three suitcases, one belonging to Sarah as well as two kitchen chairs and a pile of ex-army blankets, they've got all their worldly possessions piled in the little car.

In the trailer are three army-disposal canvas stretchers, because we've got one for Sarah. Then there's also a rolled-up narrow mattress tied with rope for Sarah because she's pregnant and Morrie says when her back gets sore she may want to sleep on the floor for better support.

A fold-up ex-army map table and three fold-up chairs, some pots and pans and quite a lot of books Morrie's collected and some of Sarah's as well. Wedged in the corner is a hurricane lantern and next to it an old second-hand Bakelite wireless Bozo's found and fixed with a new valve because Morrie reckons he learns his English from the ABC News. The trailer can't take all that much because the Austin couldn't pull a heavy load anyway. Bozo's even got shock absorbers he's built into it so the bike wheels won't have to take such a strain when they hit a bump.

Bozo's tuned the Austin 7, greased and oiled it, cleaned the spark plugs and the carburettor and checked the radiator hose and the radiator itself. The tyres aren't that good but if they don't go over 25 mph he reckons they'll be okay. If they have a breakdown, they can always camp out for the night because the weather in March is still good, nice and cool in the evenings with autumn coming on. It rained last night and it's a lovely clean clear day, perfect for travelling.

The whole idea is to get going early when there won't be too much traffic on the road and no big trucks because Sunday's not a sale day. They are going to try to make the journey in a day, same as we did in the Diamond T. Sophie's been into Melbourne three times on the train, the last time with Morrie and Sarah. They've found a terrace house in Carlton with a rent they reckon they can afford. It's near the university so they can walk and save money by not taking the tram.

That last time they were at the house, it started to rain pretty hard and the roof didn't leak except on the back porch. They think the Early Kooka cast-iron gas stove will be okay when they have the gas put back on, because the people next door are an Italian family and have got one the exact same and, although it's old, it still works like a charm.

Sarah says the lights work because they took a bulb and tried it in all the overhead sockets and every one of them worked except on the porch. The toilet is in the backyard same as us but it's a flush with a chain you pull, and all the toilet needs is a new seat because someone's took the seat and there's just the porcelain.

The bathroom is made of fibro and is at one end of the back porch and has an old green bath, a bit chipped with a deep-brown rust drip from the tap, but no hot water. We've never had any hot water so Sarah's pretty used to cold, but I don't know how she's going to go lying in a cold bath, which is different to a shower where you can jump in and out of quickly. Maybe they could boil some water on the stove so her baby won't freeze to death before it's born.

Sarah says that after a good scrub, a lick of paint and, when they can afford it, a strip or two of lino on the floor, the place will be quite cosy. She's measured the windows in the front room and the two bedrooms and she's made curtains using some of Nancy's yellow-daisy cloth. Nancy's had this big bolt of cloth for as long as we can remember and, at first, she said she got it from the clothing factory in Wangaratta when they were having a sale. But later she admitted that Tommy had nicked it somewhere. He must have stolen it from some place far away because Nancy's been advertising it daily for several years. 'Trust him to nick something that's in bad taste,' said Mike. Anyway, the daisy-pattern curtains are our Maloney gift to the new house. 'It'll be like Nancy is hanging on the windows,' Sarah laughs. 'Our mum, ever-present as always.'

There's also a fireplace, but it's been boarded up for donkey's years and probably doesn't work, so they'll have to get a heater for the coming winter. Bozo says no worries, we'll keep our eye out for people throwing out broken heaters, which is what happens after the first cold snap comes along every year. We get these heaters with broken heater bars but with the reflector and heater unit still in pretty good nick. All it needs is a couple of new bars and heater coil and sometimes a bit of new flex wire and a three-prong, all of which are easy enough to get if you know where to go.

Their place in Melbourne sounds pretty good when you think about it. Much better than the corrugated-iron garage behind the petrol station that Morrie and Sophie lived in while they were saving every penny. Better even than sharing a bedroom with Nancy or taking over ours with Colleen when Tommy's in residence. Sarah will have her *own* room, the whole of one room to herself. She says it will be absolute bliss and it looks out at an old lemon tree in the backyard that's got millions of bright-yellow lemons on it.

Sophie claims there's plenty of morning sun in the backyard and enough room for a vegie garden because that's what the Italians have got and they're growing tomatoes big as your fist. They might even get a cat.

The whole idea on the day of departure for Melbourne is to get away early so Morrie and Sophie arrive at our place in the Austin 7 just after six o'clock. Bozo takes one look at how Morrie has arranged the gear and makes us unload the lot. Under Bozo's instructions, we re-pack all their stuff, including what Sarah's taking. Bozo says it's a bloody miracle Morrie got across town without everything coming apart.

Then, from about half-past six in the morning, people start to arrive to see Sarah off. It's not as though we've invited anyone, they've just come of their own accord, not just the families that live in Bell Street but from all over town, damned if I know how they knew. They've just sort of come out of the woodwork, some of Sarah's girlfriends, but lots of grown-ups as well. Some of the women are even having a bit of a sniffle as they wish Sarah good luck.

Old Alf Darby who always gives us a pot of cream every Christmas has come all the way on the gammy leg he's got from Gallipoli to bring Sarah a big jar of cream for the journey. Reckon it will be butter by the time they arrive in Melbourne. Some of the women have brought things for the baby; booties, matinee jackets, leggings and caps they've knitted themselves. They know Sarah will have all the beautiful posh embroidered garments for her baby but these are the practical things she'll need day to day for the coming winter. There's also a giant jar of Vaseline, three big tins of Johnson's Baby Powder and two dummies and flannels as well as three bars of Pears soap and a pink rattle.

One of the men has brought a sack of potatoes and another a box of Jonathan apples. Allan Gee has come in from Wooragee, with his wife Kath driving, and they've brought along a roast leg of lamb from a sheep he's killed special for Sarah. It's wrapped in this red-and-white-checked tea towel. 'Bit of tucker for the road,' he says, handing it to Sarah through the window that's closed, and the leg of lamb bumps into the glass and Mr Gee loses it as it falls to the ground. It's happened of course because he's almost totally blind from the Burma Railway and wouldn't be able to see things like window glass easily. But the tea towel saves it and Kath picks it up and goes round to the other window and, still laughing, hands it to Sarah.

There's a bit of an embarrassing moment when there's no room for the spuds but Bozo rips open the bag and distributes the spuds in every nook and cranny he can find in the trailer, which is now pretty close to chockers. Bozo has to let a little air out of the bicycle tyres so they won't burst from the impact of the load if they hit a sudden and unexpected bump.

Mrs Rika Ray has walked in from Silver Creek and she gives Sarah a jar of light-greenish something which she says is willow bark and other bits 'n' pieces from her herb garden. 'You are promising to be rubbing this on your pretty brow and also your tummy and lower private parts when the labour pains are starting, my dear. If you are wanting, I'm taking the train to be there by your side. I am very, very qualified midwife, Indian style, which is the very best style even if I am saying so myself. My God, in India we have the most practice! Babies are popping out every minute of the day and also the night, there is no rest for the wicked who are running off their feet and smacking baby bottoms to get the crying out!'

It's not just Sarah whom the town folk have come to farewell but Morrie also, because he's become popular with a lot of the families who regard him as their own doctor. He's set that many broken arms and legs and fingers, he's lanced boils, stitched up every kind of cut, even pulled the odd tooth out and, once, on an outlying farm, he arrived just in time to deliver a baby. They've often taken his advice more willingly than if it had come from old Dr Hughes or young Dr Wallis. They all want him to come back to Yankalillee when he re-qualifies. If there is still a deep suspicion of foreigners in the town as we all know there is, it sure doesn't apply to Morrie and Sophie Suckfizzle, who've made their mark in a big way.

It's just after seven when they're all packed and ready and we're about to wave them goodbye, Morrie and Sophie in the front and Sarah in the back seat with a box of groceries, some china dishes, plates and stuff wrapped in towels and protected by three cushions and then the box of apples which couldn't go anywhere else. Lucky, like I said, the window on the opposite side to Sarah has glass in it and winds up, or the stuff packed up to the ceiling would fall out. Sarah has the leg of lamb resting on her knees because there's nowhere else to put it and, wrapped in the tea towel, it looks a bit like she's already had her baby.

There's an awkward moment when Bozo is cranking the Austin 7 and the engine won't fire and he's getting a bit sweaty because the little car is being stubborn and I can feel he's getting weary in the arm. You can see some of the older men watching are itching to have a go and I don't want Bozo's pride to be dented. But then, at the last minute, the engine turns over and there's a backfire followed by a loud cheer from everyone as the Austin 7 shivers and shakes into life. Compared to the Diamond T, it sounds like Nancy's Singer sewing machine.

Nancy is crying and Mike has got his arm around her and, just as the Austin 7 is about to pull away, Tommy rushes up and sticks his head through Sarah's side window, the one that hasn't got any glass in it, and kisses her. It's the first time he's ever done it. I don't think he's even touched her since she was a baby, maybe when she was smaller he may have hit her when he was drunk. Now he kisses her on the cheek and I can see Sarah is shocked out of her mind, then she smiles and sticks her arm out the window and grabs Tommy by the back of the neck and pulls him in and gives him a big kiss herself.

I've got to admit I'm near crying myself over what Tommy's done, but also embarrassed, a sort of mix of both things, which I can't explain. But then I see he's crying and I've never seen that in my whole life, tears running down his cheeks and out both his good eye and his bad one. He's sniffing and wiping his nose with the back of his hand before he runs up the steps into the house like he's ashamed of himself, which he shouldn't be because what he's done is very nice.

Morrie crunches the gear stick into first and starts to pull away again.

To top it all, we hear the police siren coming towards us. Morrie stops two yards further down the road. Everyone's gone silent and they look in the direction the siren noise is coming from and pretty soon Big Jack Donovan in the police car draws up and the siren dies with a sort of moan.

'Oh, shit, what now?' Mike whispers next to me.

The police sergeant has his elbow out the window as he draws to a stop. 'Mornin' all!' he shouts out. Then he grins, 'The police escort has arrived. Can't have three VIPs leaving town without an escort, now can we, folks?'

They all clap and shout, 'Good on ya, Jack!' Everyone there knows that the trailer is illegal, the Austin 7 is overloaded to buggery and the tyres aren't roadworthy. They know that Big Jack Donovan could, if he wanted to, throw the book at Morrie Suckfizzle and still be short of pages he needed to fill out.

Big Jack gets out of the car and walks over and squats down beside Morrie and I hear him say quietly, 'No more than twenty miles an hour, you hear. I've alerted the highway patrol to keep a watch out for you, look after you, see you don't get into trouble. If a policeman hasn't got the message and tries to get a bit obstreperous, you tell him to give me a call on his radio.' He rises and pats Morrie lightly on the arm, 'Safe journey, eh, Morrie.' He glances quickly at Sarah in the back. 'Take good care of our girlie.' But Sarah doesn't see him because she's crying and trying not to, but can't help herself. Sophie's also sobbing and even old Morrie is doing a bit of a sniff but knows he can't cry because he has to drive the Austin 7 and he's talking to a policeman.

With the police car leading, the siren blasting away, people cheering and waving, the little Austin 7, pumping out blue smoke, begins to trundle down Bell Street, the trailer skipping like a little kid behind it. They reach the end of our street and turn right into Dunbar Road, the road that leads directly towards the road to Wangaratta where they will join the highway to Melbourne.

Suddenly, with the last wink of the red brake light as the Austin 7 turns at the end of Bell Street, our Maloney world is empty. Our beautiful sister has gone away and our lives have a big hole in them where she's been torn out of us.

Sarah has been our everything, she's been the food we ate, the clean clothes we wore, the advice we needed, the comfort when we were sad, the scolding when we were bad, help with our homework, our moral guide and our family pride, the person that made our home hum, our sister and our other mum. No matter what happened, you knew she'd be there and no day could be all bad with her in it. Now she's gone away. We don't even know if we can be there when her baby comes.

I feel this big ache that fills my throat and chest and then begins to squeeze out of my eyes and I see dimly that it's the same with Bozo and

Mike, bright tears running down their cheeks, and Nancy's sobbing and all of our shoulders are shaking and we can't stop them even if we try.

But suddenly the air above us is filled with a high whine and then a roar and everyone looks up. Coming down out of the cloudless morning sky, like a dive bomber, is the yellow Piper Cub with Mrs Barrington-Stone sitting in the cockpit at the controls.

The Piper Cub skims over our rooftop and, with a roar, rises up into the air and banks in the direction of the highway towards Melbourne. We all see that it's trailing this long banner, clear and sharp against the clean, rain-washed sky, made up with these cut-out letters:

SARAH M. PROUD OF YOU!

Chapter Ten

Now I have to tell you about the brouhaha, which is the name Mrs Barrington-Stone gives to the unfolding of the Grand Plan between Melbourne University and Sarah.

On her enrolment day, 10 March 1956, Sarah turns up with Morrie Suckfizzle at the university. Sarah's got a bottle-green cotton dress Mike has made for her which he said was the New Look. It has a long skirt almost to Sarah's ankles and she wears it with white ankle socks and flat shoes. Mike said her tummy spoils the line and it's the best he could do under the circumstances. It is true, Sarah seems to grow larger every week and Nancy's theory of twins is being increasingly bandied about although Morrie says it's highly unlikely.

Morrie's still got his long black coat and black suit and black hat that's not like the hats Australians wear, as well as the white shirt with celluloid collar and the black tie that's a bit frayed around the edges. Morrie wants so badly to be like an Australian but this outfit is his Sunday best and he can't see that it makes him look like a scruffy little reffo.

The other students, all of them blokes, some of them smoking pipes too, look more grown up. They must think the two of them look very strange, the young pregnant redhead and the funny little reffo, because they can't take their eyes off the pair of them and there's a fair amount of giggling going on behind their backs.

Sarah's feeling pretty embarrassed at being the only girl and her being in the family way to boot. Morrie doesn't seem to notice that he's equally the odd person out. He smiles at everyone and chats to Sarah and seems very excited. You'd have to wonder a bit what there is for him to get excited about, seeing he's got to do most of the hard work to become a doctor all over again and he's going to have to get a night job as well. Morrie's passed the foreign doctors' exam they held last year in September so he can skip first year.

I wasn't there, of course, but Sarah's pretty good at remembering things and I've listened to Morrie's version of what happened that first day as well and I think I can put it all together more or less the way it happened.

Professor Marcus Block is sitting in room 18 in Medical Block 22 together with the assistant registrar, Mr Tompkins. There's sixty students to be interviewed on this day although there are two hundred and forty-eight first-year students in all. They wait in this big hallway with polished lino and white walls, where there are these little alcoves in which there are marble busts on plinths of famous medical men and women, people like Hippocrates, Sir Alexander Fleming, Florence Nightingale, Madame Curie and even Leonardo da Vinci, who I thought was an artist but must also have been a doctor. Along the wall there are benches, though not enough for everyone and Sarah looks embarrassed when two young blokes in almost identical grey suits, white shirts and ties and nicely polished black shoes, one of them smoking a pipe which keeps going out and which he has to keep lighting again, get up and offer her and Morrie their seats.

The idea is that Mr Tompkins comes to the door in room 18 and calls out a name in alphabetical order and the student whose name is called goes in to have his details ticked off by the assistant registrar and is then interviewed by Professor Block. This is the final step to being accepted into the Faculty of Medicine. You know, it's to check you haven't got two heads and you are who it says you are on the application form. Although, I suppose, in a way, you could say Sarah has two heads although one is in her stomach.

Well, the letter 'M' comes before 'S' and Sarah is eventually called in after waiting three hours. She's pretty tired and her ankles are swollen because she's been doing her share of getting the house in Carlton ready. They've been scrubbing and cleaning and even though Sophie constantly begs Sarah to stop and put her feet up, Sarah's not the sort to stand by looking on when there's work to be done. When Mr Tompkins finally calls out Sarah's name and she gets up, so does Morrie. Tompkins puts up his hand to block Morrie, 'You can't come in, sir. Your daughter must go in alone.'

'Miss Maloney, she is not my daughter, I am her friend!' Morrie pronounces, confident as all get-out. I guess he's learned to bluff his way in the concentration camp and after being pushed around by experts in refugee camps and probably at Bonegilla as well. Underneath everything, Morrie is a pretty tough character.

'Oh? Is there something I should know?' the assistant registrar now asks, looking at Sarah's stomach. You can see he's not happy as he observes this plainly pregnant girl with the little bloke who's dressed like Shylock bearing down on him. He's accustomed to having to deal with meek and mild enrolment students in grey suits or tweed jackets. Harmless boys just out of school with their heads still filled with footy results and statistics, smoking cigarettes and playing at being grown-ups.

Morrie points to the door, 'Inside we must go, at vunce!' It appears as if the task of explaining his presence with Sarah is only possible beyond the door of number 18. He moves forward, giving Sarah a bit of a shove in the back to get her going. Tompkins is forced to stand aside and Sarah pushes past him, brushing her big tummy against him, followed by Morrie in his long black coat and hat and clunky boots.

I forgot to say about the boots. When Morrie came to Australia, he was wearing shoes made of cardboard and not proper leather like ours. They were issued to him in the refugee camp and when they wore out, the bootmaker in Yankalillee couldn't mend them. So he went and bought a pair of workmen's hobnailed, steel-capped boots like Tommy's that would last a little bloke like him about a thousand years. With the long black coat and the big black hat and the Horace the Horse boots, he looks pretty strange even for a reffo. Good thing he's shaved off his curled-up-to-his-ears moustache when he changed his name or you'd never know what could've happened.

Well, the professor is writing up some notes when the two of them enter and he doesn't look up until Mr Tompkins clears his throat and says, 'Miss Sarah Maloney and . . .' He hasn't got to 'S' yet and doesn't know Morrie's name. 'And her er . . . escort,' he concludes lamely. Only then does the professor look up. 'Good God!' he exclaims.

Morrie removes his hat and does a bit of a bow, 'I am Professor Maurice Zukfizzleski, Professor of Surgery, Kraków University 1935, not registered to practise in Australia and name now changed to English, Morrie Suckfizzle pleased ter meetcha, for purpose of becoming Australian.' He says it all in one breath in the voice he's been practising that he thinks sounds like the ABC voices he's heard on the wireless. We have told him a hundred times that his English name is Morrie Suckfizzle and not 'Morrie Suckfizzle pleased ter meetcha' but he never gets it right when introducing himself. I think he just likes saying the whole thing because he thinks he's speaking fair-dinkum Australian.

Morrie now turns to Sarah, 'This is Miss Sarah Maloney, my very good friend.' Morrie turns back to Professor Block and makes another small bow then smiles, 'We have za honour and za hope, sir, to be your most excellent and diligent students.'

The professor looks confused and spreads his hands, 'I don't understand?' He points to Sarah, 'You're pregnant, young lady!'

'Yes, sir.'

'Did I hear you introduced as Miss?'

'Yes, sir.'

He looks down at the paper in front of him. 'It doesn't say you're pregnant and unmarried in your enrolment form?'

'That wasn't one of the questions they asked, sir. It only asked if I was single or married, I put single.'

'Hmm.' He turns to Morrie. 'One of my students? You are one of my students?'

'Yes, Professor, I have za honour and za privilege.' Then Morrie asks suddenly, 'You are Polish, I think?' Sarah tells later how she doesn't know how Morrie picked it because the professor had this posh accent, more English than Australian, like on the wireless.

Professor Block ignores Morrie's question and looks up at Tompkins, 'Get me Mr Zuck–'

'Suckfizzle! To suck and to fizzle, Morrie Suckfizzle pleased ter meetcha.'

'Get me Mr Suckfizzle's papers, please, Mr Tompkins.'

Tompkins goes to his table and shuffles papers about a bit and brings Morrie's enrolment form over. Attached to the form are his Polish medical papers as well as his immigration and refugee papers. Professor Block looks at the enrolment form. 'I see, you're here to re-take your medical degree.' He starts reading Morrie's papers then looks up. 'Very impressive, Professor Zukfizzleski, you taught Surgery but you also have a postgraduate degree in Gynaecology.'

'I specialise in infant and child surgery,' Morrie explains, surprised at the professor's observation. 'You read Polish, Professor?' Morrie points to his papers, 'You can read this, no?'

'My mother was Polish, my father German, I speak both,' Professor Block explains without looking up.

'Ja, I think so the accent, Polish and German, but more Polish and also Jews?' Morrie pronounces it 'juice' like orange juice.

Block looks slightly annoyed, Morrie's picked him in one despite his careful English accent. 'Yes, we are Jewish and arrived in Australia after the Great War, I was eleven. There was no hardship beyond the usual business of settling in a new country and the inevitable anti-Semitism in some parts of the community and, of course, at school.'

'That is good, there has been enough hard times already for everyone,' Morrie answers in a consoling voice.

Professor Block puts his elbows on the table and brings the tips of his fingers together and smiles. 'Professor Suckfizzle, I deeply regret what you've been through and admire the courage you show to start all over again.'

Morrie gives a little shrug, 'If I mustn't, I wouldn't. But I must, so I will do it, that is all.' Then he adds, 'I am a doctor, Professor, I do not want to be anything else in my new life.'

Professor Block smiles, 'I personally welcome you to the University of Melbourne. I also regret that, with your credentials, you must virtually begin all over again. As for my colleagues, I can't say how they will regard you as a student, they know the details of the Nuremberg trials of course, but alas, over here the recent history of the

Jews in Europe is not a burning issue.' He sighs. 'Australia is a long way away from anywhere, we are not always as interested in the Nazi concentration camps as we ought to be.'

'Thank you, Professor, I hope to be a good student.'

Professor Block now looks over at Sarah, 'What have we here, then?' He looks down at her enrolment form, having already forgotten her name, 'Sarah Maloney, that's an Irish name if I'm not mistaken, Catholic, is it?'

'Yes, sir.'

Professor Block nods his head as if her being a Catholic explains everything. 'And your relationship with Mr Suckfizzle?' You can see an idea suddenly crosses his mind and he looks at Morrie in some alarm, 'You're not . . . ?'

Morrie entirely misses the implication but Sarah doesn't and she flushes, but still manages to say. 'No, sir, it was a high-school romance, Professor Suckfizzle is a family friend and mentor as well as being my doctor.'

Professor Block looks relieved, then seems to be thinking. Finally he says, 'It's very difficult.' He looks down at the papers on his desk without appearing to read them. 'We have no precedent for the admission of a pregnant student and in my time there has only been one third-year student who became pregnant and she, very wisely, chose to discontinue her degree. It may be all right in Arts but not in Medicine.' He looks up again, this time at Morrie. 'Mr Suckfizzle, you are, or rather were, a physician and a teacher at a university, do you know of such a precedent? A Polish precedent perhaps? May I take it that, as her mentor, it is you who have encouraged Miss Maloney to take her medical degree?'

'Encouraged yes, that is true,' Morrie exclaims. 'Sarah, she will make a very good doctor. But always, since she is small, she wants to be a doctor, this idea is not comink from me! She is making up her own mind.'

Professor Block looks at Sarah and then at Morrie, 'Well, you must both understand that I think it highly unlikely that Miss Maloney will be granted permission to study Medicine in her, er . . . present state. Even if I were to agree to it, and I can't say I do, I would have to seek the advice of the Professorial Board and I cannot think of a single reason why they would consider her case to be exceptional. Quite plainly she is pregnant and that is sufficient to exclude her.'

'Let me ask you a question, please, Professor?' Morrie doesn't wait for permission but continues. 'Za boy who makes her pregnant, if he is a medical student with high marks, the highest marks of all za students for entry, would he be rejected?'

Professor Block gives a little laugh, 'I dare say if he were pregnant, otherwise no.'

'So you are judging Sarah's condition and not her intelligence?'

Professor Block sighs, 'I am doing no such thing, Mr Suckfizzle, I am simply applying the rules. Every institution has rules, without rules there would be anarchy, this is likely to be as true of this university as with most public institutions.'

'Rules? There is always rules, this is true.' Morrie appears to think for a moment, 'But you ask me if I have for you a precedent, maybe in Poland? So let me ask you, Professor, is not a precedent an example where the rules have been broken so they can be broken anuzzer time?'

'Yes, precisely. Given a strong enough precedent, it can justify changing a rule, hence my question to you.'

'So, do I have such a precedent?' Morrie spreads his hands and purses his lips, 'Not exactly, no. But maybe there is something else more important. It is breaking a rule because to keep it is to deny both humanity and justice. Just because it is a rule does not mean it cannot be challenged, cannot be changed. Also, to wait for a precedent is to deny natural justice. Maybe also it is a test of the kind of doctor you are if you have za courage to challenge a bad rule? This I can give you. I have for you such an example. In Auschwitz there is a doctor, Dr Mengele, you will hear more from this name.'

'I'm not sure I know of Mengele? A physician at Auschwitz you say?' Then he adds, 'Is it something the medical profession needs to be ashamed of?'

'Ja, every doctor in za world when they know about this Mengele, they will be ashamed to be a doctor. But never mind to be ashamed. To be ashamed means you still have a conscience, to be ashamed is not so bad; not to be ashamed, that is bad. All my life I am ashamed, you see, in Auschwitz I am the surgeon assistant to this monster, Mengele.'

'Monster?' Professor Block looks curious, 'Should I know about this?'

Morrie leans forward, 'Of course! Every physician should know this. I can tell you now za story. It was not by choice, of course, my wife and my two children have already gone to the right-hand line, to the showers, to the gas chamber. In one hour from when they are coming to that place they are already dead. But I am a doctor, a professor, and so I am put in za left-hand line, the Nazis they make me a ward assistant in the hospital where is working Dr Mengele. The Germans they know already my qualifications so when comes Mengele they are making me his theatre assistant.

'I think maybe I can save lives in this death camp, that is the job for a doctor even in Auschwitz. Soon I know I am wrong. I am working for a *malman*, a madman, who is doing experiments on twins. It is not medicine, it is not science, it is murder. I am not a murderer, I am a healer, a physician. So after za first time I wait until all have gone away from that operating theatre and I go into za scrubbing-up room and shut za door and cut my wrists.' Morrie stretches out his arms so that his wrists show beyond the cuffs of his coat and Professor Block sees the two long white vertical scars running down the centre of his arm from the butt of his hands to halfway up to his elbows just like he showed us that time at home.

'But Mengele will not kill a member of the medical profession. "We are healers, scientists, I cannot kill a healer and a scientist, it would be on my conscience forever."'

Morrie stops and looks at Professor Block, 'Dr Mengele, always he is wanting twins. Every prisoner, every Jew and every Gypsy knows that Mengele wants young children who are twins for his experiments. They also know if they find identical twins, one difference, one twin is genius, how you say?'

'A child prodigy?' the professor suggests.

'Ja, za one twin must be a true genius, a Mozart, nothing less. The uzzer one is not a genius but still identical. If such twins can be found by anyone in za camp then the prisoner who finds them, their life it will be saved in Auschwitz. They will get extra soup and bread and light duties and medical attention, blankets in za winter, a warm coat also, the guards will not beat them, they will survive. To find such a combination is a chance to stay alive. They will have life where there is nothing but the promise of death. It is a rich prize.

'Then one day is coming into the children's camp twins, but they are sick. So they are coming to me in the children's huts and to my infirmary because maybe they are infectious. Mengele does not want sick twins in his hospital, where is sent only the healthy twins. I have a small infirmary in the children's compound. These twins, they are delirious, but mostly from dehydration, though they have a fever, but they are not so sick. They are two boys, Zachariah and Emmanuel Moses, and they are eleven years old. After a few days they are getting better and one morning I am coming in the ward and the one has a piece of, how you say, wastepaper?'

'A scrap of paper?' Professor Block suggests.

'Ja, scrap of paper, from which I am writing medical reports. The Germans they want reports for everything in za camp and I am maybe throwing away this piece of paper. To save paper we must write on both sides, but one side of this paper is clean. I go to see what it is he is writing and it is music.'

'"What are you doing?" I ask him.

'"Composing, Herr Doktor, it is the first movement of a concerto for violin and orchestra," he says very quietly.

'"A concerto, you are composing a concerto for violin? Show me." I put out my hand and he gives me this paper. I know a little bit music, my mother was a teacher of pianoforte and I can read music. What this twin has written on that paper is not for children. "Which one is you?" I ask him.

'"Emmanuel, Herr Doktor."

'"Emmanuel, I will give you some more paper, you will write in my surgery, but do not show this to anyone, you understand?" Then I ask him, "Your twin, Zachariah, he can do this also?"

'"No, he can only play the piano, some Chopin, Schumann, some others also."

'I can see from his expression he does not think his brother is a great musician, but he does not want to say so. "And you, what do you play?"

'"The violin, Herr Doktor. But I am first a composer, then the violin."

'"To write down this first movement, how long, Emmanuel?"

'He smiles and touch his head like so,' Morrie taps his head. "I have it in here, Herr Doktor. I have composed it on za train, I will need three days to write it down."

'My God, Professor Block! What he shows me is not sad, the music I can see on this page, it will fall lightly under the bow. This boy is composing joyous music in his head when he is coming in za cattle train from Germany to za concentration camp in Poland!

'After three days he give me the first movement. "Emmanuel, you must not tell anyone you are a composer and Zachariah also, he must not tell. You must be *stumm*!" I take him by the shoulder and look into his eyes, "You understand? If they find out, they will kill you and also your brother."

'In Auschwitz they have a symphony orchestra. The Kommandant is choosing the best Jewish musicians and when is coming in the cattle trains they are playing at the railhead so everyone is thinking they come to a nice place where is always playing concert music.

'The conductor of the orchestra is a man who is coming from Kraków. I know him from before, but not so good. I take to him the concerto, "Can you look, please, Maestro Pietrowski? Maybe you can play this?"

'"What is this?" he ask me. "You have done this?"

'"No please, you tell me what is your opinion, Maestro." I give him a little bag of salt and some Bayer aspirin, this is very valuable commodity for him in the camp.

'The next day he sends me a message to come to where they are playing the orchestra. I come and the first violinist and the orchestra they are playing this concerto. It is very beautiful, full of laughter and joy.

'"Professor Zukfizzeski, where are you getting this music?" he ask me again.

'"I have found it inside the jacket of a young boy who has died of typhus," I lie to him.

'"But it is written on medical-report paper?"

'"This boy, Isaac Goldstein, he is working in the infirmary as a floor sweeper, I think he is stealing this paper from me."

'"You are telling me this music, it is composed by this boy? Impossible!"

'"I think so, maybe, maybe not, maybe he has learned it and is copying it out."

'"I don't think so," Pietrowski says, "If he is caught by a guard or a kapo he would be killed. Why would he copy music if such a thing will get him killed? For a boy this is remarkable, he understands everything. The violin, ja, maybe he can do it, if he plays well he can write za part, but the uzzer parts, he knows already how they work together for orchestra, the different timbres, remarkable!"

'I shrug my shoulders and spread my hands like so, "But now he is dead already it does not matter if he is a thief."

'"Professor," Maestro Pietrowski says to me, "maybe one day we will get the chance to ask the Almighty why? Why must a young Jewish boy like Isaac Goldstein die? We are His chosen people! Why must God create a boy like this and then let him die?" He is holding up the paper with the music in the air so maybe God can see it. "In Paradise they will play a concerto to welcome us when we are comink there. Maybe already they have played this one for the boy. Why not? He does not need to be ashamed of this music." He waves za music in front his face, "For a young boy to compose this, he is a genius, make no mistake, maybe even a young Brahms, no less."'

Morrie spreads his hands. You can see Professor Block and Mr Tompkins cannot take their eyes off him. 'So now I have Dr Mengele's greatest desire, twins, one a genius, the other normal, and I must keep this secret from him and also za whole camp.' Morrie looks at Block, 'I must break the rules. How can I do this? Emmanuel and Zachariah they are identical, I cannot tell who is what one, not one thing is different, not even a mole or a measurement, even the length of the forefinger is the same. Even if Mengele doesn't know he has here his greatest desire, he will still want them for his experiments, he will still mutilate them.

'So I am keeping Emmanuel and Zachariah in the infirmary until two young boys the same age die in the children's huts.' Morrie spreads his hands and shrugs, 'Ach, it is not a long time to wait, every morning we are taking the corpses to the ovens from the children who have died in the night. Then I am writing the death certificates for them in the name of Emmanuel and Zachariah Moses and I am taking the names of the two dead boys, Isaac Farfel and Mendel Horowitz, and I am giving them to Emmanuel and Zachariah. So now they must learn their new names.

'I am lucky, because Emmanuel and Zachariah are just comink from the cattle train to za infirmary, they are not yet tattooed on their arm. So I take the numbers from the arms of the two dead children and I am tattooing the same number for each one on za twins. Then I tie the dead boys in two sacks and put an infection ticket on each sack and send the death certificates for Emmanuel and Zachariah Moses to the administration with my report, which say the twins have died of typhus and they must not be examined because of infection and must be burned immediately. I tell them I have written post-mortem notes for Dr Mengele, so there will be no trouble.

'If Mengele sees this he will be very angry, he must have all dead twins identified by his administration staff, the numbers on za arms must be checked against the twin register. But he will not kill me because he has the post-mortem notes for his records of twins and also I have taken za numbers in the twin register that would have been given to Emmanuel and Zachariah Moses and I have put them in the post-mortem report and ticked them in za twin register. Mengele is a fanatick about za records, everything for twins must be written down. For him, when is written down somethink, it becomes za truth.

'Now I have still two identical boys with different surnames and it is not so hard to see they are twins,' Morrie smiles, 'that here is something funny buggers goink on. So I send Zachariah, who is now Mendel Horowitz, to one hut far away from the infirmary and I keep Emmanuel, who is now Isaac Farfel, in za hospital. I tell them they must not meet or they will die.' Morrie takes a deep breath and looks first at Mr Tompkins and then at Professor Block and then down at his clumsy boots. 'I am operating on Isaac to change his features, to make for him a new face.'

Sarah gasps as Morrie says this and she can also see the complete surprise in Professor Block's face. 'Plastic surgery? You are a plastic surgeon, Dr Suckfizzle?'

Morrie shrugs, 'At the university in Kraków before the war we have been working on plastic surgery for some years, this is well known. If you can check the record you will see it is true. I am a surgeon for children and sometimes is coming in a baby or a child with a deformity. Sometimes the knife and skin-grafting can repair this, sometimes we must break the bones and reset them, sometimes it only makes a little difference, but enough so that child will grow up a bit normal. Sometimes even, we are managing a small miracle. You know this, Professor, the most common birth deformities to the infant head are the mouth, za chin and sometimes za nose. So now I am working on Emmanuel Moses so he can be Isaac Farfel. He is a beautiful young boy and what I am doing is a crime against the work of the Creator, because he cannot keep his beauty, I must destroy it with my surgeon's knife. My scalpel must make him different from his twin, it is their only chance to survive.'

Sarah cannot contain herself any longer, 'Did it work?' she blurts out. Then she looks worried because she's not supposed to say anything. But I think Professor Block and Mr Tompkins also want to know and so she is not even given a dirty look.

Morrie bends down slowly to open his battered leather briefcase and from it he withdraws a manila folder which he places on the desk in front of Professor Block. 'Take a look, please,' Morrie says.

Block opens the folder slowly and both Mr Tompkins and Sarah instinctively move a step closer to look. Inside are what appear to be several yellowing pieces of paper. The heading of the first one, in German, reads:

MEDICAL REPORT

But the word 'Medical' has been crossed out and above it, in a childlike hand, is written:

musical
~~MEDICAL~~ **REPORT**

What follows are twelve pages of music, each of which Professor Block lifts and turns over very carefully so as not to damage them. When he turns the last page of music, underneath he finds a postcard with the same handwriting as some of the margin notes on the pages of music, though perhaps now the writing is rather more practised, the hand no longer that of a child but of a young adult.

'Take,' Morrie says, indicating Professor Block should remove the postcard. 'You can read German, Professor?'

Professor Block nods his head and picks up the postcard. Sarah can see that on the side facing her is a black and white picture of a building with what appears to be Hebrew lettering running across the top.

'You can read for all,' Morrie now says, indicating Mr Tompkins and Sarah with a sweep of his hand. For the moment he seems to have forgotten that the two of them wouldn't understand German.

Professor Block reads silently for a few moments, then nods and looks up at Sarah and Mr Tompkins. 'I will do my best to translate it for you,' he says to the two of them. He begins to read, slowly at first and then with increasing confidence.

Tel Aviv, Israel
15 May 1948

Dear Professor Zukfizzleski,

I hope this finds you. The refugee records say you have survived. Zachariah and I are in Israel (only yesterday it was Palestine) and we are well. He is now the handsome twin but I am the talented one. I have been accepted at Rubin Academy to study composition at the advanced level. Also I am 2nd Violin, Israel Philharmonic Orchestra under the great Bronislaw Huberman. I have great hope that your faith in me will be justified. I owe you my life, but my face could be better!

My deepest respect & shalom,

Emmanuel Moses
(alias Isaac Farfel)

We all laugh. Emmanuel Moses has not lost his sense of humour. There is silence as Professor Block puts the postcard back and quietly closes the folder. Then he turns to Sarah. 'I will try, Miss Maloney, you have my word. But I must ask you not to expect too much, the University Professorial Board is usually very conservative and there are those among them who may not approve of women medical practitioners or pregnant first-year students. I must warn you, they are even less likely to think of your present condition as helpful to the cause of your gender. My hands are tied, the rules specify that I cannot permit you to attend lectures until the board has met and decided your case.'

'I will teach her until then,' Morrie says, 'She will not be behind when she is comink in.'

The professor nods and looks at Morrie, '*If* she is granted permission, I must stress this, Miss Maloney.' He looks up at Morrie, 'You may consider your own interview is concluded and you may take Miss Maloney home, I'm sure it has been a long day for her. My congratulations, Mr Suckfizzle, you are accepted in the Faculty of Medicine, I only wish I could do the same for Miss Maloney, but alas, despite your plea, I must abide by the rules.'

Morrie looks at Sarah, who is fighting hard to hold back her tears. She knows she mustn't cry because that will prove something about women not being suitable to practise Medicine and, besides, she's half-expected this decision all along. A place like Melbourne University isn't going to bend the rules for any student, let alone a country girl who shows up seven months pregnant. Morrie puts his arm around her and leads her to the door, which is being held open by Mr Tompkins, who hasn't said a word all along.

Morrie turns at the door. 'When we will know this, Professor?' he asks.

Professor Block shrugs and half rises, it is plain to see that he is acutely embarrassed and has his hands folded as if in apology. 'I don't know, Mr Suckfizzle, but Miss Maloney cannot miss more than two weeks of lectures or she will not be included in this year's intake.' He unclasps his hands and shrugs.

'And za board, they will meet before this?'

'I can't rightly say, it's up to them, though I expect they'll appoint a subcommittee composed mostly of the Medical Faculty. Those are the rules I'm afraid.'

Morrie doesn't know the expression, but Sarah knows she has been caught between a rock and a hard place. But like her, what Morrie does know is that Professor Block is inferring the Professorial Board or any subcommittee it appoints isn't likely to convene within two weeks.

'This is anuzzer rule that you cannot break, eh, Professor? Two weeks then everything for Sarah is *kaput*?' He allows Sarah to go ahead of him to the door of room 18. He stops and turns, 'It is a matter for your conscience, Professor, but it is not a matter of life or death for you. Sometimes za hardest decisions are the ones that will not harm your position but only your character.'

'I think that was uncalled for, Mr Suckfizzle,' Marcus Block, still half standing, calls out, 'You are an undergraduate and are expected to show a modicum of respect!'

As they leave, Mr Tompkins, his lips drawn thin, says to Sarah, 'I have your address, Miss Maloney, you will be notified by letter in due course.'

Sarah has the good grace to say, 'Thank you, sir.' Then she turns and smiles sweetly, 'And, of course, that will be well within the two weeks, Mr Tompkins?' She tells me later that inside she just wants to crawl away and bawl her heart out.

Tompkins ignores this remark and closes the door without calling the name of the next student.

'Well, that has truly set the cat among the pigeons!' Mrs Barrington-Stone exclaims when Sarah calls her from the telephone on the corner outside their Carlton terrace. 'I can't say it comes as a surprise, my dear, we've known all along that we could have a fight on our hands. A proper brouhaha. I have made out a list and will begin calling people tonight. I shall visit you in three days, by which time we should have a plan of action.'

Sarah, despite her disappointment, laughs, 'Taking the spoon out of the sink. The beginning of the Grand Plan?'

'Spoon out of the sink?' What on earth are you talking about, my dear?'

'It's an expression we use in our family, actually it's "taking the spoon out of the sink before you turn on the tap", that's the total expression. It's a Maloney thing,' Sarah goes on to explain. 'You have to be sure you've taken all the precautions, done everything you can to ensure a successful outcome to a project, if you are to prevent an unsuccessful outcome caused by your own lack of forethought.'

'Why that's splendid, girl! I shall have to remember that. Yes, that's precisely what I'll be doing, taking the spoon out of the sink before we turn on the tap. After all, this review committee is bound to be composed of a bunch of self-important, pompous old men. The good ones never have the time to sit on committees. But they're only men, my dear, and they do have wives. It is my experience that men, even the most exalted ones, are seldom heroes to their wives, who I feel sure can be made to see the woman's point of view in all of this. Although, I must admit, I often despair at the way women simply give in to their rather stupid husbands. We'll need the review committee names though. Do you think your professor may be one of them?'

'I doubt it,' Sarah replies. 'He didn't sound as if he was, but said he'd try to help.'

'Well, that's something at least. Anyway, leave it to me for the time being, one way or another we'll ferret them all out. Nothing is achieved without persistence, eh?'

'I'm about to run out of money on the phone,' Sarah says, alarmed. 'The warning beep has just gone!'

'Quick, give me your number, the number of the telephone box, and I'll call you back.'

Sarah does as she's told and picks up the receiver when it rings a few moments later. 'By the way, we have a new recruit to the cause,' are Mrs Barrington-Stone's opening words. 'Though it's hard to see how he can help us, but such a nice man.'

'Who is he?' Sarah asks, wondering what the difference is between this particular man and the ones Mrs Barrington-Stone has so recently blitzed.

'The sergeant at the police station in Yankalillee, very fond of your family. Nothing but praise for you all.'

'I'm sure not all!' Sarah laughs.

'Well, yes, I must admit, he did exclude your father from his eulogy. Very attached to Bozo, says he'd be proud to call him his own son. I met him when he came to see me about my aeroplane. I can't imagine why I haven't met him before now. It seems I flew rather too low on the day of your departure. Against the aviation rules. I told him I knew that and that I was very sorry and it was most careless of me. I asked him if he was going to fine me.'

Well, things didn't turn out quite as easily as Mrs Barrington-Stone seemed to think they might. For a start, even though she seemed to know almost everyone of importance in Melbourne, finding out the exact composition of the subcommittee was proving to be a very difficult task. We had assumed that the committee would be made up of prominent business and professional people, which turned out to be quite wrong. Its members were always academics and in this case the Medical Faculty. A search through the members of the Melbourne Club showed several professors listed with only one belonging to the Medical Faculty. A few discreet enquiries revealed that the Professor of Medicine was, to say the least, a notorious reactionary and would never have entertained the idea of allowing Sarah to enrol. None of the other academics felt they could help, covering your own arse being the first rule of academia.

As she promised, Mrs Barrington-Stone had flown down to have a meeting with Sarah and Morrie and had brought Big Jack Donovan along for the ride. He took the opportunity to visit his mate at Russell Street police station, Kevin Flanagan, the sergeant in charge of the new Olympic boxing training venue. Sergeant Donovan had started his career as a traffic cop working out of Russell Street which is where all the traffic for Melbourne and the State of Victoria was coordinated.

Mrs Barrington-Stone managed to get to the University Chancellor, Sir Arthur Dean, who is a judge. His advice to her has been that it was not a matter for the vice-chancellor, George Paton, to deal with, that even if he were to be persuaded to admit Sarah, which, in his opinion was highly problematic, the politics involved were much too delicate. 'Medical chappies, very prickly, don't like interference' were his exact words. If the vice-chancellor interfered personally, the academics on the review committee were likely to see themselves compromised. 'Besides, madam, I'm not at all sure I approve of Miss Maloney's behaviour myself,' he'd concluded.

'I think Sir Arthur may have been the wrong man to ask,' Mrs Barrington-Stone announces at their meeting in the Carlton terrace. 'I'd quite forgotten that he is a Presbyterian and superintendent of the Malvern Sunday School as well as the chairman of the council of Presbyterian Ladies College. Not quite the background that's likely to elicit sympathy for our cause, even though he does have two daughters of his own.

'I'm also told we'll find the BMA in there somewhere among the medical academics, a reactionary organisation if ever there was one and plenty of money and clout to see off anyone threatening their nice cosy little public-school-boys' club. No, we simply have to get the names of the academics within the Faculty of Medicine and try to approach them individually. We must avoid, if possible, male doctors looking after male doctors, the closed-shop policy of the BMA I simply can't imagine what happens to nice young men when they put on a white coat, they behave like little tin gods and when they eventually become specialists and decide to do a little teaching, they are quite impossibly pompous and vainglorious. It really is time to bring more women into the profession.' She turns to Sarah, 'This Professor Block, is he on our side? You said he was, if I remember correctly?'

'I think so,' Sarah says tentatively and then gives Morrie a questioning look.

Morrie shrugs, 'All the words, za soft words, they are comink out of him. He will try, but it is not in his power to influence.' Morrie stops then continues, 'I know these politics, I am myself a professor once.' He spreads his hands, 'I think he wants to help, but maybe also he is covering his arse!'

They all laugh, even Mrs Barrington-Stone. Morrie could only have learned an expression like that from Nancy Maloney or maybe when he worked up top in the loony bin.

'Well, no harm giving him a call, is there? He may be able to give us the names on the review committee, I shouldn't think that would be such an enormous compromise.' Mrs Barrington-Stone laughs, 'Can't see how that would affect his precious little bum.'

She calls Professor Block the next morning and, after several attempts to get through to him, is finally connected to Mr Tompkins who connects her to Professor Block. He was, she later reports, 'Very polite but inferred my phone call was unnecessary interference. No, he didn't know who would be elected to review Sarah's case but yes, they would all be from the Faculty of Medicine. Then he added, "Mrs Barrington-Stone, these things require due procedure and take time, faculty members are busy men, I doubt whether the committee will even sit within a month." So, that wasn't quite what we'd hoped for, was it?' She looks at Sarah, 'I'm not at all sure he's on our side, my dear.'

So there it was again, Sarah has been played out of the game before she even gets to run onto the paddock or has handled the ball.

'The names are the key, we can't do anything until we have the names!' Mrs Barrington-Stone says, showing her frustration and stating the obvious for the umpteenth time. She turns to Sarah again, 'We're far from defeated, my dear, all the members of the Medical Faculty must be listed, I'll get the list somehow and simply call everyone on it if I have to, so that if they are chosen to sit on the committee they'll know of our concern and the opposition they may have to face.'

'Not always the best idea,' Big Jack Donovan says quietly, 'Gives them time to close ranks, take a firm position and influence those among them who are eventually chosen to sit on the board. In my experience, group decisions are almost always to keep things as they are.'

'I can't agree with you, Sergeant, it's basic politics, what is called "lobbying" in Canberra. It happens all the time amongst politicians, you scratch my back and, when the time comes, I'll scratch yours.'

'Ah yes, fair enough,' Big Jack counters, 'but we haven't got anything to bargain with, nothing to encourage them to make up their minds in our favour, no way to scratch their backs in return. Which means they've got nothing to lose if they maintain the status quo.' Unlike the rest of us, he doesn't seem to be a bit in awe of Mrs Barrington-Stone.

'Hmm, I see what you mean, Sergeant,' she replies, 'I don't suppose a clear conscience might be a suitable reward? No, you're right, that would be much too much to expect.'

Then Sarah pipes up, 'If we can get the list of names, what about *their* wives?' She turns to Mrs Barrington-Stone, 'Like you said on the phone about the Melbourne bigwigs, they're not heroes to their wives.'

Mrs Barrington-Stone claps her hands, 'Oh, well done, Sarah! You've taken the spoon out of the sink!'

'But first we must get za list, eh?' Morrie very sensibly reminds them all, 'I think this is za spoon, no?' Morrie, of course, knows our Maloney theory well, though Big Jack Donovan looks a little confused until Sarah explains it to him.

And then the very next morning something happens that makes you believe in miracles. There is a knock on the front door of the Carlton terrace shortly after six in the morning and Sophie, who is with Sarah in the kitchen having a cup of tea, looks up in alarm. She still trembles when there's a knock on the door.

'I'll go,' Sarah says, seeing the look of anxiety on Sophie's face. Morrie is still in bed, he has started a night job as a liftman in the *Age* newspaper building, working the four-to-midnight shift, and doesn't get up until eight o'clock of a morning. He's got it all worked out, being a liftman isn't a strenuous physical job and even less so on nightshift. In fact, the only reason there is a nightshift lift driver at all is because the Storemen & Packers Union have a very strong shop steward on the print floor whose name, you're not going to believe it, is Joe Bloggs.

The liftman's job allows Morrie to study as the lift whizzes up and down between floors and while he is waiting to be called. One of the staff carpenters has built a tiny desk into one corner so that when Morrie's seated on his stool he can write notes. The union justified this by saying Morrie couldn't hold a cup of tea safely and drive the lift at the same time. Joe Bloggs threatened management with a fifteen-minute smoko every two hours as the alternative to what they called the installation of a safety bracket. It's not winter yet but they've already installed a three-bar heater to keep out the cold when it comes as well as free newspapers, both concessions won by the union from management.

Morrie's job is a true miracle and how he got it was also one. They haven't been in Melbourne a week yet and Morrie is taking a tram into town. This bloke has a heart attack on the tram and Morrie jumps to his aid, giving him artificial respiration, and pumping his chest, bringing him back to life again when he was definitely dead already and all of this while the tram continues on and stops right outside the Royal Melbourne Hospital where they rush him into Emergency. Then, being Morrie, he visits the bloke in hospital to see how he's doing. It turns out the guy whose life he's saved is a high-up union official for the Storemen & Packers. Next thing you know, old Morrie is sitting pretty with the liftman's job at the *Age* in his pocket. Morrie's on a bed of roses while poor old Sarah's still bashing her way through a blackberry bush.

Sarah comes walking back down the little hallway to the kitchen. 'Who is there?' Sophie asks anxiously. Sarah is reading a letter and answers absently, 'No one, they just stuck a letter under the door. It's for me.'

Sarah can't believe what she's reading:

Dear Miss Maloney,

The review committee of Melbourne University who will hear your case is made up of the following faculty members.

Dr Keith Wearne – Paediatrics
Professor Wayne McCarthy – Surgery
Professor Henry Lenton – Pathology
Dr Alex Hamill – Biochemistry
Dr Peter Keeble – Urology
Professor Hugh Spencer – Infectious Diseases, Tropical Medicine
Dr Ivan Freys – Obstetrics
Professor Irwin Light – Physiology
Dr Nick Gleeson – Oncology
Professor Graham Butler – Biology
Professor Marcus Block – Dean of the Faculty of Medicine, Chairman.

**Sec. Minutes, Mrs Billing – Administration Dept.*

Three dates have been set aside for the Maloney hearing: 22 March, 26 March and 10 April. The review committee will commence at 9 a.m.

Due to short notice it is unlikely that the first date will be acceptable to all.

The letter ends abruptly and is not signed and, surprisingly, not typed but is written on a plain sheet of paper in a neat copperplate handwriting which seems vaguely familiar to Sarah, though she cannot think where she has seen it before. It is certainly not the hurried and untidy script of a physician. Nevertheless, the last sentence in the letter sends Sarah into a state of despair. It is obvious that the writer knows of her deadline. The first date is the only one which falls within the two-week period before she becomes ineligible for the 1956 student intake.

Getting to most of the wives of the review committee isn't difficult as most of the men on the committee are listed in the telephone directory, though some give only a city surgery number. Big Jack Donovan, who's taken a week of his leave to be in Melbourne on boxing matters, he claims, notes that they are all doctors and doctors own cars. He quickly gets the remaining home phone numbers and addresses of the unlisted academics from the records held at the Exhibition Building by the Russell Street police, where copies of all driving licences are kept and where all medical practitioners must register their home phone numbers.

Mrs Barrington-Stone then makes a call to each of the doctors' wives. She simply states who she is and asks if she may visit to discuss a matter of great importance to women, while hastily assuring the doctor's wife that it is an opinion she seeks and not a donation to the CWA. The Barrington-Stones are an old and respected grazier family as close to rural aristocracy as you can get and are well known in Victorian social circles. Any woman of any social pretension would be flattered by the call. She alerts the doctor's wife to the fact that she will be accompanied by a colleague but tells her little more.

In every instance her acceptance is immediate and at the appointed hour the best tea service is laid out with a sponge cake on its wedding-gift silver stand with the silver cake forks, polished and gleaming brightly against a background of carefully folded linen napkins.

It is decided, after Morrie makes the suggestion, that Big Jack Donovan, in full uniform, should partner Mrs Barrington-Stone to the interviews. This is not because he is a policeman and likely to intimidate the doctor's wife. Morrie points out that if a country policeman is seen to be on Sarah's side, it gives a conservative male endorsement to their cause and will help to soften the attitude the doctor's wife may have to Sarah's pregnancy.

Right off, the two of them form a pretty good team. Jack takes the role of the slightly clumsy honest country cop and Mrs Barrington-Stone needs no other endorsement than being the national president of the Country Women's Association. Because they are both from the country they are assumed to be conservative. What's more, Mrs Barrington-Stone's posh accent and obvious class puts the doctors' wives immediately at ease, she is one of them, or so they would like to think.

The initial presence of a very large policeman at their door is a bit of a shock, but is almost immediately diminished by a smiling Big Jack Donovan, who introduces himself with the words 'Good afternoon, madam, as you can see I am a police officer.' Big Jack then turns to Mrs Barrington-Stone. 'May I introduce you to Mrs Barrington-Stone, the national president of the Country Women's Association.' The how-do-you-dos then take place and Big Jack continues, 'We are seeking your cooperation in a matter involving a small country community and one family in particular. May we come in?'

Once seated, they go into their routine. First, Jack refuses the offer of a cup of tea while Mrs Barrington-Stone accepts. 'Oh, lovely,' she says, 'one sugar, please.' The one-sugar-please is a tiny gesture designed to intimate that Mrs Barrington-Stone isn't a woman who stands on ceremony. It is a woman-to-woman thing, a code designed to break the ice. For the time being, Big Jack Donovan remains the male and the outsider. Then Big Jack smiles and asks if he may have a piece of cake and immediately the hostess feels protective towards him and completely in control. All of this has been worked out by Morrie who calls it basic psychology.

Once the hospitality ritual is settled, Big Jack Donovan clears his throat and begins by describing the pretty little town of Yankalillee, which, it turns out, some of the wives have visited at some time. He goes on to talk about the role of a country policeman, which is to maintain law and order with a benign, though firm hand. After this he talks about young people and how difficult it can be for them growing up in a small tight-knit community with very little to occupy or interest them and few job opportunities. The only way out of town is to go to teachers' college or university, something very few of them achieve as it almost invariably involves a scholarship. Finally he gets to the Maloney family.

'For three generations the Maloney family have been drunks and layabouts, though, it must be said, each generation of Maloney volunteered to fight for Australia,' Big Jack sighs at this point, 'and after they returned from whichever war, they were even more hopeless than before.' Big Jack pauses while they laugh, then says, 'Until this present Maloney generation.'

He goes on to talk about the present-day Maloney family, about Tommy, the small-time crim, and Nancy, the strong woman who has kept her family together against all odds. He describes their role as the town garbage collectors where the children rise at three a.m. every weekday to man the garbage truck. Finally he gets to Sarah, 'the little mother', vice-prefect of the high school and brilliant student who, because of one indiscretion with the captain of the school football team, has become pregnant to a boy from a prominent country family. He tells how the boy has since been sent away to Duntroon by his parents, who are unwilling for their son to marry into the family of the town's garbage collectors.

Jack carefully avoids the religious issues involved and concludes his story. 'Madam, Sarah Maloney in last year's matriculation exam received the second-highest marks in the state, first-class honours in every subject, an aggregate of ninety-five per cent. She will be the first Maloney in history to go to university, probably the first to have completed high school! On her academic performance she applied to study Medicine and was accepted as a scholarship student, subject only to the enrolment interview. To be a doctor has been a lifetime ambition and on the tenth of March, just eight days ago, she was interviewed by Professor Marcus Block and told that because of her pregnant condition she would have to await the decision of a subcommittee of the University Professorial Board as to whether she would be accepted.'

Having Big Jack Donovan tell the story turns out to be a masterstroke. It gives Sarah's story the down-to-earth authority it needs. It also leaves Mrs Barrington-Stone to talk about the women's issues involved and the injustice of prevailing attitudes towards women. As the national president of the Country Women's Association her brief is to fight these attitudes, which are, in particular, to be found in the larger institutions such as banks, life-insurance companies, the public service and, alas, even in the great seats of learning such as Melbourne University.

Almost on cue comes the inevitable maternal question: 'But how will Sarah take care of her baby?'

Jack then gives them a brief history of Morrie and Sophie and speaks warmly of Sophie's desire to care for the baby during the day while Sarah and Morrie are at lectures.

With this one possible objection overcome, the doctors' wives, each in turn, agree to lobby their husbands. Not only to lobby them but to make them meet on the first of the three dates set aside for the review.

Mrs Barrington-Stone leaves them with a final injunction. 'Now, we mustn't soften our stand, this is about a lot more than pretty young Sarah Maloney, isn't it? It's about equal rights and the same justice for all. It's not as though we females haven't proven our mettle, is it? During the war women did a great many of the jobs formerly thought to be the exclusive domain of the big strong male. We worked in factories, as bus and ambulance drivers, on farms driving tractors, why, even flying aeroplanes.' She then goes on to tell them how, during the war, she found herself in Britain and, as she had her pilot's licence, she volunteered with a lot of other women pilots to ferry Spitfires from the factory to the various airfields in Britain. 'Funny how when the men returned to civilian life, all that was quickly forgotten, we women were all required to put on our aprons and go back into the kitchen.' Mrs Barrington-Stone would finally pause at the door, 'Now, my dear, you'll not let the cause down, will you?'

It was powerful stuff made all the more potent because the doctors' wives, for the most part, understood and readily responded to someone like Mrs Barrington-Stone, who was so clearly a leader as well as a pillar of the establishment. This was no young female firebrand. They all agreed that Sarah should be allowed to join the student ranks and promised that they would do their utmost to make their husbands see the light.

There remained only one more, or perhaps two more, duties to perform. The first was to get on side Mrs Billings, who had been appointed to be secretary, to take down the minutes of the meeting of the review committee. Mrs Billings proved to be easier than expected. She was an attractive widow in her mid-forties who had been in the university's employment for twenty years and, as it transpired, nursed a dozen or more personal grievances mostly involving roving hands and other blatant liberties taken by the exclusively male faculty. She was angry and hurt and ripe for the picking. As she pointed out, she regularly took the shorthand notes for the important faculty meetings and had never been asked to take or sign an oath of confidentiality, something which was required of all the faculty members. Being a mere woman, or 'dogsbody' as she put it, it hadn't occurred to anyone on the faculty that she had the intelligence to understand the proceedings or the power and influence to expose it should this become necessary. Her job was simply as a factotum, to take down words, type them up and hand them out. In the eyes of the males, unless they were groping her, she was invisible.

Celia Billings promised to report on the findings of the committee immediately a decision was made. Perhaps she was being overcautious, but Mrs Barrington-Stone didn't want the decision to be delayed, that is, only made public after Sarah's two weeks had expired. In this way it would turn a 'yes' vote into a 'no' vote, justice seemingly done and then undone, and so achieve the end purpose of keeping her from starting her course on a technicality.

'I don't mind a fight, it clears the air, stops the whispering and plotting and gets things into the open. But it has to be fair, I cannot abide cheating or manipulation and women have always been cheated on and manipulated in society. I wouldn't put it past them to delay the decision beyond two weeks, men are such poor losers.'

Big Jack objects, 'C'mon, fair's fair, they're not going to do that!' He turns to Morrie, 'What do you say, Morrie?'

'Ach, it is not so easy. In a university is always politics and ambition. I think better we know za vote before waiting for za official result.'

'If we can win this one it will mean more than simply a win for Sarah, if we do it well it can be the beginning of something a lot bigger.' Mrs Barrington-Stone smiles, 'One of the great learning institutions of the land is not a bad place to start a gender revolution.'

'Lots of luck, Mrs B.S., I don't think the blokes are gunna give in that easy,' Big Jack says in his laconic way.

'Do you think I am too aggressive, Sergeant?'

'No, but understand you're in for a real fight,' Big Jack replies. He looks Mrs Barrington-Stone in the eye, 'Matter of fact, I've had to swallow a few objections myself in the past few days, when I've got annoyed with something you've said. But I've bit my lip and then afterwards thought about whatever it was you said and decided you're mostly right. Men, for the most part, don't think women should be able to challenge their authority and they *do* think they know better, so women just have to cop it sweet.' He smiles, 'They're not going to give you an inch, you're going to have to fight to the death for everything you gain and, remember, they will be the ones to dictate the terms of engagement.'

'Oh, but I love a fight!' Mrs Barrington-Stone laughs. 'If I had been born a man I feel sure I would have been a boxer. When I was ferrying Spitfires to the various air bases in Britain, I had a burning, almost irresistible desire to join a dogfight. To get in among the Messerschmitts and give them what for. Had there been any means to arm the aircraft I was flying, I feel sure I would have joined in. Does that seem strange to you coming from a woman?'

Morrie looks at her, 'To fly is enough strange, to fight in za air is crazy.'

'Battle of Britain, eh? Always seemed like an easy way to die to me,' Big Jack Donovan observes. 'Wouldn't do it unless I had to, I guess.'

'It wasn't only the excitement it was also the injustice! I couldn't stand the injustice of Germany trying to ride roughshod over a little island, over a people who had never provoked them. That was why I wanted to fight. Bullying and arrogance and injustice. This is the same fight, Sarah like so many of our gender is being judged and possibly punished for a biological factor that is as much the male's responsibility as the female's. In the meantime, young Templeton is no doubt being heralded as a sporting hero at Duntroon. I simply cannot abide the injustice, the sheer hypocrisy and the arrogance of the whole thing.'

'Hang on, Mrs B.S., the review committee hasn't made the decision yet,' Big Jack reminds her.

'That's just it, Jack! It shouldn't even be convening. Can't you see there is no moral or ethical decision to make?'

'Perhaps a practical one?' Big Jack Donovan suggests, 'Sarah is pregnant after all?'

'No! Not even that. Sarah's pregnancy is her own concern and not theirs and she doesn't have to answer to them for the physiological changes taking place in her body. Her entrance marks have earned her the right to become a medical student regardless of gender. Nothing more should be required. Providing she observes the common rules set out and which are equal for both genders, she should have equal rights. If she fails academically, whatever the reason, then they are entitled to terminate her course, but that would be the same with a male student. There can be no practical reasons for excluding her unless, of course, she has an infectious or dangerous disease or is a disruptive influence to the detriment of the other students. What we are fighting is the seemingly God-given right of public institutions to make rules that are patently designed to militate against and to disadvantage women.'

Big Jack Donovan smiles at this, 'I must admit I've never thought about it much, but you're right, Mrs B.S. Gawd help us if you ever decide to take on the police force, now there's an institution that knows a woman's place and it certainly ain't in a pair of regulation size-twelve copper's boots!'

The first outward sign that things were working was when Mrs Billings phoned Mrs Barrington-Stone in Yankalillee to report that the first date for the meeting had been agreed upon. She went on to express her surprise, saying that this had never happened before and it was usually the last date that was reluctantly complied with.

'You know how it is? Men must appear to be too busy to serve on committees and always insist on being given sufficient time to clear their desks for the half day required for a hearing. It's all nonsense, of course, they won't be any busier this week than they will be in three weeks' time. It's all about posturing and ego!' Celia Billings pauses, 'Mrs Barrington-Stone, you've worked a miracle to get them to the hearing on the first date and I can't imagine how you've done it.'

'Ah, my dear Mrs Billings, men constantly underestimate the determination of women armed with a just cause, especially when it is their wives. And may I say, you, my dear, are an admirable example of this same quality.' It was the nicest compliment anyone had ever paid Celia Billings and as she put down the receiver she knew she would happily crawl over broken glass for her.

It was a promising start. There remained one last touch for which Big Jack Donovan was responsible. Whether in the end this was a good idea or not will never be known, it was what Big Jack called 'adding a touch of uncertainty'. He visited Russell Street police station where an old mate of his was in charge.

On the morning of the twenty-second of March, as each of the review committee members drove out of his driveway he was met by a motorcycle cop who was briefed to greet him in more or less these words: 'Good morning, sir, I am instructed to escort you to the university. Would you mind following me please.' If there was an objection or a request for a reason, the policeman was simply to say, 'I'm sorry, sir, afraid I don't know, all I've been told is that you are attending an important meeting at the university and I am to see that you are not caught up in the rush-hour traffic.'

Interestingly enough, the younger members of the review committee take it in their stride, some even thinking it might be fun. But the older ones challenge the policeman, demanding to know why and who authorised the escort and, in turn, receive the standard reply. But in the end, despite their protests, they all find themselves following a motorcycle cop who, during the busier sections along the way, uses his siren to clear the traffic ahead.

The policeman drives right up to the gates of the university and dismounts, leaving his motorcycle parked in the centre of the driveway and directly in front of the car he has been escorting. He then walks up to the driver and salutes. 'Good day and good luck in the meeting this morning, sir,' he says and returns smartly to his motorbike.

That was all that was said, no names, no pack drill, the effect of the unexpected motorcycle escort hopefully leaving the committee member more than a little bemused, not sure who might have sanctioned the police escort or why they had chosen to do so.

After all, they would tell themselves, the meeting was essentially a domestic issue involving the Faculty of Medicine and not of great importance to the university. But now they would be forced to speculate. Was it the Premier's Department? The Department of Education? The University Council? They would have to conclude that some outside authority was aware of the reason for the meeting and thought it important enough to send a police escort to ensure they were not late. There would be no time to make inquiries, they would go into the meeting with the disconcerting feeling they were being watched without knowing by whom or why.

While admitting it was a risky move, Big Jack explained his reasons. 'I reckon these blokes in the uni think of it as a sort of private club. They make the rules and they don't have to answer for the consequences of their actions, so they'll make things as easy as they can for themselves. But if they think someone from the outside, someone with the power to question them, is interested in the decision, they may just think the issue out a little more carefully.'

Mrs Barrington-Stone sighs, 'Well, it's drawing a long bow, but I can't think of anything more we can do and if it makes them think a little harder that's all to the good. It's such a pity we're dealing with doctors who are also academics. A thoroughly nasty combination if you want my opinion. They're both arrogant vocations and these two in the same individual will make him feel that he is answerable only to God.'

The morning of the review is one of those days where you know that the autumn weather has finally come. A crisp breeze is blowing in from the mountains and the first cardigans of the year are seen on the street.

Mrs Barrington-Stone wears a grey tweed suit and brown lisle stockings and what she calls her sensible shoes, plain-brown brogues.

Sarah fronts up once again in Mike's green New Look dress and pink cardigan. Only the top three buttons of the cardigan are buttoned up because the remainder can't make it over her tummy to the buttonholes on the other side. Her stomach appears as though it's forced the buttons open in an attempt to escape. If Mike had been there, he wouldn't have allowed the cardigan, pink doesn't suit redheads, he always says. Big Jack, awkward in civilian clothes, wears a white open-neck shirt with the collar turned over his Harris tweed jacket, brown trousers and black highly polished shoes. Morrie is in his Sunday best again.

They don't go through the main entrance of the university in Grattan Street but take the Swanston Street entrance, which is nearest to the School of Medicine and the Professorial Board meeting room in the Law building where the review committee will meet. It is almost 8.30 a.m. when they arrive and watch as the various members of the committee are dropped off by their respective motorcycle escorts. The younger members seem quite cheery, most smile at the departing cop, while the older professors appear grim-faced and distinctly huffy, their feathers plainly ruffled, the experience of being hijacked through the morning traffic not at all to their liking.

'Oops! Looks like it's working,' Big Jack says quietly.

Then a few minutes before nine, the four of them take up their positions on a bench outside the Law School building. Celia Billings passes them on her way in, her black court high heels going *clop-clop-clop* on the cement pathway. As has been pre-arranged, she appears not to notice them.

Professor Marcus Block, who is the last to arrive, nods briefly at Sarah and Morrie without slowing his stride. He reaches the steps going up into the building, hesitates, and walks back to stand in front of Sarah.

'Miss Maloney, I was unaware that you had been informed of the date of this morning's review committee meeting.' It was said with some annoyance. Marcus Block looks down at Big Jack Donovan and Mrs Barrington-Stone, concluding no doubt that they must be Sarah's parents and ignores them in case a casual nod might cause them to react and he'd have a fuss on his hands.

For a moment Sarah looks confused, then quickly regains her

composure. 'I went to the Admin office, sir, it was posted on the bulletin board.' Which was true, the notice had appeared the previous day and Celia Billings had alerted them to its presence in case, as had just happened, they were questioned.

This perfectly obvious answer hasn't occurred to Professor Block, who now says rather pompously, 'Well, then perhaps you should understand that as the chairman of the committee I have a discretionary vote that is never exercised.' Without waiting for Sarah to react or to introduce Mrs Barrington-Stone or Big Jack Donovan, he turns on his heel and with his gown flapping climbs the steps of the Law School building two at a time.

'What a pompous little man!' Mrs Barrington-Stone declares.

'What's he mean?' Sarah asks, 'A discretionary vote that's never exercised?'

'It means,' Mrs Barrington-Stone explains, 'that in theory the chairman has a vote but in practice he never casts it.'

'Why not?' Sarah asks.

'The idea is that he mustn't appear to take sides. We've long since done away with this silly affectation in the CWA, a chairman has opinions just like everyone else and she ought to jolly well express them for everyone to hear.'

'Politics! It is all politics. Afterwards za professor he must again be the boss of them all.' If he takes one side or anuzzer he will make enemies,' Morrie says, explaining the role of the head of department at a university from his own experience.

The morning seems to stretch into eternity but shortly before noon Celia Billings comes out of the building carrying an armload of papers. As she passes them, a small note drops from her hand at the feet of Mrs Barrington-Stone, who waits until Celia has turned and walked past the Geology building before she picks it up and opens it. Her eyes close suddenly and her hand comes up to clasp her neck as she winces. Her expression plainly tells them they've lost.

'The vote is deadlocked, five for and five against.' She looks up, 'If it's an even numbers vote, the status quo remains. We've lost, my dears,' she says, her voice shaking as she fights the urge to cry. 'Oh, how very disappointing!' She hands the note to Sarah.

Sarah looks down at the note, unable to read it through the sudden tears that well and then run silently down her cheeks. She defiantly wipes them away with the back of her hand and tries to smile. 'Thank you, thank you for being my friends and wanting to help me,' she says softly.

'Five votes for, five against, the chairman didn't bloody vote! Imagine that!' Big Jack says in disgust. 'What a piss-weak little shit!' Then he puts his arm around Sarah, 'Go on, girlie, have a good cry, gawd knows you're entitled.'

'Maloneys don't cry!' Sarah whispers, nevertheless, a single additional tear escapes and runs down her cheek and over the edge of her chin to splash and disappear into the wool of her bright-pink cardigan. 'Bugger!' she says softly and hands the note to Morrie and then clasps her hands around her tummy, as if to protect her unborn child.

'Politics! Always politics,' Morrie sighs.

Chapter Eleven

Well, let met tell you, the whole of Yankalillee was split into two sides when the *Age* newspaper, showing a pretty picture of Sarah, head shot only, reported:

**Pregnant student
refused permission
to enrol at university**

The day after the *Age* piece appeared, the *Truth* newspaper also picked up the story and headlined it all the way across the front page, showing a photo of Sarah in her New Look dress with her tummy sticking out a mile. Nancy said it was in bad taste even if it was poetry.

**Uni student's
up the duff rebuff!**

Both newspapers came out strongly against Melbourne University and both sides in Yankalillee thought it was a disgrace, but a different disgrace. The first disgrace was the university and the second disgrace was Sarah. One side wondered how Sarah could think of disgracing the town's good name by applying to be a student in her condition and as an unmarried mother-to-be. The other side, like the newspapers, thought the disgrace belonged to Melbourne University for its decision to exclude a favourite daughter who had been undone by a dastardly deed.

For once it wasn't only a Catholic versus Protestant thing. What with Mrs Barrington-Stone, a topnotch Protestant and from the richest and most famous family in the district defending one of the poorest Catholic families in town, it was difficult to turn it into a religious issue, though this didn't stop some people from trying.

The Templetons, of course, were furious because it had flared up again and their good name was in all the Melbourne papers. Unfortunately for them, a reporter from the *Argus* made a telephone call to the Templetons late in the afternoon when Mrs Templeton was well into a bottle of Gilbey's and alone at home. She proceeded to give the reporter the Templeton version of things, pointing out on the way that she was the great-grandniece of the Archdeacon of Salisbury Cathedral, the greatest Anglican cathedral after Westminster Abbey. She then told him how Nancy Maloney shamelessly used her 'harpy' of a daughter to try and trap her son into marriage in an attempt to raise their miserable station in life. She gleefully told the reporter how they'd foiled this malicious little plot by sending Murray Templeton to Duntroon and then how, out of the kindness of their hearts, they'd offered the Maloney family money, which they had the nerve to refuse.

'Offered money, what was that for?' the reporter inquired.

'To have her brat elsewhere or to get rid of it, we didn't much care which!' Mrs Templeton said, not realising in her inebriated state how that might sound to the outside world.

It was unfortunate for her that in her cups she forgot to ask the name of the reporter, who was Sean O'Conner, the features editor of the *Argus*, Melbourne's most trusted newspaper. Mrs Templeton would forever deny that she'd meant Sarah should have an abortion, insisting that 'get rid of it' meant to have it adopted. But of course it was too late and no one believed her anyway. Mr O'Conner wrote a full-page feature with the headline:

PREGNANT STUDENT

BOY'S PARENTS OFFER ABORTION MONEY!

Nothing like this had ever happened to Yankalillee.

Father Crosby came around to see Nancy and to urge her to tell Sarah to keep her mouth shut because the Bishop wasn't at all pleased with the publicity. Nancy told him to go to hell and also that after she'd read the article she knew for sure there was a God in heaven. He told her that she had committed blasphemy. She told him to add it to her list of sins. He stormed out as usual. Later it was discovered that the Bishop was on the board of Newman College, the all-male Catholic college at Melbourne University, and preached regularly at its magnificent Walter Burley Griffin designed chapel, which was supposed to be the biggest university chapel in Australia. So, as you can see, while a battle royal raged in Melbourne, it was on for one and all on the home front as well.

By this time, which was a week after the review committee decision, the name 'Sarah Maloney' was well known to most people in the city and also as far as the papers reached into the country, which was probably all of Victoria. Sarah was practically, nearly, almost famous. The Grand Plan, which had moved into what Mrs Barrington-Stone called the 'Second Phase', had got completely out of control.

'It's time to take off the kid gloves and put on the boxing gloves,' Mrs Barrington-Stone announced shortly after they'd heard the bad news outside the Professorial Board meeting room. But it had now gone well past boxing gloves and onto the bare-knuckle stage. Soon enough it would reach the knuckleduster stage or even perhaps the time-to-look-around-for-a-very-big-stick stage. Anyway, if this is what she'd meant by a brouhaha, we had a no-holds-barred one on our hands all right.

This is what happened. After Celia Billings drops the note at Mrs Barrington-Stone's feet, Morrie reports for work that night at the *Age* and tells the story to Joe Bloges, his mate, the union shop steward. Joe Bloges, naturally enough, is known in union circles as 'Joe Bloggs' and has long since given up trying to make the correction. He's pretty militant left-wing Labor and in a way his nickname suits him better than his real name because justice for the common man is what Joe's all about. He's also got three daughters so it's justice for the common woman as well. Next morning Joe goes down to the City Club Hotel in Collins Street at ten to find Ross Teasdale, who is at his usual spot in the saloon bar on the second of the two heart-starters to keep him going until noon when he'll come in for five or six more beers to get him through the afternoon shift. Joe tells Teasdale the story. The reporter, though a bit of a drunk, loves to have a go at the establishment.

'Pregnant girlie from the country smart enough to get into Medicine rejected by those old-school-tie pricks?' He thinks for a moment. 'Hmm, sounds like it's got substance, I'll make a call to the chief of staff, though we're a pretty conservative paper. He may baulk.' He bums sixpence off Joe Bloges to use the phone. Teasdale is pretty good mates with the night editor Norm Gabbage, who tells him to go ahead and see if he can get the story for the next morning's edition. He comes back to have the beer Joe has bought him. 'Miracles will never cease, old Norm's bought it. I'm surprised, women's issues isn't really the *Age*, I was expecting him to say no.'

But a columnist in the Melbourne *Sun* has recently had a go at the foreign-doctor issue so the doctor shortage is in the news and moreover newsworthy. The *Sun* is a strong rival of the *Age* and the particular *Sun* columnist is a fierce rival of Teasdale's, who's read the *Sun* article and clipped it out, thinking he might do a piece on it himself. Now he believes he might have an even better story. In part this is what the *Sun* article said:

> *I'm not becoming unduly ruffled about the stiffly starched BMA-dominated Victorian Medical Board.*
>
> *But I join the hundreds of thousands of rebels who say there should be a curb on this tight little coterie's activities . . . Consider this incredible sequence of events:*
>
> *The Commonwealth immigration policy has brought us many doctors with European training. Some are graduates of world-famous universities.*
>
> *But the British Medical Association – tightest union in the country, many people say – has set its face sternly against accepting foreigners, except on almost impossible conditions.*
>
> *At last the State Government has realised the absurdity of a virtual blanket ban and promises to pass legislation designed to ease the way for alien doctors . . . but will the BMA-sponsored members support the government? I have my doubts.*
>
> *There is clearly a shortage of doctors in Australia.*

Scores of country towns have no medical service because Australian graduates are disinclined to leave the cities.

After Teasdale's interviewed Morrie and talked to Sarah, taking a photographer with him to the terrace in Carlton, he puts a call through to Mrs Barrington-Stone, who has flown back to her property. She has a chat to him and also gives him the phone numbers of the review committee members who voted against Sarah.

'Lovely,' Teasdale tells her, then adds, 'You do know what you're up against, don't you, madam?'

'I think we're beginning to realise it is going to be difficult, doctors are always difficult, the most reactionary group I know after the Victorian Liberal Party.'

Teasdale laughs, 'Reactionary! This mob are to the right of Genghis Khan!'

'But we need more doctors? Here in the country we're screaming out for them.'

'Don't tell me, I did a piece on this not so long ago and interviewed some of the medicos on the faculty. They all said they couldn't increase their intake of first-year students, that lectures were over-crowded and facilities inadequate. "Perhaps then we should open a second medical school," I suggested to them.' Teasdale laughs. 'You'd have thought I'd used a dirty word in front of the Pope! The answer as far as they were concerned was a smaller intake, end of argument.'

'Well, I hope you give them curry, Mr Teasdale, what's involved here is more than Sarah Maloney, much more. It's about the rights of women to share equally in the system and to be entitled to observe the same rules and receive the same justice as their male counterparts.'

'I'll do my best, but as a betting man I don't like your chances, madam. I don't think you'd find a bookmaker in Victoria who would give you even hundred to one odds on a win.'

'That's all right, Mr Teasdale, Emmeline Pankhurst the great suffragette had odds greater than those against her. We're simply a very small part of an ongoing fight with a long, long way to go.'

'I hear you,' Teasdale says, 'I've got two daughters of my own.'

Although none of the review committee members will talk to him,

Teasdale has a feature story for the morning paper with the nice big photo of Sarah showing how very pretty she is and also head shots of Marcus Block, the dean of the Faculty of Medicine, and the professors who voted against her admission, all six photos obtained from the newspaper photo library taken on the previous occasion Ross Teasdale had interviewed them.

The story appears on page three. Page one features the coming referendum to extend hotel hours and the shortage of quality accommodation for overseas visitors to the Olympic Games. Anyway, by now people are pretty sick of the Olympics, which has still got eight months to go, so the Sarah story gets a lot of attention it may not otherwise have received.

The first thing that happens is that the reporters from all of Melbourne's newspapers turn up at the university to interview Professor Marcus Block, who refuses to talk to them. This goes for the other five medical men who voted against admitting Sarah as well. Block also bans the five professors who voted for Sarah from comment and now the Faculty of Medicine is closed tight as a wombat's bum. He also starts a witch hunt to find out how the reporter got the names of the five professors. Fortunately Celia Billings, having taken advice from Mrs Barrington-Stone, has taken some of her annual holidays, leaving the evening before and can't be found. Taking the lead from Professor Block, the vice-chancellor of the university decides to sit it out and say nothing, which is their first big mistake, because the newspapers can now paint them into a corner.

Then the radio stations get involved and encourage people to phone the university and the Faculty of Medicine and even the vice-chancellor, Professor George Paton, himself. It is one of the first times this has been done and there is suddenly chaos at the university. People from all over Victoria are phoning in and sending telegrams and it's soon pretty obvious that women are the majority of callers and they're mad as hell. The newspapers are beginning to say that women's voices are being heard on this issue and that they're angry and what the university has got on its hands is a public outcry. Suggestions are being made that Mr Henry Bolte, the premier, should step in and that the women's vote at the next election could be critical for his government.

Then, just as the story is getting a little soft, Mrs Barrington-Stone lets it out through Ross Teasdale that Professor Marcus Block, as chairman of the review committee, had a casting vote on the day and didn't choose to exercise it. She's done this deliberately to give him a chance to clear the air, to ask him publicly to cast his vote and bring this unfortunate business to a just conclusion. The news hits the papers and Marcus Block is back in the firing line in a big way. Hundreds of phone calls and telegrams ask him to declare his hand or resign at once. They all urge him to cast his vote and to see that justice is done. But he stubbornly refuses, saying that he won't have any part in a fissiparous Medical Faculty.

The word 'fissiparous' is picked up by a reporter and is soon used mockingly on all the radio stations and becomes a sort of in-joke, employees in companies walk around and say 'Sorry, mate, don't want to be a part of a fissiparous organisation'. The radio stations and the newspapers explain that it refers to an organism that's divided into two parts. But it's also a word that makes everyone feel that Professor Block and his cohorts are up themselves and think they're above criticism. The general consensus is that it's high time to bring them back down to earth.

Morrie likes this new 'fissiparous' word a lot and says it only goes to prove English is an amazing language because just the sound of a word people can't even understand can make them take sides.

Then, the next thing, the *Age* newspaper is onto Duntroon. Their Canberra political reporter tracks Murray Templeton down at a football game and catches him in the dressing room with the rest of the Duntroon AFL team. The interview appears in the paper the next day.

REPORTER: *Mr Templeton, do you love Sarah Maloney?*

STAFF CADET TEMPLETON: *Actually it's not mister, sir, it's Staff Cadet Templeton, sir. No, it was just something that happened.*

REPORTER: *And you personally feel no responsibility that she has become pregnant?*

(Laughter from the players around him)

STAFF CADET TEMPLETON: *Who said it was me made her pregnant?*

(More laughter)

STAFF CADET TEMPLETON: *No, I take that back, sir.*

REPORTER: *You know it was you or you take back that Miss Maloney was sleeping around?*

STAFF CADET TEMPLETON: *The former, sir, Sarah wasn't sleeping with anyone else. We only did it once, anyway. It was just bad luck.*

REPORTER: *You* did *make her pregnant and it was* just *bad luck? You don't feel any remorse?'*

STAFF CADET TEMPLETON (thinks): *Yeah, I suppose, don't know really.*

(A player offers him a soft drink.)

STAFF CADET TEMPLETON (acknowledging): *Thanks, mate.*

REPORTER: *You don't think you should have married her?*

(More laughter)

STAFF CADET TEMPLETON: *No way! Then I couldn't have come to Duntroon!*

(More laughter)

REPORTER: *That was more important to you?*

STAFF CADET TEMPLETON: *My parents thought so.*

REPORTER: *And you?*

STAFF CADET TEMPLETON: *Look, sir, I don't have to answer your questions and I'm not going to say any more!*

CHORUS FROM THE OTHER CADETS: *Yeah! Yeah! Piss off!*

This interview printed verbatim without anything added causes another public stir. The next day Duntroon is besieged by reporters from all over the nation and the Commander in Charge, Major General I. R. Campbell, CBE, DSO, refuses to allow Staff Cadet Murray Templeton to comment any further.

All this begins to add up to the fact that people are beginning to believe the elite in society are protecting themselves. Melbourne University, especially, is seen for what it is, a bastion of privilege, a power unto itself and under the control of men who are arrogant and up themselves, all of whom come from an upper-middle-class background. With few exceptions, those of the Medical Faculty have had a private education, mostly at the most exclusive schools. They appear to be men who have no interest or regard for, as the Student Labor Club puts it, the proletariat, the common people, such as Sarah Maloney who comes from a working-class background.

This is probably an unfair assessment, I mean, about them all coming from an upper-middle-class background and private schools, but it is nevertheless the public perception, so that the working-class element is very much on Sarah's side, especially those people who see themselves as blue-collar workers.

Then something extraordinary happens that throws everything into turmoil. Under construction at the university is the new Beaurepaire Sports Centre to be opened late that year. It will serve as a training centre for the Olympics and will be the most modern sporting facility of any university in the nation.

The Builders Labourers Union working on the site decide to strike, demanding that Sarah have a second hearing, this time from the Professorial Board itself with the vice-chancellor, as the chairman. The construction workers carrying out alterations to the Anatomy building also strike and this is followed by the Student Union, which decides to call a simultaneous strike demanding the same outcome. Now Melbourne University comes to an abrupt stop.

In the meantime the phone calls, telegrams and letters continue unabated and are streaming in from the other states as well. This is not a student uprising or a trade-union dispute, but an issue which is proving to have repercussions in the wider community and one which the vice-chancellor cannot continue to ignore.

Melbourne University puts on a brave face and someone purported to be from them breaks the silence by sending out an unsigned press release on university notepaper hinting that it is all a clever Communist Party plot to disrupt the university. Blaming the communists is always a pretty good way to get off the hook and Bob Menzies, the prime minister, has used it more than once in politics.

The evidence their spokesman gives for this is the activity of the Labor Club, a student political organisation which during Orientation Week had set up a table in the foyer of the university union building and sold 'progressive literature', political tracts and publications by Karl Marx, Lenin and Joseph Stalin extolling the virtues of socialism. They also handed out leaflets demanding that Sarah Maloney be allowed to enrol in Medicine. The leaflet also points out that Denis Lovegrove, the Member for Carlton in the State Parliament, an ex-Communist Party member, has raised the issue of Sarah's admission to the university in parliament. It points out that Lovegrove is also president of the Fibrous Plaster and Plaster Workers Union, the first union to walk off the job at the Beaurepaire Sports Centre.

Even to the most ardent communist-under-the-bed conspiracy theorist, the university press release, if it is genuine, is over-the-top nonsense, and only serves to prove how cynical and naive academics are, thinking they can bamboozle the media and public with such a ridiculous assertion.

Melbourne University is simply not accustomed to defending itself and is making a hopeless mess of things all round. The ABC has done a special program on Sarah's case and mention is made of the communist conspiracy. Someone from the Communist Party of Australia who is on the program takes a great deal of pleasure debunking the theory. The only one who seems willing to go along with it is Mr Santamaria from the DLP and even he isn't all that sure.

The communist theory simply won't wash. The Sarah affair, everyone knows, isn't about politics or trade unions. Even the ALP Club, the sworn enemies of the Labor Club and representatives of the right-wing side of university socialism, come out in support of Sarah. Barry Jones, a leading member, points out that the issue is one of polemics not politics and is essentially about human rights and justice for female students and is a broad and long overdue issue that needs to be brought out into the open. What he means is that it's high time women's rights are looked at in the community not as politics but as plain justice.

The vice-chancellor, Professor Paton, then makes an announcement on morning radio, saying the university has been unable to find the person purported to be on their staff who suggested the communist-plot theory and that the university does not hold this viewpoint. He claims it is a hoax and that it would be a simple matter to get hold of the appropriate letterhead. When asked what then is the viewpoint of Melbourne University, he says, 'We will be making a statement later in the week.'

In the meantime the strident and demanding voice of Mrs Barrington-Stone can be heard daily on the wireless and read in the newspapers. As the reporter on the ABC program said, 'The president of the Country Women's Association, a bastion of conservatism, can hardly be accused of being infiltrated by the communists or being in sympathy with the trade unions.' Furthermore, the program goes on to make the point that a small-town policeman who simply believes in fair play and justice cannot be accused of political manipulation.

Mrs Barrington-Stone and Big Jack Donovan stick to their guns, saying repeatedly that what the university is doing is unjust and unfair and that their attitude turns women students into second-class citizens. They demand that female students enjoy equal rights with males and that they be judged on their scholastic ability and not on whatever biological factors or on such moral judgements the male-dominated review committee care to make.

Though Mrs Barrington-Stone is the more vocal of the two of them and more attractive to the media as a protesting voice, Big Jack Donovan takes the issue away from just being females whingeing for a better deal. He is a well-remembered South Melbourne footy hero, and is known by those in a position to judge him as a damn good cop, while others who know him personally say he is fair dinkum and an all-round good bloke. The consensus in the pubs around Melbourne is if Big Jack Donovan is going in to bat for the little Maloney lass, then this is something that must claim the attention of fair-minded men everywhere.

Then the university makes its statement and it's their second big mistake. The spokesman is not from the Medical Faculty but is the registrar, a Mr Newington. He points out at the press conference that

Sarah's pregnancy was not the reason for her rejection, that the 1956 intake of medical students, due to an error in administration, was the largest ever and exceeded the quota that allowed for careful and considered tutorials and lectures and was more than the existing facilities could accommodate. To make his point he examples the intake of 1955, which was 218 first-year students, and 1954, which had 180. This year the intake has a limit of 248 places whereas, due to a clerical error, 255 students were granted a preliminary entry, subject to their final interview. In other words, the university very much regrets that seven students had to be rejected. He then goes on to say that Miss Sarah Maloney and six male students have been told they were not eligible for the 1956 intake.

Asked on what basis the rejections had been made, Mr Newington said that it had been a simple matter of taking their matriculation results in Maths, Biology, Chemistry and Physics. The seven students with the lowest aggregate in these subjects had been eliminated from the list.

Though this proves to be the case with the six male students, Mr Newington hasn't bothered to check Sarah's matriculation results, simply assuming that a girl from the bush with her working-class background would barely have scraped up sufficient marks to get her accepted at the bottom end of the admission list.

Well, let me tell you, the proverbial bowel fodder hits the rotating blades in a huge way! It is a simple matter to look up the matriculation results of every student accepted into Medicine for the 1956 intake and that's exactly what the newspapers do, showing that Sarah topped the results for the marks required for acceptance, coming second in the entire state. The bloke who came first got a scholarship to Oxford to study Law and so isn't even at Melbourne University.

Sarah's results, first-class honours in every subject, are published in all the newspapers and are read out on the wireless. So now the ordinary people in the street think even more highly of her and even less of the university. She's become a working-class heroine who is showing the world that a little country girl from a state school, with difficult family circumstances and a working-class background, can still cut the mustard.

If Melbourne University now denies that Sarah's pregnancy was the cause for her rejection and if her marks are the highest among the first-year students, then they can only be discriminating against her for being a woman and, in addition, from a working-class background. If anything, the fact that the university is making a distinction of class, as well as gender, gets them even deeper in the poo. So they are forced to go onto the wireless and say that Mr Newington was wrong about Sarah and that in the eyes of the doctors on the review committee a young woman in her advanced stage of pregnancy would be disadvantaged in her first year at the university and that they had advised her that she should apply again for the 1957 intake. At last the university has admitted in so many words that they have discriminated against Sarah for being a woman.

Perhaps we'll never know who finally brought the issue to a head. The media suggests it was the premier, Mr Bolte, who is potentially facing enormous embarrassment if the issue were brought up for all the world to see just before the Olympic Games. Then, of course, there is the question of the women's vote in the next election. Anyway, the chancellor of the university, the Hon. Mr Justice Dean, announces that the vice-chancellor has agreed to review the case immediately with a committee composed of the deans of every faculty, with the exception of the Dean of Medicine.

Morrie says that this is fair, but also a big mistake, the medical men will not be happy not being represented.

But Big Jack Donovan disagrees. 'I'll bet you London to a brick that Professor Block eliminated himself. Just think about it. If he voted "Yes", then people were going to say why hadn't he done so in the first place. But if he voted "No", everyone would see him for a woman-hater. Best keep his nose clean, eh?'

Morrie then says Big Jack's right, politics as usual.

The review committee is to be convened in the Professorial Board meeting room near the Law School at 11 a.m. on the fifth of April, but by nine o'clock there is an enormous crowd in the quadrangle nearby, with people streaming through the Grattan Street entrance.

The crowd of several thousand is made up from every element in society, though there are a great many more women than men and many carry homemade placards which say things like 'Fair go!', 'Justice for Sarah!', 'Brains don't get pregnant!' One wag even carries a placard which asks, 'If the baby is a boy, then is it all right?' A lot of the placards say, 'Women's rights NOW!' and seem to be a co-ordinated campaign by female university students.

The crowd is good-humoured but it is also clear they've come to see that justice is done and that very few among them are on the side of the university. There are a few yobbos who try to disrupt things but some of the blokes from the striking Beaurepaire Sports Centre building site soon calm them down.

After less than two hours' debate, a secret ballot is taken by the new review committee and the vast majority, though not all of the faculty deans, vote that pregnancy alone is not a reason for denying a student enrolment in any academic course conducted by Melbourne University.

Pandemonium breaks loose when the vice-chancellor makes an official announcement. Professor Paton announces that as it is already two weeks over the time Sarah would normally have been accepted as a student, the university is granting her special permission to enrol in Medicine for 1956. There is renewed cheering at this and people begin to chant, 'Sarah! Sarah! Sarah! We want Sarah!'

Morrie had already decided that Sarah mustn't be present outside as the excitement might bring on her baby. Sarah says she doesn't think she could stand to be there anyway, so Mrs Barrington-Stone arranges with Mrs Billings for her to be in the registrar's office next door. This way she can hear the crowd and get the decision moments after it is made but not be seen by anyone.

As it turned out, Sarah wouldn't find herself hopelessly behind in the lectures. What with the student strike, she had only missed ten days of lectures and not really even that many, because five of those days had been taken up by Orientation Week.

The Grand Plan had worked, though not without a great many doubts, private tears of despair and misgivings on everyone's part. It was the best example ever of taking the spoon out of the sink and then giving it your best shot while never giving up.

Poor old Sarah is emotionally exhausted from it all and everyone says they wouldn't be surprised if all the excitement made the baby come early. It's then that Mrs Rika Ray, which is now what Mrs Karpurika Raychaudhuri had taken to calling herself, appears on the doorstep of the Carlton terrace. She knocks loudly and when the door is opened she is seen to be carrying a large bottle of nasty-tasting herbal mixture in a string shopping bag. She bustles past Sophie with only the minimum of greeting and proceeds down the narrow hallway. 'Where is that child? Child, where are you? This is Mrs Rika Ray, I am making a tonic for not sliding out!'

Sarah comes to the door of her bedroom. 'Hello, Mrs Karpurika Raychaudhuri, how nice to see you.'

'Nice, we are not coming for nice. You must go into the kitchen at once, a spoon we are having.' In the kitchen she measures a tablespoon of dark-brown liquid from the large bottle. 'This is the very, very best for the nerves and babies not sliding out when it is not jolly well time. You must take three times a day, no questions asked.'

'Mrs Rika Ray, it tastes awful!' Sarah protests, pulling a face and resisting the urge to throw up.

'You are wanting I am putting in sugar and spice and all things nice and not snails and puppy dogs' tails? This I cannot do, or I am diluting the potency and you are not getting so very, very healthy that your beautiful baby pops out the right time like wet pumpkin pip between the finger and thumb!'

So that's Sarah settled down, except for her baby, of course, which is still safe in her tummy, thanks to Mrs Rika Ray's magic not-sliding-out tonic.

We still cannot entirely believe that Sarah's made it. The first Maloney in history, or the known history of our family anyway, to complete high school and now the first to go to university. Not bad, eh?

But, of course, as you will have gathered Maloneys don't do things easy. Now Sarah's known among the faculty as a troublemaker and doesn't have too many friends among the teaching fraternity. Nancy sighs and says she's a Maloney and trouble sticks to a Maloney like a bindi to a woollen sock. But then Sarah finds she has a surprising and unexpected friend. She's discovered who wrote the letter giving her the names of the review committee and I have to admit I had a bit of a hand in this.

Sarah brings home the anonymous letter when Mrs Barrington-Stone flies her to Yankalillee for the weekend to give her a rest from all the publicity. Sarah shows the letter to us. People say that I'm observant and Tommy does as well and he's pretty good at seeing things in the bush, so if he says so, I guess I must be. I take one look at the handwriting and say 'It's the same bloke wrote the P.S. on that first letter that come from the university.' Nancy goes and fetches the famous letter and there it is, the P.S.: *It can get cold in Melbourne around this time and you are advised to bring warm clothing with you*. It's a perfect handwriting match, no doubtski aboutski as Morrie would say. The guy who gave her the names of the review committee is Mr Tompkins, the assistant registrar!

Sarah can hardly credit it, 'But I always thought he was against me,' she exclaims. 'Fancy him, he's always so stony-faced.' When Sarah finally enrols, she waits until he's on his own and she thanks Mr Tompkins for his help. He turns out to be a dead shy sort of a bloke. 'It's all I could think to do at the time to help you, Miss Maloney,' he stammers. His permanent stern-faced expression turns out to be a cover up, he's a nice bloke underneath but what Sarah will later call 'socially inadequate' because he had a dominating mother and came from a poor background. He's even too shy to call her Sarah until she insists and they become friends. He fills her in on the background to all the lecturers and professors and tells her what she can expect from each of them, which of them have the capacity to harm her university career and who will give her a fair go. He seems to know everything about everybody and has been at the university since he was a young clerk.

Now here's the nice part. Mrs Barrington-Stone invites Big Jack Donovan and his wife Terri, Sophie and Morrie and Mrs Billings up to her property for Saturday to go horse riding, have a barbecue and a swim in the creek then take a joy flight in the Piper Cub with Peter Barrington-Stone, the pilot. It's to celebrate the success of the Grand Plan. Sarah asks her if Mr Tompkins can come and, of course, she agrees. She also asks us Maloneys.

Morrie, Sophie and Mrs Billings are going to take the early train and then the six o'clock from Wangaratta back to Melbourne that night, but it turns out Mr Tompkins has an FX Holden and he offers them a lift. Sarah has already taken the train on the Friday night and is at home with us.

We had a good time and could eat as much as we wanted, but that's not what I want to talk about. Mr Tompkins has been at the university thirty years and Mrs Billings twenty years and, though they've met before, have never really known each other, firstly because for the first ten years Mrs Billings was at the university she was married and so that was that. Then I suppose Mr Tompkins sort of thought of her as a married woman even after her husband had died. It didn't start in the car going up because Mrs Billings was in the back with Sophie but at the barbecue Mr Tompkins and Mrs Billings get to meet each other properly and by the end of the day they're sometimes seen holding hands and walking through the garden, back and forth past the little stone boy that's pissing in the pond. They must have walked the same path a hundred times, although Mr Tompkins keeps looking over his shoulder when Mrs Billings takes his hand in case someone's looking and twice I've seen him go beetroot. He's nearly as good as Sarah at going beetroot, though he doesn't have her red hair but, instead, is bald on top, so he goes red there as well.

On the way back to Melbourne, Morrie pretends he wants to sleep, which is half true because he's swapped his shift at the *Age* with the 11 p.m. to 7 a.m. lift driver. He only has Sunday nights off so he's agreed to work Saturday nights as double-time overtime. Well, this means Celia Billings has to sit in the front of the FX and by the time they get back to Melbourne, Mr Tompkins, whose name turns out to be Bob, and Celia Billings are going steady.

Like Nancy always tells us, we Maloneys don't take without giving in return, no handouts, thank you very much, so now Sarah has paid Mr Tompkins back for his kindness. Sarah says she didn't really plan it and shouldn't get the credit, but I reckon she did, she just doesn't want to be seen as a bossy boots. Though I don't know what we can give back to Mrs Barrington-Stone because she's already paid for her daughter's layette and it would take about a hundred million layettes to thank her for what she's done for Sarah.

It's not as though it's been easy for her, she's taken a fair amount of flak on the way, not just from the men who think she's too big for her boots and should go back to the farm, but from her own kind as well. There are letters in *Collect*, the official magazine of the Country Women's Association, which suggest that Mrs Barrington-Stone's gone too far defending Sarah.

One letter from an ex-national president said, *'Our President is defending a young woman of doubtful morality who got pregnant when she should have been home doing her homework.'* There are other letters supporting this viewpoint and there is a definite movement under way, conducted by what Mrs Barrington-Stone calls 'the old guard' and 'the deep Anglicans', who have always been a powerful and conservative element in the CWA. Both want her censured and are privately calling for her resignation.

She laughs and then tells us, 'The first verse of the CWA prayer goes:

Keep us, Oh Lord, from pettiness; let us be
Large in thought, in word and deed.
Let us be done with fault-finding and leave
Off self-seeking.'

Mrs Barrington-Stone laughs again. 'I sometimes think we women are our own worst enemies, given half a chance we spoil things for ourselves.'

On another occasion she told us, 'My dears, if my time as the president of the CWA achieves nothing other than Sarah's entry to the university I will be satisfied. We struck a mighty blow for women which may well prove to be the clarion call, the small beginnings of a gender revolution in the next few years.' She looks at Sarah, 'A cause I hope Sarah will take on for her generation in the masculine world of Medicine. There are far too many timid mice in the CWA, women who are afraid of upsetting their men. God gave us teeth to bite and throats to snarl and we've turned ourselves into pussycats instead.

'We've always done what has been asked of us and asked for nothing in return. And, my dears, that is a self-fulfilling prophecy, when you ask for nothing you get nothing. If we don't complain at injustice or prejudice or even the simple endless, daily business of being taken for granted, then men naturally assume everything is all right. I mean, why shouldn't they?'

She pauses and looks around, 'But it jolly well isn't all right! Women, all women, city and country, have to stand up to be counted.' She looks over at us boys. 'We can't depend on men to grant us our freedom. Why should they? They have everything to lose, or so they think. We have to change from pussycats to snarling tigers and wrestle them to the ground with argument and action and take our emancipation for ourselves with intelligence and passion!'

Nancy claps and says, 'Ha! Too right! You've got your first tiger wrestler, Mrs Barrington-Stone.'

All I can say listening to them two is it's a bloody good thing Tommy isn't around. He has fallen off the wagon again and is that ashamed he's gone bush. If he'd been home, we might have seen Nancy taking him apart on behalf of womankind, both country and city.

I can't help wondering what all the fuss is about. In our family Nancy's already done what Mrs Barrington-Stone wants other women to do, because she's the boss and Tommy's the drunk and, when she's not telling us what to do, Sarah is.

As a matter of fact, Mike is having a bit of a battle with Nancy at this very moment. He's supposed to do his Intermediate Certificate at the end of the year but he wants to pack it in, not go to school any more. He wants to go to Melbourne and learn to be a dress designer. Every time he brings this up, Nancy's jaw sets firm as a road-grader's blade. 'No more ignorant Maloneys!' she yells, 'Stupid has been our second name too long!'

'Mum, I'm not stupid! You *know* I'm not stupid,' Mike protests.

'Not now you're not, but you'll grow stupid! You'll stay fifteen-year-old smart and that's not clever enough to get you through the rest of your life. Mike, you have to have a proper education and that's that!'

'Mum, dress designers don't have to be rocket scientists, they just cut up bits of cloth and stitch them together so rich people will pay a lot of money for them.' That's not what Mike really thinks but he knows how Nancy is, anything she can do like sew or smock must mean it's not hard.

'Oh yeah? So if you think that young bloke Yves St Laurent, who's in Paris, didn't have a good education, you're nuts. He has to mix with all them important people with good manners and lots of money. Think they're going to be bothered talking to, much less buying their clothes from someone who didn't even finish high school?'

'Mum! Yves St Laurent started as an apprentice at Christian Dior when he was just a bit older than me. He started in a clothing factory on the Left Bank.'

'What's the bank got to do with it?'

'The Left Bank, that's a part of Paris where the rag trade is mostly situated,' Mike says.

'Never you mind about Left Bank, my boy, what I'm concerned about is "left school!"'

When Sarah's home, Mike tries to get her to talk to Nancy. But Sarah says the timing's lousy, to wait until the baby comes so that Nancy's head is full of baby. 'Nancy loves a baby more than anything else, that's why she kept on having us,' Sarah comforts Mike. 'When the baby comes, her defences will be down, that's the time to approach her.'

Sarah also promises she'll make inquiries around Melbourne, because Morrie and Sophie, particularly Sophie, are meeting other Polish Jews who have settled in Melbourne and some of them are in the rag trade. 'Could be a useful place to start asking,' she says. Then she looks at poor old Mike who wants so badly to get out of Yankalillee. 'Mike, you can stay with us, we'll get Tommy to come down and fix up the back porch, mend the roof and make it into a sleep-out.'

That's just like Sarah, she sort of paints this picture of what could happen if you're patient and Mike knows she wouldn't bullshit him, so he promises not to get cranky and give Nancy a hard time, which will only cause her to dig her heels in all the harder.

The next thing to know is that Bozo has a big fight on his hands and unfortunately the *Gazette* has got hold of the story. It doesn't seem to matter what our family wants to hide, we always seem to be found out.

Anyway, when Big Jack Donovan went to Melbourne to help Sarah he also checked out the facilities at the Russell Street gym. By that I mean he had a good chat to his mate Kevin Flanagan, the gym instructor. He tells him about Bozo and admits his age. The gym instructor says they have a young seventeen-year-old featherweight who's in line for the Olympics, fifty-two fights, no losses, eighteen k.o.s. 'You can't put your lad against someone like that, Big Jack, not unless you want him crucified, mate. Let him keep beating his age group, can't do him any harm, plenty of time, he'll be exactly right for the next Olympics.'

Jack thinks about this for a while. He doesn't pretend to be the world's greatest boxing expert and Bozo's like his son so there's no way he's knowingly going to get him involved with a mismatch. He's worried because he's already done what his mate says he shouldn't do. He says to Kevin Flanagan, 'You may be right, what would I know, but will you do me a favour, Kev?'

'Sure, what?'

'There's a Police Boys Club boxing night coming up in Albury. Will you come and have a look at my lad, Bozo Maloney?'

Big Jack then explains that Bozo is up against a young bloke who's a welterweight and considered a pretty good young fighter. Kevin Flanagan asks why Bozo's fighting outside his weight division. 'Because, like I told you, he's smacked the arse of every fifteen-year-old kid in the featherweight division in Victoria.' Then he admits what he's done. 'But he could have a problem on his hands with this young bloke from New South Wales, the kid has lost only one fight and is supposed to be pretty handy with his fists.'

But Flanagan doesn't bite. 'Who's the kid?' he asks Big Jack.

'Young Aboriginal lad, well, half-Aboriginal. Father's some sort of dago, his folk have just moved down from Dubbo to Wodonga.'

'How many fights?' Kevin asks.

'Thirty, twenty-nine wins, one loss, six t.k.o.s and one k.o.'

'Jimmy Black?'

'Yeah, how'd you know?' Big Jack Donovan says, surprised.

'C'mon, Big Jack, this kid isn't for your young bloke. He's a fighter. He must have moved up a weight division, he's seventeen, he fought our young bloke in the National Championships last year. Pretty handy with the gloves, gave us a bloody good fight. We were bloody lucky to get the decision.'

'Your boxer was the one who beat him?'

'Could have gone either way, we got lucky, got the decision on the night.' Kevin Flanagan looks at him. 'You sure you know what you're doing, Big Jack? Stepping up a weight division is never easy, a few extra pounds behind a punch can make all the difference. Two or three years more experience in the ring, that's too much for your young lad to handle. I'm telling you now, your kid, no matter how good you say he is, isn't ready to fight Jimmy Black. We're not talking about a run-of-the-mill boxer. Jimmy Black's a pretty handy young fighter, good punch in both hands, fast around the ring, a real tearaway who can box too if he has to.'

Big Jack looks uncertain, then shakes his head. 'Sorry, Kev, but it's already arranged,' he says. 'Wouldn't want to pull Bozo now, the kid wants the fight real bad.'

'Easy to get it pulled, the Victorian Boxing Union won't let a fourteen-year-old go up against a seventeen-year-old boxer, no way!'

'Yeah well, that's just it, Jimmy Black hasn't been registered in Victoria and that's why we can fight him outside Bozo's weight division, though just the once, then we'll be breaking the rules. It's our only chance to see how good Bozo Maloney is.'

Kevin Flanagan isn't listening. 'Big Jack, you can *always* pull your lad. Flu, sprained elbow, it doesn't much matter, mate, you don't want your kid in the ring with a mismatch. Later maybe, when he's stronger, it's not a bad idea to get a young promising boxer to take a few good punches, maybe even be knocked down. If your lad has had an easy run up the ladder he's probably a bit of a show pony, hasn't been tested, but now's not the time, he's too young.'

'That's my point, we don't know how good he is and I don't think he's too young, Bozo's got an old head, he's not your normal fourteen-year-old.'

'Well, you're going to find out quick-smart, cobber. From what I've seen of Jimmy Black he's a kid who doesn't take any prisoners. Take my advice, pull your young bloke.'

'Nah, Bozo wants the fight, he's getting bored, he's just going through the motions. Maybe, as you said, he's a show pony, but I'd be surprised.' Jack looks at Kevin Flanagan. 'It'd be better if he gets beat than the easy fights he's been getting.'

'Jesus, Big Jack, hope you know what you're doing, mate? These kids are amateurs, boys still growing, Jimmy Black is a street kid, hard little bugger. Getting beat is one thing, getting a bad hiding is quite another. Your lad may never be the same again.'

Big Jack grins, but you can see he's not at all sure. 'Like I said, Bozo's different, you'll see.'

Kevin Flanagan has been selected as one of the trainers of the Olympic boxing squad and he knows his oats. Big Jack feels the beginning of panic in his gut. He's never considered himself an expert at ring craft.

'Bobby Devlin reckons he's ready to take Jimmy Black,' he now says defensively.

'Jesus! Bobby bloody Devlin! Do me a favour! C'mon, Big Jack, listen t'me, will ya? That's like asking a known pickpocket to mind your wallet. Of course he's gunna agree it's a good idea!' Kevin Flanagan seems to be thinking, then he looks straight at Big Jack. 'Okay. If you won't pull your boy, I'll come, but only under two conditions.'

'What?' Big Jack asks.

'With the greatest respect, cobber, I think your lad is gunna need someone more experienced than yourself and that old RSL fight-night glove-kisser in the kid's corner.'

'Yeah, of course, be honoured to have you in Bozo's corner. What's the second condition?'

'That I be allowed to throw in the towel if I think your lad's gunna take a beating.'

'Certainly.' Big Jack puts out his hand and they shake on the deal. He's secretly relieved, knowing now that Bozo will be safe.

Jack then invites Flanagan to stay at his place for the Friday night, show him the sights of Yankalillee next morning. It's a pretty little town and this time of the year with the leaves changing colour it's about the best it gets.

The Russell Street boxing coach agrees. He tells Big Jack he's got a sister up top who's suffered a severe nervous breakdown. It will be a good opportunity to kill two birds with one stone, see Bozo fight and pay her a visit the next morning. Big Jack, of course, has known this all along. There's not much a small-town cop doesn't know in his own community.

By now Bozo's got a bit of a Saturday-night following. He's had thirty-seven fights in three years and not been beaten yet. It may be small peanuts, but Bozo's earned himself a bit of a rep in a town and district where there's not very much going on when the footy season is over. The fights, for the most part, are held in the RSL clubs in Wangaratta and Wodonga and even sometimes across the border in Albury. There's lots of old diggers who've took notice of Bozo and as well he's attracted a following of young blokes and their girlfriends.

That's the thing about Bozo, he's only fourteen so you wouldn't expect him to attract much attention, but he comes out from the bell and goes flat out, he's got an excitement about him that makes people want him to win, makes them love him. The Wodonga RSL is chocka with the Friday-night fight crowd when Big Jack, Kevin Flanagan and Bobby arrive. Old blokes, young blokes, a fair few good sorts, they've all turned up.

Kevin Flanagan is impressed and remarks on the crowd when they walk to their seats ringside, 'Pretty good crowd. Don't usually expect this sort of roll-up for amateur fights.'

'It's not the fights, it's Bozo Maloney,' Big Jack explains, 'Bozo, the Boy Boxer's got something people want, don't know what it is, but whatever it is, he's got it in spades.'

'Well, he's gunna need it tonight, mate. Tell you the truth, cobber, if he was my fighter I'd *still* pull him.'

Big Jack looks up at Bozo in the ring. He's well built for his age, strong arms, good pecs, well-shaped legs, Bozo looks older than he is. He also looks happy. It's too late to pull out now.

Big Jack turns to Kevin Flanagan, 'If Bozo's taking a hiding, better to throw in the towel sooner than later. Punters won't like it, but I don't want Bozo hurt even if he looks like he's winning.'

'That's not the problem,' Flanagan lectures him again. 'A young bloke, even a very promising one, boxes on confidence and a lot of that comes from his corner. He relies on you to look after him. It's like a young kid with his dad, once he realises his old man doesn't know everything and will send him into the ring to get his head knocked off, whether willingly or from ignorance, he's never gunna be the same boxer again. If you've got a real good 'un, you need to be all the more mindful of what you do with him. Bring him along slowly.'

By the time Bozo steps into the ring, Big Jack Donovan is shitting himself. It's true, he's become sort of Bozo, the Boy Boxer's dad in both their eyes. Now he's sent him into the ring to get the devil of a hiding from a tough kid, the street fighter from New South Wales.

The referee gives them the usual talk, no holding, break when he says so, listen to my instructions at all times etcetera, etcetera, blah, blah, blah. They touch gloves and go back to their corners.

The bell goes and the two young boxers step out into the centre of the ring. Jimmy Black has more indigenous Australian black in him than colonial white and he comes storming out of his corner, anthracite and doom. He's a tearaway and real fast and Bozo's never seen anything like him before and you can almost feel his surprise. Suddenly he's backpedalling fast as he can go until he finds himself against the ropes. The Aboriginal kid is a headhunter and Bozo covers up with his gloves, then lets out a desperate left hook under the other boxer's heart. It's a well-aimed punch, maybe even a lucky one and it stops the attack temporarily. Jimmy Black steps back and Bozo gets the hell off the ropes.

The remainder of the round Bozo tries to stay out of his way. Jimmy Black is fast and he has a jabbing, accurate left hand that hurts every time it lands and it lands more than once. Bozo, except for the one good left hook, and a good right to the jaw the other fighter brushes off, spends most of his time trying to keep out of the way. The bell goes. No doubt about it, Jimmy Black has taken the first round with heaps to spare.

Big Jack turns to Kevin Flanagan. 'What do you think, should we get him out of there?'

'Well, it was the black kid's round by a country mile but your lad can box. I'm impressed, good sound defence, let's wait and see a bit. If it's a mismatch next round, we'll do the deed.'

Meantime Bobby Devlin is in Bozo's corner because Big Jack doesn't have the heart to tell Mr Sullivan, the governor of the prison, that Bobby isn't needed, that his bigtime cobber from Melbourne is taking over the corner duties. Bobby is in for a seven-year stretch, and being made the coach for the Police Boys Boxing Club and being let out of prison for training two afternoons a week and for fight nights, has given his life a whole new meaning and turned him into a model prisoner. Bobby's taken a fair bit of shit from some of the other prisoners and also from the screws, who aren't too happy about a prisoner getting a soft option. He has to work to keep his nose clean as he doesn't want to be put on a charge and not get out to coach his beloved boxing team.

When Big Jack goes to pick Bobby up from the gaol he tries to tell him, real tactful like, what an honour it is to have an Olympic boxing coach in Bozo's corner and that he knows Bobby won't mind sharing the duties. The old lag just grunts. Either Bobby's cauliflower ears have closed down on him or, like most professionals, he has a very poor regard for amateur coaches, no matter how high falutin'.

At the end of the first round Bobby's flapping a towel in Bozo's face and shouting instructions. 'Mix it. Get stuck in! Fight him, don't step back, you can beat him at his own game,' he shouts at Bozo.

'Whoa! Just a minute,' Kevin Flanagan interrupts. 'Listen, Bozo, this guy's a headhunter, he holds his gloves high but wide, he doesn't think you can hit him, he's got three inches on you in reach but he isn't using it, he's coming in flat-footed, looking for the shortest distance to your chin. He's looking for the one shot that will hurt you. But he's leaving his body exposed, showing a fair bit of contempt, you saw that when you threw the left hook off the ropes, he's wide open down below. Keep hitting him in the body, below the heart. Don't worry about his head, worry about your own. Hook him to the body. You understand me, all might to the body?'

Bozo nods, he's smart enough to work out that Kevin Flanagan makes sense. The bell goes for the second round. Like Flanagan said, Jimmy Black is looking for the one big punch against his lighter opponent, but Bozo is now making him miss and ripping him to the body every time he throws a left and then tries to follow with a right cross and misses. Towards the end of the round, Bozo has Jimmy Black on the ropes and he puts together an eight-punch combination to the body that makes Kevin Flanagan gasp. 'Jesus, where'd he learn to do that?' The second round clearly goes to Bozo.

'You've got him where you want him, Bozo,' Bobby Devlin yells. 'Get in there and finish him off, ya hear me?' Bozo nods, but he's no fool. Kevin Flanagan's advice worked real well the second round, so he turns to listen to the police sergeant from Melbourne.

'Okay, son, he's tried fighting you and it ain't working. He's gunna try to box you next round, take it on points and get the win, if he gets lucky, get a shot at your chin. Now listen good, Bozo, what you've done to his body is going to start to count. You've hit him fifty times below the heart and towards the end of the last round he's started to blow. He's gunna try and box you out of this contest. Keep putting them into his body, they're good scoring shots. Watch him, about halfway through the round he's gunna drop his gloves. The kid's not as fit as he should be and he's gunna realise he can't outbox you, so he's gunna put everything into the last minute. Stay calm, lead with the left, keep him off you. When he tries for the big shot, set him up with the left and follow through with a right cross. Don't go too early, the last twenty seconds will do, you don't have to knock him out to win.'

Bozo knows he's getting good advice and he nods, he's enjoying the contest and is anxious to get back for the third and final round.

The bell goes and it's almost exactly how Kevin Flanagan said it would be. Jimmy Black decides to box, but Bozo proves to be the better boxer, smaller but faster, and makes the other boxer miss, then steps in fast and jabs a left into Jimmy Black's face.

Bozo's punches are pretty harmless, but they serve to frustrate the other boxer, who's aware he's a bigger man and has the longer reach. Bozo either makes him miss or takes almost all the other fighter's punches on his gloves. In the process, almost without trying, he seats five well-aimed left hooks on the button, right under Jimmy Black's heart. They are hard punches that score. Maybe with the Aboriginal kid having to move down to Wodonga, he's missed out on regular training sessions working out in the gym, but towards the end of the third round he's slowing down noticeably, his mouth slightly open, blowing hard.

Almost on cue, with less than a minute to go, the boy from New South Wales begins to drop his gloves. Bozo waits, jabbing his left piston-like into the other boxer's face.

Jimmy Black has lots of courage and keeps coming in. He's breathing fast, the punches to his heart have paid off and now he misses with a wild swing and takes a good left in the face for his trouble before he grabs Bozo into a clinch, hanging on.

The referee separates them and, as they both step back, Jimmy Black throws a left again, misses and pulls Bozo into another clinch. He's hanging on, trying to get his breathing and his timing right. The referee separates them and warns Jimmy Black against holding. Bozo moves in close and goes back down below again, seating two real good punches, a right and a left hook where all the others have landed, slap bang under the heart, pulling back, ducking, in time to see the black boy's right whistling through the air three inches above his head.

Bozo moves slightly to the left of the other boxer, planting his feet flat, fists tight, thumbs turned inward, and then throws a right cross with the full impact of his shoulder and the weight of his body behind it. It's not a punch he could have thrown in the first round, the bigger boxer would have seen it coming. But now he's slowed down, his gloves held low and wide, Bozo's right hand smashes into the point of his chin. Black goes down. Bozo goes to a neutral corner. Jimmy Black hits the deck pretty hard, but quickly gets to one knee, then jumps to his feet at the count of five, the referee counts the customary eight and puts up three fingers.

'How many?' he asks.

'Three,' the dark lad calls.

'You okay, son?'

'Yeah, lucky punch.' He's too proud to admit he was hit fair dinkum. They box on but now Jimmy Black is simply trying to stay out of Bozo's way.

With about twenty seconds to go, Bozo has his opponent on the corner ropes. The Aboriginal lad drops both his hands to cover up another left hook he thinks is coming, but it's a feint, Bozo steps in and hits him with a short right that catches Black on the point of the chin. The punch doesn't travel more than ten inches but it's got Bozo's whole body behind it and Jimmy Black tries to grab the ropes but his arms never get there and he bounces off the ropes and hits the canvas, bum first, with a thump and then falls backwards, his head bouncing against the bottom rope of the ring before hitting the deck.

It's not the first knock-out of Bozo's career, but it's his most convincing, the referee counts Jimmy Black out without him getting back onto his feet.

'Jesus!' Kevin Flanagan exclaims. 'Jesus Christ, if I hadn't seen it for myself I'd never have believed it! What's a fourteen-year-old doing with that kind of punching power in his right hand!'

'Comes from lifting garbage cans,' Big Jack says, laughing. He can't believe what happened.

The next morning Kevin Flanagan pays a visit to his sister up top. Without realising what a small country town is like, he talks to an orderly who happened to have been at the fight the previous night. Flanagan, wanting to do the right thing by a local boy, praises Bozo's win to the hilt and mentions that he is the best youngster he's seen in a while and is almost good enough to go against Rod Barnes the Australian featherweight amateur champion and Olympic triallist. Before you can say 'Jack Robinson!', the *Owens & Murray Gazette* is onto the story.

BOZO MALONEY

LOCAL BOY TO FIGHT OLYMPIC PROSPECT!

The piece goes on to question whether Bozo will be chosen to fight in the Olympics if he beats Rod Barnes. Big Jack Donovan is astonished and pays a visit to Toby Forbes and tells him he ought to arrest him for criminal neglect of truth in journalism and demands a retraction, explaining that Bozo isn't old enough to be considered for the Olympics and that the Amateur Boxing Union would never allow such a fight to take place.

'After Friday night, a lot of people would like to see it happen,' Toby Forbes counters. 'Who is young Maloney going to fight then? He's beaten everyone else in his age group. Knocked out a welterweight last Friday.'

'Dunno,' says Big Jack, 'we'll just have to wait and see.' That night he puts a call through to Kevin Flanagan.

Chapter Twelve

You know how us Maloneys never seem to do things the easy way? I mean, we take the spoon out of the sink and all that, but then the tap handle falls off or something. You take Sarah's baby for instance, safe and sound inside her tummy for nine months. Except, of course, for when she took the stuff Mrs Rika Ray gave her, but in the end that didn't do her any harm and turned out good. Nancy says she's had a dead-easy pregnancy inside her and a rotten one outside. As for the birth arrangements, the Carlton terrace isn't more than a few minutes by car from the Women's Hospital in Grattan Street and everything has been done to make sure nothing goes wrong.

Morrie has earned enough to put new tyres on the Austin 7 so it's now safe to drive in Melbourne. Bozo's been down on the train to tune the old bomb and it's in the best possible working order, oil changed, every grease nipple examined and greased, spark plugs checked, carburettor and petrol pump cleaned, radiator hose inspected for leaks. Morrie runs the engine every morning for five minutes to make sure it will start when the time comes.

Everything's perfect for a quick, trouble-free getaway. If Sarah's labour pains start when Morrie's at work, then Sophie simply has to go to the telephone box on the corner and phone him. With all that has gone on over the past few weeks from the brouhaha at the university, everyone at the *Age* knows about Sarah's pregnancy and she's now become like their own daughter. They've even got a newspaper delivery van on standby in one of the loading bays (Management think it's got a cracked crankshaft) so Morrie can be taken home the moment he gets Sophie's phone call. What's more, if the Austin 7 doesn't start, then the newspaper van's the back-up. They've even got four sixpences in an envelope drawing-pinned to the inside of the front door to use on the corner telephone.

Then there's the Italian family next door, Maria and her husband Costa are ready to do anything in an emergency. If the Queen was going to have a baby, there couldn't be much more back-up. Operation Sarah is on maximum alert.

In the last weeks of her pregnancy Morrie and Sarah drive to university in the Austin 7, so if the labour pains start during a lecture he can get her home to collect her things or if it's an emergency take her straight to the hospital, which is within walking distance. So you can see all the spoons are polished and put safely in the kitchen drawer, there isn't a one of them anywhere near the sink.

Meanwhile, Sarah is proving to be very popular with the male students. She's playing it smart because even though she knows the answers to most of the questions, she always lets a bloke go first and only answers if the lecturer or professor asks her directly. At first some of the professors pick on her because after all the publicity she's not exactly flavour of the month. For instance, when a real hard question comes up for discussion they direct it at Sarah. But they soon find out it isn't the best ploy because she usually knows the answer. They don't much like this, but they learn to respect her. The young med students soon become protective of Sarah and also, funny enough, of Morrie, whom they call 'Professor Fizz'. The baby is accepted as part of the faculty and there is a great deal of discussion about the sex and one of the more enterprising students is running a book with half the takings going to buying needed baby things when it's born.

Morrie is always willing to help anyone with an explanation of things medical. Even in his crook English, Sarah says he is a wonderful teacher who can make complex things simple to understand. Morrie really loves being a student and gets high distinctions for every paper because the lecturers can't mark him down, even if they wanted to as he can argue back and then they have to prove *him* wrong.

Sarah's nine months has come and no baby. Everyone's on tenterhooks. It's nine months and one week, May 21, and Nancy's that worried she's driving the Diamond T into things on the garbage run. Mrs Rika Ray, unable to stand the pressure any longer, arrives at the front door of the Carlton terrace pushing an old rusty pram she's found somewhere.

In the pram are blankets and a pillow and one of those thin mattresses rolled up, so the load is bigger than the pram and is tied down with string. It turns out later that under the blankets and pillow is a spare frock and some women's things. She also brings two towels as well as jars of herbs and bunches of fresh herbs and a big bag of vegies from her garden, all her bits and pieces. One of the pram wheels is wobbling like mad and it looks like Mrs Rika Ray's just made it from Spencer Street station before it falls off.

From her hut at Silver Creek to Wangaratta is about thirty-five miles and she's taken two days to walk to the railway station at Wang, camping out in the bush for the first night and sitting all the next night on the train platform so she can catch the 9.31 a.m. train to Spencer Street Station. I don't know how she got onto the train with the pram but there she is, large as life, standing at the front door.

Sarah opens the door. She and Morrie have been to a morning lecture and have the afternoon off. Sarah's having a bit of a rest because her back is hurting when she hears the knock at the door. Morrie's out somewhere and Sophie won't answer the door on her own. Sarah drags herself up wearily, she's just been drifting off. It's just a few minutes to two o'clock on the old Wesclock that rests on the fruit crate beside her army cot. She goes to the door with her hand planted firmly in the small of her back, not too happy, to find Mrs Rika Ray standing at the door.

'Mrs Rika Ray!' Sarah exclaims, surprised.

The old lady looks at her. 'One pound, seventeen shillings and sixpence. In India we are going to Calcutta to Lahore, one thousand miles, same price, three days in train!' Her hand shoots out and feels Sarah's tummy under her nightdress, her head to one side like she's listening for something. 'Thank God, not yet it is sliding out.'

Sarah looks surprised, it must be fairly obvious to anyone that her baby hasn't arrived, her tummy's sticking out halfway to the front gate.

'I am looking at your stars and I must be here by your side for the baby coming. It is Indian thing, Indian stars, not like Australian stars with shitty Southern Cross. Indian stars when they are telling me they are never wrong! I must obey or all the hell and the high water it breaks loose and I am responsible. The gods have spoken and Vishnu Himself is pointing holy finger at me. I am telling myself, "Mrs Rika Ray, don't delay, take blankets and get going, woman." So that is why I am coming to help Sarah for the sliding out and the cutting off and the tying the bellybutton perfect like a little rosebud.'

'But, Mrs Rika Ray, it's all arranged, I'm to go to the hospital, it's only five minutes away.'

'No, no, no, my dear, that is what *you* are saying and Morrie is saying and all arrangements are saying, but not the stars, they are not saying this. No, no, no, Indian stars saying, "Mrs Rika Ray, you must stay, sleep by Sarah's bed, waters are breaking and nobody there!"' She points to the pram standing in the pathway behind her. 'Look, my dear, I am bringing self-sufficiency and we are making a tonic also and fresh herbs for when labour pain are coming.'

Sophie comes down the hallway, she's heard friendly voices so she wants to know what all the fuss is about. When she sees Mrs Rika Ray, she's delighted. The two of them have got on like a house on fire ever since Mrs Rika Ray cured a bunch of nasty warts on her fingers and on the back of her right hand by rubbing them with a piece of raw steak and then burying the meat under a rock in the backyard when it was full moon. Honest, I do not tell a lie, that's what she's done and the warts, which Morrie had been trying to cure for years, disappeared in a week, never to return again.

I've got to say, Morrie was more than a little bit miffed, but Sophie said he'd had his chance and she'd had hers and Mrs Rika Ray had won. So, no point him being angry that God works in mysterious ways. I'm not sure that's how she put it exactly, that's what Nancy claimed she said, but it was all in Polish and Morrie looked pretty cross and shook his head and said, '*Znachor!*' Which, when I asked him later, he said was the word for 'witch' in Polish, only it was worse than a witch and he didn't yet have enough English to explain.

'Witchdoctor?' I suggested.

But he didn't seem to like that one bit. 'That one, she is not a doctor! How can she be a doctor? A witch is not a doctor, *Znachor*, it is word for witch medicine!' But, all in all, Morrie quite likes Mrs Rika Ray and says there's maybe a place in medicine for herbs but not for pieces of meat under rocks.

I don't think he was too happy when he comes in to find Mrs Rika Ray has arrived, but by this time the three women are in the kitchen yakking and having breakfast and Mrs Rika Ray's already got some sort of herbal concoction bubbling away on the gas stove.

Nine months, and the second week overdue is almost over and things are getting pretty tight, although Nancy says predicting a baby's arrival can be two weeks out, but not much more. Sarah calls Nancy every evening. They've got this arrangement, Sarah gets to the corner telephone booth at six-thirty sharp every night and Nancy phones her on the number of the corner telephone booth. They know that Dotty Ryan is on duty at the Yankalillee telephone exchange and that she's bound to listen in, but that's sort of okay, she's on our side and so won't spread any malicious rumours. Nevertheless, compliments of Dotty, on a daily basis, the whole of Yankalillee knows the state of play with Sarah's baby.

They've even got a book going at the Shamrock, five bob in, nearest on the day and the hour of birth plus the right sex takes all, the winner to drink out the total pot, except for a fifteen per cent fee to Mickey O'Hearn the publican, who is acting as the bookmaker. The word's got around town and blokes who drink at some of the other pubs are dropping into the Shamrock to place a bet and have a beer and Mick's doing a roaring trade.

Of course, nobody has expected Sarah's baby to be late. Men think when you say a date that's when it's going to happen and so most of them have kissed their dosh goodbye. Now they're all having a second go and the pot is getting really huge.

Tommy's back from the bush and on the wagon again, but he reckons if he wins it he'll be obliged to do his duty and stay drunk for three months. When he says this, Nancy sniffs, 'Just make sure you're sober by the time the christening comes around, I don't want Father Crosby having another go at me, bad enough no father, but no grandfather as well! Crikey, the sanctimonious old bugger will be putting me down for extra time in purgatory!'

Anyway, Nancy makes her daily phone call to Sarah and during their conversation Sarah, without thinking, mentions Mrs Rika Ray has arrived on the scene. Well, does Nancy ever go spare! It's not that she doesn't like Mrs Rika Ray. Ever since the 'bottoms-wiping certificate' episode she's quite admired her, though she's still a bit crook over the abortion attempt, even if a lot of good came out of it in the end.

Deep down, well, maybe not so deep down, Nancy's still a good Catholic. Collapsed or not, she still believes that getting rid of a baby is the worst sin out. Once when it came up and Sarah pointed out that it was her who approached Mrs Rika Ray in the first place and that it was Mrs Rika Ray who told her she didn't think it would work and didn't want to do it, Nancy said that didn't change nothing.

'Mum, don't you see?' Sarah says, 'I begged her! I went down on bended knees! It was my fault, my responsibility, she didn't charge us a penny, so it isn't like she's an abortionist or anything like that.'

'Don't you say that wicked word in front of me, my girl!' Nancy snaps. 'What if you'd gone sooner? What then, hey? You'd have blood on your hands and you'd have committed a mortal sin and would have burned in hell everlasting with the angels holding your precious dead baby up for you to see when you looked up from the flames and appealed to heaven for God's mercy!' I think she must have got that last bit from the nuns when they taught her at school.

Back to the telephone call. 'What's *she* bloody doing there?' Nancy asks Sarah on the phone, cranky as all get-out.

Sarah realises too late that she's said the wrong thing. She doesn't tell Nancy about the Indian stars or the pram or the concoction she's taking every day. 'Mum, she's just visiting for a few days!'

'Visiting my arse! She's interfering. What's she know about having babies? Has she ever had a baby? I've had the five of yiz brats and I'm stuck back here with the garbage with my very own daughter about to give birth and me nowhere to be seen and *she's* there getting under everyone's feet!'

'Mum, it's not like that at all!'

'What do you mean she's on a visit? For heaven's sake, you don't go on holiday to someone's place when they're about to have a baby. She's up to something, I'm tellin' you, girl! She's up to no good, that one, her with her herbs and magic potions. Don't you take nothing she gives you, you hear, Sarah? Nothing! Them herbs nearly killed you last time. You tell Morrie to call me, he's the man in the house, he's got to send her on her bicycle!'

Sarah doesn't tell her it isn't a bicycle, it's a pram. 'Mum, Sophie's got a whole lot of piecework from this frock factory in Flinders Lane and she's happy to have Mrs Rika Ray help out, she can use a sewing machine real well and she cooks and cleans and even bakes.'

'Cooks? What sort of food? That curry stuff Indians eat, and rice? Don't you go eating nothing she cooks.'

'Mum, it's just Australian food with some nice things, you know, flavours added.'

'What do you mean flavours added? Poison most likely! Your baby needs plain food, meat and potatoes and maybe a bit of pumpkin and peas. Think about your baby, you don't want them herbs coming through your breast milk!'

'Mum, it's nothing like that. I haven't even got any breast milk yet, I only start to lactate a couple of days after the birth.'

'Don't you start telling me about babies and breast milk, my girl! You just keep squeezing those breasts of yours, keep them nice and supple, rub your nipples, with that stuff, what's it called? Lanolin. You don't know how lucky you are, in my day we had to rub them with sheep's fat. You've got to stop the nipples cracking. I've had five, the four of you and little Colleen. I should bloody know. Nothing wrong with you lot, sucked me dry the every one of yiz, surprised you left anything for little Colleen. Don't think you know everything just because you're gunna be a doctor. I never had a cracked nipple, not even once.'

'Mum, I'm not trying to tell you anything. We're fine, honest. Everyone's fine, really! You don't have to worry about Mrs Rika Ray,

Sophie's glad to have her and she's not going to do anything bad. Morrie's got it all worked out, we're five minutes from the Women's, Bozo's fixed the Austin up a treat, we've got back-up with Maria and Costa, the Italians next door, if it's needed *and* the van from Morrie's work if the Austin 7 won't start. The Women's is supposed to be the best maternity hospital in the southern hemisphere, nothing's going to go wrong.'

'So, where's she sleeping then?'

'On the floor in my room, she brought her own bedding.'

'In *your* bedroom! She's moved in, taken over *your* bedroom! Why, the bloody cheek of the woman!'

'No, Mum, she's sleeping on the floor, there's plenty of room, she's very quiet and doesn't snore, it's nice to know there's someone there if something happens in the night.'

'You just told me nothing can happen, that it's all organised. Now it's nice to have somebody in case something happens? Right! That does it, I'm comin' down. If something happens, you need your mum not that old herb witch.'

'Please, Mum! I can't share my bed with you, it's a single, an army cot we got from the disposal.'

'We'll take the Diamond T, bring the double bed and the Singer. I'll help Sophie all she needs with her sewing.'

'What about the garbage, you can't leave the garbage,' Sarah cries desperately.

'We'll come down Saturday, Bozo and the boys can drive back Sunday, they'll just have to manage without me for a week. Tommy's back from the bush, he'll have to stay on the wagon long enough to help with the garbage while I take care of me precious daughter!'

'Mum, I don't need taking care of! What about little Colleen? Bozo hasn't got his driving licence!' Sarah's clutching at straws.

'Little Colleen? She's comin' too, bed's been big enough before, it will be big enough again. Bozo can get a note about his licence from Big Jack Donovan. Don't try to stop me, girl, I've made up me mind. We're comin' down Saturday. You send that woman packin' you hear me now? 'Cause your mum's comin' to take care of you, darling.'

'Mum, there isn't room, it's a tiny house!'

'There's room for her!'

'Mum, you're four of her! Pleeease Mum!'

Nancy bangs down the phone before Sarah can say anything else.

That night when we're having our tea, Nancy announces out of the blue. 'Indian woman's having another go at getting rid of Sarah's belly, we've got to go down to Melbourne to rescue her.'

'Whaddayamean?' Mike cries in alarm. 'Mrs Rika Ray? She wouldn't do that, she loves Sarah!'

'Huh! Loves her, does she? It was her tried to get rid of Sarah's baby the first time!'

'Mum, that's not how it happened,' I protest. 'You know it wasn't.'

Nancy ignores me, 'Bozo, better make sure the Diamond T is all right.'

'It ain't, Mum, the tyres won't make it, no way. You'll have to go by train, be lucky if I can get the Diamond T to Wang and back.'

'I can't take the train, we're taking my bed and the Singer sewing machine, leaving Saturday, you three will drive back Sunday, do the garbage run with Tommy next week.'

'Mum, I just told you, I haven't a licence, the tyres are ratshit, we'll never make it!' Bozo cries. 'Tell us, what's happened to Sarah?'

'Black woman's sleeping with her.'

'What!!' we all shout together.

'Waiting for something to happen so she can pounce on the baby!'

It takes about ten minutes to get the whole story out of Nancy and it doesn't take us too long to figure out that Nancy Maloney is not what Sarah needs in the last stages of her pregnancy.

But we also know that, come Saturday, we'll be on the road to Melbourne with her double bed and sewing machine in the back of the Diamond T. Nancy is riding to the rescue and if we have to push the Diamond T all the way to Melbourne, that's where we're going.

I quite like the idea of going to Melbourne. I've only been there the once when we went to the Show and Mike got Best of Show and Bozo fought the Aboriginal bloke. But I'm also dead disappointed, because Tommy has arranged for me to go hunting Saturday with him and John Crowe, who's going to teach me to fire a .22 rifle.

You remember John Crowe? He was the bloke who found the corrugated iron that fell off a truck for Mrs Rika Ray's hut and also helped to build it, him and Ian McTavish and Tommy and me when the bottoms-wiping-certificate fire burned her old hut down.

We're going after foxes and rabbits and feral cats. Though Tommy says not to talk about the cats because even though they're vermin and kill the wildlife, people get funny about cats, even some country women who should know better. Tommy can't teach me to shoot by example, because of his crook shoulder and his one eye missing. He can't use a rifle no more so he's asked John Crowe, because you can't be a proper bushie if you can't fire a rifle.

As you can see, having to go to Melbourne is a bit of a big disappointment as well as not a bad thing to do if we ever get there.

Bozo says we've got Buckley's, the tyres are history. Two are showing canvas and the other two are so smooth the tread wouldn't trip a bull ant up if it was running at top speed. It looks like I'm not going shooting and that we'll spend the weekend somewhere on the road to Melbourne, most likely about fifty miles down the road where we'll starve all weekend. Bozo begs Nancy to see some sense and take the train, but she won't.

Bozo's serious about the Diamond T. No ifs or maybes, it can't make it to Melbourne. We should have been on offal a month ago to save for retreads on the back two tyres, but Nancy's been so distracted by Sarah's baby that she's forgot and the tyres are on their last legs.

'We're going to Melbourne, to our darling Sarah, that's all there is to it, Bozo!' is what she says to him when he persists. By now she's convinced herself the baby's life is in danger. Sarah's tried to phone her, getting Dotty Ryan to call from the exchange, because Nancy hasn't been making her six-thirty calls since she told Sarah she was coming to the rescue. Nancy tells Dotty Ryan to tell Sarah we'll see her Saturday night. She's scared Sarah will come up with a good reason why we shouldn't go.

I tell Tommy I'm not going to be able to go shooting with him and John Crowe. He tells me I'd better go and see him, tell him myself, because the whole idea was to begin to teach me to shoot and John's giving up his Saturday because Tommy's asked him special.

'Better go see John down at the council depot, mate,' Tommy says, shaking his head, because he knows it's not my fault. I can't go against Nancy's wishes and him asking her would only make matters worse. Nancy wants all her kids around her, we're like her security blanket, she's missing Sarah something terrible, which is more than half the reason we're going.

So after school I walk to the workshops where they repair the shire trucks to see John Crowe. I ask a bloke in blue overalls where I can find him. He points to a truck in the lube bay. 'He's under the Dodge,' he says.

When I get to the truck I stand for a while. I can see this pair of legs sticking out from under it, but I don't want to disturb him. You know, just call out to him. Nancy says you have to always look a man in the eye when you talk to him and all I can see is a pair of boots with no socks on and a part of his hairy legs that are spotted with grease. There's grunts coming from under the truck like he's struggling with something, then, 'Shit! Bastard, Whore!' and a spanner comes flying out from under the truck. I think maybe I should come back later but after a few moments I cough and say, 'You all right?'

'Yeah, bastard nut on the oil sump, tight as a nun's pussy! Who's askin'?'

'Mole. Mole Maloney.'

Then there's the clatter of those little iron wheels on one of those platforms on which mechanics lie on their backs to slide under a truck. The legs become a body in dirty khaki shorts and blue singlet and then it's him. 'Gidday, Mole, what brings you to this neck o' the woods?' John Crowe says, looking up at me.

I tell him about going to Melbourne to see Sarah and that Nancy's gunna stay for when the baby comes so I can't get a shooting lesson.

'Baby! I've already lost a fortune on your sister's baby. Had three goes at guessing and the little bugger still ain't come.' He stands up meanwhile and laughs and puts his hand on my shoulder. I can only hope grease stains come off in the wash or I'm in the shit with Nancy. 'Melbourne, eh?'

'I'm sorry about not going shooting. I really was looking forward to it.'

'That's all right, mate, we'll do it another time, no worries,' he grins. 'Foxes and rabbits'll be happy they've been spared your deadly aim.'

I laugh, he's a real nice bloke. Then I tell him how it's all a bit of a waste, because we ain't gunna get to Melbourne anyway.

'Why's that?' he asks.

I tell him about the Diamond T tyres. 'Bozo, me brother, says we ain't got a snowball's hope in hell, no chance.'

He rubs his chin and I can see, even though his face is black with grease and shiny with sweat, that he hasn't shaved in a few days and has got these bristles, some of them already white.

He puts his hand on my shoulder again and now I've got two blotches to worry about. 'Hey, Mole, we can't take chances on the road with Bozo, the Boy Boxer, now can we? Bloody good fight he had with the Abo kid, won me two quid, should've bet more but the other kid looked so bloody big and strong, know better in future, hey.'

He turns to watch a truck coming in through the gate and seems to be thinking. 'Hmm, the Fargo takes the same size of tyres as the Diamond T,' he says, like he's thinking aloud. Then he turns back to me. 'Tell your brother I'll meet him outside the gates here six o'clock sharp, Friday night. He's to come in the Diamond T.'

Well, Bozo turns up at the right time and John Crowe is already waiting. The gates to the shire workshop are locked and chained with all the shire trucks, graders and tractors inside, safe for the weekend. John Crowe unlocks the gates and signals for Bozo to drive the Diamond T into the yard, then he jumps up onto the running board and points to where the Fargo is parked.

'Pull her up next to the Fargo,' he instructs. Bozo does as he's told then steps down from the Diamond T. John Crowe looks at him and laughs, 'Don't expect there's anyone gunna arrest you around here for driving without a licence, you and Big Jack Donovan being mates an' all. Bloody good fight in Wodonga, Bozo.'

Bozo thanks him and notices that he's got the big-truck tyre jack under the Fargo and one of the back wheels is already off the ground and the wheel nuts removed.

'We don't want you to get into any trouble, Mr Crowe,' Bozo says, worried. I've already told him what I think John Crowe has in mind.

Bozo's a bit of a law abider. Being with Big Jack so much, it's rubbed off on him.

'No worries, old son.' John Crowe points to the Fargo tyre, 'We're only borrowing them tyres for the weekend, do them good to get a couple of hundred miles on a straight road, warm them up, keep the rubber expanding correct. We're doing the shire a big favour, not that those bastards would appreciate it, you get no thanks around here for trying to be helpful.'

Bozo thinks it's probably bullshit about tyres needing expanding and all that, but they get to work and in about an hour they've swapped all the tyres over. The Diamond T has never had six good tyres on her at the one time since Tommy got her from the US Army disposal.

'Be bloody sure you're back Sunday night, Bozo. It don't matter how late, just get to my place before five o'clock in the mornin',' John Crowe warns and then laughs, 'or they'll have my guts for garters! Come round the back, bang on the bedroom window, the missus will wake up and let you in.' Then he asks, 'Okay for petrol? Might as well fill her up, hey? We'll call it natural dissipation, evaporation, it happens with petrol all the time, act of nature.'

I'm beginning to understand how come that corrugated iron we used for Mrs Rika Ray's roof fell off a truck.

Meanwhile, on that same Friday night, no I'm wrong, because it's already Saturday morning, isn't it, but early, before even we leave Yankalillee, things are beginning to go wrong in Melbourne.

First thing, Morrie's had to swap his shift and is doing the 11 p.m. to 7 a.m., because it's a payback for when we all went to Mrs Barrington-Stone's place. The late-night lift driver's niece is having her engagement party at the Salvation Army Hall in Fitzroy. No grog because her fiancé is in the Salvation Army band and is a born-again Christian. Morrie is dead anxious, knowing Sarah could come any time, but Joe Bloggs the foreman says it's still only ten or fifteen minutes in the van for him to get to Carlton from the *Age*, probably less that time of the night.

At least Mrs Rika Ray is there and she'll know what to do if the labour pains start to come. Mrs Rika Ray isn't taking any chances with

Sarah. On the floor beside her mattress she has a pile of newspapers. Morrie gets the early-morning edition of the *Age* for free when he knocks off every night and Mrs Rika Ray has several beside her bed. 'Newspaper very, very sterile,' she says. When Sarah looks doubtful, Morrie confirms this, newsprint ink is a powerful disinfectant he assures her.

Mrs Rika Ray also has him bring home two newspapers unopened every night and she sterilises a pair of scissors and a sort of rubber-bulb contraption she's brought with her and she boils two short pieces of string. Then she carefully removes the centre pages of the unopened newspapers and wraps the scissors and the rubber contraption in it, together with the two lengths of string. She does this all over again every night just before she goes to bed. She also has a small enamel basin, two flannels and a jug of boiled water beside her bed as well as a jar of potassium permanganate and a jar of seaweed extract and other assorted herbs.

Early on the Saturday morning we're supposed to leave Yankalillee for Melbourne, Sarah wakes up feeling strange and then she gasps in dismay, because she's discovered she's pissed her bed. The sheet is sopping wet between her legs and so is her nightie. For a moment she's horrified, then, almost at once, she realises it isn't what she thought, that her waters have broken (whatever that is). It's not her that's wet the bed, it's the first sign the baby is coming.

Suddenly she gets this pain. Later she tells us, 'It's a vice-like pain across my tummy and it takes my breath away. I want to scream, but I think I'll wake Mrs Rika Ray up, yet I can't help myself. The pain is so bad I start to sob and groan because it's getting worse and I'm sure I'm going to die.'

Mrs Rika Ray, who's sleeping on a hair trigger, hears Sarah in her sleep and she's up in a flash and runs down the passage to the door of Morrie and Sophie's bedroom and knocks loudly. 'Sophie! Sophie! Waking up please. Come quickly, we are needing boiled water and the towels!' she cries.

Sophie wakes up and sits bolt upright in bed, she thinks she's in Poland. '*O borze oni ida Maurice gestapo po nas przysli chca nas zabrac*' ('Oh God, they are coming, Maurice. It's the Gestapo, they are coming for us!'), she yells in Polish.

But then she must have realised what was happening and she leaps out of bed and hurriedly puts on this pink chenille dressing gown she's made specially, so that if she has to go to the corner telephone to phone Morrie, she'll be respectable.

'Bring hot water, Sophie! Baby coming! Put on kettle and pot also for sterilising!' Mrs Rika Ray shouts from the other bedroom.

But Sophie has been programmed for a different kind of action, one she's rehearsed in her mind a hundred times over. She's got to get to the corner telephone and call Morrie. Now nothing else matters.

She's out the front door and has reached the front gate when she remembers the sixpences in the envelope pinned to the door. But the door has slammed behind her and is on a Yale lock and can't be opened from the outside. Morrie has done it specially, because Sophie needs to know she's safe when she's inside the house. So now Sophie can't get back. It's two o'clock in the morning and she's screaming and banging on the door. But Mrs Rika Ray is busy with Sarah, who's also screaming, and so she doesn't hear her and can't come anyway.

To add to the catastrophe, Maria and Costa and their family next door have left early the previous evening to catch the train to visit her sister, who is getting married on the weekend to an Australian-Italian who owns a big orchard near Shepparton. At that time in the morning the street is completely deserted. Sophie's knuckles are practically bleeding from hammering at the door. She's panicking like mad and can't think what to do next.

Meanwhile Mrs Rika Ray can't wait for towels and hot water because Sarah's baby isn't hanging around for anyone. She lays newspaper over the fruit crate Sarah uses for a bedside table and puts all her things down on it, including the newspaper parcel she's sterilised. Then she spreads thick sheets of newspaper over the bed, lifting Sarah's legs and bum onto it. As she lifts Sarah's legs, Sarah's hit with another excruciating pain and screams out. 'I need to push, oh God, pleeeease . . . *I-have-to-push*!'

'You are calming down, please, Sarah, we are getting to pushing when I am examining sliding-out possibilities. Now, please, you must bring your legs up so.' She grabs a hold of one of Sarah's legs in each hand and bends them at the knee and pushes her legs back and then slides extra newspaper under her bum and where the baby's going to come and then has a good look-see at what's going on inside Sarah.

'Please, I have to push! Oh, oh, it hurts so much! Ahaaawha!! Shit! Shit! *Shit!*'

'My goodness gracious me, hushings please! Such language, it is not becomings a lady!' Mrs Rika Ray says calmly. 'The baby head it is making to slide out perfectly, my dear. I am putting my hand on the top and then you are pushing, Sarah. You are pushing hard and I am holding baby head, it must not come too quickly, we are not wanting tearing of perineum! Push, darling, your baby is sliding out very beautiful, like wet pumpkin pip.'

Sarah pushes hard and then lets out a scream and her baby comes sliding out into Mrs Rika Ray's willing hands. She places it between Sarah's legs and reaches for the little rubber pump contraption and inserts it into the tiny mouth and, pressing on the rubber ball, sucks out the mucus and fluid in the infant's mouth. The baby's eyes crinkle up and, balling its tiny fists, the baby starts to scream its head off. She doesn't have to hold it upside down and spank its bottom like they say you must, because it's breathing a treat and also yelling its lungs out, which requires a whole heap of breath.

'My goodness gracious me, this one she will be opera singer!' Mrs Rika Ray is ecstatic. 'It is a girl, a most beautiful very, very wonderful girl, Sarah! Very, very healthy!' Mrs Rika Ray says.

Sarah is still panting furiously but the moment she sees her daughter, she bursts into tears, trying to smile and at the same time trying to stop her panting, all of which can't be done simultaneously. So she bawls and pants. She's not crying because she's sad, but because she's so happy.

Then Mrs Rika Ray becomes aware that someone is banging furiously on the window of Sarah's bedroom. She moves over and opens Nancy's yellow-daisy curtains to see a wild-eyed Sophie outside, her nose pressed against the windowpane and the branches of the lemon tree behind her, a lemon resting on top of her head. She pushes the window up and Sophie climbs into the bedroom, gasping and falling to the floor with a thud. But she's up in an instant, even before Mrs Rika Ray can reach out and give her a hand. Mrs Rika Ray doesn't seem too surprised at Sophie's entrance. 'Hot water we are needing, a kettle to boil and a pot, you are hurrying please, Sophie.'

But Sophie isn't listening, she doesn't say a word or even glance at Sarah or see the baby but makes straight for the bedroom door and runs down the passage to the front door where she grabs the envelope containing the sixpences and flies out the door and tears down the pavement to the telephone booth on the corner. The door bangs behind her.

The scene in the bedroom continues uninterrupted. Mrs Rika Ray lifts the baby from between Sarah's legs and places her on her tummy. 'Sarah, you are holding the baby only on your tummy, you are soon seeing fingers and toes for counting, but not yet.' She takes each of Sarah's hands in turn and shows her how to hold the baby. 'Be careful, the umbilical cord we are not yet cutting, I am tying first then we are cutting.'

She reaches down to the newspaper parcel on the wooden fruit crate beside the bed and takes a single length of twine about eight inches long and ties it tightly around the umbilical cord, about an inch from the baby's navel. Then she takes the second piece and ties it about three inches further up towards Sarah's tummy. She reaches down again and picks up the scissors and cuts through the section of the cord contained between the two pieces of twine. In this way she stems the blood flow through the cord from the baby *and* the mother's end, and at the same time detaches the baby.

With the baby no longer attached to its umbilical cord, Mrs Rika Ray looks down at Sarah. 'Now you are lifting baby and holding to breasts. You are holding up baby and you are counting ten for fingers, ten for toes.' She smiles. 'If you are finding more than ten, you are telling me please and I am putting baby back quick-smart and we are asking Mr Stork for new one.' Sarah smiles weakly at Mrs Rika Ray's feeble joke as she lifts her baby up toward her face.

Throughout the birth Mrs Rika Ray hasn't raised her voice and is perfectly calm, seemingly going about her business with plenty of time on her hands, as if what she is doing is the most natural situation in the world. Which, when you think about it, I suppose it is. Sarah senses that she's in good hands and does what she's told, now drawing and clutching her daughter to her chest so that her stomach is exposed.

'My dear, we are taking out placenta. I am pressing down on your tummy, I am wanting deep breath, then slowly, slowly breathing out until next contraction is coming.' She sees Sarah's look of dismay. 'No, no, it is not hurting.'

Pressing down gently but firmly on Sarah's tummy with one hand, she proceeds to tug carefully on the umbilical cord and, waiting for the next contraction, she allows the placenta to slide out. She then checks it to see that it is intact. 'Everything perfect, Sarah, a very, very nice birth we are having, I am giving eleven out of ten, no questions asked!' She wraps the newspaper around the placenta and sets it aside for Morrie to examine. 'Now we are looking for the tearing. If the tearing has come, we must wait for Morrie to stitch.' She examines Sarah. 'My goodness, so lucky, so very, very lucky! First birth and always tearing but no tearing, only very small, not needing stitches, your perineum it will be like new in week, you are having spontaneous birth and very nice baby to boots.'

'Oh, she's so beautiful,' Sarah whispers. 'Thank you, thank you, Mrs Rika Ray.'

'Red hair she is having, beautiful like her mother,' Mrs Rika Ray smiles. 'Now, my dear, I must go to kitchen. It is cleaning up we must do, making you and baby clean like a whistle. I am boiling water and bringing basin and changing sheets. Where is Sophie? I am the complete bamboozlement with disappearance of Sophie. A very, very big mystery. She comes first through the window and then she is disappearing in thin air! Abracadabra, I am not knowing where! I must boil kettle now.'

Almost as she says this, there is a furious banging on the front door and Mrs Rika Ray goes out and opens it to find a sobbing Sophie on the other side. 'Just in nick of times you are coming, Sophie, no more midnight wanderings, we are needing boiling water in kettle and clean sheets. You must help me now please.'

'Morrie! Morrie is comink, Sarah will go to 'ospital!' Sophie says tearfully.

'Hot water and basin, Sophie! Sarah is having a baby girl. She has very, very easy pumpkin-pip special, first-class sliding out, a copying-book birth.'

Sophie brings her hands up to her lips, her eyes are wild and terrified. 'Oh my God! The Kommandant, he will kill za baby! We must hide baby, Morrie is comink, he will do it!' She starts to laugh hysterically.

'Hystericals we are not having!' Mrs Rika Ray slaps Sophie hard against the cheek and Sophie grabs at her face and sinks to her knees in the hallway, sobbing, 'I am sorry, I am sorry,' she sobs.

'No time for sorry. Boil water!' Mrs Rika Ray commands. 'I must get the herbs for cleaning and disinfecting.' Sophie gets to her feet and runs into the kitchen and Mrs Rika Ray hears the tap at the sink being turned on and then the sound of the kettle being filled.

Mrs Rika Ray sets about tidying up, removing the newspapers from the bed and the bottom sheet. It isn't long before Sophie enters with the large kitchen kettle, clutching the handle in both hands. She looks at Sarah for the first time and sees the baby, now asleep, on Sarah's breast. 'Thanks to God! Thanks to God!' Sophie cries.

'We are thanking God later, Sophie.' Mrs Rika Ray takes the kettle. 'Now we are cleaning baby and mother and you are helping me.'

But instead Sophie sighs and collapses to the floor in a dead faint.

Mrs Rika Ray brings her around and makes her sit with her back against the bed and she puts Sophie's hand in Sarah's. 'Hello, Sophie, have you seen our little girl?' Sarah says, smiling weakly. Sophie bursts into sobs. *'Ja bede kochala wiecey. Ja przyzekam.'* ('I will love her more than my life, I promise.')

Mrs Rika Ray pours the contents of the kettle into the basin and adds cold water from the jug until she judges it hot enough. Then she taps a few crystals of potassium permanganate (Condy's crystals) into the basin, turning the water purple, and adds the extract of seaweed (iodine). She starts to wash Sarah. When she's finished she takes up a jar of herbal ointment and rubs it into Sarah's thighs and girl parts. 'It is natural analgesic, my dear, for taking away pain.' After she's made Sarah comfortable, she starts to clean the baby, having first thrown the water from Sarah's basin out the window and added fresh water from the kettle and a lighter solution of the previous concoctions. Finally she pats the tiny infant dry and swaddles it tightly in one of the baby blankets Mrs Barrington-Stone has given Sarah and hands the bundle to Sarah, who draws her baby daughter to her breast. The tiny infant, exhausted from the birth, immediately falls asleep again, sucking its thumb. Sarah lifts her baby bundle gently and hands it to Sophie to cuddle.

Sophie is ecstatic. Tears once again run down her cheeks, but this time happy ones. Mrs Rika Ray makes Sarah take a tablespoon of something else she's brought and soon she too is asleep. She then changes the sheets and cleans up the room just as Morrie arrives home, banging the door behind him and running down the hallway.

Sophie's sitting there, holding Sarah's baby. She looks at him. '*All my life. All my life,*' she says quietly in Polish, smiling this huge smile.

Mrs Rika Ray takes the baby from her and puts it on Sarah's chest.

Sophie rises and rushes into Morrie's arms, 'Morrie, you have come just in time!'

Morrie laughs, 'I am in time for what? The christening?' He walks over, takes the baby from Mrs Rika Ray and places it at the end of the bed. Then he unswaddles her and checks for any abnormalities, examining for a hernia, looking to see that the spine is straight, or if there are any birthmarks. After he sees that the baby's palate is intact, he tidies up the navel. Sarah's daughter doesn't much care for all this extra fuss and yells her tiny head off. Morrie pronounces the infant perfect in all respects, then swaddles her again and hands her to Sophie.

'You hold, my darlink, we check Sarah now.' He pulls back the sheets and presses on Sarah's tummy and finds it is soft and doughlike. 'Perfect,' he says, then he examines her perineum, 'No sutures needed.' He pulls the sheets back over Sarah, who smiles, drowsy from the stuff Mrs Rika Ray has given her. 'A spontaneous birth, that is wonderful for a first child. Congratulations, my dear. *Mazeltov*!'

Sarah can't keep her eyes open but smiles. 'Mrs Rika Ray was wonder–' She doesn't complete the sentence before she's asleep again.

Morrie turns at last to Mrs Rika Ray and, moving close to her, embraces her. 'We are grateful more than we can say, you too, Mrs Rika Ray. Now you are also our Australian family. Thank you, thank you, from za bottom of za heart.'

It's been a long time since Mrs Rika Ray has been hugged by

someone who loves her and she doesn't know whether to cry or laugh. 'I also, I am happy from my heart's bottom!' she says, tears rolling down her cheeks.

About this time with Sarah's baby asleep in Sophie's arms and Sarah now a mother, the remainder of the Maloney family are on the road to Melbourne. Nancy is driving and refuses to go more than twenty miles an hour, which is twice as fast as she goes when we're collecting the garbage, so, as far as she's concerned, she's practically racing. In some places where the road is narrow, cars are banked up for a mile behind us, some hooting with the driver's arm out the window trying to urge us to go faster. You can almost see the steam coming out of their ears. We pretend not to hear their angry shouts when they eventually pass us.

Little Colleen's in front with Nancy and the rest of us are in the back with the bed, double mattress and Singer sewing machine and Bitzers One to Five, who have arranged themselves around the perimeter of the back of the Diamond T so that their noses can catch the breeze. Bozo has given them permission to bark and they're having a real nice time barking at passing cars, cows, sheep and the occasional horse grazing in a paddock.

'Should make it around Christmas,' Mike says with a sigh.

But the good thing is that the old Diamond T hasn't broken down.

'It's a bloody miracle,' Bozo declares. 'Old bugger must be showin' off with its borrowed tyres, don't tell him it's only for the trip to Melbourne.' He's got his tool box with him, a spare radiator hose, spark plugs, a tin of engine oil and a four-gallon can of water. The Diamond T is farting smoke out the exhaust like it's in a chimney-blowing competition, but that's nothing unusual, nor is the clapping of the tappets in the engine, which sound like a kid banging on a tin drum. The only mishap was when some cows decide to cross the road and Nancy slams on the brakes and the Diamond T swerves to the edge of the road and skids on the gravel and then stops with a jerk. The Singer sewing machine, which we've tied to the back with a rope, breaks loose and, because it's on these little metal wheels, it goes sliding across the end of the Diamond T and slams into the opposite side. But when we examined it, it didn't seem to be any the worse for wear, a scratch on the side that Bozo said he could get out and revarnish when we got home. Otherwise the trip was easy with no other problems.

Seven hours later we arrive with a clank and a snort and a single backfire outside the Carlton terrace. A whole lot of kids are playing in the street and one shouts out, 'Jeez, look at the old bomb!' They all rush over and stand on the pavement with their hands behind their backs staring at us and one little girl says slowly, 'Maloney & Sons – Garbage', reading the side of the truck. They all giggle.

'G'arn, git!' Mike says and they all run away, yelling 'Maloney & Sons – Garbage! Maloney Garbage!' Bozo gives Bitzers One to Five permission to bark and so everyone in the street knows we've arrived.

Suddenly the door opens and there, standing in Sophie's pink dressing gown is Sarah, smiling and holding this little bundle in a blue blanket.

Well, I've never seen Nancy so over the moon! She's grinning and laughing and holding Sarah's baby and kissing its head and making snoofy sounds and touching it on the nose with her finger and swinging around and doing a little dance.

When she hears the story of the delivery, suddenly Mrs Rika Ray and she are blood sisters forever. All is forgiven in the instant. Nancy, as the grandmother, promptly pronounces Mrs Rika Ray one of the godmothers on the spot. Sophie and Morrie are like proud parents and Sarah, who has slept practically the whole morning, gives us all a hug and I must say, I know she's my sister, but her hair is brushed and the sun is catching it and it's shining like a sort of blaze and she is beautiful. Even someone like me can see that.

Sophie's been baking all morning and there's something she calls *cholent*, which is sort of like a stew with meat and beans and Jewish stuff that she explains is cooked real slow. It's been in a low oven all Friday night and all day until dinner at noon, because Jews aren't supposed to light a fire on a Saturday. She calls Saturday '*Shabbat*'. Only, she says, she and Morrie are not kosher and they can light a fire if they want but cholent is a tradition. I don't know about a tradition, but I'm telling you, it's the best stew I've tasted in the history of the world! Then there's *latkes*, which are fried potato cakes, sort of made very light, but they taste better even than chips and she's made this apple strudel with fresh cream and we all decide that perhaps we ought to stay forever. All except Bozo, because he's et hardly anything and says he's not hungry. Sophie is a bit upset, but Bozo explains it ain't the food, it's just he's not hungry.

Nancy, who's tucking in a treat, says, 'If you're sick, you'll have to have castor oil!'

Mrs Rika Ray says castor oil isn't good for him, she'll give him something. But Bozo says, no, he's fine, just not hungry, that he'll be hungry tonight for sure.

'That's good,' Sophie says. 'Tonight we eat chicken soup and *geroicherte flaysh mit kroit* (I only learned how to say that later, but it's stew with cabbage) and *honig lekach*, which turns out to be honey cake. Mrs Rika Ray is cooking something special too.

After we've had our tea, Bozo comes up to me, real casual like. 'Hey, Mole, Big Jack Donovan's telephoned Kevin Flanagan so I can visit the Russell Street police gym. Wanna come with me?' He looks at me and I can see he wants me to come. 'We could go in a tram?' he offers, bribing me.

I'd been sort of hoping him and me and Mike could have a look around Melbourne in the afternoon. Go walkabout in Collins Street and those other places we've only heard about, the Myers shop that's got the biggest toy department in the Southern Hemisphere. We've never been in the city proper, just the showgrounds. Though, I have to admit, riding in a tram would be something else. 'We haven't got any money for the tram,' I say.

'Yeah, got plenty,' he replies and puts his hand in his pocket and pulls out two bob. 'Wanna come?' He must have sold something he's fixed up before we come down.

Then I see he's brought his boxing gloves, the ones Tommy give him for Christmas. It don't take too many brains to work out what he's got in mind. He's hardly eaten any of Sophie's champion grub, which means he's going to try to have a spar with the featherweight who's in the running to go to the Olympics. The bloke who's seventeen and Kevin Flanagan said would be much too good for him.

Chapter Thirteen

I don't know how Bozo does things, I mean he's only been to Melbourne twice, once to the Show and the next time to tune the Austin 7 ready for Sarah's getaway, but he knows exactly what trams to catch to get us to the Russell Street gym. We walk to Nicholson Street, where we catch the tram to the city and Bozo asks the conductor to put us off at Russell Street. Sounds simple enough but the thing is he took the trouble to find out before.

Bozo thinks about things more than me or Mike, even Sarah. Right from when we were small he's always had a bob in his pocket. Nancy says she doesn't know where he gets the nous from, no Maloney ever had a shilling to spare, money always burns a hole in our pockets. It was him thought about fixing junk up and selling it, he's a natural trader.

To give you an example, there's the time in January when Toby Forbes wanted a special weekday delivery of the *Gazette*. He had six clearing sales advertised for the coming weekend and came to see us about an early-morning drop when we did the garbage. He always pays on the nail, not a fortune, but there's usually five bob in it for each of us. Bozo's got three lawnmowers he's fixed and painted and then re-varnished the wooden handles but hasn't managed to sell to the second-hand shop in Wangaratta, so he says to Toby Forbes that we'll do his drop for nothing if he gives us two advertisements in the *Gazette*.

Toby Forbes agrees and Mike does up this little advertisement which is clever as anything and which says:

Bozo
'THE BOY BOXER'
BARGAINS!
THREE KNOCK-OUT
LAWNMOWERS
FOR SALE
ONLY 40/- EACH.
Hurry
DON'T LET THE GRASS
GROW UNDER YOUR
//////**feet**//////

Before you can say 'Jack Robinson!', the lawnmowers are sold and we don't even need the second advertisement, which Bozo can now use for something else he wants to sell. He reckons Joe Turkey, who has the second-hand shop and junkyard in Wang, would have given him fifteen shillings each, at the most a quid.

Bozo gives Mike ten bob because he did the advertisement, Nancy the same because he couldn't give her less than Mike, and me seven and sixpence, which is more than the pound Toby Forbes would have paid us altogether for dropping off the *Gazette*, so we're happy as Larry and he's still made an extra one pound, twelve and sixpence more than he would have made if he'd sold them to Joe Turkey. Not bad, eh?

Nancy says Bozo's the only one of us she'll never have to worry about because he's got his head screwed on right. Although she always says after, 'That is, if he doesn't get his brains mashed in the boxing ring!'

The tram ride was beaut, it sort of clanks and rattles but is also smooth at times and everything has to get out of the way. The tram is boss of the road and it feels pretty important trundling along with it swaying and clickety-clacking, coasting along and then suddenly surging. You could stay on it all day and not get tired of riding in it. I've still got to go in a train so I can't compare the experience, but it would have to be pretty good to beat the tram and we got to see a fair bit of the city as we went along.

We arrive at the Russell Street Police Headquarters and ask a cop coming out of the building to direct us to the gym. When we get there, we can hardly believe our eyes. There's five boxing rings, and boxing bags and speedballs and weight-lifting gear and stuff we've never seen before. The gym is full of boxers working out on the equipment, skipping, shadow-boxing in front of this big mirror, knocking the crap out of the heavy punching bags and blurring the speedball. Every ring is occupied. There's a helluva racket. It's not just boxers hitting punching bags and the skipping rope whipping the jarrah floor, but instructors are yelling at their boxers in the ring and there's a smell of liniment, sweat and physical exertion.

Bozo and me just stand there with our mouths half-open. We've never seen anything like this before. Bozo's got his gloves hanging around his neck and the rest of his clobber, his boxing boots and trunks together with his jockstrap, mouthpiece and a small towel, in an old sports bag he's carrying.

'Jesus, Mole, have a decko at that!' he says, almost under his breath.

'This is the big time, Bozo,' I reply. 'I suppose they're all going to the Olympics, hey?'

We're both a bit, you know, intimidated. Where to go? What to do next? It's like walking into a sort of cathedral, only with noise. Nobody's taking any notice of us, we're just a couple of kids standing at the door gawking. Then I see Mr Flanagan come out of a door at the far end and move to the ring furthest from us, where there's two young boxers sparring with another trainer in charge.

'That's him!' I say. Bozo nods and we start to walk towards the far ring, careful not to get in the way of any of the boxers, of which there must have been about thirty altogether. We get to where Kevin Flanagan is standing with his arms folded, he's got his back to us concentrating on the boxers in the ring and doesn't even see us. We know we'll have to wait until he's got a moment. Bozo's watching one of the boxers, who seems the better of the two, and he's the one Flanagan's mostly yelling instructions at.

'Box him, Johnny, go in fast, come out fast, don't mix it, move, lad!' Kevin Flanagan shouts up at the ring.

'That's him,' Bozo says, almost as though he's speaking to himself.

'Who?'

'The flyweight.'

I can see this bloke's a flyweight, 'So?'

'The one Mr Flanagan says will be too good for me.'

Just then Kevin Flanagan sees us. 'Hello there, Bozo, thought you might show up today, got a bell from Big Jack Donovan about you coming.'

'Afternoon, Mr Flanagan,' Bozo says and I say the same.

'Afternoon, lads.' He shouts to the two boxers sparring, 'That'll do for a moment, take five, stay warm.'

The two boxers stop and the bloke who's been in the ring with them puts a towel around each of their shoulders. The boxers climb down through the ropes. 'Let me introduce you,' Kevin Flanagan says. 'Bozo Maloney, Johnny Thomas and Eddie Blake.' He points to the coach still standing in the ring, 'And Mr Jones.'

'Gidday,' they both say, not too interested. Johnny Thomas doesn't even look up. Mr Jones nods his head.

'And Mole Maloney.'

'Gidday,' we say to the two boxers, then 'Good afternoon' to Mr Jones.

Thomas now looks up, 'Bozo and Mole, they your real names, that what yer was christened?'

'Yup,' says Bozo. 'What's it to you?'

I can't believe my ears, Bozo's not the sort to pick a fight, not outside the ring anyway. Besides we wasn't christened those names.

Johnny Thomas laughs. 'Bozo's a clown's name, mate. You a bit of a clown then?' He's got his head to one side and this little smile, you just know he's a real smart-arse.

Bozo looks him in the eyes. 'And a mole is a rodent.' He turns to me, 'What d'ya reckon, Mole, think we've got stupid names?'

'Whoa there, lads!' Mr Flanagan interjects. 'Steady on, Johnny, you too, Bozo.'

'Sure,' Thomas says, 'but they've still got bloody stupid names.'

'That's enough, boys,' Mr Flanagan says and turns to Bozo and me. 'Come, I'll show you around. There's everything here you could wish for, all mod cons, no expense spared, reckon we'd have got bugger-all from the government, wasn't for the Olympics. Now we just have to ask.'

Bozo looks down at his boots then up at Johnny Thomas. 'I'd rather spar with him, Mr Flanagan,' he says, pointing to Thomas.

'Now then, Bozo, Johnny here is three or four years older than you, don't be impatient, mate.'

'Who's he think he is?' Thomas says, pushing his glove out so it touches Bozo's chest.

Bozo knocks Thomas's arm away, not even looking at him, addressing himself to Mr Flanagan. 'It's only sparring, sir,' Bozo says quickly, 'If I get taught a lesson, that's why I came.'

Kevin Flanagan shakes his head, 'I dunno, Bozo, some lessons ought to wait a bit.'

'Please, Mr Flanagan, we've driven seven hours, special to get here.' He looks up at Johnny Thomas and grins. 'I'll never get another chance to get into the ring with someone like John Thomas, who's gunna be in the Olympics and who is named after a big prick.'

I can't believe I'm hearing this, Bozo taking the piss. Thomas is going to slaughterate him. (Maloney word.)

'Shit, who the fuck do you think you are? Cheeky sod!' Thomas says. You can see now he's *really* cranky. 'I'm ready, Bozo the clown, any time, mate! How about right now?' He makes as if to climb back into the ring, turning and grabbing the bottom rope.

'Please, Mr Flanagan, just give me three sparring rounds. I want to see what it's like to spar with someone who's *really* good.' The way Bozo says it you can't tell whether he's being sarcastic or means it. I think he means it, because Bozo isn't like Mike and doesn't come on all sarcastic at the drop of a hat. But you can see Thomas thinks Bozo's mocking him again.

Flanagan laughs, 'Jimmy Black was *really* good, Bozo.'

Bozo indicates Thomas with a nod of his chin, 'Yeah, but you said he's better.'

'Okay, Bozo, we'll put you through your paces, see how you go, but I'm stopping it at any time I think, you understand?'

Bozo shakes his head. I've never seen him like this. 'Give me one round first please, Mr Flanagan? One round where whatever happens you don't stop us. After that, whatever you say, sir.'

Eddie Blake, the other boxer, hasn't said a word up to this point. Now he looks at Bozo, his head to one side, and he sort of smiles like Thomas did previously. 'You'll be bloody lucky to get through it, mate.' Now he's taken his mouthpiece out, I can see he's got two front teeth missing, 'Johnny's gunna eat yiz for breakfast.'

'Breakfast's already over, it's after lunch,' I say, which is real dumb, you'd expect a little kid to say a thing like that.

Kevin Flanagan grins and puts his hand on Bozo's shoulder. 'Big Jack says you're a stubborn little bugger, more guts than is spilled on an abattoir floor. It's not always enough, son. Better think about it, eh? Johnny here is a very good boxer.'

'Then let me find that out for myself, sir,' Bozo pleads.

Kevin Flanagan shakes his head and sighs. 'G'arn then, get your gear on.' He points to the change room. 'There's headgear in the big box, wear it.' He looks up at Thomas, 'You too, Johnny, put your headguard back on when you go back in the ring and, in the meantime, stay warm.' Then he calls to Bozo again, 'When you've got your clobber on, get onto the speedball, then five minutes on the skipping rope, I don't want you going into the ring cold. Have you got a jockstrap and a mouthpiece?' Bozo nods and we go into the dressing room.

'Shit, Bozo, what the fuck are you doing?' I yell at him. 'That bastard is going to the Olympics. You heard Mr Flanagan, he's a class act and he's three years older than you.'

'So?' Bozo says.

'So he's had three years' more experience!'

Bozo looks at me and laughs, 'Mostly with his mouth I'd say. Did you see his build? He's not had my experience lifting rubbish bins. I don't suppose I'll beat him, but I reckon I've got the strength to stay in there with him. Just hope I've got the speed to hit him back. Be a bit embarrassin' otherwise. I guess that's what I'm here to find out.'

'And have him give you a bloody good hiding in the process?'

Bozo grins again. 'Mole, everyone gets to take a licking somewhere along the way. We've been fighting in Yankalillee and all the country shires since I was twelve and I ain't been beat yet, how am I gunna know if I'm any good unless I get whupped by someone I can respect? What if I've been fighting mug lairs all the way? Country bumpkins like us who don't know diddly-squat?'

'Jimmy Black wasn't a mug! You heard Mr Flanagan say so yourself.'

Bozo shrugs, then starts to pull on his boxing boots, concentrating on doing up the laces. 'Jimmy Black hadn't trained in six weeks, his timing was out, he smokes like a chimney. Someone said they saw him pissed, fallin' about outside a pub in Albury a couple of nights before the fight. Truth is, Jimmy Black ran out of puff halfway through the second round. Kevin Flanagan knew that, he just didn't say. I'm a big hero in Yankalillee for fighting an Abo bloke who was way out of condition and who beat me in the first round when he still had some puff left.'

'So now you have to show you're an even bigger hero by fighting a white bloke who's in tiptop shape and is probably going to the Olympics?' I wish Mike was here, Mike would give Bozo a real tongue-lashing.

Bozo ties the lace of the second boot and then sits up and looks at me. 'I'll be eighteen when the next Olympics comes around. If I'm going to make it, I'm gunna have to fight in the city where the real boxing talent is, where I can be seen. You know what that means, Mole?'

'No, what? You mean you'll have to leave Yankalillee? Leave us?' I can't imagine life without my brothers, Bozo in particular. There's a sort of hole in me since Sarah's gone.

'Nah, it means catching the train to Melbourne every weekend, sleeping over at Sarah's and coming back the next day. It means using all the money I can make fixing things for my boxing career, it's two pounds, sixteen shillings and threepence there and back every week.'

It's just like Bozo to have worked it all out already. To have done the sums. Now he looks at me, he's got this real serious expression on his face. 'Look, mate, now's my chance to find out whether it's gunna be worth it. Whether I've got what it takes? Find out what my chances are if I work my arse off to go to the Olympics in four years. If this bloke gives me a real good belting today and if I don't reckon I can reach his standard, then perhaps I'll be able to make up me mind, see.' He grins, 'One way or t'other, I'll know if Bozo Maloney is good enough to go all the way.'

Like I said earlier, Bozo doesn't do nothing without thinking about it first. He's the original spoon-out-of-the-sink boy. On the other hand, just going into the ring with Thomas is, in my opinion, a whole drawer full of cutlery left lying in the bottom of the sink. If he's thought this whole thing out, like he suggests, and if getting a boxing lesson is part of his plan, my only hope is that my brother doesn't get the boxing lesson of his life and gets himself hurt bad in the process.

Bozo now goes to this big box in the dressing room that's filled with headgear and gloves, all of them almost new, and he takes one out that's black.

'Take that one,' I say, pointing to this beaut-looking red headguard.

'What's the diff?'

'It'll make you look tougher,' I tell him. But really it's Mike's influence on me, Bozo's boxing gloves are red and now so is the headgear, what Mike calls colour co-ordination. Bozo's got white trunks with a dark-blue stripe down the side. So now it's red, white and blue, that's your colour co-ordination. But I can't say that to Bozo, so I add, 'I saw this picture of Joe Louis when he was heavyweight champion of the world and he had red headgear on.'

Bozo laughs, 'Joe Louis, eh? Mole, you're whacked in the head,' but he picks up the red one and I do up the chin strap for him. Then I help him with his boxing gloves. I like tying the gloves, it's sort of tough, like you belong to something that's men's business which women don't know about and if you tie them just right it could influence the result of the fight. I know that's stupid, but it's what you feel.

We leave the changing room and find a speedball that isn't being used. Thomas is close by, he's removed his gloves and is having a go with the skipping rope making it sing, *whurr-whurr-whurr*, doing twists and whirls and figures of eight and generally drawing attention to himself. You can tell he likes himself a whole heap.

Bozo goes to work on the speedball until his back and arms and neck are shiny with sweat. Then he does the skipping rope, just fast and plain, Bozo doesn't know how to show off, it's not part of his nature. He's one of those boxers the punters like straight off, all business in the ring and someone they always know is going to give them one hundred per cent. He's a pretty good-looking kid too, so the sheilas love him as well.

'Righto,' Mr Flanagan says, 'Lemme see your gloves, lads.' He examines the gloves, unties Bozo's left glove and does it up again. I blush for shame. I've done it lots of times and nobody's said anything before. Mr Flanagan looks at Thomas's gloves and nods. 'In the ring, boys. Bozo, you take the blue corner.'

The two of them climb up into the ring and so does Kevin Flanagan. Thomas is snuffling and snorting into his gloves and smacking them together and looking tough, half-spitting out his mouthpiece and then drawing it back into his mouth again, setting about the business of intimidating Bozo. He's also walking around and throwing punches in the air and looking over at Bozo's corner, trying to catch his eye.

I don't know how Bozo feels, but, I'm tellin' ya, Thomas is doing a damn good job on me, I get this real scared feeling just looking at him. I forgot to say he's got this thin moustache like Errol Flynn, which helps make him look real nasty. If Johnny Thomas is as cranky as I think he is, then sparks are gunna fly.

On the other hand, just looking at Bozo, you'd think he was half-asleep because he doesn't appear to notice Thomas. He stands in his corner with his arms by his sides, his head down looking at the floor. But that's the thing, see. Bozo standing there makes you feel confident. He's got this silence about him, no fuss . . . he's, well, just Bozo Maloney, the Boy Boxer you can trust.

Some sort of buzz must have gone around the gym because several boxers have stopped what they're doing and they've come over to watch. The thing is, they don't know Bozo is several years younger. He's got a better build than Thomas, stronger around the shoulders, and the arms and his stomach muscles can be seen, every one of them perfect, like plaited rope. There's a lot of garbage-bin lifting that's gone into making them look like that. Though mine don't. Maybe when I stop being a kid?

Bozo's father, the Yank marine, was Polish or something. Nancy was never too sure and Bozo's skin is tanned a nice brown, not like the rest of us Maloneys, who've got freckles and turn reddish-pink in the sun. Nancy says it's because we've become overcivilised, primitive Africans are black and we're the extreme opposite. Overcivilised. It don't sound like a Maloney though, does it?

For an Australian, Thomas is white as a Pommie migrant. It doesn't look like he's been out in the sun ever. There's not a freckle, nothing. He's probably spent his whole life in the gym and that's why he's so good. Even I know snow-white skin doesn't mean he isn't tough.

'This is a sparring session, understand?' Mr Flanagan says sternly. 'No funny stuff, okay?' He says this looking at Thomas. 'We'll let it go for the first round, see your form, Bozo, then I'll try to be useful. See if I can help a bit. Couple of things I saw in your fight with Jimmy Black need correcting.'

When he says the name 'Jimmy Black', Thomas looks up suddenly. You remember, Bozo and Jimmy Black had a hard fight which could have gone either way. I don't know if it's Kevin Flanagan's way of telling him that Bozo's gunna be no pushover, or he just means what he says, that Bozo needs a bit of coaching help.

'When I say "break", you break clean. Defend yourself at all times. Obey my commands. All right?'

'Yes, sir,' Bozo says, but Johnny Thomas doesn't even bother to nod, he knows the instructions are for his opponent.

Mr Flanagan takes a stopwatch from his pocket. 'Box!' he calls out.

Both boxers come out of their corners fast and get stuck in right off. Bozo's a body man and he likes to fight close when he can, going for the hook and the left and right uppercut under the heart. Thomas may be the same, but he wants to make quick work of this round when there's no interference from the coach and he's going straight for his opponent's head. Seems silly, Bozo's got a protective headguard on, Thomas must reckon Bozo's jaw is a sufficiently big target.

Both boxers are fast and good defenders. Bozo gets in a good body blow and then tries to move backwards out of range. Thomas lets him have it with a long straight right, a beautiful punch, and Bozo finds himself sitting on the deck. He's up in a flash, almost bouncing off the deck back on to his feet, but he's fooled nobody, it was a terrific punch.

'Stop!' Flanagan shouts. He asks Bozo how he feels, if he's had enough.

'No way,' Bozo grins.

Flanagan wipes his gloves on the front of his shirt and says, 'Box on.'

Thomas has got this sort of half-grin on his face and now he's showboating, his hands hanging loose, his shoulders moving up and down. He's doing a little dance and then he baulks at Bozo, taunting him. He doesn't know it yet, but he's got the wrong fighter, Bozo's not going to worry about anything like that. Bozo continues all business in the ring and he steps forward and catches Thomas with a looping left to the side of the head. Thomas knows he's been hit and he brings his gloves up high. Bozo tries to come in again and Thomas catches him with a good solid right that knocks his head back. The boxers watching wince. Bozo covers up and then steps to the left and Thomas catches him with another right that sends Bozo into the ropes.

The Melbourne boxer is getting on top. He comes in with an uppercut that misses and Bozo goes down below with two lefts followed by two rights, each side of the ribs, hard telling shots that come in lightning fast and Thomas doesn't like it one bit. Bozo pushes Thomas away and gets off the ropes. They move to the centre of the ring and Bozo keeps Thomas away with three left jabs. Thomas is still going for the head. He comes in with a big right hand over the top and whacks Bozo square on the forehead, sending him flying backwards. Thomas is onto him fast and comes in with a looping left which Bozo takes on the point of his shoulder. Then Bozo lets rip with a right uppercut that seats just under the rib cage of the other boxer. It doesn't look much but it's a tremendous punch and Thomas goes into a clinch. Flanagan separates them.

I think the Melbourne boy still thinks Bozo got lucky, because he comes straight back and they slug it out in the centre of the ring until Bozo steps away. Thomas is getting the better of his opponent, throwing more punches, though Bozo is the harder puncher and is doing a lot of damage down below yet there's no telling what effect the frequent body blows are having on Johnny Thomas.

I'm suddenly caught up in the fight, I'm no longer scared for Bozo, who's giving almost as much as he's getting. Thomas is starting to use his feet and he's clearly a very skilful boxer, making Bozo miss badly on a couple of occasions. But Bozo's fast enough to get himself out of trouble and takes a couple of glancing blows that probably would have scored but didn't do any real damage.

Thomas is slowly beginning to realise he's got a fight on his hands and the other boxers watching around the ring are grinning. I don't think Johnny Thomas is the most popular bloke in the gym. Bozo's not backing off and throwing some good hard punches that hit their mark, most of them rips and uppercuts to the body. There's an old saying in boxing, which Big Jack Donovan never tires of quoting, 'Land 'em to the body and sooner or later the head will follow.'

Thomas seems to sense that it isn't a boxing exhibition any longer, that he's got to step up a notch and he throws a left–right combination that's copybook perfect and Bozo stumbles backwards into the ropes, hanging on. The older boxer is onto him in a flash, going for the head. But he doesn't realise how strong the young boxer is. Thomas smashes a left and then a looping right into Bozo's headguard. Bozo brings his gloves up and Thomas gets a good punch into Bozo's ribs. Bozo, if he's hurt, doesn't show it and manages to push Thomas away and move off the ropes, moving laterally so that Thomas has to half-turn. Bozo's got his feet set square and Thomas swings with a big right hand that goes over Bozo's head and throws him slightly off balance, his left glove too high, exposing his gut and ribs. Using the full weight of his shoulders, body and legs, Bozo plants a tremendous left hook into Thomas's solar plexus. All of us feel it. Thomas doubles up, drops to the deck and rolls over onto his back, clutching his stomach with both gloves, his legs in the air.

There's clapping and cheering from the side of the ring. Thomas makes no attempt to get up and Mr Flanagan goes over to him. He's down easily for a ten count before he gets up slowly, first onto his knees then still half-stooping, his hands now cupped over his knackers. He spits out his mouthpiece. 'Foul blow!' he gasps, 'Bastard hit me in the balls!'

There's a howl of laughter from the boxers watching. They've all seen Bozo's punch, an absolute classic left hook well and truly above the waistline, high and hooking upwards under the rib cage, leaving Johnny Thomas with not enough puff to blow a harmonica.

'That'll do, boys,' Mr Flanagan says. 'First round's over, anyway.' His face shows nothing of what he might be feeling. He's seen Bozo twice and twice he's knocked out his opponent. An amateur featherweight can go his whole career without a knock-out. 'Go take a shower, Johnny,' he instructs.

'I'd like to go on with it, the bastard hit me low!'

'Forget it, son, you fought him real dumb! You can do a whole lot better, but that was the best left hook to the solar plexus I've ever seen. If it had been a real bout, you'd have been counted out twice over. That's enough for today, take a shower, we'll talk later.'

Flanagan undoes the lace on Thomas's right glove and pulls it off, leaving him to do the left himself. Thomas is angry and starts to climb through the ropes.

'Where's your manners, lad? Bozo's our guest, now do the right thing, touch gloves!' It's the only sign Flanagan's given that he's ropeable.

Thomas glares at him, but climbs back into the ring. Bozo goes straight over to Thomas. 'Thanks, Johnny, it was real good of you to let me spar.' He smiles at the other boxer. 'You're right, Bozo is a bit of a dumb name.' He holds out his gloves to touch Thomas's. 'But then we're Irish, what can you expect?'

'Get fucked!' Thomas spits, climbing out of the ring without touching Bozo's glove. The other boxers shake their heads. Amateur boxers are supposed to be good sports. What happens in the ring stays in the ring. They don't like what's just occurred, it's their gym and Thomas is shaming them. One of the bigger fighters, a cruiserweight I'd say from looking at him, shouts out, 'That's piss-poor, Thomas, do the decent thing. Shake the man's hand, he whupped you good!' Johnny Thomas doesn't look around but keeps on walking towards the change rooms. If Bozo ever gets to fight him in a real contest, there's gunna be no love lost, I can tell ya.

'Righto, Bozo, there's a couple of things you're doing wrong,' Kevin Flanagan now says. 'If your opponent hadn't been so aggro going in, he'd probably have put you down more than the once. You're stepping directly backwards when you're coming out of a clinch or fighting close and decide to break off, that's as good as helping the other boxer to line up a big punch. He'll cop you, mostly with a right, even a left and a right if he's got the hand speed and the bloke you've just been sparring with could have done so easily enough if he'd been concentrating. It's the easiest way to get yourself knocked out. Move to the sides of your opponent, don't let him get set. Move left or right, keep him off balance. Lateral movement keeps him looking for you, trying to guess where you're going next.

'Also, you're standing too square, you're giving the other boxer the maximum target, your whole body is exposed. Come in with your left shoulder, fight him with the minimum body exposure, make yourself small, a hard-to-hit target, the less he can see, the less he can hit. You're a good boxer, Bozo, but you tend to want to fight, to slug it out. Box smart and the hard hits will come later when your opponent is tired and starts to get sloppy.'

Funny how he never once uses Johnny Thomas's name when he's explaining things to Bozo. Flanagan goes on like this with a whole heap of things. I can't believe Bozo's done so many things wrong and still put Thomas on the deck. But when Mr Flanagan puts him in the ring against Eddie Blake, who's a pretty fair boxer it turns out, it becomes apparent Bozo's caught on fast. Kevin Flanagan stops them several times and demonstrates what he wants. He works with Bozo for half an hour, during which time Thomas has come out of the dressing room in his street clobber and walked straight out of the gym without saying anything to Mr Flanagan or any of the others. He's still pretty aggro and I think maybe he feels humiliated. It's him who's the Olympic prospect and you can't blame him for feeling the way he does, Bozo's just a kid from the bush.

When it's all over, Eddie Blake thanks Bozo and pats him on the back, 'Sorry I said what I done, I should've known better. Bloke don't ask to fight Thomas unless he knows a thing or two.' He smiles his gap-toothed smile, 'Shit, that was a good punch took him out!'

Kevin Flanagan doesn't say well done to Bozo or anything like that but in the dressing room, some of the other boxers who are showering tell him he's done good. 'You in the Olympic trials?' one of them asks.

'Nah, I'm only fourteen,' Bozo tells him.

'Fourteen? Shit, hey? You don't look fourteen. You doing weights?'

'Garbage bins,' Bozo says, not explaining further.

We go over to Mr Flanagan when Bozo's showered and changed and thank him. Bozo's got a black eye starting but is none the worse otherwise. Nancy's going to go crook on him though.

'Nice shiner comin', Bozo, souvenir to take home to Big Jack, eh. I'll give him a call, maybe we need to make a few arrangements to see a bit more of you, son. Four years don't take that long to come around.'

'Thanks, Mr Flanagan,' Bozo says, 'I've learned heaps.'

Flanagan smiles, 'There's a lot more to learn before you can call yourself a champion, Bozo. Maybe we can learn together. Australia's only ever won one Olympic boxing medal, Snowy Baker 1908.'

I'm dead-chuffed and real proud of my brother. Coming home in the tram I tell him so. 'Mate, you done good. See, you did have the speed to hit him.'

Bozo nods. 'Yeah, I was happy about that. Though when he put me on my arse, I didn't see the punch coming.'

'Wait until Kevin Flanagan phones Big Jack Donovan, maybe he'll tell the *Gazette*.'

'Christ, no! I'm not supposed to fight out of my age group, even spar with a seventeen-year-old. Boxing Union could suspend me.' He turns to me, 'Don't tell no one, Mole, you hear? Not even Mike.'

'What about Nancy? She's going to see your shiner.'

'I'll tell her it was an accident, you and I walking along looking at everything and I ran into a lamppost not looking.'

'Ha! She's not that stupid.'

'It'll have to do. You know how she feels about me fighting Thomas, she'll go spare.'

When we get home, Nancy's got a crisis. Her sewing machine doesn't work and there's a whole heap of stuff has to be done for Sophie who is doing piecework for a frock factory and has to have it done by Monday morning. She doesn't even notice Bozo's closed eye and asks him to take a look at the Singer. Bozo says he'll do it right after he's fed the dogs. Nancy has a lot of confidence in Bozo's ability to fix things so she hasn't panicked or anything. She's holding her granddaughter and cooing and bib-bib-bibbling and she doesn't even look up when we come in. Bozo makes himself scarce by going out to the Diamond T and getting the bag of bones and offcuts he's brought for the dogs.

The Bitzers have been in the backyard all afternoon and when Bozo goes over to feed them they go ape. 'It's the smells,' Bozo says, 'They don't know the local smells and they thought they'd been deserted. Dogs depend on smells almost as much as their eyes to know where they are.' Now they jump up and climb all over him, licking his face, yelping their heads off, telling him they love him, more interested in him than they are in the tucker he's putting out.

Mike, of course, sees the eye right off and so does Sarah and we know immediately there's no point in fibbing, the game's over, Sarah's as good as Nancy at not being conned by us kids. 'You tell them, Mole,' Bozo says, sighing.

So I tell them the story and Sarah says we ought to be ashamed, but you can see she doesn't mean it and Mike says we know he thinks boxing's bloody stupid, but he's glad Bozo stuck it to Thomas, who sounds a right bastard. Both of them laugh when I tell them how, after Johnny Thomas had a go at us about our names, Bozo asked how come he'd been named after a prick.

We agree that when Nancy asks, we ought to stick to the lamppost story, feeble as it is.

'It's an AC/GC,' Sarah decides.

Whenever there's general agreement over a matter between us kids, it cancels out the sin of telling a lie and it becomes an AC/GC. Sarah once told us that sometimes parents shouldn't know everything us kids know and, if it doesn't harm Nancy, then it's not a real lie. It's what she calls 'A Conspiracy for the Good of all Concerned', or AC/GC.

Mrs Rika Ray also sees the eye and soon she's back with a poultice made of leaves that look like cooked spinach. Who knows what it is, her remedies are endless. She's been for a walk and on the way she's picked weeds and stuff growing out of the pavements. She's walked all the way to the Fitzroy Gardens in East Melbourne and struck up a conversation with one of the gardeners, who has taken her to the nursery, and she's come back with an armful of herbs and cuttings. She makes Bozo lie flat on his back on the porch as she puts the poultice on his eye. Bozo's not too happy, it's drawing attention to him and he doesn't like that. It's okay in the ring, but outside he doesn't like a fuss being made. After about five minutes, Mrs Rika Ray takes off the poultice.

'We are doing same every hour, three times only, tomorrow you waking up, eye a bit red, but open and not black. Always after the fisty-cuffs you are promising to come, black eyes we are not having, cuts we are not having, bruises we are not having, one hundred per cent Indian guarantee and no arguments, full stop.' She can be pretty formidable when she carries on like that.

Little did we know at the time that Mrs Rika Ray was going to become Bozo's Number One fight fan, never missing a fight, sitting in the front row with a plastic bag of wet herbs on her lap and, whenever possible, with Bitzers One to Five at her feet watching the fight with her. In time, she and they would become almost as famous as Bozo himself.

Everything's been going perfect but we should have known it couldn't last. Now things start going wrong. The first thing is that Bozo can't fix Nancy's sewing machine. When we had to stop because of the cows crossing the road on our way down and the Singer broke loose and banged into the opposite side of the Diamond T, the wheel that holds the belt which drives the treadle must have hit the metal side of the truck and is bent. Bozo tries to straighten it, but he hasn't got the right gear and only makes it worse. There's no getting it fixed until Monday.

But that's not all. Given all the excitement of the birth and Sophie cooking all the delicious tucker for dinner and then again for tea that night, she's way behind with her piecework for the factory in Flinders Lane and, what's more, the shuttle in her sewing machine is playing up as well. It's a hand machine and very old but Bozo gets it going again, but then an hour later it breaks down proper. It's now four o'clock on the Saturday afternoon and there's four people can use a sewing machine and both machines are history.

Even though Sophie and Mrs Rika Ray had been up all Friday

night with the birth of the baby and cooking and caring for everyone the next day, it would have been easy to complete the piecework. The idea was that Nancy and Mike would work all afternoon and late into the night to allow the two other machinists to have eight hours' sleep and then take over. By Sunday morning they would have finished the lot.

Sophie has got this job with Mr Stanislaw Zelinski, who came originally from Klobuck which is in the west of Poland. She reckons she is dead lucky to get the job. Mr Stan, which is what her boss is called by everyone in the frock factory, wants his workers on the premises and except for very skilled hand-finishing, won't have a bar of pieceworkers. *What you can't see, you can't guarantee* is his motto. Sophie, on the other hand, needs piecework if she is to stay at home and look after Sarah's baby.

Being Polish, the same as him, doesn't help Sophie neither. Flinders Lane is full of Polish immigrants who are willing to put up with the primitive conditions and come into the factories to work. What gets her the job in the end, is when she mentions her cousin, Halina Jankowski, who also came from Klobuck and it turns out Mr Stan and her were childhood sweethearts.

Halina, of course, has long since travelled the way of the six million – ghetto–cattle-train–Belsen oblivion. Mr Stan is a concentration-camp survivor the same as Sophie, but so are a lot of the people who work for him, so that was no help whatsoever. For the sake of old-time sentiment and of past-sweetheart tragedy, Mr Stan makes an exception in Sophie's case and allows her to work from home. But first he tells her the rules of the establishment, which she must observe to the letter. Any cabbage must be returned to him with the completed garment. Cabbage is any material over six inches in width that may be left over when a garment is finally sewn up. In time you learn that all of Mr Stan's rules are made into slogans. If you know the slogans, you know exactly what to expect. The Australians who work for Mr Stan have this rhyme they say behind his back:

Oi vey! Stan, Stan za slogan man
Offcuts, please put za cabbage can
Please, every stitch must be on time

You comink late! Zen your pay I fine
Next time late, you not verk again
You can say cheer-o to Flinders Lane
I'm sorry, my dear, zis come to pass
Not on time, you can kiss my arse!

Now Sophie can look after Sarah's baby during the day and still earn enough to help keep the wolf from the door. With Morrie's night job, her job and Sarah's scholarship money, they can pay the rent, put food on the table and have a bit over for petrol and the theatre or the symphony orchestra once a month. Morrie's also bought the second-hand Singer machine for Sophie. The work involved in turning the handle of the sewing machine is very tiring and their very next priority is to trade it in on a second-hand treadle. It's not a bad life and Morrie says they couldn't wish for more, a little food, a little culture, a little learning, freedom from danger and a family with a child to love.

Baby or no baby, the favour granted by Mr Stan doesn't extend to Sophie not meeting her quota. Like everyone else in The Lane, he runs a sweatshop on a shoestring. Sweatshop isn't a dirty word, it just means a frock factory and the frock factories run by Jewish immigrants are always short of money. There's a joke which says they are called sweatshops because the proprietors are always sweating on orders, sweating on deliveries, sweating on credit, sweating on deadlines and a host of other intangibles. Credit is everything and prompt payment for goods is a matter of survival. Work simply can't be late.

Mr Stan has been in business eight years. To start up on his own he borrowed fifty pounds from a moneylender, a Pole called Wolski from the same part of Poland as him who came to Australia before the war and made a lot of money making military uniforms, so the interest on the money was only twenty per cent per annum on the principal with weekly repayments. There is no reduction on the principal until the interest has been paid. Banks wouldn't lend immigrants money and these were generous terms compared to many being offered the Jewish rag traders.

Mr Stan leased a factory in Fitzroy with six machines and a cutting table and two years later moved into Flinders Lane. This was not a big jump on the prosperity ladder but more an opportunity to make small economies that would add up. The conditions of most Flinders Lane premises were appalling but now he could get his buttons and binding, sequins, cottons and fabrics, beads, zips, machine parts and the mechanics to fix them, as well as his designers and pattern-cutters and rat catchers, all on the spot. What might have taken a messenger boy all morning to procure when Mr Stan's factory was in Fitzroy, now takes a matter of minutes and the messenger boy's salary is another few shillings saved.

Then, of course, there is the comfort of having his own kind around him. Everyone knows everyone, The Lane is the beating heart of the *schmatte* business. The clanging of lifts with their brass grilles gives a certain assurance that business is solid. A hundred sewing machines whirring in impossibly cramped quarters is the sound of opportunity beckoning. Trucks backing into tight spaces, the drivers yelling out warnings and hurling abuse, mean orders are completed and soon to be delivered. The squeaking of the clothes racks on the cobblestones below is continuity of purpose and recalls lives spent in other places, where their fathers and their grandfathers cut and stitched and earned a livelihood pushing the same delivery racks along more worn cobbled lanes. The smell of burnt coffee and the hiss of the steam presses remind them that life is urgent and goes on whatever happens. Even the tired ceiling fans swirling fetid air around the factory before pumping it out through the windows into The Lane below are a living, breathing reminder that you have survived another day. Despite the persistent invasion of rats coming up from Queen's Wharf and the clogged and broken lavatories and primitive facilities, they tell themselves that they are in the business of elegance, the fashion trade, a place of rags to riches, where a ball gown can take a year to make and cost five thousand pounds. If the place they work in is freezing in winter with the pecking order on the factory floor determined by one's proximity to the oil heaters, and if in summer they must resort to working in their slips because of the oppressive heat, they are still in a free land where hardship and sacrifice can lead to security and freedom from want. All it will take is work, work, work and a little *mazel*, a little luck.

Flinders Lane is not only a place of work, but also a place of the heart. The Lane is food for the impoverished soul. It is the intellectual and spiritual nourishment needed by a people who have suffered and lost everything and are once again trying to gather sufficient emotional capital together to rebuild their lives. Flinders Lane is a new place in the heart where the word 'Jew' is a description, or, at the very worst, a bigoted though harmless adjective and not a death sentence.

After eight years in the business, with, God forbid, never a debt he couldn't somehow pay, the bank is only just beginning to trust Mr Stan. But then, in Flinders Lane, everything is conditional, nothing is a certainty, trust is a compliment that has to be earned over and over again. Mr Stan has to deliver his garments *On time, every time!*, which is another of his more important slogans. Each season in fashion is a lifetime ago, sometimes even a week or a month is a different age. Mr Stan would explain, 'What was good last week or last month, next month you couldn't give it away!'

With pieceworkers anything can happen and Mr Stan knows this; children get sick, evictions take place, husbands lose jobs, get drunk and smash and bash things, including their wives, home sweet home is a constant tragedy in the process of occurring and reoccurring.

In other words, *What you can't see you can't guarantee*. Mr Stan wants his workers at their Singer sewing machines at nine sharp every morning and he shakes their hands at the front door when they leave at five. 'See you tomorrow, Mrs Kaspowitz, my compliments your husband.' Each garment worker is recognised and accorded a departing remark. 'The sleeves the crystal organza you are doing, very nice, Mrs Adams. Remind me a small bonus.' If they can't get into work because of illness or some domestic problem, Mr Stan expects his workers to call him or to send a message so he has sufficient time to bring in a freelancer for the day and get the maximum work off the floor.

In the harsh world of the *schmatte* business, everyone knows the rules. If Mr Stan doesn't deliver on time to Myers or Mantons, Darrods or Buckley & Nunn or a dozen other emporiums big and small, the entire order, months of work, can be cancelled with the stroke of a pen. There's always someone else. Competition, even with your best friend, is a no-holds-barred business. The big buyers are the whimsical gods of prosperity. They cannot be offended. *A broken promise is a business broken*.

Mr Stan is working for the most part on credit, if he doesn't get paid, his suppliers don't get paid and he's out of business. Of all Mr Stan's many slogans, one is the most important to him. This particular slogan has been painted by an expensive Italian signwriter in big red letters above the door leading to the rows of Singer sewing machines on the factory floor.

IT'S THE SINGER, NOT THE SONG.
IDLE MACHINES SEW NO SEAMS.

Promises don't make profits is another favourite.

Sophie knows the piecework rules. *Not in on the day, means sorry, no pay*, which means that the first time she's late she doesn't get paid for her work. The second time, yet another slogan, *Second time late and you seal your fate*.

Mr Stan speaks like most Polish Jews who have learned their English late. Like Morrie, he gets it right but often his words are the wrong way around. But his slogans are always in proper English and there's no mistaking their meaning.

While a few of his factory workers are Australian, most are refugees, migrant women who speak almost no English, so that the rhyming in Mr Stan's slogans is meaningless to them, but they soon catch on that the sentiments they express are not negotiable. Mr Stan is fair, pays overtime at slightly above union rates and treats them well. Good work earns a two shilling bonus at the end of the day. At Christmas he throws a party for his staff with gifts for their children, even though most of his workers are Jewish. He explains this simply as 'custom of the new land', which becomes the all-embracing explanation for anything that can't be readily explained.

Above all, his slogans are his business, break them and you break him. To show he means what he says, he works twice as hard as anyone else and puts in twelve hours a day, six days a week, and so does his family. On the Sabbath (Saturday) he does the books. *God looks when we do the books*. Often he and the family are simply too busy to go to synagogue. *God understands busy hands*. Mr Stan is credited with a famous saying in The Lane. It is supposed to have occurred outside *Shul* one Saturday when the rabbi noted, a little sharply, that he hadn't seen him in synagogue in over a month. 'Rabbi, personally I am not so worried, everyone in the *schmatte* business will go to heaven because already they have been to hell.'

Sophie, if she has to, can probably afford to lose the pay she won't get if she can't deliver first thing Monday morning. After all, a baby doesn't come along every day, does it? But she can't afford the *Second time late, you seal your fate* clause. Mr Stan makes no exceptions. 'Why you think za word sentimental got za word *mental* in it? For sentimental I got no slogan!' he would say. Sophie was simply too nervous a type of person to have the threat of instant dismissal hanging over her head if she was ever late a second time. So what to do? The answer is, there is nothing they can do, they're stuffed, might as well relax.

Bozo and me decide to take the Bitzers for a walk. We invite Mike but he says he wants to talk to Sarah when she wakes up about talking to Nancy about him working in Melbourne. On the way we gather up a bunch of young kids who like the dogs. Station Street is full of kids playing and soon there must be twenty or more traipsing behind us. By the time we get back outside the house we're all mates and just for fun Bozo puts Bitzers One to Five through their paces.

The kids love the show and the Bitzers love doing it, so Bozo keeps going. Soon, quite a crowd gathers and there are almost as many grown-ups as kids, with women in aprons and slippers coming out of their kitchens to have a squiz. Bozo's Bitzers are good performers and he's been told lots of times he could make a quid if he took the act to the RSL clubs.

Bozo's dogs are good all-round but Bitzer Five, the Silky–Pomeranian mix does this special trick that brings the house down every time. He can piss standing on his front legs with his back legs in the air. Fair dinkum, that's what he can do! So Bozo's just about finished his routine and all the dogs are sitting in a straight line in front of him, tongues lolling, waiting for instructions. Each one of them can do a trick that's his very own and you can see they're all hoping they'll be the one to be picked next. The crowd want more action so Bozo points to Bitzer Five.

'Bitzer Five, handstand with golden squirt!' he commands.

All Bozo's dog tricks have names like that, 'Roll over rover', 'See you later alligator' and so on. Some of them are also accompanied by a certain number of claps, which tells the Bitzers when to perform a particular trick. Bitzer Five jumps out of the ranks and comes and sits at Bozo's feet, tail wagging like mad. You can see he's going to do his best. Bozo claps three times and Bitzer Five is up and moves over to the telegraph pole and gives it a bit of a sniff first, sees who's been there before him the way dogs do. Sniff-sniff he goes and this gets a laugh, even though they must have seen a dog doing this a squillion times over. Then Bitzer Five turns so his bum is facing the pole and waits. Bozo claps three more times and the little dog ups onto his front legs with the back legs in the air and splashes the pole with a golden stream, holding his balance perfectly until he's finished.

The crowd goes wild. They've never seen a dog do such a thing before. Bitzer Five then rejoins the ranks, licking his chops and looking very chuffed with himself. Then this loud voice from the back says, 'You ought to be arrested, son, dog messing the pavement like that!'

Everyone parts to let this cove come through. 'Afternoon, Mr Lovegrove,' a few of the adults say, but they're smiling and he's smiling, like you can see he doesn't mean what he's just said.

Bozo says quickly, 'About turn!' and all the Bitzers up and turn, facing in the direction of the bloke coming towards us and they sit up on their bums, front legs in the air. 'Say gidday, the Maloney way!' Bozo commands and each Bitzer waves his right paw. This brings a roar from the crowd and this Lovegrove bloke breaks up. 'Stand at ease!' Bozo shouts and the dogs bring their paws down again and drop to the footpath.

'How's young Sarah?' Mr Lovegrove asks right off. 'Had her baby yet?'

I don't know how he happens to know about Sarah but Bozo replies, 'Early this mornin', a little girl, sir.'

'Congratulations, she's a tribute to the working classes. I'm glad she won in the university debacle.' Who is this bloke? I think he must know Morrie or maybe even Sarah. He's got a look of authority, like a headmaster. You know, a man who's used to talking to people and also being listened to. He must have been reading my thoughts, because now he says, 'Denis Lovegrove, Member for Carlton.' He looks at Bozo and then at me, 'And you are?'

'Bozo and Mole Maloney, sir, Sarah's brothers,' Bozo answers for both of us.

'Nice shiner, Bozo, had a scrap, did ya?'

'Sort of, sir. Boxing, sir.'

'Boxing, eh? Damn good sport for a lad. Teaches you independence. You're down from the country for the birth then, are you?'

'Yes, sir, Yankalillee.'

'Well, I can see you're a talented family, you've done a damn good job on those mutts.'

'Thank you, sir.'

'Bozo, thanks for the show, it was damned good.' He turns to the crowd, 'Wasn't it, folks?' They're cheering and clapping and one or two even whistle. Mr Lovegrove then turns back to Bozo. 'You tell Sarah we're proud of her and congratulations, she's got a lot of guts. I had a word about her situation in parliament recently, high time women stepped up and claimed their rights.' I can see he's taken the opportunity to tell this to the crowd and not to me and Bozo. There's a bit of a murmur as people realise that Sarah lives in the same street as them and a few of them clap again. Sarah's become pretty famous after what's gone on.

'Thank you, sir,' Bozo says.

'You tell her, anything I can do to help, just to give me a call,' Lovegrove looks at us, 'I mean it, lad, the working class has to stick together. Anything she needs, call me.'

My mouth falls open when Bozo says, 'Well, sir, there *is* something.'

Mr Lovegrove shows surprise. I guess he says it a lot, not expecting to be taken up right off the way Bozo's just done.

'What is it, son?'

Bozo explains about Sophie and her piecework and how, because of Sarah's baby, she's behind and also her machine has broken down and the one we brought has as well. If she doesn't get the stuff in on time, which is Monday morning, she'll be sacked. It's a bit of a lie, because it will be only her pay that's docked. 'Sir, there's four of us can sew,' Bozo continues, 'we were wondering if someone here could maybe hire us a sewing machine for today and termorra?'

'Hear that?' Denis Lovegrove yells out. 'Anyone here willing to hire their sewing machine to the Maloneys for today and all of tomorrow, they're in a spot of bother with piecework for the frock factories?'

Hire? Maybe Bozo's got some money, but I know all Nancy's got in her purse is the petrol money to get us home. Morrie and Sophie are skint and Mrs Rika Ray has done nothing but complain about the train fare from Wangaratta since she's come. Who knows what hiring a sewing machine would cost.

Two women put up their hands, then one says, 'He's a good kid, putting on a show for us like he done, he can borrow my Singer treadle. I don't want no money, done piecework meself. Kid's right, she'll lose her job!'

'Yeah, he can have ours as well,' a second woman says, 'for free also.'

Lovegrove turns to Bozo, 'Could you use two?'

Bozo grins. 'Couldn't be better, sir.'

With two treadle machines on the go and the four of them working, we'll shit it in! Even I know that.

'There you go, Bozo,' Lovegrove says, pleased. He turns to the crowd. 'That's the Carlton spirit, neighbours looking after each other, wouldn't see that happening in Toorak now, would you? The two ladies, your names, please?'

'Dot!' one shouts out.

'Betty!' says the other.

'A big clap for Dot and Betty, ladies and gentlemen! Two very generous people.'

Everyone claps and Lovegrove shakes Bozo's hand and then mine and Bozo brings the Bitzers to attention in a straight line. 'See yer later alligator!' he commands and they're up, balanced on their bums, but this time they're waving both paws at the Member for Carlton and they bark 'Whoof!', just the once in unison. Everyone laughs.

Betty and Dot get their husbands and one of Dot's sons to help us lug their sewing machines to the house.

Well, needless to say, with two sewing machines going flat-out between Nancy and Mike, who work past midnight, and Mrs Rika Ray and Sophie, who went to bed at seven o'clock with Nancy waking them at one in the morning to take over, Sophie's piecework is complete before breakfast on Sunday morning.

Nancy says to Sarah to find out if Dot and Betty have daughters or sons who are going to have a baby. You can bet your prize booties and bib there's a brown-paper parcel coming their way.

We've decided to leave for Yankalillee straight after breakfast as Bozo is dead concerned something bad might happen to the Diamond T. We have to allow time to repair it on the road, so that we can get it back to John Crowe to change the tyres on the Fargo before work.

'Can't get lucky twice,' Bozo warns. 'Somethin's gotta go wrong.'

Nancy has come to her senses and sees she's not needed and will only be in Sarah's way. Mrs Rika Ray says she'll come home with us and insists on giving Nancy ten shillings towards the petrol. Nancy feels honour has been restored. Having been up till very late Saturday night sewing, Nancy says she's too buggered to drive through Melbourne until we come to the highway where Bozo was going to take over. So Bozo takes over right off from Station Street. We're all shitting ourselves in case we're stopped by a cop and Bozo's asked for his driving licence.

But it's a magic weekend. Bozo says that after the sewing machines, we're bulletproof. First Sarah's baby, then the fight, then getting Sophie out of trouble and, believe it or not, the Diamond T holds out and we don't see a cop the whole way and get back to Yankalillee at four o'clock in the afternoon.

We unload the double bed and the Singer, and Bozo gets to John Crowe's place just as it's getting dark. They drive to the shire workshops, do the deed with the tyres, and Bozo's home by six with the Diamond T back to its old miserable self. All I can say is the Maloney luck has definitely turned. Nancy says that when a baby is born in a family, God smiles and grants you forty-eight hours' grace. I think that must be something else she was told by the nuns. But it turns out to be true, nothing's gone wrong since Sarah's baby was born.

Only thing is, Mike's not his usual self. Coming home in the back of the Diamond T, he, like Nancy, is tired from being up so late Saturday night. He's stretched out on the double-bed mattress at the back of the truck and I can see he's worried about something because there's no quips or sarcastic remarks coming from him. Something's happened but he doesn't say. Maybe because Mrs Rika Ray is in the back with us. We drop her off at Silver Creek and Nancy has a bit of a howl as she hugs poor old Mrs Rika Ray and nearly smothers her to death in the process. I reckon they're gunna be mates forever now that she's got the baby safely out of Sarah.

Then at tea, Nancy, who's slept all the way back and is now awake, says there's a family discussion on. We haven't had too many of these since Sarah left, because it was her who usually got Nancy to hold one if there was anything the family needed to discuss. Mostly it was stuff Nancy had decided on and Sarah felt wasn't the best decision, so she'd persuade Nancy to have a family discussion. The discussions were good, because we all got to have a say and made up our minds sort of together. Well, sometimes, anyway. Unfortunately Nancy could put the kybosh on anything if she wants to, with an overriding vote. But sometimes she's fair.

Tommy is home again and because it's Sunday and the pubs are closed, he can't wet the baby's head neither, so it's also good to have him in on the discussion.

'We've got two things to discuss tonight,' Nancy says, as she's cutting up this strudel cake Sophie's made for us. Mike's sitting next to her and he's pouring out our tea into mugs and still looking worried. 'First one's Mike,' Nancy announces. 'You all know he wants to pack in school and go and work in Melbourne, learn to design frocks.'

'Ladies' dresses, Mum! Frocks are not designed, they're just sewn.'

'Dresses then. As you know I'm not too happy about this, there's been enough stupid Maloneys and Mike should finish school. We didn't make the sacrifices we done so that he could go treadle a sewing machine in a stinking factory.'

'But, Mum, that's what I've been doing all my life, that and embroidery!' Mike protests.

'That's just it! We done that so you could *get* an education!' Nancy looks around at us, 'Isn't that right?' We all know her too well and we look down at our plates and don't show any expression. 'Pass your plate, Mole, and tell your mother, what do you think?'

She's starting with the youngest, Colleen is too young to get a say, and with me starting off the defence it means she's going to be tough. When I'm asked first, it's because Sarah says Nancy wants to polish up her argument against the motion. You see, Nancy doesn't listen and then comes in at the end, she argues back with everyone on the spot. She's picked me first so she can sort of limber up. It's like Bozo warming up on the punching bag. I'm on Mike's side, of course, because brothers have to be.

'They can't teach him nothing that's gunna help him design dresses here in Yankalillee,' I say, passing her my plate.

'That's not a good enough reason! Learning's not about what you learn about, it's about learning to learn.'

'How's that?' I ask, not understanding.

'It's called being educated, so you'll go on learning all your life, learning how to learn, that's the difference between us and people who are clever. Mike hasn't learned how to learn yet, but Sarah has.'

Sometimes, if you listen hard, Nancy says things that make you think she's not as dumb as she looks.

'A person won't learn if they're not interested in learning stuff,' I say, trying to defend my point of view. 'Mike's only interested in dresses, so why can't he be educated about dresses?'

'Become a stupid dressmaker, you mean? You're right, he could become that!' Nancy can be really bitchy if she wants. I can see exactly where she's heading, she's not going to let Mike go to Melbourne.

She puts a piece of apple strudel on the plate and passes it back to me. 'Thank you, Mole,' she says. That's another sign. When she's being polite, you know she's not going to take any notice of what you've said. I look at Mike and shrug. I want him to know I've done my best to help him.

'Bozo, pass your plate. And what have you to say?' Bozo doesn't muck around. 'You let Sarah be a doctor, so why can't Mike be a frock, er, dress designer? Doctors only think about cutting people up and dress designers only think about cutting material up, what's the diff?

Why's one more educated than the other? It takes six years to become a doctor, Mike says it will take him longer, much longer, to become a dress designer.'

Nancy scoops up a piece of strudel onto the knife she's using. The strudel is balanced on the blade of the knife, her thumb holding it safe so it doesn't fall off. Now she holds it in the air. 'Sarah's *going* to be a doctor, she's going to a university. Mike *might* be a dress designer if he's very lucky, he's not going to school any more!' She says it slowly so each word is pronounced clear, it's her way of trying to put Bozo in his place, act like he's dumb when it comes to such things. 'Sophie says it will be hard for a *goy* to get anywhere in the garment trade and he'll have to start as a sweeper in a sweatshop. I don't want my boy sweeping the floor for a Jew! Sophie says if he's lucky he'll learn the steam-presser, that's real clever, I don't think! I didn't bring any son of mine up to sweep floors or iron ladies' frocks!' Then she declares, 'We love Morrie and Sophie, but not all Jews are like them. Jews hate Catholics because they know we know they killed our Lord!'

'No, Mum, it's the other way around!' Mike protests. 'It's the Catholics who hate the Jews! But that's not how I feel, I just want to learn and they're the best at it.'

'Mike ain't dumb, now,' Bozo says, 'He won't be dumb later. Even if he sweeps floors when he starts out. It's better than collecting people's garbage, ain't it? Sarah's got to start by cutting up frogs, she told me so herself. Isn't that the same as Mike starting as a sweeper? What would you rather do, sweep a floor or cut up a frog?' Then he adds, 'Do you know any Catholics in the garment trade who will take him on?' He doesn't say nothing about Jews being Christ-killers. I bet there were plenty of Catholics in charge at the concentration camps. Bozo's doing all he can for Mike, but we know Nancy, she'll close it down any moment now, not even ask Tommy for his opinion because he might agree with her. She wants to be boss of the wash, show us how tough she is. She'll ask us to vote, then she'll use the overriding vote and that'll be Mike, well and truly down the gurgler.

But Tommy comes in suddenly. 'Designing frocks is for nancy boys, poofters! I'm not having no son of mine doing that!'

Oh shit, here we go. I look over at Bozo, who lifts one eyebrow. We both look to see how Nancy's going to handle this! Mike's whole body has gone rigid.

Nancy slides Bozo's cake onto the plate and hands it to him. 'Whose son did you say he is?' she says real quiet, deadly as a king-brown, you can practically see the forked tongue hissing in and out of her mouth.

'Ah, fuck yiz!' Tommy says and gets up, sending his chair back three feet before storming out of the room. 'He's a fucking fairy, ain't he?' he shouts from the kitchen door.

Jesus! I can't believe it! Game, set and match. Nancy's going to let Mike leave school, Tommy's just seen to that fair and square.

Nancy puts it to the vote and Bozo and me vote for Mike leaving and Nancy says that's okay, she's talked to Sarah, who's also voted for Mike. She doesn't even mention Tommy's conniption but she says she doesn't agree with us. However she's not going to use her overriding vote, Mike can go to Melbourne but only if he can find a job in the rag trade first and he'll have to stay with Sarah, Morrie and Sophie. 'Tommy can go down by train and build a sleep-out on the back porch,' she says, cool as a cucumber, as though what's just happened hasn't happened.

Nancy also said at the beginning that there were two things to discuss, but after what's happened with Tommy doing his block, whatever the second thing was, it doesn't come up.

It's the first time since the night Nancy went ape at the table when she heard of Sarah's pregnancy and had a go at Mike for sticking up for her, that Mike's been lost for words. He should be happy as Larry about the decision, but what Tommy's said has knocked him for a six and he gets up without even having a piece of Sophie's strudel. Then he says, 'Thanks, Mum, I won't let you down,' and he goes to our bedroom.

He's asleep, or maybe pretending, when we come in a little while later. It's garbage in the morning and it's been a bloody long day, I kid you not.

That night Tommy comes into our bedroom after we're all asleep, only I'm not, and I hear him say 'Wake up, will ya, Mike!' in a loud whisper and then he grabs a hold of Mike's shoulder and shakes it. 'Mike, wake up!'

Mike wakes up suddenly and shoots up out of his blanket, 'What?' Then, 'Oh, it's you!'

Tommy whispers, but I can hear every word. 'Mike, I'm sorry I said what I said, but it was the only way I could think to make sure she'd let you leave school to go to Melbourne to do them frock drawings.' Then he sort of hesitates before he goes on. 'Son, I don't care what you are, I loves yer. I dunno if you're a fairy and it don't matter if you are. There's plenty of turd burglars in the clink and some of them are good blokes. Just because you may be a poofter without even knowing it doesn't mean you can't be a good man.'

That's Tommy all right, he does the right thing and then he immediately screws things up again.

But I reckon Mike understands Tommy means no harm, because he reaches out and touches him on his crook shoulder. 'Thanks, Dad. Thanks for the help,' he says and then turns towards the wall. When Tommy leaves a little while later, I can hear Mike sobbing.

BOOK TWO

1961–1964

Chapter Fourteen

Templeton Maloney is five years old. Well, it's actually Lucy Templeton Maloney, the 'Lucy' is named after Mrs Barrington-Stone and the 'Templeton' for revenge. That was the second item in the family discussion all those years ago when Mike got permission to stop school and go to work in Melbourne. Nancy wanted to discuss naming Sarah's baby 'Templeton' so that nobody in Yankalillee would ever forget what had happened. Only it didn't happen at that meeting because of what Tommy said about Mike and so she went ahead with it anyway, using her overriding vote even though there hadn't been a vote in the first place. She must have known she'd never have got it agreed to by the family.

Father Crosby bloody nearly dropped the baby at the christening when he asked her name and Nancy, who was standing next to Sarah at the font, said, 'Lucy Templeton Maloney'. Naturally he was dead against it. He could hardly speak, but because there were three christenings on that Sunday and St Stephen's was chocka with everyone's relatives and friends, he couldn't make a fuss and was forced to go along with the baptism. But that didn't stop him coming around on his bike to give Nancy the usual lecture.

This time it was all about hate, how it was sinful to hate someone even if they were Protestants and Anglicans. 'Revenge to me; I will repay, saith the Lord,' he thundered at Nancy, his fat jowls wobbling. It seems as though ordinary Catholics, even collapsed ones, aren't supposed to seek revenge. 'Revenge,' said Father Crosby, 'is the Church's prerogative!'

'And what will the Church do?' Nancy asks him tartly.

'We will commend your case to God Himself, if He sees fit to visit shame and humiliation on Mr and Mrs Templeton, then in His infinite wisdom He may decide to shower them with brimstone and ashes. Metaphorically speaking, of course.'

'Can't hang around for God to make up His mind, Father, haven't seen too many cases of brimstone and ashes falling out of the sky around Yankalillee.'

'I've warned you several times before about blasphemy, Nancy Maloney! If you want to find yourself on the path to damnation, you are going the right way about it!'

Nancy flips her lid when she hears this. 'You seem to notify everyone else around here about the sins of the Maloneys, might as well tell the Pope too. And while you're doing all this notifying, Father, could you kindly notify Dora Templeton that Templeton Maloney is here to remind her every day of her miserable life that she's done the wrong thing by us Maloneys. She thinks she's so high and mighty and can just ride roughshod over us because we collect their rubbish! We collect her gin bottles as well, you tell her that! You hear me, Father, I'll not forgive that drunken bitch as long as I live and Sarah's daughter's going to remind her and her fat husband what a lily-livered, gutless little bastard her son turned out to be!'

Father Crosby clenches his teeth and raises his fist as though he is preparing to strike Nancy. Better not try, he'll be no match for her, she'll slaughterate him and then we'd have the blood of the Church on our hands. But instead he storms out. 'I'll pray for you, you wicked, wicked woman!' he yells, his fist still in the air. 'Revenge to me; I will repay, saith the Lord!' he shouts out again as he's going through the front door. I reckon he'd fortified himself with the altar wine before coming, because, even for him, saying stuff like that is a bit over the top and his bicycle is wobbling all over the street as he takes his departure. Nancy's going to cause him to have a heart attack one of these days. I must say, she's my mum and all that, but she can be a pretty nasty piece of work when she's been crossed.

If you ask me, even with revenge taken into consideration, Templeton is a pretty weird name for a girl. I guess Sarah must have agreed to it, thinking all the while her little girl would be called Lucy anyway. She'd give Nancy her revenge wish and hide the name of Templeton except for the birth certificate. But it hasn't turned out that way, people just call the baby 'Templeton' from day one. You can look like a Lucy, I suppose, but you can't look like a Templeton, so it's hard to work out how that's happened. But it has. I don't suppose Templeton is an easy name to forget when it belongs to a little girl. But that's the funny thing, at first Sarah tries hard to call her Lucy and when the girl was real small she got away with it, but Nancy's always called her granddaughter Templeton and at two years of age the child insisted on being called Templeton. Like it was her destiny or something. When people ask Sarah her little girl's name and she says 'Templeton' because she's long since given up, they look blankly at her or they go 'Huh?' or 'Beg yours?' or 'Pardon?' But when they see the child next time, they call her Templeton right off, natural as anything.

Even though Nancy did it out of sheer revenge, naming Sarah's daughter 'Templeton' turned out to have a good side to it as well. The people in our street and the Micks in town see the point and they admire Sarah for not being a victim like most of the other girls who got up the duff and ended up having their babies. It also showed Sarah wasn't ashamed. Of course, they don't know it was Nancy's idea. When Sarah comes up from Melbourne on occasional weekends or during the university holidays, she doesn't creep around as though she's committed some sort of mortal sin and has to live with the shame forever after. She's the same Sarah as always, friendly and modest and proud to show her little daughter off, and the townsfolk, except for a few diehards or friends of the Templetons, admire her and are pretty proud of what she's achieved, bringing up her daughter and taking a medical degree at the same time. They say things like 'That young girl has real character' or 'She's a credit to Yankalillee'. 'They may be from the wrong side of the tracks and Micks, but I tell ya what, wouldn't mind if she was my daughter.'

In fact, with Bozo winning a bronze medal at the Rome Olympics, there's some in town who think of us Maloneys as a family of high achievers and Bozo as the ultimate hero. There are people who before wouldn't have even crossed the street to say giddday to Nancy who now give her the big hello and want to know about the family. But Nancy's not impressed. When the Women's Auxiliary invite her to work at a stall for the Easter fete, she comes right out and says, 'No thank you very much, I wouldn't work in anything that would have somebody like me in their organisation.' It's supposed to be funny, but they know what she's saying, they've ignored her for the past thirty years and now it's too late. 'They can go to buggery!' she tells us, 'I know who our friends are and they'll see me out nicely.'

Then there's the fact that Mrs Barrington-Stone makes no bones about her affection for Sarah. Having her on our side almost makes us respectable. She finished her full stint on the Country Women's Association even though what she calls 'a reactionary element' tried hard to get her kicked out. But it turned out that most of the members were behind her and admired her for going in to bat for Sarah and winning against enormous odds. They're beginning to feel there's a change in the air for the country women's cause and that Mrs Barrington-Stone has shown the way for the older women and Sarah is the example for their daughters to follow. That is, of course, if you cut out 'the falling pregnant to the high-school footy captain' part. What Mrs Barrington-Stone has shown the outside world is that the CWA aren't a bunch of old chooks baking cakes and making jam for fetes, but one of the most progressive women's organisations in Australia. They have a long history of fighting for just causes, justice and the rights of women everywhere and it was them who started the Land Army during the war so they're no shrinking violets.

Templeton, by the way, is a typical Maloney with flaming red hair. The only thing Murray Templeton gave her is his skin so she doesn't have freckles. Nancy says she hopes it, her skin that is, doesn't turn out as thick as her father's, but otherwise not having freckles is a blessing. Except for that, she's a Maloney from her carrot top to her toenails and looks like ten-year-old little Colleen's younger sister.

There's a lot to tell you and then, on the other hand, there isn't, which is why I've skipped about five years. Television's come, but you know about that. Of course, it didn't come up to Yankalillee properly until earlier this year. We didn't think we'd be able to afford a television set for a couple of years, if even then. Then in the very first week of transmission from GMV6, the new TV station at Shepparton, a miracle happened.

We got real lucky, some rich bloke in Turnbull Street comes home pissed one night and demands his tea. It seems his wife and three daughters are crowded around the brand-new set watching Bob Dyer's 'Pick a Box'. He's told his tucker's in the oven, to get it himself. This makes him a bit shitty in the first place but he then finds that his wife must have turned the oven up too high by mistake and his tea is ruined, burned to a crisp or dried out or something. He's had a skinful and comes back into the lounge and goes off his rocker. He kicks the screen in and does what looks like irreparable damage and the set ends up in the garbage.

Goes to show it isn't just the poor and the Catholics who do irresponsible things like that. Nancy says that those rich blokes can't beat up their wives like us Catholics so he took it out on the television instead, which is our Maloney good fortune. I reckon she's wrong, just because you're rich doesn't mean you can't be a mongrel.

Anyway, there it was when we come around the next morning to collect the rubbish, a television set with a big hole in the screen. Bozo's onto it in a flash. He's since studied up on TV sets and reckons once we've got a new picture tube he has to order from A.W.A. in Sydney, we're going to have TV. Fair dinkum, a television set of our own and an expensive twenty-three-inch one to boot. If anybody else had said it, I'd be doubtful, it looked a heap of shit when we recovered it from the garbage. Bozo wouldn't say it will come good unless he was pretty sure he could repair it. The only immediate problem is that we can't yet afford the new picture tube, but when we can, it's going to be a lot cheaper than a new set. In the meantime we've got a piece of smoked glass fitted to hide the damage inside and keep the dust off and it looks pretty good in the front room sitting up on a small table we also scavenged some time from someone's rubbish.

With Mike gone to Melbourne that left only Bozo and me and occasionally Tommy to do the garbage. The old Diamond T was just about clapped out and towards the end couldn't get out of second gear even with Bozo's best efforts. The gearbox was history and there was a whine in the diff loud enough to wake the dead, no way we can afford a reconditioned one either. We didn't save anything with Sarah and Mike gone neither. Bozo and me ate like a horse, still do, and Nancy makes us all look like pikers. Only Tommy and little Colleen peck at their food and so, what with the cost of living constantly going up, things were tough. Bozo's having to pay his train fares to Melbourne every weekend meant he couldn't help out that much when we got into a pinch. The truth is the first three years after Sarah and Mike left were the worst ever.

Tommy's attempts at being on the wagon have been reasonably good by his standards, but his health hasn't held up. What with the war, prison and his lifetime of drinking, he's crook more days than he's better. He's not been up to lifting a hundred and fifty garbage cans from three in the morning until seven-thirty, so Bozo and me had to do the lot ourselves. It was hard going, just the two of us behind the truck. Bozo didn't even have the weekends to sleep in. He'd go down to Melbourne Saturday morning on the 9.13 from Wangaratta to train with Kevin Flanagan at the Russell Street gym. Or he'd have a fight on Saturday night. Sunday mornings he'd catch the train again and come back in the arvo on the 3.15 and get home on the bus from Wangaratta by nine o'clock if he was lucky, then have to be up at 3 a.m. again. If it wasn't for the fact that he could usually grab three hours' sleep on the train, he'd have been exhausted all week.

Tommy also had two more stints inside for petty theft, the first for stealing a fifty-pound bag of dog biscuits for Bozo's Bitzers. Silly bugger, got himself tanked at the Wangaratta Agricultural Show and became carried away on the spur of the moment when he saw this bag of biscuits in front of one of the exhibition stalls at the sheep-dog trials. He upped the bag and humped it towards the entrance fast as he could go. But it was open one end and he left a dog-biscuit trail to be followed and when Tommy ran out of puff he's citizen-arrested by this sheila in pants who frogmarched Tommy to the cops. She turned out to be the 'Good Dog' dog food representative from Melbourne so we couldn't even appeal to her compassion as a local. The real truth was that she might have come around but Tommy, being drunk, told her exactly what he thought of women with moustaches who wear men's khaki pants, and that put an end to any goodwill that might have been going around.

Bloody Oliver Twist, the stipendiary magistrate of ill-fame, gave Tommy six months.

The second time was equally ridiculous and is Tommy Maloney at his all-time stupidest. I think Tommy can't be a real crim at heart, just someone who gets these sudden rushes of blood to the head, because nobody can be that dumb. Not even Bobby Devlin, Bozo's old boxing coach, who's served his sentence and gone to live in Queensland. Big Jack says it's a place in the sun for shady people. What's more, I *know* Tommy isn't stupid because I go out with him in the bush and he's bloody clever the things he knows. It's what the war's done, sometimes he's really fucked in the head and I reckon that's when he commits these really dumb crimes. The second crime that gets him six months from Oliver Twist defies explanation, even for Tommy. What's more, he isn't even pissed when he commits it.

Father Crosby calls around, must have been early November 1958, if I remember correctly, and he's all smiles for a change. It seems there's a convocation of priests to be held by Cardinal Stewart in Bendigo and he's been invited. He's come to see Nancy about a new surplice, he wants all the trimmings and, of course, he wants it for free. 'A donation to the Blessed Virgin, my dear.'

Nancy will work off some of her past sins, shorten her time in purgatory, is the other subtle suggestion from Yankalillee's own Friar Tuck. Anyway, Nancy buys the deal, I mean what else can she do, even her, a collapsed Catholic, doesn't want the priest from Yankalillee to look like a dag surplice-wise. Besides, with Mike gone, we can't really afford to drop our standards because all these years people think it's Nancy's work that's winning ribbons. Mind you, Nancy's no slouch herself when she really wants to try.

Well, Father Crosby as usual leaves his Malvern Star resting against the front fence. Tommy comes home with the problem that he owes the SP bookie ten quid he's lost that afternoon betting on the St Leger, one of the big local greyhound races. He sees this beaut bike and in his addled mind thinks, 'That'd be worth a fiver at least.'

Well, to cut a long story short, he rides it all the way to Wangaratta, and tries to sell it to Joe Turkey. Only problem is that it's got *Property of the Catholic Church* stamped on the frame in three places. Joe, of course, doesn't know that Tommy is Bozo's old man, and while bicycle theft isn't exactly front-page news, stealing from the Church is not on. Joe Turkey, who's a good Catholic, dobs Tommy in to the Wangaratta police.

Nancy swears she'll never forgive Father Crosby, who, when the case came up, refused to withdraw charges.

'I cannot in all conscience go against the law of the land, Nancy Maloney. The Scriptures teach us, "Render thereto Caesar the things that are Caesar's and to God the things that are God's."'

'So, Tommy took a little ride on your bicycle, you got it back, didn't yer? No harm done!' Nancy yells.

'Nancy Maloney, I *am* the Church in Yankalillee! God's servant and representative in this benighted parish. We've got a prison up the hill, as you are well aware through bitter personal experience! Every Thursday I hear confession and distribute Holy Communion in the prison chapel. The lads inside are always contrite, but I've never heard a single one of them confess to the crime they've been convicted and sentenced for. They're all innocent, the lot of them. What comes through the confession grille is a general admission of guilt and the wish to be forgiven in the eyes of the Lord, if you know what I mean? *Bless me, Father, for I have sinned*. But the sins they've committed are always due to special circumstances. If it wasn't for a drunken father and a mother with TB and too many hungry mouths to feed and not enough money, they'd all, every one of them, have grown up pure as the driven snow to become doctors and lawyers and upstanding citizens. It's the cruel hand that society has dealt them that put them inside. Nothing to do with them or their bad characters.'

'I reckon they're half-right about that, Father, but what's that got to do with Tommy borrowing your bicycle for a few hours?'

'Theft! He stole it. Borrowing requires permission, stealing doesn't.'

'So he'd had a drop to drink, so he forgot to ask. These things happen, the Church got its property back and there's no harm done.'

'All the harm in the world, Nancy Maloney. Moral harm! Stealing from the Church is the same as stealing from God Himself. God has His hand stretched out in His infinite compassion and your husband, Tommy Maloney, has gone and bit it!'

I suddenly see the hand of God stretched out to Tommy and him taking a great chomp at His fingers and people looking up and saying, 'Look, it's raining blood!'

'Bloody hell! Here we go again!' Nancy's eyes shoot up to the ceiling and she lets out a monumental sigh. 'Father, he was pissed, stonkered, he didn't know it was your bicycle, he didn't *know* he was stealing from the Church, he was just being a perfectly common thief as usual!'

'Now that's just it, Nancy Maloney! That's my point. How would it be if the lads doing time up the hill, common thieves and scoundrels themselves, heard that Tommy Maloney, a known recidivist, was let off by their own priest who hears their confession? Good Catholic boys hearing that about one of their own! How do you think they'd feel, eh? Them innocent in their own minds and incarcerated and him, guilty as sin before God *and* man, free as a bird. No, no, not at all, I can't do it! What Tommy Maloney's done is like stealing from the Blessed Virgin Herself, we'll not be forgiving that with a wave of the hand and fifty Hail Marys!'

'What about the Lord Jesus Christ forgiving the thief on the cross when he was crucified?' Nancy now quotes the words of our Lord. '"Amen I say to thee, this day thou shalt be with me in paradise", isn't that what Jesus said, Father?'

Sometimes Nancy can leave you flabbergasted about what she comes out with. I reckon, if she'd had half a chance, she might have got somewhere in life. No wonder she's determined we've got to have an education.

'Extreme circumstances call for extreme unction,' Father Crosby says. 'Tommy isn't on Golgotha, now is he? He hasn't been nailed to the cross with four dirty big nails, now has he?'

'Three, Father, one through each hand and just the one for his feet which were crossed, the fourth one is the one *you've* used to nail Tommy!'

'Nancy Maloney, I've warned you before about blasphemy! The

Bishop simply wouldn't approve a recommendation of clemency. A bicycle is valuable property and it's on his diocesan audit. As God's representatives on earth His Holiness the Pope, the Cardinal himself, the Bishop and myself *are* the Holy Roman Church and we must see him punished and *only* then can he confess and be forgiven for sins committed.'

'Ha! *Revenge to me; I will repay, saith the Lord!* Didn't I hear you say that when it came to Dora Templeton? What was it you were going to do? That's right, pray. And in His infinite wisdom maybe the Lord would send a bit of fire and brimstone hailing down. Well, there's been bugger-all happen to the bitch that's nasty! But Tommy nicks your bike for a few hours and there's no praying for fire and brimstone, no leaving it to the Lord to decide. Instead a charge of grievous bodily harm for biting God's fingers and straight to gaol you go, Tommy Maloney!'

'Blasphemy! Blasphemy!' Father Crosby cries.

Mind you, all this is said after Father Crosby has received his fancy new surplice which Nancy does for him in less than a week. It's delivered to the priest's home before the Wangaratta cops come around to nab Tommy. I don't mean they waited deliberate, nothing like that, but stealing a bloody bicycle, even from a priest, isn't exactly urgent police business.

What's really suspicious, though, was that Wangaratta didn't inform Big Jack Donovan before they made the arrest. That's bad form. Tommy's a local crim and Big Jack should have a say, that's how the cops work in the country.

Nancy says it's not that hard to smell a rat, a nasty little Father Crosby conspiracy somewhere along the line. Big Jack came around to apologise to us, he knows how difficult things are, but there's nothing he could do about it because Tommy was arrested and held overnight in Wangaratta and went before the stipendiary magistrate, the one and only Oliver Twist, the very next morning and got six months for petty theft.

It's this last term in prison that seems to really do it for Tommy. It's not a big sentence, but I think he's had about enough. He comes out not the same man that went in. His spirit seems broken. When we go to get him, we've hired a taxi special, so he doesn't have to get into the

Diamond T which is on its last legs. Tommy comes out the gate and he's sort of crumpled and small, nothing cocky left in him. You can see his crook shoulder and his one eye and crooked jaw and caved-in cheekbone where the Jap guard smashed him with a rifle butt, something which you hardly even noticed before. I don't know how we know, but it isn't Tommy who walks out the gate, it's someone who's given up. It's not something you can explain but just something you know inside of you. Nancy takes one look and starts to cry. These days the only time Tommy perks up a bit is when we go bush.

The next thing to know is how Philip Templeton tried to get rid of us in the rubbish-collection business. Even though he'd been elected shire president twice in a row, he'd not been game to take a shot at us before. This was because Peter Barrington-Stone had been on the shire council representing the graziers. He wouldn't have had the guts to take on Mrs Barrington-Stone. When someone else took Mr Barrington-Stone's place on the council, Philip Templeton's free to have a go at us.

It wasn't going to be easy because Bozo looked as though he might get selected for the Rome Olympics and Sarah was the pride and joy of Yankalillee and has nearly finished Medicine.

But Mr Templeton is patient and waits for his opportunity and, sure enough, given that we're the Maloney family, it comes along dished up to him on a platter with sauce.

One morning in February 1959, halfway through the garbage run, the axle on the Diamond T breaks. As luck would have it, we're only two blocks from John Crowe's house and I go round and tap on the bedroom door. His wife Trish wakes him up and he comes out and I explain what's happened, thinking maybe he'll get the Diamond T going with Bozo's help, him being an expert mechanic.

But he does more than that, he comes out in the ute and looks at the broken axle. By this time the gearbox and differential, which I mentioned earlier, are ratshit and now there's the axle. The tyres are in their usual state except for one back one that's still half-good.

John Crowe crawls under the old truck and comes out a few moments later. 'Forget it, axle's snapped.' He opens the bonnet and gets Nancy to start the engine. 'Holy shit!' he exclaims when he hears the whine of the diff and the clapping of the tappets. Then Bozo tells him how it can't get out of second gear. 'I can't believe it's still going, mate, it's a bloody miracle.' He turns to Bozo. 'You keep this old lady on the road, Bozo?'

Bozo pretends he doesn't know whether he means Nancy or the Diamond T. 'Which one?' he says, laughing up at Nancy. 'Yeah, best I can,' he finally answers.

'Well, you're a better mechanic than me, mate. This heap o' rusty nuts 'n' bolts should've been retired to the scrapyard about the time we swapped them tyres around. Shit, that must've been three years ago if it was a day!'

We leave the Diamond T and John Crowe lets Nancy drive the ute. He also helps shovel the rubbish into the back from the Diamond T and, making a few extra trips, he helps us finish up with the morning's run. Bozo and me are an hour late for school and we both get detention which is small potatoes compared to the trouble us Maloneys are in with the garbage run.

But John Crowe's ahead of us and he arranges for us to use a council truck, sort of unofficial like. This is done after consultation with Macca McKenzie, the depot foreman, and involves rabbit meat for his greyhounds, a little scam I'll explain later. The shire-council trucks are parked overnight at the depot, so we 'borrow' one and have it back by seven-thirty in the morning.

This is temporary of course and as luck would have it we're only three weeks off the end of the contract with the shire council. Tommy's first contract was for five years initially, with an option to renew it every year providing the council is happy. So far the yearly renewal has been more or less automatic, nobody's ever come along with a better bid and it's pretty obvious for all to see, there ain't much of a living in it anyway.

Well, the contract comes up for renewal and we put in our offer, which is lower than ever because we ask the council to supply the garbage truck. It's all over red rover, Philip Templeton pounces, no truck no contract, simple as that. We're out of business and he puts the contract out to tender. We're in deep shit, the tender stipulates that the contractor has to supply his own vehicle, only I think it's called 'infrastructure' in the tender. There's no bank manager in the world is going to loan a Maloney money even if we put the house up as guarantee. It would take a junior bank teller who failed arithmetic at school about two minutes to see we can't pay the loan back in several thousand years.

John Crowe comes to see us and he makes us a proposition. He'll sell his ute and buy a truck, he reckons he's good for a small loan from the bank and his wife has inherited a couple of hundred quid, so why doesn't he tender and we work for him for the same take-home pay as we're making now? We'll carry on just like before, only now we've got no overheads.

'You're no worse off, better in fact because there's no maintenance expenses, I'll even supply the gumboots and shovels and whatever.' Compliments of Macca McKenzie no doubt.

Bozo feels duty-bound to tell him that there won't be all that much left over for him.

'That's okay, I'll keep working at the shire council so I've got my regular pay packet comin'. Trish and me will see this business as an investment in case we ever need it. Another thing, how much you reckon it costs you to maintain the Diamond T?'

It's a good question because the old truck these last years has been eating up the money we earn and we've been on mince and offal that long I've practically forgotten what a steak tastes like. 'About half what we make,' Bozo says.

'There's my cut right there,' Mr Crowe says. 'It ain't going to cost us a brass razoo to keep the new truck in good nick, I'll just do it myself in the council workshops after hours.'

We tell him we need to think about it and we'll give him an answer on the Monday. It just so happens Sarah and Mike are up from Melbourne, it's uni holidays for her and there's a Jewish holiday on the Friday so Flinders Lane, where Mike works for Mr Stan, is closed until the Monday. He's come up on the train with Sarah and Templeton for the weekend. So, seeing we're all at home, Nancy calls a family conference which includes Tommy, who is both sober and out of gaol. She puts John Crowe's offer to us, even though we know all about it anyway.

We haven't had a family conference since the time Tommy called Mike a poofter and I can only hope this isn't going to be a repeat performance. Before we start, Sarah says, 'As it's a decision which involves some of our futures, Mum ought not to have the overriding vote.'

It's pretty cheeky and we all wait to see what will happen. Nancy doesn't give up her power lightly and she reckons she's still our mum and warns that she always will be. To our surprise, she agrees that whatever the majority decision is, then that's what we'll do. Miracles will never cease.

It's Sarah who goes first, which is a good sign.

'Well, of course, it's easy for me to say because I'm not directly involved,' she begins, 'but it might be a good idea to take the pressure off a bit and simply work for wages. We won't be any worse off and for the next couple of years anyway with the two boys still at school, I guess it will keep the wolf from the door. Nancy's lost Mike so she can't get through the same volume of layette work and I'm not home to do the cooking, washing and ironing, which cuts her earning time down even further.'

I feel like saying it doesn't cut down Nancy's work all that much further because Nancy is a crook cook and our meals are bloody terrible. In this department we miss Sarah a lot. As for the washing and ironing, Bozo and me take turns boiling the copper out the back for the whole family and have to iron our own clothes for school as well as little Colleen's. Nancy just wears her yellow-daisy dresses, which are made of rayon and don't need ironing. It's a far cry from the old days and the hole in our lives that came when Sarah left us hadn't mended much.

'Tommy's pension doesn't go very far,' Sarah continues and then shrugs, 'so I guess, without the Diamond T, we don't have much of an alternative.'

What she's really saying is that ever since his last stint up the hill Tommy's on and off the wagon like a yoyo so his TPI pension can't be relied on and, whether we like it or not, we are more or less forced to work for John Crowe. There doesn't seem much more to add, Sarah's said about all there is to say.

Mike chips in, 'I'm working as a waiter two nights a week and weekends, I can probably manage to send home a pound a week.'

'You give that to Sarah,' Nancy says, 'to get shoes and the things we can't make for Templeton.'

'Mum, we're fine, Mike pays rent and between the four of us we're doing fine. Really.'

'Well, I disagree with you all!' Bozo says out of the blue. 'When you work for someone else, there's a boss and there's always trouble. We've always worked for ourselves and we've always managed until now.'

We all look at him surprised. 'So where are we going to get a truck?' I ask before anyone else can get in and ask the same question.

'Partnership,' Bozo says. 'John Crowe and us Maloneys.'

There's a stunned silence, then Mike asks, 'Do you think he'll buy it?'

'Can't see why not, he knows bugger-all about garbage collecting.'

'It's not exactly rocket science,' Mike says, using one of his favourite expressions.

'That's what *we* think because we've been doing it all these years. Not too many families are willing to get up at three o'clock in the morning, summer and winter, to collect other people's rubbish. There's a lot more to collecting garbage than people think. Have you ever seen anyone try to lift a bin and toss the contents into the back of a truck a hundred and fifty times every morning?'

'No, because nobody's stupid enough to want to do it except us,' Mike says.

'Maybe yes, but that's part of my point. It's a dirty job and there's not too many people willing to do it. That's one of the aces we hold.'

You could've fooled me, one moment we're on the bones of our arses and the next we're holding aces?

Nancy now pipes in, 'Nothing wrong with collecting rubbish, it's honest work.' She looks at Bozo. 'So go on, how's this partnership of yours going to work?'

'John Crowe's a decent bloke, he's also pretty street-smart,' he looks over at Tommy, 'that's not necessarily a bad thing, but he doesn't know how to run a business and he doesn't know, in particular, how to run *our* business.'

'We've got a business all of a sudden?' I ask. 'Don't we just collect other people's rubbish?'

'That's just it, Mole,' Bozo says. 'I reckon there's a real quid to be made out of the stuff people throw away. Rubbish is the one thing that's always going to be there. It's like funerals, there's always going to be dead people and there's always going to be rubbish and it can be made into a good business.'

Sarah laughs. 'I believe you, thousands wouldn't.'

She's right, if it wasn't Bozo saying all this we'd all be laughing our heads off. He's always made a bob out of what other people throw out, so you can't say he's talking through his hat. Calling what we do a business gives it sort of a respectability we never thought we had and we all perk up a bit knowing we're a business. Or could be one. Bozo goes on, 'What I reckon we should do is this, we should own fifty-one per cent and John Crowe forty-nine per cent.'

'What!' we all shout together. 'He'll never go for that!'

'Why not? We run the business side and do the daily grind and he does the engineering side.'

Sarah laughs. 'You mean he keeps the truck on the road?'

We all laugh except Bozo. 'That's what it is now, just truck maintenance, but it won't always be like that, you wait and see.'

'He'll want the biggest share,' Mike says. 'He's supplying the truck, putting his own money in, we're putting in bugger-all!'

'Bugger-all? That's our whole problem, we think what we do is worthless. Just because a Maloney does it, it can't need brains or skill or be worth anything. But that's wrong, we put in both the muscle and brains and that ain't bugger-all! They're the main ingredients in business, labour is always the highest cost and experienced management is how profits are made. We've got both and John Crowe needs both.'

Nancy shakes her head. 'In my experience the blood, sweat and tears is what everyone takes for granted. Them that work from the chin up always take advantage of them that work from the shoulders down!'

'Yeah, if we work for Mr Crowe or even are the minor partners, that's exactly what will happen,' Bozo says. 'But if we own the majority of the business, it's not the same thing. With a good reliable truck we'll do more than just collect the rubbish in the mornin'.'

'What?' Nancy looks shocked. 'I can't do more than I'm doing now. I'm getting old and tired. What do you mean we'll do more?'

'Think about it, Mum! I've got only this year to go at school, what then, hey? Mole's got two more. I don't reckon we, him and me, are the university types. I know I'm not. Mole can decide for himself later. I want to go into business, and garbage ain't such a bad place to start. We've been doing it practically all our lives and as far as I can work it out the whole world is one big garbage tip. Now, think, what's garbage as a business?' He looks around the table questioningly.

'A dirty business?' Mike suggests, smiling.

Bozo takes no notice, he's too earnest even to smile back. 'Garbage is an *early-morning* business! The rubbish is always collected in the early morning and the truck stays idle during the day. That's what's called slack time in business. Now if we can utilise this time, put the truck to work, then we maximise our effort and increase our profit. Did you know that a truck will last twice as long if the engine never cools down?'

Nancy has a lot of faith in Bozo, he's got us out of more money scrapes over the years than you can count on your fingers and toes. She says, 'Son, I don't know how much longer I can get up at three o'clock in the morning to drive the truck, I'm getting more aches and pains than you'll find in the Sisters of Charity hospice. I'm about ready for some slack time meself.'

'Just do early mornings one more year, Mum, and, you'll see, things will be different. But not if we work for wages and not if we're junior partners,' he warns. Bozo must have thought a lot about it because he's not the type to promise what he can't deliver. Next year is the Olympic Games in Rome and if he makes the boxing team it's going to be his biggest year yet. But typical of old Bozo, he has his eyes on the long term as well. It must be his American blood from the Marine boxer Bozonik or whatever he was called, anyway the bloke who's supposed to be his dad, because he sure doesn't get his spoon-out-of-the-sink-ability from the Maloney side.

Bozo finally persuades us to have a shot at his partnership proposition. We all agree that he should be the spokesman for our side. John Crowe already respects him and maybe he can pull off the deal, though in my heart I don't much like his chances.

We ask John Crowe to tea with his wife, Trish, on Saturday night so we can all be there. Sarah cooks a roast leg of lamb with mint sauce, roast potatoes, pumpkin and also some green stuff in a dish that's spinach, I think. Sarah says it's something Mrs Rika Ray has shown her how to cook, it's got peanuts ground into it and nutmeg and a dash of something called sesame-seed oil, it's the first vegetable I've ever known which you can smell before you eat it and it looks like stuff Bozo's mutts cough up after they've been chewing on a bit of green grass.

Mike has paid for the leg of lamb out of his waiter money. He reckons on a good waitering night he can make seven or eight bob in tips. He's being paid peanuts in Flinders Lane because he's learning stuff. *When you learn you don't earn, when you know you get dough*. The waiter's job only pays five bob a shift but with tips it's keeping him alive and sometimes there's stuff over at the restaurant in St Kilda that he brings home to Sophie and Morrie. We're having lamb because Mike and Sarah want it especially. Sophie's a good cook but she and Morrie have never got accustomed to the smell of lamb and so they don't ever have it in Carlton, not even lamb chops, so this is a special treat for Mike and Sarah. For us too, of course, a juicy leg o' lamb doesn't come your way every day, in fact, just about never.

To our surprise John Crowe agrees right off to the partnership. He even says he's glad we brought it up and he likes the idea of himself being in charge of the engineering side and leaving Bozo to do the business. He admits that he's been in business for himself twice and come a cropper, once when he tried to open a motor-repair shop on his own and once with a partner in breeding turkey chicks. 'Can't do them books and that bank rec stuff. I'm only good with me hands, always been like that, book learning's not my bag.' He laughs. 'Bloody failed arithmetic every time at school, couldn't do spelling neither.'

I admit, I was expecting him to say that Bozo's still a kid at school, what would he know about business? But he's done no such thing, John Crowe's treating my brother like Bozo's the boss right off.

There a bit of a silence follows and we all look into our plates and wait for Bozo to tell him about what we want in the partnership.

'Ah, we'd like the, er, partnership to be forty-nine, fifty-one, our way,' Bozo says, then adds quickly, 'We're running the business and doing the hard yakka, we think it's worth an extra two per cent.'

There's silence as we wait for John Crowe to say something. 'Now wait on. You mean you want control?' he says at last.

'Yeah, well sort of.'

John Crowe comes right back, 'No way, Bozo.' He doesn't seem offended, or angry, just acts like he's made up his mind. 'Fifty–fifty, couldn't be fairer than that now. Had a partnership the way you say once and got ripped off, lost all me dough and couldn't do nothing about it, me partner completely knackered me! Me and Trish had the clothes we were standing in, bastard took the rest. Then I got two years for grievous bodily harm, premeditated assault the judge said, and for once he was right, I should've killed the bastard!'

There's silence from Bozo, silence from all of us. What's there to say? It's clear Bozo's not going to get his way, John Crowe's been burnt before and he's not stupid.

John Crowe comes back again. 'I'm buying the truck and maintaining it, doing the engineering, without the truck you've got no business.'

Fair enough, I think.

But Bozo comes back, 'You're right, it's six of one and half a dozen of the other. Without a truck there's no business and without workers none as well,' Bozo replies. 'The two per cent isn't extra profit, we'll split that. It's in case, you know, there's a disagreement.'

'I know what it's for! There was a disagreement the last time and I ended up with bugger-all except two years up the hill.' He looks around at all of us. 'I don't see the point of not going fifty–fifty. I already said I won't interfere in the business side. Look, mate, what we've got here is a bloody good arrangement, there'll be big savings on truck repairs and maintenance because I can do them. You said yourself the Diamond T was costing you half your take-home, didn't ya? Well, that's my fifty per cent of the profits took care of already. So what's the problem with a fifty–fifty split, you ain't working any harder for your dough and I ain't interfering?'

John Crowe's got a point. I don't reckon there'll be too many bills for spare parts, thanks to the unknowing generosity of the shire-council workshop and also I reckon the truck we buy is going to have a world record for petrol economy, compliments of the very same source.

John Crowe and me are pretty good mates by now, he's taught me how to shoot and Mrs Barrington-Stone's husband, Peter, has given me this old .22 rifle and we've been out a lot of times with Tommy. John Crowe's a pretty good bushie himself, though he doesn't know as much as Tommy. Still and all he likes Tommy and it's nice they're mates and he treats me real good. John Crowe's been known to have a few but he's not a drunk by a long shot, so having him as a fifty–fifty partner seems to me to be a pretty good arrangement. Ever since we've been 'borrowing' a council truck after working hours, he takes half a dozen of the rabbits we've shot. 'They're for Macca at the depot,' he says, 'keep him sweet, like.' I guess there'll be a few more rabbits needed if the partnership ever gets going.

'Equal partners never work, Mr Crowe,' Bozo now says, 'sooner or later a decision comes up that one partner wants and the other don't. You just said so yourself. There's got to be a way to break the stalemate.'

I don't know where Bozo gets this stuff, I mean what kid would know that? I can only think that he's got it from the radio, there's a program on the wireless, the ABC, Friday nights, called 'This Week in Business', which Bozo has been listening to since he was thirteen.

'Well, sorry, mate, but I reckon it's fifty–fifty. If yiz don't trust me then I ain't good enough to be in business with yiz. Matter of fact, I'd rather not.' John Crowe looks at Bozo and shrugs his shoulders. 'Once bitten twice shy, Trish and me ain't gunna start from scratch again.' He grins. 'Besides, this time it'll be my partner that does the grievous bodily harm to me!'

'That's not what I meant, Mr Crowe. We may never have to make a decision we don't both agree on. Like I said it's not the extra money, we can split that fifty–fifty. Business decisions are liable to be more frequent than engineering decisions and I'm not going to tell you how to repair a truck or what brand of tyres to buy. Any big decision we have to make we'll make together, but, well, things happen sometimes between partners, go wrong, like.'

You can feel it's getting a bit tense and Trish Crowe is looking down at her plate, her hands folded in her lap.

Sarah jumps in. 'What about forty-nine per cent each and have two per cent held by someone we both trust, a third party?'

Yeah, good on ya, Sarah! She's got it in one. It seems like such an easy solution and I wonder why Bozo hasn't thought about it and saved us all the aggro.

'Sounds okay by me,' John Crowe says, 'What say, Bozo?'

Bozo is smart enough to look around at all of us, pretending we all have to make the decision, but we all know it's him has to. We nod, each in turn. 'Okay by us Maloneys,' Bozo says. He's agreed too quickly and I know Bozo well enough to realise that he *has* thought about this solution. It's just that he wanted to try the other because it would be the better way to go, the easier way to operate, Bozo always faces up to the hard decisions.

Well, now we have the next problem. Who do we both trust?

Nancy suggests Mrs Barrington-Stone right off. John Crowe pretends to think about it, but I know him well enough by now to know he wouldn't want a sheila and especially one that's from a posh Protestant family. We know she's not like that and would be fair, but he doesn't. Besides, everyone in Yankalillee knows Lucy Barrington-Stone is Sarah's friend and protector, so, fair enough, John Crowe can't be sure she'd be neutral in any disagreement between us and him.

'Wouldn't know her from a bar of soap,' John Crowe says, putting the kybosh on the suggestion.

'Big Jack Donovan?' I suggest.

'Bloody good idea!' Tommy says right off. 'Reckon Big Jack knows the worst and best about us all, hey Crowy?' Tommy hasn't said a word until now, though that's not unusual these days since he's back to binge drinking. The other night he stumbled home, been gone two days, and he'd shat his own pants, Bozo and me had to take him outside and clean him up.

John Crowe rubs his chin. 'He's a cop, mate. How would you be going into business with a cop?'

Quickly Tommy says, 'I dunno, most crims been in business with a cop at one time or another.'

This gets a laugh. Then Mike says, 'Well, we're both Catholics sort of, what about Father Crosby?'

'Christ no!' both John Crowe and Nancy yell simultaneously and Nancy is so shocked at the suggestion that she has to fan her face with one of the paper napkins Mike brought from the restaurant where he works.

There's a lot more laughter, then John Crowe says, 'If we have to choose between a cop and a priest, better take the more honest one.'

So it's decided. Big Jack Donovan is to have two per cent of our business. Or as John Crowe puts it, 'Two per cent of bugger-all of nothing! Might just keep him in Minties for a week every year, that is if he chews real slow.'

John Crowe puts in a tender for the shire garbage collection under the business name 'John Crowe & Partners', which Bozo registers and gets Tommy to sign because he's under age. The shire council accepts our tender which is for about fifty per cent more than we've ever asked and we're back in business. Philip Templeton even says how happy he is that a council worker, Mr John Crowe, a mechanic in the motor-depot workshop, has shown the initiative to go into business on his own. That men who show this kind of gumption should be encouraged by council. He also notes that Mr Crowe wishes to purchase one of the council trucks due to be retired from the fleet and he is sure that council members would approve generous terms of sale. Of course, he assumes John Crowe is going to give up his job, so the laugh's on him. Nancy says that while it isn't exactly fire and brimstone, at least it's a kick in the bollocks to Philip bloody Templeton.

Now, here's the funny thing. Remember the Fargo we took the tyres off so that we could go down to Melbourne for the birth of Sarah's baby? Well, it's up for sale because the shire council sells their trucks when they've got 75,000 miles on the clock. So that's the truck John Crowe buys for a song, because its logbook shows that it's clapped out from hauling gravel from the quarry.

However, it turns out that John Crowe has, thanks to the workshop's spare-parts division, replaced just about every moving part, put in new suspension, stripped the gearbox and rebuilt it, the engine's had a rebore, fanbelt, spark plugs, distributor leads, electrics, batteries. You name it, they're all brand spanking new. The tyres are also virtually new, having been selected carefully from among the entire council truck fleet, one tyre off this truck and another off that one, until six practically new tyres are on the Fargo, whereas six trucks in the fleet will mysteriously require at least one new tyre long before the other five wear out.

'That can happen with a truck, seen it plenty of times, no explaining it,' John Crowe says, grinning and scratching his head. 'One o' the truckin' mysteries of life, mate.'

For the past three weekends, John Crowe and me have been out shooting rabbits fast as we can for Macca McKenzie's greyhounds. The motor-depot foreman has six dogs and is considered a big owner as most blokes who have them can only afford one, two at the most. Macca swears greyhounds do better on rabbit meat and his lot sure get through a lot of rabbits even though they're so thin you'd think looking at them that they hardly ate at all.

John Crowe drives the Fargo up to the house and we all come out to see it. It's astonishing, he has even given it a spray job. It's dark green with a yellow stripe down the side.

'Australian colours, green and gold, for when you go to the Olympics,' he says to Bozo.

Bozo laughs, 'I haven't been selected, it's way off yet.'

'A shoo-in, mate. When you're selected we're gunna paint them Olympic rings on the door each side.'

Bozo shakes his head. 'There's lots of good boxers around in the middleweight division, Mr Crowe.'

'You been boxing a fair while, though?'

'Yeah, since I was ten.'

'And you've never been beat from before feather to bantam and now middleweight.' John Crowe laughs, 'I'll take those odds any day, my son.'

The Fargo with its green and gold paint job looks like it's new. 'It's a beauty, Mr Crowe,' Bozo exclaims, changing the subject.

I wonder if there's any other business like ours where the managing director, who is Bozo, is still at school and calls his partner 'Mr Crowe' and his partner calls him 'Bozo'?

Bozo takes us for a drive and when we get home again he steps down from the cabin. 'Drives like a new truck, Mr Crowe, nice 'n' tight, engine pulls great and the gearshift is smooth as velvet.'

'Bloody ought to be, my son! Just about the only thing that's original equipment is the mileage counter, didn't want to wind that back in case some dickhead from the shire council came and took a squiz!' He turns to me. 'You can thank Mole here, all them "minor" repairs cost us about a hundred rabbits and he shot most of 'em.' He looks at Tommy, 'Don't you go putting a quid on one of Macca's dogs in the Waterloo Cup, mate, they're fat as prime porkers, couldn't win a race if all the other mutts in it were on tranquilliser pills.'

Bozo hasn't given up on the Diamond T. He reckons soon as he's got a spare quid or two, he's going to do her up. John Crowe says he's crazy, the old girl was ready for the scrapheap years ago.

And that's how we stayed in the rubbish business and got into the road-hauling business. Bozo quit school in Leaving to concentrate on business. Nancy let him do it though she was pretty worried with Mike leaving early and then Bozo and she made me promise I'd do my Matriculation.

It's two years now since we went into business with John Crowe and there's never been an argument. What's more, he helped Bozo get the Diamond T back on the road.

Starting with the two trucks, doing the garbage early mornings then working all day after that, we're now in the short-haul trucking business. We're hauling stuff between Yankalillee and Wangaratta and the surrounding districts and to Wodonga and Albury and back. There's already talk of putting on a third truck as there's one coming up at the council that's going real cheap. We haven't had a taste of offal on our plates in near eighteen months and things are looking pretty good. This coming Christmas we're going on our first family holiday ever to Sydney, to a place called Manly which is on the beach.

Well, that just about brings us up to date. Now you'll want to know about Bozo at the Rome Olympics and Sarah becoming a doctor and Mike in the rag trade and Mrs Rika Ray becoming Bozo's Number One fan and spare-time dog handler. Also about Tommy and me in the bush, all of which brings me more or less up to the present time, which is November 1961.

Chapter Fifteen

Mike was doing it tough the first year he started work. You see, they don't do apprenticeships for men in the rag trade because a young Australian boy who wants to go past a steam-presser in the business is unheard of. Flinders Lane is a place where you have to make your own breaks but where there are no rules to tell you how to go about doing the things you need to get on.

Mike says that the workers in The Lane are almost entirely women and they come in three kinds. There are the Jews, then the Italians and Greeks with an occasional English migrant, and lastly the Australians. Though the bosses are almost all Jewish and mostly men, there are some women who run their own workshops and businesses.

The Jewish workers and the bosses have usually come from a Europe destroyed by war where most have suffered personal tragedy and some have lost their entire families. These are people who've already had two other lifetimes and now face a third in Australia. Most see their lives as contained in three parts: a home with a loving family, death and the destruction of everything they've known, where their previous lives were rubbed out by the horror of the concentration camps, and many of those still alive then found their countries being taken over by the communists who imposed a new type of bleakness and despair. Now they face a third life, in a new place where they are known as 'reffos', misunderstood, often ridiculed, at best reluctantly tolerated. For them Flinders Lane is seen as a safe haven, almost another place to hide from a world they have long since given up trying to understand.

The machinists, steam-pressers, pattern-makers, hand-finishers and the rest of the ragtag army that make up the Jewish element who work in The Lane have fought tooth and nail just to survive. There are men pressing garments who, at another time in another world, were teachers, intellectuals, scientists or businessmen who owned and ran their own factories. To have endured against all odds is the miracle, a fluke that has no logical explanation. Now they will do just about anything to keep their heads up in the sea of chance and circumstance in which they are now treading water.

They don't speak much English and the most common languages among themselves are Polish and German, or if it's a Pole speaking to a German then it's Yiddish. English is the language they must reluctantly learn and use for the trams and shopkeepers and to speak to the confident and loud-voiced strangers all around them.

Like the Jewish workers, many of the bosses have also arrived from a war-ravaged Europe without a penny to their name and have borrowed from a *landsman* to buy two sewing machines and a bit of material to get started. Though on the surface some appear to be doing well, it is a fragile, almost always undercapitalised existence and they, too, are trying not to drown. The only difference is that they've managed to swim a little closer to the safety of the shore.

The second group of women workers in The Lane are Greek and Italian migrants who have also left their war-torn countries for the promise of a better life. They bring with them no social or language skills but offer instead an ability to sew and a high work rate. They are cherished by their Jewish bosses because they work hard and never complain. They too see The Lane as a place where they feel protected from the strangeness they encounter when they leave to go to their rented inner-city homes at night.

The last of the workers are the Australians, young girls who start work at fourteen and who will leave when they get married. There is also a second Australian group, the older women who have missed the altar and have made the garment trade and Flinders Lane almost their entire lives. They are most often the senior workers, the hand-finishers, the foremen or the manageresses, and The Lane cannot do without them. Mr Stan spends a lot of time massaging the egos of these older ladies. If they got upset, they would up and go to the competition, because their special skills are always in demand.

One of them is a Mrs Wilma Pinkington, called Mrs P, but never Wilma, by everyone. Mike says she can do the most amazing and original beadwork, but only when she's drunk. She comes to work with a jumbo-size 4711 Cologne bottle filled with gin and it isn't until she's well under the weather that her best work comes out. But she gets pretty cranky in the process and Mr Stan is always having to soft-soap her and tell her how *vunderful* she is. *'Mrs P, we must have always the Pinkington look, without your genius with the beads we are not so special. You are the vun!'* Mrs P then reminds him in no uncertain terms that Mr Haskin at Henry Haskin has offered her double to work for him. *'Ah, Mrs P, you are so precious, maybe a little bonus is comink your way,'* Mr Stan says soothingly, patting her scrawny shoulder. When they're putting the **Style & Trend** summer or winter collection together for showing, he puts on an assistant specially to nurse Mrs P through the tension. Somebody she can shout at. Mr Stan then gives the assistant a bonus at the end for putting up with Mrs P's harassment and general crankiness.

Now imagine a kid from the bush with dreams of being a clothes designer coming into this strange world, this tower of Babel populated almost exclusively by female workers. If Mike's arrival wasn't so unlikely and impossible, it would be a joke, nobody's ever heard of something like this happening before. Ridiculous! Quite impossible! Women are workers and men are the bosses or salesmen, and poor old Mike, with his burning ambition to design dresses, is a contradiction in terms.

Ambition isn't something most workers in The Lane think much about. The best possible outcome most can imagine is to try to stay alive and out of trouble, to be permitted to grab onto the passing flotsam and then hope it will carry them to the safety of the beach.

Then swimming in from nowhere, from a country town nobody's heard of, comes a boy who has a complete family, every one of them alive and breathing God's fresh air. A young man who wants to design beautiful clothes, whose heart hasn't been broken, who is possessed of a mind not tormented by memory and whose stomach has never cramped in fear or his bladder or bowels lost control.

The men who work in The Lane, those who are not bosses or sales representatives, are mostly messenger boys, dispatch clerks, steam-pressers, sewing-machine mechanics or truck drivers. They think Mike wanting to be a dress designer can only mean one possible thing, he's a fairy and when they see what he's prepared to do to get on, they conclude he must be a bloody drongo and halfwit as well.

Mike is pretty tough. Collecting other people's rubbish all your life isn't exactly dainty work, but he's not come across anything quite like The Lane before. For a start, there's rats, hundreds of them. Apart from the work he has to do, which is made up of all the tasks nobody else is prepared to tackle, he is made the official rat catcher for Style & Trend Pty Ltd, Mr Stan's business.

Mike laughed when he first told us, 'One day when I'm a famous designer and people ask me how I started in the *schmatte* business and I tell them I was a rat catcher, they're not going to believe me.' He said it like it was funny but we could see he's paying heaps for his ambition and inside him it was hurting like hell. All I can say is that us Maloneys don't quit easily and Mike is a Maloney even if he is also half-Italian.

When the rats get real bad they call in the proper rat catcher, but for the regular nightly rat visits Mike is the designated rat man. He has to put out a rat cage last thing, usually baited with a few bits of bread, crusts and scraps of food the workers bring for the lunch they must eat at their sewing machines.

Then in the morning Mike has to reach into the cage and grab the rats and drown them in the hand basin in the toilet. Rats are good swimmers so he has to hold them down until they die. There'd be at least six every day, big buggers that come up from Queen's Wharf. He wears rubber gloves and, as an extra precaution, bandages his gloves with strips of cloth so he's wearing a sort of bandage a rat's teeth can't bite through; you never know what diseases they're carrying. When they're drowned he puts the rats in a canvas bag, goes down The Lane and empties it over the Queen's Wharf into the Yarra River.

You'd think they'd put down rat poison but the trouble is, the rats crawl into dark places to die, like under floorboards where you can't find them and they stink the place out so that's not on. Catching them is the only thing you can do.

In the winter when there isn't a lot of food in the drains and gutters, the rats get really hungry and they'll have a go at anything they can find, like the sequins off the expensive gowns, the fur trimmings on coats and horsehair shoulder pads. When this happens, Mr Stan and all the other owners have to go to the extra expense of calling in the official rat catcher who comes in of a Sunday. He'll arrive with five or six little Fox Terriers and the whole lane will be filled with their yapping and the squeals of the rats getting slaughterated.

Mike says the whole of The Lane is one big stinkhole, that the conditions for the workers are terrible and that factory workers in any other industry wouldn't work there in a fit. The seats the women sit on behind their sewing machines are old and broken so they make cushions to pad their backs and bring a blanket from home to drape over their knees to keep themselves warm in winter. In summer it is so hot they take off their frocks and work in their slips and brassieres.

The toilet is old and broken, without a seat, and is always clogging with you-know-what as well as the women's monthly rags. That was the first time I'd ever heard about such things and I think it was for Bozo too. There's one toilet for the fifty women machinists and it's so dark in there you can hardly see, with just an old smelly cloth to wipe your hands. There's a bin for where they should put the stuff that shouldn't go down the toilet but they don't always do the right thing and emptying the bin is also Mike's job. Poor old Mike says he can't go in without first tying a hanky around his nose and mouth.

Of course, Mike only tells Bozo and me about this, because he doesn't want Sarah and Nancy to know what he has to do. He just tells them that he has to clean the lavatory once in a while, which doesn't sound too bad when you think of city lavatories like the ones they have in the Russell Street gym. You know, white porcelain and shiny white tiles on the walls and red tiles on the floor and a chain you pull so everything disappears in a rush 'n' gurgle of water and is the very meaning of cleanliness itself.

Because we don't have that sort of posh toilet in Yankalillee we can't even imagine what it is that Mike's describing. Things like proper flush toilets being cracked, broken and old, clogged with stuff, just isn't in our experience yet. But anyway it's not the sort of thing you can tell Nancy or she'd go spare and march on Melbourne and down Flinders Lane and up the stairs where she'd wallop Mr Stan with an uppercut and grab her son back from the brink of disaster.

'All the Jewish-women machinists suffer from nerves and they're not the only ones,' Mike says. 'In the toilet there's a jar about this big,' he indicates a jar about six inches high. 'I fill it with Bex every morning and by the night it's empty. Sometimes you see them taking five or six at a time when the tea lady comes around. You can't blame them, there's fifty machines going all at once on an old wooden floor and the din is something terrible.' He says that you can cut the air with a knife, it's that stale and stinking with sweat and bodily odours, which Mike calls B.O.

The Greeks and the Italians are the worst, because they don't shave under their arms and eat stuff called garlic and they can really pong the house down! But then, on the other hand, Mike says they are the nicest to him and bring him things to eat from home that taste delicious, little flaky pastries soaked with honey called baklava and there's a delicious sweet stuff called halva the Jewish women bring in. He says he's also learned to eat sort of berry things called olives and little parcels of rice wrapped in grape leaves. Both sound weird. They also laugh a lot and flirt, but the Greek women are completely dominated by their men, who on pay day wait outside and, as soon as the women come out, take all their pay to gamble with and drink something called ouzo.

Mike explains that most of the women, not only the Jews, have had a terrible time during the war, so that their nerves were already shot before they came to Australia. If a small thing goes wrong, they just stop and cry and after a while they start their machine again. Everybody understands this and if one worker can't cope, the others finish her work for her, or if a young girl seamstress messes up her bundle they all help to unpick it and then fix it for her.

'It's like a big family, even though there's the three kinds. It's like we belong to each other, we're all part of a glamorous world that gives us our identity,' Mike says.

Mike works in Lancashire House at 36–50 Flinders Lane and he says there are forty-two rag traders and twenty dress factories in the same building. He says when you walk through the place with all the sewing machines going, the building vibrates and you have to raise your voice to be heard. When you walk down The Lane during working hours with more than two thousand industrial sewing machines going from the various garment-makers, the whole Lane has this rumble like a train approaching in the distance.

'This Mr Stan doesn't sound like a very nice boss,' Nancy says, without having heard the half of what poor old Mike has to do. 'Can't you get a job in one of the other firms?'

'Mum, Mr Stan is one of the best. It's Flinders Lane, it's all like that, it's the rag trade.'

'Collecting other people's rubbish is bad enough, but at least it happens in the fresh air! I don't want my son to be cleaning other people's lavatories and catching their rats!' she snorts, 'Mike, I think you ought to seriously think about doing something else. We haven't sunk that low yet, even though if Tommy'd had his way we would have been nightsoil carriers as well as rubbish collectors! You can always go back to school and end up being something decent like Sarah's going to be.'

Mike looks shocked. 'I am gunna end up doing something decent! Mum, I love it! I love Flinders Lane. Not doing stuff, like toilets and the rats, of course, but what I'm learning. The trade, how to make beautiful gowns, you can't believe the beautiful dresses and things that can come out of such a crap hole.' He sees our doubtful looks. 'F'instance, yesterday Miss Australia came in for a fitting, she's modelling an evening gown for us. Imagine that, Miss Australia in one of our **Style & Trend** evening gowns! And then the other day Mr Stan said to come with him and we went over to Henry Haskin and Hartnell, who are the big boys in the trade. I thought maybe Mr Stan wanted me to carry something back, but when we arrived, there were people from some of the other factories there as well and Mr Haskin had this curtain drawn across part of his showroom. I'm standing with Mr Stan, who knows everybody and is shaking their hands and chatting on. I'm feeling a bit of a galah, wondering what it is Mr Stan wants me to do. Then he turns to me and says, "You want you should be a dress designer, now you will see a dress, my boy." And then Mr Haskin draws the curtain and there's a model and she's showing the dress Henry Haskin has designed for Lady Brooks, the wife of the Governor. It's the gown she's going to wear to open the mannequin parade in the Myer Mural Hall.' Mike's eyes are excited as he describes the dress. 'It had this wide skirt of magnolia satin, embroidered with deep rose shading, palest pink to red with traceries of green leaves. It was the most beautiful gown I have ever seen!'

I tried from Mike's description to imagine what it looked like but couldn't so I said, 'I bet you could have done the embroidery better!'

Bozo, who probably couldn't imagine what the dress looked like either, came right out and said. 'But, Mike, you're not making beautiful frocks for Miss Australia or Lady Brooks, you're cleaning the shithouse!' He's angry that Mike has to do such things. 'Is it that you're not Jewish they make you do all the dirty work?'

'No, nothing like that!' Mike is adamant. 'Nobody's like that in The Lane. It doesn't matter what your religion is, the Italians are all Catholic anyway and so are a lot of the Australian girls and the Greeks have their own church called Greek Orthodox. It's just that I'm a boy who wants to be a fashion designer. They don't understand that. Not even Mr Stan. There's never been a male fashion designer in Australia. In Paris, yes, but that's different because they're French. I'm Australian and male so it doesn't make sense to them. If I want to be a steam-presser or a truck driver or a clerk in the dispatch department, that's okay, but nothing more than that.

'Mr Stan says in the old country a boy who wanted to be a tailor started at the bottom because you had to know how to do everything. He and the other owners did the same, they started sweeping the floors and running messages and slowly worked up to be skilled machinists, then tailors.

'Mr Stan calls me the *shammes* and when I asked him what it meant he told me the *shammes* in the old country is sort of the dogsbody in the synagogue, the bloke who keeps the synagogue clean and warm, calls the village to prayers, looks after the Torah, which is the Jewish Bible, only it's in a big scroll, announces the official sunset time on the Sabbath, runs the messages for the rabbi, does the repairs around the place. Mr Stan said, "Without a *shammes* in the synagogue nothing can happen, Mike, you are the *shammes* for Style & Trend."

'So when Mr Stan agreed to take me, he's done what they've always done, make the boy start as the *shammes*.'

'But you're already a skilled machinist!' I point out, 'why do you have to start from the bottom as a dogsbody?'

'And finisher and embroiderer,' Nancy butts in.

Mike shakes his head. 'Can't tell 'em that. The women wouldn't have it. Sophie says to keep *stumm*, keep quiet, about that until later. If I was a trained tailor then I'd be allowed to know how to use a sewing machine, but then I'd be the boss and not one of them, so that's okay again. But a man shouldn't be on the assembly line or seated with the girls, they just won't have it. It's like their nerves couldn't stand it. It's not *kosher*.'

'And in the meantime you're cleaning the shithouse?' Bozo says again.

'Yeah, only after I've drowned the rats and dumped them in the river, it wouldn't be hygienic otherwise.' Mike laughs at his own small joke. 'Then I'm the delivery boy and the floor sweeper and I collect and match the cabbage from the bin and fetch Mr Stan's morning cappuccino from Pelligrini's and push the clothes racks down The Lane and load the vans and write out the delivery tags and fetch a bolt of cloth from the wholesale warehouses with a handcart if we run short. After that, I oil the Singers and change the bobbins, and at the moment I'm learning how to use the steam-presser and I've persuaded Wally Simons to teach me how to be a pattern-cutter in my spare time.'

The amazing thing is that as he says this, you can see he's happy. Mike who won Best Embroidery at the Royal Melbourne Show for his Bush Blossoms is drowning rats and cleaning shithouses and learning how to use a steam presser and he's happy.

Mike laughs and tells us how Sophie says he must be careful to brush all the scraps of cotton off his clothes before he gets on the tram to come home so people won't know a fine boychick like him works in a clothing factory. 'But I tell her, "Sophie, I'm not in a factory, I'm in the fashion trade!"'

Mike tells how Mr Stan goes to Paris every season to attend the fashion parades. In Paris they don't allow you to take a camera or a sketchbook into a parade so Mr Stan has a taxi waiting outside where he keeps a sketchpad and then has the taxi drive around Paris while he frantically tries to remember what every dress looked like. He also spends a fortune on calico toiles, which are patterns for dresses made from calico that you tack together and can then try on a model to show a buyer from a department store before they order.

'Mr Stan can't even draw well,' Mike says. 'I reckon sometimes he just guesses how something goes on a dress because the result is awful. One day I'll be in Paris and London and I'll do my own fashions without having to rip off someone else's.'

It seems a long way from shithouse to fashion house, but Mike knows where he's going and Sarah says that's half the battle.

So there's Mike away to a bad start which he says he loves. That's the funny thing about Flinders Lane, the workers are happy despite the conditions, they like the bosses, like the business of being in the fashion trade, take great pride in their work and don't even mind when Christmas comes and Mr Stan says, 'Sorry, girls, we finish today, come back January.

Have a Merry Christmas Day
I'm sorry, girls, no holiday pay
Have a nice rest please, my dear
See you again in za New Year.'

Nobody grumbles like they would in a normal factory and they wouldn't ever think of reporting this to the union. Mr Stan is like a father, they're his family, and before they break up for the Christmas holidays, he brings in a piano and a piano player and they have a great party and everyone brings a plate. This is not because Mr Stan is mean, he'd supply the food if they wanted, but it's a chance for everyone to show off with their national food, Jewish, Greek, Italian and even Australian, which is always lamingtons and pavlova with passionfruit topping.

Mike says all the girls have been up half the night cooking and it's the best spread you'll ever see with foreign things he's never tasted before that are simply mouthwatering. Mr Stan puts on the booze and you can drink as much as you like because afterwards he calls taxis to take them all home. When January comes, everyone returns and signs on again.

Mike says he doesn't mind not getting holiday pay because in his first year he's only paid three pounds a week and during the Christmas holidays the restaurant he works in needs him full-time and with tips he can make eight quid a week, so he's laughing all the way to the bank. He also has time to sew, and he's beginning to build up his collection, which means with scraps of material he's saved, he's experimenting with ideas he hopes some day to use on the clothes he designs.

That was Mike's first year and his hardest because he had to be accepted. Nobody thought he'd stick it out, but by the second year they were beginning to take him seriously. They've thrown everything at him, all the worst jobs, and he's never complained and did them as well as he could so that he earned their grudging respect. They knew he was in the rag trade to stay and so he started to get a few breaks. Now he's been there five years and has learned everything there is to learn.

In his second year Mr Stan put in a word and Mike was allowed to attend fashion school at the McCabbe Academy. He was the only boy and this caused a few giggles at first among the young female students, some from the rag trade and some straight from school. But that soon stopped when they saw him on the sewing machine and when they were being taught the rudiments of hand-finishing. Mike the needle wizard left them all, including the teacher, gasping. He also knew how to work with a pattern and even how to cut one out. After two weeks, their teacher had him moved up into the second-year class. He only lasted there for three months before he was moved up again to the third year. In other words, he did the three-year course in one year and still got the top marks. I don't want to skite or anything, but you have to admit that's pretty good and had never been done before and now it's been done by a boy. Admittedly, Mike's been at this sort of thing since he was seven years old and I suppose it's not that unexpected that he'd do well. Nancy's pretty proud of how well he's doing and I think she's beginning to believe that her dream of dragging the Maloney name out of the dirt is beginning to work.

There are others in town, of course, who won't have a bar of us, who point out that the eldest Maloney got herself up the duff when she was still at school, the next one is a fairy who makes frocks with the Jews in Melbourne, the third one is a brawler who started making trouble when he was still at primary school and keeps a vicious pack of dogs and has gone into the rubbish business with a man who's spent time in gaol for near beating his business partner to death.

As for me? 'Don't be fooled by him being the youngest bushfire fighter, he's a kid who is a bit too handy with a rifle, if you ask me. You mark my words, there'll be trouble there sooner or later! Goes bush with his father, who's a well-known crim and alcoholic. They're supposed to be shooting rabbits and foxes, wouldn't be surprised if the rabbits grow a nice warm winter fleece and the foxes have cloven hooves and both turn up in a butcher's shop in Albury looking remarkably like legs o' lamb and best quality chops.'

Nancy is convinced, of course, that the main source of all of this scuttlebutt comes from Dora Templeton, but really it's just small-town stuff. There's always those who think only ill of everyone else and, like I said before, most of the town is pretty generous in their attitude to us Maloney kids and Nancy gets a fair bit of praise for bringing us up, so she shouldn't whinge.

Anyway, Mike's doing pretty good and from the second year on he's been designing his own clothes, though not for the factory, except for bits and pieces. Mr Stan uses overseas patterns and designs and then lets Mike modify them for him, but not too much. **Style & Trend** is at the expensive end of the market and makes evening gowns and women's suits and cocktail dresses. These are pretty traditional Paris fashion rip-offs and he won't let Mike have a real go to give them a different look. Can't blame him I suppose, last year they made an evening dress that took two thousand hours of beading, most of it done by Mrs P, and it sold for five thousand pounds.

They have a second label, **Collection**, at the less expensive end of the market that works mostly with the new synthetic fibres from America. The label 'Sanitised' in a garment was good news to the average buyer with the promise that the garment didn't pick up body odours. Drip-dry meant no more slaving over a hot iron. Fabrics such as bri-nylon, high-bulk orlon, banlon brocade, and terylene quickly entered the everyday vocabulary of The Lane. The New Look, introduced by Christian Dior in his glamorous expensive dresses, has now moved into the American wash 'n' wear fabrics at the cheaper end of the market. With its tiny, pulled-in waist and long wide skirts, the new design seemed the height of luxury to the average working girl without the usual labour-intensive care required of long, wide, often pleated skirts.

This was followed by the H line, the A line, the ballerinas, the frou-frou and the tulip skirt, all of which now came in the cheaper non-iron, drip-dry, easy-care fabrics. It was here that Mr Stan allowed Mike to innovate, though not as much as Mike would have liked. The rag trade was a conservative business and if something didn't happen in Europe (mostly Paris), it couldn't possibly be any good. Most of the buyers for the big department stores were cast in the same mould and too much experimentation was frowned on. It was a part of our cultural cringe, Australians couldn't possibly do things better than they were done in Europe.

Last year Mike came home on the Queen's Birthday weekend, he'd been in the rag trade four years and was nineteen. He'd changed a bit and seemed more confident with people, especially females. I suppose it's because he's worked with them for so long, he isn't afraid of them like Bozo and me and can charm them, twist them around his little finger. He's also earning good money now and sends Nancy five pounds every week which means we're in clover. The rubbish business is going well and Bozo's branched out into general transport and that's breaking a bit better than even. The offal days are well and truly over and Nancy doesn't have to work so hard at the layettes. In fact, she can pick and choose what she wants to do. I'm still up at three for the rubbish truck but I'm that used to it now that I don't suppose it's a hardship. The winter mornings are still pretty bloody awful.

On the weekend Mike was home, we went to see Mrs Barrington-Stone who invited us out to dinner and she asked Mike to tell her about the fashion industry. 'Quite a mystery to those of us in the bush, my dear, another world completely, though you certainly seem to be thriving on it.'

But, to our surprise, Mike isn't his usual bubbling-over self about the job. 'Things aren't too good at the moment, what with the credit squeeze and people in the rag trade saying it's the end of the boom-time fifties. But I disagree,' Mike says. Hearing him speak like this seems amazing. Mike's never been interested in business, which has always been strictly Bozo's department. Bozo used to say he doubted if Mike could count change.

'You don't agree, why is that?' Mrs Barrington-Stone asks. 'There's certainly a recession on the way, wool prices are down again.'

'It's not just that,' Mike says. 'They can't see what's obvious, they make clothes for the ladies in Toorak, married women who are rich and fat! Then they make the cheaper versions of the same clothes for everyone else and they call it fashion and everyone's supposed to kowtow!'

'What else could they do, people follow fashion slavishly, don't they?' Nancy asks. It's a funny statement coming from her, she's still wearing her yellow-daisy dresses. I definitely know she has six that are identical, because it's me does the washing now that Bozo's running a business.

'Times are changing, you can feel it in the air. Young office girls don't want the same clothes as a Toorak matron. They want something different, they're tired of wearing stockings and hats and white gloves and conservative colours. They want exciting, bright colours, something that shows their figures, you know, a dress or a skirt that's, well, sexy, that shows off their tan. We should be making bikinis.'

'Sexy? In the office? Oh, I don't know about that,' Mrs Barrington-Stone laughs.

Mike tells us how he tries to persuade Mr Stan to make a new young label called 'Frock 'n' Roll', a skit on the young music that's come out of America, but he doesn't want to listen. Mr Stan's made quite a lot of money in the fifties which he's put into real estate but, now, in the early sixties, with a downturn in the economy, he isn't taking chances. *A man who pisses into the wind better have a good umbrella!* Old Polish proverb. 'Mike, now is not the time, now is the time to be nice to the buyers, I want you take Miss Harris to have a nice dinner.'

Miss Harris isn't a dragon like some of the older female buyers, she's in her early thirties and is already the chief buyer for a chain called Country Stores. She is no pushover as Mr Stan well knows, having tried the chocolates-and-flowers routine and finally what he calls 'A little smile in the hand, darling', which, when translated out of rag-trade language, means a bribe. She's been in to see the summer collection and, according to Mr Stan and Mrs P and the two models hired to show the dresses and coats, couldn't take her eyes off Mike. She hasn't made a decision and Mr Stan thinks a little Mike Maloney with the Italian looks might do the trick.

'You show her a good time, Mike, be nice to her, go along, drink some champagne, take her to Florentino's. I phone Mr Luigi, I book the best table. An orchid, you take an orchid, the biggest, no expenses spared, compliments Style & Trend. Here, take the phone, call.'

Well, Mike does the deed and he's got taxi money from the cashier and picks up Miss Harris who is wearing a Hartnell cocktail dress and Charles Jourdan high heels. To his surprise, she's not wearing a hat or the mandatory gloves and her hair is cut in a bob and, all round, she looks pretty good, even to Mike who isn't all that taken with girls except as clothes horses. But it turns out Miss Harris is a pretty good clothes horse and Mike, who can talk the hind leg off a donkey, keeps her laughing in the taxi. She's wearing the orchid and he's told her how pretty she looks. He's also confident about his table manners, having worked in a quite nice restaurant in St Kilda Road and, anyway, Mrs Barrington-Stone has shown Sarah how to eat properly and what all the knives and forks and spoons and the different glasses are for and Sarah's taught us, so Mike knows he won't make a fool of himself or appear to be too much of a country bumpkin.

However, Mike's not sure Mr Stan is getting his money's worth because there's no mention on the way to the restaurant about the **Collection** range. The head waiter at Florentino's, Mr Luigi, greets them personally at the door and makes a fuss over Miss Harris. This is mostly because earlier in the afternoon, he's received an envelope with ten pounds in it from Mr Stan and the instructions that no expense is to be spared and to send the bill to the factory, where it will be paid in cash. He flicks his fingers once Mike and Miss Harris have been seated and a waiter wearing what looks like a tablecloth around his waist brings a bottle of French champagne.

'Compliments of Mr Stan of Style & Trend, who sends his best wishes, Miss Harris,' Mr Luigi says, pouring the champagne.

They order oysters and then the veal scaloppine and a bit more French champagne and they're chatting on a treat about this and that, all the rag-trade goss. But every time Mike mentions **Collection**'s summer range, Miss Harris shrugs and changes the subject. He keeps trying so eventually she says, 'Mike, I'm not at all sure, the summer range is . . . well, frankly, it's uninspired.' Mike doesn't know what to say because he agrees with her. Then, halfway through the main course, she leans over and puts her hand over Mike's. 'Why don't you call me Sally?'

'Righto, Sally,' Mike says, real confident, because the champagne has gone to his head a bit and he's feeling pretty relaxed.

'Now!' Sally Harris says, 'Tell me about the **Sarah Maloney** label!'

Mike, even with the champagne in him, is completely gobsmacked. 'Huh? Beg yours?' He's suddenly forgotten all his fancy language and is talking pure Maloney.

'The **Sarah Maloney** label,' Sally Harris repeats.

'Ah . . . how'd you know about that?' Mike says, trying to recover his dignity.

'Let's say a little bird told me.' She smiles. 'No, I've got a sister who's a lecturer in Arts at the uni and she bought the pink and green bolero jacket and skirt, very risqué wearing it with matching bra. Pink and green though? Isn't that a touch *outré*?'

Mike is immediately on the defensive. 'You mean, in bad taste? It was bottle-green,' Mike says, 'Pink lining and green jacket, like a watermelon, with a pink cummerbund tie to the green skirt. Nobody says a watermelon looks wrong, do they? You look at a watermelon and you think it looks sexy, clean and crisp but also full of sunlight. You couldn't grow a watermelon in the cold, could you?'

'Well, it's certainly a different approach with the short skirt as well.'

'It's time we gave up these silly notions about colour, that blue and green should never be seen, that sort of crap, it's a load of rubbish.

Most of the earth is blue and green, blue sky, green grass, God seems to have done okay using those two colours. It's not the colours, it's how you use them, put them together! It's also the fabric. Does the fabric feel pink, if you know what I mean?'

'And the length of the skirt, just below the knee?'

'It's summer, brown legs without stockings, open sandals with a heel, that's what being an Australian is all about, isn't it?'

'I like that,' Sally Harris says. 'Tell me more, please.'

'As I just said, we're Australian, look at the light, bright sunshine, sharp colours. The shade under the trees is black, everything's definite, red soil, acid-green gum trees, yellow wattle, blue sky, azure sea.'

'Some might say we're lacking in subtlety,' Sally Harris suggests.

'That's just it! I never thought of it like that, but that's precisely it. Why should clothes, I mean their colours, be subtle?' Mike doesn't wait for a reply because an idea occurs to him. 'Yes, yes, that's it all right! Grey skies, cold climate, short summer, long autumn and miserable winter, trees losing their leaves, witches' brooms against a grey sky, wind howling, that's Europe, ain't it? Rug up, protect yourself. Wrap, wrap, wrap. They have to be subtle, clothes have to wrap and hide, browns and russets and greys and blacks, maybe a touch of orange, occasionally a tinge of red for a dying sunset. That's them, and that's okay, but it's *not* us. Why must we, a people of the sun, wear what Europe decides is fashion!'

'Because we're snobs?' Sally laughs, 'Scared to be different.'

'Maybe some of us are. For most it's because we're told how to behave by a bunch of people who can't get Paris or Europe out of their minds. People who were born in Europe and, despite what's happened to them, still think of Europe as their heartland.'

'You mean the Jews?'

'Well, yes, but only because most of the bosses in the rag trade are Jewish and Europe's mostly where they were born. But what gets me is this. Six million Jews died at the hands of the Germans and those that managed to escape the concentration camps still think Europe is the intellectual, emotional and aesthetic centre of the world, I mean, c'mon!'

'Old ways die hard,' Sally says.

'I know, it's not really their fault. They can't help it. People like

Mr Stan think Australians are peasants and not only in a fashion sense. They may be right, I'm a peasant, but only because I've never been given a choice. We're told what's right and what's wrong. We're terrified of making a mistake or appearing to be gauche. We're wearing Europe on our backs and it's time we stopped being copycats. Mr Stan and Hartnell and Harry Haskin and all the rest of the rag-trade bosses here make their annual pilgrimage to the Paris fashion shows and sit up and beg for scraps like Bozo's Bitzers, and whatever they bring back becomes the fashion law for the season.'

'Bozo's Bitzers?'

'Bozo's my brother, he has five dogs that do tricks, you know, sit up and beg for scraps.'

'Mike, you can't blame them.'

'You're right again, I can't. It's what they know, what's safe, what they can steal and then sell to the buyers.' Mike is so carried away he forgets where he is. 'It's the buyers who think it's sophisticated to genuflect at the altar of European fashion, who demand more of the same every year.'

'Oops, that's me,' Sally Harris says, reaching for her glass of champagne.

Mike realises what he's just said. 'Present company excepted, of course,' he says, but much too late.

Sally Harris takes a long, slow sip from her champagne glass, looking directly at Mike. She's pretty with blue eyes and dark hair. 'Have you been to Paris, Mike?' she asks, probably knowing full well that he hasn't.

Mike laughs, colouring. 'No, I haven't even been to Sydney,' he admits.

'Well, I have. The Wool Board invited me to the Paris fashion shows last year. It's hard not to be impressed with the French. They have an assurance and a sense of style that leaves you feeling you've got two left feet and a rubber mouth. I felt dumpy and parochial even though I was wearing a Chanel original, paid for by the firm of course, and a pair of handmade Italian alligator pumps with the sheerest nylons I could buy from Schiaparelli.' Sally laughs. 'I'm supposed to scrub up reasonably well, but I felt like a country bumpkin, Paris does that to you, it's the easiest place in the world to get an inferiority complex. We're at the launch of the Christian Dior collection and one of the hosts, the usual tall, beautifully dressed and urbane Frenchman, hands me a glass of champagne. It looks like liquid gold and comes in this tall fluted glass, like an elongated tulip. "Oh what a funny champagne glass," I exclaim, looking up at my French host. "Is this part of the show, you know, some sort of a gimmick?" I don't allow him to answer as I gush on, "No, don't tell me, let me guess, it's the shape of the year's Dior skirts, how very clever!"

'All I'd ever seen are these.' She points to the shallow and wide-brimmed champagne glass she's holding and laughs. 'He looked at me, I think a little amazed, not quite sure he'd heard correctly, what with my Australian accent and all.'

She now imitates the Frenchman talking in English, 'No, no, Mademoiselle Arass, champagne is, how you say, wine for beautiful bubools to play, they must not escape before they have danced to make za champagne.' He stops, searching for a word, 'Sparkling! Za glass and the champagne, they are partners, like a good model and a beautiful gown, where one begins and za other ends, who can tell this mystery?' Sally Harris looks at Mike. 'We still have a lot to learn, but you're right, it's time we took a few steps out into the Australian sunlight.'

'Of course we have lots to learn!' says Mike. 'But can't we use their knowledge and our light? The sun is shining, the birds are chirping and what's more, they're rosellas, blazing with colour, the wattle is a riot of yellow blossom against an impossibly clean blue sky and our leading fashion magazine has just declared that the colour for Summer 1961 is navy and white! Navy bloody blue and white and go easy on the white! Let me quote: *Navy blue is the colour this season with a soupçon of white around collars and cuff, any more than the lightest touch would be deemed vulgar*. Deemed vulgar! Who does this "deeming"? Who writes this shit?'

Sally throws back her head and laughs, 'I think I'm falling in love with you, Michael Maloney.'

Mike blushes. He's accustomed to the factory girls having a bit of a go. They can be a fairly rough mob sometimes and indecent suggestions are not unknown, in fact they occur on an almost daily basis, the Greeks being the worst, closely followed by the Australians. But Sally Harris is an ex-model and, well, she's been around and is very sophisticated and there's no shortage of men who dream about getting into her pants. In fact, it's almost a total preoccupation with most of the sales reps in The Lane. They'd rather have her than any of the models because they reckon she's 'experienced', a woman of the world. Sally now sees Mike's embarrassment and reaches over and places her hand over his. 'It's okay, Mike, I'm not going to seduce you,' she looks up and grins, 'not just yet anyway.'

Mike forgets he's supposed to be a poofter, but what he really is, is a virgin, though he's not sure he knows the difference. He's been that excited that someone in the fashion industry is prepared to listen to him that the other thing hasn't even occurred to him. Someone is listening at last, someone who isn't consumed with her own importance like most of the buyers who require truckloads of chocolates and flowers and an anthology of ego massaging, *'Darling, you look vunderful, the suit, sensational!'* to some fat frump with upside-down legs and an order book in her crocodile-skin handbag.

'Mike, I know why we're having dinner, it wasn't your idea, was it? Mr Stan's?'

Mike nods, 'But that doesn't mean I'm not enjoying it, Sally. It's the first time I've been able to talk to anyone in the trade about how I feel about clothes design.'

Sally sighs. 'I'm enjoying myself as well, but yeah, all right, you work for Mr Stan and he wants you to flog the **Collection** 1961 summer range to Country Stores, that's about it, isn't it?'

Mike looks at Sally Harris sheepishly. 'Yup.'

'So tell me, Michael Maloney, what is the major colour component of the **Collection** range?'

Mike blushes violently. 'Navy blue with a soupçon of white.' Now they both fall about so that the entire restaurant is looking at them, but they're so obviously enjoying themselves that Mr Luigi doesn't come over, and most of the people in the famous restaurant don't seem to mind. A waiter walks over and sees that the champagne bottle is empty. Mike orders another. The kid is learning fast but it may not have been the smartest thing to do.

Sally, still chuckling, glances sideways at Mike. 'Now, tell me about the **Sarah Maloney** label.'

The **Sarah Maloney** label has been going for more than three years and is the reason Mike can send Nancy five pounds a week. It's also paid for two professional Singer sewing machines, one for Sophie and one for himself, as well as for the fabrics that go into Mike's designs. It all started after Templeton was born and Sarah got her figure back, which was always slim, with long legs and a narrow waist.

Sarah had nothing to wear, I mean she was feeding her baby and her breasts were larger than normal and none of her old clothes really fitted her. Not that she had that many in the first place. So Mike started to make her clothes, him and Sophie, with Mike buying the fabrics and doing the designs. At first he simply followed the fashions of the day but after about a year things started to change. It must have been about the time he went to the McCabbe Academy when he started to be different.

It began as a bit of fun, something for Mike and Sophie to do together. It worked real good because Morrie was working at the *Age* and Sarah would come home at night and look after Templeton so that Sophie could finish her piecework if the baby had kept her from it during the day. On the weekends, Morrie and Sarah would study together and Mike and Sophie would design a dress for Sarah or, if Sophie needed to catch up with her piecework, Mike would hop in and help her.

It was a crowded little house but somehow it worked. Tommy and John Crowe came down one weekend early in the piece and turned the back porch into a sleep-out for Mike, as well as a workroom large enough so that when they eventually got two professional Singers they would be able to work in it together. It wasn't exactly what you'd call spacious and Mike would laugh and say to Sophie, 'What are you complaining about, they're better working conditions than The Lane.'

Mike would look around while he was doing messages or things in The Lane or elsewhere for offcuts, fabrics that were different. He might find a scrap here or a small length of cloth somewhere else and he'd offer to buy it. Sometimes the owners would let him have the scrap of cloth for nothing. The girls in the factory started scrounging as well.

Word would get around that someone was using a light wool in brilliant scarlet for the lining of a winter coat and, mysteriously, half a yard would be handed to Mike by one of the factory girls, who said it had been given to her by a friend in another firm. Mike also discovered furnishing fabrics, beautiful brocades imported from Europe, cottons for curtains in colourful designs nobody would have thought to use in the fashion trade. Even the tiniest scraps of velvets and other precious fabrics too small to be useful to anyone would be cherished for appliqué work. The miracle of Mike's designs was in the use of scraps, bits of material inlaid or used as a contrasting pocket or a collar or even a belt. The result was that the fabrics used were of a very high quality and the clothes beautifully made but they cost much less than the expensive labels.

Soon Sarah was going to lectures at the university in a new dress or outfit every week. At first it was only the male med students who noticed, but being men it was more a matter of seeing how very pretty she was. However it didn't take long for the female students on campus to take notice. One thing led to another and Sarah would be asked where she bought the fabulous new dress. The first time this happened, it was a third-year student doing Arts, whose parents must have had a quid or two because she was always dolled up to the nines.

'That's a wonderful dress, what's the label?' she asked Sarah.

Sarah, without really thinking, grinned and replied, 'Oh, it's a Sarah Maloney', gently sending her up.

'It's fabulous, where is the shop? Toorak Road? I simply must have one of her outfits.'

Sarah couldn't explain it's a joke but had enough nous to say, 'No, it's . . . it's a private collection, I'm glad you like it, I'll tell him.'

'Him? I thought you said the label was **Sarah Maloney**?'

Sarah's got herself into a bit of a pickle. 'Yes, that's the label, the designer is a male.'

'Well, does he sell?'

'I'll ask him,' Sarah replied.

And that's how it started on campus. Mike who knew one of the label-makers in The Lane, had him make up a roll of **Sarah Maloney** labels to sew into his garments. Morrie was roped in to do the measurements and each lunch hour in the little garden outside the

Zoology labs Morrie would take careful measurements and Sarah would write these down along with the colouring of the student or any special feature, eyes, hands, shoulders, legs, if the student wanted an original **Sarah Maloney**. Otherwise it would simply be the dress of the week or of previous weeks made to a particular student's measurements.

Morrie, who would fuss around in his white lab coat, looked just the part of the busy little tailor as Sarah, looking beautiful in the dress of the week, wrote down his instructions and measurements on a notepad. They both loved taking the measurements, as it took them outside the Medical Faculty and where they could meet other female students. Sarah discovered she was already a bit of a hero to most of the female students, who now pestered her to stand for the student council. Sarah felt, with Templeton and her studies, it was more than she could handle, but eventually she stood as a third-year student and was elected, gaining every female student vote in the university and most of the Medical Faculty votes, although Engineering let it be known that they were voting as a block for anyone as long as it wasn't a female or Sarah 'trouble' Maloney.

Mike's clothes aren't cheap because he uses expensive fabrics and they are so very well made and hand-finished. However they aren't beyond the means of some of the students from wealthier families. Some designs sell well and Mike and Sarah could make up fifteen garments in a week.

It worries Sarah that there are students who can't afford a **Sarah Maloney** even though they'd practically kill for one. So, for his Summer 1959 collection Mike designs a day dress in three styles made from tablecloth American gingham in the most outrageous fluorescent colours, pinks and lime greens, blues, purples and yellows. He got the cloth cheaply from the importer because none of the linen departments of the retail stores were willing to order the cloth, thinking it too bright for Australian dining and kitchen tables.

He also designs his 'watermelon' dress with the little bolero top and cummerbund for *après*-beach and summer evenings. The summer dresses are priced at three pounds ten shillings and the female component of Melbourne University goes berserko kaperko! (Maloney word.)

Over three weeks, orders for two hundred and seventeen fluorescent gingham dresses, which Mike has called 'Broadway Lights', are taken and also for fifty 'watermelon' designs, that sell for four pounds and ten shillings.

By rag-trade standards these are not big numbers, but what it is allowing is for Mike to build up a collection to ultimately show to the big buyers. The dresses that sell easily are photographed by a friend of Mike's, a young German photographer named Helmut Newton, toiles are cut so that the pattern exists, and one dress is made up for racking and showing.

The lovely thing is that Mike is also designing clothes for Templeton, which Sophie is making. She makes up a few of the designs as samples and visits Toorak Road, pushing the stroller with Templeton in it as the model and with a whole heap of samples in a canvas bag she's made that is attached to the stroller. The designs are an instant success and Sophie starts to get more orders than she can cope with. Mike's infant designs are like his other clothes, lots of colour and imagination.

Next thing, Nancy and Mrs Rika Ray are hauled in to help with the appliqué work, smocking and embroidery. The little garments get sent up on the train to Yankalillee and are collected at Wangaratta by Bozo. Anyway, Sophie's flogging her kids' clothes and getting ridiculous prices for her **Suckfizzle** label. 'Suckfizzle' turns out to be just about the best name possible for infants' clothes.

In 1960 the buyer from Georges in Collins Street asks Sophie to come in and see her, she wants an exclusive range made specially for Georges under the Georges label. It's a big temptation, Georges is the establishment shop where the rich and famous go. But Mike, following consultation with Bozo and Sarah, advises Sophie not to lose her label, her name is everything and what's to stop Georges from terminating her contract one day and ripping off her designs. So Sophie says no to Georges, who are pretty miffed, because they're not accustomed to being turned down. Then Mike has this idea and Georges buy it. Sophie's label says '**Suckfizzle at Georges**', which is to be an exclusive line not available elsewhere.

By the sixth year Mike, Sarah, Morrie and Sophie have been in Melbourne, which is 1961, and by the time Sally Harris and Mike are having dinner at Florentino's, Sophie has three women doing piecework for her and she can't keep up with the orders coming in.

Nancy is now getting ten pounds a week from Mike, who is earning fifteen pounds a week at Style & Trend but is pocketing fifty pounds from his **Sarah Maloney** label and another twenty from the **Suckfizzle** kids' range, all of which, except for what he sends to Nancy and a bit for Sarah's and his lunches, goes into fabrics and building up his sample collection.

With the good money Sophie is bringing in, Morrie could easily give up his job as a lift driver at the *Age*, but won't. He says he's getting fluent in Australian, a language he recognises as quite different to English, and also he has lots of good mates dependent on him, who bring their families in with all their medical problems. In fact, some nights, the Morrie lift-clinic is so busy, the union is considering whether they should demand an assistant lift driver from Management. Besides, he says he can't study at home because of the din of the sewing machines, which he calls 'The second industrial revolution already!'

Sarah doesn't mind the noise. With Nancy and us kids, she's always had chaos around her. Morrie, of course, is killing it at university, in fact, most days he tries hard not to be a smart-arse, because he often knows more than the lecturer about the subject being taught, but Sarah is also thought to be a brilliant student. 'It's not me!' she protests when she's congratulated on her results, 'It's Morrie, he drills me day and night until I know everything.' She laughs, 'It's not the university exams I find difficult, it's the bloody Suckfizzle ones I dread.'

All this is the background to Sally Harris asking Mike about his **Sarah Maloney** label.

Well, two bottles of champagne, a bottle each, is just a tad too much for Mike, who doesn't really drink and it's Sally Harris who orders the taxi and next thing Mike knows he's in this flat. At the time he doesn't even know what suburb it's in, but the lounge room has a picture window that looks over the Yarra and it's pretty posh.

I'm not sure I should tell what happens next because I can't really put it in the right words. They should be good words because what happened Mike said was very, very nice. But I'll just tell what he remembered and told me, well sort of, because I can't get Mike's words exactly any more because he now talks differently, he knows things we don't and he uses words I don't use or even know.

Sally Harris talks to him about the **Sarah Maloney** label. She says she thinks she can get Country Stores to back him, for a percentage of the action of course. She wants to see his samples, but she thinks she knows enough and has seen enough to be pretty confident that she can sell her directors on the project. Country Stores will then launch the **Sarah Maloney** label as a winter range in 1962.

Mike's pissed but he can't believe his ears, the money to go his own way, to do the things he wants to do. He sits there pretty stunned, with the room sort of going round and the ceiling tilting and him trying to get what Sally Harris has just said fixed in to his champagne-soaked brain.

'Thank you, Sally,' he manages to say. 'Thank you, but why? What can I ever do for you?'

Sally laughs. 'We're about to find out, Michael Maloney, come with me.'

She takes Mike by the hand and leads him into her bedroom. Even smashed, Mike remembers how it looked. Big double bed with this brilliant old-fashioned quilt, every colour in the world in the squares and all the other furniture white, with a large picture above the bed of yellow wattle blossom with rosellas frolicking among the blooms. I could have told him this was a most unlikely situation and the artist couldn't have known the bush very well. Rosellas like fruit and a bit of nectar, they're not going to bugger around with wattle blossom that's got neither. But I don't, because I want all the juicy details and I don't want him distracted from the main subject at hand.

Sally makes him stand at the end of the bed and she starts to undress him, kissing him as she removes his tie then his jacket and then his shirt, so he's standing in his strides. She's kissing him all over his chest and neck and on the mouth and Mike says she tastes of champagne and smells of rose petals, but it's really Chanel No. 5 that's worn out a little. Then he becomes aware that she's put on some music, or anyway there's music coming into the bedroom, something classical, soft and romantic. She goes down on her knees, unlaces his shoes and takes them off and his socks. He's got a hole in one sock, which he remembers too late.

Now he's standing in his strides, bare feet on the carpet. He knows what's coming next and he's shitting himself, because he's got this raging hard-on and he knows he should but at the same time he knows he shouldn't. Him being what Tommy said he was and all. But she doesn't go for his belt or unzip his fly.

'Stand there,' she commands. Then, slowly, standing in front of him and never taking her eyes off him, she undresses herself like some sort of ritual. The room is still going round and round, but sometimes it stops long enough for Mike to see how pretty she is. She's still got her model figure and long shapely legs and pert breasts and Mike thinks she'd look wonderful in his watermelon outfit. Then suddenly she's standing in the nuddy in front of him.

'Your move next,' she says.

Old Mike can't get his strides off fast enough and then his underpants, but they don't come off smoothly, there's this resistance pointing up to the ceiling and getting in the way.

Now they're both standing naked and Sally Harris melts down onto her knees (Mike's words, I swear!) and she takes him in her mouth and starts to stroke his old fella with her lips. I admit, I've got a hard-on with Mike telling me all this. Mike then says it was like going to heaven twice over and he thinks he can't hold on, any moment he's going to blast off and there'll surely be a crack in the roof. The ceiling and the walls are still going around but it doesn't seem to have anything to do with him, it now seems part of the whole experience like she's made that happen as well. But she seems to know exactly the right moment to stop and she takes his hand and makes him lie on the bed and she climbs on top of him and kisses him all over. Then their lips and their tongues sort of mingle and she's rubbing herself, breasts and things, all over him and he's moaning and crying for mercy. (Oops! I may have put that last bit in myself.) Sally Harris sits astride him and comes up to rest on her knees, leans forward and kisses him and, at the same time, she produces this rubber from nowhere and slips it onto his old fella in a flash so neat-o that Mike doesn't even feel it going on and only discovers it afterwards. Then she takes him in her hand and pushes him inside her and there's nothing more he can do, she's completely in control.

'Now, darling,' she says to Mike, 'we're going to ride a cockhorse to Banbury Cross!' and she starts galloping and starts to moan and gallop faster and faster until he bursts open and it's all over red rover and Mike says it was wonderful and afterwards Sally said he had the makings of a stud though had a lot to learn but luckily he'd enrolled at the right academy. How's that for brilliant, hey?

That's more or less how Mike told it to me, though maybe I let my imagination get in there a bit, with things like Mike crying for mercy, but I don't think so. Anyway, Mike's told me, which I suppose he shouldn't, because Sally Harris is a real beaut bird and he likes her a lot. The offer she made, though, turned out to be a disaster, which I'll explain later. But the way Mike tells me, their lovemaking, it's not rude or anything, Mike's a pretty gentle sort of bloke when he's not being sarcastic or witty. He just told how he lost his virginity which is something that has still to happen to me and probably never will, even though I dream about how it will happen most nights before I go to bed and sometimes while I'm asleep as well. The way Mike told it was better than I just did, because he said it soft and nice and not like he was boasting or anything, I was forced to take myself away to the dunny out the back for a private consultation with what Nancy calls 'Mr Trouble'.

Chapter Sixteen

The generous offer Sally Harris makes to Mike sits on his conscience for a few days. He's gone out to dinner with her admittedly on Mr Stan's orders, but Style & Trend paid for the night out and the end result was that she's turned down Mr Stan's summer collection with the exception of three styles, all three of which are Mike's designs.

Mr Stan gets Sally Harris's phone call and he isn't a happy man. He's got sixteen styles in his range and she's ordered only fifty of each of the three styles. He's not stupid, it takes him about two seconds to realise that these are Mike's creations.

He calls Mike into his office, he's sitting behind his cluttered desk in an old captain's swivel chair. There's only one other chair in the tiny room, a bentwood upright such as people have in their kitchens sometimes. It's got several garments piled on it so Mike has to stand, but he would anyway until Mr Stan told him to sit, which, on this occasion he doesn't. Also, he's not told about the dud order from Miss Harris at Country Stores.

'So Mike, you have a good time za other night, Florentino's?'

'Yes, thank you, Mr Stan.'

'No, no, thank you is not necessary, you are working for Style & Trend, the summer range, how goes it?'

'You were away three days last week and then the weekend. Today's Monday, I asked first thing to come and see you, sir.'

'Yes, I go to Sydney, za overnight train to get the Farmers' order. No good.'

'Oh, I'm sorry, what about Grace Bros?'

Mr Stan shrugs, 'So, so, not good not bad. They want cheap, I told them I don't do rubbish, they want *chozzerai* they go to Sol Epstein in Sydney, he got plenty rubbish.' He pauses, then looks up at Mike. 'So tell me, my boy, Miss Harris, it went okey-dokey?'

'The dinner, yes . . . I don't think she likes our summer range, Mr Stan.'

Mr Stan looks sternly up at Mike. 'Oh? So tell me, please?'

'The navy and white, she . . . she thinks it's a bit dull, the word she used was "uninspired".'

Mr Stan doesn't say anything, he picks up a gold Parker 51 from the desk and, with the cap still on, uses it to tap the top of the desk, looking down again. 'Yes, I know this, she calls on za telephone this morning.' There is a long pause when he continues to tap slowly, deliberately as though the pen is somehow counting down, then he looks up at Mike. 'So, tell me Michael, she's put in an order, hundred fifty dresses, one day, two days the machinists, maximum, an insult!'

'I tried to influence her, Mr Stan, but I think she'd already made up her mind. The dinner, it turned out a bit of a waste, I'm afraid.'

'Waste? What you mean waste? Did you *shtup* her?'

Mike has picked up enough Yiddish to know what this means and he blushes violently. But before he can say anything Mr Stan barks, 'You're supposed to *shtup* her, Michael. What are you? You *shtup* her, then we get a big order!'

'I . . . I don't know what you mean, Mr Stan. Miss Harris, I don't think she's like that.'

'Miss Harris is a woman and a buyer!' Mr Stan shouts, 'You are a boy, a nice healthy boy, take my word, she's like that! It is *you*! Are you a *faygeleh*?'

Mike's never heard the word, but it's immediately clear what Mr Stan means, it's more Tommy talk. 'I resent that, Mr Stan,' Mike protests.

'Resent away, a fact is a fact! If it isn't a fact, what's to resent? Now tell me, a coincidence maybe? The three styles she orders, they are za ones *you* designed.'

Mike looks surprised. Then says, 'Mr Stan, I didn't know that! I promise you I didn't tell her I'd had anything to do with the range, I'll swear it on the Bible!'

'The Bible? *Your* Bible maybe! You think I am stupid? A *shmuck*, you think Stanislaw Zelinski is *meshugge*?'

Mike knows both words well, they're used all the time by the Jewish workers and mean 'You think I'm a fool? You think I'm crazy?'

'No, Mr Stan, but I didn't tell her any of the styles were mine.'

'Deduction! You know deduction? Let me show you deduction! When we are ordering the fabric for the summer range, you tell me you think navy and white is not right. You remember that?'

'Yes, but . . .'

'No, no, let me finish, then you talk. When we cut za patterns you come to me, "Mr Stan, these patterns are not right, they will not sell." You remember that also? I say to you, "Mike, you know from nothing. These patterns they are from Paris, the latest no less, navy blue and white, that is the summer colour!"' He looks at Mike. 'I am right so far, yes?'

'Yes, sir, but about the patterns. I pointed out to you the article in the American *Vogue* which said they'd bombed in New York and the American Midwest. Macys couldn't sell the Paris look, the style or the navy and white summer colours!'

'Who cares from New York? This is Melbourne, Australia, what do we want to know should happen in New York!'

'Yes, that's exactly what you said then. You also said that Australians would do what they're told. "They're *shmucks*, Mike! Tell them here comes from Paris the latest and they will wear sacks with holes in it,"' Mike says, using Mr Stan's precise phrasing.

Mr Stan ignores this last remark and, raising the pen into the air above his head, continues. 'Deduction! Then you say to me, "Mr Stan, please let me design some of za range."' Mr Stan shrugs, lowering the pen and placing it on the desk. 'What the hell, I am a nice man, I like to help. The boy he wants to design, be a little kind, what harm can come, two, three dresses in the samples. Buyers always they like to reject something, better not the Paris, better the regular genius.'

Mr Stan picks the pen up again and points it at Mike's chest. 'So you think I am stupid.' His eyes light up suddenly and he throws down the pen and grabs his head in both hands. '*Feh*! I *am* stupid! You did *shtup* her! Then afterwards, when all is lovey-dovey, you ask she should buy anyway your designs!' He pauses to catch his breath, 'You know what is a designer in Australia? A designer is a glorified cutter! A nobody!'

He bangs his fist down onto the desk, 'Now I see, now I see.' Then he looks up at Mike. 'What you done, it shouldn't happen to a dog! You put on za *kibosh*. I gave you a chance, you have betrayed me. I pay the entertainment, you *shtup* the buyer, you win, I lose. Go, see the cashier! You are sacked!'

Mike is both furious and close to tears, he's trembling but doesn't know if it's from fear or anger. He takes a deep breath and tries to speak calmly. 'Please, Mr Stan, you've got it all wrong!'

Mr Stan half-rises in his chair and points to Mike, 'No, *you* got it all wrong! Go!' he roars.

And then Mike loses it and blows his top. 'Mr Stan, your bloody summer range is crook, so are my three designs! I'm not proud of them, *you* kept bloody fiddling with them, adding a flounce, taking away the high collar, fucking them up! Maybe you shouldn't have sent me to try to sell the range. I'm not a salesman, *you're* the salesman, you and Mr Green! I did my best! You wouldn't have sent me if you weren't desperate! If you didn't know the summer range is a heap of shit! *Please*, Mr Stan, listen to me, I have a proposition!' It all comes out half-shouted and fast, one sentence bumping into the next.

'Proposition? My God! *You* have a proposition? Let me tell you something, young man, I have a proposition! Get out my office, out za factory, out my life!'

Mike turns and walks to the doorway. He suddenly realises that the factory is silent, all the workers have stopped, everyone has been listening. Mr Stan's office is right next to the factory floor so he can see what's going on. Now Mike has the presence of mind to stop and face Mr Stan. 'Mr Stan, I want you to remember I said I had a proposition, I still have. Take my designs for the winter collection.'

This piece of blatant and mistimed arrogance is the final straw, Mr Stan goes bright red and Mike thinks he's going to have a heart attack. 'Get out! I call za police! Get out! Get out!'

And so now Mike is out of a job, which he doesn't really mind because he can sell more than he and Sophie can make of his own designs and he doesn't need Mr Stan's fifteen pounds a week. What worries him is his standing in the rag trade. Flinders Lane is a close-knit community and much of the business is done on a handshake. Mr Stan is not only popular but also has an impeccable reputation. In the early days he'd sometimes fall behind, but in the end he always paid what he owed. A quiet word in a supplier's ear from Mr Stan and Mike is in real trouble.

Mike returns to Station Street and the Carlton terrace feeling pretty glum. He tells Sophie and Morrie what's happened. They already know half the story because Sophie was terribly excited about Mike going to dinner with Sally Harris and she'd fussed around him, ironing his white shirt with the starched collar, pressing and brushing his sports jacket several times over and tugging on his tie to get the knot right. She even wanted to polish his shoes but Mike wouldn't let her and did them himself.

When he returned early the next morning looking somewhat dishevelled and with a terrible hangover, Sarah soon pried the story out of him and she and Sophie both laughed, giving him a glass of Andrews Liver Salts, and sent him off to work holding his head. Sarah and Sophie retired to the kitchen and made a cup of tea and, without saying anything to each other, raised their cups, Mike wasn't what Tommy'd said he was. Mike had slept with his first woman and, it seemed, had come out of the experience with flying colours and a French-champagne headache.

Over the next few days Mike would tell them the story of the Florentino's dinner, without placing too much emphasis on the later visit to Sally Harris's flat, which by common consent becomes a subject of some delicacy not to be mentioned other than as a sly glance or a lift of the eyebrows across the kitchen table. Mike ruefully confessed how neatly Sally Harris had trapped him when he'd gone on about navy and white and she'd asked him, knowing of course because she'd already seen it, what the **Collection** summer colours were. They'd all laughed uproariously at this except Morrie.

Morrie, listening, clasped his head in his hands. 'A designer yes, definitely. A salesman?' He shrugs and spreads his hands, 'What can I say, mate, couldn't sell snow to Eskimo.' Morrie likes to call everyone 'mate' now he's an Australian. Only he still pronounces it 'mite'.

Now, after Mike's been sacked, they listen tremulously to the rest of the story. Mike has a good ear and he tells it pretty well exactly how it occurred. There was silence around the kitchen table when he'd finished.

Morrie turns to Sophie and says, 'This is not right, we go see Mr Stan tomorrow. Explain to him.' Sophie nods in agreement.

Then Sarah says, 'No, wait on. Mr Stan is not entirely in the wrong, Mike has to share the blame.'

Mike is indignant. 'Why?'

Sarah sighs. 'Talk about not taking the spoon out of the sink! For a start, you were there to try to sell Miss Harris the **Collection** range.'

'I didn't ask for the job, I was given it. I've never pretended to be a salesman!' Mike protests.

'No, but you're not stupid either. And you accepted the task. You happily went to dinner in a posh restaurant, drank French champagne, all of which, I remind you, Mr Stan was paying for. Then you got tipsy and carried away with your own self-importance, telling Miss Harris all your theories and you forgot about why you were there in the first place. Next thing you've condemned the **Collection** summer range out of hand.'

'Hey, wait a cotton-pickin' minute!' Mike yells in protest. 'Sally, Miss Harris, had already said she didn't like the **Collection** range. She'd already decided to only give us a small order. She said it was uninspired.'

'Uninspired? That's not how I heard you tell it,' Sarah says. 'What you said was that she had serious doubts, that the range was uninspired.'

'Well? That's the same thing!' Mike turns to Sophie, 'Isn't it, Soph?'

'Listen to Sarah,' Morrie says quietly.

'No, it's not the same thing, Mike! Serious doubts suggests that she wants to have those doubts eliminated. If I recall correctly she said, "Mike, I'm not at all sure, the summer range frankly is uninspired," or something close to that. She wanted you to tell her why she might be wrong.'

'But I couldn't do that, the colours *and* the style hadn't gone over in America, it had bombed! It was obvious the fashion wasn't going to work here as well.'

'Oh, who says? You? But you don't *know* that will happen here, do you? Mr Stan is right, America isn't Australia and Michael Maloney is not an internationally recognised arbiter of fashion trends.'

'Whose side are you on anyway?' Mike bursts out.

'Nobody's,' Sarah says. 'But if Morrie and Sarah are going to see Mr Stan to explain, to clear the decks, then they have to know the whole story so they can be fair. Otherwise Mr Stan is going to make them look like fools.'

'But Mr Stan doesn't know about the conversation with Miss Harris, I told him that I hadn't tried to sell my ideas to her and that's true. For Christ's sake, I was only talking, just telling her how I felt about design coming from Australians. I didn't know she was going to make me an offer. I didn't know she knew about the **Sarah Maloney** label. I was just, just . . .'

'Putting yourself first and the **Collection** range last,' Sarah interrupts.

'Look, I haven't done anything wrong! I didn't say a single bad word about Mr Stan or Style & Trend or about the **Collection** summer range!'

'No, not in so many words, but you didn't leave Miss Harris in any doubt about what your personal feelings were about the Paris choice of style and colour, did you?'

'Well, I wasn't being disloyal. I love Mr Stan. He gave me my first break in the business, I wouldn't do anything to hurt him, would I?'

'No, Mike, I don't think you would. But you've let your ego get the better of you and Mr Stan has every reason to be disappointed in you.'

Mike looks at each of them in turn, his expression pleading. 'But Sarah, Morrie, Sophie, don't you see! I'm right, he's wrong! Things are changing, look at Norma Tullo and that girl not long out of RMIT, Prue Acton, who's wowing the buyers. They're both doing what I'm doing, ignoring Paris and European design and designing for young Australian women! Prue Acton's hand-painted bikinis are sensational and the Catholic Mothers' Association has come out against them, which has to be good. She's using dog collars as belts and making hats in nylon, in hot pinks and oranges that she's spraypainting.'

'Mike, that's not what we're talking about, or whether you're right or wrong about the trends. We're talking about you and Mr Stan!' Sarah looks at Mike, 'It's about doing the right thing.' She tilts her head to one side and smiles at her brother. 'It's the Maloney way, you know that.'

Mike makes one final protest. 'But I have! I *have* done the right thing. I offered my designs to Mr Stan. Sally Harris offered me a chance to get my designs into their shops, to finance a winter collection. I could have just said thank you very much and resigned from Style & Trend and next thing they know I'm in bed with Country Stores!'

'I think you are already in bed with Country Stores,' Morrie chuckles in a clumsy attempt to calm the atmosphere.

But the joke is ignored by Mike, though Sarah smiles in recognition. She sighs, 'You don't offer your designs shouting at him from the door, it was arrogant. No wonder he went berserko-kaperko! The *shammes*, the boy he employed to drown rats and clean the dunny and who has barely completed his training as a cutter, now offers him the exclusive use of his designs for his winter collection. Don't you think that's just a little bit cheeky?'

'How else could I have done it? I didn't mean to shout at him like that. I didn't know he was going to sack me, did I? I thought I could tell him about the Country Stores' offer and then say, why not him and me do the winter range?'

'Mike, even now you're not being completely honest, are you?'

'What now?'

'Well, the offer from Sally Harris means you'd get your collection into fifteen shops, of which only two are in the city, one here in Melbourne, the other in Brisbane. If Mr Stan accepted your winter range, you'd be selling to the retail trade all over Australia. It would be by far the better deal for a young designer wanting to earn himself a reputation in a hurry.' Sarah, as usual, has read Mike's mind and Mike is too stunned to reply. She's done it to us all our lives and it can be bloody annoying if you're on the receiving end.

Sarah then says, 'We may still be able to get him to look at your designs, Mike. If Morrie and Sophie see him and explain the whole thing and then you go in and apologise to Mr Stan.'

'Apologise?'

'C'mon, Mike, you have to, then maybe he'll be receptive, or at least hear you out.'

Morrie calls Mr Stan from the corner telephone booth; they've applied for a phone, but the waiting list is still six months long and even then the PMG won't guarantee it. Mr Stan agrees to see him and Sophie. Morrie misses out on the morning lectures to go and reports back lunchtime that Mr Stan has agreed to see Mike, but that he hasn't done so with a lot of good grace and during their conversation has never once referred to Mike by name but instead has called him 'the regular genius', which in Yiddish is a disparaging way of referring to someone.

'Mike you have to tell Mr Stan everything, I mean about the conversation at Florentino's with Miss Harris. Don't leave anything out, don't try to make excuses for yourself, come clean, okay?'

'Sarah, you don't know Mr Stan, he'll slaughterate me.'

'That's okay, he's already sacked you, the worst that can happen is that he can say no to using your designs for his winter collection. You've still got Miss Harris up your sleeve and anyway, having been straight with him, Mr Stan won't be able to badmouth you to the suppliers.'

Mike agrees to do his best. 'But I'm not eating humble pie.'

Sophie kisses him, 'Sometimes this pie, it can be healthy to eat, to make you strong, Mikey darlink.' Sophie loves Mike and he knows she's always on his side.

Mike tells Mr Stan everything, the whole Florentino-dinner conversation with Sally Harris. Mr Stan hears him out and turns him down flat.

Nor does he offer him his job back, not that Mike would have accepted it unless his designs were involved and Mr Stan has never taken him seriously as a designer. As Mr Stan had earlier said to him, designers are regarded in the local rag trade as glorified cutters. A designer is only a somebody if he lives in Paris, Milan or London. In Australia, the major credit for the Gown of the Year always goes to the owner, never to the designer, who will get about the same mention in

Australian Fashion News as the model, machinist and the person who did the beadwork or the hand-finishing. So Mike's proposition that he design a range of Australian-inspired fashions doesn't exactly make Mr Stan jump up and down. In fact, to tell you the truth, he is less than polite about the concept.

'So let me see, the regular genius makes some designs. Colours the Australian land, wattle flowers, the budgies . . .'

'Rosellas,' Mike corrects.

'Leafs from the gum tree! Let me tell you something for nothing, Mr Regular Genius. We got such a wattle tree in za garden, every year you should clean up the mess! If you ask people what does a parrot, they tell you it shits the bottom the cage. And leafs? The gum leafs, you got a cold you rub za oil on your chest. From the landscape you want to know what you got? You got brown, you got bulldust, you got ashes! From this you want I should make dresses!'

'Mr Stan, Norma Tullo is in all the good shops, her stretch pants are selling like hot cakes.'

But Mike doesn't get any further. 'Don't tell me Tullo! Tullo, shmullow! A flash in za pants!' Only he pronounces it 'A *flesh* in za pants', which is pretty witty and he's got it right by mistake. Or perhaps not, Mr Stan is a famous wit in The Lane. As Mike explains later, it's the very '*flesh* in the pants' that makes Tullo's invention of the stretch pants a sure-fire winner. Mr Stan continues, 'Next year who is Norma Tullo? Let me tell you, from stretch pants she goes bottom up!' He grins at his own joke.

'I don't agree, Mr Stan, her other styles are selling well despite the recession.' Mike doesn't want to tell Mr Stan that Georges and Myers, and David Jones in Sydney, have gone big for Tullo, who has turned the proverbial little black cocktail dress into the little yellow, orange, blue, red, green, in fact all the rosella colours, cocktail dress. What's more, according to Sally Harris and later confirmed by a visit to Georges and Myers, because of the sexy cut and wonderful body-clinging fabrics Tullo is using, she's even selling more little black dresses than anyone else in the rag trade. Young Australian women like wearing clothes a matronly figure couldn't get away with.

So Mike is sent away with a flea in his ear, but at least Mr Stan won't make it difficult for him to use the suppliers from The Lane. What Mr Stan doesn't tell Mike or anyone else is that he personally thinks the boom in the garment trade is over. That the good years are gone and the recession Australia is going through is yet another sign of the bad times that lie ahead. Over the years he's made some very prudent investments in real estate and that's where he sees the future. He wouldn't have gone into partnership with Mike even if he'd thought he had a chance of succeeding, which, of course, he doesn't. He has decided to get out of the rag trade and people would later remark with some surprise that he, of all people, hadn't resorted to the mandatory fire to collect a fat insurance cheque as a departing bonus. This, especially as it was strongly rumoured in The Lane that his summer range was a dud, better going up in flames than on the racks of retailers.

Flinders Lane was notorious for its fires, the conditions were primitive and in the winter the heating on the factory floor would usually consist of half a dozen kerosene heaters or small open radiators the women would bring in to warm their legs. The danger of a fire starting was always present. The flimsy materials that were being increasingly used at the time for the cheaper end of the summer dress market, bri-nylon and terylene and the other synthetics, were highly flammable. The point being that the summer fashions were being produced in the winter months. A garment brushing against a heater could go up at a touch, simply exploding into instant flame.

The fire hoses were never maintained and in one case, when Bradford House burnt down, the flames at first might have been manageable but when they tried the fire hose there wasn't any water. In truth the fire hose had never been connected to a water pipe but had simply been installed in case an inspector from the fire brigade came around. Eventually all four floors and the twenty-seven factories and businesses in the building were completely destroyed.

Whenever a fire occurred and, as Mike tells it, they were not infrequent, the immediate gossip in The Lane was that it was deeply suspect. When business is crook, a sudden fire can help no end, the insurance assisting greatly to balance the books. People will point out the strange coincidence that most of the fires occur at night. Invariably it will be put down to one of the workers leaving a radiator on near a pile of fabric. Very convenient these piles of synthetic fabric left lying around near a radiator after everyone's gone home.

Even *Australian Fashion News* would occasionally have a go. '*Heard of a flustered maker-up in The Lane the other day. Seems he had taken out a new insurance policy covering him against fire and flood. He was trying to find out how to start a flood.*'

There was also the story often told: Hymie is walking down the lane and he's looking pretty glum. Moshe comes up to him and puts his arm around his shoulders. 'So how's it going, Hymie? They tell me things are not so good za business. I'm sorry to hear about the fire in your factory.' Hymie whirls around and clasps his hand tightly over Moshe's mouth and whispers urgently, 'Shut up, you fool, that's only next week!'

Well, Mr Stan does no such thing. He announces that he's closing down and Friday will be the last pay envelope. Everyone is invited to the farewell party and with their notice of termination comes the last of Mr Stan's rhythmic couplets, printed on special imitation vellum paper and made into a scroll and tied with a red velvet ribbon. Every worker receives one as a keepsake. It is the longest and saddest poem he's ever written and many a tear is shed upon reading it.

Sorry girls, but we're closing shop
Za last pay's Friday, three o'clock
We'll have a party, so bring a plate
A piano, free booze, let's celebrate!
Style & Trend is now no more
All grows quiet on za factory floor
So now, my dears, I wish you well
In life what happens, who can tell?
Like my own family you are to me
Cheers, let's drink to za memory!
Goodbye, adieu to Flinders Lane
AND
To za Buyers who know no shame
I wish only bad luck comes to pass
From now on, you can kiss my arse!

Mr Stan even finds a position for Mrs P, which isn't with Henry Haskin as she'd so often threatened since the news of the contents of Wilma Pinkington's jumbo-sized 4711 bottle has preceded her, but he finally gets her placed with a small factory that specialises in wedding dresses and ball gowns at the expensive end of the market where beads remain the big thing. He also finds jobs in other factories for five of the old-timers, people who had been with the firm from almost the beginning. Surprisingly, Mike is also invited to the farewell party. He doesn't want to go, but Sarah insists and he returns happy as a sand boy because he and Mr Stan have made up their differences.

After his virginity was lost Mike had hoped for a few more lessons under the direction of Miss Harris, but she says nothing can happen until the deal with Country Stores has been settled. She points out to him that if they find out she is having an affair with him they will be reluctant to make him an offer. 'Our MD's very big on morality and is on the committee of the Anglican Cathedral Restoration Fund,' Sally Harris says, 'The first whiff of a scandal and it's all over.' This is fair enough. Mike is quite glad actually, because he doesn't know how he'd be in bed when he's sober, you know, whether he'd be able to perform to her Banbury Cross galloping expectations.

Sally Harris makes an appointment for Mike to see the managing director and chairman of Country Stores, who is the same person. It's for ten on the Wednesday morning, some weeks after Mike has been sacked from Style & Trend.

Mike turns up for an interview accompanied by Sarah, who is dressed in a light khaki gaberdine suit with a nicely tailored look. 'Casual & Business' is how Mike has named it. The khaki is quite severe but is offset with large bright-green buttons and a green breast pocket. It's a pretty daring fashion statement, nobody has been game to use khaki since the war. Under the jacket, Sarah is wearing a matching green polo-neck sweater in a synthetic material. Another cheeky touch, combining synthetic with natural fibre. The skirt is plain khaki but cut to show Sarah's figure and is about three inches shorter than the prevailing fashion, so that the hem is just below the kneecap to show off her excellent legs.

Sarah wears no stockings and has on a pair of high-heel strappy

Ferragamo beige sandals, which Mike has bought in Georges for her birthday. They were horribly expensive and Sarah wants him to take them back, but he persuades her that they're an investment, a beautiful prop for when she's showing off his gear at university.

Fortunately, it's a warm day and she can get away without stockings. She wears neither hat nor gloves and her hair, now cut into a bob, is pure molten copper. She wears a touch of black eyeliner to emphasise the sharp blue of her eyes and a fairly light lipstick, red with a tint of orange.

They've taken a taxi to the Country Stores' main Melbourne shop which is at the lower end of Elizabeth Street, where Mr Pongarse, the managing director, has his office.

'Now remember, Mike, you pronounce it Pon-garse, not Pong-arse,' Sarah giggles. 'If you get it wrong it could be the shortest interview in history.'

From the moment they step out of the taxi onto the busy pavement outside the shop, all eyes are on Sarah, both male and the younger females. The males because she looks dead sexy and the younger women because her outfit is so stunning and they can immediately envision themselves in it. They haven't gone ten feet before the first young girl comes up.

'Excuse me, miss, I don't mean to be rude, but where did you get that beautiful suit?'

Sarah smiles, 'It's a new label, a **Sarah Maloney**.'

The store is fairly busy but Sarah has the same effect inside as on the pavement, shoppers and shop assistants alike stop and stare. As they walk to the lift, Sarah, talking out of the corner of her mouth, says to Mike, 'Well, we've either got it very right or very wrong.'

They take the lift to the fifth floor, which is Administration, and go to a window at the Credit Department and ask for Mr Pongarse.

The clerk behind the window looks momentarily surprised, 'You mean, Mrs Pongarse?'

Which is the first big shock as Sally Harris simply referred to 'Erica Pongarse, our MD' and they'd both thought Erica must be some European way of pronouncing Eric and assumed he was a man. A thought flashes through Sarah's head that maybe she's dressed a little too provocatively for a woman, even though the suit is intended as a stylish work outfit, but the no stockings, hat and gloves and the strappy sandals are definitely a tad risqué.

The clerk now says, 'Wait on, I'll take you over.' He leaves the window and a few moments later comes through the door of the Credit Department and signals for them to follow. They cross the floor to an anonymous brown-stained door. The clerk knocks politely, then calls out in a brisk voice, 'Visitors for you, Mrs Pongarse!'

'Come!' a voice calls back. The clerk opens the door and leaves them to enter the rather dark interior of Mrs Pongarse's office on their own. A lady of about fifty is seated behind an incredibly cluttered desk. She's wearing thick horn-rimmed glasses and her greying hair is pulled back into a tight bun. There's not a skerrick of make-up on what they can see of her face which is half in shadow. She's rather overweight and is wearing a fairly shabby-looking, plain black dress of no distinction whatsoever and no jewellery, not even a brooch. Her legs, which can be seen under the desk, show that she's wearing sensible black shoes and elastic stockings. She looks up from whatever she's writing as they enter, takes off her glasses to have another look at Sarah and at the same time stubs a cigarette into an ashtray that's overflowing with butts.

'Who are you?' she asks, but doesn't wait for an answer before turning to Mike, 'You are Mr Maloney, the designer, I take it?'

'Yes, madam, er, Mrs Pongarse, and this is Sarah.'

'Is she your sample?' It is said on the edge of rudeness.

'I beg your pardon?' Mike says, not understanding.

'That suit, your sample on a model.'

'Sarah is my sister,' Mike answers.

'You are a mannequin, Miss Maloney?' It is clear from how she says it that she doesn't think very much of the modelling profession.

'No, madam, I'm a medical student in my final year.'

'Medicine? University? Sarah Maloney, Sarah Maloney,' she repeats, then looks at Mike and Sarah. 'Weren't you the one that made all the fuss at the university, let me see, about six years ago, wasn't it?'

'It wasn't us that made the fuss, madam,' Sarah says.

'I'm not so sure about that.' Erica Pongarse has a deep voice, which if you heard first over the telephone, you might easily mistake it for a man's. The room smells of stale tobacco.

Mike and Sarah are confused. They don't know what to expect, but certainly not the cold welcome they appear to be getting. Sally Harris had been so positive and enthusiastic about the meeting – a complete contrast to the reception they were now receiving from the Country Stores' managing director.

'Barrington-Stone, wasn't it? Yes, I remember it clearly, she made quite a to-do in the papers and on the wireless. Always sticking her nose into everyone's business, that one.'

'I don't think I can accept that, Mrs Pongarse. Mrs Barrington-Stone is a personal friend,' Sarah's colour is still up.

Mrs Pongarse ignores Sarah's protest. 'Country Women's Association, interfering bunch, that lot. I suppose you'd better sit down.' She indicates the chairs placed in front of her desk. Like her office, they are not in the least pretentious but standard upright office chairs. If Mike and Sarah hadn't been so young and inexperienced, they might have reasoned that something must have happened to have caused Mrs Pongarse to become so antagonistic. Instead they sit silently, thoroughly confused. Mike looks about him, trying to make sense of what's happened.

The office too looks like Mrs Pongarse's desk, there are samples of clothes all over the floor and cardboard boxes, some opened, others still sealed. The walls are painted a dirty cream, and the skirting boards and picture rails as well as the door are stained in a deep mahogany brown. There is not a single picture on the walls and the overall effect is depressing.

Three large military-green filing cabinets rest against the wall to the right of Mrs Pongarse's desk. Judging from the heavy maroon brocade curtains, which are drawn, a large window is situated directly behind her. Mike imagines it must look out onto Elizabeth Street. The floor covering, like the curtains, is in a well-worn maroon with the thread showing through on a spot directly behind the chairs, indicating that generations of minions have stood on this spot to take their orders and that the offer of a seat is not the usual courtesy.

In the centre of the ceiling hangs an old-fashioned, very ugly, six-stemmed chandelier, shaped like a spider's legs and ending with bell-like shades in opaque glass. Of the six lights, three of them are not working and the remainder cast a low, depressing light, so that the office appears to be in a sort of permanent twilight.

A modern desk lamp with a green metal shade rises above the clutter on the desk and casts a circle of yellow light into the layers of paper scattered around it. The light extends far enough to include Mrs Pongarse's torso, neck and half her face, ending in a sharp line under her nose so that the remainder of her face is in shadow. When she talks, you can see her mouth moving but it's difficult to interpret what her eyes might be indicating.

It is obvious Mrs Pongarse is quite unaware of her surroundings or how they might affect her visitors. This is an office created without sentiment, made for work, it is a neutral environment that would operate regardless of the time of day or night, sunshine or rain. It made Mike think of a rather large cave and Mrs Pongarse as a bear with a very sore tooth which doesn't much welcome intruders.

Mrs Pongarse removes several sheets of paper to the side of her to reveal a squawk box. She leans forward. Pressing the button she barks, 'Miss Harris come!' in what is clearly a command to be instantly obeyed.

Sally Harris must have been waiting close by, though where the squawk-box voice ended was anyone's guess. There had been no sign of a secretary when they'd been ushered in by the credit clerk. The door opens almost immediately to reveal Sally Harris, who, smiling pleasantly as she walks towards them, first greets Mrs Pongarse with a polite 'Good morning, Mrs Pongarse' and then says 'Hi' to Mike. Mike rises from his chair and introduces her to Sarah, who stands up to shake her hand.

'What a lovely suit, a **Sarah Maloney** I take it?' Sally Harris says. Her pleasant welcome is a contrast to her managing director's coldness and Mike suddenly feels better.

Sarah smiles and nods and they all sit down. There is a moment of awkward silence before Sally Harris smiles and says, 'Well?'

Then Mrs Pongarse starts right off, 'Miss Harris has told me what you want, Mr Maloney, so we don't need to repeat any of that. You are a young designer and you need backing to get started. Am I correct so far?'

Sally Harris looks over at Mrs Pongarse in some alarm as she picks up the abruptness, even rudeness in her manner.

'Yes, madam,' Mike says. Though he is somewhat surprised, he is under the impression that Sally Harris was the one who made the proposition to him. Still, he keeps his mouth shut. He looks over at Sally and sees that she too is confused.

Mrs Pongarse now looks over at Sarah, 'Why have you brought your sister?'

It is the squawk-box voice, a business voice, a voice accustomed to the sort of authority that might be exercised by the headmistress of a private school for girls and one which is clearly intended to intimidate.

It is a manner which would have worked with ninety-nine per cent of young blokes, especially those from the bush, but Mike has spent the last five years in Flinders Lane among some pretty feisty women. While most may have been factory workers, nonetheless, some, such as Mrs P with half the contents of her 4711 bottle down her gullet, the manageress and even some of the Jewish workers, many of whom had come from privileged backgrounds before the war, could and often did put a flea in your ear as effectively as any boss. What's more, if you got an Italian or Greek worker riled, you knew about it soon enough and in no uncertain terms.

'There were two reasons, madam,' Mike answers politely. 'Sarah is the cleverest and the wisest person in our family and I asked her to be present.' Mike tilts his head slightly, looking into Mrs Pongarse's eyes and smiles, 'We've never done something like this before.'

'And, of course, what a lovely way to show off your talent,' Sally Harris says, 'Sarah's suit is stunning.' Mike can see she's trying to show him that she's on his side.

Mike smiles. 'Yes, I admit, I wanted you both to see one of my garments being worn. I thought it might be useful to see that my work is practical.'

It's not a bad answer for a young bloke. Mike has learned heaps about the rag trade and in particular from Mr Stan, who often smiled when he was in a tight corner and was always polite to buyers or debt collectors, but who never took a backward step and was a master of the counter punch.

He'd once told Mike that the only time you kneel is when you know that the bloke who holds the gun at your head will pull the trigger if you don't. 'But even then, don't beg, it is much easier to kill a man who stands and pleads for his life than one who kneels because not to do so will show him to be a fool. Believe me, I know.' Mr Stan then quoted one of his lines. *When you play the game, don't justify, don't complain, only explain.*

There is nothing in her manner to suggest that Mrs Pongarse is impressed with Mike's reply, and she completely ignores Sally's remark about the suit. In the light, the line of her mouth remains tight. 'I'm not at all sure that the garment Miss Maloney is wearing is suitable for our clients. We have fifteen stores, thirteen of them in the country. I can't see young people in the country wearing a suit like that, they have no money and even less fashion sense.'

'But, Mrs Pongarse, we talked about a young women's shop in the arcade,' Sally Harris protests. There's talk of Myers opening a Miss Melbourne shop in Bourke Street and at the Chadstone Shopping Centre, all the signs indicate that the time is right.'

'That will do, Miss Harris, that was only an idea, *your* idea as I recall.' It is clear she wishes to diminish Sally Harris's involvement, though Sarah picks up on this immediately.

'You're quite right, Mrs Pongarse. I come from a small country town and I'm sure if I walked down King Street in Yankalillee with this outfit on, someone would call the superintendent from the mental asylum up the hill to come and fetch me.' Sarah smiles, trying to lighten the mood of the interview. 'I seem to recall you have two shops in the city, this one and one in Brisbane. A Country Stores Young Shop, perhaps within the confines of the two city shops, could work very well.' Sarah says all this in a rather la-di-da voice which Mike hasn't heard before. Medicine isn't the only thing she's learning at the university.

'Thank you, Miss Maloney, for teaching me my own business. What are you saying?' She doesn't wait for an answer, 'Are you suggesting our clothes are too conservative?'

Mike jumps in at this point, 'Yes, for the younger market! Not just yours, *everyone's* styles are too old! The rag trade isn't catering for young Australian women, madam. Norma Tullo is the only one out there.'

'He's right, Aunt Erica,' Sally Harris says, forgetting to address her aunt formally as she'd previously done. 'Tullo's doing very well with the younger set.'

Mrs Pongarse turns, her lips drawn even tighter if that's possible, 'And *you'd* know, of course!'

'I am the buyer after all,' Sally Harris protests. 'I should know what's happening in town.' She's clearly annoyed and not a little confused at being given such short shrift from her aunt.

It is becoming clear to Mike and Sarah that while Sally Harris may be all-powerful outside the environment of her aunt's office, Country Stores has only one boss and a pretty grizzly one at that. Mike hadn't known that Sally, who was the youngest buyer in the retail industry, was Mrs Pongarse's niece, which he now thinks may explain her elevation in the business at such a young age. But right now Mrs Pongarse is treating her like a schoolgirl.

Mr Stan, of course, would have known of the relationship and this might also explain his seduction ploy. Sally Harris was clearly good at her job. Unmarried and in her early thirties, she'd also grown accustomed to the good things in life but was dependent for them on a domineering aunt and an ultra-conservative retail organisation. Seducing a young and talented designer and then becoming his champion was a way of striking back, showing her aunt that she too had ideas. Perhaps the seduction was unnecessary to bring all this about, but, what the hell, Mike was young, good-looking and there to be plucked, a leaf from the virgin creeper.

Who can say how much of this would have gone through Mr Stan's mind? Probably not the part about Mike being a young and talented designer. But you can bet he'd worked the rest out and thought it was worth a try. If he could get his summer range out and paid for before he closed down, he'd be a happy man. As it happened, he sold all but eight hundred dresses to Grace Bros in Sydney. He complained bitterly about the discounts he had to offer them, but you can bet your baby booties he came out of the deal on the credit side of the ledger.

'Mr Maloney, if, and I emphasise the "if", we decide to support you in a partnership, what is it that you expect?' Mrs Pongarse asks.

Mike is no businessman, but he's discussed the likelihood of going into business with Country Stores with Sarah, Morrie and Sophie, and made a long-distance phone call to Nancy and Bozo. Morrie isn't much help, but Sophie is the one who turns out to have the strong opinions. She's running the **Suckfizzle** kids' label very well and is proving to be an excellent businesswoman; the children's garments are beginning to make them more money than the **Sarah Maloney** label.

'Mikey, darlink, you must have za . . .' she appears to be searching for a word, then adds, 'power!'

'Power?' Mike doesn't understand.

'Za power the designs. You make, they take.'

'You mean Mike must have the right to design without interference?' Sarah interprets.

Sophie nods. 'No change, also fabric, always Mikey chooses.' Sophie's English is getting better but it's not a patch on Morrie's, who would be speaking very well if he didn't try to include every piece of slang he learns from the workers at the *Age* in his sentences. 'Fair dinkum, very bonzer, struth, bewdy bottler, stone the crows!' he'd exclaimed recently after seeing Sarah model one of Mike's creations.

'I don't think you can expect them to simply take Mike's designs,' Sarah replies. 'They'll want to have an opinion. I mean, wouldn't you? Mike's just starting out, he hasn't got a reputation yet, they'll feel that they're the ones who are taking a punt, they're not going to let him have carte blanche.'

'Half! He make ten design, they take za minimum quantity five!' Sophie says, quite decided. 'Minimum quantity' is a phrase she's learnt from dealing with the shops that sell kids' clothes. 'One from two they can throw away.'

Mike accepts this idea with some difficulty, he thinks he's worth more than a fifty-per-cent success rate. But after some argument he acknowledges that people don't yet know what he's capable of and they'll want to mess about with his stuff, thinking they know better. I'm not saying Mike is a big-head, or anything, but he's always been confident about sewing and if you take his embroidery as an example, with all the ribbons he got, he's probably got every right. Sarah says they're raving at the university about his clothes.

Then he phones Yankalillee to discuss the Country Stores offer.

Expecting a long call, he's got a whole pocketful of sixpences for the phone box. Nancy, for once in her life, doesn't have a lot to say, but it is her suggestion that Sarah accompany Mike and that she wear one of his outfits to the interview.

'You must speak to your brother, he's the businessman' is what she finally advises.

However, Bozo plays the same old record, 'Mike, you must have control of your own stuff, you must have fifty-one per cent at the very least. But I don't like it the way it is. They're big and you're a nobody. Why don't you set up a design and manufacturing company and they buy into your company, say twenty-five per cent, that's what they get for financing your first two ranges.'

'I'll need more than two ranges to get going.'

'How many?'

Mike thinks, 'I reckon four seasons, two summers, two winters.'

'Okay, they get an exclusive range for four seasons and say twenty-five per cent of your net profits until the money they've loaned you has been paid back plus some interest.'

The figures and business ideas Bozo's spouting are gibberish to Mike. 'But what if I'm not successful?'

'It's a business risk they'll either take or reject. You have to bet on yourself, Mike, and they'll have to take a punt on you as well.'

'I don't think they'll be in that. It's their money and they know they've got me by the balls, they'll want me exclusively. Miss Harris says there's room on the sixth floor for a factory which would cut down the overheads. They can also buy fabrics at a highly competitive price.'

'Don't sell yourself short, Mike,' Bozo warns. 'If you go into their organisation, sooner or later they'll swallow you up. What did you say, they've got fifteen stores, thirteen in the country? How are you going to earn a reputation as a young and exciting designer when your stuff is being sold in the bush? Not much use being a big fashion statement in Coonabarabran, is there? It will take years, mate. That is if you do it their way. You've got to be able to sell to everyone, all the big city outlets.'

Mike sighs, Bozo's got a point. In the back of his head he can hear Mr Stan again. *If you work for the classes you eat with the masses. If you work for the masses you eat with the classes.* 'Bozo, what do I know about running a company? I don't know anything about business!'

'You're running a business right now, Mike. What do you think the **Sarah Maloney** and the **Suckfizzle** labels are?'

'That's a backyard operation, just me and Sophie, we sew things.'

'So?'

'So we just make a few dresses and kids' things, I design them and Sarah and Morrie sell them at the uni and Sophie flogs the kids' stuff to the shops.'

'How do you know whether you've made a profit or a loss?'

'Sophie does all that, she's very good. She gets that narked if I don't tell her exactly what I've spent. Even if I buy a piece of velvet the size of a small hanky for an appliqué from Buckleys' remnant tray, she wants to know and writes it down in a notebook. One pice velvit one shilling,' Mike says, pronouncing her spelling.

'You mean a ledger? She writes it in a ledger?'

'No, a notebook, a Croxley pad.'

'And the money you make?'

'She keeps it in a bag.'

'A bag! What sort of a bag?'

'A sort of body bag, she's made this bag with its own straps and she wears it around her waist.'

'What, for everyone to see, like a tram conductor?'

'No, of course not! She wears it under her dress and she even sleeps with it under her nightie.'

'What's she do when Morrie, you know . . . wants a naughty?'

Mike grins. 'How would I know? Uses it as a cushion under her bum, I suppose. I think it's all a part of what happened to them in Poland before they came here. She doesn't trust banks and she says if there's Nazis, that's what she calls burglars, this time they're gunna have to kill her first to get the money.'

Bozo laughs, 'Well, why don't you just do as you're doing now, mate. Make Sophie your partner and register a company with both of you as shareholders with you owning fifty-one per cent.'

'Mate, I couldn't do that to Sophie, we'd have to be equal, we're mates and she works harder than me.'

Mike can hear Bozo sigh at the other end. 'Mike, in money terms, forty-nine and fifty-one are equal enough, you must maintain the major equity.'

'I'll try,' Mike says, then a thought occurs to him. 'Hey, if we have a proper company, we'll have to pay income tax!'

'That's right, everyone has to in the end.'

'Well, we don't now. Mr Stan doesn't with the stuff he makes and sells from cabbage.'

'Until they catch up with you and him.'

'Me yes, him *never*!' Mike laughs, then sounds serious again. 'Yeah well, I think it's all pretty academic. Like I said before, I don't think Country Stores will buy us being a separate company.'

'Maybe they will, maybe they won't. I'm warning you, Mike, if they have the control they'll eventually blow you out of the water. Don't let them turn you into what amounts to being one of their employees with a small share in the profits they make from your exclusive-to-them designs. It's selling your talent far too cheaply.'

'Sophie says to ask for total design control and choice of fabrics and the proviso that they must accept five out of every ten designs I do.'

'In your dreams, Mike! You've got half a chance of that happening with your own company, you've got Buckley's if *they* have control. Mike, listen to me, for Christ's sake!'

Bozo reads all the business magazines and now gets all the Melbourne newspapers every day and cuts things out of the financial section and pastes bits into a big art book he's bought. If Bozo could've worked with Mr Stan for five years and not Mike, imagine what he'd know now. But I don't think Bozo wants to work with anyone. Funny that, he's always been in control, even fixing up junk. He ran things and we just helped, doing what he said.

After the telephone conversation with Nancy and Bozo, Mike reports back to the others and they agree Bozo's right. Mike and Sophie should legitimise the organisation they've already got and offer their design and manufacturing services to Country Stores. Sarah suggests they might offer them exclusivity for three years.

Mike seems to understand. 'If we outsource the work and they pay for the manufacture of the ranges and pay the design company for quality control and supervision. Of course, they'll also have a twenty-five per cent partnership until they've got their original investment back. Then there's the normal retail profit they'll make for themselves in the stores from my exclusive ranges.' He's got it down pat for the interview and Sarah's there to correct him if he makes a mistake.

So now Mrs Pongarse asks Mike what he wants out of a possible partnership, that is, if they, Country Stores, are interested in the first place. Mike and Sarah have rehearsed the whole thing with Mike doing the talking and Sarah coming in if she's needed.

Mike starts selling the idea of a design and manufacturing company with the majority owned by him and Sophie. The first indication they have that things are going wrong isn't very long in coming and it's plain from Sally Harris's expression that it's not how she saw things happening. Her mouth has fallen open and she can't believe what she's hearing. Sarah can hear that Mrs Pongarse is breathing faster, her bosom going up and down, but her eyes can't be seen because of the light and her lips remain in a tight, straight, blue line. Now she's folded her arms across her ample breasts, which isn't a very good sign.

It doesn't take all that long to outline the proposition and when they're finished Mrs Pongarse ignores Mike and Sarah and turns instead to Sally Harris. 'That's not how you put it to me, Miss Harris. What have you to say?' She's pretty cranky.

So is Sally Harris, who turns on Mike, 'Michael, that's not what I suggested!'

'No, I know, but it's a reasonable proposition and me and my family think what you wanted wasn't in our best interest.' He's practising what Mr Stan said, explain but don't justify.

'I've never heard such impertinence!' Mrs Pongarse says, looking at Mike and Sarah. 'Who do you think you are? If there is to be any decision on this matter I shall be the one to make an offer, not you or Miss Harris!'

'You asked what we expected, madam,' Sarah says quietly, 'and we told you.'

'You again!' Mrs Pongarse snorts, 'You may have won with the university but you won't put one over me, my girl. You, in that *ridiculous* outfit!'

There's some of Nancy in Sarah, only she knows how to stay calm and Nancy doesn't, but both can fire a verbal bullet and score a bullseye. 'Mrs Pongarse, when I wear Michael's clothes I feel like a princess. I dare say you've never been quite young enough to have had such an exquisite experience or you'd know immediately just how wonderful my brother's designs are.'

There is an audible gasp from Sally Harris, who can't believe her ears. It's probably been years since anyone has talked back to her aunt, much less insulted her in such a calm and dignified manner.

Mike looks at Sarah and she smiles at him. He can see she's not afraid and this gives him the courage to say, 'I suppose that's it then?'

'No, it's not!' Mrs Pongarse shouts out. She points to Mike. 'You thought that by seducing my niece, you could influence us to help you to go into business for yourself! You impertinent young scoundrel!'

Mike's jaw practically hits his knees and he looks over at Sally Harris, who seems equally flabbergasted.

'Aunt Erica, how dare you!'

Sarah looks at Sally Harris. 'You *told* your aunt my brother seduced *you*?'

'She did no such thing!' Mrs Pongarse says, pursing her lips, 'I heard it elsewhere.'

'Well, who did then?' Sally Harris demands. 'Because it's not true!'

'Oh?'

'I am entirely responsible for the seduction. Now tell me, who told you?' Sally Harris demands a second time.

'It's none of your business, Miss Harris.' The old lady wears a smug look.

Mike shakes his head, the penny drops at last, the interview was doomed from the start. 'Oh, Jesus, Mr Stan!' he exclaims.

Sally Harris turns furiously on Mike, '*You* told Mr Stan?'

'No, of course not. He's made an assumption, taken a punt in the dark, then come to see Mrs Pongarse.' He turns to Erica Pongarse, 'Did Mr Stan come to see you, madam?'

Mrs Pongarse looks pleased with herself. 'I can't deny that.'

Here was the master at work, because Mike now guesses that Mr Stan has sold his last stock to Country Stores. 'And he sold you eight hundred dresses because he said I'd . . .'

'Eight hundred dresses on the strength of his accusation!' Sally says, furious. 'You've gone against my recommendation?'

Mike realises that the dresses can't have been delivered yet or Sally would have known about them.

Mrs Pongarse sighs and looks over at her niece. 'I had no choice. Mr Stan pointed out, quite correctly, that you had taken a piddling order of only one hundred and fifty garments in three specific designs, all of which were the work of his junior cutter, Mr Maloney.' She now looks at Mike and then back at Sally Harris. 'Mr Stan was kind enough to say that Mr Maloney's designs were in the range for a singular purpose, to be rejected. He confided in me that it is common practice in his trade to give the buyers something to reject. It gives them a sense of being in charge.' She points a finger at Sally Harris, 'And *you*, Miss Harris, were sufficiently naive to buy the rejects!'

'Naive! How dare you! Can't you see the Jew has conned you?'

Her aunt ignores this remark like all the others. 'What am I supposed to think? It was obviously a conspiracy between Mr Maloney and you. Either that or blatant incompetence! Though now I'm inclined to think, both. I had no choice but to put things right for the good of this company and our reputation in the trade.'

'Reputation? We've just become the laughing stock of the trade!' Sally shouts.

'You have shamed me, Miss Harris! My own flesh and blood has shamed me and put the company at risk with this whippersnapper, this . . . er, junior cutter!' She pulls back, reaches out to put on her hornrims, and sneeringly says, 'Go into business with this little twerp. You really *must* think I'm a fool!'

Sally Harris leans forward in her chair, now she's spitting chips. 'Let me put a few things straight as well, Mrs Pongarse! The dresses won't sell, not even in the bloody bush! I made a professional decision not to order them and a private one to sleep with Michael Maloney! Who, I think, may just one day save the moribund Australian fashion industry from Parisian sycophants like Mr Stan and his cohorts!

I agree, the decision not to buy his summer range very much concerns you and this company and, speaking frankly, you've been gulled! As to the second decision I made, to make love to a beautiful young man, I count myself fortunate to have done so. So why don't you mind your own business! I'm sick and tired of having to kowtow to you, you're a stupid, dried-out, old harridan!'

'I beg your pardon!' Mrs Pongarse points to the door, looking directly at Sally Harris. 'Miss Harris, you may leave. At once! I shall discuss this with you later. Now leave at once!'

Sally Harris jumps to her feet, 'You can have my notice as of now, Mrs Pongarse!' She turns to Mike, who can see she is very close to tears, her bottom lip quivering. 'I'm sorry, Mike, very, very sorry! I apologise for my aunt who has used you shamelessly to get at me!' Then she storms, sobbing, towards the door.

'Did you know you slept with a Roman Catholic, Miss Harris?' Mrs Pongarse shouts after her niece. 'That's disgusting *and* degrading!'

Sally Harris opens the door and whams it after her, practically slamming it off its hinges.

'It's just Catholic, Mrs Pongarse, not *Roman* Catholic, we're Australian, not Italian, have been for five generations,' Sarah says. Then she rises from her chair. 'And you, madam, *you* are a bigot.' She turns to Mike, 'C'mon, Mike, this disgusting old woman doesn't like us and the feeling is entirely mutual.' To Sarah's credit she doesn't raise her voice even once, she's calm as early-morning Mass.

Outside on the footpath Sarah grabs Mike's arm, 'Oh, Mike, I'm so sorry, but I couldn't help myself, the old bitch was *horrible*. You couldn't really have worked with her, could you?'

Mike laughs. 'I think we grabbed the spoon out of the sink in the nick of time.' He wipes the front of his jacket as if wiping himself down. 'Though I reckon we got splashed a fair bit in the process. It really should be pronounced *Pong*-arse, she's a nasty smell all right.'

Sarah then says, 'Anyway, one thing is for sure, she never intended to make us an offer, she was using us, the entire interview, to punish Sally Harris for sleeping with a *Roman* Catholic!'

Mike grins to himself, 'Mr Stan, the rotten old bastard, got the better of us all in the end. There's a lesson in that alone. *When you play the game, don't justify, don't complain, always explain,'* Mike quotes, then says, 'What he didn't say is that the art is in the way you explain things to your own advantage. He sure took that old lady for a ride. Jesus, eight hundred navy dresses with, I quote *Fashion Week*, "just a soupçon of white, anything more would be deemed vulgar".'

'And in the process he's wrecked things for you,' Sarah adds, looking soulfully at Mike.

'Let's be fair, he couldn't have known about the proposition Sally Harris and Country Stores made to me.' Mike thinks for a moment, 'Nah, he didn't wreck nothing,' he says, reverting to Maloney English. 'We couldn't have worked with the old bag anyway. Good thing she had it in for us right from the start. In a sense Mr Stan did us a big favour. Bozo's right, she'd have eaten me alive.'

Sarah turns to Mike and says earnestly, 'But what will you do now? This is my final year at uni, I can't exactly model clothes as a resident in the Royal Women's Hospital.'

Mike doesn't reply right off, but says instead, 'Look, we're not far from Bourke Street, let's go to Pelligrini's and I'll buy you a cappuccino, then I'll tell you exactly what I'm going to do.'

Sarah grabs Mike's arm, 'Good, I've never had one of those.'

'There's another reason for going.'

'What?'

'Well, about this time of the morning most of the factory owners in Flinders Lane either catch a tram or walk up to Bourke Street to Pelligrini's to have a cappuccino and a *dolci*. I want them to see what a beautiful woman looks like in a Mike Maloney original.'

Sarah laughs, pleased with the compliment. 'What's a *dolci*?'

'It's like a small cake, only in Italian. The bosses are mostly overweight, see. On a constant diet and under the beady eyes of their wives and so they always say, "Such a little cake, so tell me already, how can such a small thing hurt a person?"

'Then someone says, "It hurts, believe me, it hurts."

'And someone else says, "Only the conscience. It hurts only the conscience. On za other hand, in za rag trade, tell me please, where can you find a conscience?"'

Chapter Seventeen

Well, there's not a lot happening in Yankalillee that you should know about us Maloneys. I'm in my last year at school, which isn't exactly shattering news, though I think I'm doing okay, not like Sarah or anything, but okay. School hasn't started yet, it's the hottest January since the bushfires of 1952 and everyone's talking bushfires.

Since coming back from the Rome Olympics, Bozo's going gangbusters in the cartage business, which he calls the trucking business. It's an American expression but he says cartage sounds like it's done with horses and drays. The business had to be called John Crowe Transport because when they went into it Bozo was too young to be a company director and have his name on a business. They've even got a logo. It's this crow that sits on a box which is wrapped like a parcel with string and above the crow it says 'John Crowe Transport' and below the box it says:

As direct as the crowe flies

Which is Mike's work again, that bloke's a genius. Already the transport business is showing a small profit and earning a bit of a reputation around the place even as far as Albury across the New South Wales border.

Now here's the juicy bit of gossip that's got the whole town looking shocked and indignant and up in arms. You're not going to believe this, but I promise you it's true. Do you remember Crocodile Brown, my teacher in primary school and also Anna Dumb-cow-ski, the reffo girl who was in a concentration camp in Pooland? You will recall how Crocodile Brown always used to be nice to her because of what she'd suffered and all that? Well, she's turned out to be the ace student in the school, even better than Sarah was. But that's not the scandal, the scandal is that Crocodile Brown has left his wife and fallen in love with Anna and they've eloped and taken the boat to England where he comes from.

Crocodile Brown never had any kids so at least that's something. Anna's mum died a year ago and her stepdad, who she married after they come to Australia, says ever since Anna's mum died there's nothing he could do with her, she wouldn't listen to him and he's not surprised what's happened. It turns out he's a bit of a drongo anyway and gets pissed most nights and everyone says they don't know how a nice woman like Mrs Dombrowski got involved with a no-hoper like him in the first place. Loneliness, I suppose.

So there's Anna, who they say might be the brightest student in the state, with old yellow-teeth Crocodile Brown on their way to England. Big Jack Donovan went to see her stepdad, whose name is Barnes, Chicka Barnes, and he's *not* a Catholic, thank gawd, and works at the abattoir. Big Jack explained to him that Anna was under-age, just seventeen and was, according to the law, under his protection, that they could have her sent back, extradited from Great Britain if he gave his consent. But Chicka Barnes said, 'No way! If she was old enough to screw a school teacher, she was old enough to stay away permanently.' Only, in the *Gazette*, he said 'old enough to have an affair with a school teacher' but everyone knew what he meant because Tommy says 'screw' is what he said to all of them in the pub.

Then, of course, the rumours started. People said that it was Barnes who'd been playing sticky-finger and other things more drastic with Anna and that she'd really run away from him and it's him who doesn't want her back because there's a thing called carnal knowledge in the law. It says that if he was the first to have a go at Anna, he'd be guilty of an indictable offence that could get him up to twenty years in prison. No wonder he doesn't want her back.

Crocodile Brown was the only one who'd always been kind to her, which is true, if you remember. All this came from the *Gazette* where Big Mouth Saggy Tits, Vera Forbes, the ace reporter, had her finest hour reporting the entire episode.

Nancy read every word for two weeks and after every article said the same thing, 'Isn't it nice, for once in our lives, it isn't a Catholic that's done the bad deed and, what's more, there isn't a Maloney anywhere in sight.'

She spoke too soon. Old Saggy Tits found Anna's diary when she was in primary school. She made it sound like it was a discovery as important as *The Diary of Anne Frank* because it was written when Anna and her mum had not long come from Poland to Yankalillee. She printed a page from the diary which said:

> *Today in our class Mister Brown stopped Jografee to have a lesson on birds. We all don't know so much about birds, excep Mole Mulonee who nose everythin and watchs birds but don't took the eggs because it's krool. He is a nice boy and I love him. But some time he fall asleep in class and Mr Brown beats him with a stik. Mister Brown is krool. I love Mole Mulonee who piks up rubbish in the mornin so is always tide.*

So there we go again, a Maloney's in the middle of 'The Diary of Anna Dombrowski', which is what Vera Forbes has as the headline when she writes the article for the *Gazette*. Nancy's ropeable and can't believe her eyes, 'Y'know, I think a Maloney must have stepped on the head of the serpent in the Garden of Eden. Doesn't *nothing* happen in this gawd-forsaken town that our name isn't in it somewhere!'

Of course Father Crosby comes around and wants to know what's going on? How come I'm mixed up in the affair of the *Jewish* girl and the *Protestant* school teacher and choir master at the Church of England. For once in his life he thinks he's in the clear; there's a scandal in town and there's no Catholic involved. Then this happens and, say fifteen-Hail-Marys-before-you-go-to-bed, the bloody Maloneys are back in the bad news.

'Fer Christ's sake, Father! Mole was nine years old at the time!' Nancy protests.

'That's blasphemy, Nancy Maloney, you'll not be taking the Lord's name in vain! And as for the other, the Church teaches us that carnal knowledge, which is a part of original sin, exists in the very young, all of us being born with it.'

I think the next real big scandal in Yankalillee will most likely be about this three-hundred-pound lady garbage collector who strangles the local Catholic priest with her bare hands in broad daylight and then pleads temporary sanity.

Nancy can't believe the old priest. She's often wondered why the Bishop in Bendigo sent him to Yankalillee. 'Could be that he thinks we must all be as stupid as Father Crosby!' she sighs. Now she looks at him and shakes her head, 'Father, Mole had nothing to do with it, it's only stuff in a little girl's diary. At nine, Mole wouldn't have known that little girls don't have peckers the same as little boys.'

That's not true, I'd seen little Colleen in the nuddy often and I wasn't stupid enough to think that you grew a willy later on in life. She has a point, though, the only thing I can remember thinking about Anna at that time was that she'd been sent to concentration camp to learn how to concentrate in Pooland.

I have to confess, things have changed. Anna isn't only the cleverest person in school, but in this year and for the last two years in high school she's been the most beautiful as well. There's not a bloke in class who wouldn't do it to her if he got half a chance. I know I would, no questions asked, and I wouldn't even have time to think about using a rubber because I'd be that carried away.

But Anna isn't a cockteaser, not like some of the girls in class. Everyone likes Anna, she's a real beaut person but all of us thought she was a bit too serious, only interested in getting a scholarship to the university and reading books, that all that beauty was going to waste. In the meantime, while all our tongues are hanging out from lust, old Crocodile is doing the dreaded deed. I've got to be honest and say that I've taken myself to the dunny on more than one occasion on Anna's behalf. I just can't believe that an old bloke like Crocodile Brown with his big yellow teeth could pull a bird like Anna. It makes you think there's no justice in this world.

So, in a strange way, Father Crosby is right, only he's eight years too early for the accusation. I've had all the carnal thoughts it's possible to have over Anna Dombrowski.

Now I need to talk about Bozo's boxing career up to the time he won his Olympic medal. There's not much to tell after that because he's given up boxing even though lots of people thought he should turn professional. When Bozo got back from Rome, he had this long talk with Jimmy Carruthers, an ex-Olympian who was the professional bantamweight champion of the world in 1953 and after the Rome Olympics came down to visit the Russell Street gym. Jimmy's fallen on hard times and it seems he's made a few bad investments and is just about broke and runs a fruit-juice bar in Sydney. After the discussion Bozo had with the ex-world champ, to everyone's surprise, except Sarah, Mike and me, Bozo announced that he was giving up boxing for business. Nancy would have danced on the table if she'd been able to climb up on it in the first place because now she knew Bozo was going to use his brains instead of having them scrambled. It was always her greatest fear that Bozo would end up like Bobby Devlin, even though we'd told her it wouldn't happen, not with Bozo, no way.

Bozo's amateur career up until he won a bronze at the Rome Olympics can't be separated from Mrs Rika Ray. She's his number-one fan but much more than that as well because there's also her and Bozo's Bitzers, they took to her like she's their mum and Bozo's their dad. It's uncanny. I mean, Bozo's dogs have always liked us, the family that is, they'll wag their tails and jump up and let you scratch behind their ears, no problems. They're nice mutts every one of them, but they won't take food from us or go for a walk or do any of their tricks unless Bozo first gives them permission. No way otherwise. But with Mrs Rika Ray they're different. She even teaches them *new* tricks and they say you can't teach old dogs new tricks. Well, she did. She also gets three new dogs from the pound at Wangaratta, so now there's eight, Bitzers One to Eight, though some of them are getting a bit long in the tooth so they only do the easy stuff because they're semi-retired.

So every fight Bozo has, except the National Championships and the Olympic trials, Mrs Rika Ray is there with Bitzers One to Eight. At every other fight the Bitzers put on a show before Bozo's bout. It's Mrs Rika Ray who takes them through their paces: jumping through fire hoops, climbing ladders, keeping this big ball in the air with their noses so it goes from dog to dog and never touches the deck, marching in line on their back legs, doing a tug of war with people making bets, dancing as couples to square-dance music, playing cops and robbers where Bitzer Three stands on his hind legs and points a paw at Bitzer Seven and there's the sound of a gun going off and then Bitzer Seven leaps in the air, does a backward somersault and plays dead, sprawled on his back.

Mrs Rika Ray is dressed in this sari dress made of gold silk and she wears earrings that are miniature red boxing gloves as well as a rhinestone tiara that spells 'Bozo'. The only pity is that Bitzer Five can't do his handstand piss against the corner post, which is reasonable enough, but normally the highlight of the show. Now he's the dog that can't do anything – the dumb dog, he falls over when they sit up or salute, baulks at the fire ring, falls off the ladder, gets knocked arse over tit by the ball, and he's out of step in the square dance. People love him the most. The whole Bitzer routine runs about ten minutes in the ring before Bozo fights his opponent and is an absolute crowd-stopper.

Bozo's always been called 'Bozo, the Boy Boxer' in Yankalillee, but the *Truth* newspaper does this article on Bozo's Bitzers and they call him Bozo 'Dog Boy' Maloney and it kind of sticks with the crowds. Big Jack now uses it to get Bozo's name in the papers because he reckons it's good publicity and will help Bozo get noticed for the Olympic trials. In truth, it nearly backfires because the Olympic Committee think Bozo's being promoted like he's a professional and it will bring a bad name to amateurism and is against the Olympic spirit. Nancy says they're a bunch of silly old farts and must all be related to Philip Templeton. But I'll tell you about that later.

In the meantime, it turns out that what Mrs Rika Ray has done for Sophie's warts, as well as being the midwife at Templeton's birth, is child's play compared to what she does for Bozo.

The health part is weird Indian stuff that Bozo swears works a treat. Bozo's not the sort of bloke that goes for mumbo jumbo like that, so if he says it works, then you can bet that it does. It's called Ayurveda and it's an ancient Indian type of medicine which is all about poking out your tongue and seeing things on it that can't be revealed elsewhere. There's other things as well, of course, but the tongue is one of the most important, in fact, probably the most important.

Mrs Rika Ray explains it like this. 'We are sleeping the night and breathing out all the time and all the poisons are coming out from inside and the tongue is catching them like sticky flypaper, then we are waking up with mouth like Indian lavatory, which is a very, very bad thing we are now fixing!'

Every morning Bozo has to examine his tongue in the mirror. 'We are looking for white coat like a bunny rabbit on the tongue. This is breathing-out fur we are making and that is very, very bad.' Bozo has this tongue scraper, I'm not kidding. It's a thing made of metal with tiny burrs on it like a carrot grater and he has to use it to scrape off 'the breathing-out bunny fur' on his tongue.

'If it's already on the tongue when he wakes up isn't it too late? I mean the poison's already been inside him doing its deadly best?' I once asked Mrs Rika Ray.

'No, no, no, no! Poison coming up is going down again, same as Mr Newton's Law, what comes up must come down. We are making the scrapings so the poison buggers can't go down again!'

It's all pretty complicated but Mrs Rika Ray says it's been around about five thousand years and comes from the ancient Sanskrit texts and has been passed down by word of mouth, which is probably why the tongue is so important. Though I reckon it must be okay or they'd have found out by now, unless of course Indians are very stupid, which we know they're not. It's not just the tongue but Ayurveda has lots to do with herbs and massage, exercise and the stuff you eat. There's even a bit of yoga thrown in for good measure, but not the sort that has a man with a turban and a flute making snakes come out of baskets, it's a sort of exercise of mind and body. Or is the snake bloke a yogi?

So there's old Bozo training for his fights and dreaming of being chosen to go to the Olympics, with Mrs Rika Ray giving him herbs and almost no meat and massaging him before and after every fight, and him scraping away at his tongue and her looking for tell-tale indentations to see if he's digesting his food properly, Bozo doing a thing called 'meditation' where you cross your legs and close your eyes and look at what Mrs Rika Ray calls 'inner self', which is not the same inner self that breathes out the poison, but the inner self that makes you strong and unbeatable.

If you think that's complicated, how about this. 'We are dividing into three and then much overlapping is happening quick-smart, *vasta* is overlapping *pitta* or *kapha* or other way round, the overlapping is going on and on like bloody Dagwood sandwich!' Mrs Rika Ray brings her hands up to either side of her face. 'Oh, my goodness, who can be telling the combinations! Impossible, only I can do it, no other in Australia!'

Well, if only Mrs Rika Ray knows how to work it out and Bozo's got her, I suppose we can count ourselves lucky. I don't know how this helps him to be a good boxer but he's that focused on going to the Olympic Games that he'll try anything. He says, no doubt about it, if he listens to Mrs Rika Ray he's full of vim and he's got something left at the end of a fight. Morrie says it's all in the head, if you believe something hard enough, the head does the rest, it's basic psychology. Me? I don't know, I'm just glad I don't have to give up meat like Bozo almost has.

Whatever it is, it's working, Bozo keeps winning and getting closer and closer into contention. As I said, he's no longer a featherweight but is now a welterweight. Now here's the thing, who do you think he meets in his first fight in the National Championships? You guessed it, John Thomas, the big prick Bozo sparred with in the Russell Street gym the weekend Templeton was born.

John Thomas has also moved up in the weight divisions and the Victorian amateur welterweight title is up for grabs and, as they're the only two Victorians in the division at the Nationals, the fight is billed not only as the quarterfinals for the national welterweight championship, it will also decide which of them is to be the next state welterweight champion.

John Thomas has become a police officer, which Big Jack says is a pity because you don't need that type in the force, they've got too much aggro. Anyway, when Bozo started coming down on the weekends to Melbourne to train in the Russell Street gym, Thomas got real angry and told Kevin Flanagan that it was either Bozo or him. To choose, because he wasn't going to fight for the same club.

Remember, Thomas went to the Melbourne Olympics and, although he didn't win a medal and was eliminated in the first round, he's a big name around the place. Being an Olympian isn't chicken-feed, especially around Melbourne where people are still basking in the glory of having pulled off the Friendly Games. Even though when the Hungarians played the Russians in the finals of the water polo and the pool was red with blood, it wasn't all that friendly, I can tell ya. Anyhow, Thomas being in the Russell Street Police Boys Club is a big deal for the club so you can see he's carrying a big stick to threaten Mr Flanagan.

Big Jack says Kevin Flanagan sort of stands there looking down at his feet and rubbing his jaw before he says, 'Well, son, you'll be twenty for the Rome Olympics and I reckon you might get a medal this time, but only if you're properly prepared, if you're good enough. The kid from Yankalillee also wants to go to Rome real bad and he's the only one in this state, possibly in the country, who can match you. Fight him, spar with him regularly and you'll be that much better off.' He looks into Thomas's face, 'Son, it's not me has to make the decision, it's you.'

Well, John Thomas goes to the Police Academy and after that he's posted to Geelong so he uses this as his excuse to leave the Russell Street gym even though Geelong is only a hop, skip and jump from Melbourne and, because he is an Olympian, Big Jack says they would probably have arranged for him to use a police vehicle from the car pool.

The two of them, Bozo and Thomas, haven't met again until the 1959 Nationals in Brisbane, which is billed as 'The Carnival of Swat & Fist Fiesta'. This is mainly because Bozo was in the under-seventeen junior division until the August before the championships on October 28 and 29, so they couldn't have met before this. Bozo's got to be a welterweight just by growing and Thomas has got there by doing weights in the gym and doing a bit of general body building.

Of course, the interstate people at the championships don't know it's a grudge match though some of the Victorians do. The story of Bozo, the Boy Boxer, and John Thomas the Olympian has been retold so many times that it's become an almost legendary fight even though it was never really a full fight, only a bit of a serious spar.

Now Bozo is seventeen and Thomas twenty and of course those in the know want to see what's happened to them in the meantime. The news soon gets round the championships that this just could be a ding-dong scrap, that the two fighters hate each other and that there's a real donnybrook in the making as they're well matched in height and reach and both are fast as buggery.

It's not true about them hating each other. John Thomas may hate Bozo, but Bozo's not the hating type and, under Mrs Rika Ray's treatments, which teach that hate makes a person weak, Bozo's sort of super calm when he goes into a fight. 'Totally focused' is how Kevin Flanagan describes it. Bozo comes into the ring very quiet and doesn't jump around or fist the air or even give his opponent the evil eye. All he does is sit on his stool and listen quietly to Mr Flanagan and Big Jack and sometimes he nods his head. Bozo looks like he's about to fall asleep most of the time, which must be the meditation Mrs Rika Ray has taught him. It probably gives his opponents the shits seeing him like that all cool, calm and collected. Bozo says he just doesn't see any purpose in huffin' and puffin' and blowin' the corner posts over, and all that shadow-boxing is just boxing bullshit.

The welterweight division is about where you start to attract attention in a national championship, though the real crowd-pleasers are the cruiserweights and heavyweights, who get most of the limelight. The fight between Bozo and John Thomas is scheduled to start at ten o'clock, when the hall would usually be almost empty except for a few fighters and their trainers working out. But on this particular morning there's more than five hundred fight fans and all the other fighters are there to watch as well. This is not a lot of people. For the finals there will be five thousand people in the Brisbane Festival Hall, but it's a lot more people than would normally be watching the preliminary fights.

Thomas, it seems, hasn't been backwards in coming forward and has been saying a few things about Bozo 'Dog Boy' Maloney that are not very polite. He has every reason to be confident, he's got the Melbourne Olympics under his belt and he's become a much harder, tougher, physically stronger and more skilled fighter since the two of them last met. Besides, there's always the possibility that he didn't take

Bozo too seriously the first time and Bozo got a crack at him before he woke up to what was happening. This time there will be no surprises, except of course that Bozo might have learned a bit more as well.

I'm sitting in a ringside seat with Mrs Rika Ray who's wearing her gold-silk sari dress, her Bozo tiara and her boxing-glove earrings that hang down on a little chain from each ear.

Sarah, who's also come to Brisbane, is wearing a Mike outfit that causes all the boxers to wolf-whistle when we come into Festival Hall. It's a pair of hipster pants made out of sort of rust-coloured Thai silk and very tight. With them, Sarah wears a simple short-sleeved cream cotton shirt cut like a man's, with the first three buttons undone. She wears a green scarf tied around her neck, not a long scarf, sort of like a bandanna, and Mike has spraypainted a pair of ordinary sandshoes the same colour as the bandanna. Mike calls it 'Casual Dazzle'.

Morrie's come with us as well. We've driven up from Yankalillee in the second-hand Volkswagen Kombivan Bozo's bought for the business. It was in an accident and consigned to the wreckers and Bozo got it for fifty quid. John Crowe panelbeat it and put it together again. It's got seats in it like a small bus and although Bozo's going to take the seats out to turn it into a parcel van, he hasn't done so yet and we all fit in, with room for our sleeping bags, blankets, cushions and cooking stuff. Morrie and Sarah take turns driving, because Bozo of course hasn't got his licence yet. Big Jack turns a blind eye to this in Yankalillee but we can't take a chance on the open road. Anyway, it gives Bozo a chance to have a bit of a rest on the way up to the championships.

It took us three days to get to Brisbane and we camped out beside a different river on the two nights and then, when we arrived in Brisbane, we went to the Brisbane City Caravan Park, which is alongside the river and not that far from Festival Hall. Talk about modern. It had hot and cold water in the shower block, which was clean as anything, with even septic toilets. There was a modern laundry with these Bendix washing machines you put a shilling in and you could do your whole wash and, then, for another sixpence there were dryers, so you didn't even have to hang your clothes out on a line. We're snug as a bug in a rug because we're in the tropics or subtropics and very warm at night. Morrie's been enjoying the fights but now is dead worried because he's been told that it's a grudge fight between the two boxers and he wants to be there in case Bozo gets hurt.

Sophie is back in Carlton looking after little Colleen and Templeton while Nancy's stayed home in Yankalillee because she's got a crook back. Tommy's been on a binge and gone walkabout so couldn't be found. Mike's never been with us to a single boxing tournament and he maintains his record by remaining with Sophie to sew. Sophie's a very nervous type and Morrie wouldn't let her be in the house alone because she's frightened of Nazis, but with Mike there as well it's okay. Mind you, he probably couldn't protect her against a determined house fly. Mike's funny like that, he's got a mouth full of razor blades if he wants, but he can't stand violence and he'd faint if he saw blood. He once did when I cut myself badly on a broken bottle while we were doing the garbage.

There's a bantamweight fight going on between a Queensland boxer and one from New South Wales. Bantamweights are usually nice to watch because they're fast and generally pretty cocky, but these two have way too much respect for each other. For the three rounds they're either standing off, throwing punches that are seldom landing, or they're locked into a clinch so that the referee is constantly telling them to break. The New South Welshman gets warned in round two for headbutting but I don't think it was on purpose. In the final round, with the crowd having lost interest and talking to each other, the ref warns them halfway through the round to get on with the fight or he'll stop it. So there's a bit of action at last with the boxer from Queensland using his left quite well and only just getting on top, though it's a boring fight which could have gone either way. If the Queenslander comes up against a good boxer in the quarterfinals, he's going to get slaughterated. It's funny, you wonder why boxers like that want to get into the ring when they're so reluctant to have a go. I reckon that was why I gave boxing away, though I told myself it was because of the garbage, and me being too tired.

The referee announces Bozo Maloney and John Thomas, but not like it's a big deal, not the way it would happen in the finals with a ring announcer doing the honours. He just says, 'The next fight is a welterweight contest between John Thomas and Bozo Maloney. Will their seconds prepare their corners and the two boxers get up into the ring.' Then he announces, as sort of an afterthought, that the fight will be for the vacant Victorian welterweight title. But there is a fair bit of excitement in the crowd because, as I said, the word's got around this could be a good fight.

Bozo does his usual sleep act in the corner while John Thomas is snuffling and punching the air. Not much has changed in this department since the last time. Thomas tries to lock Bozo into the big stare but Bozo takes no notice and drops his eyes as the referee goes through the usual stuff. He examines their gloves and tells them to break when he says 'break', in the case of a knockdown, go to a neutral corner, blah, blah, blah. 'Okay, shake hands, come out fighting with the bell,' he says finally. Bozo looks up for the first time and the two boxers' eyes lock. Thomas grins. Bozo's expression doesn't change, he's focused, ready to go. Big Jack slips Bozo's mouthpiece in. Thomas is standing in his corner punching his gloves together, anxious to get going. He's in good shape and you can see the results of the weights, his pecs show clearly and, unlike last time, he has a tan and looks sharp.

The bell goes for the first round and it's on for one and all. Both boxers move quickly towards the centre of the ring and the stoush is under way. Thomas leads with a left that misses, but follows with a right that hits Bozo high on the forehead, the punch throws his shoulder up a fraction and Bozo puts a left hook into his opponent's rib cage. The two of them stand there, matching blow for blow, both of them taking most of the punches on the gloves, though Bozo is also hitting Thomas hard on both arms, high up on the biceps. Then Thomas hits him with a simply beautiful left uppercut and knocks Bozo into the ropes and he's onto him, seating a left and a right into Bozo's stomach. The uppercut and the two punches to the gut are enough probably to win him the round. Bozo hangs on and then goes into a clinch and the referee has to separate them. The uppercut and the left–right combination have slowed Bozo down and he dances around Thomas, more interested in staying out of the way than hitting his opponent. Thomas is on top and manages to land a hard straight right into Bozo's face. In fact, Bozo seems to walk into the punch and his nose starts to show a fair bit of claret.

The bell goes and Thomas is well ahead, he's outboxed Bozo and is giving him a lesson.

Mrs Rika Ray is beside herself. She is accustomed to Bozo winning the first round and getting on top of his opponent and she's never seen him outboxed like this. Even Morrie, who knows nothing about boxing, is looking worried and wants to know whether he should go up and see if Bozo's nose is okay.

Thomas is sitting in his corner and his second is yelling out stuff but you can see he isn't listening. He's drumming both feet on the canvas and looking towards Bozo's corner, he wants to get going, certain after such a good round that he's got Bozo's measure. Old Bozo has his eyes closed while Big Jack stems the blood from his nose, Kevin Flanagan is talking to him softly because he never yells, and Bozo is nodding. With the bell about to go, Thomas stands up and so does Bozo.

The bell sounds and Thomas comes out of his corner like he's got a rocket up his bum and it's a repeat of the opening round, they're slugging it out in the centre of the ring. Thomas hasn't changed all that much, he's still a headhunter and Bozo is still a body-finder. Bozo always says, 'Why would you hit the smallest and hardest object when there's a bigger one just as vulnerable right in front of you?' Bozo hits Thomas with a nice left and right. They're scoring shots but they're taken on Thomas's biceps, rips that dig deep but it's hard to see if they do any damage. Thomas backs off and into the ropes. Bozo hooks him with a left to the jaw and Thomas's hands go up. Bozo territory! Bozo's right uppercut slams in under Thomas's heart and he follows it with a left and another right and then with a left hook. The punches are so fast you can hardly see them coming. Mrs Rika Ray is screaming with excitement, 'Bozo, Bozo, kill him!' which I must say isn't very yoga-like.

Thomas comes off the ropes, he's been hurt but he doesn't do like Bozo's done in the first round, moved away, stayed out of harm's way, until he's regained his strength. Instead, he seems to lose it and comes tearing in, angry. Bozo backpedals, keeping him off with a left jab, then he suddenly moves laterally, plants his feet firmly and throws a swinging right hand that catches Thomas on the side of the jaw, which makes the audience gasp and yell as Thomas hits the deck at almost the same moment the bell goes.

The ref starts the compulsory ten count but at seven Thomas is back on his feet. The ref shows him four fingers and asks him how many and Thomas must have said there were four, to prove he wasn't concussed. But then Thomas's trainer and his assistant are in the ring, saying Bozo hit Thomas after the bell and he should be disqualified. The ref says that's not the case and so does the crowd, but Thomas's trainer is still shouting and waving his arms and the ref tells him to get back to his corner or he'll stop the fight and award it to Bozo. So the trainer goes back, but still protesting, and the ref asks Thomas if he wants to go on and he says yes. The ref walks over to Thomas's corner and asks the trainer who must have said yes because he's nodding his head but you can see he's still bloody angry. We couldn't really hear all this because the crowd is booing Thomas's trainer. It was clear as daylight that Bozo's punch had landed before the bell went. Bozo said afterwards that's what happened. So now the time out between rounds is almost four minutes and John Thomas has had plenty of time to recover. Thomas's trainer took a chance challenging the referee like that but he's given his boxer an extra two minutes to recover and Thomas is right as rain when he comes into the final round.

People who were there would talk about the last round for years. The classic battle between the boxer who was Bozo and the fighter who was Thomas. The two boxers just stand toe to toe in the middle of the ring and slug it out. Thomas the headhunter looks to be throwing better punches because Bozo's getting hit lots and his left eye has closed. But Bozo hasn't forgotten his craft, and the rips to the body, under the heart and into the rib cage, are landing time and time again and when Bozo isn't down below, he hits Thomas's upper arms.

I'm getting scared that the ref and the three judges will see all the head shots Thomas is landing and not the body damage Bozo's doing, which means Thomas won the first round and Bozo the second, but Thomas could be given the last round. There's less than thirty seconds to go when Bozo rips a tremendous right under Thomas's heart and the other boxer buckles up and backs into the ropes, bringing his gloves up to cover his face and tucking his arms in to protect his heart and stomach. Bozo follows with a left and then another hard right to Thomas's upper arms and Thomas grabs him in a clinch. The ref tells them to break and Thomas comes off the ropes but suddenly he can't raise his arms; they're hanging by his side, and Bozo smacks him with a tremendous left hook to the jaw, following with a straight right to the side of his opponent's head with Thomas already going backwards. I reckon he was out before he hit the canvas. 'Timber!' Mrs Rika Ray shouts. She's out of her seat, dancing with her arms in the air, and we all feel a bit embarrassed, but it's okay because the crowd is cheering and whistling.

So there's the old law proved again, when the body goes, the head must surely follow. The ref's count reaches ten before Thomas starts to move up onto his hands and knees, shaking his head, trying to clear it. He'd fought a damn good fight and, whatever you may think of him as a person, he has to be given credit for that. Bozo comes over and helps Thomas to his feet and half-carries him to his corner. But as he reaches Thomas's corner, the trainer, who's a big bloke with a fat gut, pulls Thomas to his chest and with his free hand pushes Bozo away so that he nearly loses his balance. The crowd boo him again. Later, Big Jack says the trainer is a cop nicknamed 'Banjo', though his real name is Nick Patterson and he's a mug lair and a bully.

Mrs Rika Ray fixes up Bozo's eye so that by the following morning the eye is bright as the other with only a little patch of purple in the corner of the lower eyelid. Morrie examines his nose and swabs out a bit of blood with cotton wool on a small stick and says there's nothing broken, Bozo's going to keep his nice straight nose.

Meanwhile, there's a bit of a conniption going on in the championships when everyone getting into the final night was expecting to fight their three fights in three days. The officials, as usual, screw things up and the boxers are told if they get through their preliminary fight and into the semifinal they're going to have to fight twice on the same day, once in the morning or up until two o'clock in the afternoon, and then the winners will have to fight again that night for the title.

Kevin Flanagan is disgusted but says it's a typical cock-up, that the Amateur Boxing Association couldn't run a chook raffle in a hungry pub. There's even worse to come. When it's time for the doctor to examine every boxer fighting in the semis, there's no doctor, someone's forgotten to book him. So the boxers have to jump into taxis and are told they have to pay their own fares to the Brisbane General Hospital. Well, the hospital's got a fair bit of work on and the boxers don't get priority treatment and it's 1.45 p.m. by the time they get back to Festival Hall. The lunchtime crowd is pretty aggro because they've missed seeing any fights and they demand their two shillings entrance fee back. So now Bozo and the others have to fight in the afternoon and then again that night. Bozo's fight takes place at 4.30 p.m. and if he wins he's on again at seven.

Fortunately Bozo easily wins the semifinal without having to expend too much energy and that night is introduced on the microphone as Bozo Maloney, the welterweight champion of Victoria.

It's a one-sided fight which Bozo wins again on a t.k.o. in the second round and so, in a bit of an anticlimax, he wins the national title. Everyone says the final should really have been between him and Thomas because the other two fighters couldn't hold a candle to either of them. The ring announcer then says into the microphone, 'The winner is Bozo Maloney, the welterweight champion of Victoria and now the national title holder in the welterweight division.' He also announces that Bozo has been selected for the Olympic trials to be held in Melbourne in March during the Moomba Festival.

There's not much point going through the Olympic trials because Thomas has broken his hand and can't fight in the trials and there isn't too much competition left because no dark horse has come through since the Nationals the previous year. Bozo gets his Olympic blazer and Yankalillee has its first Olympian and, guess what, it's a Maloney!

Nancy is completely over the moon, not because of Bozo's selection though that too of course but because the *Gazette* calls for a civic reception and Philip Templeton is the shire president and so nothing is done. Then Toby Forbes runs a piece in the *Gazette* which says it's a disgrace and if people will write in or phone to say they think there should be a civic reception for Yankalillee's first Olympian, he'll print their names in the paper. He also says if they object, they can send in their names and he'll print them as well. In the next edition there's hundreds of names, not only from Yankalillee but from as far as

Wodonga and Wangaratta and all districts in between. There's not one name printed as an objection, which doesn't mean there aren't some since there always are, the Templetons for a start and their mob on the council, but because they were scared they'd be seen for what they were, bloody-minded and mean-spirited.

The council issues a statement to the *Gazette* to say that they were conscious of the honour of having an Olympian from the town but that a civic reception in sport is only held when something is won, like the footy competition or a medal. They don't even mention Bozo's name in the statement. It's all utter bullshit of course and Toby Forbes loses no time saying so, pointing to various precedents. He's called three towns in the bush that have someone going to the Rome Olympics and all three have held a civic reception to honour their athlete. Toby writes a blistering editorial pointing out that the people of Yankalillee clearly want to do the right thing and the council just as clearly doesn't. Toby later tells us that several of the council members threaten to stop advertising in the *Gazette* if he doesn't let up. Toby's a pretty fearless sort of bloke and he keeps the war raging and certainly Philip Templeton's Holden dealership advertisements stop appearing. The council stands firm. Tommy comes home and says the blokes in the pub are pretty pissed off about it and there's no other conversation going on except how Bozo's been treated.

Then Nancy says at tea one night, 'Bozo, you better go win us a medal so I can stick it, ribbon and all, up Philip Templeton's fat bum at the civic reception he'll be forced to have!' Not that she has any right to comment on someone's fat bum, but we all laugh anyway. Bozo says thank gawd it's happened because he'd feel a real drongo standing in the back of a ute waving to the crowd. Without knowing it, Philip Templeton has done him a big favour.

This is true when you think about it, because them not doing it, like refusing to have the reception, has made people much more interested and aware of Bozo's achievement than any silly parade down King Street, where Bozo would only have got another bottoms-wiping certificate on the town-hall steps like the one I got for the rescue that I didn't really do of Mrs Rika Ray.

By the time of the Rome Olympics, there was television in

Melbourne and Sydney but not too many places else and certainly not in Yankalillee. So we all went down to Melbourne and stayed at the Carlton terrace and Morrie got permission from the shop steward at the *Age* to invite us to see it on the workers' set at the newspaper. They couldn't send the pictures as far as Australia and so the opening of the Olympics and all the events were taped and put on a Qantas plane and were shown on TV two nights later. We also went to the movies and saw some of it on the Movietone News.

We're watching the opening ceremony at the *Age* with about two hundred other people, the workers and their families. They've got the set high up on a special stand so we can all see. When the Australians came marching into the main Olympic stadium, we cheer like mad and then, suddenly, out of the blue, they do a close-up. There's Bozo with a row of marchers, waving into the camera and walking beside Murray Rose and Dawn Fraser, both of whom won gold medals in the swimming and went on to be all-time champions. Bozo's waving and looking the full part, proud as anything. Nancy's bawling and stuffing her gloves in her mouth and little Colleen's screaming out and I'm a bit choked up meself and I think something in my chest is going to burst I'm that proud. I look over at Tommy and the tears are running silently down his cheeks. It's a moment I don't suppose our family will ever forget.

When a thing like that happens in your family, it makes you think not only how hard Bozo's worked, but also how other people have given up a lot to help him. Big Jack Donovan and Kevin Flanagan and Mrs Rika Ray and even Mrs Barrington-Stone, who's flown Bozo to Melbourne on lots of occasions for a fight, using the excuse that she's going to see her daughter but then flies him back the next day so he can get a decent sleep before doing garbage of a Monday. The blokes at the abattoir, who don't know that Bozo's on a practically meatless diet, set aside a couple of big, juicy steaks twice a week so he'll have only the best. They've been doing it for the past two years and I've practically forgotten what offal tastes like. Even Bobby Devlin, who started Bozo off in the fight game, sends Bozo a postal order for twenty pounds with a letter that said:

Dear Bozo,

I'm not much of a hand at letter writing. I don't think I've wrote more than two in my life. Once to the army to say I had flat feet, but they didn't believe it and I had to go to Egypt. Stinkin' hole! Then the other when my mate was kill'd and I wrote to his mum and said how sorry and all that, what a good bloke he was.

Now this one, to wish you luck in Rome. I'm very proud of you, Bozo, and can't take credit because you're a natural, always and was willin' to work hard even as a little bloke. But you made me time in prison a pleasure and I'd do the stretch all over again if you was there. I'm sending you twenty quid. I-talians are cowards and I captured 20 meself in Toobruk and I didn't even have a live round up me barrel when I come across them behind a sand dune. They dropped their rifles and put their hands up and one already had a white rag tied on his rifle barrel. I reckon'd, for sure, I'd get a gong or something, but lots of blokes did the same thing and some brought in 200 prisoners of war single handed. But it's the I-tie sheilas the money's for. There's no better, take my word, son. Spend it wise on one of them but take a rubber. Never can tell, eh!

Yours faithfully,

Bobby Devlin

P.S. Ask your mother has she still got the gold bracelet, she'll know what I mean.

Bozo couldn't even write to thank him because there was no address, but the postmark said Tweed Heads. Bozo wrote anyway, care of the Tweed Heads post office but we never heard if he got it.

Bozo isn't like Sarah or Mike who can tell you sort of blow by blow what happened. He's always been a modest sort of a bloke who doesn't like talking about himself too much so when he got back from Rome I had to interrogate him for weeks to get the story and some of it has taken years, bits coming out here and there.

Bozo said the preliminaries were all pretty tough fights as there were thirty-three welterweights in the first section. According to Ray Mitchell, the great Australian boxing expert, there were some pretty weird decisions at the Rome Olympics. It seems that sometimes you weren't only fighting your opponent because some of the referees and judges were pretty one-eyed, and there was a fair bit of aggro about it among the boxers and the team managers. Not just the ten Australian boxers, some of whom felt they were the victims of a bad decision, but a lot of the other teams as well.

The Eastern Bloc officials were pretty keen to see their boxers come home but so were some of the judges and referees from the free world. The Italians, whose games it was, wanted to see the local boxers come good even if they didn't always have the talent and if they needed a nudge or two on a scorecard, well, so be it.

Bozo said that after the first section of fights when it became pretty apparent that it wasn't always a case of the best man wins, there was a pretty bad spirit among some of the teams and you couldn't help feeling it. You knew you had to beat more than your opponent in many cases and a lot of blokes, to make sure they'd beat their opponent convincingly, were encouraged by their trainers to start off a lot more aggressively than was maybe their natural way of fighting.

When I asked him if he'd done the same, he laughed, 'Mate, I just kept thinking of Big Jack and Kevin and Mrs Rika Ray and even Bobby Devlin and what they'd taught me and I reckoned that if it wasn't enough I wouldn't win. No good trying to change your style going into the most important fight of your life.'

There definitely were some very weird decisions given and one of them was when our Australian light heavyweight, Tony Madigan, fought Cassius Clay and the crowd booed after the verdict was given to Clay.

From outside the ring it appeared that there was very little between the two boxers in the first two rounds. Clay used the ring very well and scored on the back move, keeping the fight at long range. You see, Madigan had knocked out his Romanian opponent, Negrea, when the Eastern Bloc fighter made a careless mistake in the second round and led with a right and, *boom*, Madigan let go a left hook followed by a right to the head and dropped Negrea cold.

So Clay's corner are anxious not to get too close to Madigan. But

Madigan keeps coming in and in the first two rounds it would have been hard to separate them.

In the third and final, Madigan steps up a notch and goes for Clay, who tries to dance out of the way and keep the ferocious Australian at bay but Madigan's got a gold medal in mind, which means he has to get into the finals and he's showing tremendous aggression. His constant attack takes the fight to close quarters where Clay can't escape. Madigan has Clay holding on desperately as he whips punch after punch to the American's body. Ray Mitchell says that unbiased and good judges of boxing rated the decision for Clay. The crowd was very vocal and hooted the verdict, but Bozo disagrees, he saw the fight and he reckons Cassius Clay always had the fight under control. It was just that Madigan was a fighter who looked very good in the ring, a bit like the contrast in styles between Thomas and himself.

Yet you can't help thinking about what happened afterwards with Cassius Clay, who became Muhammad Ali, world heavyweight champion and one of the greatest boxers the world has ever seen. What if our own Tony Madigan had won? Christ. I don't suppose Madigan, who was a Catholic, would have said anything like that in a hurry.

The Italians won an amazing thirty-three bouts counting all the preliminaries, that was more than anyone else. A great many boxing experts came away from Rome saying that the sport of boxing had not been well served at the 1960 Olympic Games.

When all was said and done, Australia did okay in the boxing though, considering they were a very inexperienced team and most of the fighters from Europe and America had over a hundred amateur fights under their belts. Except for Tony Madigan, the rest of our boys didn't even get near that figure. The flyweight, Rocky Gattellari, who later ranked number five in the world when he turned professional, went to Rome with only twenty-seven amateur bouts behind him. So bronze medals also coming from Madigan and Ollie Taylor in the bantamweight division wasn't a bad show and the best we'd ever done in Olympic boxing.

While we didn't win as many medals in Rome as we'd done in Melbourne, Herb Elliott's win in the 1500 metres by twenty metres, which is about twelve yards, was one of the greatest 1500 metre races ever! Some people say he may even give up running because he is bored with winning and he's won everything there is to win anyway. You'd think that sooner or later he'd have an off day, a cold or something, but he hasn't.

We also did much better in swimming than in Melbourne. Murray Rose and Dawn Fraser, whom Bozo marched next to in the opening ceremony, both won gold medals, so did John Devitt and John Konrads and David Thiele. I think Rome was where Australian swimming really started to come into its own and look at it now!

As far as I can gather, Bozo's fight with the boxer from the Soviet Union was almost a duplicate of his fight in the 1959 Nationals with John Thomas, only this time the other fighter got the decision.

The Soviet boxer was another headhunter like Thomas, though he knew a fair bit about going for the body as well. He was tough as teak and was prepared to take a few good punches so that he could get in close where he preferred to fight. In the first round Bozo did a lot of backpedalling, keeping his opponent at bay with his left hand and, every once in a while, throwing a beautiful straight right that kept him in contention. Like the Thomas fight, the more aggressive Soviet fighter seemed to take the first round. He'd landed two good right hands of his own, a straight right to Bozo's head and another right hook when on a rare occasion he had Bozo on the ropes. Both punches hurt Bozo, and his opponent seemed pretty pleased with himself when the bell went, smacking his gloves above his head on his way to his corner. The judges might have given him the first round, they probably did.

Thinking that Bozo lacked the punch to hurt him, the boxer came in very aggressively, chasing Bozo all over the ring. But it was Bozo who'd worked his opponent out and in the second round Bozo boxed beautifully and scored well, counterpunching when the boxer went on the attack. Bozo took most of his punches on the gloves and, regular as clockwork, planted his signature with a rip to the body, most of his punches going into the same spot under the heart. Bozo was working to his plan, not allowing the Russian to dictate the fight, though to someone who wasn't an expert, the Soviet fighter's aggression may have fooled them into thinking he was gaining the ascendancy when just the opposite was true.

In fact, Mitchell says he thought at the time the fighter from the Soviet Union had lapsed in the second round and that Bozo's hard and accurate punching had sapped some of his opponent's strength and he was now fighting in flurries and breathing heavily from the mouth, his punches mostly missing. It became clear from the number of times the Russian threw the same punch that he was hoping he might get a good right cross to Bozo's jaw and put him down. But towards the end of the round, uncannily like the Thomas fight, Bozo moved laterally after his opponent had thrown a right cross and missed, putting a perfect straight left into the point of the Soviet fighter's jaw, which dropped him to the canvas as the bell went.

The Soviet fighter was tough and proud and he took the compulsory count on his pins before going to his corner. There was no doubt that Bozo had hurt him and comfortably taken the round. One round each with one to go.

In the third round, the superbly conditioned Soviet boxer was ready to fight. He was throwing punches from every direction of the compass and Bozo was tying him up so that the ref warned him on one occasion. Then the Russian was warned for a headbutt, which may or may not have been accidental. But he kept coming and Bozo had to withstand a desperate onslaught. I keep repeating it, I know, but Bozo kept those rips going in, landing them close up, short jabs that went under the heart. They may not have looked much but Bozo was a very strong boxer and the short punches had the full weight of his shoulders and body behind them and each time he landed one, you could hear the Soviet boxer grunt, they were hurting bad. With thirty seconds to go in the final round, Bozo had done enough to win but he wanted to make sure so he hit the boxer with a beautiful left and right that should have put him down. The boy from the Urals was tough as they come, though, and hung onto the ropes for dear life. Bozo went for his heart again and the Soviet fighter grabbed desperately at Bozo, locking his arms and holding on for grim life. The referee didn't tell them to break and the crowd started yelling, but the other boxer kept hanging onto Bozo's arms. The few seconds Bozo needed to make the break and then put in the decider, the knock-out punch, was gone. The final bell went.

The decision in favour of the Soviet Union boxer was jeered at by the crowd. Afterwards, the trainer of the Soviet Union team came up to Bozo in the Australian dressing room and, in front of all the other Australian boxers, raised his hand above his head, before walking out again without saying a single word. Bozo laughs when people say he could have won a gold if he'd been given a fair go. 'Nah, the Italian, Nino Benvenuti who won gold was in a class of his own, I couldn't have taken him,' he'd say. Bozo's always been a straightshooter and he was right, Benvenuti went on to become the world professional middleweight champion.

So Bozo Maloney became an Olympic bronze medallist and he said later it was the happiest day of his life. All the hard work was rewarded and Big Jack Donovan's faith in him justified.

Toby Forbes at the *Gazette* goes wild. He has a special rotogravure colour front page printed in Melbourne on high-quality paper. It shows a picture of Bozo stripped down to his boxing gear with the red singlet and white shorts that are the Yankalillee colours and, of course, his red Tommy Christmas-gift boxing gloves and, as well, his bronze medal big as a side plate with the ribbon trailing across the page with the five Olympic rings across the top of the page. In two-inch letters, in the alliteration Toby Forbes is so fond of using, the headline says:

SOUVENIR EDITION

BLOODY
BEAUTY!
BOZO'S
BRILLIANT
BOXING
BRONZE!

In the editorial, after he's said how fantastic Bozo's win was and how proud the town of Yankalillee is of him, Forbes gets well and truly stuck into the shire council.

Every dog has his day and Bozo 'Dog Boy' Maloney's is well overdue. Refused a civic reception when he was chosen to represent Australia, he has now returned from Rome with a bronze medal. A brilliant result for a local lad fighting the world's best. But, it seems, he can win in the international arena but not in his own backyard unless he brings back the spoils. Now Yankalillee's shire council and the men who run it must keep their promise and give this upstanding young boxer the civic reception and the honour that goes with it that he so richly deserves!

He goes on a lot more and quotes the article from *Australian Ring Magazine* that says Bozo should have got at least a silver and that who knows where he'll go in the 'world of fights and fists' but everyone knows that he is a credit and always has been a credit to Yankalillee and so on.

So now, of course, the shire council and its president, Philip, with one 'l', Templeton, are forced to give Bozo a civic reception. Bozo's not that keen, but Nancy wants it more than the crown jewels. The town clerk comes to see her and says they'll have a parade down King Street with all the trimmings. They've decided to borrow the Rolls-Royce from the mayor of Albury and Nancy and Bozo will sit in the back seat and the town band will lead them to a reception at the town hall.

Nancy won't have a bar of this. 'We all go in the parade or nobody, this family does things together,' she tells him.

'We could get a ute from Mr Templeton's dealership and you could all stand in the back.' The silly coot must be away with the fairies or something.

'I'd rather be pushed down King Street in the nightcart than go in a Holden ute belonging to Philip bloody Templeton!' Nancy protests. Then she has her sudden inspiration. 'The Diamond T!' she screams out. 'We'll do it in the Diamond T!'

She goes on to explain that the whole family will be in the back of the Diamond T. Bozo in his Olympic blazer, tie and hat with the special khaki flannels. Sarah in one of Mike's outfits, me and little Colleen, Morrie and Sophie as well, because as far as us Maloneys are concerned, they're family as well. Tommy will be the front passenger with Templeton, Sarah's daughter, on his lap waving to the crowd and reminding everyone who sees her who she is, and Nancy will be there, behind the wheel.

Nancy knows that this way everyone in town will know that she's sticking it up Philip Templeton good and proper and that doing the parade in the Diamond T, the town's clapped-out old garbage truck, shows the Maloneys are not stuck-up and are proud of who they are. Which isn't exactly one hundred per cent true, but we're getting prouder by the year, with Sarah nearly a doctor, and now Bozo, and no doubt Mike will come good. Of course, there's always Tommy to remind us not to get too cocky.

The shire council are not too pleased with the arrangement, but there's not a lot they can do. With the band, led by George Fisch playing 'Waltzing Matilda', 'Colonel Bogey', 'When the Saints Go Marching In', as well as other things, the parade goes down King Street. The Diamond T is decked in gold and green crinkle-paper streamers and the council gives those beaut long-throwing streamers to the crowd, which is most of the town. By the time we reach the town hall, we're all covered in streamers and you can hardly see us, and Tommy's lettering on the side, 'Maloney & Sons – Garbage', is obscured by the streamers.

The reception is on the steps of the town hall so everyone can see and Nancy, Tommy and Bozo are seated in a row of chairs on the top step along with all the councillors and their wives. Philip Templeton, with his chain of office round his neck, is in the middle. There's a microphone standing in front of him but placed on the first step down.

Nancy is wearing her yellow-daisy dress and a big white hat and white gloves. Mike has begged to make her a new frock instead of what he calls 'the garden tent', but she won't hear of it. 'This is how folks know me and they know it's clean and neat. Besides I'll wear that hat Mrs Barrington-Stone give me and gloves and stockings.' Mrs Barrington-Stone is seated next to Nancy with her husband, Peter, who is back on the shire council. Big Jack Donovan sits on Tommy's left.

It's Templeton that's the dolled-up one. She's four years old and she's wearing this **Suckfizzle** little-girl outfit that makes her look like she could be Alice in Wonderland in Australian colours, with yellow socks and little-girl shoes, with the one cross-strap and button, a green dress and little yellow pinafore with a green ribbon in her hair, which is the exact same shade of copper as Sarah's. The green suits her hair colour and she looks beaut because she's a really pretty little girl anyway. What's more, she's seated on Nancy's lap for all the world to see though Mike says the daisy-dress garden-tent is the worst backdrop possible for Templeton's outfit, but what can you do.

All the councillors are wearing suits and ties, Big Jack is in civilian clothes, a tweed sports coat and his South Melbourne club tie, but Tommy has on a white short-sleeved open-necked shirt and brown daks, though his shoes are polished. That's because they're my school shoes, he only wears workman's steel-cap boots. I'm the one wearing his boots, which is a bit of an embarrassment, but I'm in the crowd and I don't think too many notice.

Tommy's probably never been in such distinguished company in his life and, with what's left of his hair glued to his head with Brylcreem, one eye closed and his dented cheek and crook arm, he looks bloody miserable. I reckon he'll be in the pub right off afterwards to wash away his embarrassment with a dozen or so cleansing ales and probably stay at it for a week. Nancy's insisted he be with her on the podium for her hour of triumph over Philip Templeton, but I can tell you he's not a happy man sitting there among the nobs. Sitting next to Big Jack Donovan, if you sort of squiff your eyes up a bit, Tommy looks like one of those ventriloquist dolls with Big Jack about to make him say something.

I've got to say this for Philip Templeton, who some people thought might not even show up on the day, he did a very good speech. He said how proud Yankalillee was of its favourite son, Bozo Maloney, an outstanding young man who had earned the respect of the community even before he was chosen for the Olympic Games. He lays it on really thick so nobody can say he hasn't done the right thing by us, though, of course, he doesn't mention Sarah or any of us. He ends up by saying he's sure that whatever Bozo does in life he will be successful. Nancy's mouth is pulled down to the left and her nose is in the air like she'd been forced to sit through a bad smell. The crowd claps when Philip Templeton announces that the shire council has agreed to honour Bozo with the keys to the city, which has only been done twice before, both times to the men returning from the world wars.

But, trust the shire council, the key to the city doesn't turn out to be a key at all, but a bottoms-wiping certificate with a cut-out picture of a key in gold foil stuck on it. At least this time it's framed. Philip

Templeton then calls upon Bozo to accept the freedom of Yankalillee and to make a speech.

Bozo's a pretty shy sort of bloke when it comes to that sort of thing but he surprises us all with his speech. He must have learned something in Rome, because he speaks quietly but well and you can hear every word on the microphone. He turns around to acknowledge Big Jack Donovan and then turns back to the microphone, thanking him for everything he's done. He also mentions Bobby Devlin and gets a bit of a laugh when he says he was also one of Yankalillee's citizens, although he didn't enjoy the freedom of the city all that much as he was doing a stretch up the hill. This brings a real big laugh. Bozo also thanks Mrs Barrington-Stone for all her help and all of us in his family, even Tommy, mentioning that it was Tommy gave him his first pair of boxing gloves. He thanks the crowd for supporting him and says the medal really belongs to all of them because if it wasn't for all the garbage bins he'd had to lift since he was nine years old he probably wouldn't have been strong enough to box at the Olympics. 'So, thank you everyone for putting out so much garbage!' he says, grinning. The crowd claps and whistles and he's won them forever.

Bozo shakes the hands of all the councillors and their wives and I wonder what's going to happen when he gets to Dora Templeton. But he shakes her hand and to my astonishment seems to be talking to our mortal enemy, saying something more than thank you before he smiles and moves on.

Later, when we're home and all having tea, Nancy has a go at Bozo. 'You should've given Dora Templeton a snub, Bozo, 'stead of stopping to talk to her like you were grateful or something.'

Bozo smiles. 'I simply thanked her politely for staying sober for the occasion,' he says.

Chapter Eighteen

It's been some time since I've talked about fires and the bush. While there have been a few fires in the district and we've even been out as far as the Snowy Mountains for two of them, they were scrub fires, not the sort of big blaze that you'd hear about in the news. Anyway, you'd probably be a bit bored reading about them, fighting a fire is different for a firefighter, who knows that no two fires are the same, but to people who don't know, a fire is flames and bush and more of the same, scary if you're in one or if lives and houses are threatened, but otherwise it's ho-hum.

Over the years and since I attended my first fire with Tommy, I've learned a bit about the behaviour of bushfires. The first thing to learn is that you may think you know all there is about the nature of a particular fire, and then it will spring a surprise on you. If you're arrogant, you're going to get yourself burned and your pride dented, there's many a silly coot who thought all was going well and so he'd take a bit of a short cut in procedure and the next thing he's in the deepest kind of trouble.

A bushfire, even a small one, is not something you can take for granted. Most of the smaller district bushfires are started by farmers who reckon they'll do a bit of burning off, get rid of the rubbish and get some green grass growing when the autumn rains come. A bit of burning to keep the grass down late summer can't do too much harm.

Next thing the house is threatened, or a couple of thousand acres goes up in smoke and with it his neighbour's haystack, or you're piling up burned dead sheep and pouring a tin of kero over them and having a second fire to mark the stupidity that caused them to die in the first place.

The Yankalillee Bushfire Brigade is a bit of a Dad's Army, with a fair amount of quarrelling going on amongst some of the old-timers and some of the younger blokes who want to introduce new methods. As far as I can see, the aggro's been there for a while and Tommy says it goes way back to just after the war when the Country Fire Authority was formed after the Royal Commission into the January 1939 fires in Victoria where seventy-one lives were lost. The war got in the way and the CFA only really got going just before the war ended.

From day one there was resistance to change, the 'landed gentry', that is the big graziers, had always been the boss cockies in the bushfire brigade and they reckoned they knew how to fight a fire. They learned it from their fathers and their fathers learned it from their fathers since time out of mind. They reckoned the government couldn't teach them nothing.

They were wrong, of course. Just because your family has been on the land for a hundred years doesn't make every generation an expert firefighter. But you couldn't tell them that. Besides, it was sort of prestigious to be the big boss in the bushfire brigade, you'd go to meetings dressed in your moleskins, tweed jacket, old school tie and big hat and people would say 'There goes the bushfire boss.'

So when one of the recommendations of the Royal Commission was to appoint a salaried fire chief, to be called a regional officer, the cow cockies and the graziers didn't like it one bit. Losing control over firefighting operations meant, in their eyes anyway, that they were losing their power and influence in the community.

Tommy and John Crowe reckoned it was a bloody good thing as the graziers who put themselves in charge were generally a bunch of old farts. What made it worse for these elder statesmen in the brigade was that many of the new regional officers were ex-servicemen. The old-timers couldn't come right out and be critical, though privately they reckoned the ex-soldiers were given the jobs because of what they'd done in the war and that they knew bugger-all about fighting fires. So it was a sort of Mexican stand-off, both sides reckoning the other side were a bunch of bloody wankers.

Mr Reed was our regional fire officer, he was known as Nick to one and all, except to me and a few of the other young blokes. Like Mr Gee and Tommy, he'd been a prisoner of war under the Japanese but his real sin was that he lived in Wangaratta, which was a big mistake. You see, Wang wasn't a little town like Yankalillee and it had its own municipal fire brigade and everyone reckoned you had to be a real bushie to know about fires.

As far as I was concerned, Nick Reed was a pretty good bloke and he and Tommy worked well together. He respected Tommy for being 'the real maloney' and Tommy said he was a sensible sort of bloke who wasn't likely to make too many mistakes and didn't big-note himself.

He'd always be out there for the real big fires but the small local ones, like the one where we rescued Mrs Rika Ray, he'd leave to Tommy, who could always reach him on the HF radio when he was needed or if the fire got out of hand. The old blokes would say it was a conspiracy between war veterans, which was pure and utter bullshit. Nick Reed trusted Tommy's judgement and his ability to get on with the job.

It was just that some of the older blokes never got used to taking orders. They'd been a law unto themselves for so long they resented anyone but their own. So the Owens Valley CFA weren't always happy little Vegemites. For days after fighting a fire there would be post-mortems in the pub, mostly about what an idiot Nick Reed was and where he'd made his mistakes. It wasn't true and was just the usual whingeing and big talk and thinking the old ways were the only way.

Tommy, being like a petty criminal, couldn't stand up and tell them they were talking shit. When a fire was over, his standing in the community vanished with the last embers, except for those who knew a bit about fires and that certainly wasn't the majority.

For instance, when Tommy first got back from the war, he wanted the Owens Valley Brigade to buy up six army-surplus high-frequency radios to be used for firefighting. To raise the money, the bushfire brigade would have had to have a fete as well as raffles in the pub, cake stalls and that sort of thing. The people who were against having the radios, which they called newfangled nonsense, were mostly Church of England and among the toffs, some of them on the shire council. Their catchcry became 'You can't put a fire out with a bloody wireless set, boy!' And since their wives were all in the Anglican Women's Guild and many also members of the Country Women's Association, who would also have needed to be involved, all it took was for the men to put the kybosh on their wives' involvement with the fundraising.

Tommy, who at the time wasn't into crime and wasn't yet known as an alcoholic, put it to Nancy that the Catholics could do something similar to raise the money. 'Show them toffee-nosed Anglicans the Micks can do it without 'em, hey?'

Nancy reckons that's fair enough, time the Catholics took the initiative, and she takes the proposition to Father Crosby, suggesting they run their own fete and raffle.

Father Crosby isn't so sure. Privately he isn't game to take on the powerful elements in town and he ums and ahs before he finally says he'll have to refer the matter to the Bishop. Well, he's back soon enough with the Bishop's opinion, though Nancy said she doubted he'd ever asked for it, just drank some altar wine and cogitated in the priest's house and as usual took the coward's way out. She said having Father Crosby on your side was like having a large thorn in the sole of your foot at the start of a race.

'The Bishop is of the opinion that the purchase of five wireless sets is not an issue that is sufficiently important to disturb the good relationship which exists at the present time between Catholic and Protestant in Yankalillee.' Just to come out with a dumb sentence like that shows Father Crosby's invented it. Then he goes on, 'Besides, there are some very important people in the district, all of them experienced in firefighting, who see no value in acquiring these wireless sets.' He didn't even know that they were *radio* sets, not the wireless sets like you hear the ABC on at home.

'Yeah, all of them Protestants and all of them bigwigs!' Nancy replies. Remember this was way back in 1946 and she wasn't a fully collapsed Catholic yet and still had some faith in the Church and didn't yet have the goods on Father Crosby like she does now.

Father Crosby then points out that the last big fire happened in 1939, before the war, and that a lot has been learned since then. Which was a whole load of manure. It was funny how everyone seemed to think, because there had been a war, a lot had been learned. In fact, Tommy said bugger-all had been learned, that just the opposite had happened. The war sort of put all civilian things on hold, and bushfires are a voluntary civilian occupation left to the volunteers to fight and so things hadn't improved one bit since the tragic fires of 1939.

Father Crosby's cautionary words, after *supposedly* consulting with the Bishop on the matter, were, 'The fifty pounds you'll need to buy the wireless sets with the installation and the power packs to make them work, which I am told on good authority will cost the same again, is a poor use of such a large sum of money.'

He'd wagged a finger at Nancy, 'Are you aware, Nancy Maloney, that's the cost of feeding a hundred orphans at the St Vincent de Paul's Boys Orphanage in Melbourne for three whole weeks?' Father Crosby looked accusingly at her, 'The Bishop has chastised me for my lack of priorities and my diminished sense of where God's charity should be placed! He has pointed out that we are in the business of avoiding hellfire and not bushfires!' He also said that the Bishop had recommended that the Catholics of Yankalillee contribute the selfsame sum of money to the saving of heathen souls in New Guinea.

'Now, Nancy Maloney, where are we going to get such a sum of money, I ask you?' His manner suggested that it was Nancy's fault and that she'd compromised the Catholics of Yankalillee.

All Nancy could manage to say in reply was, 'Father, what about the seventy-one souls that died in the Black Friday fires of 1939?'

'Ah, my dear,' Father Crosby replied, 'they were souls already saved and only ten of them were Catholics, all of them elderly and granted the last rites and absolution by special dispensation.'

Anyway, the end result was that there were no radios in the Owens Valley Bushfire Brigade even after the disastrous 1952 bushfire hit north-eastern Victoria. The old-timers won out and we still don't have them. Some of the old blokes are proud of the fact that they've fought off 'the radio gimmick'. One old codger said to me, 'Mole, the fires ain't changed none and we've fought 'em before and won without them stupid things crackling away confusing matters. Government's now talking about bombing fires with aeroplanes, water bombs, next we'll have pelicans trained to do the same thing, never heard nothing so stupid in me life. Radios and water bombs, that's Canberra for yer, pure mahogany from the bloody neck up.'

In the end Tommy shrugs and says it would be good to have radios, cut some of the danger out, but it's how well you know the bush that counts. He even admits that the radios have a problem. When there's a lot of static around, it's because of lightning and thunder, the sort of weather bushfires bring. In other words, in bushfire conditions, HF radios often prove difficult to use and sometimes you can't hear a word for the static and interference. Sometimes you can hear people talking in South-East Asia but not ten miles away where a fire is raging. But on the other hand, the radio can save lives and get people to a fire as well as direct them when they get there.

That's what I've been learning since my twelfth birthday and Tommy reckons I've picked it up a fair bit, although in five years you can't even begin to know all there is to know and every time we go out I learn something new that's important.

One thing that's happened is that Big Jack Donovan has spoken to Mr McDonald, the District Forestry Officer at the Forestry Commission, and since I've been thirteen he's taken me on work experience for three days a week during the summer holidays and taught me their side of things. It's okay by Tommy, but some of the others in the volunteer brigade reckon I'm consorting with the enemy. The bushies reckon the Forestry Commission is up its own arse, but Tommy says to take no notice, to ignore them, the Forestry Commission has facilities and practices any firefighter should know about and fuck the silly bastards that think different.

They've got high frequency radios and all sorts of gear and I reckon I now know just about the lot. One of the things I've been trained in is fire spotting from a fire tower. There's eight Forestry Commission towers all around, in places you can see a fair distance, like about thirty miles. So you'll spot a fire no matter where it starts. The tower I use is called Mt

Pilot and it stands just above a large forest of Scribbly Bark and has a good view of the flat land and to the north. On a good day you can see the heavy eucalyptus forest that follows the meandering Murray River.

I know how to read all the instruments, like the relative humidity, wind speed, the temperature and the extent and nature of the cloud cover. I know all the HF-radio call signs to the district fire brigades and exactly how to report the presence of a fire. All this is theoretical, mind you, I've never really been in the tower when a big fire happened and I don't know how I'll go if I'm there and there's fires to report. A person can panic and do it wrong so I hope I won't.

Tommy and John Crowe and myself are sort of a team when it comes to working with fires and John Crowe reckons Tommy knows more than any professor of botany about things like eucalyptus trees and what to expect from a big burn.

I don't want to go on too much about things, but if you're going to be a bushfire fighter you have to know a fair bit about what's burning and, if it isn't a grass fire, it's usually eucalyptus and the stuff that lies under the forest canopy. So I'll need to tell you some of the history of this remarkable tree for you to understand how a fire works on the driest continent on earth.

If you get bored just skip this part, though that would be a pity, because all Australians should know why we're a different country to anywhere else and that's mostly because of eucalyptus and fire.

I'm going to sound like I know more than I do because Tommy's the one that knows most things about the bush and fire. I mean he's uneducated and probably a bit thick with some things, but when it comes to the bush he uses the right terms and likes to get things correct and goes crook when I don't learn the Latin names for things.

John Crowe laughs and says he's always been like that. They're real good mates and have been since they were kids and he tells how when they were just little nippers and they'd go out shooting birds with slingshots, he'd be aiming at a regent honeyeater and Tommy would fire a stone into the bush and the bird would fly off. 'Why'd you do that?' John would yell at him, really pissed off.

'Don't see too many of them around here, best not kill it,' Tommy would say. Even then he was a conservationist without knowing it.

'He showed no bloody mercy on crows though, even this one,' John Crowe laughs.

Tommy and John Crowe are a funny pair together, sort of a contradiction in terms. Tommy looking the way he does and such a little bloke who never says boo to a goose and John Crowe a big bastard and the full operator, real quick on the uptake and not scared to get into a donnybrook if he has to. He's always got a scam he's working on and an opinion on just about everything.

Funny that, small ratty blokes are supposed to be the lightning lips and the big blokes the slow ones, but Tommy and John Crowe are just the opposite. Though nobody says nothing bad about Tommy Maloney in John Crowe's presence if he doesn't want his nose broken. He's the one who most often brings Tommy home when he's been on a bender and is down at the lake with the other deros.

Sometimes he has to carry Tommy over his shoulder like a sack of potatoes and throws him in the back of his ute because he stinks to high heaven. John Crowe then takes him to the abattoir, undresses him, hoses him down and makes him sit in the sun in the nuddy so he can't escape. Little Tommy sitting in a corner with his broken face resting on his clasped knees, all hunched up, drying out in the sun. John Crowe leaves him there while he comes home and gets a clean shirt and trousers then goes back and dresses Tommy before he delivers him to us in some sort of respectable shape.

Other times Tommy's gear is that ratshit, that John Crowe just throws it in the abattoir furnace and buys new stuff. He never lectures Tommy, they're mates, that's all. He doesn't judge him or try to change him. I reckon Tommy loves him more than a brother, even more than us. No, a lot more than us! Tommy doesn't have that much reason to love his kids and only Sarah and little Colleen are his anyway. Nancy, though, doesn't work things that way. As far as she's concerned, for better or worse, Tommy's our dad.

When Tommy's been up the hill, John Crowe visits him every day, come rain or shine, he never misses. We're his family and have to keep to the visiting hours, which are once a week and strictly observed unless an inmate is sick or something and even then he has to be practically dying for them to let you in.

I dunno how he does it. John Crowe just walks in every morning on his way to the shire workshops, says gidday to the warder at the gate, who waves him past. Some people say he's got something on Mr Sullivan the governor but they don't say what it could be, because the boss of the prison is a pretty respectable bloke and well regarded even by the Protestants.

Anyway, John Crowe sees that his old mate is okay and usually brings him a bit of tucker, a couple of Vegemite and cheese sandwiches or a homemade rissole and a roast potato. Tommy eats like a bird anyway. John Crowe always brings in a packet of twenty Turf cigarettes and the book Tommy's asked for. The librarian, Mrs Botherington, must think John Crowe is just about the best reader of things about nature in Yankalillee. He's never explained to her that the books are for Tommy. She's a bit prim to say the least and he doesn't want to take any chances.

'Mate, never know how people in this town think,' he once said to me. 'Maybe she'd reckon a bloke doing a stretch couldn't be trusted with books. Can't take no chances, if the little bloke couldn't read, he'd go round the twist in there.'

Tommy reads a book about, say, the various types of native grasses to be found in Australia and in the book will be a reference to another book about some aspect of flora and he'll be onto it. John Crowe will then ask Mrs Botherington to get it in from the State Library in Melbourne. Sometimes she kicks up a stink but John Crowe's got her twisted around his little finger and he looks after her little Morris Minor so she'll usually make the effort. 'I wouldn't do it for anyone else, Mr Crowe, but I know your bushfire research is very valuable, one day perhaps you'll write something we can be proud of?'

'Sure thing, Mrs Bother,' he'll laugh, 'Maybe a whole library to make you even busier, eh?'

When he told me this, he chuckled. 'Last time I wrote something real serious was this heart I carved into the trunk of a Scribbly Gum and carved me initials and the initials of this sheila I was in love with, Elizabeth Logan.'

We were sitting down and he drew this heart in the dust at his feet with his finger and added the initials:

J.C.
L
E.L.

'I got to kiss her once but that was about it. I used to dream about touching her tits but she'd never let me. She married some bloke over in Bright and had seven kids, every one of them got plenty of what I got nothing of. There's been a kid hanging on them beautiful boobs for bloody years.'

When we are in the bush together, John Crowe knows Tommy's safe from the dreaded grog and, while they don't say much, you can see them both sort of relaxing, enjoying being together, having a smoko next to a creek or laughing when they find a wombat hole or come across a veined sun-orchid tucked away under an overhanging rock. Or they'll be sitting on the bank of a river fishing, even John Crowe not chatting on for a change, the two of them watching a white-faced heron land in the reeds and, turning and grinning, sharing the moment, saying nothing but knowing something together only they know.

I'm the kid with the .22 rifle who tags along and who is being taught things. And a lot of what I'm being taught is about eucalyptus trees. 'Know your eucalyptus and you'll know your fire,' Tommy says. I also do the rabbit shooting and an occasional fox. Sometimes the cow cockies ask us to cull the roos, but Tommy won't, even when their numbers have grown to plague proportions.

'It's not them that's grown to plague proportions, it's us! Rabbits and foxes are vermin, introduced by the white settler. The kangaroo and the wallaby were here before us, fuck the sheep and the cattle. Far as I'm concerned the wildlife's got the first right to the grass!' I guess Tommy, like Mr Baloney before him, would never had made a living on the land, both too interested in allowing the wildlife to have a go at surviving after the white man cometh.

Tommy also reckons that DDT and Dieldren used by farmers are doing a lot of damage to the wildlife, specially birds. 'You don't hear the birdsong like you used to and some species I haven't seen around for a few years,' he'd say when we were out and about.

He'd make me climb up a tree and look into a bird's nest. 'How many eggs?' he'd shout up at me. Most often it'd only be one, sometimes two. 'Should be three.' Once when we found a little, cracked egg on the ground, Tommy held it up ever so gently to the light, 'See that, Mole,' he said, 'the shell's so thin it's almost soft, shouldn't be like that. It's pesticides doing that.'

You couldn't prove any of this, of course, and anyway nobody would have listened to Tommy. They think DDT is one of the great inventions of mankind and don't care if all the birds go and the little bush animals as well, as long as the lucerne, tobacco and fruit isn't eaten by pests.

Tommy said when he was a kid, it was the Chinese mostly who grew the tobacco and vegetables and they used herbs for pesticides and the birds were okay and so was the tobacco.

'Only thing that's different now is the pesticides, so it stands to reason that's to blame.'

Now let me tell you just a little about eucalyptus trees and how they came about in Australia and no other place in the world. First thing to know is that during the last 730,000 years Australia has been through eight major climatic changes from glacial, which is real cold, to interglacial, which is warm. Each time it's returned to warm, two types of trees returned, rainforest and sclerophyll (hard leaves), each fighting the other for dominance. Both managed to hang on until about 130,000 years ago when the sclerophyll won the battle and took over as the dominant species, forcing the rainforest into wet gullies and into some of the more tropical rainfall areas.

There's one thing to be said for being in prison, Tommy gets to read stuff brought in by John Crowe that he'd never normally have a chance to read. He may not know a whole lot about some things, but when it comes to the Australian bush he is a walking encyclopaedia. He can make it interesting too, so you don't get bored. Like for instance the human hair. He was talking to me about early times when Australia was drifting away, having broken off the main crust of what was the earth at that time.

'Think about this, Mole, Australia broke away from Antarctica and drifted north at the rate of the growth of a human hair!'

That's not the sort of thing you hear every day. 'So what stopped it so it's where it is?' I asked.

'Nothing, it's still doing the same.' Next time you need a haircut, just remember the amount the barber cuts off is how far Australia has moved since the last time you had your hair cut.

'Then, as Australia drifted further and further north, undergoing prolonged periods of drought,' Tommy explained, 'only the tough and the opportunistic trees and bushes could make a go of it and the toughest of all these hard-leafed trees were the eucalyptus.'

Remember when he took me out that first time and went crook when I didn't know the name of a gum tree? At the time I supposed I was pretty dumb, but I reckoned there'd maybe be, you know, half a dozen types and he'd teach me their names. Well, it isn't like that, there's over six hundred species, all of which evolved and adapted brilliantly to the particular terrain they happened to find themselves in.

Tommy lets you have bits of information, never too much at one time, so over a long period you remember all the bits because it's like only one thing to remember at a time. I recall we were sitting beside a creek near an old mining camp near Woolshed called Hopeless Dig. There'd been a bit of a bushfire in a small stand of gum but the rains had come and Tommy pointed to the canopy of a Scribbly Gum, how it was green with new leaves.

'This fire's come through only three days ago and already the new leaf is out, there's been almost no rain, but enough to get them going. If the same amount of rain had fallen but there'd been no fire, the tree would still be sitting tight. That's the eucalyptus for you, the great opportunist. You see, way back in the dawn of history they couldn't beat fire so they decided to co-operate with it, to make fire a part of their personal survival technique. They took fire head-on and won, so that they are no longer scared of the flames. Clever, eh?'

'Just them, I mean only the eucalyptus?'

'Some other trees and plants do a bit of this as well, but the old eucalyptus has elevated nutrient scavenging and hoarding to an art form no other genus can begin to match. In fact most species of eucalyptus are not only fire-co-operative and adapted but also fire-dependent. Fire is what makes them what they are and even keeps them alive.'

Tommy doesn't speak like this when he's normal, only when he's explaining things in nature, then he uses words like 'fire co-operative', 'genus' and 'fire dependent'. I think he likes the language of the books and wants to get things right.

Everyone knows that Australia has the most impoverished soil in the world. It's stuff you learn in geography at school. But lots of people don't know that this is because we've experienced almost no volcanic upheaval. Volcanic eruptions serve a purpose, they recycle the soil and make it rich again. Put this absence of volcanic activity together with the wet periods and the dry, the cold and the hot, and most of the nutrients in the soil got used up or washed away long ago and the soil became impoverished.

Tommy was explaining all this to me when he said, 'Now this is the clever part, this is where fire and the eucalyptus come in. When fire burns natural fuel, like dried bush and undergrowth, twigs, bark, seed capsules and the like, they release nutrients which would otherwise be locked away in the unused fuel material.'

'How come, locked away?' I ask.

'Well, these nutrients are stored in dead wood, which is like stockpiling fertiliser in a farmer's shed. It's no bloody good there, you've got to take it out of the shed and spread it around, see. Fire does that, unlocks the wood shed and the nutrients are in the ash. If there wasn't any fire to recycle these precious nutrients, the supply already in the soil would eventually be used up and we'd become one great big desert. We've got enough of that anyway, being the driest land on earth.'

Tommy then explains how the eucalyptus has become the supreme opportunist and has found a way to grab a hold of these nutrients not only for immediate use so that they can recover from the big burn or live through the next drought, but also to store them for later use in prolonged drought periods.

Talk about survival, how's this? Say for instance a wildfire, which is a fire that's started with lightning and is out of control, kills or severely weakens a patch of old-growth eucalyptus forest. Immediately after the fire passes, the seeds rain down from the scorched crowns onto the burnt forest floor below.

Once we're walking along in the forest when Tommy bends down and picks up this little gum pod. You know, the ones you see lying around and don't even bother to notice. 'See this, Mole, empty.'

'What's empty?'

'This gum capsule.'

'It's a seed, isn't it?'

'Nah, it's a fireproof container, only it's called a capsule. Your actual seeds are stored in its little fire-resistant chambers. I reckon this one come down in the 1952 fire.' He pointed to several trees not as big as the others, 'Could be those came from one of these. Almost certain; if there'd been a fire through here since '52, then this capsule wouldn't be lying around . . .'

He hands me the little capsule and I realise that it's hard as cement, which is what Tommy means about them being fireproof.

'That's the amazing part, son, the capsules grow high enough up in the forest canopy so the seeds inside them aren't scorched by the radiant heat from the bushfire passing underneath. The heat generated is sufficient to open them after the fire has passed to allow the seed to rain down onto the newly burnt forest floor. Here's the extra smart bit, the warmth of the soil from the spent fire will stimulate the germination of the seed and seedlings will rapidly push their roots down through the nutrient-rich ash.'

Tommy reaches out and breaks off a eucalyptus leaf and rubs it into a little ball in his hand. I think he's going to ask me to smell it, like we've all done a thousand times, but he doesn't. He makes me touch the wet spot that's left in the centre of his hand. 'Feel that, it's oily, ain't it?' I nod and he says, 'The eucalyptus species is even designed to attract fire, the highly inflammable oils in the leaves is just one example.' He points to all the dry twigs and things that are nearly always found under a eucalyptus tree. 'See that, that's the tree laying its own fire. It's called litter-fall and it's mostly fibrous bark the tree's been dropping on purpose. Those are the dried twigs and leaves the tree has got rid of so it doesn't need to feed the leaves in a drought. Mate, you couldn't lay a better fire if you tried, it's perfect for quick combustion. When the flame hits, it will create a high-intensity fire that will quickly clear the forest floor and allows the seeds to germinate.'

'You mean it's made its own kindling and is just waiting for someone to come along and light it?'

Tommy grins, 'Well, these days not somebody but something, usually lightning.'

Talk about well thought out! Then there's the way the seedlings store these nutrients for when times get really tough.

'The eucalyptus seedlings have a root system which has these little bulbs called lignotubers, which are tiny storage tanks for nutrients that they don't need right away. When a drought comes along, they stop growing and use only enough nutrients to stay passive.'

'How do they know there's a drought coming?' I ask and then realise what a bloody stupid question that is.

'Because the bloody rains don't come!' Tommy can't believe his ears.

We walk on and he's silent for a while because he expects better from me, I suppose. But he's spent too much time in a prison cell studying up and I know he's not going to let it hang in the air like that. Tommy's got to tell this stuff to someone and the only someone he has is me. Eventually he says, like there hasn't been nearly twenty minutes of no-speak going on, 'When the drought is over and the rains come and conditions become right for growth again, the tree has enough nutrient reserves in its storage tanks to blast off. The clever thing is that they can acquire far more nutrients than they need for normal growth and store the surplus, if necessary, for years.'

'What about the grown-up tree?'

'Mature-growth eucalyptus! Trees don't grow up, people do! Yeah, well, the mature tree can do the same and also has a rapid recovery system, known as epicormic buds, which are buds waiting to happen on a thin stalk found at the axil of every eucalyptus leaf.' He tears off a small branch and shows me these hard little knobs. 'If the going gets tough, like in a severe drought, the tree drains the nutrients in a percentage of its leaves to store them for use later. At the same time, this tiny little bud just sits tight and hangs on waiting for when times are good again and there's a bit of rain. Then they sprout and produce new leaves at a very rapid rate.'

After a drought when the rains came and we'd go into the bush, Tommy would say if you watched carefully enough you could actually see the eucalyptus growing. Which is a bit of an exaggeration but they sure can get a new canopy of leaves going in a hurry. One week there's nothing, then a fall of rain, and the next weekend the bush is green as anything and you wouldn't know there'd been a drought.

So that's the sort of thing I learned when I was with Tommy and afterwards studied up a bit myself. The point is that a bushfire is a natural happening and is the reason why Australia is the way it is and so very different to other countries. It's also why the early navigators called Australia 'the burning shore'.

When you're fighting a bushfire, you're fighting something that knows what it's doing and is very good at its job and has had 130,000 years of practice with the trees actually on its side. You have to pit your brains and your skill against nature, and nature is no dummy, with a whole heap of tricks up her sleeve that you don't know about.

When the Aboriginal people came, some say around forty-five thousand years ago, some say long before that, they learned to use fire for themselves. They were hunters and gatherers and used fire rather than ploughs to live off the land. This is sometimes known as firestick farming.

Even though the continent was subject to a high natural-fire frequency due to lightning strikes, the Aborigines increased this natural phenomenon to create more of the natural woodland so they could hunt and forage more easily in the clearings under the trees. By the time us white people arrived, they'd done such a good job that some say they were actually managing the land with lots of small fires. In doing this, they prevented the huge build-up of dry fuel that, if left alone, would lead to conflagrations such as would have happened in prehistoric times, where the whole continent was consumed in one great roaring flame and people and animals couldn't have survived on it.

Firestick farming was such a part of the Aboriginal way of life that it became a duty, a custom, to clean up the country. They thought land that was unburnt was poorly managed and that when it was covered with litter, it was dirty and disgraced the tribe to whom it belonged. Unburnt or dirty land had to be cleansed with their firesticks or it would harbour evil spirits.

Of course, when we came along and brought sheep and cattle and general farming, we changed everything and now Australians see a bushfire as a terrible thing that must be prevented at all costs. The funny thing is, by no longer managing fire like the Aborigines did, we have now returned to unmanageable fires. Some people think that's what nature intended and that's the way things ought to be. However, the Aboriginal way of fire-farming has been going so long that a great many Australian mammals are very dependent on it and at least seventeen species of mammal have become extinct because we've chased the Aboriginals off vast stretches of woodland.

What's more, the build-up of debris under native trees now allows the large unmanageable fires to start, like the great fires of 1939 and 1952 here in Victoria. When the Aborigines were chased from the good land and firestick farming stopped, the undermanaged woodland forests caused huge fires to start again. While these fires may not have harmed the eucalyptus all that much, they reduced a diverse and comparatively rich environment to an unstable, oversimplified and often plague-species-ridden system that was useless for anything even the wildlife.

So now we've got people we call bushfire fighters to stop fires, which is like a contradiction of terms when you think about it. People like Tommy and John Crowe and me are fighting nature to the death and Tommy reckons nature will win in the end as the soil can't take the punishment it's getting because there's not sufficient managed fires to keep our ecosystem going.

He says that fire is vital to many native animal species that depend on the landscapes, which routine fire replenishes with food. Kangaroos, wallabies and wombats prefer the nutritious new growth that springs up following a decent sort of burn. Tammar wallabies need the dense scrub for shelter and green foliage for food. These thickets degenerate over several years and need fire to regenerate them. Koalas need fire to bring out the young eucalyptus leaves they need to feed on and there's lots of little mammals like the rat kangaroo that can only be perpetuated through some process of burning taking place in their natural habitat.

Then there's termites that live in the cavities carved by fire in big old eucalyptus trees and which are essential as food supply for birds, rodents and reptiles. Tommy was showing me how, after a fire, the bark is sort of loosened and this is when the termites can get in under it.

'Termites are good things, Mole.'

'No they ain't, they eat people's houses!' Sometimes you can't let him get away with things.

'Yeah, but that's civilisation for you. Did you know that the weight of the termite population that lives under the Australian soil is greater than the weight of all the creatures that walk upon the surface of our land?'

I wanted to shout out that was the biggest heap of bullshit I'd ever heard. I think he must have read that in *Ripley's Believe it or Not*! I looked to see if he was pulling my leg but he was busy digging away at the termites, exposing them under the bark.

Now, I'm not saying this is true, it could be another story like the fish. You remember the fish that appeared in a ditch they dug in Borneo when it wasn't anywhere near a river. But if it *is* true, that's a humungous lot of termites living under our feet.

'That's why the Australian desert is the richest desert ecosystem in the world,' he suddenly continues. 'It's because the termites are the only things that can eat the tough spinifex grass, which is pure cellulose. They come out of their mounds at night to feed and the small reptiles, like the many varieties of lizards and goannas, are dependent on them for food. They come after the termites and the bigger reptiles and birds eat the little reptiles and so on, which is how the whole desert food chain begins.'

There could be something to this theory, which is a bit more understandable than the fish. Remember how we couldn't tell anyone at school about the fish from nowhere for fear of them making us Maloneys a laughing stock?

Well, that's enough lecturing. It's just that I thought you'd like to know some of those things, about fire in particular. The way fire is essential to us goes on and on and you begin to understand that fire on our landscape means life, not death, even though we have come to fear it, even more than floods or any other form of natural disaster and always equate it with, you know, destroying things.

This summer is not looking good, the spring rains haven't arrived and here it is early January and temperatures have already risen above one hundred degrees most days and it's getting hotter. The worst part is that the winds have been coming from the north, which dries out the north-western slopes of the hillsides and that's real bad news if a fire starts in the valley. Tommy says that in the January 1939 fire seventy-one people died in Victoria.

The rural bushfire brigade has two tankers. Ford and Chevrolet ex-army 'Blitz' trucks equipped with four-hundred-gallon tanks and fitted with Grazcos Mk 25 pumps. The only problem with the trucks is that they are ancient, ex-army and petrol-driven so in bushfire conditions suffer severely when the petrol turns to vapour in the fuel lines and stalls the engines.

I reckon this was one of the main reasons John Crowe got to be our fire captain this year. He can get the trucks going again quicker than most of us. He'll use one of the fire hoses to cool down the fuel line and engine manifold and then tinker a bit and away she'd go again. It was always dicey and you don't want a fire truck that you can't trust, but what can you do? The government doesn't spend enough on bushfire prevention and we just have to do the best we can in the volunteer brigade. The urban brigade that looked after the town had these smart Austin tankers that worked a treat, but of course that had nothing to do with us.

Then there is the usual stuff to be maintained, none of which has changed a lot. The thing that worries Tommy a lot is the maintenance, which he reckons isn't as thorough as it could be. He'll go around himself on a Sunday to try to do something and he'll find a battery is flat in one of the trucks or it won't start for some reason or another. He'll get John Crowe in to fix it, but he always says there should be a weekly maintenance roster. Yet no one seems interested and nobody ever thanks him for his opinion or his efforts on the occasions that we do meet.

The equipment we have are knapsack tanks, hand pumps and fire brooms, which are beaters made of leather or canvas, you had to know how to use them or they'd spread the fire faster than put it out. Tommy would also check the fuel tanks and rope-start the two BSA motors on the pumps to make sure they were going. Sometimes they'll start with the first pull of the rope and, then again, sometimes you'll pull and pull and the buggers won't start and you can't help thinking how would it be if this happened in an emergency.

We're all volunteers in the rural brigade except for Nick Reed, the CFA regional officer who came in from Wangaratta the second Saturday in November to say that the long-term weather forecast is for a very hot summer with heatwaves in January and February. He said it has something to do with a thing that happens in South America which raises the temperature of the Pacific Ocean and causes drought and heatwaves in Australia.

None of us could quite understand what he was saying and I don't think Nick could either, because he read a lot of it from a paper he'd been sent by CFA headquarters. Anyway, he warned that the fires might be worse than normal and to have everything in tiptop condition, which is a bit of a laugh when you think of the age of the two trucks.

Like I said, John Crowe has been elected fire captain because of the two old tanker trucks. Tommy, who knows the most, could never be our fire captain because of his drinking and his record. John Crowe is pretty good at it anyway and has lots of experience and everyone's confidence, especially since he's gone into transport and become a bit of a businessman. A mechanic at the shire-council depot is one thing, the owner of a trucking company is quite another, even if it's only two trucks. Out on the location of a bushfire, him and Tommy will work together. They always have and together they'll get the best results with our volunteer firefighters.

Being a volunteer firefighter is the one thing in Yankalillee that sort of evens things up for everyone. Sure there's still quarrels but there are whole families who dedicate all their spare time to the needs of the brigade and raise money in raffles and bush dances and fetes and some have been doing it for generations. Without the women helping, not just catering, but manning phones and directing fire information from one place to another, I reckon we could never exist. Mrs Barrington-Stone says it's yet another example of how country women just shut up and get on with it. If you're in the volunteer brigade, people reckon you're fair dinkum because it takes a fair bit of dedication but I reckon they don't give the women the respect they deserve. Even Tommy, as the real maloney, is respected in bushfire circles for his knowledge and because he's a third-generation firefighter.

It's weird how that happens. He's highly respected at a Saturday morning meeting and when out fighting a fire, but come Monday or the day after the fire, he's a dero and crim for the rest of the week. I must say it hasn't rubbed off on me, though. People have always been real nice and point out to visitors that I'm a fourth-generation firefighter and haven't missed a fire call since the first one I went on with Tommy, John Crowe and Ian McTavish for my so-called rescue of Mrs Rika Ray. When you're out fighting a fire, religion doesn't come into it, you're just a bloke doing his best for his community.

Because it's the school holidays and the fire danger is so high, I'm helping the Forestry Commission to man the fire towers, the one I told you about earlier on Mt Pilot. It's a ten-hour shift and I'll come straight from collecting garbage and a quick plate of porridge. I make myself four cheese sandwiches and hope there's a couple of apples around and take two big bottles of water. I'm doing my matriculation this year so I probably won't do fire-tower duty later in the summer so this will probably be my last bit of fire-watching for the year. Of course, if there's a fire that threatens your town, even in the middle of the exams, you wouldn't worry too much about your matriculation, would you?

Bozo's put together another bicycle and made this kind of basket on the back where you can put your things. The tower overlooks a large stand of Scribbly Gum, *Eucalyptus haemastoma*, on the slopes of Mt Pilot.

It's called Scribbly Gum because it's got this yellowish, whitish and sometimes grey bark and has what looks like a little kid's scribbling all over it. Bozo's bicycle is fairly hard pedalling, but Mt Pilot isn't a huge mountain or anything, just the highest hill around with good sighting north, south and to the west. Hard pedalling or not, it's better than walking in this heat, I can tell ya.

I take a book along. I don't know if that's allowed, I've never asked, but it gets pretty boring in a tower for ten hours at a stretch and I've become a bit of a reader over the years. The one I'm reading at the moment is by Alan Moorehead and it's about fighting in Egypt. I'm very interested in military stuff, wouldn't mind being in the army, though Tommy says I've got to be fucking crazy, over his dead body!

When I ask him why, he says, 'F'chrissakes, look at me, will ya, Mole!'

My hope is that some day Tommy will tell me about what happened to him in Borneo.

I've searched the library and nobody has written a book about being a prisoner of war in Borneo. Maybe they have but it's not in the

Yankalillee library and Mrs Botherington isn't going to ask Melbourne, not for the sake of a kid. I thought of asking John Crowe to pretend it was for him but she knows he only reads books about nature and she'd be suspicious.

I haven't stopped trying to question Tommy about the war, though every time I bring it up, he says, 'Let it go, Mole.' He's not cranky or anything, just won't talk about it. Once he said, 'That's another life I want to forget.' It was like he was saying he didn't want to live through it again by telling me about it, but you can sense that he hasn't forgotten and that most of what's happened to him and why he is how he is may be because of the past. I mean with his shoulder and jaw, and one eye missing, how'd that happen? He's never said, was it a bullet or what?

With the experience I'm getting working for the Forestry Commission, Mr McDonald says he'll be happy to recommend me for a job when I've finished school. He says they're looking for bright young blokes they can send to university, because forestry is becoming more of a science. But I dunno, I've seen what Sarah's been through to get a university education and I don't think I'm up to it. Probably haven't got the brains anyway.

This is also Sarah's final year at university. She's kept on being brilliant. Meanwhile, Morrie's just become a doctor for the second time.

Mike is thinking of going to London, but I'll tell you about that later because we're all worried and not sure he should do it and Nancy starts to bite her fingernails whenever the subject comes up. She can't tell Mike he can't because he's been away in Melbourne too long and has his own life to lead and is no longer dependent on us. But she doesn't want him to go. She wants to know what's wrong with what he's doing now? Him and Sophie are going really well, especially the **Suckfizzle** label for kids. But all Mike says is, 'Mum, I'm a glorified dressmaker, no one will take me seriously here until I've been overseas and come back as a designer.'

When I'm up in the fire tower reading away and stopping every once in a while to scan the horizon and take the measurements for the log book, wind directions, relative humidity, cloud condition and the temperature, Anna Dumb-cow-ski will come into my mind. I can't help thinking about her and that she's somewhere in England with Crocodile Brown and won't be studying for her matriculation with our class this year. I try to imagine what she'd be doing. I mean Crocodile Brown isn't a very interesting bloke and he must be at least thirty-five years old!

Everyone thought Anna would be one of the top students in the state, like Sarah was, and now look what's happened. Perhaps Crocodile Brown, being a teacher, will see she goes to school and does her final exams in England, though it would be pretty weird, I mean, you know, with him doing it to her and her being a schoolgirl in her spare time, wearing her sports uniform. When I think about all this, I get this big, almost physical, shock, I just can't believe she was on with Crocodile Brown all of last year.

Nancy says that with this weather, anything could've happened. It's the heat and that bastard Chicka Barnes that's turned Anna's mind, the poor girl, coming from Europe originally. Maybe Chicka Barnes, yes, but the bad heat only really started in November and Crocodile and her must have been on together long before that.

I sit there looking over the Scribbly Gum thinking, unable to get Anna out of my mind, not only the lust factor, which I admit is always there when I think about her and her being so beautiful as well, but also her, little Anna Dumb-cow-ski. Sometimes sitting alone in the tower thinking about her, I have to whip the old man out to get a bit of relief. But Anna's more than that, it's her, she was about the nicest girl I've ever known. Everyone loved her, grown-ups as well as us kids and she was going to be the head prefect and everyone thought she was the perfect choice, the best any of us could remember. I'm sure she could've done better in life than old Yellow Teeth, Crocodile Brown. I keep asking myself why, why, why?

Tommy and me went out on Saturday. Despite the heat and it being blackfella weather, Tommy wanted to check on the combustible fuel that's lying about within a large stand of Mountain Swamp Gum, *Eucalyptus camphora*, growing at the base of some hills about eight miles from town. Later, if we've got time, we'll also check the *Eucalyptus camaldulensis*, River Red Gum, running along a dry watercourse into Reedy Creek. Tommy says a fire starting here among the bigger trees and running along the dry course would be just about the worst thing you could imagine happening. There's tall grass on either side and what with pasture improvement the fire danger is way up. The gully would be like a lighted fuse heading up towards the town and the grass fires would be like a pincer movement on either side.

Yankalillee is set among the hills so that fire can travel at a fair pace. It's been months since there's been any rain and the natural fuel in the two forests we check is that dry, it cracks like a rifle shot underfoot. It's been like this since Christmas. The grass in the open country and on the north-western hillsides is completely cured, all it needs is a spark and it will go up in a huge swoosh, then practically nothing will stop it. Tommy reckons the grassland carries about one ton of fuel per acre but the fern gullies and the western slopes of the hills carry as much as three tons. The two forests would easily average ten tons per acre as well as the burning bark that can be carried away in a convection column sometimes for miles to start new fires. It's the worst imaginable situation. We get home and Tommy goes straight off to see John Crowe.

For once in our lives we know everything's ready at the fire station because we've been through all our drills last Saturday and checked the gear. I know it sounds silly but I even check the rope on the fire bell, which you can hear all over town and every firefighter knows its sound. When that rings it's never good news. Fire bell's only rung for one thing, fire. Once a group of yobbos rang it in the middle of the night and Jack Donovan somehow got a hold of them and they got three months on the hill. There can be no mucking about when it comes to fire.

Well, the weather yesterday cooled down a fair bit and was down to eighty-five degrees Fahrenheit with a light north-westerly blowing, which sounds pretty good after the heat we've been through. But if you're an experienced bushfire fighter, a cool day in the middle of a heatwave is not necessarily good news.

So last night, as usual with periods of high fire danger, Tommy and me listened to the national weather report on Bozo's radio and what we heard filled us with a sense of dread. There's a cold front that's made its way across the south-east of South Australia and is coming towards Victoria. 'Oh shit!' we both exclaimed.

Today it's hot as hell again, but the first four hours pass uneventfully. The temperature at noon when I do my routine measurements is ninety-seven degrees. The cloud cover is cumulonimbus, people call it cumulo around here but Tommy says we've got to say it right. The wind direction is north-west with a Force Three wind with occasional gusts to Force Four.

These sudden gusts are what drives a fire faster and makes it unpredictable. There's not a lot else happening but the interference on the radio is building, that's always a sign that there's worse to come.

It's been bad news from dawn when Bozo and me got up to do the garbage; already the wind was blowing hot and strong from the north-west. About half-past seven, when we got home from washing the truck at the abattoir, the ABC news predicted thirty mile per hour winds for north-eastern Victoria and said that bushfires had started in the Chiltern bush overnight. They issued the usual high fire alert for the whole state, which was the same as they've done every day since mid-December. The Chiltern fires are not good news and Tommy looks at me and says, 'London to a brick, it's our turn soon, Mole.'

The day starts with a clear sky the colour of pewter but around nine-thirty cumulo clouds begins to form in the west. I watch as the clouds grow up into their towering anvil shapes that you know come before a thunderstorm. What the cloud means is the atmosphere has become unstable, anything could happen. Hopefully it will be rain, lots of the stuff.

The cloud doesn't tell you too much either. For the past two weeks there's been cumulus come up in the right direction for rain and there's not been a drop fall anywhere in the district. When I get to the tower, I heard on the HF again that fires had broken out in the Chiltern bush during the night. About ten in the morning, the smoke from the Chiltern fires about ten miles off starts to make visibility difficult from the tower.

After doing the noon schedule I call on 2792 KCS, which is Mr McDonald on the HF radio, and give him the report. He'll call the brigades in the CFA region and pass on the information. The crackle on the radio is pretty bad so I can only just make out his return report to me. He asks me if I could give him any accurate information on the Chiltern fire and I say it's hard to tell, the smoke is coming directly towards me and reading the distance is difficult. He says they hope the back-burn being set to the north of Chiltern will protect the town, but it's a big fire, to keep my eyes peeled.

I don't need to be told that real shit could hit the fan any time now, the conditions are just about perfect for a bushfire of major proportions. With the bush at Chiltern already a big blaze and several smaller fires started in the district, our turn could be next. I scan the horizon with my binoculars and my heart skips a beat, I think I've seen something. So I have a look through the telescope, which isn't that crash hot, being war surplus and probably as old and worn as the Diamond T. The visibility isn't good, maybe ten miles, not much more, but it turns out simply to be drifting smoke from the Chiltern fire or maybe one of the smaller ones, there's nothing new.

At one o'clock I check all my readings and see that the temperature has risen to 102 degrees and there's a rapid fall in the humidity to nine per cent. The cloud cover is now beginning to really build up, though still slowly and there's been a change in the wind speed.

I start checking on the Chiltern fire and move around about ninety degrees scanning the horizon but I'm having difficulty penetrating the haze. There's a fair bit of dry lightning around and I think briefly how lightning is attracted to the highest point in an area, which is the tower I'm standing in. It all seems okay but then I lower the binoculars a little and, there, to the south-east, I see the small unmistakable plume of new smoke.

I know the area the plume is coming from pretty well, Tommy and I have passed through it often enough. By my calculations, the fire seems to be in the vicinity of a small tributary of Reedy Creek close to Hopeless Dig. Jesus! It's about the one place you wouldn't want a fire to start! I take the bearing which is at 220 degrees and, with my heart pumping, I get onto the HF.

'VL3FD Mt Pilot calling VL3FD Yankalillee. Do you read me? Over!'

'Yankalillee to Mt Pilot, reading you 3 by 4.' It's a woman's voice. The girls at the Forestry Commission headquarters operate the incoming network.

'Smoke report Mt Pilot. Bearing 220 degrees. Approximate distance ten miles. Location in the dry tributary which runs into Reedy Creek, near Hopeless Dig. Over.' It's how you're taught to do it, each piece of information separate so it doesn't become confused.

Then Mt Stanley cuts in, 'VL3FD Mt Stanley to VL3FD Mt Pilot. Affirmative smoke report. Bearing 340 degrees. Over.'

It is nice getting the affirmation from Mt Stanley, it means I've got it right. The girl at the Forestry Commission repeats my message, which she gets correct. 'Affirmative. Over and out,' I say, feeling pretty pleased with myself.

But the feeling doesn't last long. I'm conscious that the Forestry blokes will all be out at the other fires and that we'll have to call out the CFA volunteers and it looks distinctly like we'll have to go it alone.

I hope to God that Tommy isn't in the pub, though with fire around he's usually pretty good. I'm yelling at the radio operator at the other end, hoping she'll hear me through the interference, the static is terrible. I'm busy plotting the fire on the map as I talk and check the wind direction. It's blowing the fire in a direct line to Yankalillee, no mistaking it. I check again, trying not to show the panic in my voice.

'This is Mt Pilot Tower to Yankalillee, do you read me? Over.'

There's crackle, then nothing so I call again. A faint voice comes through the static, 'Go ahead, Mt Pilot.'

'Fire in the vicinity of Hopeless Dig along Reedy Creek, 220 degrees, Mt Pilot Tower. The wind direction puts Yankalillee in its direct path, wind velocity thirty miles an hour,' I shout, even though we're taught to talk normal because that will cut through the static better, I'm that nervous I can't help myself. There's a lot of crackle and I repeat the message twice over until I finally hear, 'Wilco, over and out.'

Suddenly Bill Breadcake at Mt Stanley Tower chips in, 'I see it, Mole! Good on ya, mate, the bearing here is 340 degrees.' Then Mr McDonald confirms, 'You've got it right, Mt Pilot, Hopeless Dig, we'll need all the volunteers we can get, there's River Red Gum right along that tributary, there'll be a lot of fuel. Mole, there's a fair bit of lightning around, you better come down.' The amazing thing is that this all comes through pretty clear, which is the HF for you, sometimes calling in is terrible but the receiving can be clear as a bell.

'Please, Tommy be sober,' I beg aloud, looking to the heavens. 'Mate, we're all in a lot of shit, the bastard is heading directly for us.'

I can hear the wind beginning to pick up as I get onto Bozo's bicycle.

Chapter Nineteen

I reckon I've never pedalled this hard in my life, my legs are history by the time I get to the brigade headquarters and, as I get off my bike, I topple over. I don't mean faint or anything, it's just that my pins don't want to hold me up. I guess the adrenaline rush is all but used up.

John Crowe and Tommy are already at the bushfire station sorting things out and I give a sigh of relief when I see Tommy is sober. He watches me get up from the dirt, brushing my backside with both hands, looking sheepish. 'Gidday, what kept ya?' he says. 'Thought we'd have to leave without yiz.' I can see he's proud of me for being the one to spot the fire.

I look over to where a bunch of kids are quarrelling about who is next to ring the fire bell, 'Bell's still goin', calling fighters in.' I grin, 'You old blokes need a bit of time to get goin'. Did ya bring my overalls?'

'In the ute,' he says, nodding to the direction of John Crowe's utility. Then he looks up at me real serious. 'What ya reckon, son?'

'It's in among the River Red Gum, looks like a tributary of Reedy Creek, maybe two hours away, heading straight for Yankalillee, could be a big 'un.'

'We'll make a stand at Hopeless Dig,' he says immediately, 'be our best chance.'

Tommy's good like that, he's known exactly where I'm talking about and sees the surrounding country in his mind's eye. 'Yeah,' he says, spitting into the dust at his feet. 'Reckon you're probably right, there's a lot of fuel in the creek bed.' He goes over to talk to John Crowe, who listens then nods.

The men are beginning to come in fast now, utes lined up. Most are already in their overalls and broad brims, many bringing their own shovels and rakes. We never have enough of these in the fire shed, some have their own knapsack tanks and hand pumps, they don't trust the maintenance crew (don't blame 'em). Several utes and a couple of four-wheel-drive, ex-army jeeps are towing a furphy, bringing their own water supply. Be great if every ute was towing one. The messenger's jeep is standing by with its engine running, Hugh Spencer, the driver, standing next to John Crowe.

Everyone knows his team and they wait for their mates to arrive, anxious to get going. No point in hanging around when there's an angry fire coming your way. It's usual to send a scout out in a jeep to check the extent of the fire and confirm its whereabouts, but that can take anything up to two hours. Often, with a midafternoon fire like this one, the fighters only get to the fire just before dark. Fighting a fire at night is an even more dangerous business and John Crowe decides to wait no more than another half an hour for everyone to assemble.

John has complete faith in Tommy and he knows that I also know the area, the chances are we've got the location exactly right. Besides, it's already been confirmed by the Mt Stanley Tower. He'll leave the map reference with Mrs Thomas, the switchboard operator, and Marg O'Loughlan, the 'hello girl' at the telephone exchange, for any latecomers and for the Eldorado mob if they come in to help. Both women will be staying on duty until the last ember is out and they probably know more about the communications needed to direct a big fire than we do.

Mrs Thomas and Marg are just two of the remarkable country women Mrs Barrington-Stone often talks about who don't expect any praise at the end when us black-faced firefighters come in exhausted and get all the pats on the back.

It's the same with the Red Cross Catering Group and the CFA Women's Auxiliary. Nobody ever stops to think that they've been up eighteen or twenty hours fighting the fire as well. I have to admit I didn't think about it until it was pointed out by Mrs Barrington-Stone.

It's always women who make the sandwiches and the hot soup and cups of sweet tea, grill the snags, take the messages and co-ordinate the various brigades.

Then there's the wives of firefighters left on lonely farms who have to care for the kids and dogs, the stock in the paddocks and, if they're in the path of the fire, prepare the house and stay put until the fire has passed over or organise the evacuation. It's only when you start to think about all this that you realise there's more to fighting a fire than smacking its bum with a fire-broom.

We hear the cop-car siren, which means Big Jack Donovan is on his way. I reckon we should have a siren instead of a bell as a fire alert, an air-raid siren like the ones you hear in movies of the war when the Germans bombed London. They sound like there's a real disaster on its way and it could be the end of the world and you better get ready to meet your Maker. Any bell sounds like a church bell even though the fire-station bell has a different sound and you can't mistake it, but it's still a bell. You know what I mean? Bells don't sound urgent enough. Or anyway I don't think they do.

When I hear the bell at St Stephen's going for Mass on a Sunday morning, I imagine Father Crosby standing outside the church in the dawn light. There'll be frost on the bit of lawn and he'll be in his soutane ringing the bell for early Mass, unshaven, bleary-eyed, with a hangover from too much altar wine or from drinking someone else's whisky. He's probably still got his pyjamas on underneath his smelly soutane and his balls will be freezing, like ours are most winter mornings doing the garbage. Meanwhile, all the old biddies in their scarves and woolly underwear and knitted gloves are making their way across town to the church. If you ask me, the church bell's about the least-urgent bell you can possibly think of for something like a bushfire that could be threatening the whole town.

Big Jack's job is to direct the traffic if there has to be an evacuation of the town and he will already have phoned Wodonga and Wangaratta in case he needs extra police to help him, though Chiltern will get first pick. He is also in charge of the St John Ambulance and the Red Cross emergency units and, if things get really out of hand, he can ask Mr Sullivan, the prison governor, to bring out the prisoners to help.

We can take six men on the back of each old 'Blitz' fire truck and two in front. It's a helluva squeeze and a big load, what with knapsacks and fire-brooms and a big pile of pre-soaked hessian bags and the tanks carrying four hundred gallons of water. We never get much above twenty miles an hour out of them, which is enough to stay ahead of a bushfire on an open road but in rough country it can get dicey. Anyway, it doesn't get you anywhere in a hurry, that's for sure. Then, if we reach any sort of incline, we all have to hop off and walk.

The main bulk of the teams will go ahead in someone's ute, which is much the better way to get to a fire. They'll all have filled up their knapsack hand pumps, which will last them until we arrive. Driving the two ex-army 'Blitz' trucks, the Chev and the Ford, is important, but no honour I can tell you. You're the first to leave and the last to arrive. They only do about four miles to the gallon so you have to take extra petrol as well.

Tommy drives the Chevrolet because he's doing a favour for his mate, and the other truck is driven by Whacka Morrissey, an old-timer who knows its ugly ways. Both trucks are manned by Catholics and Nancy says that's because the Protestants are not stupid enough to be caught in the two slowest vehicles in the bushfire brigade. She may have a point.

We're all standing outside in a widish circle getting a briefing from John Crowe. There's five brigades in the Owens Valley Group. There's Yankalillee of course, then Wooragee, Bowmans–Murmungee, Gapsted and Mudgegonga, altogether about three hundred volunteer firefighters. There must be over two hundred already here and the others will turn up pretty soon.

John Crowe clears his throat, he's got a big voice that carries so nobody has to draw that much closer. 'Well, boys, this has all the makings of a big bastard. Nick Reed has just phoned from Wang, there's fires reported bloody everywhere. Chiltern bush is up in smoke, threatening the town, that's where the relief brigades are heading from Wodonga and Wang. I told him we didn't know the extent of the fire Mole's reported and we'll give him a bell if it's bad.' John Crowe laughs, 'He said he didn't like our chances, there's fires at Mount Buffalo and the Myrtleford boys have got their hands full.

Bright's got the same problem and we can't expect any help from the Forestry boys, they've got more than they can handle as it is.' He looks around, taking in most of the circle. 'He's got Eldorado on stand-by, but we can't count on them, they may be needed elsewhere. Looks like we're on our own, it's volunteers alone for the time being at least.' He shrugs, 'Don't need to say much more, you all know the drill. Anyone here that's new?'

Two blokes put their hands up. A young bloke from a farm near Allan's Flat, who gives his name as Lindsay Jarvis, and an older bloke, Michael Mooney, a Collins Street cocky who's big in insurance and has bought a place near Myrtleford and is probably going to prove to be more of a hindrance than a help. Tommy sighs next to me, nobody wants to have to keep an eye out for a rookie. All of us have read Mooney correctly, or anyway, we reckon we have and so there's no immediate volunteers. Inexperience is one thing you don't want fighting a bushfire.

'Righto, we'll take Mr Mooney,' Tommy says, breaking the ice. Tommy doesn't want the poor bloke to be standing there like a shag on a rock.

Quick as a flash Alan Phillips from the Wooragee Brigade says, 'Old Merv O'Hare carked it two nights back, we'll take the young fella.' There's a bit of a laugh among the men, Alan isn't known for his subtle approach. The Jarvis family are well known in the district and they're all bushies and he knows this well enough, he wouldn't have a bar of the Mooney bloke on his team. If the Jarvis boy proves a keen youngster who can take orders, he'll stay with the Wooragee Brigade permanently.

'Okay, boys, let's be off then, we're heading for Hopeless Dig.' John Crowe tells us to meet half a mile across the bridge over Reedy as most would know roughly where it is. He says all this matter-of-fact, like it's a cricket match or something.

It all sounds pretty reasonable, like we'll just go in and douse the flames. But it ain't. Fires don't work like that, even small ones. With fires things change so quickly, you've got Plan A all worked out and next thing you have to change everything, and not to Plan B because you can't anticipate what that is. Firefighting is about quick judgement coming from experience and that's what makes a good fire captain, some bloke who can call a fire more or less right. Nobody gets it exactly right.

With John Crowe and Tommy both on the job, I feel a lot safer. To be in Tommy's team, even though it's on one of the fire trucks, is a great honour. I haven't always been with him because he wanted me to gain experience with other teams, he still thinks that maybe one day I'll be the real maloney. Now I'm with him and it's good because I've never fought a fire that could be as potentially big as this one.

I'm excited, of course, fighting fires sort of gets into your blood, but you're not stupid enough to be disappointed if it turns out not to be as bad as you thought. There'll be three hundred fighters out there before long and, if Eldorado joins us, that's another fifty. It's not very many if a bushfire gets out of hand. Everyone knows it's up to them to do their best.

The good thing so far is that we know where the fire is coming from and that it's following the dry creek bed. As yet it hasn't hit the open grassland that's stacked with high-combustion fuel. It's midsummer and the grass is up to your knees and sometimes well beyond, and all of it tinder-dry. If the fire stays the way it is (fat chance), we can fight it on a fairly narrow front and concentrate all our efforts in more or less the one place.

The big problem is that this is a eucalyptus fire and that can travel fast. What we'll be looking for is a break in the trees growing along the creek, some area where the creek bed is bare of any growth for maybe a couple of hundred yards. What we'll do then is back-burn the grass beyond the line of trees on either side of this bare strip a hundred yards or so and hope that the burnt ground will halt the fire spreading into the grassland beyond. Also, the hope is that the gap in the creek between trees will be extensive enough so that the fire can't jump the bare earth and connect up with the trees on the other side.

If we get that lucky and the fire doesn't get into the grass and doesn't jump, three very big 'ifs', then we've got a real chance. The chances of finding a break in the tree line with bare earth in between is not zero but we'll be bloody lucky if we do. Yet that's what we'll be looking for.

If the River Red Gum stretches uninterrupted along the creek we've got Buckley's trying to stop it until we get to the gorge just outside of town. Even then we'd be in trouble because the gorge runs right through the centre of the bushland reserve, which carries a lot of big old eucalyptus trees and there are houses right up to the edge of the reserve.

There are two major types of bushfire, a forest fire and a grassfire. What we've got on our hand so far is a forest fire. A grassfire is probably the more dangerous because it can change direction on you in a second or combust behind you and trap you, but it's fairly slow, travelling around seven miles an hour. A good forest fire can go twice that speed, which means if we can't stop it somewhere along the creek, it could be on the outskirts of Yankalillee in less than two hours. By my reckoning, the fire is approaching at around six miles an hour with wind gusts of about thirty miles an hour. It doesn't sound fast but over rough terrain the two fire trucks will have a lot of difficulty staying ahead. We try to keep the Blitz trucks together, it's safer that way, what with the vaporising always being a problem.

Since the fire trucks are so slow, John Crowe goes ahead with the teams in the other utes and we follow behind. The story of Hopeless Dig goes that a bloke named Simpson found a gold nugget worth a thousand pounds there in 1865 and sparked a bit of a gold rush to the site. The creek must have been running that year because the miners set up camp beside it and chopped down all the trees and dug up the ground so thoroughly that not even the River Red Gum came back. Except for a little alluvial gold panned lower down in Reedy Creek, Simpson's site was as barren as a nun's tit and yielded not an ounce of gold and so was named Hopeless Dig. Had Simpson been around, the mob would have strung him up on the spot since it was clear that he had found the nugget elsewhere and was protecting the original site. However, by that time, he'd already cashed in his nugget and bought dry goods and was last reported to be running a store in Gulgong, New South Wales, where gold had been found, and was making a packet.

We get to Hopeless Dig at half-past three, about half an hour after the utes carrying the other firefighters. Tommy's guess is right and it looks pretty good, the fire is less than an hour away and the old gold diggings carry a bit of low bush and a few isolated Red Spotted Gum,

Eucalyptus mannifera, a small, stunted tree that grows in really poor soils and in gullies and is easy to cut down with an axe or saw. With the old digging and a fair bit of soil erosion, all the topsoil has been removed so the River Red Gum have given it a big miss, its seed carried by the wind over the gap to continue along the course higher up. The gap without any meaningful trees is over a hundred and fifty yards long. All I can say is that Tommy's a bloody genius.

The boys who've arrived earlier have formed teams and constructed a trail. Trail-making is real hard yakka and is an attempt to create a section of cleared ground similar to a dirt track. The other name for it is 'making a firebreak'. Working smoothly, the leader of a fire crew heads off, removing a narrow strip of all vegetation, with the rest of the team following, chipping and raking and widening the trail. They chop out all the low scrub and rake the debris from the forest floor, alternating the lead every few minutes so that the bloke in front gets a blow. We have to hope the trail is wide enough, there's no time to keep at it, the approaching fire is already too close. So John Crowe spreads the men out along the newly made trail and, facing into the wind on the edge of the trail, he gives the order, 'Light up!'

We set fire to the low scrub, back-burning from the edge of the trail, which has been made on both sides of the banks. This is known as a controlled fire, or at least you hope it is. Back-burning in the heat of the day is taking a huge risk but we can't wait for the temperature to drop. We are pretty tense, a single gust of wind can undo all the work and send the fire out of our control into the grass beyond and out of reach. The point is that Tommy's picked the only real place we have a chance to stop the fire. If it doesn't stop here, next stop is Yankalillee with a few farmhouses in the Woolshed Valley threatened in between.

We back-burn as carefully as we can, hoping the wind won't change direction. Several of us are beating out and dousing sparks that fly ahead of the back-burn, keeping the fire in more or less a straight line. We're at it about three-quarters of an hour and have barely done a hundred yards on either side of the creek when the fire is almost upon us. The radiant heat is already intense and we can feel the oxygen being sucked from the air and we know it's time to pull back. So far our luck is holding. Although the wind is blowing almost parallel to the creek bed, the fire hasn't blown sparks nor has any burning bark been caught in the convection current into the grass beyond the back-burn.

We're lucky in another sense as well. Soil erosion and past floods through the old diggings have had the effect of sinking the creek bed maybe a further ten or fifteen feet so that the River Red Gum canopy is only about thirty feet above the flat ground we're standing on, with a few taller trees sticking out a few feet further. This means that the larger percentage of the trees are contained within the confines of the creek bed. It's like the fire is burning in a long trough. The bad thing, of course, is that this narrow trough makes it like a flue, with the wind driving it forward, so the fire is travelling faster than it would in an open forest.

Tommy pats me on the back and nods towards the fire truck, time to get the hell out. The utes are all beginning to pull back, nothing we can do now but hope the fire doesn't jump the gap. There's simply no time to cut a trail on the other side of the gap and back-burn.

We reach the truck and Tommy is about to climb into the driver's seat when he turns to take a final look and shouts out, 'Oh shit, the canopy!' Almost in front of our eyes the fire rises into the forest canopy. The River Red Gum has heavy twisting branches and a spreading open crown and once the fire reaches the canopy the updraughts and the convection current created by the fire has plenty of space to move through. The effect is a bit like a blowtorch, with the heat of the fire driving it higher and sending burning bark and sparks into the atmosphere to be picked up by the wind.

All our work is for nothing. With the wind parallel to the flames, the burning bark and sparks in the air will jump Hopeless Dig without too much trouble, but worse than that, the convection sends the sparks every which way and high up into the sky so they're going to fly way past the back-burn we've just completed and into the open grassland. Bark capable of igniting a grass fire can travel a mile or more ahead of the main fire and can start a new fire just about anywhere. We can kiss the containment goodbye.

The thing about fires most people don't realise is the noise. It's deafening so even if you shout, you can't be heard three feet away. You can never quite get used to the fury of it, it's like a mighty roar of anger that just keeps going. I suppose flame is beautiful, the way it leaps into the air like it's free to do what it wants. Other elements are also free and I guess the sea can be pretty awesome, wind too, and lightning, but fire has a mind and a determination. You don't see it as a blind raging thing, which I suppose it is, but something that attacks and thinks and changes tactics. It has a malevolence that uses surprise, dirty tricks, cunning. You get to think of it as someone, not something, and it's someone you have to beat, but right from the start you don't like your chances because it's so big and unpredictable and can do so much harm.

In fact, you never really beat it. You may eventually slow its progress, but even that is debatable. Tommy says a bushfire will stop when it's starved of fuel and he's yet to see one that's been tamed by man. 'No way yer gunna make it stop, mate,' he explains, 'Best you can hope for is to try to direct its path until it's had enough and used up all the available fuel.' The back-burning we've done is just such an attempt, futile as it's proved to be.

With the fire in the canopy of the River Red Gum, it's time to move out. The fire's not only going to jump Reedy Creek, it's also going to spread to the grassland. It's the farmhouses in its path that are our immediate worry, then the houses on the outskirts of Yankalillee. We'll try to stop the fire before it reaches the gorge. Don't see how though. Maybe Tommy and John Crowe have an idea, but I can't for the life of me think what it might be and I reckon the others feel the same.

We load our gear and jump onto the back of the tanker and Tommy starts to move out even before we see John Crowe standing on the roof of his ute, signalling for all the teams to get going.

We haven't gone more than a couple of hundred yards when we see the first small spiral of smoke rise in the grass in open country about twenty yards to our right. Tommy keeps driving, it's important to get to open ground where there's low grass so that we can park the tanker and back-burn a parking spot quickly. Without water for their knapsack pumps, there's no chance of putting out the spot fires.

I jump off the truck, my knapsack pump on my back, and move through the grass to the spiral of smoke, it's only just beginning to take and I douse it quickly. Another minute and it could be well on the way and hard to stop. Tommy's slowed right down, we're only crawling along as it is, but the knapsack pump is heavy and I can't move all that quickly. I'm pretty puffed by the time I catch them again and the other blokes grab a hold of me and pull me up onto the back of the tanker.

By this time, the utes carrying the men are beginning to pass us. We learn later that John Crowe has decided he can't do anything about the grassfire and he's sent the message carrier ahead in his jeep to Yankalillee to warn them to get ready. Also that the houses on the edge of the Historic Park are to be evacuated and hosed down thoroughly, drainpipes blocked and gutters filled with water, sprinklers going wherever possible and any inflammables, especially petrol and kerosene, taken from the sheds and garages. Many a house would have been saved except that there's a drum of petrol or kero in the garage or someone's drained the sump of their car or ute and the oil is left in an open container.

We're undermanned anyway and the chances of finding another place to make a stand is remote. Every district bushfire brigade has to attend to its own town when it's threatened, that's the code. Tommy says later that John Crowe made the only decision he could, there was no stopping this fire.

The idea in the meantime is to try to protect the farmhouses and property in the path of the fire. There's a number of farms in the Woolshed Valley that are directly in the path of the grassfire and they're going to need help before we fall back to a last stand in Yankalillee.

What most people don't understand about fires is that if a house is properly prepared before the fire strikes, it's just about the safest place to be. Fleeing a house when a fire is approaching can be a disaster. A fire feeds on oxygen and even though a fire can be a fair distance away, it has created sufficient radiant heat so that you may even see birds falling out of the air, though I've never seen this myself, but Tommy says he has.

Remember how I told you about the folk who ran for the dam thinking they'd be safe in the water but never got there, that's because of the radiant heat and smoke. So the drill is fairly simple, though I admit it takes courage. Stay in the house. Do what I said before, water down everything, fill the gutters, wet the roof, clear the outhouses and sheds of any inflammable liquid, seal all the homestead windows tight as you can so there's plenty of oxygen trapped in the house. Then soak all your wool blankets in the bath tub and leave the tub full of water and anything else, buckets, the kitchen sink, so you can douse a small flame if it gets inside. Wrap yourself in the wet blankets just before the fire reaches you and wait for it to pass over.

Even if the house eventually burns down, it will only happen long after the fire has passed and you'll usually have time to escape into the burnt and blackened, but safe, world outside. Fire travels with wind, wind and fire are natural partners so the fire moves on. Remember, a fire starting inside a house is quite different from one that starts on the outside and is trying to get in.

Well, you can only hope all the farmers and the property owners know this, they've certainly been told often enough. It's not hard to understand the temptation to bundle the kids into the car and get going. That's fine if you're well ahead of the fire, though not such a good idea if you have to drive through one.

Also, if you're heading for a main highway, the chances are that it might already be blocked by others trying to do the same as you. All it takes is for a couple of breakdowns or an accident and you're stopped with nowhere to go and with the possibility of the fire catching up with you. If this happens, stay in the car, wind the windows up and hope that the fire will pass before the car goes up in smoke, which is almost always the case. Getting out and running for it is not a good idea, the radiant heat and smoke will get you before you've gone a hundred yards.

With the fire now in the open grassland and the wind blowing in a north-westerly direction, it's not hard to see where its most likely path will lie, and the first farm is Woolshed Park, the property of Tom and Edie Park.

John Crowe now draws up alongside and he signals for Tommy to stop. 'Mate, how much water you reckon you've got left?' he shouts over.

'Fair bit, about half-full or thereabouts.'

'Yeah, okay, looks like Woolshed Park is gunna cop this lot first off, we've still got the other tanker for the knapsacks. Head over there, see what your crew can do to get the farm ready. I'll send crews over to the other farms, you handle this one.'

'Righto,' Tommy calls back.

'Don't wait for the fire to come, I want you back with us as soon as possible. Bring Edie Park and the kids with you if you think you have to. Tom Park is with the Chiltern Brigade and has been gone since yesterday, Edie's gunna need a hand.'

Tommy nods and we turn in the direction of Woolshed Park, which is a big property, with both sheep and apple orchards and a fair bit of hay and lucerne. Tom Park is a bloody hard worker and he's built it bit by bit and it's not come easy.

The track's not too bad except that there's gates to open every few hundred yards. It's muggins has to do this as the older blokes reckon opening farm gates is kids' work. I leave the gates open because there's stock, mostly sheep, in some of the paddocks and, when they sense the fire, instinct will take over while there is an escape route and they'll try to stay ahead of the fire. The survivors end up gawd knows where, but that's something that gets sorted out later in a communal muster between neighbours.

We open the last gate to the Woolshed Park homestead, which is a mile or so further up the track, and see the little Park girlie pedalling her bicycle as fast as she can with her school bag still on her back. In fact the tanker can't move a lot faster than her furious pedalling and we've gone three hundred yards up the road before we catch her.

The wind is making such a racket we've come right up to her before she realises we're there and when Tommy blows the horn she gets such a fright she skids and falls off her bike. I jump down from the tanker, pick her up and dust her off. Her eyes are brimming with tears and she wipes them with the back of her fist.

'I'm sorry we frightened you, hop in the front, we'll get there faster!'

'What about my bike?' she says tearfully, then adds, 'We got out of school early, Miss Lenton said it was because of the fire.'

She's come from the Woolshed Valley Small School about five miles down the road. 'No worries, we'll take it in the back.' Then I say, 'My name's Mole.' I smile, trying to reassure her, 'What's yours?'

'Ann,' she says, her eyes are still wide but the tears have cleared. I see that she's scraped her knee and there's a trickle of blood running down her shin and not quite reached the neat little white ankle socks. 'It doesn't have an "e" on the end, my dad says it cost more to put an "e" on the end of Ann and we couldn't afford it at the time because fat-lamb prices were down.'

I don't laugh because she looks so serious. With little Colleen around, I'm used to kids. 'You think that's bad! I'm called Mole because as a baby I used to burrow down in my cot and get lost.'

She laughs. 'That's funny, Mr Mole,' she says.

'It's just Mole. What say we get moving hey, Ann? We ain't got much time.' I jerk my head in the direction of the rolling clouds of black smoke towering above the horizon. The wind is blowing something fierce and there's dust everywhere.

Ray Davis, who, like John Crowe, is a mechanic, works at Philip Templeton's used-car lot. He's sitting in the front with Tommy and stretches his hand out to grab little Ann's as she climbs up into the Blitz cabin. She sits on his knee and after I heave her bike up onto the back, we're off again.

Directly above us I hear the birds – magpies, crows, galahs, sulphur-crested cockatoos, rosellas – heading away from the fire-filled sky. They seem to be calling frantically to those of their kind lagging behind.

The smell of burning leaves fills our nostrils and there's floating embers landing around us that have blown miles ahead of the fire. A patch lights up, ignited by an ember, and Tommy slows down and two of the blokes hop off with their knapsack pumps, killing the smoulder before it gets a hold. Bad enough waiting for the big bastard coming, no point in having a dress rehearsal. The heat has increased noticeably, so that we're all soaked through and I can feel my overalls clinging to my back and the sweat running down my neck and down the inside of my legs.

Edie Park comes out to meet us, the wind whipping at her cotton dress; she's shielding her eyes against the dust. The party-line phone has run hot and news that the fire has beaten the back-burn has spread terror through the women of the valley. All their men are gone and it's up to them to cope. Most of the younger wives haven't seen a big fire like this.

'We can take you out with us, Mrs Park,' Tommy says, 'you and the kids?'

'There's only me and Ann,' Edie replies, 'No, we're staying put. There's everything me and Tom have worked for here, we built the homestead with our own hands.' It's sandstone and brick with a bullnose iron-roofed verandah. The posts may go, but it's solid right through.'

Tommy looks around quickly, there isn't much time. 'The orchard's a bit close, that'll go, looks like a good crop of greengages, won't get any apples this year.'

'Yes, the plums are good this year,' she laughs, 'We're down to the last barrel of last winter's apples.'

Tommy looks about him at the outhouses, all solid brick. Tom Park has done his thinking ahead of time. The only things that are wooden are the hayshed and the shearing shed some distance from the homestead, no hope there.

Ann has run inside and I take a quick look around. In the horse paddock nearby, there's a dozen cows and two rams in one part and, in a separate area fenced off from the others, is a big Hereford bull.

Edie sees me looking. 'That's our investment, we've had the sheep eat that paddock clean as a whistle all summer.' She points to the stock nervously milling about. 'They're all "boxed" into the one paddock, those were Tom's instructions. The cows and a prize calf, the bull and the rams won't be able to keep ahead of the fire, we have to take the chance the fire will burn around the paddock.' She shrugs her shoulders. 'It's all our capital. Tom sold a truck to put down the deposit on the bull and we still owe the bank for him *and* one of the stud rams.'

Tommy doesn't try to dissuade her, Edie Park is a country woman who knows her own mind. 'What about the kid?' he asks.

There is a slight hesitation before Edie Park says tight-lipped, 'She's country-bred, she stays.' Then she looks at us, 'I'm scared, Mr Maloney, and I don't suppose I have the right to stop Ann going, but this is our life, this is everything we are, I've got to try and save it.'

I think to myself, if it were little Colleen or four-year-old Templeton, I'd have her out of there so fast you wouldn't see our dust!

'It's no problem to take you both?' Tommy tries again.

There is still the hesitation in Edie Park's eyes, but then sudden resolve. 'It's happened once before to me, when I was Ann's age. I still have nightmares about it but my parents saved the farm and if we'd moved out that time it would have all gone. I can't take that chance, Tom's worked too hard.'

I wonder if Tommy has the right to force her to come, this is a crown fire and anything could happen, I wouldn't like to be in their boots. But I guess not because Tommy says, 'We left the gates open comin' in, what about the other paddocks, any stock?'

'Yes, sheep and cattle.' Edie points to a Welsh mountain pony standing in the yard still saddled, its flanks wet from hard riding. 'I've just got back in, I've opened all the paddock gates.' She smiles, but it's a sort of sad smile. 'Let's hope some of our stock make it out ahead of the blaze.'

Tommy doesn't waste time on sentiment, 'Righto then, let's fix the house.' He glances around, and his eye fixes on the shearing shed about two hundred feet from the house. 'The shearing shed, what's in it?' Tommy asks.

'Nothing much, but the tractor's under the lean-to at the back, the keys are in it.' Then she adds quickly, 'I was just about to go for it.'

'Any fuel?'

'No, Tom emptied the drum two days ago.'

Tommy nods. He's calm, completely in charge, his voice flat, like he's chatting about the weather. I must say I admire Edie Park, she's tough all right and though she's frightened she doesn't show it. The point is that we're all frightened, scared shitless as a matter of fact, but you'd expect a woman to show it, only she don't.

'Mole, get the tractor out, park it in the paddock with the cows and the rams, don't forget to turn off the fuel taps.'

In the meantime most of our crew have spread out with their knapsack pumps putting out little fires everywhere. Two of the blokes are on the roof, they've blocked the downpipes from the roof gutters with tennis balls. They've started the tanker pump and Ollie Brook, who is too fat to do much running around, is feeding the hose up to them and they're splashing down the roof and filling the gutters with water. Tommy doesn't bother to tell them what to do, they know the drill backwards. He now has to make sure Edie Park has things inside the homestead organised.

Little Ann is no fool either, she's led the pony down to the paddock where I've just parked the tractor. She and the pony are nearly blown over by the wind, which is howling at gale force. I help her unsaddle and I carry the saddle back to the homestead. 'Mr Mole, are you related to Mole in *Wind in the Willows*?' she asks, shouting against the noise of the wind.

'Me great uncle,' I shout, 'Not a bad old rodent, as I recall.' It's a book Sarah read to us when we were small, so I know what she's pulling my leg about. We're running back up to the house, her two kelpies yapping at our heels, the wind behind us this time. I'm that hot I think I'm going to burst open any moment, the dust is irritating my eyes like hell.

'Can you take the dogs and put them in the separator shed with the saddle?' she asks. I'm beginning to wonder who's in charge around here.

'Where's that?' I shout.

'Where we separate the cream, silly!' Fortunately she points to a small solid-brick structure about twenty yards from the homestead.

'Oh, okay,' I say, 'What's their names, the dogs?'

'Toby and Lassie, they'll come if you call. My dad says working dogs have got to be obedient.'

I call the two kelpies and, to my surprise, they follow me. Bozo and Mrs Rika Ray are not the only dog trainers in the world. I lock the dogs in the creamery together with the saddle and come out to see little Ann carrying two very large cats into the laundry behind the house. Later I learn that they're called Blackie and Sooty, both of them being pitch-black, only difference between them is Blackie, or is it Sooty?, has one eye missing.

The wind has risen a notch again. Fires make their own wind and it's unpredictable, we can see it gusting and swirling across the paddocks coming towards us and ahead of the fire. The whirlwinds, seemingly starting from nowhere, are gathering momentum, collecting everything in their path, dancing like dervishes across the paddocks, spreading the spot fires until they look like some sort of disease visited upon the land. The cows and the bull bellow in terror, milling about, going in circles while the two big rams simply jump out of the way of the terrified cows, afraid of the fire and the cattle around them. One ram, in a panic, jumps up onto the tractor engine, then slides down and falls to the ground sprawling on its back, hooves frantically thrashing. The high-pitched whinny of the mountain pony cuts through all the other animal sounds. Soon they too are drowned by the howling of the wind.

We can see the fire now, great orange streaks of light against the black smoke, leaping up and momentarily dying down before rising higher. It seems to be positively galloping towards us, malevolent, anxious to get at us. Already the sound of its fury is reaching us.

'We're out of here,' Tommy yells. He looks at Edie Park, 'Comin', Mrs Park?' he asks again.

He's done all he can, everything that can contain water inside the house has been filled, the bathtub, kitchen sink, wash troughs, every available container. Blankets have been soaked, he's left a knapsack pump full to put out any fires that might start inside and I've got mine as well. There's a pile of blankets soaked and the new carpet in the lounge room is saturated. All the windows have been shut and any gaps stuffed with rags, the outside gutters are full and the outside front walls hosed down.

Edie Park shakes her head. 'We're staying, Mr Maloney, we'll be needed after the fire has passed over.'

Tommy can't stay to argue. He's cut things fine as it is and he has to think about the greater good, which is trying to save Yankalillee.

Then little Ann comes up to me and hugs me round the waist. 'Please stay with us, Mr Mole, I'm very frightened. Please, please, Mr Mole!' she begs.

'Ann, pull yourself together!' Edie says sternly.

But little Ann hangs onto my waist, her eyes pleading. I'm feeling pretty guilty leaving two women alone in an isolated farmhouse and I look at Tommy. Whatever he says, I have to obey, that's the code. 'Can I stay?' I ask.

I've never seen Tommy's face, I mean his expression, like it is now. I can see he can't make the decision, his bottom lip is trembling, he's fighting something inside himself. I can't bear to see him like this. 'I'm staying,' I say, helping him out. He nods and turns away, not looking at me again. Something's been stirred inside of him, something old that's damaged him. I mean our chances of survival are pretty good, but that's not what I've seen in Tommy's eyes. It's a kind of pain and defeat and even hatred, I dunno, something like all them three things.

'Oh, thank you, thank you!' little Ann says. 'Thank you, Mr Mole!'

Mrs Park turns away, but not before saying to her daughter, 'That was not necessary, Ann, we could have managed perfectly well.' But I see it in her eyes, just before she turns, the relief that there's someone else going to be with them. I reckon I'd feel the same.

We watch as the Blitz moves away. The old tanker had better not stall in the heat or they'll have no chance. Hell is on its way and it will gobble them up, licking them off the landscape like a cow at a salt lick.

It doesn't take long before the dull roar becomes deafening and drowns everything out. At any moment the fire will be upon us. We've wrapped ourselves in the wet blankets and we're lying on the floor in the bathroom where there are no windows. I've talked about the roar before, but I've never ever been in the middle of a fire, inside a box enveloped by roaring flame. I've never been this close to my own death. If the fire gets into the house, like blasts out the front windows, it will fill every room, roar through it, looking for a way to escape.

I have everything covered with the wet blankets, my head as well as my body. Mrs Park and Ann are the same, I've seen to that myself, the mother clasping her little daughter to her breasts while I cover their heads and put more wet blankets over them. If we're going to die, she wants her little girlie in her arms. 'Thank you, Mr Mole,' Ann says, then she smiles, 'See yer later alligator.'

'In a while crocodile,' I say back. It's the last thing anyone says. The roar and the fire hit us. Of course we don't see the flames grab a hold of the house, but they're driven by a tornado-like wind and the whole house shakes as if any moment it's going to be ripped off its foundations and take off into the burning sky, a part of the debris being hurled forward by the monster consuming us. I've never heard a sound that's to be compared with it, express train is the one most often used, but that's not right. There's a sort of high-pitched wail along with the roar and the fury, as if the house itself is screaming at the touch of the furious flames. I'm finding it difficult to breathe, but I'm not game to put my head out of the blankets. The roar is so intense that it's become more like deep silence than sound, nothing comes through, we can't hear if the windows are popping and if flames are already inside looking for us. The holocaust isn't just physical, it is everything, it consumes my every thought, enters my mind so I know that if we escape I'll never forget it, it will haunt me for the rest of my life.

Then it's gone. The all-consuming sound has gone, diminished; all there is now is a dull roar in the distance, which does sound like an express train.

I rip the blanket from my face and body, struggling to get out, the wet blankets now steaming. It isn't easy. I've wrapped myself in a sort of cocoon and the more I struggle to get free the tighter it seems to pull. Breathing hard, I tell myself to take it easy, unwrap slowly. Don't panic, Mole, it's over.

By the time I'm free, I can see Mrs Park and Ann moving and I unwrap them, their dresses are soaked and I can see Edie Park's breasts showing through the wet cotton of her dress. 'Outside, quick,' I instruct, 'keep a blanket wrapped around you.' I grab the knapsack pump, sling it on my back and lift a bucket of water. The two of them follow me to the kitchen door. There's tiny whiffs of smoke coming through the cracks in the door and I tentatively touch the door handle and, to my surprise, it isn't that hot. I turn it but the door won't budge, so I kick at it and it flies open and we're hit by a wall of heat, but that's all it is, a blackened landscape and the heat leftover from the fire. I turn and see that the outside surface of the door is alight, the green paint bubbling and the wood only just beginning to catch. The six verandah posts are all burning vigorously, more than the door, and I douse them first with the knapsack pump and then return to do the door.

Edie has gone inside to grab two buckets of water. There is surprisingly little smoke about, what's burnt has burnt clean with almost nothing left behind. I check for fire in the eaves but the water in the gutters and the hosing down of the outside wall seems to have done the trick, the bullnose roof has also protected the eaves. Tom Park and his wife have built a house that can protect itself from a fire. Now it stands alone with only the two outhouses, the creamery and the laundry, sitting on blackened desolated earth as far as the eye can see. The neat garden has gone, nothing, not a single bush or shrub left behind. Then I see the apple orchard. The trees still stand, they're leafless, branches bare to the sky, the fire has moved through so quickly that the apples and greengages are still hanging from the branches. Later we will discover that every one of them has been roasted, the greengage plums turned into sort of prunes.

Little Ann wants to go to her pets, the dogs and the cats. 'Better check the house first,' I suggest, 'don't want to lose it now, do we? You go check inside with your mum and I'll do the outside.' I can see the anxiety in her eyes, so I point to the creamery and then to the outside laundry where she's put the two cats. 'See, the roof is still on both, the doors are not alight, they're safe enough for the moment, Ann.'

I don't think she believes me, she hesitates but then she goes back into the house with her mother. She's strong-willed, just like her mum. I walk around the house, the heat from the fire-scorched earth making the soles of my feet burn through the leather of my boots. There's half a dozen windows cracked but none are blown, which is a miracle, the fire must have been moving at a terrific speed. A dry-burning branch from an old lemon tree at the back of the homestead has fallen onto the roof of the sleep-out and hangs over the side so that one of the window frames is smouldering, not yet alight. I pull the branch down and spray the window with a shot from my knapsack pump. Otherwise there's nothing to be concerned about, the roof is iron and probably bloody hot at the moment. I walk into the burnt-out vegie garden until I can see if any of the corrugated sheets have lifted, none have.

Edie is coming out of the house as I walk around again from the back. 'The cow! She'll cut herself to pieces!' she yells. I've already looked down at the paddock and the tractor is untouched and the stock, still bellowing and panicky, seem to be okay. Now I look again, one of the cows has been caught on the barbed-wire fence. Her calf has escaped the paddock and would be prime roasted veal by now. We've got wire cutters on the Blitz of course, but not on me. 'Pliers! Have you got a pair of pliers?' I yell out. She waves her hand and I see she's already thought of that. Farm women are different, even Sarah wouldn't have known what to do.

Little Ann is heading for the creamery and Mrs Park and me run down to the paddock. I know bugger-all about cows and it's threshing around with its back leg caught in the wire, the leg is already a bloody mess where she's been struggling to free herself.

'Cut the wire, I'll hold her by the horns!' Edie Park instructs. The cow must have been a favourite or something because the moment she touches it, it seems to calm down. I quickly cut the wire and the leg is free and the cow pulls away as Mrs Park lets go of its horns. It looks like a pretty bad cut to me but Mrs Park says she'll dress it later, not too much to worry about, it should heal quickly.

Little Ann comes running up, sort of jumping from one place to another to avoid the hot, still-smoking patches of ground and the dogs yelp after her. 'Back!' Edie Park shouts, 'Send them back, Ann, their paws will get badly burnt, we'll need them for the muster!' Ann stops. Chastised, she runs back, calling the dogs after her. 'Take them to the house!' Edie yells. Then she turns to me, smiling. 'Thank you, Mr Mole, thank you from the bottom of my heart.'

'It wasn't nothing, Mrs Park,' I say, feeling a bit foolish. 'I just lay in the blankets same as you two.' It's another Mrs Rika Ray situation where I've done nothing much. I hope I don't get a bottoms-wiping certificate out of all this.

'It was knowing you were there, it was a great comfort to us both.' She's walked over to the pony and has pulled its head against her chest and is stroking its nose, making comforting noises. I look over to where the shearing shed and the hayshed once stood and which have been completely razed to the ground. You can see the set of harrows I left behind when I took the tractor from under the lean-to. Now it looks like the skeleton of some strange creature that met its end in the fire, the leaves are its fleshless ribs.

'Well, it could have been worse. We've got the bull, the rams, the cows and the tractor, the house is safe, my pony hasn't come to any harm. Maybe even some of the sheep and cattle have made it out of their paddocks to safety.' She smiles, 'There won't be an apple crop this year and we won't be building a haystack, that's for sure.'

It's like she's doing an inventory in her head, then Edie says, 'I suppose we should count our blessings.'

Just then Ann comes running down to the paddock again and hugs her mother around the waist, 'Do you think Daddy is still alive, Mummy?' she asks.

Suddenly it's all too much for Mrs Park. She hugs her little daughter and both of them begin to sob. I don't know what to do, so I grab them both and start up as well, the three of us howling, holding each other, with the smoking earth all around us.

Then I think of Nancy and it stops me bawling. If it were her standing there in Edie Park's boots, she wouldn't be counting her blessings. She'd be yelling up at God and shaking her fist at the heavens, letting Him know He's not gunna get away with this. Father Crosby would be yelling at her for the thousandth time not to commit a blasphemy.

Edie is made of sterner stuff and she knows better than to blame God. Fires happen, nothing you can do about that. I think her tears are just relief that they've come through safely. She's got guts and I admire her a lot.

It's almost sunset and with them two safe, I've got to think of a way to get back to Yankalillee where the fight will still be going on. The party-line phone isn't working, I guess some of the poles have been burnt.

'I've got to get to Yankalillee, Mrs Park,' I say. 'Can I use your tractor?'

'If it's got any petrol, yes, of course.'

Oh shit, she's right, the drum in the shed has been emptied and there's precious little in the tractor.

'You can take the pony,' she suggests, 'but I don't think he'll be that good with fires and the smoke still around. He was pretty jumpy when I took him over to open the paddock gates.'

I don't tell her I've never been on a horse in my life, much less one that's going to shy at every patch of smoke and falling tree. 'No, you'll need him,' I say, 'you'll want to get around the place first thing tomorrow.'

'Won't you spend the night, you're very welcome to stay, Mole?'

'Thanks, Mrs Park, but I've got to try and get back. If Yankalillee's threatened I've got to be there to help and be with my folks. I can walk it in just over two hours if I get going now.'

'There's always Ann's bike? It's a bit small, but it's quite sturdy.'

So there I am with me knees pumping way above the handlebars of the little girl's bicycle, dirty, tired and moving through a completely blackened landscape. In the pocket of my overalls, I've got a bottle of water and four apples Mrs Park has pressed on me from a basket in the kitchen. I dare say they're the last apples they'll get from their orchard for a year or two.

The light is beginning to fade even though it's summer and it should stay light until nearly eight o'clock, but there's that much smoke about it's going to be dark pretty soon. The fires, both of them, must be getting close to the gorge, coming like a pincer movement, the one in the River Red Gum moving remorselessly up the Reedy Creek tributary and the grassfire coming up the other end of the gorge.

There's a bit of lightning around and with nothing else to hit but the blackened earth, I think of myself riding along the rutted farm roads, the only metal object likely to attract it in these desolate surroundings. Just my luck, escape a bushfire and get struck by lightning. There's been lightning this time of the afternoon for weeks and it doesn't mean there's going to be rain, which, if there is and it's enough of a thunderstorm, it will save our lives. As Tommy always says, 'Hope is a whore with a bad nature' and is not to be taken into consideration when planning anything. 'Always look for the dirt behind the shine' is definitely his motto.

What I'm going to tell you now is hearsay because the time it's happening I'm pedalling across the scorched earth towards Yankalillee on a child's bike, my knees practically brushing the sky.

It seems that after John Crowe and the rest of the brigade left Hopeless Dig, there was some discussion about trying to back-burn from Boundary Road, which is not far out from Yankalillee. John Crowe wasn't that keen on the idea and wanted to head back to Yankalillee and put in as much time as possible getting ready for the fire. But a number of the fighters insisted Boundary Road was worthwhile, so John decided they'd stop there first and check it out. Tommy got there from where he'd left me at Woolshed Park just after they'd left, having decided back-burning from the road wasn't an option, just like John Crowe had maintained.

While they were making the inspection, one of the utes coming in after protecting a farm reports to John Crowe that the Ford Blitz tanker being driven by Whacka Morrissey has stalled in the heat and the old bloke can't get it started again. What's more the stubborn old coot has refused to come with them and said he'd get the fucker started if it killed him. They've brought in the rest of the crew, who are jammed into the back of the ute like sardines in a can.

John Crowe asks where the tanker is and he's told about two miles back, about a hundred yards in from the start of the eucalyptus forest. With Tommy gone to Woolshed Park and the time of his return not known, John Crowe knows he'll need the second tanker when they reach the gorge. He also knows Whacka Morrissey, an old-style firefighter, won't take instructions from anyone except the fire captain. He glances at his watch. 'Fuck, it's cutting things a bit fine! Righto, you blokes push on into town, you know what to do, I'll see you there later.' Though it isn't necessary, he adds, 'Make sure every house is evacuated three streets back from the gorge.' He knows that Big Jack Donovan will have seen to it already, but he'll have his hands full with other things and people can be bloody stubborn when it comes to leaving their homes and possessions, and often it's only when the fire brigade arrives that they'll take moving out seriously.

John Crowe also knows what the problem would be with the Ford Blitz. Even more than Tommy's tanker, it is prone to stall in conditions of extreme heat. Using one of the fire hoses to cool down the fuel line and engine manifold, he'll be able to tinker a bit and away she'll go. Whacka's no fool, he would have done all this, but would have failed in the tinkering department. John Crowe reckons to himself that it shouldn't take long to get the Blitz back on the road. Anyway, if he fails, he'll bring Whacka out with him in the ute. 'Be back in twenty minutes,' he tells them, 'You'd better be getting a move on.'

There were people afterwards who claimed that John Crowe should have tried to stop the fire at Boundary Road and not at the gorge. After a fire, post-mortems and know-alls always abound. Hindsight has twenty–twenty vision. When I asked Tommy later, he said John Crowe made the correct decision. He pointed out that between the grassfire and Boundary Road was the eucalyptus forest going right up to within twenty yards of the road, with Yellow

Box, Red Stringy Bark and White Box mostly, and Casuarina in the understorey.

'Trees like that and you've got yourself a crown fire that wouldn't be stopped by any road, no way. If we could've back-burned far enough, maybe half a mile or more on the Yankalillee side of the road, we may have had a chance. It'd take a day to do that, John Crowe had less than an hour. No way the fighters could have done the job properly with the men available. He done the right thing pulling back to the gorge, there wasn't no other option.'

Not that meeting the fire at the gorge on the edge of town was much of an option anyway. Once the fire got into the gorge there was no going in after it. What's more, it would soon enough climb out the other side and across a narrow strip of land that formed part of the Historic Park and then it was into the town proper, with nothing to stop it and with buildings and gardens to feed its fury. In other words, the brigade was caught between a rock and a hard place. If they stopped at Boundary Road to back-burn and the fire jumped the road, they'd have lost valuable time. If they went on to the gorge, it was going to be almost impossible to stop the fire at that point. The only realistic choice was to try to save as much of the town as possible. It's little wonder there was a fair amount of heated debate afterwards. These things are never cut and dried.

So the crews get back to find the whole town has already been alerted. Houses near the rim of the gorge have been evacuated after they've been treated. Cars are packed with things the families want to preserve at all costs. In other words, all the usual stuff that's supposed to happen with fires but which the locals haven't experienced in the lifetime of any of its citizens.

Tommy arrives not long afterwards and takes over until John Crowe gets back, hopefully with Whacka Morrissey following behind in the Ford tanker or with him in the ute.

In the meantime I'm coming in behind the fire. The ground temperature is blistering and the smoke-filled air makes breathing hard. At one stage I take off my overalls and bunch them up and, using a bit of string I find in one of the pockets, I tie the bundle to the frame of the bike. I take a drink of water and eat an apple. My clothes cling to my body and, while I don't realise it at the time, my eyebrows and my hair are already singed. There's still sparks flying around and every now and again one lands on my bare arms and burns like hell.

I can see the fire way ahead and observe as the grassfire reaches the eucalyptus forest that starts about two miles back from Boundary Road. One moment the fire is racing close to the ground, feeding on grass and shrub, a brilliant orange and magenta line stretched across to the immediate horizon, and then it disappears into the dark line of the forest.

For a moment it seems as though it's just been snuffed out, then, even where I am half a mile back, I hear the roar as the flames leap into the air. Within moments the crown canopy is alight, flames licking skywards, then a blast of heat hits me in the face and damn nearly knocks me off the little bike. The combination of eucalyptus oil and 4000-degree heat driven forward and upwards by a Force 6 wind makes it crown with a demonic ferocity. The volatile gas causes the fire to burn in the air above the canopy. It hovers, or appears to do so, petrifying the leaves in the upper canopy, sucking all the oxygen out and, in moments, large trees are reduced to blackened candlesticks.

If there was a house or anything in the way it wouldn't be like Woolshed Park, where the grassfire roared over the building and raced on. I reckon a forest fire would take everything with it, explode the windows and be inside the house in moments, the fire roaring through the rooms and out the other side like Red Box roaring in the furnace of a Lux stove. Despite the intense heat I shudder at the thought. A fire going through a eucalyptus forest must be the land equivalent of a tidal wave, there's nothing going to stop it and nothing in its path it can't destroy.

Then I see something I've only heard about in stories. It's called the Red Steer and is a phenomenon that old-timers sometimes talk about, tall stories you think of as old men's dreaming. One of those things they talk about in pubs when they've had a few and they all claim they've seen, but you know they haven't. You know it's just bullshit, legends passed on, spooky stuff, because men have to have stories larger than their lives.

As I watch, the fire in the forest gains even more intensity. Its roar, even half a mile away, is now deafening. Then a huge fireball rises above the canopy, it's maybe fifty yards across and, in a split second, the hair on my arms and legs disappears and the heat on my face and uncovered skin feels as if boiling water has been poured over them. Later my face, arms and legs will blister.

The fireball rises above the burning canopy and, as if gathering momentum, swirls in the air like a catherine wheel sucking up oxygen into its furious belly. It moves higher still and seems to hesitate a moment. Then, with a roar that cracks open the surrounding air, the huge, balled inferno shoots forward in a flaming arc to land in the forest a mile ahead of the fire itself.

It is exactly as if a monstrous bomb has hit the forest. Huge uprooted trees fly high into the air as the eucalyptus explodes with flames leaping higher above the forest canopy than I've ever seen. A mushroom cloud of smoke, like the pictures of the atom bomb on the Bikini Atoll, rises into the towering clouds above. It is as if the entire bushfire has consolidated into one huge ball to hurl itself forward. I shall forever think of it as being alive, a creature beyond all human reckoning. I have seen the Red Steer. I shall never forget the sight for the remainder of my days upon this earth. I have stared into the eyes of hell.

The following day we will find the spot where the Red Steer landed. The remainder of the forest stands blackened and charred. The forest where the Red Steer has been is totally destroyed, everything in a circle two hundred yards across is gone. Not a single tree stump stands as witness to the holocaust. Large rocks have been reduced to gravel and sand, the charred and blackened forest floor is fourteen inches deep in ash. After searching through the residue, we find a few twisted metal parts from the Ford Blitz tanker and some yards further on what looks like the remains of John Crowe's ute chassis and, beside it, two feet of stainless-steel chain, the links welded into the shape of a hunchback's spine.

There is not the slightest trace of John Crowe or Whacka Morrissey, they have been cremated, disappeared in a furious puff of smoke, reduced in an instant into being a part of the burning, malevolent air.

I suppose I must have been in a state of near collapse by the time I got to Yankalillee where the fire has arrived before me, though not yet into the town proper. It has now reached the outer rim of the gorge and is beginning to enter the town itself. The firefighters have given up any further hope of stopping the fire before it tumbles into the gorge. Yankalillee cannot be saved.

Tommy must have pulled them all back into town. The streets are strangely quiet as I enter the outskirts. On the hill I can see the gaol and, further up, the loony bin. I think of the twin aunties, confused, fingering their rosaries, their thin lips supplicating. There is no movement, no cars and the King Street I cycle down on little Ann's bicycle is completely empty. There are no lights on in the post office, which means Mrs Thomas and Marg O'Loughlan have been pulled out. I pass the deserted service station and wonder about the petrol bowsers. Will the underground tanks explode, a Red Steer of man's making?

I'm too tired almost to think. I suppose that everyone's gone, Nancy and Bozo and little Colleen, the town empty except for those volunteers who remain, though I can't see any of them about either. Many would have left when things became hopeless at the gorge, they'd have gone to salvage what they could from their homes and to get their wives and children to safety. Then I think of Lake Sambell, the only decent stretch of water anywhere near. Big Jack would have moved them all down to the lake shore, which is the furthermost point from the fire.

Somewhere there is a bell ringing, not the fire station bell, it's St Stephen's. It's near the rim of the gorge and will be one of the first buildings to go as it's constructed almost entirely of ship-lapped wood. What would Father Crosby be doing ringing the church bell? Too late for that! My mind is too tired to figure things out. Should I rescue him? How could I do that? Imagine a bottoms-wiping certificate for rescuing Father Crosby! Nancy would never forgive me. It's suicide to go down there anyway. Maybe it's the wind? There's a Force 7 blowing, driving the fire up to and into the gorge, maybe it's catching the bell tower, ringing the bell of its own accord? I can't be bothered to think it out. Anyway Father Crosby, being a priest, will probably go to heaven. Nancy says priests don't have to qualify first, which is all wrong, and they should change the law.

The streetlights are on but they're not helping a lot, the acrid smell of fire is everywhere and the sky is filled with billowing black, white and grey smoke mixing with the low cloud. I think this must be what the last day on earth will be like. The air crackles and explodes and is filled with sparks, crazy fire embers darting everywhere. You can sense that death is on its way, it fills my nostrils. There's rolling thunder and a streak of lightning crosses the tumbling sky, a closer burst of thunder follows. I look to the west where the rain should come if ever it does. The sky is mocking us, it's been like this for weeks, growling, taunting us, dry-eyed and uncaring. I glance back towards the gorge and see the orange sheets of flame rising up out of it and St Stephen's is briefly caught in its light. In my mind's eye I see the statue of the Virgin Mary behind the altar enveloped in flames, the Mother of God burning in an Australian hell.

It's downhill to Lake Sambell and the last bit is a fairly steep incline. My legs are so tired, they'll barely move but from now it's coasting all the way down, with the road ending in a small pier right at the lake's edge. The fierce wind is behind me, increasing my speed, and the air in my face is like a constant slapping from a hot towel. I try to put on the brakes but the heat pumping through the blackened fire country has long since melted the brake pads and I'm going at a thousand miles an hour and out of control. The little bike reaches the end of the pier and takes off and I'm flying through the air and come crashing down into the lake. The water embraces me in a gargle of bubbles and I've never felt anything so lovely in my whole life.

When I surface, I can see hundreds of townspeople gathered on the shore. They've seen me coming and it's the only funny thing that's happened all day. They're still laughing as I struggle out of the water, which isn't much higher than my waist. Then Bozo comes running, knees high, splashing through the shallows. He grabs my outstretched hand, pulling me against his chest, he's crying and hugging me in the water. Then the first drops of rain fall and you can see them sizzling on the shore, each drop like a tiny explosion. There's a cry from the crowd, then a clap of thunder to drown it, then another. People have their faces to the sky, you can see them in the orange glow from the direction of the gorge. The drops come harder and faster, beating the surface of the lake. Bozo hugs my head, 'You've brought the rain, Mole, you've brought the fucking rain!' He's bawling his head off. The rains have come at last.

Chapter Twenty

Funny that, a fire, so big there was no way of stopping it, is about to gobble up a town and all it takes is one downpour, one big thunderstorm and it's not only tamed but it's effectively out. Yankalillee is saved, people can go back to their houses and climb into the same beds as they got out of this morning.

Most of the men head for the pub, six o'clock closing ignored. If a bloke can't have a drink after he's fought a fire then the government can get stuffed. They'll have to arrest the whole bloody town is the general sentiment. Anyway, Big Jack Donovan is the law around Yankalillee and he's the one going from pub to pub, thanking everyone for a good job done. So while the women are busy unpacking their precious things from the car or the ute or the council trucks Big Jack's organised to take the possessions of people who don't have their own transport, the men are busy getting well and truly pissed. By morning the tales of derring-do will have reached mythical proportions.

Tommy isn't with them drinking, though we don't know this at the time. The firefighters and townsfolk are offering him drinks but he refuses, it's probably the first time in his life he's knocked back a free drink. Meanwhile he's asking anyone who will listen if they've seen John Crowe or Whacka Morrissey. He's been told about his mate going back to help start the Ford tanker, but he has to make sure nobody's seen the two of them since.

There's been a lot of confusion and the gorge is fairly long so he may have missed John Crowe, Tommy thinks. Or he may have returned after they'd pulled back into town and he's missed him in the crowd. His commonsense says they are not reasonable assumptions, John Crowe would make his presence known. In his heart Tommy hopes what he's beginning to fear isn't what's happened.

It's not that the other fighters are not concerned, they've had a long day and fought hard and they reckon, quite correctly, that John Crowe is an experienced firefighter and knows how to look after himself. Moreover Whacka's a stubborn old bastard, but he'll listen to John Crowe and do what he says. 'They'll be right, mate, no worries. Take more than a fire to get them, they'll turn up in the mornin', you'll see' is the general tenor of the replies Tommy receives.

Tommy's been to the post office, where Mrs Thomas and Marg O'Loughlan are back on duty, trying to contact the surrounding farms. If John Crowe hasn't returned, maybe he's taken shelter at one of the valley properties. Mrs Thomas tells him the Woolshed Valley line is still down and they can't send a linesman from Wodonga until morning. She tries places nearer to Yankalillee but comes up with no news about the two firemen.

While all this is going on, I've been taken home from the lake by Bozo, with Nancy and little Colleen and all the Bitzers in the restored Diamond T. The old truck is packed with our precious stuff. Nancy's sewing machine, embroidery materials, one small suitcase containing all Mike's blue ribbons, the family photo album and the scrapbook.

The scrapbook has a lot about Nancy winning ribbons at the various shows but Nancy has carefully scratched out her name whenever it's mentioned. In her neat handwriting she's written 'Michael Maloney' above her scratched-out name. There's also the clippings on Bozo's boxing career, the Olympics and the Key to the City Parade down King Street to the Town Hall (ha-ha, Yankalillee a city!). There's all the stuff in the *Gazette* about Sarah's pregnancy, and the university brouhaha takes up nearly half the scrapbook. There's even a little bit about me. Mostly the bottoms-wiping certificate episode and the latest, 'The Diary of Anna Dombrowski' stuff by Saggy Tits, Yankalillee's smut-rustler and fearless reporter.

When you see it all together like that, it's amazing how much trouble us Maloneys have caused in our time. Nancy's even cut out and pasted in the bits about Tommy being sentenced for this or that misdemeanour or petty theft over the years.

She's also got all the pots, pans and dishes in a big cardboard box, another large suitcase is full of her yellow-daisy dresses, then there's the TV set and a heap of blankets and cushions. Later, Nancy explains her choices, 'Gotta have a dress to wear that fits (daisy dresses), gotta eat (pots, pans and dishes), gotta make a living (sewing machine), gotta have a bit of relaxation (Bozo's still-to-be-fixed TV), gotta sleep somewhere (blankets etc), but most of all, gotta have our memories (scrapbook and photo album).'

Bozo's taken his old radio, his boxing gloves and his Olympic medal. There is nothing little Colleen and me have that's precious so they don't bother, except for little Colleen's doll which Tommy gave her with the money from his Christmas heist six years ago and it's beginning to look a little worse for wear. Bozo's also taken the old .22 rifle Mrs Barrington-Stone's husband gave me, plus a packet of ammo (defence?).

They've taken me home to dress my burns and because there's not much left in me to celebrate the end of the fire, I don't see Tommy to tell him about the Red Steer.

Of course, I know nothing about John Crowe going back into the forest after Whacka Morrissey and the Ford Blitz, so I haven't put two and two together either. I don't even know John Crowe's missing. All I want to do is to get out of my wet clothes and go to bed. It's still raining cats and dogs anyway so there's no danger of the fire reigniting. In the morning I'll get little Ann Park's bicycle out of the bottom of the lake, polish it up a treat and put in new brake pads. What I know for sure is that I'm going to sleep for about a thousand hours. I doubt there'll be a garbage run tomorrow anyway and if there is, the town can get stuffed, this Maloney isn't participating.

Fortunately Nancy didn't take all the blankets and pillows from the house when they evacuated, because the ones in the back of the Diamond T are soaked through from the rain. I've already had one wet-blanket episode for the day.

I haven't eaten all day and my throat is so sore and raw from breathing in hot smoke and stuff in the air that I can't bear the thought of swallowing. Besides, I can barely talk. Nancy's smeared a tube of Savlon all over my arms, legs and face, with me ouching at her every touch. My ears sort of naturally stick out a bit and they feel like someone's ironed them with a flat iron. I'm so tired Bozo has to help me undress and pull off my boots and socks. The soles of my feet are one big blister, which I haven't even noticed as separate from all the other sorenesses. It's been a long day since we did the garbage run before dawn and the coming of the great Yankalillee fire.

First daylight's coming through the window when I feel someone shaking me. I don't want to open my eyes because the pain has already hit me. The skin on my arms and legs seems to be stretched tight and it hurts like hell, my face feels like it's been clawed by a cat.

'Don't touch me!' I yell out. My eyes are burning inside their sockets and feel swollen and when I open them they sting bad. It's Tommy standing beside my bunk.

'Wake up, Mole,' he demands. There's enough light in the room for me to see that he looks like shit, but I don't smell any alcohol on his breath. It takes only a moment longer to see that he's sober.

'Wha', whazza matter?' My voice is hoarse.

'The eucalyptus forest, before you get to Boundary Road, you see anything coming in?' I can't think, I'm hurting and still half-asleep. He grabs me by the arm and I scream.

'John Crowe, the Ford Blitz in the forest?' Tommy asks again.

'What's he doing there?' I ask stupidly. Well, perhaps not so stupidly, no firefighter would have stopped in the forest with the fire approaching like it was.

Tommy doesn't answer. 'Did ya, Mole? Tell me!' There's panic in his voice.

'I didn't get that close, I took the back way, the forest was burning.' Then I connect and make sense of what he's saying. 'Oh shit!'

'What, what?'

'I seen a Red Steer, an explosion, it was like an atom bomb!' Tommy doesn't seem to understand. 'Big ball of fire, jumped maybe a mile, trees were thrown up above the canopy.'

'Come!' Tommy says. 'Get yer gear on.'

'Don't think I can, I'm burned bad!'

'Fuck you, Mole! Now get your gear on, yer hear me!'

Tommy can say things like that to us when he's drunk, we don't take no notice, but it's not the way he'll speak when he's sober. Bozo's suddenly awake and leaning on his elbow, 'He's not going, he's crook. Leave Mole alone, I'll go.' He doesn't call him 'Dad' or anything, just gets out of his bunk and stands in front of Tommy in the nuddy.

Tommy suddenly crumples to the floor and covers his face with his hands. He's sobbing. Then he gets to his knees and brings his hands together like he's begging and starts jabbering to Bozo in some strange language. He grabs a hold of Bozo's ankles and starts to kiss his feet, sobbing and jabbering away, shaking all over, looking up pop-eyed, frightened, then down again, kissing Bozo's feet, pleading.

'Shit!' Bozo says, looking down at me, 'What's he saying?' He's trying to kick out of Tommy's grasp but Tommy's holding on for dear life, his hands, surprisingly strong, like manacles around Bozo's ankles.

Suddenly Tommy jumps to his feet and he runs like hell. We hear him crashing through the house. Next thing there's the sound of an engine starting and a car pulling away. Bozo runs to the window to see a dark-green ute taking off, skidding, spraying mud in the puddled street.

'Jesus!' Bozo says, turning from the window, 'What happened there?'

'It's John Crowe, he's dead, the Red Steer got him.' I explain it to Bozo, what I've seen, 'Can't be certain, of course, but what else? He hasn't come back.'

Bozo seems stunned, 'John Crowe?'

'It's only a guess, but if he was in the forest, anywhere near, there's no way he'd be coming out.'

'Christ, I hope you're wrong, mate,' Bozo says. 'Can't be, he'd be too smart to get caught in the forest with the fire approaching, surely?'

'It wasn't like that, he'd have thought he was well ahead of the fire, still a mile away.'

He nods, thinking, then says, 'He had our ute, didn't he?'

'Yeah, I reckon that would be gone.'

Bozo doesn't dwell on it, just shakes his head. 'Let's hope you're wrong about both,' he says again. Then being him he gets down to practical matters, 'We'll wait until seven o'clock and go see Big Jack at his house. Reckon you can get up? Walk?'

Big Jack's wife, Terri, brings her hands up to her mouth when she sees me. 'Oh, my goodness!' she exclaims. I haven't looked in the mirror so I don't know what she sees, but if it looks like it feels it can't be too pretty. She goes to the first-aid box she keeps in the back room and gets some ointment and pretty soon I'm ouching all over again. Then she cooks us breakfast, scrambled eggs, my throat feels a little better and I wait until the eggs are not too hot, can't come at the toast and tea though. I tell Big Jack the story of the Red Steer.

'The Red Steer, you saw it?' It's the police officer in him asking. He nods, 'Hmm, heard about them, never seen one myself, don't know anyone who has.' You can hear the doubt in his voice. I begin to wonder if I saw it myself, you know with everything that's gone on before.

'Mole wouldn't make it up,' Bozo says, also picking up on the doubt in Big Jack's voice.

'No, of course not. Tommy was asking everywhere last night. Not like him to refuse a drink. We all thought John Crowe would show up eventually, if not last night, first thing this morning. Never know, still may, hey? Mind you, not too many of the fighters were in a fit state to go looking for him in the rain and even less so after it stopped.' He smiles slightly. 'About midnight I could have arrested the whole male population of Yankalillee for drunk and disorderly conduct.'

So Bozo and me get into the police car with Big Jack Donovan and drive to Boundary Road and turn into the dirt road running alongside the eucalyptus forest. Everywhere we look it's just blackened stumps and trees on the one side and blackened earth on the other with the ash stained dark by the rain.

I think to myself, this time there won't be any regeneration, this eucalyptus forest ain't coming back to life, no way! The road turns into the forest and everywhere we're surrounded by trees that look like spent match sticks. About three miles in, we spot the ute where the road turns again suddenly. 'There's his ute!' we both yell out, thinking it's John Crowe's Holden, but almost at the same moment we realise it's not, it's the right colour, green, but it's an International.

'It's Tommy's,' Bozo says, 'the one he used this morning.'

'Tommy got a ute?' Big Jack asks, surprised.

'Nah, must have borrowed one,' I say quickly. Bozo glances at me, we both know that Big Jack reckons the same as we do, that Tommy's pinched the ute, desperate to find his mate.

'We'll get it back to its rightful owner soon enough,' Big Jack says quietly. 'Probably some bloke too drunk to drive, Tommy's done him a favour.'

We pull up to examine the International but there's nothing in it except some firefighting gear in the back. Big Jack writes down the registration number. After that, we carry on in the police car, take the bend and then into a little dip when Big Jack suddenly slams the brakes on. 'Holy Shit!' he exclaims. For a hundred yards or more in a rough circle there is nothing, not even a stump, nothing. After a few moments Big Jack Donovan turns to me, 'I'd never have believed it unless I'd seen it with my own eyes, Mole! Sorry if I sounded doubtful earlier on, son.'

I've already described what we saw when we got to the spot where the Red Steer landed, but there's no Tommy to be seen. We see his footsteps in the wet ash and then out again and heading away down the road in the opposite direction to the ute. The road leads out of the forest and towards the hills. It's the best thing could happen, Tommy going walkabout. But what his footsteps do say to all of us is that he knows John Crowe is dead.

Bozo found the bits of the Ford tanker and then the part of the chassis from John Crowe's company ute we still owed a lot of money on. Later Bozo will tell me he had insurance built into the hire-purchase price and I'm glad he's taken the spoon out of the sink as usual. If we had to pay for it without having its use to make the payments, I suppose it would send us broke. Big Jack takes the twisted length of welded stainless-steel chain and puts it in the boot of the police car. He turns and looks at the devastation all around us. For a long time he says nothing, then he sighs. 'The worst part is knocking on the door and telling the wife,' he says, then he shakes his head, 'It's always the good ones that go!'

Which is a pretty strange thing for him to say, him being the law and all, and with John Crowe no angel and giving him a fair amount of aggro in the past. Maybe he meant Whacka Morrissey? If I don't sound choked up about John Crowe, it's because so much has happened and I haven't grasped it all yet. He was a good bloke and always kind to me and I liked him a helluva lot. Him and Tommy were like brothers and they may not have been angels but they never hurt anyone and he was the only person who could make Tommy laugh. I'm going to miss him an awful lot.

In the wash-up from the fire, there's four houses burnt down as well as the picnic rotunda in the Historic Park, St Stephen's and the priest's house. Father Crosby is without a place to sleep and the Catholics of Yankalillee are without a place to worship.

'Ha!' Nancy says, 'Just goes to show, don't it? Protestant church didn't burn down, did it? God was sending out a message to Father Crosby to mend his ways, nothing's more certain!' The proof she offers is that the baptism font is the only thing left standing. It was full of rainwater the next morning. 'Clear as the nose on your face,' Nancy points out, 'First the baptism of fire to cleanse his wicked ways and then a new beginning, the font filled with God's tears!'

No use pointing out to her that the Church of England was in our street and the Presbyterians are practically in the middle of town and the Congregational Church up the hill a bit, all of them are well away from the gorge. Also that the font was made of sandstone. Nancy doesn't put much store in sheer logic. 'Tell me anything in this world that's been brought about with logic alone?' She always challenges when we've got her cornered. 'Bollocks to logic! If logic had anything to do with it, none of you would be here!'

As it turned out, the Virgin Mary didn't get consumed in the flames of an Australian hell. What's more, Father Crosby ends up getting a bottoms-wiping certificate from the shire president, Philip Templeton, and, as well, a commendation to Rome from the Bishop.

Nancy says you couldn't have expected better from Philip Bloody Templeton and the shire council, but the commendation to Rome just goes to show how corrupt the Holy Church has become in the twentieth century! Also, what a miserable opportunist the Bishop is, licking the boots of His Holiness the Pope.

It wasn't any use pointing out to her that the shire council were all Protestants and so Father Crosby would have had to be pretty worthy in their eyes to get any sort of praise from them.

Nancy's never forgiven the Bishop for chastising her about the radios Tommy wanted for the bushfire brigade in 1946. How they had to collect the same amount for the Missionaries of the Sacred Heart in New Guinea so that the Yankalillee Catholics could be seen to have their priorities right. When we remind her that it was her said she doubted Father Crosby even consulted the Bishop, she says, 'Yeah, well, same difference, it was him, the Bishop, who also opposed Sarah going to university. He's tarred with the same brush as Father Crosby!'

This is what happened to bring Father Crosby his new-found fame. Remember when we were being briefed by John Crowe at the fire station and there were these two new volunteers and Tommy said he'd take the Collins Street cocky, Michael Mooney, because he knew nobody else would. Then Alan Phillips shouts out that old Merv O'Hare has carked it, so he'll take young Lindsay Jarvis in his team?

Well, old Merv is due to be buried and naturally enough with a name like O'Hare he's one of ours and so there's a grave dug for him in the churchyard. Normally he'd be buried in the Catholic section of the cemetery, but because the family has promised Father Crosby a nice little cheque for the stained-glass window he's been on about for years, he's being buried next to the half a dozen tombstones of prominent past Yankalillee Catholics who have, no doubt for the same reasons, been given the privilege of a churchyard burial.

The fire gets in the way of the burial and when it threatens the town, Father Crosby is told to pack a suitcase and someone will come and pick him up. Well, the someone arrives and Father Crosby puts his suitcase in the boot of their car and then says he'll be using his bicycle to get out himself. But he doesn't. He stays and rescues the two silver candlesticks and the three-foot-high gilt crucifix that stands behind the altar and the silver incense burner then dumps them all into Old Merv O'Hare's empty grave.

After that, Father Crosby spends an hour trying to get the carved wooden statue of the Virgin Mary down from the wall at the back of the altar. He's dragged a mattress from the priest's house next door and put it on the floor directly below the Virgin and somehow he's unscrewed the Mother of God from the wall and she's fallen, face-first, onto the mattress but only her nose and crown have broken off. Then Father Crosby somehow dragged the three-hundred-pound, six-foot-high carving out of the church, across the lawn to the grave, and dropped it in there with the other church treasures.

By this time, the fire is into the gorge, soon to be coming out the other side as a roaring furnace, with St Stephen's directly in its path. With the flames in sight and him near exhausted, Father Crosby grabs a shovel and pours dirt over the grave covering the church artefacts to protect them from the approaching fire. The flames are now practically licking at the clapboard walls of St Stephen's.

Maybe it was stupid, but you've got to admit it was pretty brave. Folk said he only just got away in time and that the hem of his soutane was burning when he arrived at the lake on his Malvern Star. Which is bullshit. If it had been alight, he'd have let it go for a while and then doused it and he'd never have taken it off again. Anyway, Nancy says his order doesn't always need to wear a soutane and it's pure affectation on his part. 'There'll be no stopping him now. Can you imagine? Father Crosby, Priest of the Flames!' she says, disgusted with the whole thing.

Anyway, now he's a hero of the church and they'll probably make him a saint when he's dead. Him saving The Blessed Virgin from the flames of an Australian hell! So much for Nancy's saying that few things in this world are brought about by logic alone. Of course, Nancy doesn't see this saying of hers working in Father Crosby's particular case. Far as she's concerned, what's happened shows what an irresponsible idiot our priest is, wearing a dress when he doesn't have to and putting his own life in danger for the sake of a wooden statue.

Later the Italian migrants build a new church out of stone, which the Catholic community pays for. All the Catholics help a bit with the work, but mostly the Maltese and the Italians. It takes more than a year to rebuild and it's now called 'St Stephen's Church of the Flames' and the baptismal font is placed in the very centre of the new church rather than in a corner like in the old one.

The Italians also fixed up the Holy Virgin and carved a new crown and nose. They've done a really good job. With it back on the wall high up, you can't tell it's been damaged. They've added this wooden plinth that's got flames carved around the edges at the Virgin Mary's feet and they've painted them gold and now she's called 'The Virgin of the Flames'. Nancy says it makes you want to puke.

There's also two stained-glass windows, one on either side of the Virgin. One window shows eucalyptus trees on fire with Christ's ascension up into heaven, you can see the three crosses on a hill through the flaming trees. Looking at it, little kids are bound to think that Christ was an Australian who went to heaven when he was caught up in a bushfire. The other window shows the baby Jesus lying in straw in a horse trough with a donkey in the corner. There's a star up the top of the window shining down. The window isn't big enough to show Joseph and Mary and the Three Wise Men, but I guess everyone knows they're there from Sunday School.

The gilt crucifix is not so lucky. If you look at it carefully and close one eye and squint, you can see it's dented in the middle. That's where the Virgin hit Jesus in the guts when she toppled into Merv O'Hare's grave and not even the Italians have been able to restore Him perfectly.

There's a new brass plaque on the baptismal font that says:

'The Font of the Flames'
Yankalillee child, thou art
born knowing Original Sin,
condemned to the eternal
flames, the furnace of Hell.
Thou shalt be redeemed,
by an all-forgiving Saviour
and baptised in holy water,
these blessed Tears of God.

It just appeared there mysteriously one Sunday shortly after the new church was consecrated by the Bishop, a shiny brass plaque, properly drilled and screwed into the sandstone base which had been left blackened by the fire and is now known as 'The Font of the Flames'.

I reckon Catholics are their own worst enemy because soon enough the story gets about that the rainwater that fell into the baptismal font on the night of the fire is inexhaustible and the font never gets empty. So every new baby is now baptised in the original rainwater that everyone calls 'The Tears of God' from the great Yankalillee fire.

What's more, Father Crosby does nothing to contradict this. In fact, there's no holding 'The Priest of the Flames' back and Nancy says, far from repenting, he's a worse bloody hypocrite than before, if that's possible.

After the inquest, when the coroner finds John Crowe and Whacka Morrissey died by misadventure, there's a memorial service held in the churchyard next to the burnt-out St Stephen's. Sarah, with Templeton, Mike, Morrie and Sophie, come from Melbourne for the funeral. Almost the whole town turns out on the day, Catholics and Protestants, and they've rigged loudspeakers up on poles so everyone can hear the funeral service. The crowd is so big they spread to the Historic Park right along the gorge.

The entire shire council is in attendance, the Bishop comes from Bendigo in a big black Buick and the Cardinal sends a message of condolence to both families and so does Premier Bolte. The deaths are even mentioned in the State Parliament. The bushfire brigades from all the surrounding districts including Wangaratta, Chiltern and Wodonga attend, almost a thousand men come dressed in their firefighting overalls.

Both John Crowe and Whacka Morrissey were pretty ordinary blokes who, under normal circumstances, would have had a box and a few members of the family and friends, with a bunch or two of flowers at the graveside and that would be it. So it's not a bad way to go with over three thousand people attending and a heap of wreaths you couldn't pole-vault over.

However, other than his wife Trish, John Crowe's most important mourner is missing. Tommy's been gone a week. Nobody says anything but lots of people know how close Tommy and John Crowe have been since they were kids, the only time they've been separated was during the war when John Crowe was sent to Darwin in the quartermaster-general's outfit to dish out boots, shoelaces and socks for the use of, to the troops. He admitted to me once that it was a scam he'd worked out to avoid active service. 'No point in getting your arse blown away by some harakiri Jap, is there, Mole? Wars come and go but I've only got the promise of three score and ten, don't want to put that at risk, do I?' Some of the folk at the service come up quietly to shake Nancy's hand and wish her well.

Father Crosby is in a new surplice that has these red and orange flames appliquéd on the back. He must have reckoned his chances of getting Nancy to embroider them weren't good, because he's got a dressmaker or someone to put on the flames. Nancy says it looks vulgar and is machine-stitched and in typical bad taste, but, after all, what can you expect from a Diocesan priest.

All the same, I reckon she's pretty insulted that he didn't come to her and ask. They may be mortal enemies but that's not the surplice's fault. 'A job worth doing is a job worth doing well,' she says as her final bitter comment.

I must say that the Priest of the Flames has prepared a nice sermon, which he concludes by saying, 'John Crowe and William Sean Morrissey have gone straight to Heaven as they've already done their time in the terrible fires of Hell. I commend their immortal souls to Almighty God and ask Him to embrace them in His love everlasting.' Then he stops and sort of looks into the distance:

'May the road rise up to meet you
May the wind be ever at your back
May the sun shine warm upon your face
May the rain fall soft upon your fields
And until we meet again
May God hold you in the palm of His hand.'

I tell you what, there's a few tears about, and not just the women.

A big wake is held at the Shamrock by the Yankalillee and Eldorado firefighters together with the family and friends of both the deceased. Trish Crowe announces that she's going back to look after her ailing mother in Shepparton. She says if Bozo's willing to shoulder the debts in the business, she'll be happy to sign John Crowe Transport over to him. Bozo thanks her and says he agrees to be responsible for the money owed and we won't change the name of the company. He'll always be proud to have been associated with John Crowe, who was the best business partner anyone could have had.

Since coming back from the Rome Olympics, Bozo has been pretty confident with people. He's still the same quiet person who doesn't have any tabs on himself and is a real good bloke, but now he can handle himself in any company. I reckon he could meet the Queen or the Governor-General or even maybe Bob Menzies if he had to, and still look calm. I'm proud that I'm his brother, not because of what he's done but because of who he is. It's nice to know we've made a Bozo in our family.

I forgot to say that I was pretty sore coming back from the forest where John Crowe and Whacka Morrissey died and so I didn't go out to the lake to fetch little Ann's bicycle. I doubt I could have walked the distance from home with the blisters on my feet. Next day, though, I made it and changed into my cossie behind some bulrushes. It took me ages to find the bike, even though I knew exactly where I'd landed coming down the hill. But when it and me were back on shore, I saw that all the paintwork had been damaged, blistered by the heat from the fire. The little bike was a mess. I wheeled it home because I was still too sore to ride it.

That night I told Bozo my problem. As you know, he's built several bikes. He comes out and has a look at it and says, 'Leave it to me, Mole.'

Anyway, a couple of days later he delivers it back. In the meantime I'm feeling pretty guilty, little Ann uses it to ride to school. Edie Park hasn't called, which is what I've been expecting. You know, 'Fair go, Mole, Ann needs her bike!' She's got every right.

Well, Bozo takes it down to the shire-council workshops where John Crowe used to work and explains everything to Macca McKenzie the depot foreman, the bloke who takes the rabbits I shoot for his greyhounds. Macca says he saw me crashing into the lake, she'll be right, no worries. Next thing, the spraypainter at the workshops strips down the bike and sprays it a brilliant fire-engine red with shiny black mudguards. They take up a bit of a collection among the mechanics and truck drivers and they put on new tyres and brake pads and a light with a dynamo running off the back wheel. It never could have looked as good when it was brand new. Talk about posh! I'm that chuffed and owe Bozo and them at the depot heaps. From now on Macca McKenzie gets regular rabbits for his dogs.

Bozo drives me out to Woolshed Park and you should have seen the little girl's eyes when we unloaded her bike. She can't believe what she's seeing.

'We didn't like to ask about the bike,' Edie Park admits, 'Not after what you did for us, Mole.'

'I didn't do nothing, Mrs Park,' I protest.

'That's what you think,' Tom Park says, 'You stayed with my two girls, you'll do me, Mole Maloney.'

'We've put you in for a commendation. We wrote a letter to Philip Templeton,' Edie Park adds.

No point in telling her that's the Protestant equivalent of spitting on your mother's grave. She must have forgotten all the stuff in the *Gazette* about Murray Templeton and Sarah. Anyway, Tom Park comes back with a leg of lamb and says they've got most of their stock back in the general muster and he can't thank me enough. No point in telling him that all I did was lie next to his wife and little daughter, wrapped in a wet blanket.

Ten days go by and I'm back at school and to my astonishment, with Anna Dombrowski gone, I'm elected vice-prefect. It's a big surprise because there's lots better than me should have got the job. I've always been a bit of a loner and I'm not so sure I'm as happy as I'm supposed to be over the big honour.

Nancy is over the moon. I think she thinks because I'm the one with male Maloney blood in me I could be a bit of a throwback, it being not very far to throw back. Nancy reckons that the Maloney women she's met from the Irish-Australian tribe have been good to middling, it's the men who turn out, one and all, to be absolute bastards. Even though I'm not Tommy's son, I'm still a Maloney and the only Maloney male in this new generation. So maybe, going on past records, she's a bit worried about how I'm going to end up.

After two weeks, I'm getting worried. Tommy's stayed away longer in the past but not a lot longer, and I'm concerned that he's gone off somewhere and killed himself. We don't talk about it among ourselves because it's sort of an unspoken thing amongst us Maloneys that when Tommy's gone walkabout, he just isn't there and we all get on with our lives. So we behave as if everything's normal, which we all know it isn't. This isn't like the other times, sooner or later we're going to have to go to Big Jack Donovan and report him as a missing person. It's funny that, Tommy's been a missing person since he came back from the war.

Then three weeks after the fire, he turns up on the Friday night.

Now, Tommy Maloney isn't what you'd call a handsome bloke, he's not even an ugly-looking bloke, he's a real hopeless mess. Now he seems to have lost at least a stone in weight, maybe more, which in Tommy's case is bloody nigh impossible to speculate upon. He's thin as a rake anyway and now he's back to being the drover's dog, all prick and ribs, Nancy told us about when he come out of the prisoner-of-war camp under the Japanese. His eyes are dark hollows sunk deep into his head and you can see the break in his jaw where the bone has knitted and grown crooked and his bad shoulder is jammed up near his left ear and against his neck. He makes Quasimodo look like Cary Grant.

'Jesus!' is all that Nancy says when he comes through the front door, 'Look what the cat brought in!' She sits him down in the kitchen and makes him a cup of milky tea with six spoons of sugar and fetches him a cigarette. Tommy never stinks when he gets back, but now he smells to high heaven, I doubt if he's washed in the three weeks he's been away and his hair is matted and wild, his skin is black from the fire, worse even than when he's been on a binge down at the lake. Nancy hands him his cuppa tea and says, 'Take it out the back and then when you've drank it, get going to the shower, Mole will bring you a towel and clean clothes. When you get back, I'll cut your hair and give you some grub. You look a right mess, Tommy Maloney.'

That's the funny thing, Nancy still loves Tommy and you can see she's happy to have him back. 'We gave your mate a right proper funeral, you should've been there, you'd have been proud of this town for once.'

'Funeral? What, you find something?'

'No, it was a memorial service.'

'That don't count,' Tommy says and takes his tea and goes out the back. I expect he'll clean up and then go on a binge. For once he's got a right, though from the looks of him, if he abuses his body much further, he'll be joining John Crowe pretty soon.

Tommy comes back from his shower and Nancy has a kitchen chair out the back and an old towel and she's got the barber's clippers out. 'Christ Almighty!' she exclaims, you've got nits, where have you been?'

'Dunno,' Tommy says. He's always like this for the first few hours he gets back and talks in sentences of one or two words, possibly because he hasn't talked to a single soul for three weeks and has temporarily lost the knack of conversation.

'I can do two things,' Nancy suggests, 'blast you with DDT powder every day for the next week and comb out the lice, or I can shave it all off. Make up yer mind, handsome.'

'Shave,' Tommy says, 'DDT's fucking up nature, hair won't grow back.' It's a long sentence for him under these circumstances.

'Tommy Maloney, you'll not use that word in this house,' Nancy remonstrates, but she's got a bit of a smile at the corners of her mouth.

With all his hair shaved off, he looks even worse. While he was taking a shower, I walked into the shed out back to bring him his clean clothes. He was soaping his face and I could see he was all ribs with his gut sunk right in so you could see the lumps in his spine through the skin. His legs and arms were like sticks and his donger looked the only normal part. He's gunna die soon, was all I could think.

At the end of the first week, though, Tommy's looking a bit better, not great, but compared to before, there's a human being in there somewhere and, more importantly, he's still sober, he hasn't touched a drop. He also goes out with us on the garbage run, picking up his fair share of rubbish bins. To look at him, you'd say he couldn't pick up his knife and fork, yet he'll heft a full bin into the back of the Diamond T, which is now doing the garbage run again, with the other truck, the Fargo, doing contract work for the shire council.

Funny thing that, the council sell us the Fargo because they think it's clapped out, then they hire it back to do the work it did before they sold it and pay us for the privilege. Bozo says it's economics, don't have to pay a driver and maintain his vehicle and then there's all the hidden costs the government says you have to pay, like payroll tax and all that sort of stuff.

We're in a bit of trouble. Bozo hasn't got John Crowe to keep the vehicles on the road any more and they're not exactly new, the lot of them. Even though the two trucks are in good nick they're old, and the VW Kombi, because it was put back together after a bad prang, has constant problems. Without John Crowe to maintain them, it's an expense we've never allowed for. Then there's the missing ute, the one John Crowe was driving in the fire that got disappeared by the Red Steer. The insurance said it was not covered for natural disaster, which is flood, fire and earthquake, so they're not paying out. It and the Kombi are the backbone of the freight-delivery business we're building up. There's more money in small parcels to the towns in the district than bulk cartage in the big trucks and Bozo's dead worried because he has to have a ute to cope with the business we're getting.

We're in a real pickle, when I suddenly think of Michael Mooney, the Collins Street cocky Tommy took into our team for the fire. For a while, when we were fighting the fire out at Hopeless Dig, Tommy said I must look after him. He turned out to be a decent sort of a bloke and did what I told him. He could have easily thought I was just a kid but he tried hard and obeyed my instructions and didn't whine or slack off even though he was puffing furiously after a while.

Mr Mooney works in Melbourne during the week and comes up to his property on the weekends. So the next Saturday I get on Bozo's bicycle and go out to this big property he's bought about six miles out of town. He comes out to see me and is really nice and we sit on the verandah and he asks me if I'd like a beer. Neither Bozo nor me drink because there's enough of that going on in our family history anyway. So he has the cook bring out tea and scones with cream and homemade strawberry jam, which are nearly as good as the ones Mrs Barrington-Stone's cook makes.

I tell him about the insurance and he asks what company. I've brought all the papers to show him. To cut a long story short, I leave the insurance policy with him and on the following Monday he phones from Melbourne and says there'll be a cheque in the mail. Talk about pulling strings! Sure enough, two days later, the cheque from the insurance company for the full amount arrives and with it a letter that says it's nice to do business with us and they'd like to continue the relationship. Nancy says, 'Just goes to show, it's not what you know, but who you know.' She says I showed real initiative and looks pleased that I'm showing signs of not being a male Maloney throwback.

We don't forget however that it was Tommy's kindness that done it for us in the first place. But here's the joke, the letter is signed 'Michael Mooney, Chairman'. The following weekend when Bozo and me drive out to thank him, he looks serious before he says, 'No, no, lads, it's me who has to thank you. It's easy to forget other people's circumstances when you're sitting in the chairman's chair. For once in my life, I saw things from the client's side. I'm ashamed we treated you like that.' I reckon he can stay on in our team. In time he'll make a pretty good firefighter.

After he's been home a month, Tommy comes to me after school on the Friday afternoon. 'Bring your sleeping bag and the rifle, we're going bush, Mole.'

'But you've just got back!' I protest.

'This is different.'

I don't want to upset him and I've been meaning to tell him, so I say carefully, 'Dad, it's my matriculation year and I'm vice-prefect of the school, I can't go bush except maybe a few days in the school holidays.'

'But it's the weekend, no school.'

'I've got to study, I've got an essay and a Maths test coming up.'

He looks at me. 'You'll not go because of an essay and sums?' I can see he can't believe his ears.

''Fraid so,' I say, biting my lip.

He's silent for a long time then he says hesitatingly, 'I thought it's time you saw the Alpine Ash, *Eucalyptus delegatensis*.'

This time it's me who can't believe his ears. 'Yeah? The Maloney tree?'

Tommy nods.

'I'll go get my sleeping bag,' I say.

'Better take some flour for damper, and tea, we'll live off the land the three days we're away.'

I hesitate. 'I can't, Dad. I've got to be back at school Monday!'

Then I think a moment. All they can do is take my vice-prefect's badge away, I haven't waited five years for that. 'Ah, bugger it! I'll fetch the flour and tea.' At the door I turn back to him, 'If she asks, don't tell Mum we'll be away three days.' It's a silly thing to say, Tommy wouldn't tell her anyway and I'll tell Bozo so Nancy doesn't get worried when we don't return on Sunday night.

I can't believe it, I've waited ever since I turned twelve and I think he's mentioned that big old tree maybe three times and that's only because I've brought it up. Every time I've done so, Tommy's said, 'Not yet, Mole, there'll come a time when it's right to go.'

I can't understand what he means. Once I protested, 'It's only a big old tree! How come there has to be a time that's right?'

'If that's all you think it is, then the time isn't right yet,' he replied.

I often wonder if that's where Tommy goes when he goes walkabout? The Alpine Ash isn't the biggest hardwood tree in the world, because that's the Mountain Ash, *Eucalyptus regnans*, which can grow to near three hundred feet with a trunk ten feet across and it can live up to eight hundred years. But the Alpine Ash, the eucalyptus Tommy's going to show me, can live four hundred years and grow to two hundred and eighty feet with a trunk nearly as large as the Mountain Ash. I can't believe it, the time is right at last!

Chapter Twenty-One

Tommy surprises me when he says we're off to Mount Buffalo, which is sort of the beginning of the high country before you get to the Snowy Mountains. I'm surprised, because we've been in the area often enough and he's never mentioned the big Alpine Ash. Where we're going is only about an hour's drive from Yankalillee, though we'll be going on foot more or less as the crow flies. I'm a bit disappointed because I'd always imagined the big old tree would be growing further up on the Snowy range. I should have known better, Alpine Ash can't grow all that high up, but when a picture, a thing you want to believe, is stuck in your head, you don't ask it to make sense.

'We'll see where the fires went, eh? Should be a fair bit of regeneration,' Tommy says, then adds, 'We'll go the German bloke's way.'

The German is a man named Ferdinand von Mueller, Victoria's first government botanist, who travelled from May Day Hills, which is more or less where Yankalillee stands today, to Mount Buffalo during the gold rush in 1853. We'll follow Myrtle Creek through Buckland Gap to Myrtleford and then on to the little town of Ovens and from there into the national park to Porepunkah and up the slopes of Mount Buffalo. In all, it's a distance of about thirty-two miles, which is a fair bit shorter than going along the Ovens Highway. Though, even if the highway was shorter, Tommy never takes a major road. 'No point, is there? Don't see nothing but trucks and cars.' Anyway, the countryside in the direction of the mountains is a bit up and down and, in good weather, it's a full day-and-a-half trek and then maybe some.

We're travelling light but we've both decided to take our sleeping bags and groundsheets, it can still get cold at night in the mountains or it may rain. I'm carrying a bit of flour and tea and a couple of carrots in my knapsack as well as lugging the .22 and a billy to make a rabbit stew which we'll eat both nights. I've also cut some cheese sandwiches and six hard-boiled eggs to keep us going on the way.

For once I don't forget to take mosquito repellent, as the mozzies can be real bad up the various creeks, though for some mysterious reason they never bite Tommy. I'm the big feast. Mozzies see me coming and right off they send out this high-frequency message, the *zzzzzzzz* you hear that's their HF radio and can be picked up by every mozzie within miles, 'Mole Maloney heading your way, prepare for a banquet!'

'It's because you don't smoke,' Tommy claims. 'You should smoke, cigarette smoke keeps them away.'

'You don't smoke in your sleep and you don't get bit,' I point out.

'Yeah, that's because I sleep next to the fire, smoke there works the same.'

It ain't true, I also sleep next to the fire and the mongrels still get me. I reckon it's because they can't take the alcohol that's built up in Tommy's system over the years. One bite out of Tommy Maloney from a mozzie and I guarantee it drops dead of alcoholic poisoning.

One of the things we had to do last year in English class was to write a poem and I wrote this one, which I admit is a bit cheeky because it comes right out and says that Tommy is an alcoholic. But as there isn't anyone in the whole town that doesn't know this already and talks about it behind our Maloney backs, I thought I'd just bring it out into the open. This is because The Parrot, our English teacher, her real name is Mrs Barrett, told us that poetry could express your innermost and secret emotions and desires, that poetry was the purest form of the truth. The baring of the human soul.

I reckoned Tommy being a drunk is our family's most innermost emotion and wanting him to get better is our greatest desire. That's baring your soul, ain't it? But you can't write something like that and be serious at the same time, can you? You know,

Woe is me!
Got a drunk for a dad.
I'm all screwed up,
Isn't that sad?

So I reckoned I'd do it from a mosquito's viewpoint. It took me ages and ages to get right and then I only got a B+ rather than an A+, which was what I was expecting, because The Parrot said that while the rhyme structure worked well and the theme I chose was worked to its proper conclusion, it was disrespectful of our elders and 'in bad taste'. Nancy said, 'What can you expect, she sings in the choir of the Church of England.'

Anna Dombrowski asked me what I got for my poem and when I told her B+ because it was 'in bad taste', she begged to read it. I showed it to her and she laughed and said it was brilliant. She looked real serious into my eyes and said that she wished she had the courage to write something like that about Chicka Barnes, her stepdad, though she wouldn't know how to make it funny the way I did with Tommy and myself. I should've known then that there was something going on in her life that wasn't nice.

I asked her what she got and she said A+ but that her poem was a con job.

'Why? How can a poem be a con and get A+?'

She shrugged, 'Easy, I didn't have time to write a proper poem so I wrote a bad one about the concentration camp and The Parrot was forced to give an A+.' She grinned, 'If she didn't, it would have been in bad taste on her part!'

Clever, eh? You can see why Anna's top of the class and could've been top of the state if she hadn't run away with Crocodile Brown. I miss her a lot.

Anyway, I showed my poem to Tommy and he laughed and said I was a flamin' genius, that I was a poet and didn't know it, and a chip off the old block because Maloneys have always been bush poets. He took it to the pub to show all his mates and came back and said he wanted ten copies because they all wanted one to keep for themselves.

Mozzie lemonade

All you mozzies gather around
Mole Maloney has been found.
He's what all mosquitoes crave
His blood is mozzie lemonade!
Avoid the father, enjoy the son
Tommy is the dangerous one!
A million mozzies are his toll
Tom's blood is purest alcohol.
You'll have a very nasty death
A single sip your final breath.
Sip the Mole and stay frisky
Nip his dad and you are history!
A mozzie moral has been made
Stay sober, stick to lemonade!

Bushwalking with Tommy is never a hurried experience. It's the process of wandering about that he likes. This is the first time I can remember where the destination was of some importance to us. This doesn't mean, though, he's in a hurry and we stop to examine everything of possible interest as we follow the creek down to the little town of Ovens.

This time our major interest is the recovery after the fires, it's only a matter of weeks but since the rain, the ground cover is already a carpet of green and the eucalyptus canopy is awash with new leaf. The leaves are not yet the army-green of their maturity but come in pale orange, white, yellow and scarlet. It's almost as if the leaves have retained the colours of the fire as a tribute to the renewal of life that it brings to each eucalyptus tree.

There are lots of rabbits around, they too have responded to the fire and I guess their burrows are full of kittens being suckled by the doe in the nesting chamber, which is a sort of side-alley maternity section off the main burrow. They're blind when they're born so can't come out to nibble on the new grass, but in a month they'll be weaned and the doe will get pregnant again and so the cycle begins all over. Once when Tommy explained this to us, Nancy said, 'It's not that different to the Maloney women, no sooner is one brat off the breast when there's another in the oven.'

For once in his life Tommy's got a comeback. 'Don't look at me, woman!'

I reckon Nancy had that coming to her.

While we know rabbits are a plague and I should shoot the females, do a favour to the countryside, later I'll salve my conscience by shooting a couple of bucks in the late afternoon, taking them off the breeding cycle. One buck probably accounts for about a thousand rabbits born in his lifetime and, anyway, in a stew the tougher meat doesn't matter much and I reckon is tastier.

We follow Myrtle Creek and by mid-afternoon get to the little town of Ovens, about twenty miles from Yankalillee. 'Forget the bunny chow, what say we get a couple of steaks for tea tonight?' Tommy says.

It's not like him to suggest something like this, he believes we should live off the land as much as possible. 'I'm skint,' I say with a shrug.

'She's right, I'm payin', he says, 'couple of bottles of lemonade'll go down good as well.'

There's definitely something up. It's not as though he's mean or anything, Tommy will always pay his share and then some, it's just that he's always separated bush and town. The only compromise is a small packet of White Wings for damper and half a packet of Bushells tea and half a jam jar of sugar and a bit of salt. He's even been known to go without flour, tea and sugar and then he'll hunt out a bush called Alpine baeckea. It has a little white flower with scented leaves, which make a sort of lemon-flavoured tea that is drinkable, though you wouldn't want to make a habit of it. Tommy says it's good for rheumatism but I'll have to wait until I'm a grandfather to find out. So why is he offering steaks and lemonade all of a sudden, I ask myself.

'We celebrating something?'

'Nah, not exactly.' He doesn't explain further.

I don't want to show him how impressed I am. 'Suits me, bloody sight better than rabbit stew,' I mumble.

'Have that termorra night, bit of rabbit will go down a treat then.'

Well, we buy a couple of enormous T-bones and two large bottles of lemonade. It's a special treat so I don't mind carrying them. Anyway, with his crook shoulder Tommy can only just manage a small knapsack without the strap on the one side falling down.

From Ovens we walk a little way down an old dirt road, maybe two miles and into the Mount Buffalo National Park. I reckon by sunset we've covered about twenty-three miles and, if we start early, we'll get to the big old mountain about noon tomorrow.

We find a campsite, an old picnic clearing on the banks of Buffalo Creek, and I build a fire, letting it burn down to the hot coals before I make a bit of damper with flour, water, and a sprinkle of sugar and salt. I let it cook on the coals until it's black and burnt on the outside, you only eat the inside. I also do the steaks and boil the billy for tea.

By the way, there's a knack to making billy tea a lot of people don't know. You bring the water to the boil with the lid on, then lift the billy off the fire with a stick, remove the lid and let the water stand maybe a minute. Put the billy back on, but without the lid this time, so it can absorb a bit of the smoke from the fire. Bring it to the boil again and remove it a second time, then add a handful of tea and let it brew until you can't see the bottom of the billy. Toss in a couple of gum leaves at the very end just before you pour it.

A man can't ask for much more. A bit of a rub with repellent to keep the mozzies away, a juicy steak and a piece of damper swilled down with the last of the lemonade and finished off with a mug of hot, sweet billy tea. I reckon life doesn't get much better even if you are the King of England.

The birds are coming in to roost, a kookaburra close by letting everyone know who's the boss and the currawongs, as always, having the last word before all the birds come to silence and the frog and cricket choruses begin.

Tommy's done me a great favour teaching me to love nature and I reckon I've got to respect him heaps for that. No matter what happens to me in my life, I've always got the bush and that's like having a friend you can rely on forever. It's his gift to me and I'm grateful.

It's not long dark, we've eaten and we're into our sleeping bags.

The mozzies are gone with the last of the light, they'll be back again just before dawn. The moon is still hidden behind the trees and the only light is from the fire. There's a bit of a fresh breeze blowing off Mount Buffalo so we've spread our groundsheets at opposite sides of the fire and are snug as a bug in a rug. I've thrown a heap of wood on the embers to build it back up into a fire in an hour or so, this way it should last until around midnight.

The last thing I remember is Tommy sitting up in his sleeping bag, his knees up against his chest, having a final fag. I watch as every time he draws, the tip of his cigarette lights the end of his broken nose. Poor little bugger, he probably wasn't that handsome to start with, but the Japs sure as hell done a good job of smashing up his face.

I wake suddenly. The moon is high above me and it's bright enough to see clearly. The fire is not completely down to embers, a few small flames still lick up, which means it's around eleven o'clock. Then I see Tommy across from me, he's still sitting up in his sleeping bag and he's crying. Not bawling or anything, just quietly sobbing. I'm not sure what to do. Tommy is a pretty private bloke and it would take a fair bit to make him cry. He hasn't cried for John Crowe yet, or if he has, it was when he went walkabout in the bush straight after the Yankalillee fire.

There's been a small marble memorial made to John Crowe and Whacka Morrissey, which has been placed next to the war-memorial names in the rotunda wall. Big Jack Donovan gave Tommy the stainless-steel chain that had its links welded when the Red Steer hit and it's been incorporated into the plaque. When every fireman in the district attended the memorial ceremony and Nick Reed read out the eulogy, I could feel Tommy shaking beside me, his lips trembling, but he didn't cry. Now he is sobbing in the moonlight and I don't know what to do.

I lie there for maybe an hour, playing possum until the fire burns down, almost out. At last I hear Tommy pull the zip on his sleeping bag and lie down. Next thing it's morning and he's shaking me, holding out a mug of tea.

There's been a fair bit of dew on the ground and the grass around is wet. There's also a bit of a chill in the air before sunrise. The currawongs are carolling in the trees beside the river, so it must still be early, they're usually up a good half-hour before the other birds and always well before sun-up. I don't have a watch nor does Tommy, no point in the bush anyway.

'Better get going, Mole,' Tommy says. He waits until I sit up and unzip the sleeping bag, then hands me the mug of steaming tea. I take the mug and place it beside me on the ground and search in my knapsack for the four hard-boiled eggs left over from yesterday and hand him two.

After we eat I go down to the creek where there's still a wisp of mist above the water and have a bit of a wash and clean my teeth. Then I clean up the camp site and make sure the fire is completely dead and we're on our way just before sun-up.

We should be able to make Mount Buffalo a little before noon, though I don't know where the big old Alpine Ash is situated on the mountain or how high the climb to find it. Can't be that high.

I still can't quite believe it's only Mount Buffalo we're heading for. In my imagination I thought the tree must be some place far away. That we'd have to walk days and days and climb over towering cliffs and pass through rough country, mist-filled valleys and over snow-capped mountains, in and out of dark ravines, to finally reach some secret place known only to a Maloney. But no such thing. Mount Buffalo ain't exactly the world's best-kept secret and it's hard to believe there's some place on it no one's been.

Over the years Tommy and me have done this area a good few times and the Alpine Ash could have been reached on any of those occasions, no problem. So why has Tommy always avoided showing me? What's he mean about me not being ready before now? I haven't changed. Sure, I've got a bit older, but I'm still the same Mole Maloney. Seeing the tree now that I'm seventeen or seeing it at any other time, what's the big difference? I sometimes wonder what goes on in Tommy's head and I prepare myself to be disappointed.

We don't mess around too much this morning and only really stop when I shoot a couple of rabbits for our tea, a pair of big bucks, two clean shots through the head. They're handsome fellas a doe would really go for, given half a chance, so I reckon I've taken a couple more bunnies out of the breeding cycle.

In 1863 twenty-four rabbits, brought into Victoria by a homesick Englishman and held in a pen on his farm, escaped during a bushfire. By 1940 after good rains, you could pass by a paddock and it would move like tall grass blown in the wind, only it was rabbits. They covered every inch of the land far as the eye could see, this great bunny rug stretching to the horizon. Rabbits are randy all right, but myxomatosis soon took care of all that. It was released into the burrows along the Murray River eleven years ago and it wiped out ninety-eight per cent of the rabbit plague by making them blind, which is a pretty horrible way to die even for a rabbit; they now had to make love by feel. Tommy reckons they're staging a comeback and that they'll soon enough become immune to myxo and then we'll find something else to kill them off with, which will probably get into the native creatures as well.

I skin the two bucks and bleed them quickly, leaving the innards and the heads for the ants and the crows, and take a muslin bag out of my knapsack, drop them in and we're on our way again. I'm carrying the empty lemonade bottles, no point filling them with water until we get to the mountain as we're following Buffalo Creek all the way. Tommy can get a fair pace up if he wants to and, as I'm carrying all the clobber, I'm fair whacked by twelve o'clock when we finally get to the lower slopes of the mountain.

We stop to boil the billy when Tommy points out Goldie Spur about a mile away. 'We'll have to climb that to get to the first of the Ash,' he says.

'And then?'

'You'll see.' He swirls the bit of tea with the tea-leaves on the bottom of the mug, hurls them out and hands the mug to me. 'Let's push on, mate.'

The spur is pretty steep and bushy but Tommy seems to know a way up, there's no path but I can see he knows where he's going. We're climbing more or less parallel to a fall of water. It's not exactly a waterfall, because it never falls that far without changing direction, and it's not a creek either but I guess just a bit of water falling down the edge of the spur. Though there's a fair bit of fern and water plants about, which tells you it's been around a while and isn't simply seasonal. Since everything's got to have a name, I say to Tommy, 'What's the creek called?'

'It don't have a name, just a bit of water, a leak in the mountain.'

'A leak in the mountain?' I say, surprised at his answer. It's not like Tommy to describe something like that, he likes to know where things come from, you know, cause and effect. What I would have expected him to say is that there was a bit of a catchment area above and why it resulted in this more than a trickle and less than a stream.

'Wait and see,' he calls back.

We get to the top of the spur and we're in among the Alpine Ash, big trees all right but nothing to write home about, I've seen as big as these before a few times.

'This it?' I ask, the disappointment showing in my voice.

Tommy doesn't answer, instead we follow the little stream as it winds down among the Alpine Ash. Easy to see why the Ash are here, they like a bit of water and this little stream would suit them a treat. We follow the stream to the beginning of the spur and the point where the mountain suddenly starts to rise steeply. Another cliff to climb, I think to myself, though I know we're unlikely to find Alpine Ash higher up. The spur we've just climbed onto is about max for them. They might not even grow this high if it wasn't for the little mountain trickle they're living off. Then I see what Tommy means by a leak in the mountain, the stream is coming out from under a large rock at the base of the sheer cliff facing us.

'This is where it gets a little rough, Mole,' Tommy announces. 'What you got in the knapsack?'

I tell him and he says to leave the two empty lemonade bottles, they could smash, that there's plenty of fresh water where we're going. 'Give me the billy, mate, and the mugs, you'll have enough trouble with the rifle.'

I take the two bottles out and leave them where I can find them on my way back and hand him the mugs and the billy. He puts the two mugs in the billy, puts the lid back on, then fixes the billy to hang from the bottom of his knapsack. 'Keep your knapsack flat as you can, nothing hard in it, is there?'

'Nah, except a few .22 bullets and the rabbits.'

'They'll tenderise nicely on the way through,' he says, casual as you like. 'Okay, follow me.' To my surprise, I see he's got a torch in his hand. 'Keep right onto my heels, shout out if you can't touch me boots. Okay?'

'Yeah, but where are we going?'

He doesn't answer, instead he parts some fern and I see a narrow opening where the water trickles through. 'Yiz'll have to leopard-crawl to get through.' He's down on his stomach and starting to worm through the hole. 'Wait on and hand me the gun before you come after me,' he gasps.

'We could leave it here, we've got our tucker for the night,' I shout out.

'Nah, bring it, never know,' he shouts back.

So I wait until he disappears and then push the .22 through the gap. I feel him grab the butt and pull it inwards. I follow on my stomach, which is immediately immersed in the icy-cold stream. I crawl forward and feel my knapsack and sleeping bag catch on the edge of the rock but by wiggling a bit I manage to get them through. I see what Tommy means by tenderised rabbit.

Inside is a cavern only big enough for the two of us to sit in and it's dark and because I'm wet it's cold. Tommy shines the torch and I see the stream is coming from an underground passage that is so narrow I can't believe Tommy expects us to crawl down it. 'It's only about a hundred yards but it's gunna take us a good hour, air's okay though, just take it easy,' Tommy advises. 'Shout out if you need a rest.'

'I've never done nothing like this before, sure it's okay?' I ask him. Far as I can see, if I panic and want to go back or if something happens, like I break a leg or something, there isn't any way we can turn around and get back, not in the part the torch shows anyway.

'Not afraid of the dark, are you?'

'Not when there's plenty of space around me.'

'You'll be right, just take it easy, slow and easy, it's like climbing up the mountain's arse and the rocks you come across are its haemorrhoids!' That's Tommy's humour, which is never very subtle and generally a bit on the nose.

'Jesus, how'd you find this place?'

'Didn't, your great-great-grandfather did.' He laughs. 'The German bloke reckoned he was the first to climb Mount Buffalo. Got the credit for it in the history books. Which is bullshit, of course. In them days ordinary blokes didn't get the credit for nothing. Old Patrick Maloney climbed it eight or nine times. I can't remember exactly. That was around 1840 when he'd first got his ticket-of-leave. The botanist bloke did it thirteen years later. Better get going, eh.'

So there we are up the arse of the mountain and after a few minutes I realise Tommy wasn't kidding. I bump against rocks almost every time I crawl a couple of feet forward and I reckon I'm bleeding like a stuffed pig; the stream must be running red with my blood. I'm effing and shitting until Tommy says, 'Save your breath, Mole, it gets worse, just mind your scone and watch my torch.'

Hah, what torch? I'm seventeen years old and I'm finding it difficult so I don't know how Tommy keeps going with his crook shoulder and arm. It's pitch-dark crawling up behind his boots and the gap is so narrow I only occasionally glimpse the beam of light the torch throws.

After what must be at least an hour but feels like a bloody eternity we emerge from under a rock into quite a sizeable pool where we can stand with the water up to our knees. I see we're standing on the wrong side of a waterfall. Again, that's a bit of an exaggeration because it's not exactly a cascade of water, but it's coming straight down from some place higher up and looks like a fine lace curtain.

Tommy motions me forward and we walk through the curtain of water and emerge on the other side. We're in a kind of natural bowl with the walls too high to see over and the water is falling from a steep cliff that rises up on one side of the bowl. We're both soaked to the skin and, I can tell you, Mole is not a happy little Vegemite. But Tommy grins, 'Cheer up, mate, we made it, didn't we? That's the thing, once you're in, there's no turning around, if there'd been a sudden shower up top, we'd be dead meat by now.'

I think about this for a moment. On a mountain like this, clouds can gather in a matter of minutes. Even out of a clear blue sky, you can get sudden rain on the summit and in a moment there'd be a torrent thundering down the cliff into the tunnel. We'd never know what'd hit us.

I check the rifle and see that the front and back sights have been bent, but the bolt action still works. There's a couple of nicks out of the stock but nothing to worry about. My knees and my elbows are bleeding and Tommy says I've got a cut above the eye which I can't feel but it must have stopped bleeding because nothing is running into my eye.

'Careful when you climb out of here,' Tommy cautions, 'it drops real sudden the other side.'

I've got a bit of rope out of my knapsack I sometimes use as a sling on the .22 and I fix it to the rifle and throw it across my back and over the knapsack. Lucky I've bled the bunnies, they'll be mince by now, good thing we're having stew.

I follow Tommy up the side of the bowl, which is a bit of a scramble, clinging onto bushes, holding on for dear life. I come over the top and I can't believe my eyes. There's a sheer drop into a ravine that's got to be a thousand feet down, it's a cleft in the mountain that's no more than maybe two hundred and fifty feet wide and half a mile long, like someone's just gouged this narrow slit into the side of the great mountain as if to mortally wound it. You might be able to see it from the air but it wouldn't be observable from any point on the ground or even from the top of the mountain. About eight hundred feet below from where Tommy and me are sitting is the dark canopy of the trees growing in the cleft.

'Shit, where'd that come from?'

'Look closer, Mole, look at the canopy,' Tommy replies.

I scan the canopy, which seems pretty even and flat, looking down at it like we are. And then I see it. Standing maybe two hundred feet above the rest of the canopy is a single tree. 'Holy shit, is it as big as I think it is?' I shout out.

'Wait and see,' Tommy says.

I look at him, afraid, 'No way! We can't get down there, not from here anyway,' I protest.

Tommy shrugs. 'There ain't no other way, Mole, except maybe if you've got a spare pair of wings.'

'You've done it before then?' He knows I mean, has he done it since his shoulder, since he come back from the war, not just as a kid.

'Yeah, no worries.' He looks up at the sky, 'It's about two o'clock, must make it before five, it gets dark down there early.'

Tommy and me have done a few difficult climbs, but nothing like this. 'Is there a best way?' I ask fearfully.

'Yeah, if I can remember it,' he says, pretty nonchalant. I look to see if he's kidding, but I can't tell because he has started to move over the edge.

I can't describe the going down, except to say that if I hadn't first come through that tunnel I would have shit myself. Almost every step I think will be my last, one slip and you'd fall all the way down. It's a matter of grabbing onto bushes and digging a footing with the heels of your boots and clinging on to clumps of grass.

Tommy's a little bloke and pretty sure-footed, his legs are the only part of him that aren't stuffed, but he's doing it tough and I'm doing it tougher. If I had the time to think about it, I'd admire him. All I can think is, if this is bad, then how the fuck are we gunna get back?

It's going to take a full day's climb just to get to the basin and the waterfall. We'll be much too whacked to do the tunnel after the climb, that's for sure. We'll have to spend the night in the little waterfall basin. What's more, there's no way we're going to be back home by Monday night, Tuesday night maybe. Nancy's going to slaughterate me! Good thing I told Bozo we wouldn't be back Sunday night, though I don't know what he'll do when we don't show Monday or even Tuesday morning.

In about three hours we reach the bottom of the ravine, which is the wrong word because there's no outlet like a ravine should have, just this deep wound in the side of the mountain. We're in among the Alpine Ash, all of which are big trees, bigger than the ones on the spur, and a couple we pass are at least two hundred years old. If Tommy had stopped at either one of them and declared we'd reached the big old tree, I'd have thought, fair enough. But he doesn't and we press on. There's been a fire through here maybe two years ago so the undergrowth isn't too bad and we can make our way along pretty steadily. It's twilight down here, even though it's summer and it can't be much more than about half-past five, with the sun not yet set.

Then we come to a clearing and there it is, the biggest tree I have ever seen. It's as though no other tree dare take any space around it, the trunk is easily fifteen feet across and the clearing in which it stands is quite light because the canopy of the other trees hasn't crowded in and its own canopy is pretty sparse, so the light streams down from above like it's an altar or something. This old fella has to be three hundred feet high! I stand gobsmacked. I can't say nothing, this is the biggest growing thing I have ever seen and only a Maloney has seen it. This must be true, because if someone else had been here then they'd have said so. You'd have to skite about it. The only reason we haven't is because to us male Maloneys this is a sacred tree, this is the God Tommy worships, and so did Tommy's father and grandfather.

I look over at Tommy, who is now sitting on a rock completely knackered. I'm young and the sight of the tree has sent my blood racing and, all of a sudden, I don't feel the weariness in me. Now I see dark patches of blood through Tommy's shirt. He's also got a nasty cut along the neck and the skin on his legs is rubbed raw.

I don't know what to say, he's done this for me when physically he was well past such a climb. 'Thank you, Dad,' I say. Then I can't help myself, I run over and take his head in both my hands and kiss him on the forehead. 'Thank you, thank you,' and I start to cry.

'She's right,' Tommy says quietly, he nods towards the tree, 'I did the same first time I saw it. But you've got to be ready, it's not something you can see if you're not ready.' He doesn't explain what he means and I don't understand. Does he think the tree is invisible? You could easily think something like that, you know, you can only see it when things are right in your mind and soul? But it's there all right, this mighty Alpine Ash has been standing here for at least four hundred years.

Tommy has got his elbows on his knees and he's looking at a spot between his legs. After a while, he looks up slowly directly into my eyes. 'I'm that proud of you, Mole. You're the best son a man could ever wish for and that's why I'm gunna tell yer.'

I knuckle back my tears, I'm his son even if I ain't. 'You mean, show me the tree?'

'Nah, tell ya.'

'Tell me what?' I sniff.

'Everything, mate. Everything what happened.'

'You mean the Japanese?'

'Yeah, them mongrels, Malaya, Singapore, Changi, Sandakan, all me mates long dead, Gunner Cleary!'

I've heard of Changi but never of the other place, 'Sandakan? Where's that?'

'Borneo.'

I can see he's exhausted, even deciding to tell me, spitting it out, has taken something out of him. There's a stream nearby so I say, 'Better wash them wounds, get the dirt out. I'll make us a fire and boil the billy, we'll have a cuppa, then I'll make us a nice rabbit stew.'

'You're a good son, Mole,' he says. That's the second time he's said it in a matter of minutes. It's something he's never said to me in my whole life.

'Better wash them scratches in the stream, get the dirt out,' I repeat.

He gives me a tired smile. 'It's better than that, Mole.' He points to a large rock about forty feet to my right and on the edge of the clearing made by the big old tree. 'There's a hot spring behind that big rock, I reckon we're closer to hell than we know.' I look over and see there's a wisp of steam rising from behind the rock, then another. 'What say you, Mole, we'll have a cuppa, take it with us and have a good soak.' I walk over to the little stream. Above the rock it's icy cold and below it's lukewarm. 'The hot springs is what's helped the great giant grow so big, kept its roots warm in the winter,' Tommy shouts out.

There's plenty of dry wood lying around and I gather an armful and cut two long green twigs. I build the fire and bend the twigs, on either side of the fire, so that the points are pushed into the ground. 'Take your gear off, I'll dry it,' I say to Tommy and start to undress. Tommy hands me his wet clobber.

I never cease to be astonished at Tommy's body, his shoulder is sort of crushed in and one arm is thin as a stick and he's sort of a bit lopsided and thin as a rake. If you look at him in the nude, you'd think he was a broken man but he can go all day and walk the legs off any of us. I think I should wash the bloodstains and the dirt out but I know Tommy wouldn't want me to do that, he'd think I was demeaning myself. Instead, I drape both our gear over the looped sticks to dry and set the billy to boil.

So there's Tommy and me having a cup of tea, sitting up to our necks in hot water, letting all the aches and pains flow out of us. After a while Tommy clears his throat, 'I guess you know some part of it, eh?'

'Not much.'

'Malaya?'

'Nah.'

'Singapore?'

'Only the poem you told us which says it was like a fortress that couldn't be took, only the Japs captured it in a week.' It's not strictly true, I know a bit more, but I want to hear Tommy's version, the way a bloke who was there would say it.

'Singapore don't make sense unless you know what happened before, what happened in Malaya.' Now Tommy laughs. 'Only the bloody Poms! They've got this idea that no army can cross Malaya. The jungle's too dense, the swamps too deep, it's what they maintain all along. They should know, they tell everyone, they've been in Malaya for donkey's years, planting rubber and running the show, they know it inside out. Can't tell them nothing.

'The suggestion is that if the Brits can't do it, march an army from the north to south, no bastard can. Simple as that. So they prepare Singapore with their big guns armed with armour-piercing shells to be used against invading warships. Only problem was, the Japs took no notice and decide to come overland instead, ride in on bicycles down from the north of Malaya, down the pensinula to the southern tip.

'The intelligence coming through from Malaya says that's what the Japanese plan to do, Thailand has given them permission to march across its territory. Bullshit, says the British High Command, we're not stupid enough to fall for that old trick, nobody can get through that jungle.

'Later when we are on Singapore Island, the Brits shell Malaya. We hear the shells passing over, even saw one or two, but being armour-piercing when they landed in Johore they didn't detonate. Right idea, wrong shells, another Pommie fuck-up.'

'Dad, I want to know everything!' I burst out suddenly, 'Everything that happened, don't leave nothing out!' I tell myself even if it's stuff that's a bit technically wrong but is what the ordinary soldiers believed was happening, that's okay. I also know that Tommy's telling it from the Australians' side and that he might be a bit one-eyed.

'Tell you the truth, I'm whacked, mate,' he says. 'Been a long day. What say I'll tell you about Malaya, then you make us a bite of bunny stew and we'll have a few hours' kip and then I'll carry on with the rest?'

We sit in the pool nearly an hour as Tommy tells me the story of his battalion, the 2/19th, and how they fought in Malaya.

The fire has burned down to embers when we get back from the hot pool and our clobber is dry again. We dress and I set about making rabbit stew. But first I cut two sticks that branch into a Y and put them in the ground either side of the embers, then run a long stick through one of the rabbits and place it on this bush spit to roast. I take the other rabbit and cut it up for stew with a bit of salt and the two carrots I've brought. One rabbit isn't going to make much of a stew, but I reckon we'll have a little less to eat tonight and save the other rabbit roasted. We'll need to eat tomorrow night as well and there'll be nothing to be taken off the land until then.

We wash down the stew with another mug of billy tea and it can't be much later than about half-past seven when, after building up the fire so it will last until about midnight, I crawl into my sleeping bag.

There's still a little light coming through because of the missing canopy to the massive old tree. That's the thing with truly old trees, after about three hundred years they lose most of their canopy, I guess it's a tree's version of going bald. Anyway the birds have all shut up and the frogs have now took to croaking and I reckon I'll be dead to the world in a matter of minutes. But not before I've made Tommy promise to wake me at midnight to go on with the story.

However, tired as I am, I can't go to sleep. What Tommy's told me sitting in the hot pool is working itself out in my memory. I hear his voice, the way he says things, going on and on in my head like it's a record playing back to me. I suppose I've waited so long that my mind doesn't want to lose a single detail, even though I know a fair bit about Singapore and even Changi, because that's history you can read and Mrs Botherington has let me take books about it out of the library.

I tell myself, history is one thing, telling's another. Tommy was there and he saw it like an ordinary bloke sees things and not like the writers who write it from the general perspective or like the generals in their memoirs, who want to cover their arses and come out smelling of roses.

So there it is, Tommy's voice. 'Mate, Singapore was a complete shambles, a stuff-up that you wouldn't believe unless you were there yourself. I heard tell about a wireless broadcast from one of the Pommie military big shots to the civilian population that happened before we get there. He's said we might get attacked from the air by day, but the anti-aircraft guns were strategically placed to give the Nips hell if they tried, but not to worry about night attacks, because the Japanese pilots all suffer from poor eyesight and it is a fact that the Japanese can't see in the dark.' Tommy chuckles, 'Maybe they didn't eat raw carrots like we did when we were kids, eh?'

I laugh as well, I don't know if it's a true story, but I've heard it before, maybe read it somewhere. 'Must have been the same bloke fired the shells that wouldn't detonate.'

'Could've been, though there weren't that many in top command had a bloody clue. Too many gin slings before curry tiffin at the Singapore Club, I reckon.

'Well, the Japs weren't taking no notice of what they were supposed to do and at last the blokes in command realise that we've got a very likely invasion on our hands, jungle or no jungle. So, we're sitting there waiting for the Japs to get in among us, there's not even a roll of barbed wire on the island to stop them. We've been fighting in Malaya, back-pedalling all the way, thinking that once we get to Singapore they'll have had time to get ready and the defences will be in place and we can stand and fight for a change. Not a sausage, mate. They done bugger-all!

'General Wavell, who's in command of all the troops from Burma to the Philippines, and that includes us and the Americans, the Dutch and the British, goes over to Singapore to take a look-see. He finds there's no defences anywhere.

'"Where's the defences?" he asks General Percival.

'"We ain't got none," Percival replies.

'"What do you mean you ain't got none? Fucking Japs are on the way!" Wavell shouts.

'"Yeah, well, we thought it would be bad for civilian morale if we started building bunkers and stuff," says General Percival.'

I guess that's Tommy's version of the conversation between Wavell and Percival, but I reckon it amounts to the same thing. The English generals may have said it more posh but the records show that Percival did say he thought it would be bad for civilian morale when Wavell questioned him about the lack of defences. The point is they've been sitting on their arses in Singapore, spouting about the impenetrable virgin jungle being the natural enemy the Japs can't defeat and suddenly the Japs are knocking on the back door.

Tommy continues, 'We expect to see these massive concrete fortifications, anti-tank traps, pillboxes and weapons pits. Gawd knows they've had all the time in the world to construct them. There's nothing! Sweet Fanny Adams! Like I said, not even a strand of barbed wire.

'Our own general, Gordon Bennett, is a pretty good bloke and we're happy with his leadership but there's bugger-all he can do. He's under the direction of General Percival of the low-morale quip and also General Wavell, who finds himself retreating fast as his troops can go.

'The Brits have been fighting in Malaya long before us, starting right up in the far north at Jitra and Kota Bahru when the Japs first landed. I don't know that much about their part, except I heard how at Kota Bahru way up north, the Japs attempting to land were met by Indian troops under Brigadier Key who fought with great gallantry but, despite holding the high ground, were eventually hopelessly outnumbered by the Japs coming ashore.

'Far as I know, it was much of the same elsewhere, they fought best they could but the odds were too great. Percival, gawd help us, is in charge at this stage and when the Japs cross Thailand into Jitra, the defences aren't organised, the anti-tank mines are laid in clumps dead easy to avoid, the trenches aren't wired for communications and, besides, are waterlogged. Well, the rot sets in right there at the very beginning and from then on they're chased all the way down Malaya until they're in the south. That's when the Australians are brought into the fray.

'The 2/19th, which is us, is on the east coast way down south with the rest of the Australians in Johore, we're supposed to be the last-ditch stand. After Johore there's the straits separating the mainland from Singapore Island, at low tide you can practically spit across it. Judging from the way the Japs are moving, it ain't gunna take too long before we're tested.

'When we were first brought across from Singapore to the mainland, we know bugger-all about the jungle.'

'Wait on!' I say to Tommy. 'How'd you get to Singapore? I need to know everything. Can you start at the beginning?'

Tommy grins. 'You'll probably be one of them historians or something when you grow up, Mole. Never known nobody who has to have all the facts like you do. That's nice, that's an inquiring mind.' He pauses. 'Okay, let me see. Well, I'm in the permanent army, not long trained when it's known to one and all there's gunna be a war. I'm not yet attached to a battalion and me and a sergeant and a captain are sent up to Delegate on the New South Wales side of the border to help start a recruiting drive up through Goulburn, Bombala, Cooma and Queanbeyan.

'The drive works pretty good and eventually there's about one hundred and forty recruits, which become known as the Snowy Mountains contingent. I like these blokes so I put in for a transfer and join the 2/19th Battalion, which is a New South Wales unit and is known as The Riverina Battalion cause most of the blokes come from Griffith, Leeton, Wagga, Hay, Cootamundra and then there's us from the Snowy area. The 2/19th is one of three battalions in the 22nd Brigade, the other two are naturally the 2/18th and 2/20th.

'We done our training and on account of me being already trained I'm made a corporal, which don't mean a lot. I'm sort of the spokesman for the troops to the platoon sergeant and that's about it. Corporal ain't a rank really, all it means is you're the senior shit-kicker among the troops and are equally despised by the sergeants and warrant officers.

'In February 1941 we board the *Queen Mary* for destinations unknown. Some of the blokes think we were going to Egypt, most think Europe.' Tommy shrugs. 'Why not? The Japs ain't in the war yet and we know bugger-all about Asia. I reckon you could have asked any bloke in the battalion to pick out Singapore Island in the atlas and he wouldn't have a clue. I know I didn't.

'We arrive in Singapore and entrain for Malaya and we're stationed first at Seremban and then at Port Dickson. That's where Bennett's good. He spends what time he's got training us in jungle warfare, so we're not completely raw and, besides, we're pretty well-disciplined troops before we leave home, so we can act like soldiers, or think we can. We're a cocky lot and by now we know the Japs are preparing for war. "Just wait till the Japs have to fight real soldiers, eh?" we tell ourselves.

'We're at Port Dickson from March to September and in May our platoon sergeant is killed by a truck while we're out on manoeuvres and we get a replacement, a bloke named Roger Rigby. He's a big bugger with knife scars all over his arms and chest. I don't know how he got them, but about a week later he's got these truck springs, you know the steel blades used on a truck. He's got us all together and he points to the truck blades.

'"Righto, them's reinforced steel them blades, best metal there is to make a fighting knife." He looks around, "I'm willing to teach you stupid buggers how to fight with a knife because I reckon you're gunna need to know. But it ain't compulsory, you have to volunteer and there's a catch."

'Some bloke in the platoon says, "So what's the catch, Sarge?"

'Rigby picks up one of the springs, "Make three fighting knives out of one of these, but it's gunna cost. I've got a mate in Malacca reckons he can make them according to my specifications for two quid each." He reaches into a knapsack at his feet and brings out this knife. It's a thing of beauty but dangerous-looking and I'd shit myself if someone pulled it on me. "This is a fighting knife, blade seven and a half inches long, handle, solid, tapered at the end, grip serrated, one inch at the widest point, copper crossguard slightly 's'-shaped, three inches long. Personally I think you can do without the heavy crossguard, we'll leave it off, leather sheath fourteen inches long." He flips the knife in the air and catches it by the handle. "That's the weight and size of this knife, but we'll make them tailor-made to fit the size of yer hand and the weight of your body." He points the knife at the steel springs at his feet. "It began its life as one of those, high-tensile spring steel, so make up yer minds."

'I look around at the faces of the men and I can see they're not too sure. Who is this bloke anyway? He's only just become our sergeant, we ain't done any real work with him. Seeing I'm the corporal, I guess I have to say something.

'"Sergeant, we've done our jungle training, there's no knives mentioned. Bayonet and grenade is for close-up work, no knives are issued as standard equipment."

'"Maloney, you ever fought in the jungle?"

'"No, Sarge."

'"You ever been in the jungle?"

'"Just around here, Sarge, also the bush at home."

'"Where's home, North Queensland?"

'"No, Sarge, Yankalillee, north-eastern Victoria."

'There's a bit of general laughter, most of the blokes are from the bush. "Must be tough goin' hackin' through the blackberry and all," he says.

'I'm real embarrassed, "Yeah, tear yer to pieces soon as look at yer, Sarge."

'He grins, paying the reply. "Okay, Corporal Maloney, fix bayonet." I do as he says. "Righto, try and kill me." He puts his knife back in the knapsack and he's standing in front of me empty-handed.

'The platoon laughs, thinking he doesn't mean it. I've got this stupid grin on me gob. "You for real, Sarge?"

'"Never more serious in me life, son, go ahead, kill me," he says again.

'I shake me head and look down at me boots. "Couldn't do that, Sarge." See, I fancy meself a bit with a bayonet and I've put in a lot of extra practice with some of the city blokes who don't come natural with a rifle.

'Sergeant Rigby is suddenly aggro, "Dammit, try and kill me, Maloney. Yer know yer fuckin' bayonet drill, don'tcha?"

'I can see he's not fooling and I charge him in the regulation manner. Course I'm not gunna kill him. Next thing I know I'm on me back and he's got my own rifle and bayonet pointed at me chest. If he's the enemy, I'm dead meat.

'"Okay, get to yer feet, Corporal. Don't mean to make a fool out of you in front of the men." Then he turns to us all, "There ain't a Jap soldier don't know how to do that. A bayonet is a big knife at the end of a very clumsy stick named a rifle. You can jab it in the enemy's gut providing he gives you permission or ain't lookin', but that's about all. The only advantage is that, if you manage to do it, the enemy is three and a half feet away from you. But first you've got to stick him and he won't be standing there like a sack of sawdust waiting to be pricked."

'Then Rigby picks up the knife again. "The human arm isn't as long as a rifle and bayonet, but even in a bloody midget like Maloney, it's two foot long. On your average Jap that's not much more than he can manage with a bayonet. Now some Japs have this thing called jujitsu and you better hope you don't meet one, because he'll disarm you before you even decide where you're gunna stick him. But, thank gawd, most don't have the skill, so if you know a bit about handling a knife you just may have the advantage in a close encounter. In the jungle you can be two feet away from the enemy and not see him. When you do, you just may have to be quicker than him and that's where the knife comes in."

'"What's wrong with a bullet from your rifle?" some bloke asks.

'"If you have time and see him coming, sure." He looks at us, "But I promise, you won't, he'll be behind the next branch you part, or jungle tree you pass, little yellow bastard comin' ter kill yer."

'I'm still not entirely convinced, using a knife to kill, well . . . it ain't Australian, is it? But I can see the rest of the platoon are now pretty keen even though two quid is a big ask, so I go along with the ploy and we all agree to take knife-fighting lessons.

'Next time we get town leave we take the springs and we're down to the native quarter in Malacca to see the smithy that's gunna make the knives. He's an evil-looking character, the colour of old tabacca leaf with a dirty turban and a big curled-up-at-the-ends moustache, his face is pretty scarred and he's only got one eye, there's this big scar runs from above his eyebrow across the left eye socket and right down so you can see it, a white line through his dark beard. Sergeant Rigby and him embrace and they chat on in some lingo that ain't Malay, Hindi or something like that. It seems they're old mates, and they suit each other, a more evil-lookin' pair o' bastards would be bloody hard to find.

'Then after a while each of us has to stand in front of Ali Baba with the turban. First off we have to pay him the two quid. "How do we know we can trust him?" I ask, once again being the mouth for the troops.

'"With your flamin' life, Corporal," Rigby says. "He's been in the army himself, he's an Afghani and comes from generations of blade-makers." I can't help wondering to myself what Rigby's cut is, he's not the sort of bloke who would do things out of the kindness of his heart, or, I'd vouch, someone who'd step back if there was a dishonest quid to be made.

'Well, Ali Baba picks each bloke up, grabs him by the side of the arms and lifts him, sort of weighing him. Then he writes something in a dirty notebook and measures each bloke's knife-fighting arm with a tape measure and writes that down as well. He's got several short pieces of copper pipe, about four inches long, each one a different diameter. He makes us close our hand around them and when he thinks one of them fits our grip, he marks it in the spiral notepad. Last thing, he takes a spring and with white chalk carefully measures a bit of the spring and writes on it in this squiggly writing.

'"He's making your knife to order, the right fighting weight and grip for your size. If a knife's too heavy you can't get the most from it, too light and it don't cut right. It has to be properly balanced for your size and strength, grip must be perfect," Rigby explains.

'Couple of weeks later the knives are ready and, I have to admit, I pick mine up and take it out of its leather combat sheath and it's beautiful. Lethal and beautiful and, what's more, it feels like it belongs in me hand. We compare our knives and it's true, no two are exactly the same and everyone feels the same way I do.

'Next four months Sergeant Rigby, who is now known as "Blades" for the obvious reason and because everyone in the army has a nickname, trains us in how to use a fighting knife in combat. I'm a reasonable good shot and I can use a bayonet as good as the next man, but I have to admit the knife gives you a lot of confidence. It's a very personal weapon, not like a rifle or a bayonet. After a while you get to think of it as an extension of yourself, your hand don't end at the tips of yer fingers no more, it extends to the tip o' the blade.

'In September we move to Kluang and then in October to Jemaluang on the east coast. All of it is jungle training and with it, Sergeant Rigby's knife fighting. We've become a bit of a joke with the other platoons, but our lieutenant, who's also joined in the training, gets special permission from the colonel for us to carry our knives in combat as part of our personal kit.

'In December the Japs enter the war by bombing Pearl Harbor, but even before this they're already on their way to invade Malaya. We're pretty excited and then dead disappointed because we're not sent north to stem the invasion. We reckon it's unfair keeping us down south while the Poms and the Indians get all the glory.

'Well, it don't turn out that way. Like I told you, the Japs are no pushover and there's no stoppin' them. The Brits and the Indians are retreating and eventually try to hold the rapidly advancing enemy at Kuala Lumpur, but can't. After this we get our chance.

'General Bennett sends us into new positions west of a place called Bakri, which is near the Muar River that is being defended by a battery from our 2/15th Field Artillery regiment and the Indian troops, who've taken a fair old battering. As I said, the Brits have withdrawn from Kuala Lumpur and are in no shape to carry on, so the Japs have got a free run to Muar River where the Indians waiting there are no match. Our 2/29th and an anti-tank mob are sent to shore them up. Meanwhile we're ordered to Parit Sulong a little further east.

'So much for being cocky. The Poms are retreating and the Indians collapse, so now the 2/29th and the anti-tank go into battle. Soon they're taking a terrible hiding and we're told to go to their aid. So we leave a platoon to defend the bridge at Parit Sulong and move over to the west of Bakri to join in the fighting.

'We discover that we can't get to the 2/29th because the road is blocked by the Japs. We send the armoured cars in but the Japs drive them back. Then two platoons, ours is one of them, and a mortar detachment, have a go. This is what Blades has trained us for, I guess, and we're in among them. I've never seen a Jap before and now they're fuckin' everywhere you look, but they must have seen Blades coming at them with a knife because they're soon routed, though we corner them and I reckon it wasn't a day to take prisoners. We're on to the next group of Japs and to our surprise they up and scarper, abandoning their positions and leaving behind a number of their wounded. When the smoke clears we have one bloke who's got a minor neck wound.

'We say to ourselves, that weren't too bad, fuckers may be able to fight but then so can we. We've forced them back and are feeling quite pleased with ourselves. Most of our platoon have blooded their knives and we're like a bunch of schoolboys who've won a footie game.

'In the meantime the 2/29th, the mob from Victoria, are in the thick of it, but they've also had their moments. The Japs send their tanks in against them and they fell trees and drop them between the ranks so the tanks are stuck. There's eight tanks and they're sitting ducks and the blokes in the 2/29th finish them off with anti-tank guns, rifles and grenades. The Japs try to infiltrate their positions that night but they're driven off with automatic fire. During the early part of the night there's a fair bit of shelling that's directed at our positions. Still an' all, as far as the 2/19th are concerned it ain't been a bad day's fighting.

'Next day we've not long ate our rations when the Japs attack us, we reckon there's about three hundred of them but we outmanoeuvre them and we get stuck in. They're badly bunched up and easy pickings and in the wash-up we kill a hundred and forty of them and ten of our blokes are killed. It's here we learn a new Jap trick, many of the wounded Japs play dead and when you walk past them, the corpses come alive with a grenade in their hand. So it's a matter of putting a bullet into every Jap lying down dead or alive. I fire at one "corpse" and he must have had the pin out of his grenade already because his head is blown off his shoulders by his own grenade.

'Then we learn that our rear is cut off and that the transport group in charge of the ammo and food has been attacked by four hundred Japs who have set up roadblocks both sides of their position along the Parit Sulong road. The Jap artillery start pounding the Brigade HQ and score a direct hit. Just about all the senior officers there are killed. We're close at the time and a truck containing about thirty wounded men from the 2/29th has taken a shell and there's bits of body everywhere.' Tommy pulls a face. 'Just beside the road I come across one bloke, or what's left of him, there's a naked waist with two legs twisted and black dangling from it, a few feet further there's his head and neck with half a chest and one arm. It's total fuckin' carnage everywhere you look.

'The Japs are between us and the 2/29th again but we manage to infiltrate their positions and drive them off. At long last we're within reach of the 2/29th, who've by all reports taken a lot worse than us. The Japs attack again and we hold them off with rifles and Vickers and Lewis guns and pound them with mortars. It's every man we can spare and even the padre is hard at it. He's a real decent cove, Wardale-Greenwood, he's pumping two-inch mortars at the enemy, goin' at it hell for leather. Can't fault him, his technique is perfect and he don't stop for a breather neither. The attack keeps up until nightfall and it's only then that the 2/29th reach us.' Tommy reaches for a cigarette and lights it, taking a long draw and then exhales. 'Mate, poor bastards have had the shit well and truly kicked out of them. Out of around a thousand men there's only two hundred reach us. Their C.O. is shot dead while riding on the back of a motorbike when he's returning from a reconnaissance the day before.'

'What was his name?' I know I shouldn't interrupt, but I can't help myself.

'Mate, I wouldn't remember. No, hang on, Robbo, no Robbie, Colonel Robbie, probably stands for Robertson, he wasn't our C.O. so I can't be sure.

'Then the new C.O. of the 2/29th is killed and as the Indian's Brigadier Duncan has concussion, our bloke, Lieutenant Colonel Anderson, is now in charge of what's left of both battalions and also the 2/15th Field Regiment and what's left of the Indian Brigade.

'Anyway it's us and the rest of the 2/29th copping constant artillery shelling during the night. We plan to withdraw in the morning and get back over the bridge at Parit Sulong, where we started from just fourteen miles away. There's this long causeway we're gunna need to cross that's eight miles across with no protection and swamp on either side. The good thing is that the Japs can't attack us on the causeway because they can't come at us through the swamp on either side. They can hit us from the air, of course, but the plan is to cross at night. It's getting to the causeway that's going to be the problem. Once we get to the bridge at Parit Sulong we'll be okay, because the Norfolks, who replace our blokes, are holding that.

'Come first light and the Japs go ape-shit. Mortars and shells rain down on us. Thank Christ, we're in this rubber plantation and a lot of the shells and mortars hit the trees and explode before reaching the ground. Pretty soon it looks like a tornado has hit the plantation, there's practically no leaves left on the trees, trunks are split open and branches lie everywhere. The white rubber latex bleeding from the trunks and branches makes everywhere you move sticky. The Japs come at us and we're fighting desperately to hold them back. Down the road a bit, our transport units have been attacked and are fighting a ferocious battle.

'B Company, that's us, leave at 0700 hours as an advance guard but we hit a roadblock and are pinned down. A Company comes in to help and, I do not tell a lie, they're singing "Waltzing Matilda" as they attack a small group of Japs, killing twelve of the bastards. But we're still pinned down by machine-gun fire and in no mood to join the singing. Our C.O., Lieutenant Colonel Anderson, joins us and leads an assault on the Japs, he's no slouch with a grenade and he takes out two enemy machine-gun posts and shoots a Jap coming for him in the head. Anderson is a South African who's in the AIF and who fought in the first world war. He sets great store by grenades and, as I just said, he could throw a Mills grenade good as any of us.

'It's a big setback and when we reach the transport unit it's too late, there's only dead men there. When we do a body count, though, we see that some must have escaped because it's not everyone accounted for. The only consolation is that the food and ammo is still there, the Japs haven't had time to take it.'

Tommy looks up at me, 'I'm learning that this isn't a nice tidy war, the enemy is everywhere, in the trees, strafing us, pounding us with mortars, mounting sudden attacks so you don't know where the next assault is gunna come from.

'General Nishimura and the Imperial Guards Division advancing have blitzed us with their armour and nailed us from the air. Everywhere we look there's Japs comin' at us and, although we ain't doing that badly, we also ain't winning the contest.

'We're clearing one roadblock with axes when, from out of nowhere we're attacked by a platoon of Japs at close quarters. It's axes, bayonets and knives, man on man.

'We're under constant attack all day and hit several more

roadblocks, Japs have felled trees or used broken-down trucks to block the road. They keep coming at us and we keep driving them off, but we're losing men all the time and Brigadier Duncan is killed. I tell you what, I did more ducking than shooting, every time I looked up there was a Japanese plane coming down out of the clouds to get me personally. By nightfall when we finally get to the causeway, I've had enough. If I could have, I would have resigned on the spot, handed back me rifle and gone home.

'We cross the causeway after dark, our trucks in single file, us also in single file on either side, and that fills all the space. If we'd tried to cross during the day the Jap planes would have destroyed us. But for the moment we're safe. It's been three days since I've had more than half an hour's sleep at a time and there's been precious little of them half-hour kips as well. We have a brief rest on the causeway and something to eat. I have to say the morale is still pretty high in the 2/19th and the blokes in the 2/29th, who've taken such a pounding, are still resolved to fight on.

'I think about how I could've easy been there with them. The 2/29th is a battalion from Victoria. Lots of them recruited from around Yackandandah, Wangaratta, Wodonga and, of course, Yankalillee. Luck of the draw, I suppose. Later we hear how in one attack the Jap artillery go in among them. When the big guns get into a unit, it's fucking carnage. They've been blown to bits. There's intestines hanging like strings of sausages from the branches of trees and bodies sliced in half, it's like a mad butcher has been among them. I could've easily been one of them bits hanging up on the branches.

'Amazing what a rest and a bit of tucker does, we're feeling not too bad. We march on into the night and halt about a mile from the rubber plantations which are about four miles from the bridge at Parit Sulong where we'll join up with the Norfolks.

'As there's fairly good cover in the rubber, our aim is to occupy it before dawn. Anderson gets the bad news, the Norfolks have withdrawn, they haven't received any supplies for two days and they've been cut off. They've abandoned the bridge and the Japs now hold both. We're back up shit creek.

'It's the twenty-first of January, my birthday and I'd been hoping to celebrate it by having a good night's sleep when we got to Parit Sulong. It would've been the best birthday present anyone could have given me, no risk.

'Instead, we meet the fiercest resistance yet. We get to within about six hundred yards of Parit Sulong village. We mount attack after attack but there's a solid rain of lead coming back at us. The Japs have turned some of the more solid houses in the village into machine-gun nests and they're hitting us from everywhere. They own the high ground on the bridge beyond and their main force is safe from attack on the other side and there's no chance to get at them with bayonet and grenades and they're too well entrenched for mortar or our artillery to do much good. We, on the other hand, are sitting ducks. We have to somehow break through, the Japs are behind us and in front of us and they're hitting us from the air, strafing the bejesus out of us. There are men dying everywhere and the condition of the wounded is pitiable. We've already lost most of our platoon and I know this is the day I'm gunna die. I can't stand the idea of dying on me birthday, it's too bloody neat, born and died on the same day, there's never been a Maloney got things done that neat before!'

I laugh at this, Tommy can be a funny bugger when he gets going.

'By now the Japs are having a go at us from the rear as well, we're the meat in the Japanese sandwich and it's only a matter of time. We can't fight them from both ends of the column and our flanks are exposed. Every man is put to fighting, the truck drivers, those not too badly wounded, we reduce the gun crews where we can and use the gunners to fight on our flanks.

'The wounded and dead are piling up. Anderson decides to move two ambulances containing the hopelessly wounded out so they can get treatment, or at the very least morphine to put them out of their misery as our own supplies are long used up. He sends a deputation with a flag of truce and the two ambulances up to the bridge and asks the Japs for safe passage for his wounded. "No way!" say the Japs, "You've got to surrender first."

'But Anderson won't. "Okay," say the Japs, "then piss off and let's get on with the stoush, but leave the ambulances where they are. Try to move them back, we'll machine-gun them."

'So we go back to fighting, leaving the two ambulances containing the worst-wounded men, with the poor bastards inside them dying without help. The Japs send in tanks in the afternoon. They should've learned by now, tanks is the one thing we can still do well. The enemy bring their tanks up at night but we stop the leading tank in its tracks with hand grenades and anti-tank guns. The others are blocked and can't get past. The fighting goes all night and once it passes midnight, I give a sigh of relief, I ain't gunna die on me birthday.

'During the night a Lieutenant Austin, who's with the two ambulances and is gravely wounded in the neck, him and a wounded driver release the handbrakes and under cover of darkness roll the ambulances backwards from the bridge. When they get to the bottom of the slope, they start the engines, which can't be heard in the din of the battle and drive them back to our lines.

'I reckon the Japs have got to be really pissed off. As long as them ambulances are there, we're not going to be firing at their men on the bridge in case we hit our own. I reckon they should have given Austin and the driver a couple of VCs.'

I laugh to myself, the old Tommy is fond of handing out VCs but I reckon the top brass wouldn't be quite so generous.

'Mate, they're slaughtering us and we know it's only a matter of time. Anderson sends a message to Bennett, asking if an aircraft could be used to bomb the approaches to the bridge at dawn and, at the same time, drop food and morphine as we're just about out of rations and the wounded are suffering something terrible and need the morphia real bad.

'It seems the code books have been destroyed earlier when the Brigade HQ had been wiped out so the bloke sending back his confirmation to Anderson can't use code and if he sends it in plain English the Japs will know what's gunna happen. So he sends this message in Australian, "Look up at sparrow fart!" and of course we know there'll be a plane over at dawn. The Japs' code breakers are probably scratching their heads wondering what the fuck farting sparrows have got to do with anything.

'At dawn we look up and there they are, two Albacores escorted by three Buffalo fighters from the RAAF station at Sembawang. Them Buffaloes are well named. They're old and they're slow but the Japs are caught by surprise, they own the air and they're not expecting nothing like this so they don't have time to scramble their fighter planes.

'The Albacores drop their much-needed supplies, three food canisters and the morphine, then decide to go on a bit of a bomb run at the same time. They drop two bombs on the village, two more on the Japs in the rear and the last two into the rubber where we've got our Battalion HQ and they kill and wound seventeen men. We only hope they did more damage than that to the Japs.

'Well, the fighting continues fiercer than ever and we're getting nowhere, the only blokes not fighting are the ones so seriously wounded they can't lift a rifle or carry a mortar shell. We're trying to push out the perimeter at the bridge but the Nips ain't giving an inch. They send in their tanks again, which close in and this time there's not enough of us to stop 'em getting in amongst us.

'We're now the same as the 2/29th were when they reached us two days earlier, we're down to around three hundred men. But they've copped the same hiding we have and have now got, at a rough count, around a hundred and fifty men left. The 2/15th Field Regiment are down to about a hundred and the Indian brigade have got less than five hundred survivors and are in terrible shape and in no condition to fight much longer. It's as plain as the nose on your face we can't go on. There's no given way we're gunna take the bridge or the village on the other side. I'm gunna die the day after my birthday, which ain't so bad, I suppose. At least I get to live a year longer.'

That's Tommy again with what Nancy calls Irish humour. Which is humour that shows how dumb the Irish really are. If it's true then she's of Irish descent and so is Tommy and me, don't know why she thinks being Australian for five generations is going to make us any smarter than we were before we came here.

Tommy goes on. 'Anderson is buggered if he's gunna surrender but decides instead to withdraw to the east. There's been no contact with the enemy in that direction for hours so he reckons it's the best way to go. The idea is to circle around the Jap positions and make for Yong Peng, which is fifteen miles as the crow flies but a whole lot longer the way we have to go to avoid the enemy. It's all on foot through swamps and jungle so we sabotage what trucks, carriers and guns we've got left and prepare to move out in small groups. It's like every man for himself, with Yong Peng the destination.

'We also have to make the hardest decision you can make in war and that is to leave your wounded behind. There's one hundred and fifty can't make it. We make them as comfortable as possible in trucks and fill them with morphine and leave what's left for them to use as well as enough rations.'

Tommy pauses, looking down into the water between his feet, the fire in the distance is now down to a glow, perfect for the rabbit. I hope the clothes are dry enough to put on before we turn in for the night.

'Mate, I'm saying goodbye to blokes I've trained with, some of them we picked up at that first recruitment drive and who are part of the Snowy Mountains contingent. We've been real good mates and shared many a beer and a laugh together.

'One bloke, Lofty Mason, gives me his fighting knife, "Take it out, Tommo," he says, meaning for me to take the knife out of its combat sheath. I pull it out, "Look on the blade." I do as he says, he's got the name "Garth" embossed on it. "It's me small lad at home in Cooma. If you come out of this alive, mate, can you get this to him, tell him it's took more than one Jap in his name. Then tell him I love him, the same to his mum."

'"Don't you worry, mate, I'll hand it back to you personally," I say, trying to sound a bit cheerful.' Tommy looks up. 'What else could I say? It turns out the Japs herd them all together and bayonet them and then make this big funeral pyre and douse it with petrol and set it alight.

'So, we're out of there and the Japs see us going but maybe they've also had enough because they don't come after us. Later they send planes over to strafe us but we're in the jungle and they can't see us and we're not too concerned. The going is really rough, there's times we're wading up to our waists in swamp and then thick jungle and up and down mountains. Some blokes arrive at Yong Peng several days later but we make it by late that night.

'There's the six of us, all that's left of our platoon, Blades Rigby, the other four and me. We've become a small independent unit and we vow we'll stick together, come what may.'

'That's only six out of thirty men, one-fifth, and you had knife training?' I say, though maybe I shouldn't, I don't mean to suggest how come the casualties are so high with them being so highly trained and having knives an' all. I just want to know what happened, but Tommy thinks I mean the knives.

'Yeah, the fighting knives. Blades Rigby was exaggerating a bit when he said every Jap can disarm you if you're coming at him with a bayonet on the end of your rifle. It's still the standard way to fight 'em close up, that and the hand grenade. If it sounds like we're in control and each of us is a sort of superman, that's bullshit. Mate, no way! I know it sounds a bit gung-ho, the knives and all. I mean it ain't in the official war history or anything. But I have to say, I don't reckon I'd personally have come through the war without what Blades Rigby taught us. I owe him a great debt.

'But, for the most part, we fought just like the other platoons, only on three occasions I come suddenly upon a Jap and I used me knife.' Tommy squints up at me, 'Okay, that's three times I could have been dead. Far as I'm concerned, you only die once and I've been given three extra lives because of Blades Rigby's constant knife drills. Fair enough?'

'I didn't mean to criticise,' I protest. 'I just wanted to know what happened to your platoon.'

'About the same as every other platoon, I guess. When we get to Yong Peng there's 499 Australians left, and our platoon is doing slightly better than average. Like Lofty Mason said, he'd also taken three Japs with his blade before he copped a Jap bullet. Maybe the knives helped a bit, eh?'

'So what happened next?' I ask, knowing Tommy's kind of put me quietly in my place.

'From Yong Peng they wait for the stragglers to get in and they truck us back to Johore Bahru. We're too bloody exhausted to be happy we've survived. Besides, with most of your mates dead, you don't want to celebrate nothing. Blades Rigby is the only bloke that's happy, he's off his head most of the time, don't know what it is he's on as there's not a drop of grog out here in the jungle, but he calls it "jungle juice" and he must have personally killed twenty or more Japanese. Later he called what we were doing "bravely running away" and I reckon he was right, though I don't know so much about the brave bit. I was shitting my pants most of the time. More than once I said goodbye to all the Maloneys whose names I could remember, because this particular Maloney was on the way out, convinced he wouldn't make it through the day's fighting.

'Well, we eventually get to Johore and they give Anderson the VC after that. Some say that because of the gallant resistance of the 8th Division at Bakri/Muar River and the bridge at Parit Sulong and Anderson's refusal to surrender, General Yamashita, "The Tiger of Malaya", had to abandon his plan to invade Australia. If it hadn't been for the way we fought the Japs and held them up, in all likelihood Australia would have faced invasion from the north-west.'

Tommy scratches his head and takes a sip from his mug, though his tea must be dead cold by now, he's been talking a good hour. 'To tell you the truth, I dunno about them being held up that long, or if it's correct what they said about us saving Australia. All I know is the Japanese crossed Malaya from north to south in fifty-six days, a feat declared impossible by the British High Command in Singapore.

'Their soldiers were lightly equipped and whole divisions were mounted on bicycles. The Brits also said they didn't have good maps and would get lost in the virgin jungle. That's a laugh, there were fifth columnists everywhere. They even had the smaller jungle paths flagged. You can ride a bike as good as you can walk along a jungle path.

'So now we're about as far south as you can get in Malaya and we're set to hop over the causeway to Singapore. They've made up our battalion numbers with over seven hundred new blokes, all recruits, a lot of whom haven't been in the army much more than a month and don't know their shit from a tin o' brown Kiwi.

'Because I'm a corporal I'm made a section leader to train a third of the platoon.'

'Congratulations,' I say, grinning in the dark.

Tommy holds up his hand, restraining me. 'It's no honour, I can tell yer. I've got blokes in my platoon who still call a rifle a gun and it's my job to pull them into shape before the next attack. Give you an example, I take them onto the makeshift shooting range one day and each has ten rounds rapid fire at a hundred yards. Not one of the silly buggers even hits the flamin' target, which is roughly eighteen inches across. When I bring out a knife and demonstrate how it goes into the gut and how to bring it out in one movement, a bloke from Sydney faints. I reckon the Nips must be quaking in their boots when their intelligence tells them the fighting shape we're in.

'We've now been fighting the Japs for less than two months and they've come right across Malaya with us retreating all the way. I'm not so sure about the impregnable-fortress theory. Still and all, I hope to Christ the British High Command are right, I can do with a bloody good rest.

'I'm one of the lucky ones, I haven't been wounded, only a bit scratched and cut about, everything festers in the jungle anyway, so we're all wounded in different ways. We've got a touch of the squits and various other complaints, tropical ulcers starting, infections. Most of all, we're completely knackered. A bit of a rest in Singapore city would be just what the doctor ordered. So when in late January we withdraw to Singapore from the shithouse they call Malaya, Tommy Maloney is one happy little soldier.

'Mate, if I'd only known, Malaya was to be the dress rehearsal and the shit is about to hit the fan in a big way. We're in Singapore and from here there's no place to go except into the sea.' He sits back and reaches for a Turf, the packet with a box of matches is resting on a rock beside the hot pool. The way he's smoking I hope he's brought an extra packet. Usually it's only three or four a day when we go bush, back home he's puffing all day. He lights the fag and then I see his hands are shaking and he has two goes with a match. He's been telling things pretty calm-like, but now I see the memories flooding back are taking their toll.

I can't help myself, though I know it's like showing off and I'm not usually like that, but I want Tommy to know how interested I am. I want him to know before he gets into his sleeping bag that I've waited a long time for this night, this moment. That he's taking a battering telling the story and it's not for nothing. I really care and his time ain't wasted. So I decide right off to recite it, the poem he taught us when I was six years old.

*‘**Singapore***
A mighty island fortress
The guardian of the East
Impregnable as Gibraltar
A thousand planes at least
Simply can’t be taken
Will stand a siege for years
We’ll hold the place forever
And show our foes no fears
Our men are there in thousands
With defences quite unique
The Japanese didn’t believe us
And took it in a week.’

Tommy laughs, ‘Jeez, Mole, I must have told you that one when you were knee high to a grasshopper. Good on ya, mate.’

So we’ve had our meal and another brew and then we’ve crawled into our sleeping bags and I reminded him again to make sure he wakes me. Now, when I think back, I wonder why the urgency? After all, when we eventually come back out the tunnel again it’s going to be a full day and probably half the night to get home, plenty of time to tell me the whole story on the journey back.

I tell myself at the time that he may change his mind. Tommy’s a funny blighter, better get him now, here at the big old tree that’s become a sort of spiritual home for four generations of male Maloney. He’s brought me here as a sort of initiation, something only he can give me. It’s a precious gift, a secret place, a kingdom of our own. It’s only fitting that he tells me his story here. I tell myself he’ll say things here beside the mighty Alpine Ash, the Maloney tree, that he won’t elsewhere. Now I’ve been initiated, there’s another knowledge I have to acquire and my greatest fear is that once we’re back in the outside world, Tommy might clam up again. Tommy’s spent too much time alone in the bush and in a prison cell so when there’s people around they seem to diminish him and he goes quiet and almost completely disappears.

I think about the tree again. It’s stood tall two hundred years before the white man came and chopped down all the great monarchs of the forest and sawed them into planks from which they've built their shitty little homes and bred their snotty-nosed, barefoot kids, just like what we've done. Except that it's a Maloney that's saved one old tree, to remind us all that when we cut down the great trees, we cut down the anchors of the earth and allow the broken land to crumble and wash away forever.

Now Tommy's telling me that I'm its guardian. That, while the Maloneys may have amounted to nothing much in the past, stayed the lowest there is, they have nevertheless been entrusted with this one great task and they haven't failed in three generations. He's saying the secret has become mine and he's going to have to trust me to keep it safe, the fourth-generation Maloney, the next guardian of the mighty Alpine Ash.

Tonight he's been yacking away, a Tommy I've seldom heard before, except sometimes when we're alone and he talks about nature. Now he's talking about himself, that's different, Tommy is unlocking his heart. He's digging up memories that haven't been aired since he come back looking like a drover's dog, a bag of bones that lay on the soft pillow that meanwhile Nancy had become. It's stuff I need to know urgently. Maloney stuff. If you know the past, you may just figure out what it is that makes you who you are. I only wish I'd brought the alarm clock from home.

Then, in a sudden panic, I tell myself, 'What if Tommy doesn't wake up till morning?' I think about trying to stay awake, building the fire up, sitting in the hot pool, thinking about Anna Dombrowski.

Tommy's snoring away. At least there won't be any tears tonight. Poor little bugger's dead to the world. Now that I've been over his story in my head so I've got it down pat, my eyelids are like lead.

I look up one last time, along the mighty pillar that rises from the forest floor, the massive trunk of the old man Ash. My eyes follow up the great stem and, through its missing canopy, I see there's stars pinned to a sky that has become its rightful roof.

Chapter Twenty-two

I don't know how but I wake up. Sometimes your mind has its own alarm clock. The moon overhead is pouring silver light through the canopy. Tommy is snoring away. We've never known Tommy when he didn't snore. Nancy says it's because of his broken nose and his sinuses and his battered jaw. I glance over at the fire, which is down to a few glowing embers. Somewhere in the trees to my left I hear a mopoke, then another answering, the real name is boobook owl, but what they sound like is 'mopoke' so that's how come they get that name. The frog chorus has stopped.

Judging from the position of the moon it's around midnight. I crawl out of my sleeping bag, my body stiff and aching from the cuts and bruises I've copped in the tunnel and from sliding down the waterfall. I collected wood to build up the fire before going to sleep and, soon enough, bring the billy to the boil.

Tommy isn't all that happy being woken up. I guess he's hurting even more than I am. He grunts when I shake his good shoulder and groans when I shake him a second time. He opens his eyes, sits up, and I hand him a mug of tea. I've put a bit of extra sugar in to perk him up a bit. 'I'm sorry waking you, Dad.' I really am because Tommy needs the sleep, though I can't take a chance he'll clam up on me once we get off the mountain.

'Nah, 's all right.' He remains sitting up in his sleeping bag and takes out a Turf cigarette. Most working-class blokes smoke roll-yer-own. Far back as I can remember he's always smoked Turf. John Crowe used to say it wasn't a bad name for them because they were made from pure horseshit. Tommy takes a couple of puffs to help him wake up, then a sip from his mug and sighs.

I wait for him to say something but he doesn't so I say, 'I suppose I could have waited and you could tell me on the trip home.' I'm apologising to him, because in the light from the fire I see he looks like absolute shit, as if he's whacked beyond belief.

'Nah, it's okay, I couldn't do it nowhere else, it's partly why we come here.'

'Doubt we'll get home by temorra night. Climb out's gunna take us five hours, I reckon,' I say, for want of a reply.

'Yeah, sorry about that, Tuesdee late.' He gives a weary grin. 'Yer mother's gunna be ropeable.'

'Yeah, well, it's been worth it, you telling me the war stuff and the tree and all.'

Tommy doesn't say anything for about two minutes, just takes sips from his mug, puffs on his cigarette and looks into the fire. I decide to climb back into my sleeping bag, sit up nice and cosy, hugging my knees, and wait for him to talk.

'Well, we're in a right pickle, mate,' Tommy begins at last. 'The Japs have chased us across the causeway onto Singapore Island. Not only do they now control all of Malaya, they've got the food they need growing on the land and what we've left behind during the retreat. There's so much stuff we haven't taken, food, ammo, equipment, that the Japs call them "Churchill Supplies". Now they got airfields to bomb us from, what's more, they control the water supply that is piped over from Johore Bahru to Singapore. Although they have far fewer men than us, they're well trained and battle-hardened.

'That bloke Winston Churchill never could get it into his head that the Japanese just might be good soldiers. Far as he was concerned, they were a bunch of midgets with buckteeth wearing glasses thick as the bottom of a Coke bottle. He reckoned they'd be a pushover. He kept all his trained Pommie soldiers to fight the Germans and, same as we done, sent the raw recruits to the Far East as reinforcements. Some bloody pushover! I hate the Japs, can't never forgive them for what they done, but they were bloody good soldiers. A man would be stupid to say otherwise.

'Anyway, we blow up the causeway between the mainland and Singapore, which any galah can see is basically a waste of time. They also blow up the water supply, which comes from Malaya. Percival reckons there's plenty of big reservoirs on the island but he doesn't reckon on two things; the Japs overrunning them or bombing the pipes at that end. That's exactly what happens and one of the reasons for the final surrender was the lack of water for the one million civilians in the city.

'Anyway, Bennett wants to destroy the entire causeway but there's old Percival at it again who overrules him. In the end they blow up the first seventy feet or so. As the water at low tide was only about four foot deep, the Japs simply waded across until they repaired it. They'd have come across easy enough even if the causeway wasn't there. F'instance, some of our blokes who got left behind in the final withdrawal from Johore waited until low tide and then swam across. At best, blowing it up was a minor inconvenience. The Japs rebuilt it, good as new, in a couple of days.'

'But I read there were around 120,000 soldiers on our side, more than three divisions,' I say.

'Yeah, on paper! On paper it all looks dinky-di, we should've been able to make a go of it.'

'Just bad leadership, you reckon?'

'Can't say that, mate. I'm only a corporal, a shit-kicker, trying best I can to stay alive. The real point is we've got no air cover and a huge number, about half, of the men available to us were Indians. I don't want to heap shit on the Indians, some of them fought like tigers in Malaya, but many were fresh recruits who'd had hardly any training. Like our own reinforcements, they were raw as butcher's mince. The Pommie 18th Division arrived in Singapore in time to see us crossing the causeway. They'd just spent eleven weeks at sea and hadn't acclimatised to the heat and humidity. They'd expected to be sent to the Middle East and what training they had was for the desert, not the jungle. The experienced blokes like us who fought in Malaya were exhausted, especially those of us who'd fought at Parit Sulong.

'We left Johore Bahru on the tip of the Malay peninsula and marched across the causeway to Singapore with the Japs hot on our tail. The Australians and what was left of the Argyll and Sutherland Highlanders were the last to come across. The Jocks are a crack outfit, the only one of the Pommie battalions to train in jungle warfare. The English garrison troops thought they were crackers. Us and the Jocks are supposed to be the seasoned fighters, just in case the Japs surprise us from the rear, they said.' Tommy chuckles at the thought, 'We were that knackered I doubt we could have fought a boy-scout troop. But the highland pipers weren't beaten yet, they played "Hielan' Laddie" and "A Hundred Pipers" as we marched across. It was grand after the horror of fighting. There's this story I heard told of the Argyll's drummer, a bloke called Hardy.

'It seems Hardy ain't never been known to run and he's at the very end of the rear guard and he's taken his usual measured step as we're retreating across the causeway. His C.O.'s getting just a tad anxious so he yells to Hardy to get his arse into gear, the Japs are on the way and the engineers want to blow up the causeway.

'Hardy takes no notice, he ain't never run from the enemy to date and he ain't gunna start now. The engineers are looking at their watches, waiting to push the plungers, and Drummer Hardy is still beating his drum to the same measure, increasing his pace not one inch, and while we cross the border the last two pipers alive in the Argylls play "Blue Bonnets over the Border".' Tommy laughs and so do I. 'Finally he crosses the Straits of Johore and the C.O. gives Hardy a proper bollocking for being so bloody slow. But Hardy answers, "Sir, Japs are only Japs and it is undignified for an Argyll to take any notice of them."

'I remember looking about me at the blokes who fought at Parit Sulong and on the way, and you can see in everyone's faces they've had enough. We weren't cowards, nothing like that, we were just bloody exhausted. Up ahead there's new recruits, young kids just out of school, some of them singing "Waltzing Matilda", thinking how good it will be to fight the Japs, the job they've come over to do.'

'Another cuppa?' I ask Tommy. He nods and I get out of my sleeping bag and put a little more wood on the fire, empty the tea-leaves out of the billy and go down to the stream to fill it, then set it back on the fire.

Tommy lights another Turf. 'Moon's clear enough, should be a nice day termorra.'

I think about how we've only had a few hours' sleep and we'll be spending the better part of tomorrow morning trying to get up the mountain. 'Keep talking,' I say to Tommy, 'I can hear you okay while I make the tea.'

'Nah, wait till it's done, I need to clear me mind a bit. Should have known yiz would've wanted to know all the details, it's how yer mind works, don't it?'

'It's just that I want to hear it the way you did it, Dad.'

Tommy doesn't reply and goes on smoking, staring into the night. I make the tea. We're running out of sugar so I leave off putting some in my cup. I don't really mind it without anyway. 'There yer go,' I say and hand him his mug.

'I've never told any of this before,' Tommy begins, holding his mug in both hands to warm them, the cigarette hanging out the corner of the broken side of his jaw. That side doesn't work that well so he can talk almost perfect with a cigarette in his mouth. 'When you listen to the blokes on Anzac Day after they've had a pot or two and the bullshit begins waxing lyrical, you'd think the lot of us were heroes.'

'You were, Dad.'

Tommy shakes his head. 'No, mate, it was just that there was no place to hide.' He takes the fag that's down to no more than half an inch out of the corner of his mouth and repositions it to the front, then draws it down to his fingertips and flicks the last quarter of an inch into the fire. The tops of his finger and thumb are stained dark from nicotine.

He takes a sip of the hot tea and then gets going again on the story. 'As you say, there's about 120,000 Allied troops and it looks dinky-di, but we don't amount to what you'd call a fighting force in any army's manual. The Indians have just about had it, the Pommie reinforcements have just arrived and our reinforcements are wet behind the ears. On the credit side there's six 8th Division battalions, a good part of whom have had jungle experience, and the Jocks who can acquit themselves same as us, we're the old hands who now know how to fight the Japs.

'Anyway, we cross onto the island and, with the 2/20th and 2/18th and blokes from the machine-gun battalion, we make up the 22nd Brigade and are told to take up positions on the north-west coastline. That's where Bennett reckons the Japs will invade, though Percival disagrees and thinks the attack will come from the north-east and that's where he puts his main thrust.

'We're told to dig in. Our platoon draws the short straw and we get the position well forward as the greeting committee for the Japanese coming across the Straits of Johore. "To dig" is also a bit of a joke, we're situated in the middle of a mangrove swamp. We tell ourselves that at least the going is gunna be as tough for them as it is for us and the Japs have to come and fetch us while we only have to wait. It's small comfort, we've seen how the Japanese come in, stepping over the bodies of their mates.

'Maybe the Japs decide to give their men a bit of a rest. We have to wait a week before they make their big move. Meanwhile they're shelling the daylights out of us. A week sitting in the middle of a mangrove swamp isn't exactly homey. It's the eighth of February, right in the middle of the monsoon season, it's been raining all afternoon to make us just a little more uncomfortable than we already are. Don't know why, but we sense this is the time they're gunna come.

'Darkness comes suddenly in the tropics, one moment you can read a map, the next you need a torch to see your own feet. We're sitting there quietly shitting ourselves, each man thinking about what's about to happen, feeling a bit sorry for himself. We've just fought ourselves to a standstill in Malaya and deserve better.

'They've told us all to write letters home, which is not a real good sign. Letters home are generally followed by a telegram from the War Office to your next of kin.

'Anyway, we're sitting biting our knuckles when the shelling really steps up. There's a total barrage coming at us, sixty to eighty shells a minute, in the area where we're dug in. There's huge sprays of mud and shit every time a shell lands. You can't see them in the flash made by the explosions. Lumps of mud thump down on the ground beside you and hit you so we're all covered in shit. Something hits me in the neck and fair takes me head off. "Jesus! I'm done for!" I grab my neck but there's no blood. Then something starts flapping at my feet.' Tommy laughs and looks at me. 'It's a bloody great fish, not a mark on it, we would've cooked it for tea under different circumstances!

'Next to me is an old bloke, first-war veteran, name of Tony Freeman, and in between the explosions and the shells whistling above his head, he says to me, "May as well take a smoko, Tommy, no point ducking. If your name's on one of them mortars or heavy artillery shells, you won't know nothing about it anyway. They'll keep this up a while, it's when it stops you've got to watch out, that's when the buggers will come at us."

'He's right. Eventually the barrage stops and we get ready for the fray to come. But there's nothing, not a sound. After a while I reckon the silence is worse than the shelling. At least in the jungle you're fighting on equal terms, they don't know where you are and you can't see them. Here we are sitting ducks, we're not goin' nowhere and they know where we are.'

Tommy glances at me. 'You see, I've changed me mind about them having to come to us across the mangrove, which don't seem the better option any more. We're sitting ducks, all I can see is the black strip of water in front of me. After a while, I pick up the faint splash of oars and then shapes of boats and barges. Black shapes are moving towards us in the water, now there's bloody hundreds o' them. I hear Tony Freeman say "Here comes the fucking Spanish armada!"

'We wait until they hit the shore on our side and our machine guns open up. I guess they're dropping like flies, but who knows, there's no encouragement to be taken, it's dark. I think to meself, I've seen this before in the jungle, they're dying for the Emperor God and no machine-gun crossfire ain't gunna stop the fuckers. Soon they're close enough so we can hurl grenades at them or pick off their dark shapes with a rifle.

'It don't make no difference, they run over their comrades' bodies, wave after wave. There's not enough of us to cover the whole perimeter and there's gaps between our various units which they find out soon enough and our crossfire don't keep them out.

'We're expecting our own artillery to start hitting them any moment, but no such thing happens. Later we find out that the communication lines have been cut by the Japanese bombardment and, with no orders, our artillery blokes are helpless. Eventually a runner gets to them and gives them the orders. The artillery are told to bring down fire everywhere, so they give it all they've got. A total of 4800 rounds fall and now there's bodies landing with a thump in front of us.

'Soon enough the machine guns are out of ammunition, their barrels red-hot from continuous firing, and the Nips are still coming, shouting out in the dark, splashing through the mud and the water, happy to die in the name of Nippon. The machine-gunners fix bayonets same as we do and we're in among them hand-to-hand. We are outnumbered eight to one and haven't a hope in hell of stopping them.

'Did you kill any?' I ask, excited.

Tommy stops. 'It's not a question you ask a soldier, Mole.'

I bow my head. 'I'm sorry.'

'No, don't be. If you didn't kill the enemy, he was gunna kill you. The answer is you don't count, it's your bayonet or his, your knife or his, you do the best you can to stay alive. Killing don't really come into it, just staying alive is what it is all about.' He grins, 'Mate, when you've got yourself an enemy who don't seem to care if they die, you've got your work cut out just staying alive. We fought hard as we could and we retreated hard as we could without ever turning our backs.

'Eventually, at dawn we get the message to withdraw and by morning it is all over for the advance defence, which, of course, is us. The Japanese make one last assault before they finally halt the main attack. They've won the foothold they needed to take on the rest of the island and now need time to gather their forces.

'We withdraw to the other side of the Tengah airfield, that is, what is left of us. Our dead are now in Jap-held territory, we've had to leave them where they'd died.' Tommy sighs, 'A more sorry-looking bunch of blokes you wouldn't want to see at a school reunion. We're covered in blood and mud, some of the machine-gunners have no skin left on their palms, it's burnt off from the red-hot barrels.

'The 20th, 18th and ourselves have ceased to exist as battalions, the majority killed or wounded, or they've been cut off, routed, wandering about in the dawn light not knowing what's hit them. I doubt we could have made up one battalion out of the lot of us. But one thing's good, there's still the six of us together under Blades Rigby. We're beginning to think we must be leading charmed lives, Malaya, now this. I'm the only one that's copped something, which is only a bloody awful headache where the fish hit the back of me neck, the other blokes are untouched.'

Tommy reaches out and picks up one of the sticks I'd cut earlier to dry our clothes and he pokes at the fire, turning the logs, bringing it to life. I get out of my sleeping bag and put a dead branch over the top of the fire so it will catch in the renewed flames.

'Remember before we went to sleep, I told you about the padre with the funny name, Wardale-Greenwood, how he helped lay on a mortar attack?'

I nod, 'I don't reckon you'd get Father Crosby doin' that, eh?'

Tommy grins, 'Don't suppose, though you never know, he did rescue the Virgin in the fire. Well, the padre's still with us and if it weren't for him, I reckon a lot more blokes would have died. He takes no notice of the enemy fire, mortars landing, shells exploding, don't seem to matter to him, he's hopping from one wounded bloke to another, applying field dressings and comforting the dying, saying final prayers when it's needed. Then he wades up to the waist through a swamp to help get forty wounded men to safety. Reckon he should've got the VC, no risk.'

I smile to myself, Tommy's handing out VCs again.

'From the airfield we move back to Brigade HQ at Bulim Village. Much later the same day, a Captain Richardson arrives with some blokes from the 2/20th and a few machine-gunners. Poor bugger was in charge of a forward post and didn't get the signal to move out when we did. Just about dawn, when we're in the process of getting the hell out, they get the full brunt of the final Japanese attacks and somehow they hold them out until about ten-thirty, most of it hand-to-hand combat.

'Eventually the Japs withdraw and the blokes that are left, because most of them are dead, pull back to where their HQ should have been. All they see is dead bodies. The captain decides to try to make it to

Tengah airfield, a fair distance across country, hoping to find out where the commander, Brigadier Taylor, has his HQ.

'That's easier said than done. There's Jap snipers infiltrated everywhere and the enemy seems to control the intervening country. His blokes are on their last legs. Soon enough they're ambushed and Richardson breaks them up into two small groups and tells them to try and make their own way back.

'What's ahead is jungle, river and swamp, where a rifle isn't all that useful, so most of them chuck their rifles and any other kit that's heavy and just keep their bayonets. Eventually some of them, including the captain, make it to Bulim Village hours after everyone else. There's nothing said about their lost rifles and kit, they're not the only ones done that.

'Then at Bulim Village we move by truck to the base depot, where we're hurriedly formed into a scratch battalion that's got no real name. They simply call us X Battalion. There's some few of us know how to fight but the remainder are untrained reinforcements who couldn't fight their way out of a wet paper bag. There's only about two hundred of us all up and those who haven't got rifles and kit get reissued. We're told to take a couple of hours sleep then to move back into the line.

'I can't believe my flamin' luck, a man couldn't take a prize in a one-man raffle, we've jumped out of the frying pan into the fire. Like I said, we've got a bunch of no-hopers, drongos who couldn't fix a bayonet and charge if their lives depended upon it, which sooner or later it will. If I'm gunna have to fight, it would be nice to know the bloke next to me knows which end of a .303 is up!

'Having routed the 22nd Brigade the night before, the Nips now come after the 27th. Thank gawd, X Battalion isn't included with the 27th. I don't think I can take another helping of last night. Instead, we're held back in reserve.

'Poor bastards in the 27th cop the same as we done, first the shelling, and then the Japs coming at them in their hordes. They manage to hold on and repulse the first attack but their commander reckons they're in danger of being cut off. He decides to withdraw to a more defensible position about three miles to the rear. Fair enough, but that's when he makes his one big mistake that, in the end, may have cost us the battle for Singapore.

'In the 27th sector are these huge storage tanks that contain oil and aviation spirit. The brigadier decides the fuel shouldn't fall into enemy hands and he orders the cocks opened and the fuel set alight. Though he probably hasn't planned it that way, a river of fire flows to the exact spot the enemy has been trying to infiltrate and incinerates an entire Jap battalion.

'But now comes the disaster. It seems we've made such a good job of repulsing the Japanese invasion that General Nishimura, the Jap commander, overestimates the numbers he's against and decides to call off the attack. But the flames from the storage tanks light up the whole area and Nishimura sees the Aussies retreating so he takes the initiative and continues the attack. The sector is lost.

'That afternoon, X Battalion is ordered to move into position to mount an attack. The one day we've been out of the attack, we've been instructed in weapons and kitted out and kept on our feet. It's been two days since those of us who have survived the first night's fighting have had any sleep, except for a couple of hours, and we're like zombies. The walking-dead. The bloke in charge of us is Colonel Boyes and towards sunset he's told to advance to high ground a little beyond the village of Bukit Timah, slightly further on from where a unit of Indian troops is positioned.

'It's coming on dark, we don't know the area and we stumble forward and get to the village just before dark. The whole place is up in flames and we skirt the village and come across where the Indian troops are supposed to be, only there's hundreds of dead bodies and no live Indians. From the look of the bodies and the fresh blood, the enemy isn't that far away. There's a smell of roasted flesh in the air and I feel like puking.

'We reach our designated position and we're told to dig in.' Tommy grins, 'Well, there's no way that's going to happen, it's now nearly three days since we've slept and the troops in X Battalion drop to the ground where they're standing and are asleep in a matter of minutes.

'At least the six of us stay awake long enough to find a deep ditch and slide into it and bivouac under a rocky overhang, just in case the Japs send in a few mortars. I reckon I've never been that tired in me life. Blades Rigby says he'll keep watch. He's the only one who's got the stamina.' Tommy laughs, 'It must be the hashish. He was always chewing it in Malaya and it kept him going when the rest of us were completely rooted. He said he loved to kill the little yellow men and the *ganja* helped him to stay awake and get a few extra notches on his knife.

'There's no denying it, he was always in the thick of the killing. I dunno how he ever made sergeant because he was a law unto himself and completely unpredictable. But if it wasn't for the knife drill he taught us, I'd have been long dead. As far as I know, knife drill don't come out of any army instruction manual neither, so where did he learn it, eh?

'There's no way a mere mortal could have stayed on guard after three days of fighting without sleep, unless he was on something. With him it was hashish or maybe something else he'd found. He spoke fluent Malay and some of the Chinese lingo and was always talking to the locals, scroungin' information, bartering something.'

'What's hashish?'

'Hashish? It's a drug they use in the East, the resin of marijuana, which is a plant. There's lots of ways you can use it, smoke it, chew it, put it in food. In prison, some of the crims smoked the marijuana leaf when it could be smuggled in, it's much weaker than hashish, which comes from the blossom. The leaf can be rolled like tobacco into a cigarette called a roach, these days it's a joint.'

'Have you? I mean have you smoked it?'

'Yeah, makes you feel relaxed. Some blokes smoking it start to giggle a lot. If a screw finds it on you or in your cell, you get seven days solitary. The official name is cannabis.' Tommy reaches for another Turf. 'Personally I prefer these coffin nails.'

He lights up, draws back and exhales. 'Where was I?'

'You've just fallen asleep, Blades Rigby is on guard.'

'Righto. Well, I don't know how long we're asleep when he shakes me and whispers urgently, "Japs! Wake up, Tommy!"

'The Japanese 18th Division have found X Battalion asleep, though I only know this afterwards. The six of us just sit tight and from where we are in the monsoon ditch under the rock overhang, we can't see nothing. They've simply come up and bayoneted most of the blokes in their sleep. Those who woke in time had a go but most don't have a hope. Most are not fighting men anyway. We learned later that Captain Richardson managed to get away with a handful of troops. I reckon he should have got the VC.

'Anyway, we play possum until we hear the Japs have all gone and then we come out of hiding. Everywhere we look there are dead Australians, some blokes left over from our battalion, not that that's a lot. They're mates you've shared a beer with. Worst thing is there are no Japanese dead. Either they've caught us completely by surprise or they've taken their dead and wounded with them. It's the perfect ambush, the whole of X Battalion caught napping.

'"Christ, I should've been fuckin' there!" Blades shouts out, real angry.

'"Remember, you were, mate, playing possum," I tell him, "And thank gawd for that!"

'"If I'd been up top, I'd have heard them coming, given a warning. Even if I'd only got two or three of the murdering sods!" The bastard's off his scone.

'What can I say? I know he's saved my life. If it wasn't for him, I would've been up top asleep. I'm getting a bit tired of Blades Rigby saving me life.

'Can't really call the Nips murdering bastards in this case. I reckon we'd have done the same if we had come across them asleep. Ambush is a part of war. I guess the sentries Colonel Boyes posted must have fallen asleep. Can't blame them neither. Anyway, he was dead as well.

'But it don't take that long to find out that the Japs *truly* are murdering bastards. Remember, we only found out later what they did to our wounded at Parit Sulong, bayoneting them, then setting them alight. Until now, we'd thought of them as pretty worthy warriors.

'We make our way back towards Bukit Timah, using whatever concealment there is.' Tommy stops and looks at me. 'Bukit Timah isn't like a native village, it's a small town with streets marked, sort of half-native and half like one of our towns. There's a Catholic college and a post office, some administration buildings and shops owned by the Chinese that haven't been destroyed by artillery fire. We're creeping along a road named Jurong Road which is leading in the direction of the village when we come across this monsoon drain.

'There's sixteen Australian bodies lying in the ditch. They've been taken prisoner by the Japanese and they've been trussed and made to kneel above the drain. The Japanese have beheaded some of them and used their bayonets on the others. Their wrists are still tied behind their backs, some are without heads, their heads scattered willy-nilly in the bottom of the ditch like they've been kicked into it afterwards.

'Later I meet a bloke in Changi named George Plunkett, who it turns out was in that ditch in Jurong Road. There was twenty of them taken there by the Japs and trussed up and executed. He told me how one of his mates, "Titch" Burgess, regained consciousness. In the killing frenzy, a bayonet thrust that was meant to kill him had severed the rope they'd used to tie him up. Badly wounded, Burgess managed to untie Plunkett and three others. They all had deep stab wounds and sword cuts to the neck. Plunkett had been bayoneted thirteen times in the back. They managed to somehow get themselves out of the ditch and a Chinese family took them in. Three of them survived, but "Titch" Burgess, the bloke who'd saved their lives, had lost too much blood and died.

'Soon enough we come across what was left of Brigadier Taylor's Infantry Brigade HQ. They were strung out along Reformatory Road Ridge above Bukit Timah. We'd no sooner reported in when the Japs attacked and every able-bodied man, including the staff officers, were ordered to counter-attack across Reformatory Road.

'Let me tell you, it was on for one and all. Up to now the Japanese had always been the enemy, you know, the other side, I even had a grudging respect for them. But after seeing them blokes in the ditch, I now hate the little yellow bastards. I reckon the others feel the same because now it's a matter of grenade and bayonet. Only with us six, it's the knife and we get stuck in. We cut our way through the buggers and have the rare satisfaction of seeing them running backwards. I'm no hero but there's six Japs coming at me, and me and Blades Rigby with a knife coming at them. They take one look at us carrying nothing but a blade and they turn and run for their lives. I'm convinced after that that Blades is crackers, stark starin' mad. The bastard just ain't scared of no one and they've seen it in his eyes.'

I'm smiling inwardly at this, little Tommy and his mates mounting a knife attack and the Japs, all bug-eyed, seeing their fierceness and running. I can see it in my mind and I admire him. But then he's squinting at me, reading my thoughts.

'Mate, you're probably thinking it's like the films, Errol Flynn, blokes fighting hand to hand, knives flashing. It ain't like that. You're in there and you can't think. If you think, you'll run, so you just charge and fight and hope your training and instinct will take over. It's a sort of fighting frenzy you're in, afterwards you're so scared you can't lift your arms and you're sobbing and can't stop shaking. I remember sitting on a forty-four-gallon drum after that fight, me arms like lead, shaking like a leaf and I look down and, right up to the elbows, I'm covered in Jap blood and it's still wet.'

'But you didn't run away, you fought them, didn't yer?'

Tommy doesn't reply. 'Next day Brigade HQ, which is where we now are and where I meet a few other blokes from in the 8th Division, retreats down Holland Road and then we move to the outskirts of the city. What's left of us, that is the 22nd Brigade, are hardly enough to form one battalion of three hundred soldiers. Let me remind you, a brigade is around three thousand men and now there's two hundred, maybe a few more stragglers comin' in every day.

'The rest are all dead, wounded, lost or cut off. Transport, supply and service personnel are now making up the numbers. Like X Battalion, they know bugger-all about hand-to-hand fighting. That's the point, sometimes the front between the enemy and us is twenty yards. It's not difficult to see we're pushing shit uphill with a broken stick.'

Tommy pauses and I can see he's wearing out but I don't want him to stop, there is so much telling yet to be done. 'You're tired, Dad, would you like to stop?' My heart is beating faster. 'Please, please don't let him stop,' I think to myself.

'She's right, mate, just need to take a piss, too much char.'

Tommy returns a couple of minutes later and settles back into his sleeping bag. 'Now, where was I? Oh yes, we're into the outskirts of the city. If I make it through the day, I'm gunna sleep in a dry place, maybe even a bed. It seems a funny thought, our chances of seeing the dark of another night are pretty slim but you can't think about that. What's it Nancy always says? Yeah, that's right, "Hope springs eternal".

'We enter the outskirts of the city and it's a repeat performance, the Japs just have too many fit fighting men and us too few. Their artillery is pounding the shit out of the city and bombs are falling everywhere. The Japs own the skies and it's a considerable advantage. Pretty soon they overrun our hospital at St Patrick's College at Katong and we set up two makeshift ones at St Andrew's Cathedral and the Cathay building, both of which are well within the Allied perimeter. Later we learn that when they take Alexandra Hospital they murder the wounded along with the doctors and nurses. Some of the wounded men were taken outside and used as bayonet practice while the Jap soldiers laughed at the fun of it all.

'We were beginning to realise that the Japanese take no prisoners. That they regarded surrender as cowardice, which was a bloody good reason to keep fighting. I reckoned at the time I'd rather die facing the enemy than be trussed and on my knees so some little yellow rice-munching midget wearing thick spectacles can behead me with the family sword. No, that's a lie! You don't think like that. That comes after.

'But we knew in our hearts it was only a matter of time before it was all over, there's nothing we could do to stop the rampage. On the afternoon of the fifteenth, General Percival surrenders. I don't know why he bothered, we were convinced we'd all be killed one way or another. But at 8.30 p.m., on the fifteenth of February 1942, the guns stop and hostilities cease. The fortress that couldn't be took has fallen in just seven days. We'd seen enough of the mongrels to know that whatever was to come it wasn't gunna be no Sunday School picnic.

'What followed was this big Japanese parade with their soldiers marching or riding in trucks or tanks or in streams of cars taken from the civilian population, every vehicle bedecked with the flag of the rising sun. They're yelling and blowing their hooters and laughing, like a bunch of larrikins outside the movies on a Saturday night. We watch them, too tired to look away. If, during that week of fighting, I slept in a dry place I don't recall it, mostly because I don't ever remember sleeping except under the rock when X Battalion was ambushed.

'But now, with the surrender, the real slaughter starts. To the Japanese everyone is the enemy, even the civilians and in particular the Chinese. They hate the Chinese something terrible, more even than us. The poor buggers had already suffered enough. The city was a bloodbath, 70,000 civilians were killed. The bombing had been responsible for a lot of the destruction but once inside the city the Japs are merciless, rounding up women and children and lopping heads off looters and anyone they don't like the look of.

'There are bodies and parts of bodies lying piled up in the streets, infants, women and children as well as men. They lie on front lawns, on the steps of the bigger buildings, the monsoon ditches are piled full of them. In some streets and pavements the surfaces are so black and slick with congealed blood, from the blood oozing from bodies piled up to make roadblocks or to be burnt, that you didn't dare walk there.

'Pretty soon the bodies start to rot in the tropical heat, the gases bloating the corpses. The Japanese would wait until the stomachs were huge, blown up like a balloon by the gases roiling inside the dead, then they'd hurl a hand grenade in among them or pepper them with bullets so the bloated stomachs would explode and spray intestines and everything else thirty or forty feet into the air. Bits of body hung off roof gutters and telegraph wires. They thought this was huge fun. There was shit and human parts, blood and rotting human flesh everywhere you turned. We had no hope of burying the dead. We had to leave the job of cleaning up to the maggots and flies. All we could do was try to care for our own wounded.'

Tommy is silent and I've got my head bowed. My imagination is working overtime to try to understand what Tommy's just told me, to try to see it in my mind's eye. I'm glad we haven't eaten nothing because I reckon I'd be sick. I can't offer him another cup of tea because if I do there'll be nothing left for the trip home. 'A mug of water?' I ask him and he nods. I rinse the mugs, then fill them at the cold part of the stream. I know that what's next is Changi, I've read a bit about Changi where the prisoners were taken and I'm expecting more of the same. Maybe it was Changi where Tommy got his shoulder and jaw and eye bashed.

To my surprise Tommy now says, 'Mate, tell you the truth, the march out of the city to Selarang Barracks at Changi I hardly remember. We were that happy to be alive and getting out of the stinking city, away from the smell of rotting corpses, I reckon my mind drew a blank. I was that exhausted anyway, probably didn't even know where I was. We'd scrounged a bit of gear here and there and I'd changed my uniform for one on a dead bloke as mine was in tatters. I took his kit as well, keeping only me slouch hat which had a bullet hole through the crown where a Jap rifle had come close to parting my hair. I remember finding this pork-pie hat somewhere, so I stowed mine in my kitbag and wore the pork-pie. Lots of the blokes were wearing civilian headgear, pukka-sahib helmets and one bloke I saw was wearing a female wig. We was laughin' and jokin' as we marched, Christ knows why, there wasn't nothing to laugh about, 'cept of course we were still alive when a lot of our mates weren't. But the six of us are still there and unhurt, which is a flamin' miracle and good reason to be happy.'

I find it strange that in all Tommy's telling and with what all them six have been through together, he's never given their names, except for Blades Rigby. 'You've never mentioned the names of your mates, why's that?'

Tommy looks up, 'Suppose you think it strange, eh? I've only named the one, Blades Rigby?'

'Yeah, you seemed to be good mates?'

Tommy nods his head, 'Never any better. Only mate I ever had better than any one of them was John Crowe.' He squints, 'I'm scared to say their names or how they died, they's locked into me head, if I say their names they might fly away.' He looks up, 'It's not something I can explain.' He looks down again between his hands which are resting on his kneecaps, his legs inside the sleeping bag, his arms out, one hand holding the mug of water. 'I've never done no mourning for them, see. Never put them to rest in me heart.' He says it softly so that I only just hear him. Then he looks slowly up at me, 'After them I knew I could never make a new friend, that if I did, he would die violently before his time, just like they done.'

I can't say anything to comfort him, to tell him it ain't true, that it's all in his imagination, because of course I think of John Crowe, Tommy's oldest and only real friend in Yankalillee, someone who had known him as a kid and had been there for him after he came back from the war. John Crowe has died violently, the Red Steer wiping him off the face of the earth. Shit! Tommy thinks John Crowe's death was because of him, because of their friendship. I have to say something to try to help him.

'Dad, it doesn't work like that!' I protest. 'They were soldiers, they knew they could be killed any day!'

'Yeah, I know.'

'It's just in your mind! You have to let it come out. You have to say their names!'

Tommy doesn't look up for a long time, then he does. 'You know something, Mole?'

'What?'

'I've tried, I can't remember them. I can see them plain as anything, their faces, the way they laughed.' He looks up, there are tears running down his cheeks, 'But I can't remember their fucking names! Them blokes saved me life more than once and I can't remember their names!'

I get out of my sleeping bag and sit down beside him and put my arm around him. It's the first time I've held him in my whole life. He's still skin and bone, still the same drover's dog Nancy met at the railway station when he come out of the repat hospital. I can feel his thinness against my chest and along the inside of my arms, the bone through the sinew and skin. 'I'm sorry I said that, you don't have to do nothing. Let your mates stay buried in your heart, best place for them to be, best memorial they could have.'

Tommy sniffs and pulls away, 'Christ, a man's a bloody sheila. Can't even tell a story proper without blubbing.' He wipes his hands across his eyes and then his fist under his nose.

'There's a bit of rabbit, it's cold but it's something to chew on. You'll feel better with something to eat.'

Tommy sniffs again, 'Nah, better keep it, need it termorra.'

'I seen a couple of possums earlier, ringtails, I'll go get 'em when it's first light. What say, a bit a possum stew make a nice change, eh?' I know Tommy isn't into shooting the wildlife but we've had possum in an emergency before and it tastes good if you cook them real slow.

Tommy laughs, then sniffs, 'You're a bonzer bloke, Mole.'

We chew on the rabbit and I decide to make another billy. It'll leave just enough tea to make him a mug in the morning, though there'll be no sugar. The moon is now past the canopy opening and it's pretty dark, the bush around us is silent except for the burble of the water in the little creek and the occasional crack of a log on the fire where the flames throw yellow slabs of light onto Tommy's broken face.

The cold meal, hot tea and a cigarette seem to pick him up a bit. 'You know when you read about Changi in books and that and on the films, it looks pretty terrible. But after what we'd been through, Malaya, Parit Sulong, that and the past week on the island, Changi was a doddle. There's nearly 15,000 of us and another 37,000 Poms, local volunteers and some Dutch prisoners of war down the road a bit and, what's more, the Japs decide to behave themselves a bit better now they've got the Chinese civilian population to kill.

'There's one bit of good news. Our commander Major General Bennett's escaped. He's got away in a small boat after the surrender. Most of the officers think it's a poor show that he blew through, leaving them to face the music. Also, some of the blokes are pretty pissed off and are calling him a yellow-belly. But that's not how most of us feel. He fought hard as any of us and was a bloody good leader. By escaping, far as we were concerned, he'd set a good example. What's the point in putting a crackerjack general in a concentration camp for the rest of the war?

'Later we heard that when he got back to Australia he copped a fair amount of shit for deserting his troops. But that was bullshit, it's everyone's duty to escape and I reckon the top brass just made a scapegoat out of him to cover their own backsides for the debacle of Singapore. It was them that decided to send raw recruits to fight. If Bennett hadn't trained us in jungle warfare, Christ knows what would have happened. Maybe those blokes are right, Australia may have eventually been invaded. I still reckon if the recruits that came after Malaya had been trained better and the same with the Brits and the Indians, we could have defeated the Japanese. As it turned out, we bloody nearly did anyway.'

'I thought you said the Japs were better trained and good fighters. How could you have beaten them?'

'True, but what we hadn't realised was that they'd crossed Malaya in fifty-six days, fighting some of the fiercest battles in the war. The Muar River and Parit Sulong battle, where my battalion was all but massacred and where an ambush by the 2/30th had taken a heavy toll and, like us, the Japs were exhausted.

'We had more troops on Singapore Island than the Japs, but the difference was that many of ours were fresh to combat and just didn't have the required training. If they had, we'd have won easy. But anyway, I'll say this for most of them, they were learning fast and if Percival had held out another day, we might just have turned it around. Towards the end we reckoned we had their measure and a lot of the blokes who'd fought tooth and nail for a week were very bloody bitter when Percival, who we all thought was a fair dinkum fool, threw in the towel when there was still a bit of fight left in all of us.

'Anyway, suddenly we're POWs and are being taken to Selarang Barracks, which before the war was the home of the Gordon Highlanders. It has been bombed and ransacked and all that is left are the shell of the barracks, cement floors and holes for windows but the roofs are okay, made of flat concrete, so we can sleep on them. There isn't enough room for everyone so some of us build humpies out of scraps, coconut fronds, stuff we scrounged, and we settle in nice and cosy. Escaping isn't a possibility, Malaya is held by the Japs one side, so is Indonesia on the other, the Philippines also. Escaping and living in the jungle isn't an option, be dead in a month trying that on.

'The Japs soon started sending us out as working parties, burying the civilian dead and clearing up the city. It was shit work but they paid us and gave us extra rations. As a corporal, I got fifteen cents a day in Jap occupation money and we receive four ounces of meat and extra rice.

'Then they started to build a Shinto temple in the MacRitchie Reservoir–Bukit Timah area and soon after that the Shonan Chureto War Memorial at Bukit Batok not far from the Ford Motor Factory, where Percival signed the surrender. There were thousands of us working on those two projects, which was better than staying in Changi, though I didn't get onto one o' them projects but worked in the city, then the wharves.'

'Funny, the Japs have got a religion. I mean, building that temple. If they killed people the way they did, how come they believed in God?' I ask Tommy.

'Not just one, they've got lots a gods, must be that some of their gods say it's okay, tell them they can do cruel stuff to other people as long as they're not Japanese. The Japanese think they're a superior race anyway. That all other races are inferior. Now we've surrendered they think we're lower even than dogs.'

'You must've felt pretty bad building a war memorial to them, like honouring the blokes who've been killing and chopping the heads off your mates.'

To my surprise, Tommy chuckles. 'Like I said, I wasn't on that project. Mate, you gotta laugh, the Jap war memorial is this wooden obelisk rising around sixty or seventy feet. One of the blokes working on it told me the story of how he'd gone into the bushes for a crap and he sees this termite nest. "Whacko, what's this?" he says to himself, "Termites eat wood, don't they?" So, over the next few days, he and his mates dig up the nest and cart the lot over to the obelisk and bury the termite nest nice 'n' cosy under it and the termites are set to munching. "We reckoned it would take about a year to bring it topplin' down," he says.

'"Big nest?" I ask, "How big was the queen?"

'"Queen? What queen?"

'"Mate, every termite nest has to have a queen. Big fat white grub, can get up to two inches in length."

'"Shit!" he says, "I saw that! We thought that were just some fat caterpillar that lived in the soil, threw it aside when we're digging up the nest."

'"City blokes, is yiz?"

'"Yeah, mate, most of us on my work gang are from Melbourne, two blokes from Geelong, we didn't know nothing about a fucking queen."

'I explain to him that the termites will die without their queen in the nest, that what they done was no good. He looked that disappointed that I promised I wouldn't tell nobody so they could skite about what they done and everyone would think the war memorial was slowly being sabotaged by them termites. Stories like that are important and are good for morale and here I am playing the spoilsport, being a smart-arse from the bush.

'Years later in the pub in Yankalillee I hear one of the blokes tell the story of the termites. Only it's now complete. The Jap war memorial has collapsed, eaten away at the foundation, he says, toppled down, nothing left and all of it done in no time flat! He even claims he was one of the original work gang that found the termites. He was a bloke from Bright I've known all me life, went to school with him. He worked on the Singapore wharves with me and then went on to the Burma Railway. He wasn't nowhere near the Jap war memorial, though I don't remind him.' Tommy chuckles, 'I reckon if you can't bullshit a little on Anzac Day, what's the point, eh?

'The Japs work us hard but the grub's just okay and I've got enough pay for fags. Apart from the odd bout of the squits, I'm doing okay. Naturally, we all feel a bit ashamed about being captured, being prisoners of war, like, with other blokes still fighting elsewhere. We comfort ourselves that while it's our duty to escape, the problem is where to? No use escaping unless you can become useful to your own side again. I reckon that's why the Japs were so relaxed. Short of an uprising to overthrow them, we were trapped on the island for the duration.

'Then I come down with dysentery real bad and I'm sent back to Changi where I meet a bloke who's got the dreaded lurgy, name 'o Tom Burns and he tells me he's with a working party on a small island off Singapore city named Pulau Bukum where things are good compared to anywhere else. It's an island where there's about a billion gallons of oil stored in these big concrete tanks. All they do is roll drums of oil to be loaded onto the Japanese tankers arriving every few days. He reckons it's easy enough work once you get used to it and the rations are real grouse, lashings of condensed milk, twenty-five ounces of rice daily, all the bread you can eat and a meat stew for breakfast every morning. It sounds like paradise to me.

'So I get a message to Blades Rigby and the four others and soon they're sent back to Selarang Barracks for insubordination and general bad behaviour, the only way except for sickness you can get back to Changi in a hurry. The colonel sentences them to be put on the Changi trailer for two weeks. The trailer is a stripped-down truck chassis with tyres down to the canvas and is known as 'the cart' and is used to haul wood and water and anything else that has to be moved around the camp. It's pulled by POWs who usually turn out to be one of the larrikin mob on report. Eight blokes are harnessed to the front by traces attached to steel hawsers. It's back-breaking work, I can tell yer and Blades and the rest o' them ain't too happy doing a stint while I'm recovering, sitting back like Jackie in the hospital, munching boiled rice one end and shitting what looks like camp curry out the other.

'With a little help from Tom Burns, we get ourselves onto the island in the harbour and it turns out everything he said is right. The tucker is first class though rollin' drums is bloody hard work at first. But once you get the knack and with the good grub, our bodies build up to it. Anyway, the Japs give us a smoke every half hour when we were loading a tanker, so it isn't too bad. We can swim to cool off and we go fishing every day after work. Provided we gave the guards a small part of the catch, most nights we'd have a good feed o' fish and Sundays we'd have off. Don't have to do a thing, because the guards want to go off to Singapore to get among the whores so they leave us with our own officers. They even give us mosquito nets and a mattress each to sleep on.

'But all good things come to an end and, for once, it ain't the Japs' fault neither. Blades Rigby is a pretty good fisherman and one day he catches this really big fish, maybe twenty pounds, and he wants to trade it with one of the locals for hashish. There ain't no locals on the island because it's an oil depot, but sometimes a sampan passes and Blades makes contact by yelling out at the fishermen in their own language. Now he's got some sort of arrangement he don't talk about and I think he's getting something stronger brought in. When you ask him, he just says he's doing a bit of trading with the nig-nogs, though we never saw anything he bought from them. It isn't too hard to put two and two together.

'Well, this Jap sergeant sees the big fish and wants it for his mess. He points to the fish, "*Morta coy*!" he shouts at Blades, which means "bring it here". Blades doesn't want to give it to him. I'm nervous because I know Rigby's nerves are a bit frazzled as he hasn't had the stuff he uses for a few days and we're all staying out of his way.

'The Jap sergeant insists and starts to shout, takes out his bayonet and, walking right up to Blades, pushes the tip of the blade into his gut. I shout out, "Give him the fuckin' fish, mate!" because I know what's about to happen. Blades has a knife he's made out of a bit of steel from an oil drum. I told you before how he tipped me over when I come at him with a bayonet. If he flips the Jap, it will mean the sergeant has lost face and we'll all be in serious trouble. You just don't muck about with the guards.

'I give a sigh of relief and I'm not the only one, because Blades nods and smiles at the Jap and he makes to hand the fish over. It's heavy and has this bit of twine through its gills to carry it. So the Jap puts his bayonet back and takes the fish by the twine. He's holding it and he's smiling, then he does this little bow and says "*Ichi ban number one*", which means "good on ya" in POW Japanese. Blades grins back and next thing the Jap corporal sinks to his knees with his throat cut. I reckon he's well dead before his head hits the ground.

'Our officer is told to call a parade for that evening and Blades is brought in front of us. His hands are tied behind his back and he's made to kneel in the dirt, then a Jap officer starts to rant and rave in their lingo. We don't understand a word, but he's practically foaming at the mouth and we get the drift all right.

'He takes out his sword and executes Blades Rigby. It takes him three blows to hack off his head while we're all standing to attention. Then this Jap sergeant brings the officer a ceremonial cloth and he wipes the sword and puts it back in its scabbard and marches off.

'We're known to be Blades Rigby's mates and the Japs reckon we might make trouble so the five of us are sent back to Selarang Barracks and put on the cart. Even though we'd done nothing wrong.'

I think to myself, that's another of Tommy's mates that's died a violent death. No wonder he's all screwed up. Once you get something like that in your head and think it's you that's put the curse on them, there's no stoppin' your imagination. Tommy feels guilty, he thinks it's him. That's why, except for John Crowe, he's always been a loner.

Even with us kids. We always thought it was him and the grog. We thought he didn't love us, didn't give a shit about us. When he took me into the bush, he was more a teacher than a father and he never hugged me or showed me any affection. Now I see it's not that at all. In his head Tommy reckons he's protecting us if he stays away. If he doesn't show us he loves and cares about us, then we're safe.

Tommy continues on, 'Reckon, if we weren't so fit and built-up from rolling oil drums and the good tucker at the oil depot, the cart would have done us in. There's supposed to be eight harnessed in, but they've cut it down to us five and a bloke from the 30th Battalion who turns out to be a real pain in the arse. Anyway, with two men short, by the end of each day we're well and truly buggered.

'After we come off the cart, we work on the construction of a poultry farm. We're up to our ankles shovelling chicken shit and if you so much as look sideways at an egg, you're put on report. Things are getting tedious now that we're no longer in the workers' paradise on Pulau Bukum. I forgot to say, before being kicked off the island, we tried to bury Blades Rigby but the Japs wouldn't give us his body. Who knows what the bastards done with him, probably dumped him in the harbour for the sharks to feast on.

'Anyway, around the end of April the Japs want three thousand men for a working party. Word has it that it's away from the island and the facilities are good and there's plenty of food and the work is easy.

'We volunteer straight off for the Jap working party, but are turned down on account of being branded as larrikins. A Force, which is the name of the mob that went away, are put together like a mini brigade with three battalions, the correct number of officers and with Brigadier Varley in charge. They parade and march off happy as Larry 'cause they've got it made. It turns out later they're sent to Burma to work on some railway the Japs are building.'

'You mean *the* Burma Railway? You know, where Mr Gee was?' I ask Tommy, excited.

'Yeah, mate, the selfsame, though we didn't know it at the time. The Japs made it sound like them blokes were going to a holiday camp for retired soldiers.

'It's now early July, we're fed up with the Selarang Barracks diet of rice and a bit of veg, that is if you're lucky. In all the time we were there I never tasted an official AIF egg, even though the hens in the new poultry farm were popping their bums off daily in front of me very eyes.

'Privately it was another matter of course, an omelette wasn't entirely unknown back in the humpy. But still, there's a principle involved, ain't there? A man shouldn't have to risk the cart for stealing the odd egg when he's working on a flamin' poultry farm.

'With everyone out on working parties, there's 3800 of us left behind. Those of us in Selarang are not exactly the pick of the crop neither.

'There's the old blokes, nothing too much wrong with them, most are damn good soldiers from the first world war who do the administration duties. Then there's those not fit enough for a working party who are running the camp, the cooks, the kitchen hands, cleaners and general rouseabouts, a more lazy mob would be bloody hard to find. There's us so-called larrikins, or what is known as "the less well-disciplined", doing hard yakka, working in the vegie gardens and poultry farm, pulling the cart and other unpleasant tasks. There's the real hard cases doing latrine duty. Then there's the sick, of course, who can hardly wipe their own bums, and those convalescing on light duties. After that, there's a whole bunch of useless bastards called officers and warrant officers, who are not required to do an honest day's work and who are probably the ones scoffing all the eggs.

'So when the Japanese say they need another two thousand men for a second workers' paradise, which they describe as a rest camp suitable for older men and convalescents, we're there boots an' all. They conduct a medical inspection to choose two thousand fit men but there's no way they're gunna get them. They change it to 1500 and even then they're scraping the bottom of a very battered barrel. We're called B Force and one thing is certain we ain't no force to be reckoned with.

'All the old blokes are comin' along, a lot of them from non-combatant units so they're soft as plum duff. The walking not-so-sick are included and the late recruits who never really knew what had hit them when they went into battle and are still wonderin' how they got here in the first place.

'Then there's all the officers and warrant officers who have been doing bugger-all for the duration. In the history of military organisations, I'll vouch no group ever had a bigger officer-to-private-soldier ratio. There's one officer for every ten men. Of a final count of 1494 soldiers, there's 143 officers. In one unit, the 4th Anti-Tank Regiment, or what's left of them, there are twelve officers, two majors, one captain and nine lieutenants responsible for thirty-three men. What's more, nine of the men are NCOs!'

Tommy looks at me, 'Mole, maybe you think because I'm a corporal I'm heaping shit on officers and higher rank. Mate, I'm not. A good officer is the salt of the earth. Our C.O. Anderson at the battle of Parit Sulong, you'd have given your life for him. And, as I said, we weren't exactly God's gift ourselves. But with some exceptions, like Ken Mosher and Lionel Matthews, both outstanding officers a man would be proud to fight under, about twenty per cent of the officers in B Force were a heap o' shit. I don't mean only their personalities, there were some really useless bastards you wouldn't feed in any army! Two out of ten don't sound that much but out of 143 officers there were twenty-eight officers you wouldn't pay to pimp in a brothel. There were blokes with one and two pips on their shoulders who'd arrived just in time to go into the bag and who didn't know their arse from their elbow when it come to being an officer responsible for leading men.'

'No, you're right,' I now say to Tommy, 'I read in this book where it said the officers in POW camps in Asia ranged "from cream to sour milk". I guess you got the sour milk.'

Tommy nods, 'You can say that again! But at the time we think it don't matter that much. We're going into semi-retirement, us and all the old blokes and the convalescents. The five of us Young Turks reckon we've done good getting in on this lurk. After the cart and the chook farm it's time for a bit of a spell, you know, lie on the beach eating coconuts and mangoes, taking it easy for a change. May even be some of the local sheilas around. The Asian women ain't a bad lookin' lot, some of them are real crackers and used to takin' good care of their men.'

Tommy is silent, poking at the fire with the stick. Then he glances at me and looks away into the embers. 'If I'd known what was gunna happen to us, I'd have volunteered for permanent duty on a six-man harness on a Changi trailer! Better than that, I'd have gladly done latrine duty for the rest of the war. Emptying shit buckets would have been a privilege.'

Chapter Twenty-three

It's getting pretty late but Tommy's still talking and I'm still listening, though for a while he's gone silent, thinking, looking into the fire.

Having four hours' sleep after our tea was a good idea and I'm hoping he can go for the duration. I can see there's worse to come and I don't want him to run out of steam and leave it for another time.

It's funny, as the night goes along I begin to see Tommy in a different way. I've always known him as a bloke with a bad side and a good side. The bad side is that he's a drunk and a crim and doesn't love us. The good is when we're in the bush, he explains things to me just like an ordinary bloke, even sometimes a bit like a father. Now I begin to see how he got to be who he is. Nancy always says, 'Your father's damaged, you can't expect more from him.' When you're a kid, you don't understand and you *do* expect more; well, not expect, but *hope* for more.

Even the kids in Bell Street, most of whom have an old man who comes back home drunk a couple of nights a week, skite about their dad. Sometimes they get thumped, come to school with a black eye or a thick lip, having run into the same neighbourhood door knob everyone runs into if you live in our street. But the thing is, they don't hate their old man and they tell how he does things with them, comes to the footie matches, takes them to the beach once a year, and they go on picnics and camping and fishing for fun.

I've been lucky to have the good side of Tommy, the bush side, but the others haven't experienced that and they only know the bag-of-nerves Tommy. Bozo ignores him and gets on with his life. Mike despises him. Little Colleen is terrified of him and Sarah tolerates him if he stays away from her. Only Nancy tries to pretend he's a proper member of the family and has the rights of a real father.

The way Tommy is telling me the story of the war I can see he isn't trying to big-deal himself. I've heard lots of blokes talking about the war and after a while they've picked up everyone else's bullshit and mixed it with their own so when they tell it, you'd think they'd won the war single-handed.

As Tommy speaks, I see him differently to before, now he's just an ordinary bloke who's not going to get past the rank of corporal. He can be trusted to do what's asked of him but he's not going to volunteer for any extra, even if it could make him a hero. He's doing his best to stay alive and that's all. What's coming through, without him having to say it, is that he is a pretty nice bloke and not really a larrikin. Tough maybe, a bushie and a survivor, someone you could trust if the shit hit the fan.

He's also a pretty good observer of things and can put two and two together, like he remembers the names of places and the numbers involved and what was going on in the big picture. I suppose that's the same reason he's so good in the bush, he knows the little bits as well as the big, he can see the overall picture as well as the detail.

Now I'm about to hear what happened to change him into the man he's become. The bloke who can't remember the names of the four mates who fought with him, who he claims saved his life on more than one occasion. The man who can't be a father because he thinks it will damage his family if he loves them. I'm almost scared to hear the rest of his story, afraid to find out what it takes to turn a good man into a drunk and a thief who is terrified to love. In my heart I hate the Japanese, because I know it's them done this to him and it's his family that's had to suffer.

I wonder about all the other blokes who come back from being POWs and their families. There's Mr Gee and his family, he's got Bruce, the son, and then there's two girls, twins. How'd they be? His wife, what's she had to put up with? Nancy wears the pants at our place but even she gets very frustrated with Tommy and reckons she could sometimes wring his neck. There's others also. You never know, do you? Families don't talk about those things. They've just got to cop it sweet because the old man is a war hero. I think of Mr Baloney, Tommy's old man, comin' back from the Great War. Tommy doesn't talk about him much, could be he got a fair shovel of shit thrown at him from his father.

Tommy looks up from the fire and starts talking again. 'I remember, the rise 'n' shine bugle at five o'clock on the morning of the eighth of July, the day B Force leaves for the workers' paradise, wherever that may turn out to be. All we've been told is we're going on a boat. We pack our gear, have a breakfast of rice porridge, milk and sugar, half a slice of bread and a mug of tea, not too bad by Changi standards. No eggs, of course! Though they give us a dollar note each and a cigarette ration. I'm all for the easy life, I think to meself, I'm even a bit excited about the boat trip that lies ahead.'

Tommy shakes his head, 'Mate, we should have known that very morning that the Japs, who've treated us not too bad since the surrender, were mongrels underneath. Some of the B Force are put into a convoy of trucks to drive to the wharves and some have to start marching and they'll be picked up by the first trucks returning from the wharves. We're lucky and get on a truck and on the way we have to pass through part of the city.

'On street corners are stakes pushed into the ground with freshly severed heads rammed onto the top of them. There must have been dozens of the poor sods. Then on either side of the Anderson Bridge, displayed on long tables, are more freshly severed heads, the tabletops are stained dark with blood drying in the morning sun. Most of the heads look to be Chinese. I mean, fair go, it's not like the Nips have just taken the city and they've done this in the heat of the battle. It's bloody five months since there's been any resistance and these animals keep on killing the civilian population. I should have known it would only be a matter of time before they got back to us again.

'The hell begins the moment we step on board ship, which is a laugh in itself. It's a small and very rusty tramp steamer named the *Yubi*

Maru' (Tommy pronounces it 'Yoo-bee'), 'which turns out was sold to Japan by Australia before the war.

'Bob Menzies, the Australian prime minister, thinking he was making a really good deal, sells the Japs all our clapped-out ships for scrap metal. He don't ask what the scrap metal is for. Which, of course, is to melt down to make bullets and shells and tanks and trucks to use against us. Up top for thinking was our Bob.

'I suppose the *Yubi Maru* was still more or less seaworthy, it was an Australian wheat carrier before it was sold and the Japs must have turned it into a coal carrier because when we boarded, we found the centre hold has been divided into two iron decks covered in two inches of coal dust. The poor bastards who were crammed in and come out of there at the end of the voyage all looked like boongs.

'The ship has three holds, for'ard, aft and amidships. Only way you could get in was by a vertical steel ladder. Being a wheat carrier, there's no portholes and air is blown in through a canvas pipe that only works when the ship is moving. We're packed in like sardines. I'm not kidding, we're forced to sit with our knees tucked up under our chins. There's no lying down, so you sleep, if you can in the terrible heat below, leaning against the bloke next to you.

'Like a lot of the blokes I've got the squits, I've never completely got over the dysentery and all it takes is one crook meal and it's on again. The food on board can't be et, it's watery rice with weevils floating on top and, I swear to God, there's grass chopped into it. Occasionally a tiny lump of rotten meat floats by and it all smells something terrible, like rotten eggs, as if lime has been added. It's a worm-ridden mess we only eat because we're bloody starving. With it is a pan of brownish liquid that's supposed to be tea. Mare's piss would taste a whole heap better. Only thing we can stomach is the pint of water we each get a day, which in the heat ain't near enough and a lot of the blokes are suffering from dehydration.

'I don't spend a lot of time hugging me kneecaps below decks because I join the long queue to use the latrines. Each day the queue grows longer as men suffer from diarrhoea because of the grub, and then come down with dysentery because of the conditions. The latrines are a series of small platforms constructed out of old packing cases that extend beyond the deck so that they hang over the sea. There's no real hole to shit through, just a gap in the planks, and you squat on this contraption and hang onto the ship's rails and hope for the best. I'd get to the front, have a crap, and then I'd move to the back and start queuing all over again.

'Then dysentery breaks out in a big way. While the deck and the latrines are hosed out with sea water early every morning and again in the evening, the holds and the ladders leading down into them are not. There's no place to wash your hands after a shit and some of the blokes below have shat their pants so that the stench is unbelievable. One good thing, the Japs don't come down and they keep their distance. It says in the Bible that hell is burning in flames, but let me tell you I'd take that any day to the overwhelming smell of shit, chunder and sweating, dirty men jammed against each other in heat above one hundred degrees.

'There's ten days of this, every one o' them hell on earth. The ship travels at about six knots and it's so stinkin' hot you could fry an egg on the decks during the day, and it don't cool down much at night neither. At dawn on the tenth day, we round the north-eastern coast of Borneo and set course south to a place the Japs say is Sandakan.

'It's the first time we've heard the name and it don't mean much at the time. Anything to get off this shit-hole called a ship that our bloody prime minister sold to Japan. I once saw the bugger, with his bushy black eyebrows and snow-white hair, in Melbourne. People were cheering and calling out, "Good on ya, Bob!" All I could think is "You bastard, I'd like to have you spend just one night on the *Yubi Maru* you sold so happily to Japan!" The profits probably went into perks for politicians.'

I laugh at this, because Nancy thinks Bob Menzies is an ace bloke, even though he loves the Queen and she doesn't. It's a contradiction in terms because she doesn't even vote Liberal. She says it doesn't matter, the buggers are all the same anyway, but that Bob Menzies is a nicer type of person than Arthur bloody Calwell! So she admires Menzies and votes Labor, though generally speaking her opinion of all politicians isn't any different to Tommy's.

'It's hours before we go ashore,' Tommy continues. 'Most of us are in pretty bad shape. Ten days of starvation, diarrhoea and dehydration can make a mess of a strong man and there ain't too many of those in B Force. Us young blokes are only just hangin' on, the older blokes are doing it tough. When we come down the gangplank, the Japs spray our feet and legs with a solution of carbolic acid. One of our officers demands to know what they're doin'. "Dysentery!" the Jap sergeant yells. "Dysentery no more!"

'We're standing on the wharf, being counted and recounted when we get our first look at the Nip who is gunna be commandant of Sandakan POW camp, Lieutenant Hoshijima. He's tall for a Jap, nearly six feet, and his uniform is very clean, his boots polished to a high shine. He walks down past us and I think he's an arrogant-lookin' cove if ever I saw one. "Wouldn't expect no mercy from him," one of me mates says through the side of his mouth. The Jap officer's lip is half-curled up and it's not hard to figure he don't like what he sees. Mind, I can't blame him. We're black from the coal, smell of shit, we're filthy bloody dirty, sick as dogs, and we can hardly stand up, but we're hoppin' from one leg to the other like chooks on chicken wire because the dysentery-curing carbolic acid is stinging like buggery.

'Later we learn that, in Japanese terms, Hoshijima is like a high-class Jap. He's gone to Osaka University and has been personally appointed by General Maeda, who's commander-in-chief of Japanese forces in Borneo.

'Being the commandant of a POW camp don't seem like a great military honour, but the fact he's only a lieutenant and got the job means he's got a big future in the army. Which is something we're all beginning to think don't apply to us.

'Some of the blokes are marched up the hill to spend the night in a church but the rest of us stay on the *padang*.'

'What's a *padang*?' I interrupt.

'Well, like the town square or the cricket oval. We're camped there, and the mosquitoes coming in from the swamps bite me half to death but I don't give a stuff. For the first time in ten days, I can lie on me back and stretch me legs out. It don't matter the grass is wet and it rains during the night, compared to the *Yubi Maru* it's paradise!

'At 4 a.m. the Japs wake us up. We're starvin' hungry but the food they serve for breakfast is just slush, last night's leftovers that smell even worse than on board. We've got to eat something or we'll be too weak to carry on, but there's not just a few who throw it all up again.

'We've got an eight-mile march to the camp ahead of us, which don't seem a lot, I suppose, but in our condition it's gunna feel like fifty.

'The first three miles is uphill and a bloody hard slog. They give us a smoko at the top though, and after that it's more open, undulating country, leading to the beginning of the rubber plantations.

'Our pace gets slower as the sun climbs and exhaustion begins to set in. The Jap guards get impatient hurrying us along, beating at us with sticks, kicking us and prodding us in the ribs and the back with the butts of their rifles.

'One poor sod near me must have had the trots bad, because he suddenly breaks out of line and, tugging at his shorts, he heads for the bushes. He never makes it before a Jap guard, thinking he's trying to escape, takes a pot shot at him. Thank Christ, he misses and the bloke hits the ground. Poor bastard is lying there quivering and then I see he's shat his pants. We're beginning to realise that we're in a whole heap of trouble in the workers' paradise. It's midafternoon and the rain is falling in torrents but the heat ain't let up.

'At least the heavy rain cleaned us up a bit and eventually we come to these two large timber-framed gates crisscrossed with barbed wire, with more of the wire stretched at an angle above the top frame of the gate to about eight feet. The two gates are fastened with a length of chain and a large padlock. A high crisscrossed barbed-wire fence stretches away on either side of the gates and there's another inner fence made of plain barbed wire running parallel a few yards further back. A hand-painted timber sign on one of the gates says "No. 1 Prisoner-of-War Camp North Borneo". Also in English, underneath, in smaller letters: "POW Administration HQ Kuching". We've reached the workers' paradise at last.

'There's a young bloke about the same age as me standing two from me, we'd shared a cigarette at the three-mile peg and we've introduced ourselves. Me four mates were off having a Jap-supervised shit and there's just me not needing one for a change.

'"Cleary," he grins at me, offering me a fag, "Albert Cleary."

'"Tommy Maloney," I say back. "Thanks, mate."

'"Gidday, Tommo," and we shake hands. Cleary's got a cheeky grin and you can't help liking him right off. Now as we're standing outside the gate, he says, "Reckon I could open that lock with a rusty nail, shouldn't be too hard to get out of here."

'"Know a bit about locks then?" I says to him.

'"Enough to know that's a crook one," he grins.

'"Won't be locks keep us from escaping, mate, where'd we escape to?"

'"Hmm, you could have a point, where are we?"

'"Sandakan."

'"Yeah, I know, but where the hell is that?"

'"Buggered if I know, Borneo somewhere," I say, "Just another place where they've got heat, jungle, rubber trees and Japs." I don't know it at the time, but him and me are gunna become good mates.'

'What did the camp look like?' I ask.

'I was hoping you wouldn't ask, there's a lot to tell and it's getting late.'

'Sort of the general idea then,' I suggest to him. I've got to know what his surroundings were like so when he tells me things I can visualise the scene. It's Tommy's fault, he's taught me to always note the details within my surroundings.

'Righto then,' he sighs. 'One thing I will tell you. There's a tree just inside the gates, a huge Mengarris tree.' He looks up at the dark shape of the Alpine Ash, 'It's nearly as big as this old fella. I loved that tree, I reckon it kept me from going bonkers. The honey bees used to use it for their hives. They're dead smart, see. Apart from the massive buttress, the trunk is straight up to the canopy, there's no branches so the wild bears can't climb it and raid their honey. Though the big tree stands alone within the compound, we are surrounded by dense jungle and swamps. I can't see any trees as big as the one in the compound, but this is the tropics one hundred per cent, and the big hardwoods are everywhere, much more so than where we were fighting in Malaya and Singapore. But the one big tree is an exception, it's the big daddy of them all, and must have been why them that built the compound saved it. You'd have to be a moron to cut down a tree like that.'

Tommy, ever the naturalist, looks at me. 'Can you imagine what the ancient jungle with trees like that must have been like, Mole? I saw it the first time, the tree that is, miles from the camp, standing high above the jungle like a great arm, its canopy the spindly fingers stretched up to God. When we got closer, I seen that its canopy's been ravaged by lightning strikes, some branches blackened, others split. It's a natural target, tallest thing around as far as the eye can carry.'

I nod, for once impatient. I'm more interested in the layout of the camp than the Mengarris tree. 'You said "Whoever built the camp", you mean it wasn't the Japs?'

'Nah, the Brits or the locals working under them and they done a damn good job. It seems it was built as a pukka barracks for Indian troops and their British officers and when war broke out in Europe, they used it for Italian and German internees working in Borneo at the time. Then the local Japs caught short when war was declared were interned there. They didn't stay that long because the Jap army invaded Sandakan in January '42 and, of course, it was them that now had a ready-made POW camp with all mod cons. It had a water and power plant, a small weather station, officers' houses and quarters, and barracks for the men. The whole site was nearly five acres and, looking in from the gate, it appeared very neat and in good shape.

'The huts near the gate were solid enough, six on either side of the gate and each made of timber, with palm-thatched roofs. They look like pretty comfortable quarters and we begin to think things might not be too bad. I should've known better, shouldn't I?

'There's a sort of a pond, more a muddy pool, in the far-left corner, at the bottom of a slope. It was once an elephant watering hole, then used by water buffalo, now it's just a muddy sink.

'There's a couple of dozen closely spaced palm-leaf huts that straddle the slope to the right of the pond, five huts to a line, in four lines, the one behind the other, and a last line of only four huts. They are also on stilts and because of the slope, some of the ones at the bottom are perched way up in the air. You could see that these twenty-four huts don't belong to the original barracks. They are native style with walls of nipah palm called atap. When atap's dried and shrunk, it makes a damn good building material that's waterproof and can take a hammering from the fiercest storm. This atap is tied to a rough timber frame in overlapping horizontal layers and the whole lot is secured to a timber floor built on top of the stilts.'

I have to laugh. At first Tommy doesn't want to be bothered explaining the camp layout, but when he gets started, he can't help himself, he has to explain everything in detail. Most blokes wouldn't bother to know about a thing like that.

'Each hut was about fifty feet long by about twenty feet wide and contained three or four separate rooms. More like compartments really, because the walls dividing them were only waist-high, though each had a separate doorway to the verandah that stretched the length of the hut, with a set of steps leading to the ground from each of the compartments. No glass in the windows, but some were fitted with hopper-style wooden slats. There's sixteen men to a compartment and up to sixty-four men to a hut.

'It only took the first night to realise they're not fit for human habitation. Nothing to do with keeping them clean, we done that, but there's this single electric bulb hanging from the ceiling and a few minutes after lights out, we hear this rustling in the atap roof. Someone switches the light on and everywhere we look is rats, dozens of the buggers!

'Then some bloke yells out, "Fuck, a snake!" He's pointing to the rafters above our heads and we see this dirty big python moving along one of the rafters hunting for his supper!

'"It's a python, it won't hurt ya!" I yell out. But I don't think too many of the city blokes are convinced and they're crowded on the side of the room furthermost from the big snake. I'm all for keeping the python to keep down the rats, but the others ain't none too happy. They may have been right, there's so many rats, we'd have needed half a dozen pythons to patrol the hut at night, which is not a great thought. Then we soon discover there were other kinds of snakes coming in for a feed, ones that maybe weren't quite as friendly to humans as the python.

'There's some among us that know a bit about rats, young fellows that have been branded "Dead End Kids", mostly from the city. They are among the larrikin element in B Force, good enough young blokes, but a bit wild and always getting into trouble. They're the experts at "scrounging", which is the camp word for stealing stuff from the Japs. They organise a rat-killing competition among the huts and each hut has their own method of doing the deed. In our hut we switch out the lights, having first accumulated sticks, water bottles and boots, then our rat catchers would wait until they heard the telltale rustling and on would go the light and the air was suddenly filled with flying missiles. I don't know that we killed that many, but rats are by nature domestic creatures who, like us humans, prefer a bit of peace and quiet around their nests. They weren't getting none of that, so they packed their suitcases and migrated out of the unfriendly neighbourhood. As soon as the rats departed, there was no tucker for the snakes and they scrammed as well.

'Truth is, I'd have gladly kept the rats and snakes if it meant getting rid of the lice and bedbugs. I've experienced the odd bedbug before in me life, but the tropical version are a new and ferocious breed. You'd wake up in the morning and it would look like you had the measles, you'd be covered head to foot with these itchy red bites that added to your misery. As for the lice, if you were able to borrow someone's razor and shave your head and the hair on your body, it helped. Though we soon enough stopped that because a favourite Jap punishment was to stand you out in the sun for hours in the one spot without a hat, and if you were shaved up top, you'd end up frying your brain. So, in the end you just copped the fact that everyone was lousy the same as you.

'Well, me new mate, Gunner Cleary, may have been able to pick the lock on the gate, but first he had to get to it,' Tommy explains. 'The fences around the whole compound are tight strung and crisscrossed same as the gate and then there's the angled bit at the top, same as you see in prisons. There's no getting through them and the gate is guarded twenty-four hours a day. Any approach you care to take is in the direct firing line of a machine gun. Whoever done the security done a bloody good job.

'They let us through the gates and what looked pretty neat and tidy from a distance, we now recognise is a compound that hasn't been lived in a while and is in pretty shithouse shape. It's still pouring down with rain and hot as buggery and we're dead tired and, as usual, half-starved.

'The accommodation is allocated by Colonel Walsh and his officers, who naturally get the bonzer buildings the Poms built, with the wooden floors and ceilings and a sleeping platform with a woven mat for each man. When they've made themselves comfy, the NCOs get what's left of the good billets and what's still over, they turn into the hospital and the quartermaster's store. The camp kitchen is already there on the far left and is a pretty good set-up with its own water-storage tank and two large cast-iron cooking woks in brick hearths. They look a bit like yer mum's copper in the laundry back home, only bigger.'

I don't mention to Tommy that Nancy never done the laundry. It was Sarah at first, then after she'd gone to Melbourne, it's us three boys taking turns. I must have stirred her yellow-daisy dresses a thousand times with the wooden copper stick. There'd be our stuff, three shirts and shorts, underpants, little Colleen's gear and then the rest would be yellow daisies filling the copper. Sometimes there'd be Tommy's filthy gear, after he got back from being down at the lake for a few days, drinking sweet sherry with the other drunks. That was when John Crowe couldn't get to him and wash him down at the abattoir first and buy him new gear, putting the shit- and vomit-crusted old stuff in the bin.

'There's 143 officers and about 300 NCOs who got the barrack buildings to themselves and around 1100 men who get to make the huts their home sweet home.'

'But you're a corporal, that's an NCO?'

'Corporals don't count, they've got more o' them than arseholes, there's not enough room or so they say. Anyway, I wouldn't pull rank on me mates. It's dark by the time we get into our huts and it's still raining and still steaming hot. The rain don't cool you down in the tropics, it's like ready-made sweat on yer skin. We go to bed hungry and tired and the next morning we set to work getting the camp back in order.

'The latrines are stinking and in a bad state of repair. They're like our dunnies in the yard with the same removable shit cans, only they're four-seaters. After the *Yubi Maru*, I've seen enough shit to last me the duration of the war, but the five of us cop latrine-repair duty and we spend the next four days repairing and cleaning up, gagging and feeling bloody sorry for ourselves.'

Tommy looks up and laughs, 'I once put in for a contract with the shire council to do the nightsoil, must have had a memory lapse or something. When it come to the part in the application where it asks if I've had any previous experience I wrote "Prisoner of War Camp, Borneo". The bastards didn't give me the contract. I know for a fact two of the blokes on the council at the time hid and picked fruit and said they had flat feet staying home while we were fighting for our lives. Maybe I touched a nerve, eh?'

I think for a moment about the story Nancy told us about how poor old Fred Bellows, the Yankalillee nightsoil collector, died when the rusted-through bottom of a latrine can he was carrying on his head caved in and the full can o' shit jammed onto his shoulders and smothered him. What a crook way to die, eh?

'It takes us about four days to get the camp into some sort of order and during this period the Japs leave us more or less alone. There's been plenty of rumours why we're here but nobody knows for sure. One thing is certain though, it ain't gunna be a workers' paradise.

'Then, the fifth day I think it was, we assemble under the big tree for a *tenko*, which is Japanese for rollcall. It's the first time since docking at Sandakan off the *Yubi Maru* that we've seen Lieutenant Hoshijima, who is going to address us. He's dressed up to the nines in his officer's dress uniform and is wearing his sword and, as well, an Italian-made pistol with a wooden holster that doubled as the stock to make the pistol into a short rifle. He was pretty proud of the pistol because whenever we saw him, he was wearing it. He's standing on a platform that's been rigged a couple of feet higher than us and next to him is Mr Ozawa, a Formosan civilian, who acted as his translator.

'Of the two of them, Hoshijima spoke the better English. Ozawa would babble on and Hoshijima would constantly stop to correct him in much better English. It was bloody funny, Mr Ozawa stopping, then Hoshijima telling us in English what he'd just said to Ozawa in Japanese and then Ozawa telling us again in English what Hoshijima had just told us in English. But the two of them never saw the humour of it and took the whole thing deadly serious.

'So Hoshijima starts this harangue at the first *tenko* which, because of what I've just said was so funny, I don't remember all of, but

I remember the one bit.' Tommy's voice changes so that none of the words are pronounced quite right, like he's having trouble getting his tongue around them. '"Japan will be victorious even if it takes a hundred years!" Albert Cleary's standing next to me and he says out the corner of his mouth, "And that's just about how bloody long it's gunna take you, mate!"

'The camp working routine really starts from after that *tenko*, and at first it ain't too bad. The guards can't help themselves, they'll give you a whack with a pick handle soon as look at you, but the work is no worse than we done back in Singapore. We construct a bridge across the creek that runs past the compound, build these deep monsoon drains because the monsoon season is on its way. We go as working parties into town to load bags of rice and other heavy goods. We work on the guards' and Japanese officers' quarters in town, which must have once been private homes. And the one thing that never stops is the wood detail. The old boiler at the camp is responsible for sterilising the drinking water and driving the generator and it never stops, and needs constant feeding. The cooks go through a fair amount as well. With the monsoon coming, we need to build up supplies of wood, so we're always out in the jungle chopping and carting.

'That's also the time that Hoshijima makes his smoking rule. He would decide every week when smoking could begin. He'd start and stop it on a whim so you'd never know when it was going to happen. I think he thought it was a constant demonstration of his power and influence and I reckon he was right. Not being able to have a gasper when you had tabacca in your pocket was a real bastard! Not only that, but smoking could only take place in specially designated "smoking places", which were small pits about the size of your mother's double bed and dug about a foot deep in various places around the compound. They were all clearly marked and after the weekly smoking permission was issued, you'd grab your ashtray and run for one of these pits. If a prisoner was seen smoking outside a pit or if he forgot to bring his ashtray, which was a cut-down tin filled with a little water to catch his cigarette ash, he was severely beaten.

'The smoking pit would be jammed tight with blokes, each holding his ash tin close to his chest, with the other hand holding the cigarette, thumb and forefinger up to his mouth, his elbow tucked firmly into his side so as to allow space for the bloke next to him to do the same. To get a smoke in was bloody hard work and there'd always be blokes waiting, lining up outside the pit, to take your place the moment you'd finished. The men would keep a pin or a bit of wire, which they'd stick through the end of their fag so they could grab a hold of the pinhead and they could smoke the butt down to the very last puff possible. The only good thing about the smoking pit was that the little tabacca you had lasted a while and smoking was a true luxury.

'The officers received permission from Hoshijima to start a vegie garden outside the compound. He also gave them an advance on their pay to start an officers' canteen and the canteen officer was allowed to go into Sandakan to buy stuff. This allowed the beginnings of an intelligence ring in the camp. Getting information in and out of the camp was a great morale boost to the men. We felt we were still in the war doing something useful, this was more true when we began to build the airfield.'

'Pay? The Japanese paid you?' I ask.

'Yeah, occupation money, the men got ten cents a day and the officers twenty-five. We called it banana money because there's this picture of a bunch of bananas in the centre of the notes. Don't sound like much but it could buy the odd necessity that made a lot of difference to our general state of misery.

'It was the fifteenth of August that we finally got told what we come there for. Hoshijima calls us altogether for another *tenko*, he's just been promoted to captain and at the same time his position as commandant has been confirmed, so he's full of himself and polished from his bootcaps to eyeballs.

'"You have been brought here to Sandakan to have the honour to build for the Imperial Japanese Forces an aerodrome. For this you will be paid ten cents a day. You will work. You will build this aerodrome if it takes three years!"

'"Shit, what are we gunna do for the other ninety-seven years?" Cleary says next to me.

'There's laughter among the men, because we don't reckon the war will last another three years. Hoshijima waits for our laughter to cease then starts to rave in Japanese. Mr Ozawa gets out his first words which are, "I tell you . . ." But then Hoshijima, who's pretty bloody upset, stops him with a wave of the hand, takes a step forward and, waving his finger at us, says in English, "I tell you! I have the power of life and death over you. You will build this aerodrome if you stay here until your bones rot under the Borneo sun!"

'You don't forget words like that and suddenly there ain't no more laughter and that's when our miseries truly began.

'Some of us had already had a taste of what was to come. I was a member of a working gang who first brought back the news of the proposed airfield. So, when Hoshijima finally announced it, all he did was confirm what we'd already known. How we found out was like this: two days after we'd arrived in the camp, those of us younger, fitter men were roused at dawn, then marched off, supposedly to build a road, a road, which at that time seemed to lead nowhere.

'I remember it was bucketing down, but this made no difference to the Japs. The rain wasn't any worse than the first two days in the camp, just wet, miserable and steady. At first we slogged down a track in the jungle that wasn't much more than an overgrown path that soon petered out, ending nowhere we could see that was important to anything. Then the guards handed out parangs and told the front blokes to start cutting the path onwards and the rest of us slosh along behind. It's all going reasonably well when the worst thunderstorm I have ever witnessed in my life hits us.

'The bloody sky opens, there's thunderclaps to take your head off and lightning bolts hitting the earth with a fizzing sound, all of it fused together so we know it's striking down real close, maybe onto us. Giant trees that have stood fifty years come crashing down in the forest around us, the lightning splitting them like matchsticks, leaving only their splintered stumps standing. Mate, I kid you not, it was worse than any of the fighting I'd been through in Malaya and Singapore and I'm certain this time I'm gunna die. We're lying in the mud, holding onto bushes for grim death as a torrent of water sweeps down the path.

'The storm don't last that long but it's done more damage in ten minutes than a heavy artillery battery could do in ten days. Suddenly, it's all over except for distant rumbling thunder and a few sharp flashes of lightning. With the storm passing, the rain eases off and there's even a bit of blue sky above.

'Now there's more water around than the earth can absorb and the path we've cut turns into black mud that sucks the boots off our feet, but the Japs make us get on with the job. It soon becomes apparent we can't continue. We've stopped at what looks like a large clearing in the jungle about two miles from the camp. "No more!" the Jap sergeant in charge of us yells, waving his arms. "Stop now! We work aeroplane place!"

'That was the first time we realised that we'd come to Sandakan to build an airfield. The Jap sergeant decides if we can't work on the path we might as well get started on the aerodrome. It doesn't look much like a place to build anything, much less an airfield. The ground undulates ahead of us like a series of soft-backed waves.

'Each of us is given a hoe known as a "chonkol" and a wicker basket. The sergeant positions himself on the top of one of these undulations and issues his instructions. The sun has come out but that only makes things worse. Steam rises from the ground and the sergeant, half-obscured in the rising steam, uses a pick handle to indicate the area he wants levelled. "Hill here go in valley over there!" he shouts out. He speaks pretty good English for a Jap sergeant. Most of them haven't a clue, they know one or two words and work on the principle that he who shouts loudest is best understood and, with a pick handle in his hands, he speaks perfect English anyway.

'We get stuck in, first clearing the tangled mess of secondary growth and discover the ground underneath is composed of a coral-like substance, probably some distant volcano eruption that deposited its ash in this area. The ash has become a form of white porous rock which we learn is called "tufa". It's hard to see how it can sustain any vegetation.

'It turns out tufa is easy to work when it's hard but when it's wet it's a real mongrel. It becomes jelly-like, so when you scoop out a bit, the hole you've just made fills up again, a bit like a kid digging a hole on the beach with the waves pushing in every few seconds and washing the sand back into it.

'We're now standing up to our ankles in this white jelly-like substance and spend the next three hours trying to scoop it into our baskets. The work is backbreaking and we're tired and haven't eaten nothing all day because we've been marched out of camp before breakfast.

'The idea is to chop at the tufa with the chonkol and then scoop it up and into the baskets with our hands and carry it over to the sergeant's valley then tip it out of the baskets again. But the valley doesn't fill, the tufa simply disappears, washed away by the run-off from the storm. After several hours the world around us remains exactly the same. The only way you'd know we'd been there is the pile of secondary growth we've hacked down. The Jap guards get real angry and we're taking a hiding from their swinging pick handles.

'A guard comes up to me and he's jabbering away, "More! Work more!" and he lets go and cops me in the ribs with his pick handle. I fall to the ground, more angry than hurt. I point to where I've been working, "You have a go, you bastard!" I shout at him, "See fer yerself!"

'He must have worked out what I'm saying, 'cept he probably don't know the word "bastard" yet, or I'd have got more than a pick handle in me ribs. He throws down the pick handle and grabs the chonkol and sets to work. *Whack* goes the chonkol and its head sinks into the tufa up to the haft. He tries to pull it out but the suction in the tufa holds it firm, just like our boots in the black mud a bit earlier. In a minute or so, he's puffing like a sumo wrestler and he hasn't got any tufa in the basket yet. He grunts and throws down the hoe and tries to scoop the stuff up with his hands. It's no good, it's like picking up that stuff Sarah sometimes makes when your stomach is crook.'

'Blancmange?'

'Yeah, it's like that. Then the guard throws down the chonkol, picks up the pick handle and storms off. It must have done some good, because pretty soon he's consulting with the sergeant and some of the other guards and there's heads shaking in agreement. Then the sergeant gets up on the rise that's not grown any smaller and waves his arms across his chest. "Fineesh! No more!" he yells, "All mens go back now!"

'Some of the blokes who saw me get clobbered, shout over, "On ya, Tommo!"

'So having done bugger-all except find out that we're here to build an airfield, we trudge back to camp down the muddy black path we'd previously created through the jungle.

'So, I suppose I can claim I was one of the first to start on the new Jap airfield in Sandakan. Not that that's an honour, far from it. We know we're building an airstrip from where the Jap aircraft can bomb and strafe the Allies. That's gunna be our job for the duration of the war, that's why we come to Sandakan in the first place. But we're not proud of what we're doing and it's common practice to steal tools and material and bury them in the fill to slow things down and sabotage progress any way you could.'

Tommy looks at me. 'That's a funny thing, some of the blokes on the Burma Railway were dead proud of their achievement. They suffered something terrible, we all did and in the end, ours was the worst fate of all. Some of the Brits who built that bridge on the River Kwai were dead chuffed at what they'd done, bloody engineering marvel, they boasted. What we done, building an airfield in the middle of the jungle, was maybe just as remarkable. It's now the Sandakan civil airport but nobody even fucking knows how it's come about!'

Tommy's voice is suddenly bitter, 'Sandakan is the war's best-kept secret, there's families don't know what happened to their husbands, brothers and sons. They just disappeared into thin air, it's as if they never existed. I once asked our local member to find out about Sandakan. He come back to me and says nobody knows anything, nothing he can do, it's government policy and he's hit a brick wall. It's a bloody conspiracy of silence if you ask me. All the families know is that they get this telegram, "Your husband is missing, believed dead", nothing more. Can you imagine how they feel?

'Anyway, we wasn't none of us proud of the so-called engineering feat we performed even though it was thought to be impossible to do in the time. I'm just bloody sad that nobody gives a bugger for the men that died. Because there's nobody to march on Anzac Day, the public don't even know about us, about me mates, who, in the end, were as good as any Aussie soldiers who ever fought. There's lots should have got medals, the MC, even the VC, for what they done but because they all died there's nobody to do their citations. Can't be giving medals out, can yer, people would start asking why, wanting to know the full story, so the government put it in the too-hard basket and forgot all about the families.'

Tommy stops a while, hanging his head, thinking, not wanting me to see how upset he is, trying to regain his composure. Eventually he speaks.

'You see, the Japs need oil and they come to Borneo eight days after they attack Pearl Harbor because they need the oil that's buried along the island's west coast. Oil means fuel for their tanks, trucks and planes, they can't fight the war without it. Besides this, their aircraft can't fly non-stop between Singapore and the Philippines, or even to the most distant part of the Dutch East Indies. They have to stop to refuel and Sandakan is gunna be one of the places they'll do it. What's more they're in a flamin' great hurry to get going.

'But in early September we're woken in our huts at dawn with rifle butts in our ribs. The Jap guards are fully armed, screaming, shouting out and having a go at anything that moves in the dark. It's not what we've become accustomed to, we've settled down to POW life and everyone sort of knows the rules. Sure, we get beaten for the smallest thing or even for nothing, but it's individuals do that. Not since the second morning when we went out to make the road and ended up at the airfield, have we been rousted out like this.

'This time it's not to make up a working party, or even just the young blokes, it's the whole camp and involves a full kit inspection and hut search. We're stumbling about in the dark getting clobbered and wondering what the hell it's all about. Must be something pretty bloody important, something's happened we don't know about, most likely an escape.

'At the end of July, eleven POWs escaped and the Japs went berserk. They eventually caught them and sent them to Outram Road Gaol in Singapore, all except one who died in Kuching. We all copped the shit for that escape and as a consequence, we now have to wear a square of white cloth on our hats with a personal identifying number.

'At first light, *tenko* is called beside the big tree and we assemble on parade with full kit and a Jap warrant officer screams "*ki wo tsuke!*" which is their word for "attention!" We all do as he says and Captain

Hoshijima, accompanied by his escort of guards plus the bedraggled-looking Mr Ozawa, march into sight.

'The captain as usual looks as if he's attending a trooping of the colour ceremony, with his immaculate uniform, Eyetalian pistol at the hip, boots shining like polished glass. Him and Mr Ozawa mount the platform where there's a table been placed and both stand behind it. Then right off, Ozawa, as if he's had the words waiting in his throat for hours, shouts out, "*Ze oase!*" which is how it will be pronounced ever after. He's got this piece of paper in his hand and begins to read. For once Captain Hoshijima doesn't interrupt, I suppose because the words written down are probably his very own.

'"One!" shouts the Formosan. "We abide by ze rules and regulation of ze Imperial Japanese Army!" He stops and looks at Hoshijima for approval. The captain nods for him to continue.

'"Two!" the little man shouts out. "We agree not to attempt to escape!"

'There is this murmur from the men who suddenly cotton on to what's happening, "*ze oase*", is supposed to be "the oath", something we are all collectively taking. The guards move forward, and the warrant officer shouts for us to be silent. Susumi Hoshijima nods to Mr Ozawa to go on.

'"Three! Should any of our soldiers escape we request that you shoot him to death!"

'There is this stunned silence. Nothing moves. It's like time stands still. "Shit, what's gunna happen?" I think to meself. I can't believe what I've just heard.

'Suddenly our most senior officer, Colonel Walsh, breaks rank and mounts the platform. He reaches out and takes the piece of paper from the startled Mr Ozawa. You can hear a pin drop. I remember the birds were just beginning to sound in the jungle, nothing else can be heard, just the birdcalls at first light, the cook-a-rooing of wild doves and the sound of the breath in my chest. Walsh is a mild bloke, but we don't know how he's gunna react.

'"Gentlemen, I for one will not sign such a document!" he shouts out, so we can all hear him plainly. Then he throws the paper down and it flaps and lands on the edge of the table and slowly slides off. We see it land at Captain Hoshijima's feet.

'There's a gasp from the ranks and then cheers. "Shit, the old man's got guts," Cleary says next to me, "Good on ya, mate!" he shouts out and immediately cops a kick from a guard standing nearby. The guards start kicking all and sundry, to stop us cheering.

'Next thing, the Jap guards surrounding Hoshijima drag Walsh from the table and frog-march him out the gates. There's a post just outside the main gate and they tie him to it and Captain Hoshijima goes up and slaps him across the face. Then the guards line up into a firing squad and pull back the bolts of their rifles and take aim. Meanwhile the machine guns are trained on all of us in case there's an uprising. The men are shouting and bellowing and the Japs are in danger of losing control of the situation.'

Tommy looks at me, 'Christ, I dunno what would have happened if they'd shot him, there'd have been a riot. There's fifteen hundred of us and we greatly outnumber the Japs. If they'd shot the C.O., I reckon we'd have broke ranks and gone for them. They'd have massacred us with the machine guns but we'd have got a few and Hoshijima would have been one of them.

'One of our officers breaks ranks, it's Major Workman the 2/IC and he goes up to Hoshijima and tries to calm him down. I don't suppose Hoshijima being only a captain was all that anxious to assassinate a colonel. He'd probably have some explaining to do at the Jap High Command at Kuching. The Japs respect rank and shooting Walsh without a trial wouldn't have been a good move. Hoshijima's a young bloke and educated and he's in a jam. But Japs can't afford to lose face and Hoshijima can't be seen to back down in front of his men. So a way has to be found to calm him down and save his honour and, at the same time, save Walsh's life.

'Eventually the major comes up with the suggestion that the wording of the document be changed slightly so that it isn't a collective statement taken on behalf of all the men by their commander. The suggestion is that the words are changed to read "we individuals".

'At first the Japs have a bit of trouble understanding this. They don't go in for individuals in the Imperial Japanese Army. Not that we do a whole lot neither, but their troops can't say boo to a mouse. With them it's total obedience, or death. They've all sworn an oath to die for the Emperor which covers bloody everything. Eventually Hoshijima, who understands Western ways, agrees and "*ze oase*" document is changed, the Jap captain's face is saved and so is Walsh's life.

'So now we've all got to sign the document personally by writing down our names. Hoshijima changes the words on the document with his fountain pen and the guards distribute enough blank sheets of paper to hold all the signatures. They keep us on parade for six hours in the hot sun while the guards ransack our huts and the officers' quarters, stealing anything they can find.

'They're supposed to be looking for contraband, but it's just an excuse to help themselves. They find bugger-all that's a punishable offence because we've got all that sort of stuff well hidden, but a lot of personal things go missing. Among them is the post office clock Johnny Moule-Probert pinched from the Bukit Timah post office on Singapore Island and lugged in his kit all the way to Sandakan. It's been hanging in our hut, tick-tocking happily away. When you wake up from a nightmare and you hear it going tick-tock-tick-tock, like time isn't taking no notice of what's happening, it's comforting, and helps to keep you calm when you're a long way from home and you're lying there in the dark, rats scuttling, wonderin' if you'll ever get back.

'Now it's bloody gone. Some Jap's nicked it and it's probably ticking away in his house in Osaka, with his kids thinking their old man is a war hero and the clock was given him by grateful citizens for saving their lives.

'While all this ransacking is taking place, there's blokes dropping like flies in the ranks, but they just lie there at our feet and we are forbidden to help them. One of the blokes who was on the far side of the mob told me later that one of the God-botherers had broken ranks, defying the guards to beat him. He's gone and got a kerosene can made into a bucket, filled it with water, and a tin mug and he's going from man to man lying on the ground lifting their heads and making them take a drink of water.'

'What was his name?'

'I couldn't say, just one of them padres.'

'Wardale-Greenwood?'

'Could be, yeah I think it was him,' he says, still not sure.

Tommy squints up at me, 'It was bound to be him, he was fearless.

Maybe he was a proddo, but I tell you what, he was a bloody saint. He should have got the VC.

'When it come to signing the document, I doubt there was a proper name used among the entire B Force. On the sheet where I sign "Mickey Mouse", I count eight Ned Kellys and six Bob Menzies and one "Up the Hawks!" Cleary signs "Fatty Finn" because there are already several Ginger Meggs. Me other four mates make up something equally bloody stupid, one I remember was "King George" and another "Captain Cook", although there was a real Captain Cook among us and I'll tell you about him later. I don't reckon there's one bloke wrote his birth name down.' Tommy stops and thinks a moment, 'Yeah well, I suppose there's a few who did. Some of our blokes were pretty bloody stupid. If the Japs catch on to this lurk, they don't say. With them it's all about not losing face.

'We started to work on the airfield ten days before "*ze oase*" fiasco. At first the work isn't too bad, it's hard and punishment is severe for the slightest mistake, but the rations are enough to keep our bodies reasonably strong so we're coping okay. Some of the coves doing the heavy labour get twenty-six ounces of rice, the others eighteen ounces, with a little fish or meat and some vegetables and a couple of cigarettes. To be fair, we had it pretty easy the first twelve months. We got flogged a fair bit, though when you're a POW I suppose it's to be expected but we had enough food and cigarettes. In fact, some of us had enough rice over to trade with the locals at the airstrip. Ten cents a day for working on the airstrip doesn't sound like much, but you could buy a coconut or a fair-sized banana or a turtle egg for a cent from the natives. The best was a banana fritter, you could get one for two cents and it was a special treat. We'd sometimes find a bee's nest and have a feast of honey and when we felled coconut palms, at the heart of the palm is this tender green centre which was pretty good to eat and which we called rich man's cabbage, because you had to chop down the whole tree to get it. There was also a canteen in the camp where you could buy a bit of medicine or razor blades or extra cigarettes. It really wasn't too bad at first.

'The work on the airstrip was simple enough, digging up the tufa on the rises, filling up skips with it and then pushing them along a system of portable rails to the dips in the ground, tipping the skips and levelling the spill. Our biggest problem on the airfield was our eyes. Like I said earlier, the tufa is easy enough to work when it's hard, but it's almost white as snow and in the tropical sun, just like snow, it kicks back this blinding light your eyes can't stand. So we invent these special "glasses" to stop the glare, two slivers of bamboo, or two sticks placed together with just the smallest gap between them to see through, with a piece of cord or plaited grass rope tied to either end of the sticks and then brought round and tied at the back of the head. Simple stuff, but it worked a treat. Only problem was that you ended up with pretty limited vision so you never knew if a Jap guard was creeping up on you. Sometimes you'd stop a moment for a breather and next thing you'd cop a pick handle across your back that would knock you to the ground.

'The other problem we have is Lieutenant Okahara, the Jap in charge of the airstrip project. He is the original comic-book Jap, about five feet two inches tall with buck teeth and bottle-bottom glasses. Okahara is one of the cruellest bastards it is our misfortune to come across, a sadist who loves to inflict pain. The only time you ever saw him smile was when he was ordering someone to be beaten. He tells us he wants the first landing strip completed by December 1942 before the monsoon rains and that it's got to be 850 metres long and 50 metres wide and he'll get it whatever it takes.' Tommy stops and thinks, then says, 'In our measurements that's approximately 930 yards long by about 55 yards wide. There's only a limited number of skips and rails and with two working parties of three hundred working six days a week, it's a bloody big ask. The rest of the prisoners are working on camp duties, the roads, driving trucks and loading supplies from town, others are collecting wood. But Okahara has a little trick up his sleeve to make sure the airstrip is completed by Christmas. It comes in the form of a "basher gang".

'I haven't told you about the Formosan guards, have I?' I shake my head. 'Yeah, well, they're conscripts from the island of Formosa which is part of Japan's empire. Thickset powerful little blokes who the Japs regard as a second-rate people. They've joined up or been conscripted, willing or not, thinking once they're in the Imperial Japanese Army they'll be treated the same as the Jap soldiers but they soon find out that they are there to do the dirty work and their only outlet is to take it out on us.

'Lieutenant Okahara picks four of the worst for his basher gang. Their leader is a mongrel named Kada. Built like a brick shithouse, he never tired of inflicting pain. He was known to us all as "Mad Mick". I reckon he was genuinely off his rocker and when he was in a rage, which was daily, he'd foam at the mouth and his eyes would bulge out of his head like a bullfrog. The basher gang and the guards are under the supervision of another thoroughgoing bastard, a Jap officer named Lieutenant Moritake.

'There was no way of escaping Mad Mick and his gang. They'd be armed with pick handles fashioned like swords which could be grasped in both hands. Any sign of slacking or if he imagined you were slacking or didn't like the expression on your gob, Mad Mick and his boys would get stuck in, not only into the bloke they picked first off, but also his entire working gang.

'One of their favourite tricks was to pit us against each other, mate on mate, and if you didn't wallop your mate hard enough or he you, the guards would really have a go, knocking many a bloke into a state of unconsciousness. I remember one of our blokes, a mate of mine who was at Pulau Bukum, you remember the island off Singapore where we loaded oil drums and Blades Rigby got lopped?' I nod, it's not something you could easy forget. 'Well, Richie Murray was a bloody good welterweight in civilian life and the first time we are made to go one-on-one, it's me and him. Well, he's clobbering me something terrible, though he's pulling his punches and I'm missing him with just about every attempt. So Mad Mick sees this and stops the so-called fight and makes Richie keep his hands behind his back and tells me to beat the crap out of him. Richie's a real game bugger and he's that good on his feet and at keeping his head out the way, ducking and weaving, I still can't hit him. So Mad Mick comes up from behind and clobbers Richie Murray with the pick handle. After that Richie Murray and me became mates.

'Another little invention of Lieutenant Moritake was known by the men as "Flying Lessons". For no reason whatsoever we'd be stopped and lined up and told to remove our hats and our eye protection and to stand with our arms extended at shoulder height to either side, like a kid playing at flying, using his arms as wings.

'We'd be ordered to stand like this, looking up at the sun, and if a guard copped you with your eyes closed or shoulders slumped, he'd thump you with the pick handle. We'd stand there for an hour without moving, though we'd seldom know the reason for the punishment. This particular exercise would strain your muscles to the point of collapse and even though you closed your eyes every moment there wasn't a guard nearby, the sun would burn the retina of your eyes so you couldn't see properly for hours later and the bloody headache would last all day.

'Any bloke who collapsed, and there were a lot of them, myself included on more than one occasion, got the full attention of the basher gang. But you didn't have to do nothing, you copped it anyway, the guards would walk down the ranks hitting out willy-nilly into the rib cage under your extended arms. These whacks left livid marks across the ribs and back and if you only got one, you didn't bother to mention it, two and you could claim corporal status, three and you'd hear blokes saying, "I got me sergeant's stripes at flying practice today."

'Although there were incidents and constant beatings, while the Japs thought they were winning the war, the first year wasn't too bad. Seven blokes died that year in B Force and none that I recall from torture. But already there were signs of sickness that would later cause havoc among the men. We'd been in the tropics now nearly a year and POWs more than six months, and the tropics under the conditions we were in is no place for the white man. Some of us were starting to develop tropical ulcers, you've seen the scars on me legs, but there's other things, not bad at first but later, dysentery which I'd copped in Singapore, malaria, beri-beri and, in the heat and humidity, rice balls.'

'Rice balls! What's that?'

'Mate, it's a fungus, an infection you get in the tropics and it leaves the skin on your balls raw and bleeding and it's so itchy you'd happily rip them out and throw them to the shithouse if you could! Then later there's deaths from malarial meningitis. Later still, when we're starving and most of us haven't got no boots and walk around barefoot, we pick up hookworm and various types of intestinal worm as well from trying to eat stuff we find. There's bloody nothing good to say about the tropics, the blackfellas can keep all of it as far as I'm concerned.

'Being a bushie I'm a bit interested in the environment and whenever I get a chance I have a bit of a fossick around, seeing what can be et, what can't. I don't mean bandicooting, that's different, I'm looking around in the jungle seeing if there's wild stuff you can eat.'

'What's bandicooting?'

'Bandicooting? Yeah well, after a while we find a way to get under the wire at night and into the vegie garden, which the Japs reckoned belonged to them. We'd go looking for tapioca mostly. The trick was to dig under the plant and pinch a fair amount of the tapioca root and then cover where we've disturbed the soil so the plant is still standing, and there's no evidence it's been tampered with. That's bandicooting.

'There's been no successful escape from Sandakan but it's always on yer mind. I've took the trouble to learn a fair bit of Malay from the native workers and the blokes who come to trade with us at the airstrip and I'm good enough for some of the other blokes to let me barter for them. So I'm fossicking in the jungle working out what can be et. In the back of me mind is that maybe if things get too bad I may try to escape someday.

'We're doing okay at the airfield, falling behind schedule, and then in October, there's this big parade, some Jap bigwig, a Major Suga, is due to make an inspection of the airfield. You'd have thought he was a general, the Japs are running around like chooks with their heads cut off, getting everything ready. Hoshijima is shitting himself, thinking something will go wrong and there's warnings every day that if any of us fuck up we're in for the high jump. Well, the major turns up and we're paraded and it's blah-blah-blah but then he says in English, "All Japanese officers – Samurai. All Japanese officers – honnable. You work hard, finish airfield, you be fine!"

'Then next morning at *tenko* we are told that the airstrip has now been increased to 1400 metres, which is about one mile, and that it still has to be ready for a trial landing before Christmas! Mate, those of us working on the airstrip don't reckon it's humanly possible. The monsoon season is just about on us and there's no beating that.

'Then the Japs in their wisdom decide we'll work better without our senior officers interfering and trying to look after the welfare of the men. So Colonel Walsh our C.O. and some of the other senior officers are sent to Kuching. Seven majors and officers of middle rank remain. A year later, at the end of 1943, they clear them out as well and all but eight officers from our camp are sent to Kuching, leaving us with one officer for every two hundred and fifty men.

'The Japs reckon the best way to work us harder is to beat us harder and we're now working seven days a week and copping more shit than ever. We've built the whole strip layer by layer, a layer of river pebbles and a layer of tufa, but the Jap officers decide that drains are not necessary though Blind Freddy can see what happens every time it rains. Well, it's not our job to tell them, is it? There are blokes among us who know a bit about engineering and reckon as soon as the monsoon season comes it's bye-bye no more aeroplane fly.

'The first early rains come and nature as usual proves who's the boss. It's November, not even the proper monsoon season yet, and there's this dirty great bog appears just where it shouldn't be on the strip and soon it turns into a shallow lake. Tufa is still the boss and the Japs bring in this ancient wood-fired steamroller to try to squeeze the water out and, as well, a Ruston-Bucyrus 10-RB Universal Excavator. It's the first real machinery we've had up to now and, except for the skips and the rails, Sandakan must be the first airstrip of any size in the world that's been built entirely by hand with hoes and shovels, wicker baskets and hand-pushed skips.

'The excavator gives up on the first day. The Japs move it to the boiler house near the camp, hoping one of the POWs can fix it. It gets fixed all right. A POW named Stevens fills its sump with sand. The steamroller is then used to try and squeeze the moisture out of the strip. It keeps getting bogged but we manage to pull it free and it's doing all right until it hits the boggy patch. It's going puff-puff-puff, shooting clouds of blue smoke into the air and then it kind of slows down a bit, but still keeps going and we're all watching cause we know what's going to happen. It hits the boggy patch, falters and stops, and, still upright, sinks slowly into the tufa bog and disappears.

'The Japs are ropeable, like it's our fault, and Mad Mick and his gang go troppo, all of us close by cop a bashing and there's more "sergeants" made instantly from the flying pick handles than at any flying practice I can remember. They beat us until they can't raise their arms. Then they decide they need drains after all, so we're set to work to dig a network of drains across the strip. The steamroller is *kaput* so now they make us stamp the surface with our feet, which works pretty well.

'Somehow we've completed enough of the first landing strip to allow for the official opening in early December. On the day, a lone bomber lands and you'd have thought the Japs had won the war. There's extra rations all round and we have a sports day to celebrate. Not a rest day, a day of runnin' and jumpin' and boxing and wrestlin' and a cross-country race around the perimeter of the camp with guards stationed all the way. The trouble was, those blokes who'd been excused from work because they were supposed to be sick couldn't resist joining in, so from then on you had to be bloody sick to stay in the camp.

'There's not a lot more I can say about the airfield,' Tommy continues, 'except we're way behind schedule and even the Japs can see that beating us harder ain't gunna work and that there's more men needed. So in June 1943, just about a year after we come to Sandakan, five hundred blokes from E Force arrive. They've first been sent to an island called Berhala and then later on to us and they've come to work on the airfield as well. They're separated from us in a different camp and in a different work gang on the airfield. Don't know why that is, we're all Aussies.

'Hoshijima makes all of them shave their heads so that the guards will know they're members of E Force and not confuse them with us. At the same time, just to make life bloody impossible, guard dogs are introduced. With the dogs patrolling the fences, getting out at night to scrounge for food is now more difficult. In October '43, the Japs move all but eight officers to Kuching and the E Force blokes move in with us.

'One of the E Force blokes in my hut, Nelson Short, is a bit of a songwriter and musician. He's made this ukulele from some scrap three-ply timber and signal wire; he's used part of a broken comb for the frets, and the pegs he's made from ground-down glass. He's got a real good voice like a professional singer and often when we're feeling low he'll reach for his ukulele and sing for us some of the good old songs and some he wrote himself. One of his own songs was so good that we all learned to sing it. We even got a bit of harmony going.'

I know Tommy's got a good ear for poetry so I ask right off, 'Can you remember the song?'

'Of course.'

'Couldn't sing it for me, could ya?'

'Christ, mate, you don't want to miss nothing, does yer?' Tommy starts to sing, it ain't much of a voice and I reckons it's probably been a while since he's done any singing.

'I'm dreaming of Australia,
The land we left behind,
Dreaming of the loved ones,
We could always bear in mind.
Although it's only fancy,
Our hearts within us yearn.
But we'll make up for lost moments,
When to Aussie we return.

'There'd be sailing on the harbour,
The Showboat our first choice.
Or maybe we'd be dancing,
Listening to our sweetheart's voice.
Although it's only fancy,
Our hearts within us yearn,
But we'll make up for lost moments,
When to Aussie we return.

'We had a few good concerts in the camp right up to July 1944 when things started turning really bad and the Japs banned concerts. By then, we didn't feel much like singing anyhow, apart from Nelson who seemed to think it was his duty to keep our spirits up. I heard from someone that he was a really crook soldier. If it was true, he made up for it in the camp a hundred times over.

'The officers remaining in the camp after October '43 must have been chosen personal by Hoshijima with the help of the Australian liaison officer, Captain Cook. The first thing that happens is that some of the senior NCOs who've been receiving extra rations for doing bugger-all are elevated to the status of what the Japs call "Camp Masters".

'What's more, Captain Cook and one or two others are having their tea at night in Hoshijima's quarters. Can you bloody imagine, they're eating tucker from Hoshijima's table! There's no bones showin' through their flesh, I can vouch for that, their stomachs are full, tight as a drum and it ain't from beri-beri neither. Among ourselves we refer to them as "White Japs" and we're not gunna take orders from scum like them.

'There's Brit officers done the same before they were moved to Kuching. Twenty-five o' them would march out of the camp with polished boots and best khaki drill to eat at Hoshijima's canteen. It's like they're on their way to the regular officer's mess in peacetime. They get stuck into bananas, pineapples, doughnuts, toffee, coffee and lots of other good tucker and this feast costs them the grand total of seventy-five cents each and at the end they do a mass salute to a Jap second lieutenant who's on canteen duty.' Tommy turns to me, 'I must say it wasn't all their officers done that, some o' them refused Hoshijima's invitation to use his "Friendship Garden", which is the Japanese canteen.

'The worst of our lot is Captain Cook, he's as plump as a Christmas chook and the longer he stays fat, the less authority he commands among the men. Cook isn't an officer's backside, he's never been to battle and has a temporary rank, he's an administrator, a pen-pusher. He was originally the liaison officer but now he's the commandant of the camp, selected personal by Hoshijima to the disgust of the officers who were sent to Kuching. He can't get the respect of the men and in July '44 he starts reporting his own men to Hoshijima for punishment. Next thing the toadying bastard does is ask Hoshijima to build a bigger punishment cage to be positioned next to Esau.'

'Esau? What's that?'

'Oh, I forgot to say about that, didn't I. Esau is the original punishment cage and you could be put into it for doing the smallest bloody thing wrong. It was an agonising form of punishment too. They placed it near the big tree facing the guardhouse. All it is, is a little oblong wooden cage made of wooden slats so you can see out. It's on stilts about two feet off the ground with a solid floor and a solid ceiling made of planks, there's a little door on one side you have to crawl through and once you're inside, all you can do is sit with your knees up against your chest. The ceiling is so low you can't stand up, you have to sit at attention through the heat of the day. At night the mosquitoes bite the living daylights out of you. Do something to annoy the Japs and you'd find yourself in Esau. They even put Padre Wardale-Greenwood in.'

'Oops! Here comes another VC,' I say to myself.

'He's caught taking the place of one of the blokes in the work gang at the 'drome who is sick. He's been doing this quite often and eventually the Japs find out. They confiscate his Bible and other religious books and put him in Esau for thirty-six hours.

'Well, now Cook's decided he needs a bigger cage.' Tommy looks up. 'Can you imagine an Australian officer putting in a request to the Japs to make more of these punishment cages to hold his own men?

'Most sentences are now from a week to a month. You got nothing but a little water to drink for the first week. Twice a day you were pulled out of the cage and given a severe beating by the guards and then returned. A lot of men sent to the cage died.

'Right off, Cook's got seventeen of us in his new cage. We're there for insubordination. He'd ordered us to go clean out the latrine pits, but we'd done it the last time and it was another hut's turn so we objected but he didn't give a damn. He reports us to Hoshijima and demands that we be severely punished. We get forty days, with no water for the first three days.

'On the third night they make us drink water until we're sick. "Clean yer gut out so you don't shit in a pit that's full," Cook says as he passes us that night. He's with Warrant Officer Sticpewich, another bastard who most of the blokes think is a collaborator. Though it's never proven, we were pretty certain among ourselves. We ask ourselves how come him and Cook are not losing any weight and we're all starving. They're both the same in 1944 as they were in 1942. Also, Sticpewich ain't an officer, so how come, eh? You don't have to be a genius to work it out.

'For the first seven days in Esau, we get no food and are not allowed to talk. At night they take us out and the guards beat the bejesus out of us, which the Japs call physical exercise.'

Tommy turns to me. 'What you gunna hear next, you're not gunna believe. The Pommie cooks who have been sent to work in the kitchen can't do nothing for us, but they time it so when we're out of the cage and we've been beaten up, they come out with the swill, the kitchen rubbish. It's supposed to feed the guard dogs, which are penned up near the cage and are starving same as us. They pour the swill into a trough and we all go for it together, us and the dogs. We fight the dogs for the scraps.

'If you've ever tried to take a bone out of a starving dog's mouth, you'd know what it was like. You'd wrestle the dog to the ground and grab the bone and he'd bite onto your wrist, but you didn't feel nothing. It was you or him and usually you'd win. The guards would stand around, holding their bellies, they're laughing so much, we're the evening entertainment, a huge joke. Then the guards would herd us back into the cage for the mozzies to feast on during the night. That was all Cook's doing and he done worse than that to some of the other men. What kind of a low-down mongrel is that, eh? I'm ashamed to think that him and the rest we named "White Japs" are Australian.'

Tommy pauses. 'Where was I? Sorry about goin' on like that! Yeah, that's right, back to the airfield.'

I'm amazed how Tommy can keep it all going, the story I mean. It's like he must have gone over it in his mind hundreds of times all these years and to my knowledge told nobody. Just bounced it around in his head. Maybe he's told John Crowe, but he's never said. Now it's coming out, I can't believe he remembers it so clearly, like it's all happened yesterday.

'It takes us nearly a year after E Force arrive to complete the east–west strip. Though what we've done is sufficient to be used by Japanese fighters and bombers. Then in September 1944 we start the north–south runway,' Tommy sighs, 'Yer know something, Mole?'

'What?'

'Humans are creatures of habit. We love habit. We wake up every morning feeling sick and hungry, but we don't think, like how are we gunna survive today or that we're prisoners of war. We wake up thinking today's gunna be the same as yesterday and tomorrow and the day after tomorrow. It's just work and you can't escape it. After a while you don't ask yourself no more questions. You just close down and do what you're supposed to do and hope you don't get Mad Mick's pick handle this shift or the next. Life narrows down to staying alive just the one day, there's no past or future, just today. It's an instinctive thing.

'Smiling at the guards and nodding yer head, that's automatic. You get so good at it you can read the mood of a guard just by his expression. It's like you know instinctively what to do to get through the day without creating any flak. You know the rules. No matter how unfair they are, you know them. Later you think what a weak shit you were, but at the time, it's all about avoiding trouble, about not using up the thin thread of life at your disposal. Every blow, every bruise, makes you that much weaker. So you've worked out how many you could take before you are in the hospital or on the way out.' Tommy looks up at me, 'After a while, you become an expert on measuring the amount of life you've still got in you.

'You calculate the price of everything you do, because the one thing you learn as a POW is that everything has a price. Nothing is done without a consequence. There's four hundred men in hospital with all the things I mentioned before. There's maybe the same convalescing, which is another name for dying slowly. You don't try to get into the hospital if you can manage to stay out.

'One of me four mates is forced to go into hospital, he's got a severe ear infection and his whole body is covered in a weeping tinea. There's nothing he can do except report sick. When he got into the camp hospital, he found the whole joint overrun with bedbugs and scabies. If you've ever had scabies, you'd know it drives you mad with irritation, there's some blokes got hundreds. Hospital is no rest cure. It is something you try your best to give a miss. Hospital is one of the certain steps towards the end, it's a qualification for death.

'Sometimes I'd be that buggered, scabies driving me crazy, ulcers eating both me legs away, rice balls so I'm tearing at me scrotum, Mad Mick and the basher gang having a go, so everything hurts, yer bones and muscles and sinews, and you want to rip yer skin off. The one thing that saves you is that you've forgotten how to cry, forgotten how to feel sorry for yerself. Any bloke who felt sorry for himself just had to take a look at his mate. When it got so bad I reckoned I'd chuck the whole thing in, I'd stand under that great tree and think about this Alpine Ash, this Maloney tree. The one good thing we Maloneys done, keeping this tree a secret. I'd look up into the canopy of that great jungle tree, struck by lightning, battered but not broken, same as this old tree, and I'd say to meself, "Them fuckers can't beat me. They can smash me, do what they like, but they can't break my spirit. I will survive, I have a purpose, I have a tree and we both have to anchor the earth."'

I listen to Tommy and I can't really believe what I'm hearing. It's like he's writing some poem in his head and he doesn't quite understand it's beautiful. He's saying things it's going to take me years to understand. Then in the middle of everything, he stops and goes on with the story, like nothing's happened.

'By January 1944, there's no more electricity and water in our camp. The Japs have took the cables and the pipes to run into their own barracks and there's nothing we can do about it.

'We collect rainwater and we have to wash in the swamp, which by this time had become badly polluted. The latrine buckets have rotted and we have to dig pit dunnies, but as soon as they're full, the Japs don't let us dig new ones and we have to empty the pits by hand and dump the shit onto the tapioca patch and the swamp nearby. Pretty soon dysentery and skin infections become a truly major problem. Many of the blokes are now walking around barefoot in a bit of a loincloth that looks like we're wearing a baby's nappy, and everyone's got tropical ulcers.'

Tommy looks at me, 'You've seen the scars on me legs, Mole. Let me tell you, they're nothing, some of the men had 'em so large their entire leg bone could be seen from the ankle to the knee.

'We had no medicines to speak of by this time, only copper sulphate, and then after that was finished, hydrochloric acid. Some blokes carved these syringes from wood and would line up of an evening in front of an orderly, who'd use these syringes to suck the pus out of the ulcers. Blokes also came in for treatment before they reported for work, hoping to get through another day on the airfield and not die.

'Then, after he'd sucked out the pus, the medical orderlies each had a spoon with one edge sharpened and they'd cut away the dead flesh around the ulcer and paint the wound with a copper-sulphate solution.

'Mate, the pain o' the solution was something terrible, bloody near unbearable, until later when the copper sulphate run out, they used hydrochloric acid to do the same! Jesus, now that *really* hurt!

'By October '44, the Allies are bombing the airfield, which is good, because in the end the Japs could only use it for three months, but we're sent out to fill in the craters and our own planes come over and strafe the camp, thinking it's a Jap barracks. That's happened a good few times and there's a good few of our men get killed in these raids.

'Things are turning against the Japs and now there's no mercy shown. There's a few of them know their turn is coming and they'd as soon kill you as look at you.' Tommy stops and then says, 'I can remember some of their names, the worst ones. Let me see, there's Boy Bastard, Ming the Merciless, Mad Mick of course, Gold-Toothed-Runt, Gold-Toothed-Shin-Kicking-Bastard, Duck's Arse, Black Prince, Stutterer, Sourpuss, The Indian, Coffee King, Panther Tooth, Black Bastard, Moritake the Butcher, and heaps more I don't recall right now. They were all killers, the whole lot of them, and they took great pleasure in cruelty.

'When we wasn't working on the airfield, repairing it, we was burying the dead because at the beginning of 1945 we're starting to die in increasing numbers. At first we had coffins, boxes made of crude planking, but then the wood started to run out so we'd nail some planks together to make a platform and put it inside a coffin with a false bottom. We'd cart the coffin, with the body inside, to a burial hole, undo the hinged false bottom and drop the body into the pit. It was the best we could do.

'Catholic blokes had no priest. That was Cook's doing as well. He sent Fathers Rogers and O'Donovan to Kuching even though they pleaded to stay with the men. So our blokes couldn't receive the last rites and be granted absolution.' Tommy turns to me, 'It don't matter none, wherever we ended up, purgatory or hell, it couldn't have been worse than where we'd come from. But we had second best, Padre

Wardale-Greenwood made a special point of saying the prayers for the Catholic boys. He'd apologise at the graveside, "Sorry, lad, your own priest can't be here, but I've asked God if He minds if a Protestant sends you into the arms to our Lord Jesus Christ, His son, whom we both share. He reckons it will be all right, He'll fix the books up when you get up there." Then he'd say a prayer in English and a blessing in Latin. That bloke should have got the VC,' Tommy says, forgetting that he's given it to him two times already.

'Wasn't there, like, some sort of underground resistance?' I ask Tommy. 'Like the blokes on the Burma Railway who built a radio and could get news of the Allies.

'Yeah, that was the main reason the officers were moved out to Kuching. We done the exact same as the railway mob in Burma. Our organisation was run by an amazing bloke, Captain Matthews, who was called "The Duke". He was awarded the Military Cross in the Malayan campaign and he should've got the VC for what he done here, only he couldn't because he was a POW so he got a posthumous George Cross from the King for gallantry. That's sort of the civilian VC,' Tommy explains, though I already know about the George Cross. 'The officers who survived in Kuching called him "the bravest man we ever knew".'

'So what happened?' I ask, anxious for the details.

'Mate, I wasn't a part of the underground so I didn't know all that was going on. But there was plenty, we'd joined with a civilian underground movement run by civilians of all races in Sandakan and they'd helped us to smuggle in radio parts and gave us news of the outside world. It ran for nearly a year until it all come unstuck because a Chinese collaborator and Indian informer working on the airstrip betrayed the set-up to the Japanese.

'The Japs found the radio and arrested Captain Matthews, Lieutenant Rod Wells and Lieutenant Gordon Weynton, the three of them were the main operators of the radio and the camp underground network. Then they brought in the dreaded *Kempei-tai* to find the civilians involved in the town operation.'

'*Kempei-tai*, they were the Japanese military police, weren't they?'

'Yeah, murdering bastards the lot of them, the *real* experts at torture, we were very frightened of them. They eventually arrested fifty-three civilians they reckoned were involved with the espionage ring though our blokes never told them anything. I never heard what happened to the civilians, but I know eight of them were eventually executed with Captain Matthews.

'They took our three blokes, Matthews, Wells and Weynton, first to Sandakan, where they tortured them, and then to Kuching, where they were tried at a Japanese court martial and found guilty of plotting against the Japs.'

Tommy pauses and picks up the stick and moves a few embers about, then says, 'Some blokes are just unbelievably brave, like you can't understand how they could do what they did. Remember Richie Murray?'

'You mean the bloke you couldn't hit, the welterweight boxer?'

'Yeah, that's him. He's a lowly private and a bit of a larrikin but one of those blokes you'd follow anywhere he said, a natural born leader, and blokes looked up to him. Later, when we were at another camp at Ranau, Richie Murray and his best mate Botterill and two other blokes went under the wire and down the track a bit to where there was this Japanese food store. I agreed I'd be cockatoo, you know, watch out to see there are no Japs coming. They were planning to escape and needed the food to take with them. They stole rice and some small calico bags containing biscuits. When they get back they give some of the biscuits to the sick blokes, which is just about everyone in the hut, I cop a couple for being a look-out and they hide most of the rice in the jungle, but also some rice and the rest of the biscuits under the floor of the hut.

'About a week or so later a guard finds one of the empty bags and the Japs then knew they'd been robbed. The whole group, thirty POWs, were lined up in front of Lieutenant Suzuki, the commandant at the Randall Camp. He's a pretty aggro sort of bloke even for a Jap and he rants and raves and demands the guilty blokes confess. Stealing rice is a capital offence so we don't move and Suzuki threatens to have the lot of us. Still nobody moves and it's getting pretty dicey. Then Murray steps forward, 'I done it,' he says. He tells the Jap commandant he did the raid on his own and then afterwards gave the food to the men, who, he said, didn't know where it had come from.

'Suzuki handed him over to Kyoshi Kawakami, known to one and all as the Gold-Toothed-Shin-Kicking-Bastard. Kawakami took Richie

Murray down a jungle path with four other guards and bayoneted him to death. They came back wiping their blades and boasting they had blooded their bayonets.

'We were all heartbroken, he'd died for us. It could easily have been me if they'd found out I was part of it. I owe my life to Richie Murray. Keith Botterill, his best friend, was in complete despair. He didn't even know where his mate was buried. He spent days searching for Richie Murray's body but he never found it, the Japs had buried him somewhere in the jungle.'

Tommy is silent for a moment and is thinking, then he says, 'But what happened to Captain Matthews and them two others was different. We heard first about Lieutenant Rod Wells from a Chinese boy who did odd jobs around the camp and who before that worked as a yardman at the *Kempei-tai* headquarters in Sandakan. That's where the Jap military police put Wells into solitary confinement for three weeks on starvation rations. He was only permitted to wash when they returned the latrine bucket, which was emptied every few days.

'There he was given the usual floggings to try to get him to give the names of the civilians involved in the intelligence ring. When that didn't work, he was handed over to Sergeant Major "The Bulldog" Ehara, one of the *Kempei-tai's* most vicious torturers.

'Ehara rapped him repeatedly on the head with a hammer until the top of his head was a bloody mess. Then a thin bamboo skewer was tapped into his ear canal, perforating his ear drum and destroying the nerves in his middle ear. The pain was so horrific, Wells lost consciousness. When he came to, he was forced to eat four cups of raw rice washed down with a gallon of water. The rice in his stomach absorbed the water and swelled, distending his stomach to the point that his lower bowel pushed out of his arse. He pushed his intestines back in with his fingers but still he didn't talk.

'Two days later they put him on the Japanese version of the rack. He was handcuffed and suspended by his wrists from one of the verandah rafters, his legs were bent behind his knees and tied so that his knees were about six inches from the floor. Then they jammed a long plank of wood about four inches square and five feet long behind his knees and two men stood on either side of the plank and racked him, tearing the tendons and muscles of his upper body. After that, the plank was placed behind his heels and the flesh torn away from his ankles. He became unconscious and in his delirium kept calling for his mother, but still he didn't talk.

'The Japs hoped it would make Gordon Weynton talk when his turn came, but the sight of Wells's ruptured bowel and broken body only made him more determined to keep his own mouth shut. They repeatedly beat him around the head and shoulders with a riding crop until he bled profusely, pressed burning cigarettes into the flesh of his armpits and used him for jujitsu practice, but he kept his mouth shut, the bastards couldn't break him either.

'Captain Matthews was kept in solitary confinement, flogged, beaten and tortured repeatedly but he too never said a word. After this he was brought to trial, or the Japanese version of a military court, which is that you are guilty and can't be proved innocent. The trial lasted less than one hour, the penalty decided before it began and handed out by a panel of judges. There was a prosecutor but no defence counsel. Matthews was sentenced to be executed. Wells, also expecting to die, got twelve years and Weynton got ten years.

'Matthews was bundled into a prison truck with eight civilians also condemned to die. He could be seen with his face to the grille and as the truck moved off, he shouted, "Keep your chins up, boys! What the Japs do to me doesn't matter. They can't win!"

'They were driven out to an isolated clearing in the nearby jungle, where there were nine posts erected along an open pit. The nine condemned men were tied to the posts and a mark was made in the centre of each man's forehead. There was one executioner for every prisoner. Matthews refused the blindfold he was offered. His last words were shouted out, "My King and God forever! My King and God forever!"

'That night as the stars came out in an ink-blue tropical sky, the shadow of a lone piper could be seen standing on a slight rise at Kuching POW camp. A hushed silence came over the camp as the strains of "The Lament" filled the soft night air. Men stood to attention wherever they were, the camp brought to a complete standstill. The bravest man they'd ever known had died for them and for his King, his God and his country.'

Chapter Twenty-four

Tommy has been speaking for more than four hours and I expect him to want to give it away, but he's in a groove and I can feel he's getting more and more emotional, the words almost coming out by themselves. It's as though he's reached some point in the story where there's no turning back. He must go on now.

'By January 1945 the Japs know it's all over for them. The airfield is no longer in operation and it's doubtful they have the planes left to use it. The Yanks control the skies and they've wrecked the airfield with their bombing.

'With no airfield, they had no more use for us and the rice ration stops and we have to rely on the little we've stored ourselves. The daily ration is now two and a half ounces per man.' Tommy cups his hand in the firelight, 'Boiled, that wouldn't fill me hand, you could gulp it in two mouthfuls and that was it for the day. We got no pay, no cigs and we were slowly dying, every day a little more.

'Each morning there'd be fewer blokes at *tenko* and the pretend coffins were working overtime. It took all our strength to carry the bodies to the burial ground. Then one of my mates, part of the five, couldn't go on no longer. We're on one side of the coffin doing burial duty and we've dropped the body into the grave and we're sitting down having a smoko. I've got a bit of a cigarette which I've saved and I light up and take a puff, then hand it to me mate who's sitting on the ground opposite me. But he don't take it and says nothing. "Here, have a drag," I say to him, because he seems to be looking over me left shoulder. Again he don't move to take the gasper, so I tap him on the shoulder and he keels over, he's dead. Me mate died sitting up without sayin' a word.'

Tommy looks up. 'There's no crying, there's no tears, just that thread I told yiz about, it stretches just a bit tighter, death is comin' closer, you can feel it crawlin' into you, comin' to stay, be with you permanent, eat at you from the inside until you're hollow and there's nothing left and you die lookin' over your mate's shoulder, not saying nothing, not even cheerio.'

Suddenly I'm crying. I can't help myself. The thought of little Tommy with death crawling inside of him is too much and I start to bawl. Tommy's out of his sleeping bag and over to me and he's holding me. He's never done that, not even once, now he's got his arms about me and I'm blubbing into his chest. 'There yer go, Mole. Steady on, mate. I'm here, ain't I? Made it, didn't I, eh? Got yiz to the tree.'

'Shit, I'm sorry,' I blub, 'It's not me should be doing the crying!'

'Cryin's good, mate, get rid o' the shit inside, like rain after a big dry.'

Just how he says it, I realise that he's never cried for himself, only about John Crowe and when he couldn't remember the names of his mates. I stop after a while and apologise again, but now I'm scared he won't go on. 'Please, Dad, don't stop now, please finish!'

Tommy is silent for a moment, 'Can't stop now, Mole.' He pauses and looks into the dark. 'This is a once and only, mate. It can never come out again.' Then he starts up again like if he doesn't, he can't. 'On the twenty-sixth of January, Hoshijima tells us we're leaving Sandakan, going to another camp where there is plenty of food. There's nine groups in all, each group leaving one day apart. We're told the journey will take three weeks.

'Me and me three remaining mates, Richie Murray and his mate Botterill, them two are never apart, Albert Cleary and his mate Wally Crease, are in the third group to go on the first march out. We stick together. The Japs have issued us with just four days' rations, three pounds of rice, two and a half pounds of dried fish, an ounce o' salt, the same of tabacca, which is enough to make one smoke a day, and they kit us out with an old pair of shorts and shirt, because by now we're all down to them loincloths I told you about that look like a nappy.' Tommy grins, 'There's dysentery all round and there's more than one bloke where it's had to work like a nappy as well.' Tommy is trying to cheer me up from my bawling bout.

'They also give us these shoes to wear because our boots are long gone. They're made of latex rubber and they're sort of slip-on, no laces or anything, the Jap name for them is *jikatabi*, I don't know why I remember that. Problem is, it's the middle of the rainy season, pissing down for most of every day, sometimes for days without a stop and the ground is mud and bog and more mud and the shoes ain't got no grip and keep slippin' and we're fallin' arse over tip. Soon as you stand up, you're down again, but when we took the bastards off, our feet were cut to pieces on roots, stumps and stones.

'Our group leaves Sandakan on the thirty-first of January, there's fifty of us. About a mile down the road we are joined by Lieutenant Toyohara and forty-seven soldiers. We're loaded down with our own baggage and the Japs' personal belongings, as well as ten sacks of rice, ten bags of ammunition and a dismantled mountain gun. We're like bloody pack horses with an average of about fifty pounds per man on our shoulders.

'After a few miles the track becomes very muddy and we're slipping all over the place. When a bloke falls with a fifty-pound load, he stays fallen until his mates can get him back onto his feet. We're doing that every few minutes. Then we hit the mangrove swamps of the Labuk River basin which are flooded and the bloody place is infested with huge crocodiles. There's not even a thought of escaping. There's the crocodiles in the swamps, and in the jungle we've been bit by every manner of insect, we've seen elephants, wild boars and that many poisonous snakes that most of the blokes are terrified.

'We're four days into the march when I see something that's gunna become a very common occurrence. One of our NCOs, whose name I don't recall, is bloated with severe beri-beri, his legs are that swollen they're like they'd belong on an elephant. He can't go no further and he calls out, saying he's fucked. Lieutenant Toyohara tries to jolly him along, but it don't help. The NCO goes completely berserk and he's pleading for someone to shoot him. All this is happening just a few yards from where we're standing and I seen it all. There's this Jap sergeant major whose name is Gotunda, who agrees to put the Aussie out of his misery, but he wants an authority to do it from the senior Australian present. This is a warrant officer, name of Warrington, Clive Warrington, and he writes out the necessary authority. The Jap goes up to the NCO, who's now raving and threshing about hysterically, and points his rifle at the NCO's head. We turn away and wait for the shot to go off. Can't look at somethin' like that. But the Jap sergeant major can't do it. Fuck me dead, there's one Jap in the whole war don't take a delight in killing. Warrington tells him it's okay, he has permission, so put the poor bastard out of his misery. Those of us looking on want the same, the soldier is a goner, nothing can keep him alive, best to make it short and painless. But in the end Gotunda can't do it, he shakes his head and turns away. So Warrington takes the rifle out of Gotunda's hands and goes over and pulls the trigger and we all give this sigh of relief. Poor bastard's out of his misery at last. When my turn comes, my hope is some bloke will do the same for me.

'It's not the last time we'll hear of Gotunda, the only good Jap I ever met in the war.' Tommy stops and looks at me. 'That's the thing, mate, good men don't just come because they're of your kind. It's like we have our saints. I reckon there's just some good men born, can't help themselves. They's there to make up for the rest of us. As it turns out, Gotunda, he ain't the enemy, he's a good man, can't help himself.

'Though I must say, them Japanese soldiers on that march were just blokes, just soldiers, like most of the blokes marching with us. They didn't give us a hard time. They were split into three groups, one up front, one in the middle, and one behind us, trying to keep us going at a reasonable pace. They don't bash us and they'll even light a fag for you and always stopped us for a ten-minute rest period every hour.

'It's not all that great for them neither, they're slipping and falling, though their boots have got more traction than our latex slip-ons. They're doing it tough. But they're a pretty disciplined mob all round. At night, camped in some filthy swamp, with swarms of vicious mosquitoes eating us alive, they'd sit there with needle and thread, sucking on the end of a bit of cotton, squinting to thread the needle. Then they'd mend their shirts and shorts where they'd been torn along the jungle track. They'd wash them out and hang them on bushes to dry next to their fire and they'd put on spare ones in the meantime. Last thing, they'd polish their boots and clean their weapons. Next morning they'd line up for inspection, same as if they were in a barracks. We were lucky, we didn't have no Formosans with us. Those who did took a beating whenever they fell over or slowed down a bit.

'But now at the forty-nine-mile peg we reach a so-called food dump to find nothing there. The blokes in front of us have taken the lot. But here's where Sergeant Major Gotunda comes in again. He takes a boat down river to a native village and manages to get seventy pounds of rice for us and a huge bag of vegies. It ain't much for fifty blokes and had to last us for days but it's the difference between life and death. We pool our rice so we each get exactly the same and make it last. We cook it in a five-gallon billy, adding fern tips and anything else we can find like grubs and insects we've learned to eat before.'

Tommy glances at me, 'I don't want to sound like it's big-noting meself or nothing, cause it ain't, but I'm a bushie from way back and, like I've said before, I've took an interest in the jungle at Sandakan. Scrounging around in the bush is what I've always done.' He looks at me, 'What I've taught you to do. Keeping a sharp eye out you see things others don't. It's not much, but I can spot a bit of *kang kong*, which is a kind of wild spinach that grows in the swamps. There's fat grubs that live under bark, jungle fruit, wild chillies, fern tips and lots o' other little bits and pieces you wouldn't eat in a fit but now they mean everything. Sometimes you'd come across a bit of open country, a bit of sunshine, and we'd hunt for grasshoppers or lizards taking the sun. In creeks we'd look for freshwater shrimps, frogs, even tadpoles. Anything that had a body that was soft was good for the rice pot.

'The rain doesn't stop and the jungle keeps going on and on, it's rainforest so thick that no sunlight penetrates its canopy. Finally we're out of the mud and reach the sixty-mile mark, but it ain't that much better. We have to cross several rivers where there's leeches thick as pencils that get stuck into what little blood we've got left. The march flies attack us and the mozzies are always there, swarms of them so thick that sometimes you can't see through it. At night we pack mud all over our skin, thick layers of it, so they can't get through. In the morning we break the crust off our skins and wash.

'After about twelve days we reach the mountains and the next scheduled food dump. There's no food here neither except for six cucumbers and a tiny bit of rice. There was no way the Jap guards were gunna share their emergency rations of dried buffalo meat and bean powder and the next food dump is about forty miles away. We're on a tributary of the Labuk River and the jungle is thick as ever when we climb the Maitland Range. Every step is uphill and we lose five men on the mountain. They can't go on and the Japs have got their orders so they bayonet them or shoot them, then roll them over the side of the track and leave them there to rot. We don't see death like it's a tragedy. It's just your time's come up, the wheel has turned and the peg come to rest on your number. We've lost six blokes so far, it don't seem that much considering what we've been through.

'With no food, except them six cucumbers and a handful of rice each, it looks like the rest of us won't make it neither. Now here's a good thing we didn't expect. We're sloggin' through in the jungle and, out of the bushes on the side of the track, comes an arm and a hand holding out a piece of tapioca or sweet potato. I swear you couldn't see them, dark hands holding the food and we'd grab a hold of them, desperate. You'd see nothing else, a hand darts out, gives you somethin'. We don't know where they come from, we're miles from any native village. It turns out they're jungle people, like pygmies, small as children, but they knew we were starving and they come to help. I didn't think it at that time, but later I realise all people are the same. Given their natural instincts they do two things, they kill or they care. Them little people in the jungle, they didn't have nothing to gain, they could have stood back, but they done what's right. They're probably still exactly the same as they were then, still minding their own business, doing what they've always done. Far as I'm concerned, they're the salt of the earth. We heard later they're called the Murut people. What can you say?

'We finally make it to Ranau in mid-February with only ten dead on the way. The two groups ahead of us have lost thirty-five men between them. The guards have their orders, if anyone slows down or can't continue they must be shot or bayoneted. We'd be walking along and you'd see a bloke beginning to slow down. If he was close enough you'd try to help, put your hand to his back, tell him it's not too far to the next smoko. But those who died on the march and later when we were carrying rice from Ranau to Paginatan, where groups six to nine stayed for a few weeks, would just come to a stop. You'd see in someone's eyes he were good as dead. You'd shake his hand, tell him, you know, that she'll be right, then move on. You'd just hope he'd die before the killing squad arrived. If they were kind, they'd shoot him, but mostly they'd use the bayonet or the butt of their rifle so they didn't have to worry about cleaning their rifle barrel. They'd shoot or stab or beat the poor bastard to death and drag his body a few feet off the track and leave him there. There's no time for a burial and there's no padre with our lot so there's no prayers, just a carcass left to rot in the jungle. There's only one thing we all knew for certain, once you stopped, you stopped for good.

'Conditions at Ranau Camp are terrible, we're not supposed to stop here. We're meant to be going to Jesselton, but the Allies are bombing the crap out of it. Our accommodation, if you can call it that, is a long open-sided hut. Dysentery breaks out and soon three-quarters of the living space is filled with blokes sick or dying. There's shit and dirt and flies, lice and bugs and fleas, mites and crabs, there's plenty of them, only thing that's scarce is hope.

'There's no room at Ranau, the blokes in groups six to nine are still at Paginatan, which is also a staging post for Japs using the track. They've all got to be fed, so now we're in rice-carrying work parties to Paginatan, twenty-six miles away. It's a track through the jungle and it's hell, there'd be twenty of us in a work party, each with a sack of rice on our backs but one thing this does, it gives us a chance to get extra food from the natives and we also manage to steal a bit of the rice. The thing is, if you're strong enough to make the distance, you have a better chance of survival than those back in the camp. If a bloke died on the way or was bayoneted because he couldn't keep up, we had to carry his rice bag, taking turns between us.

'Then one night Albert Cleary says to me, he and Wally Crease are planning an escape, do I want to come?

'"Tommy, we're gunna die anyway, might as well die in the jungle, bloody sight better than a Jap bayonet. Then again, we might make it." I'm sorely tempted but I tell him I can't.

'"Mate, you're a good scrounger, the best of us all, we'll get there, you'll see," he says to me again. "The natives know the Japs are on the run, they'll help us, it's in their interest now."

'"Mate, it's not that," I tell him, "It's me mates, the three of them and me, we've been together since Malaya, I can't leave them now."

'"Bring 'em then, they're good blokes," he says.

'"They'd never make it, mate. All three o' them are pretty crook. It'd only stop you and Wally getting away."

'I've managed to find a sweet-potato vine and I give him the two sweet potatoes I've dug up, shake his hand and wish him luck. Cleary's a real good bloke, the best kind of digger you can find. I don't ask him which way he's going in case the Japs have a go at me, knowing we're mates. Best I know nothing, then you can't get into trouble.

'On the third of March, Cleary and Wally Crease do a runner into the jungle from camp. Lieutenant Suzuki is off his skull, even one escape and the world will know what's been happening and he's in disgrace with his superiors. He knows there'll be trials at the end of the war and, with witnesses, he's going to be hanged for sure. The guards on duty who allowed them to escape are sent on a three-mile run with full kit, rifle and bayonet and then they're lined up for a bout of face-slapping, which is the worst disgrace that can happen to a Japanese soldier.

'Nine days later Cleary is caught, betrayed by some native villagers for the reward the Japs offered. Cleary was wrong, the natives are still hostile, or some o' them anyway.

'The guards who've lost face over his escape and are humiliated take it out on Cleary. They tie his hands behind his back and make him kneel, then they tie his ankles and place a ten-foot pole behind his knees and pull his legs back so his ankles are touching his arse and they tie them around the top of his legs so the pole is jammed behind his knees. After that, they jump on either side of the pole. Poor bastard is crying out in agony, screaming from the pain, but they keep on and on. Every hour or so, they untie him and force him back to his feet, causing him terrible pain as the blood runs back into his legs. They leave him lying there all night and we can't get to him because he's being watched by the guards.

'Next day the guards, led by Kawakami, The Gold-Toothed-Shin-Kicking-Bastard, start all over again. He's still tied to the log and they bash him something terrible. Grabbing and pulling his head back, they punch his throat till the blood pours from his mouth, they kick him and smash him with the butts of their rifles, slowly reducing him to a pulp. They don't want to kill him straight off, they want his death to be slow and as painful as possible, so each time they untie him they give him some water to drink so he won't die of dehydration.

'About noon we see the *Kempei-tai* arrive in camp and they've got Wally Crease, he's also been betrayed by the natives. Crease gets the same treatment as Albert Cleary with the log and they're both tortured at intervals right through the night. We can hear them screaming.

'At about 7 a.m., the torture stops for a little while because the guards have to organise the day's working parties. Crease, who's been untied to get a drink of water, realises the guards are busy elsewhere and ain't looking. Christ knows how, but he can still walk and he makes a second run for it. He tries to hide in the jungle but a few hours later a search party spots him and they shoot him dead.

'This time Suzuki is mad as a cut snake and he goes ape-shit, the guards are severely punished and there's more face-slapping and now there's even more guards been humiliated and Cleary cops more torture. They've tied him to a tree with a rope around his ankles and his neck and every time a guard passes he kicks Cleary or smashes him with his rifle butt, spits on him, or takes out his cock and urinates on him. They won't touch him with their hands, afraid they'll get dysentery. Cleary's out there in the blistering sun all day and no shelter from the mosquitoes at night. He's covered in his own shit and blood and he's got no face left, there's nothing you can see, just pulped and purple flesh with a hole for his mouth where his face once was and where a Jap guard pours a bit of water twice a day to keep him alive.'

Tommy turns to me, 'I can't do nothing for him. I feel it should be me there, or maybe if I'd gone with them, it might have been different. I speak the native lingo real good by now and maybe I could have persuaded the villagers who turned him in that they would've got a bigger reward from the Allies or explained how the Japs were being defeated and, if they helped them, we would've come back and got them afterwards. All these things go through my head as I'm watching my mate dying. I feel terrible guilty, like it's me that's let them down. I know it don't make sense, but the route they took was wrong, maybe I would have persuaded them to go another way. One mate is dead and another is dying in front of my eyes and I'm praying to God to let him die. But the guards won't kill him off, they want him alive as long as possible.

'Cleary suffers eight days of torture. He's only semi-conscious and I dunno how he's still alive, but he's dying. His body, that part that ain't covered in purple bruises and blood blisters, is a sickly yellow colour. The tropical ulcers on his legs have eaten to the bone and the pus runs down his ankles. He's always only worn a *fondushi*, a loincloth, like the rest of us and it's soaked with muck and blood pouring out of his bowels.

'Then on the twentieth of March the guards cut him down and dump him like a dead dog beside the Meridi track. It's the first time we can get to him and we pick him up and take him to the creek, where we tenderly wash away the shit and the grime and encrusted blood from his battered and broken body. Thank gawd, Cleary's unconscious. But we hope he knows it's us come to care for him, that his mates love him. I've got him in me arms and someone else has got him by the legs and we take him back to the hut, tender as we can, and we're not long back when he dies in me arms. He's twenty-two years old and one of the nicest blokes you'd ever meet.'

Tommy is silent for a long time and I hear him sigh a few times. I've got this lump in me throat big as an apple and there's tears running down my cheeks but I don't want Tommy to see I'm crying again. After a while he starts off again.

'The Japs wouldn't let us bury him with his mates, they said he was a criminal and so we had to put him in a lonely grave away from the others. It's such a small thing but it broke our hearts.

'A fortnight after Cleary died, the blokes who had been kept at Paginatan, or what was left of them, arrived. Dysentery and starvation had knocked them off like flies. Of the 150 men who'd reached the village six weeks before, now only fifty were alive. There was plenty of room in the hut because there was only about a hundred of our lot left as well.

'Those of us still on our feet could only watch as our comrades wasted away. You can see two kinds of dying in the eyes. There's the eyes of the blokes dying of dysentery, the skull clear through the stretched skin, all except the eyes, which are popping out like they're gunna burst out the sockets, the white part is yellow and the colour of the eyes is gone and looks like muddy water. Then there's the blokes with beri-beri, the face is swollen like a balloon with the eyes just slits in skin that looks like suet pudding.

'You'd wake up of a mornin' not believing you was still alive, the thread in you hangin' on ain't broke yet, not sure you're glad it's still holding, you've got another day to get through. You look to one side to see if the bloke next to you is still alive and then the same to the other side. If one or both are dead, you roll them over a bit to see if he's got anything you can use or there's anything in his belongings might be handy. You'd leave him there, hoping you wasn't picked for the burial party.

'There would be a burial party every morning though this time there wasn't a coffin or even a bamboo platform. The dead were stripped naked and we'd tie their wrists and ankles together and we'd put a bamboo pole through them and carry them like you'd carry a dead animal, like a dead dingo. There'd be no padre and we'd scrape a ditch six inches deep because we didn't have the strength to dig a grave. Then we'd stand back and spit on the body before we scraped the soil back over him.'

'Spit!' I shout out. I can't believe it's what I've heard Tommy say.

Tommy shrugs, 'It was a mark of respect, leaving something of yourself with him, it was the soldiers' way,' he explains.

'We don't know it at the time, of course, but there's an order that's come through to all the Jap-controlled POW camps from the Japanese High Command in Tokyo. It says that every prisoner of war held by the Japanese must be killed, there must be no survivors to tell the stories of the atrocities the Japs have committed. The camps must be burned down and any evidence destroyed that can implicate them.

'What's happening to us is that they're allowing us to die as fast as we can manage on our own by starving us and holding back the medicine that's been supplied by the Red Cross to Sandakan Camp. There's plenty of rice because we're carting it to Paginatan and the Jap soldiers are getting a full ration of two pounds a day. The plan is that whoever is left at the end they're instructed to kill.'

Tommy gives a little laugh, 'Our side is doing its level best to finish us off as well. The camp is close to a small airstrip, nothing much, just a bit of grass in the jungle, but they strafe and bomb it. A couple of POWs and a few Jap soldiers staying in a temporary barracks nearby get killed, so Lieutenant Suzuki decides to relocate. We pack up and move to a bunch of native huts in the jungle that's not too far away but can't be seen from the air.

'By this time, it's late April and there's only fifty-six of us left. Two weeks later when Richie Murray gets murdered, there's only about thirty of us, we're falling like nine pins. A week or so after that, the Japs say they need seven men to carry rice to Paginatan. They're expecting a mob of blokes there pretty soon and the village is out of rice. What we don't know at the time is that the new arrivals are another lot of our Sandakan mob who've left on a second march at the end of May.

'We're all in pretty bad shape, half the blokes are on the way out and can hardly stand up. Lieutenant Suzuki calls out seven names. Me and me three mates are among them. Me mates are just about hanging on and I see that Kawakami, The Gold-Toothed-Shin-Kicking-Bastard, is assigned as a guard. I plead with Lieutenant Suzuki to let them stay back. He's shaking his head and pushing me back into line, but I won't let up. I can speak enough Japanese so he knows what I'm on about but he won't relent. He's angry and says something to a guard, who knocks me over with his rifle butt. I get up and tell him he can shoot me, but just don't let me mates go on the working party. Then I realise who the guard is who knocked me over, it's another evil bastard called Suzuki Saburo. His favourite trick during burials was to follow two prisoners carrying their dead mate on the pole, like I explained earlier. He'd stick his boot out so one of the carriers would trip and the body on the pole would crash to the ground. Suzuki Saburo thought this was huge fun.

'Counting the previous rice trips, this is my fifth trip to Paginatan, but I knew it would be me last, we were buggered, me mates even worse than me. We were still within sight of the camp when a bloke who's suffering from beri-beri can't go any further. Suzuki Saburo drags him to the side of the track and kills him with a single shot through the head. He comes back cursing and swearing because he's got a few spots of blood on his uniform. Kawakami is laughing and that makes him cranky as hell.

'Two more prisoners are murdered before we get to Paginatan, but somehow me mates have held on and we get a night's sleep before the journey back, which without a load is a lot easier. The four of us are still standing, still together next morning, though, as we set out, I can see they're very weak and more than once along the way I've had to take each of them around the shoulder and urge them on. I'm not much better meself. We're all reduced to shuffling along, leaning on sticks, we can't lift our feet more than half an inch and the trail is rough and sometimes slippery. We get to a hill just a little higher than the others we've crossed and all three of me mates make it a couple of hundred yards up the track and stop. They can't make it no more.

'I can't believe it's all three. I urge them on, but I ain't got a lot left in the tank meself. I can see they're barely conscious, I try to grab a hold of one and urge him forward and he sinks down to his knees and then falls on his face. I look at the other two, they're out on their feet, then one sits down, then the other. By now I'm screaming at them, "Get up, you bastards! We can make it! Please, please get up!" But I'm wasting me time, they've both got their eyes closed and then one keels over. Oh Jesus, don't die on me, don't die. All three are gunna die on me, I'll be alone. I don't want to die alone. Rigby's dead, Murray's dead, Cleary's dead, I should've somehow persuaded Lieutenant Suzuki to keep me three best mates off the work party, it must be me done this to them! First Cleary and Crease not speaking the native lingo, going the wrong way, Richie Murray for stealing the food, now them three. Oh shit, what am I gunna do! is what's going through me head.

'Then Kawakami comes up and smiles, his gold tooth showing. He kicks at me mate sitting up, who keels over and lies there. The three o' my mates are just lying there now. "Smoko!" I say, "Rest! They'll be all right, you'll see!"

'"Finish," he says, grinning, "No go."

'I sink to me knees and grab him by the ankles and kiss his boots, "Please, please, smoko, rest time!" I beg.

'He kicks me off and I'm still on me knees. He's grinning down at me. Suzuki Saburo has come to watch Kawakami, who has his rifle pointed at the head of me mate. I say each of their names, I tell them I'm sorry. Kawakami suddenly pulls back his rifle and says something to Suzuki Saburo, who drags me to my feet. Kawakami's laughing. "You shoot!" he says, pointing to me mates, then hands me the rifle. Suzuki Saburo has his rifle pointed to my chest.

'"No!" I scream. "No, no, no!" Suddenly I'm blubbing, I ain't cried yet in all the time, not for Rigby, not for Cleary, not for me mate who died sitting up, now I'm crying.

'"You shoot!" Kawakami screams at me.

'One of me mates who's still conscious opens his eyes, his voice is barely above a whisper, his lips just moving, "Please, Tommy, you do it, mate." Then he closes his eyes and he don't move no more, he's passed out.

'"Shoot!" Kawakami screams.

'Now I've got the rifle in me hands and I do it, three shots, the rifle bolt clicking back each time. The clicks and the shots I still hear in me head every day of me life. The three shots that murdered me mates, the sound of a flock of birds rising from the jungle canopy at the first explosion . . .'

I'm crying again, but again not so he can hear, tears rolling down my cheeks and over my chin. I'm glad he's never said the names of his mates so I don't have a picture in me head. But Tommy ain't crying. He just sits there and then he sighs. 'Kawakami takes his rifle and knocks me to the ground and last thing I feel is the butt in me face, me jaw breaking. He's beaten me severe so I'd die slowly, he ain't gunna waste a bullet on me, it's the Japanese way of insulting the dead. But I didn't feel the most of it, only the first, 'cause the blow to me face knocked me unconscious.

'It's dark when I come to. They've pulled the four of us off the track, left us on the side of the mountain. I lie there in the jungle and pass out several times during the night. It ain't the rainy season but it rains early morning and I force me mouth open to let me get a drink. Daylight comes but I must have passed out again, because when I wake up there's these snuffling sounds and grunts. I manage to get up on me good elbow, it's a wild boar, he's ripped open the stomach of one of me mates and is eating his intestines. I can't shout, me jaw and cheekbone is broken. I can't do nothing. I lie on me back and with me good arm feel around me till I find a small rock, I sit up slowly. The boar ain't noticed and he has his snout buried in me mate's gut. I throw the rock and hit the bastard on the top o' the head. He looks up, there's intestines hanging from his pig mouth. When he sees me, he runs into the jungle, carrying the string of sausages with him.

'After a while I manage to get to me feet and I totter over to the body of one of me mates and somehow manage to get his loincloth off his body. I dunno how I done it, but, using it, I make a sling for me broken shoulder. I can feel me face and neck and chest is crusted with blood, and the pain in me jaw and shoulder is almost more than I can take. I'm terrible weak and I shuffle back on to the path, finding the spot where I've killed me mates, and pick up me stick.

'I don't want to die here, there's a big tree back down the hill, I've seen it on past occasions we've carted rice, it's a jungle giant, as big as the one at Sandakan. If I can make it to the tree I can die there. I don't want the pig to eat me. I want to be cradled in the buttress of that big tree.' Tommy looks at me. 'It's not that I'm thinking them thoughts at that very moment, it's just that they're returning to me then. I've thought it all out before. Every working party that goes out carrying rice loses men and I know my time will come. I've already thought that if it does, somehow I'll manage to last until I get to that big tree and they can shoot me there. It's the last thing I'll see and I'll remember the Maloney tree as me last thought, remember these great giants are the roots of heaven. Now it's just me instinct working, telling me this stuff, because I am in too much pain to think straight. I don't know yet that I've lost me eye and think that maybe it's just closed from Kawakami's rifle butt.'

Tommy pauses. 'When I'd escaped and I was getting better in the hospital, I'd have nightmares about the pig, that pig eating me mate. I'd wake up screaming and it would be hours before I'd be calm enough to go to sleep again. Then when I was testifying at the War Crimes Tribunal, I heard about the group left in Sandakan, there's over two hundred of them too crook to go on the second march. One of the Japs, Lieutenant Moritake, and a guard named Hinata murdered a POW only known as Honcho. I never knew this Hinata when I was in Sandakan, but we all knew and hated Moritake, who was called "The Mad Butcher". Although he was an officer, he loved to slaughter the Japanese officers' pigs, hanging them up alive by their front legs, then butchering them slowly, keeping them alive as long as possible.

'Anyhow, Honcho has managed to steal one of these pigs which he killed and shared with the other starving men. Like I told you, stealing food was a capital offence and Honcho doesn't stand a chance. He was taken to a large wooden cross which Moritake has ordered erected in the grounds of the Jap barracks. Moritake instructs Hinata to lift the prisoner so his feet can't touch the ground and then to press his body against the pole and hold the prisoner, who is too weak to resist. Moritake, a short-arse, stands on a small stool and drives a six-inch nail through the palm of Honcho's outstretched right hand and then through the other. Hinata tells how he stuffed a piece of rag in Honcho's mouth to stop him screaming. After that Moritake nails both his feet to the horizontal board Honcho's standing on. He steps off the ladder. Hammer in hand, he examines his handiwork before he climbs up again and drives a six-inch nail into the centre of Honcho's forehead.'

Tommy can hear me gasp, 'Mate, you ain't heard nothing yet,' he says. 'Moritake slips on a rubber glove and, taking a butcher's knife, he cuts two pieces of flesh from the abdomen and puts them aside before he slits the torso from neck to navel. Sticking his hand with the rubber glove in the innards, he tears out the heart and the liver. Those are the only parts he wants, the remains of the corpse is left hanging on the cross.'

I can't believe me ears. 'You mean . . . ?' I don't want to say it.

'Yeah, mate, towards the end it was not unusual, the official war instructions the Japs got from their general and the war cabinet in Japan was that they could eat their enemy but they must not do the same to one of their own. Anyway, when I heard that at the Tribunal, I said to meself, shit, I'd rather be eaten by a wild pig than by a Jap and from that time on the nightmares about the pig stopped, never come back neither.'

I want him to tell me how he escaped, so I ask, 'Was it all jungle when you were escaping?'

'Mostly, that and the rivers. Weren't for the river, I'd never have made it. I can't stay on the track it's too dangerous, so I spend the next three days in the jungle looking for the big tree. Mostly I'm delirious, lurching about, not knowing where I am, not caring neither. I'm terrible weak and I've got a bout of malaria and, of course, the dysentery is always there. I'm sitting on a log and I'm quite lucid, must have been on the third or fourth day. I can see these insects crawling everywhere, but there's nothing I can eat. I'm sitting still as death and this large snake goes by and past me toes. I reckon it's time to die and I move me foot, but the bugger don't strike, he moves off fast. It's then that I think to meself, I'm such a useless bugger I can't even get meself properly killed, might as well have a go at staying alive.

'So I get up from the log and I ain't moved three feet when I come across this little pool, it ain't more than maybe a foot across and stagnant, the water's black. I realise it's swarming with tadpoles, yiz can hardly see the water for the tadpoles. I ain't eaten much, I can't chew because of me jaw though I've found some fern tips and crushed them in me hand, pushing them in me mouth very slow and tried to swallow. It weren't enough to keep me alive much longer. So now I feast on them tadpoles, cupping them in me good hand and ramming them in me mouth, some spilling, but some go in and they slips down without me needing to chew. After that I drink some of the water. I reckon I must have had live tadpoles swimming around in me guts for hours.

'If it weren't for them tadpoles, I don't reckon I could have gone on. Not just me eating them, it was like a sign. So I stumble on and then I see a wild pig and I'm angry. It's bloody stupid I know, the pig could've killed me sooner than me it. But I hate the bugger and I lurch after it, following the sound of it crashing through the undergrowth. Suddenly the jungle parts and I'm by a river. There's a small stony beach where I can lie. I spend the night by the river and in the morning I see this canoe coming towards me. I can't shout, I can't even speak. In me head I'm callin' out "*Abang!*", which is the Malay word for "older brother" but nothing's coming out. I'm waving my good arm, hoping the native in the canoe will see me. He sees me and comes over. His name is Ackoi and he signals for me to get in, but I'm too weak so he gets out of the canoe and helps me. It turns out Ackoi's the headman from Tampias Village. He speaks in Malay to me as he soon realises that I understand him but I can't talk back.

'He says the villagers hate the Japs and are in contact with the local guerilla leader, who he promises will help me. I don't know if it's a con, but I don't care no more, nothing I can do. I'm dead meat anyway. Ackoi don't give me the name of the guerilla, which is good or bad, I'm not sure. Good if he's protecting his identity, bad if he's made the whole thing up and he's taking me back to the Japanese for the reward.

'But he's good as his word, the people of Tampias look after me. An old woman uses herbs and stuff on me eye and I learn that it's dead, that I'm blind in that eye. They can't do nothing about me jaw or cheekbone, but they make a sort of wooden splint for me broken shoulder and the top part of me arm. Every day a young girl sits beside me and feeds me tapioca and sweet potato and bananas mashed up, once or twice a turtle egg. She can't get a spoon in me mouth so she puts a little of whatever it is on the end of her forefinger and works it slowly into me mouth and laughs every time she done it. She had lovely white teeth. Them villagers were so kind to me I want to cry just thinkin' about them.

'Then after a week, when I'm a bit stronger, Ackoi himself takes me down river in his canoe to Telupid, where, after a day or two, I am transferred by another head man down river in another canoe. By now my shoulder is never going to be right again, I know that for sure. As for my face, well, it was never much anyway. I'm still in a fair bit of pain from both and, once, when we hit some rapids with the canoe jumping up and down in the water, I pass out from the pain. Tell you the truth, I don't remember much about the rest of the trip because when I'm not out of it with the pain, I'm delirious with malaria. Apparently they keep passing me from village to village, and by the time I've come to my senses, we're at a place called Muanad, about fifty miles from Sandakan.

'I reckon I must have come a bloody long way from Telupid, the last place I remember clearly, because the river is now very wide. The headman here is Kulang, chief of the Dusans, who hate the Japs with a passion.

'As soon as it's dark, Kulang takes me to a new village, deeper into the jungle, which they have built to avoid harassment from the Japs, who regularly patrol this part of the river.

'At Kulang's house I have a bath. Can you imagine, it's me first bath in over three years. I'm also given some clean clothes and a bowl of soup. They give me a shave and a haircut, which Kulang, laughing at my long beard and hair, does himself with an ancient cut-throat razor, though I must say it's sharp enough and he's skilled enough and doesn't nick me too bad. I begin to feel like a human being again.' Tommy looks up, 'I mean that, we were reduced to animals, wild animals just trying to stay alive. Now, for the first time since I escaped, I think I might make it. I'm skin and bone and with me ulcers, which Kulang also treats, and me bunged-up eye and gawd knows what me gob looks like, though I know how it feels, which ain't good.

'I stay there a few days and then Kulang decides it's time to move again. We're going to some place called the Bongaya River. It's got to be to buggery down the river because we're in a big canoe and we're taking quite a lot of tucker with us. We set off before daylight just in case the Japs are on the prowl.

'Kulang's got me lying under banana leaves in the bottom of the canoe, but it wouldn't have been much use if a Jap river patrol had stopped him. We're going with the flow and moving along at a good pace, but it takes us three days to cross the estuary and another three to reach the Bongaya River.

'About six hours later, Kulang gets me from out the banana leaves and tells me we've got about an hour to go. After a while I look up and, there, standing on the bank, is a bloke dressed in jungle greens. He's wearing a slouch hat and he looks about nine feet tall standing like that at the edge of the river. He's an Aussie from a Special Ops unit, which has been working behind enemy lines. Kulang is waving madly and shouting to attract the soldier's attention as we come into the riverbank.

'Two blokes come out of a tent and come down to the water.

They're both six-footers and healthy as sin. One's a sergeant and the other a lance corporal, don't know why I remember that. The first words the sergeant says are, "Christ, look what the cat brought in!" Then him and his mate and the first bloke we saw are running, they're splashing up to their waists in the water, coming for me, pulling the canoe into shore. The sergeant lifts me out like I'm a small child, later I find I weigh sixty-eight pounds, and I'm shaking like a leaf from malaria.

'The lance corporal who is splashing through the water beside me is saying, "She's right, mate. It's all over. You're going home." I can't make no sound, but there's tears running out me eyes, the good one and the bad. The big bloke carrying me keeps saying, "The bastards, the dirty, fucking bastards! Look what they've done to you, digger!" I can't believe it, he's crying. He's crying over me, Tommy Maloney.'

Don't know about them, but I'm crying again as well. I must have let a sob go or something because he looks up, 'Ah, mate, it was all a long, long time ago.' He looks up into the giant Ash. 'In the history of this tree it ain't nothing, things go on.' The white bark of the Alpine Ash can be seen clearly, even in the dark of night. 'There's not many like it,' Tommy says, trying to change the subject and calm me down. 'Most Alpine Ash have got the tough fibrous black-gum bark we seen on the spur, not too many like this old fella, white, smooth all the way up to the top.'

But then he goes on. 'They do the best they can for me at the camp, but they've only got a medical orderly and he gives me morphine for the pain, quinine for me malaria, pills for the dysentery and fixes the sling and dresses me eye. Funny that, first meal they bring a plate of food, best tucker I've seen since leavin' home. I smell it and I throw up. Just the smell is too rich for me stomach. Some weak tea and them plain digestive biscuits, it's all I can take, with a bit of banana and tapioca, which they get from a nearby village.

'After two days they take me out to sea and a seaplane flies me out to a Yank aircraft carrier that's anchored off the coast. They've got a hospital on board and I'm took good care of, like I'm a hero, the Yank sailors saluting me and calling me "Sir!" When they reckon I'm strong enough, they fly me to the Philippines and eventually to Darwin and, later, home to the repatriation hospital.' Tommy stops briefly. 'Of the

1793 Australians who remained at the workers' paradise all but six of us are dead, the six of us that escaped. Counting the Brits, there's 1381 died at Sandakan and 1047 on the death marches, at Ranau and on the rice-carrying track to Paginatan.'

Tommy looks over at me, 'That's it, mate, that's the story of me war. It's near dawn, Mole, forget them possums, we'll find something later, reckon we should both kip down a bit, maybe sleep until well after sun-up, eh?'

I nod, then I say, 'Thanks, Dad. Thank you for telling me.'

Tommy's silent a moment. 'Yer know, Mole, it's you done me the favour. I've never told nobody the story, except a bit as testimony at the War Crimes. I've never told nothing about how me mates died. Couldn't face it. Couldn't face the shame of it.'

'There's no shame, Dad. You did the right thing for yer mates. I hope I'd have done the same.'

Tommy doesn't reply. Just digs down into his sleeping bag and pulls the zip up, lies down and turns away from me. 'Sleep well, Mole, no point in hurrying home, mate. Few hours won't make no difference, yer mum's gunna go ape-shit anyway.'

I get up and put the last of the wood on the fire and get back into my sleeping bag. It's always cold that time of the morning, an hour or so before dawn. My head is spinning, but I'm also exhausted, glad there'll be a bit of a sleep-in. Eventually I fall asleep crying for my old man, who isn't really my dad but is and always will be. I'm proud to be a Maloney, proud to be a part of Tommy.

I wake up suddenly, like you do in the bush. The sun is high, though I can't see it properly through the trees, I know it's late, maybe ten o'clock. I lie there a moment, stretching in me sleeping bag, working my arms out, yawning. I think, should I make Tommy the last of the tea, there's no tucker to give him? I turn to where Tommy is, but he ain't there. His kitbag is there and I can see the groundsheet strapped to the bottom, the sleeping bag will be packed inside its cover. My rifle is also gone. He's gone to find some breakfast, I think. Tommy's much better than me at tracking possums, he'll find where they have their lair. Only needs to look up into a tree trunk or hollow log and knows they're there.

I climb out of me sleeping bag. The fire is dead but the ashes are still warm, a tiny wisp of smoke curls up. I'll make another fire so when he gets back we can have a brew. I've decided to use the last of the tea and cook whatever he's brought for breakfast.

I walk towards the big tree to start gathering wood. Then I see that into its smooth white bark Tommy has carved a list of names. It's been done careful, the names cut real deep, past the bark into the wood fibre, each about six inches high so they'll stay put and scar over permanent. He must have waited until I was asleep and somehow taken the torch or waited for first light and done the names. There's eight in all.

Blades Rigby

Troppo Smith

Froggy Marsh

Curly Francis

Dunno Watt

Richie Murray

Albert Cleary

Wally Crease

1942–1945

R.I.P.

Tommy has remembered the names of his mates and carved them into the roots of heaven.

I laugh, pleased as punch. Tommy's got over something very important in his mind. I feel a bit proud that I've been a part of it. I think he'll be back at any moment so I can tell him how happy I am. I'll build up the fire meanwhile, boil the billy. I'm expecting to hear a shot when he gets a ringtail. Or maybe he'll just find the possums asleep in a hole in the hollow of a tree, they're pretty dozy in the day, and he'll grab a couple and wring their necks, save the bullet. He won't want a ranger coming after us. Mount Buffalo is a national park, we're not supposed to use firearms except for rabbits and foxes, even then you need permission.

I fetch water from the creek and put the billy on. I'm dead proud of Tommy carving those names in the tree. Normally I'd think it was wrong, but not this time. This time it's right. It's a Maloney thing that's had to be done. I wonder to myself if it will be a part of him getting better. If things will be different when we get back home, now he's got all the shit off his liver. All that stuff he's been living with, the terrible guilt he's felt and told no one.

I wait another hour, it must be near eleven o'clock and Tommy ain't back. That don't make sense, he'd have wanted to get going by now, he'd never leave it this late. Something's happened. He's fallen or something, knocked himself out. Maybe tried to climb up a tree with his crook shoulder, he can do it too, I've seen him lots of times. It's not a long gorge we're in and I start to look. But I soon see that the undergrowth hasn't been disturbed, twigs ain't broken, the daisy musk bushes and blanket leaf haven't been pushed aside. Then I go towards the way we came in. I soon see Tommy's gone out this way, I even pick up his tracks one place. I follow until I'm out of the gorge and I can see where he's started to climb back up the mountain.

So I go back to the camp site and put out the fire and I'm ready to leave and go over to get Tommy's knapsack. I can't understand why he's left it behind. It doesn't make sense. Him taking the rifle and leaving without me don't make sense either.

Then, sticking out of the top of the knapsack, I see this piece of paper. It's from one of those small spiral notepads people keep in their shirt pockets, I can see the paper even before I open it, the torn, ragged holes on one edge. I open the note and in pencil Tommy's written:

Dear Mole,

I have gone under the wire, mate.
Look after the Maloney tree.
I am sorry what I done to you all.

I love you kids and Nancy.
Tommy Maloney (Cpl.)
2/19th Btn, 8th Div. AIF

I think my heart is going to stop. Then that it's going to jump out of my chest. I think, I ain't heard a shot, even a .22 you'd hear it all over the mountain. I've seen his footsteps out, I can catch him. Tommy's had no sleep, he doesn't climb fast with his bad shoulder, steady but not fast. It's a four, five-hour climb to the top and through the waterfall and the tunnel out onto the spur. I know what he's done, he wants to get clear of the tree, keep the Maloney secret. I convince myself I can catch him.

Now I've got a plan, I'm a bit more calm. 'I haven't heard a shot, I haven't heard a shot, I haven't heard a shot,' I keep repeating in my head. Tommy's still on the mountain, still not dead. I put on my knapsack and start moving out. Then I begin to think more calmly, 'under the wire' that's the term the POWs used for escape. Maybe he's just going away, leaving us to get on with our lives. He thinks he's created enough misery, it's time he got out of the way and let us grow up respectable.

I feel tremendous relief as I convince myself that's what it is. I'll find him, catch up, tell him we don't want him to go. Tell him he's as much a part of our family as anyone, it doesn't matter no more what he is, now we know why, the others will understand, even Mike.

I reckon I get up the mountain to the waterfall in about three and a half hours. If Tommy started an hour before me, even an hour and a half, then I can't be that far behind him. The spray from the fall splashes over me and then I wade through the pool and get down onto my hands and knees and enter the narrow tunnel. Soon it's pitch black and I can't hurry. I have to feel my way every few inches. I smash my knuckles and I think I've broke one finger and cut me head open again.

In the dark you can't tell time, I must have been in the tunnel half an hour. With Tommy and the torch it took an hour. I ain't going any faster than we did before. Maybe not even as fast. There's the sound of the water running over rock in my ears and there's my own breathing, nothing else. Then a shot. It's faint, like it's far away, but maybe it isn't, sound travels outwards. Maybe not even a shot, a rock tumbling down the mountain.

There's nothing I can do. So I just keep going, but my heart is pumping, beating in my chest so hard I can't hardly breathe. Then I see a small dot of light and soon it grows larger and at last I squeeze into the little chamber at the entrance to the tunnel and I knock straight into Tommy. He falls face-down and all I can see is the back of his head which looks normal. I have to push at him to get past. 'Tommy! Tommy, you all right?' I'm crouched beside him, the little stream is damming up, blocked by his shoulder, then it starts to run over his shoulder. I roll him over. He's put the barrel to his crook eye and pulled the trigger. He's done it first thing he's out and safely away from the Maloney tree.

Chapter Twenty-Five

Nancy is just not the same since Tommy's death. Not quite her old self. That's the funny thing, you'd have thought with all the trouble he caused in her life, in ours as well, that she'd be better off with him gone. But now it seems she really loved him, little Tommy was loved by great big Nancy, which is something we'd never have guessed. But on the other hand she never turned him away. Bell Street was always his home, come what may. We always thought it was because she'd cheated on him during the war that she felt maybe guilty. That wasn't it at all, Tommy was her first love and stayed that way.

The other funny thing was that she even seemed to miss being looked down on by those who would see Tommy drunk in the streets or with the other alkies down by Lake Sambell or working in a prison work party. 'With you lot all grown up except for little Colleen and Tommy gone there's nothing to hang on to,' she said shortly after the funeral. She must have temporarily forgotten about Father Crosby because he was still there large as life.

The news of Tommy's suicide brought him riding down to Bell Street pedalling his Malvern Star fast as his fat gut could carry him. And what a stoush that turned out to be. Him shaking his head, getting even redder in the face. 'Nancy Maloney, your husband has committed a mortal sin taking his own life, the Church cannot condone his behaviour!'

'What's all that mean? The Church has *never* condoned his behaviour, so what's new?'

'Ah, being a drunk and a thief, that's one thing, that's quite all right, he's from Irish stock, the Lord has long made allowances for that. But taking your God-given life with your own hand, now that's quite another matter, that is.'

'Oh? So what about Father Maximilian Kolbe? They're thinking of making him a saint.'

Father Crosby looks bewildered, it's obvious he hasn't heard of this particular priest but he isn't going to admit it. 'That's entirely different, for sure now,' he splutters.

Morrie told us about Father Maximilian Kolbe, who should be a saint. How he was put into a concentration camp by the Germans and then gave his own life to save a man who had a number of children. I think to myself that it's not quite the same thing, the priest gave his life to save someone else, same as Jesus did. I've got to say this for Nancy, she can twist a fact around as good as anyone. Besides she'd have invented a saint if she had to, she'll do almost anything to get the better of the Priest of the Flames, who is beginning to think of himself as practically a saint for rescuing the Blessed Virgin and the Christ on the Cross with the dented belly.

Since Father Crosby's got his stained-glass windows and the Italians have built him a new brick church, there's no stopping him. Nancy's still mad as hell that he didn't come to her for his fire vestments, she can't believe the appliquéd rubbish he's wearing, a big orange squiggle running up his back, twisting around a cross and other bits licking at the base of the cross. 'If that's fire, then my bumhole is a rosebud!' she says.

Big Jack Donovan reported that Father Crosby has been seen sneaking over to Wodonga and taking driving lessons from Cec and Lyn Clark who run the Hume Driving School. 'Typical!' Nancy snorts when she hears this. 'You'll see, next thing he'll be wanting the community to supply him with a car!'

'Why's it different?' Nancy now asks. She points her finger at his chest. 'You explain it to me, Father. He did the same as that Polish priest to save a family! The Pope should make him a saint and Tommy does the same and all of a sudden he's committed a mortal sin!'

'All of a sudden!' I think Father Crosby is going to have a heart attack right on the spot. 'The Church doesn't do things *all of a sudden*! And that's blasphemy, comparing the one to the other!' Father Crosby has caught on to the explanation that Maximilian Kolbe gave up his life for another man's family. 'That's not the same as committing suicide,' he says triumphantly.

'I beg your pardon, the suicide note Tommy wrote, he said he was sorry what he did to the family!'

'*His* family! That's not the same as someone else's family!'

'Ha! That's where you're wrong, Father! It *was* for someone else's family! What about Bozo, Mike and Mole? They ain't his family. He did it for someone else's family the same as the Polish priest did.'

'Nancy Maloney, you'll not be getting away with specious arguments, not this time, the laws of God are sacred, we can't be tampering about with them, twisting them around to suit your own purpose. Tommy's committed a mortal sin and that's that! There's to be no more argument!'

'Okay, what about Judas Iscariot then?' Nancy says, not finished with him yet.

Father Crosby sighs, exasperated, 'What about Judas Iscariot?'

'Well, he committed suicide.'

'Ah, but Christ would have forgiven him.'

'So, why can't Christ forgive Tommy then?'

'Tommy didn't confess his sins, he didn't receive the last rites, extreme unction. The Scriptures are quite clear on that matter!'

'So what does that mean?' Nancy asks, she's suddenly not so bolshie, and says it with her eyes downcast and her voice gone quiet.

'I'll not be giving him a funeral, his body cannot be permitted to lie in sacred ground.'

'You mean he can't be buried in the Catholic cemetery?' Nancy asks, aghast.

'You can bury the deceased anywhere you like, but there can be no mention of his name in the Church and the grave site will not be consecrated, I'll not be conducting the burial. I'm sorry, but God does not permit me to do so.'

Nancy is silent for a long time, I can see she is close to tears but she'd rather die than cry in front of Father Crosby.

Then Father Crosby says in a not unkindly voice, 'Nancy Maloney, I'll tell you what I can do. I shall conduct a nice little Requiem Mass.' He looks happy with this decision, but adds, 'Mind, there'll be no body of the deceased present and we'll not be mentioning his name and we'll not be saying anything about how he came to lose his life.' He folds his hands across his belly, pleased with himself. 'Now that's the very best I can do, my girl.'

When she looks up, Nancy's eyes are fiery, the weepies gone. 'Let me understand you clearly, Father. You'll have a Requiem Mass for somebody who isn't there, who you can't name and are unable to mention how whoever it is has come about needing to have the Requiem Mass in the first place?'

'Well, yes, something like that. It's the best effort I can make, Nancy Maloney.'

'Well, you can go to buggery, Father!' Nancy yells, 'You and the Church, you're a bunch of bloody hypocrites! You're as bad as the Protestants!'

'Now *that's* blasphemy comparing the Holy Church to that lot of misbegotten heathens! You'll not be saying that, Nancy Maloney, or we'll be thinking excommunication!'

'I'll be saying a lot worse if you don't bugger off!' Nancy yells at him.

I reckon for a collapsed Catholic we've just seen the final collapse between Nancy and the Church. Father Crosby gets back on his bicycle and, even from the back as he's wobbling to gain traction, you can see he's real huffy. Nancy's finally gone too far.

Tommy's funeral was quite big, but, of course, he couldn't be buried on the Catholic side of the cemetery and in the family plot Tommy bought with Mr Baloney's inheritance. Nancy simply couldn't bring herself to bury him on the Protestant side so she managed to get Big Jack Donovan to find a compromise with the shire council.

The Chinese part of the cemetery still has the two old Chinese porcelain burning towers standing. There has always been a wide gap between the Catholic gravestones and the Chinese section, a good twenty yards or so. The Chinese came to the goldfields in the mid-nineteenth century and helped to build the town, but as the last family left in 1885, there wasn't going to be any problems here. So Tommy is buried in no man's land, between his own kind and the infidels. Nancy says, 'I'd rather Tommy was mistaken for a Chinaman than a Protestant and at least he won't have to put up with Mr Baloney and Grandmother Charlotte's constant quarrelling all the dark hours through.'

By big funeral, I don't mean, like huge, not like John Crowe's and Whacka Morrissey's after the big fire, but a bigger one than we'd expected for a nobody in the town like Tommy. Nancy said it was the suicide caused that, all the stickybeaks came to take a ghoulish delight in a Maloney tragedy. 'Don't know what the nosyparkers expected to see, one coffin's much the same as the next. He wasn't the Pope put out on display!' she said.

But the twin aunties *were* on display, brought out of the loony bin for the funeral. I'm not sure they knew what was happening but they liked the flowers a lot. Nancy said, 'That'll show people the Maloneys aren't through with being themselves in this town.' Though after the last episode, when Auntie Gwen escaped and walked down King Street in the nuddy saying her rosary, I was a bit nervous having them around. It turned out they were nice as pie and at the wake afterwards they sat out the back of the pub and drank four lemonades and ate three chops each. Both exactly the same, they even had tomato sauce spilt on the same place on the front of the floral summer dresses Nancy made for the occasion.

Nancy's still pretty bitter, because Catholic families have a right to keep suicides quiet and not even to tell the priest. 'They all come to gawk because of what that slag Vera Forbes wrote in the *Gazette*. But that isn't quite fair, among the mourners are a good few ex-crims and most came up to us afterwards and said Tommy was a good bloke, never ratted on anyone and kept his nose clean.

John Sullivan, the prison governor, attended and he came up and said it was always a pleasure having Tommy up the hill, that he was a model prisoner. Big Jack Donovan offered his commiserations and said that, underneath, Tommy was a good bloke and meant no harm and of all the petty crims he'd met, 'Believe me, Nancy, there's been a few and Tommy Maloney was the most likeable of them all and never whinged or made excuses for himself.'

Bozo, Mike, Morrie and me carried the coffin and Nick Reed, the regional fire officer, came from Wangaratta and did the talk at the graveside. It was instead of having the funeral director doing it, which none of us wanted because we didn't even know him. Mr Reed said Tommy was the best firefighter he'd ever known and like his father before him and his father and probably his father, was a real Maloney. He was completely reliable and there was more than one fire brought to an early standstill with his skill at calling it right. A lot of the firemen present were nodding their heads when he said that and if it hadn't been such a solemn occasion I reckon they'd have clapped.

All the district bushfire brigades came from as far as Albury and Wangaratta and wore their Sunday suits and ties. Afterwards they formed a long line and each one shook our hands and wished us well. Other people came up and said nice things, most of them from Bell Street, and even the poorest families in the street sent a wreath or picked a bunch of flowers. So you can see it was quite a crowd. Tommy would have been flabbergasted.

Nancy said afterwards, 'Father Crosby may have sent Tommy straight to hell, but at least it was six fire brigades gave him a send-off!'

The whole of Bell Street threw in a few bob and so did the firemen and there was a real nice wake at The Shamrock with Mickey O'Hearn donating a keg and the abattoir supplying chops and steak for a barbie out the back. A good time was had by all, except halfway through Father Crosby turns up and the whole pub goes silent as he walks in. Mickey O'Hearn pours him a beer and Father Crosby raises his glass and says, so we can all hear, 'To the dearly departed!' So we all have to do the same. Then he takes a long swig, about half the glass, puts the glass down on the bar and walks out of the pub. We all watch as he gets on his bike and goes down King Street.

'Cheeky bugger!' Nancy says to nobody in particular. But I don't agree. I reckon it took a lot of courage to do that.

Mickey O'Hearn, ever the diplomat, tries to comfort Nancy. 'Never seen him waste a perfectly good beer like that before. Left damn near half the glass full for sure. He must have been very upset, Nancy.'

When Sarah and Mike came up from Melbourne for the funeral

with Morrie and Sophie, I told them Tommy's story three nights in a row. There were lots of tears, Nancy and Sarah wept and even Sophie and Morrie, who'd been through so much themselves.

Morrie said later it was like the concentration camps in Germany, only no women and children, that Tommy had it just as bad as they did and if you take the tropical ulcers and the dysentery and malaria and other tropical diseases, there were some things even worse.

It was a nice thing to say and we appreciated it, but I don't think you could compare it. In the concentration camps there were innocent women and children dying of starvation and that's a different matter altogether.

Nancy said Tommy had never told her anything about Sandakan and the death marches. Every time she'd ask him, he'd say, 'Maybe some time, eh?' But the some time never came.

I also told them about the Maloney tree. Tommy didn't ever say I couldn't; it's just that because I'd never seen it all those years, I'd not said anything. To tell you the absolute truth, I was never quite sure it wasn't like the fish that appeared in the rainwater ditch that wasn't anywhere near the river in Borneo. Tommy never cleared that one up, even at the end. I should've asked him, but there was so much to take in, I forgot.

Bozo came to me afterwards and asked if I'd take him some day to see the tree and I said I would. I'm sure Tommy wouldn't have minded. Mike, of course, wasn't interested, but said afterwards that he felt a bastard saying all those things about Tommy. I'm glad he did. I mean, I'm glad he said the things he did because when it got really bad with Tommy, Mike's remarks about him were said for all of us. At the time, it really was what we felt and Mike could make it sound funny so we'd grin and bear it once more.

I don't want to go into what happened after Tommy shot himself. I left him at the entrance to the tunnel and walked to the police station at Porepunkah and reported it to the policeman there and asked him to phone Big Jack Donovan. Big Jack raced over in the police car and him and the local cop went up the spur with me, back to Tommy. In Tommy's shirt pocket they found the notepad he'd used to write me the note and in it he'd written:

Affydavit

I Tommy Maloney of me own free will have took me own life. I took me boys rifle and left the camp we was at. I have died at me own hand by shooting meself. I have had enuff. I am very sorry for what I done to the family and they will be well rid of me. That's all.

Yours truly,
Tommy Maloney

Funny that, Tommy read so many books and remembered all the Latin names for trees and plants but he couldn't write properly. When I thought about it, I'd never seen him write anything in my whole life, not even a note. Vera 'Big Mouth Saggy Tits' Forbes got hold of the suicide note at the coroner's inquest and printed it on the front page of the *Gazette*. She said a few other things about Tommy, the worst being this: *'Tommy Maloney was a well-known character around town for reasons well known to most Yankalillee citizens where for years he has been associated with the town's garbage!'*

Nancy said Saggy Tits might think she's clever, but ambiguity like that was just not on, that she was going after the slaggy bitch. I wouldn't want to be Vera the fearless reporter coming down King Street with Nancy approaching from the opposite direction. Nancy would bump her shoulder so hard, Vera's saggy tits would fly up like a helicopter's blades and wrap around her neck and strangle her to death.

But, what *really* upset Nancy was her printing Tommy's suicide note, showing all the bad spelling and grammar. 'The garbage crack is fair enough, Tommy was no angel and maybe in some eyes he was town trash, but showing him up like that with the note, that's going too bloody far!' she screamed.

I reckon Vera 'Big Mouth Saggy Tits' Forbes is right up there with Philip with one 'l' Templeton as public enemies one and two. In Nancy's terms that's 'Watch out, Mrs Forbes, you may be a Protestant but you're in a whole heap of trouble with the Catholic bitch!'

Nineteen sixty-one was a big year, not just because of Tommy's death, but lots of things happened to our family. The first was that after the funeral

Mike announced that he was off to London. Nancy just can't understand this, he's been designing clothes in Melbourne and selling them and making good money, even sending some home. What's more the **Suckfizzle** kids' label is growing in leaps and bounds and Sophie's turning out to be an astute businesswoman. With Mike designing the children's clothes from layette to teenybopper and Sophie supervising the factories making them, it's early times yet, but everyone can see they've got a big future. They don't owe any money to the bank and most of the factories will give them three months' credit because they realise **Suckfizzle**'s got a future worth investing in. Nancy wants to know why, with so much going for him, Mike wants to throw it all away and go to London.

'Mum, I'm just another dressmaker here. Until I have London or Paris experience they'll never take me seriously.'

'But the young people are buying your clothes, they're taking you seriously?'

'That's not enough. I've got to show the fashion industry I know what I'm doing. That I'm not just a flash in the pan.' He looks earnestly at Nancy. 'Mum, they think I'm just a country bumpkin, the boy from the bush trying to show off by making a few silly dresses for the goofy teenagers dancing to Johnny O'Keefe on 'Six O'Clock Rock'. Besides, there really are lots of things I need to learn that I can't learn here.'

Nancy hates to lose her children, but Mike's been away from home almost as long as Sarah and she's now more used to not having him around. The first year he left for Melbourne she almost went into mourning. She missed all those afternoons they'd sit and do the layettes together, he was the closest to her, more than the rest of us, even Sarah. They'd yak on for hours like a couple of old hens.

Anyway, Mike's been independent for the last five years, so there's not much she can do. The money he sent home each week was important but now we don't need it so much, so even that's okay.

Mike has saved enough for his fare on the P & O ship and has enough to live on for a month when he gets to London. He's the first Maloney for a hundred and fifty years to leave Australia's shores without a rifle in his hand and army boots on his feet. He's going abroad to fight the rest of the world with a sketchbook. It's the big time or oblivion, that's always been Mike's way.

Then the next big thing that happens is Sarah becomes a doctor on Saturday, 16th December 1961. I forgot to say that Morrie had become a doctor for the second time the year before, winning the university medal for the most outstanding results. He gave it back and said it should be given to a first-time student. They took it back but they said he was going against the traditions of the university. Morrie then politely pointed out that he had been forced to do his medical examinations all over again. 'Now you give me this medal for what? I tell you for what I get this medal. It is for being za best student, for learning what you are teaching! *Pffft!* That is not right. You have given me this medal for teaching me what I already know before I come to the university. To take this David Grant Scholarship Medal for 1960, this is not fair dinkum. I want you should give it to a student who is learning something from you!' Then he said there were one or two things in the curriculum that he believed should be changed as they were no longer relevant to modern medicine. He offered to help, but his offer wasn't taken up, although they did give the medal to another student.

We all went down from Yankalillee to Sarah's graduation ceremony. Nancy, Bozo, little Colleen and me, Mrs Barrington-Stone, Big Jack Donovan and Mrs Rika Ray.

Morrie, Sophie and Templeton, of course, were in Melbourne. The *Age* sent a photographer and a reporter and there was a picture of Sarah on the front page of the paper, wearing her cap and gown, with Templeton, who is five, standing next to her. The caption under the photograph says: *Dr Sarah Maloney and five-year-old daughter, Templeton. The controversial 1956 first-year medical student graduates with top honours. See Page 3 for full story.*

The story, which fills nearly half a page, reminds people of what happened back all those years ago and calls it a total vindication of her fight to be admitted as a pregnant student and that the whole thing is a triumph for commonsense and for women everywhere. Sarah says she doesn't think very much has changed and if someone pregnant turned up next year, she doubts the Professorial Board would be any different from the last time.

To tell you the truth, the ceremony was really a bit boring. All these professors marched into Wilson Hall wearing these long gowns and sat up on the platform. Then Sir Arthur Dean, who's the chancellor, called us all to stand up and sing the National Anthem. Then after God had saved the Queen, we all sit down, and blocks of students in alphabetical order are called out to stand in line. They'd read out a name and a student would go to the podium and have their hands shook by the chancellor, who gave them their degree, which is rolled up and tied with a ribbon.

Then Sarah gets called back and it's announced that she's won the university medal for 1961, the medal Morrie gave up the year before. Morrie is so proud he bursts into tears. Nancy and Sophie are also crying buckets and so is Mrs Barrington-Stone, they're blubbing away, saying 'Oh dear' and blowing their noses and looking at each other and then bursting out all over again, Morrie going at it with the best of them.

When it's over, the professors march out, only in the reverse order to the way they came in. We all have to stand and watch them do this. That was it. I was expecting bands and singing and stuff like that. When the professors have all left the hall, we go over to Union House to have afternoon tea. If you ask my opinion it was a worse ceremony than prizegiving at the end of the year at school, because they didn't even have an end-of-year concert like we do.

But, of course, we were very happy. Mrs Rika Ray, who had a new gold sari specially made and was wearing her red boxing-gloves earrings, said, 'My goodness, our Doctor Sarah is getting the biggest bottoms-wiping certificate in the whole world and a medal also she is getting so we are very, very happy!'

Then she goes all teary and walks over and gives Templeton a big hug and practically kisses her to death and we all know why that is. If the abortion had worked, she and Templeton wouldn't have been there and she'd be Nancy's mortal enemy. Now Templeton and her are a part of our lives and we love them both heaps and so do Bozo's Bitzers which are now more hers than his.

Mrs Rika Ray has become Bozo's operations manager in John Crowe Transport and she's tough as nails and the two temporary drivers who drive for Bozo call her 'The Old Crow' because she really cracks the whip and they can't get away with anything.

She's also the company bookkeeper and Bozo says they're beginning to have a real business. She's got the bank's trust and they'll give her an overdraft, which he doubts they'd do for him if she wasn't there. Even though the bank won't lend money to a woman without her husband's approval, they think very highly of her.

Bozo tells how Mrs Rika Ray's got the bank to eat out of her hand. She'd been at John Crowe Transport about six months when they suddenly found themselves in financial difficulties. What's happened is this, a contract they'd been promised has fallen through and Bozo has already paid cash for a second-hand truck they were going to need to do the work involved. Mrs Rika Ray goes through the books and says, if they're super careful and don't try to expand too fast, they can scrape through for another six months. What this means, Bozo says, is that they won't have a brass razoo to invest in infrastructure if something big comes along.

'What's that mean, infrastructure and something big comes along?' I ask him.

'Well, say some company needs transport for the goods they sell and don't want to own a fleet of trucks, so they put out a tender, just like the council did for the garbage collection. Then it's up to us to put in a price for doing the job,' Bozo says, 'You don't just get the job because you put in the cheapest price. You also have to prove to them that you've got the organisation and the trucks to do the job. That's called your infrastructure. Well, we don't have the infrastructure if a big chance comes along because we've got no investment capital and no chance of borrowing from the bank.'

So they're existing on the smell of an oily rag and things are pretty shaky back at the ranch. Then Mrs Rika Ray comes in one morning and says, 'Bozo, we are asking the bank they must jolly well lend us five hundred pounds pronto, we are giving them collateral all the trucks, they will not refuse, you will see, it is guaranteed in the cards, which I am throwing every day now for one week only.'

Bozo panics. The Diamond T and the old Fargo truck John Crowe bought from the shire council and the VW van and the new second-hand truck are all they've got and worth altogether, at the most, about eight hundred pounds. If they can't repay the loan and have to sell them to repay the bank, they'll probably get six hundred, maybe six hundred and fifty tops for a quick sale. They'll be broke and out of business.

'But you said we could hang on for six months and hope things will get better? We're doing okay really, there's money coming in and we're paying our petrol bills at the garage. It's just that contract falling through has mucked things up a bit,' Bozo protests.

'Bozo, I am looking at the tarot cards, once I am looking, twice I am looking and then I am looking again and again until I am going blue in the face, every time the same, they are saying we are getting very very lucky, very very soon!'

'Or we'll be going very very broke, very very soon, Mrs Rika Ray,' Bozo says reluctantly.

Bozo does business by the business book and Mrs Rika Ray does business by the tarot cards and the two don't really mix that well. Only so far she's been right in almost everything they've done. It was her said she didn't trust the people who pulled out of the contract and maybe they should wait before they bought the extra truck. That was also the tarot cards told her that, so it's not as though they're all the one way.

They go along to the bank manager and Mrs Rika Ray is very persuasive and the bank has the trucks valued on the second-hand market and there's a bit to spare on the conservative evaluation they get, so they know their money is safe as a house.

Anyway, Bozo is still a bit of a hero around the place because of his Olympic medal. Mrs Barrington-Stone has given Bozo a reference, which is another of Mrs Rika Ray's ideas. So the bank manager, Mr Fred Mullins, who is new in town, asks a few more questions around the place. Again they get lucky with the people he asks, like Big Jack Donovan and Mr Sullivan and then, *oops!*, Magistrate 'Oliver Twist' Withers. Much to Bozo's surprise, he says the Maloney family are extremely hardworking and trustworthy and he gives Bozo the big thumbs up.

It just goes to show you shouldn't always condemn people just because they're not the same as you. Well, they get the loan which Mr Mullins says must be repaid in six months or the bank will foreclose on them. 'There'll be no excuses acceptable,' he warns.

'This is your first loan and if you're late in your repayments, I can assure you, it will be your last,' he says to Bozo. He also gives them a bit of a lecture about how he's taking a big chance on them, which he shouldn't really be doing as they have no history of borrowing blah-blah-blah and so on and so forth.

Mrs Rika Ray takes the cheque and has Bozo drive her into Albury where she puts the whole kaboodle into a three-monthly interest-bearing deposit with the Bank of New South Wales. That's the whole thing, see. They don't touch the five hundred pounds but struggle along to make ends meet like she'd originally said they could.

Then three months later they phone up and ask the original bank manager, Mr Mullins, if they can have an appointment. He says yes, then there's a pause on the phone and Bozo hears him clear his throat, 'I hope you are not going to disappoint me and ask for more money, Mr Maloney. I have taken a chance on you and it's my reputation that's at stake. I just want you to know that I meant what I said.'

Bozo then says, no, it's nothing like that, they don't need a new loan and want to see him about another matter.

They arrive at the bank for the appointment and, to cut a long story short, Bozo hands Mr Mullins the five hundred pounds in cash plus the interest on the loan for three months, which isn't a lot more than the interest they've earned from the Bank of New South Wales anyway. Then they thank Mr Mullins for his help.

The bank manager is that chuffed that he's been paid back three months early he offers them another loan. Mrs Rika Ray says, 'We are thanking you very, very much, Mr Mullins, but we are not needing it. We are very, very grateful to you for helping us. Now, we are thanking God and the little fishes, because we are doing quite well also.'

Six months later they get this chance of landing a big contract with a new supermarket chain that's starting up in country centres and they need a local transport company to do the grocery cartage for all of north-eastern Victoria for them. Bozo puts in a tender and he's told he's won the contract, but has to have three dedicated trucks to handle the work. Of course, they've got Buckley's.

Mrs Rika Ray then says the tarot cards are saying good things again. So off the two of them trot to the bank manager and show him the confirmation from the supermarket chain and they ask for a thousand-pound loan. 'Certainly,' says Mr Mullins, 'you have an excellent record for early repayments with us, will a thousand pounds be sufficient?'

Now that's how smart Mrs Rika Ray turned out to be. Bozo says he couldn't run the business without her. Like I said, she's also taken over the Bitzers which are now Bitzers One to Twelve. Even though Bitzers Three and Five have since died, she's topped them up and called the two new doggies by the old numbers and added the others, and now she's got herself a complete dog circus with a whole lot of new tricks she's taught them to do. Whenever there's a charity fete or something going on, they're the star performers, jumping through fiery hoops, boxing each other. They wear these tiny little red boxing gloves on their front paws and jump up on their hind legs and people bet which dog will fall over onto his back first, which is counted as a knockout. If the fight goes on too long, Mrs Rika Ray says a word and one of the dogs falls onto his back and is knocked out. The dog boxing alone makes a small fortune.

By the way, Bozo still has to drink nasty green herbal stuff which she brings to work in the mornings. She still lives in the hut and bathes in the stream but it's got an annexe built onto it for the dogs who are not allowed into her humpy. Once a prisoner from the gaol escaped, hid all day and went bush at night. He saw this humpy in the moonlight, but he never got within spitting distance before the dogs got him. Next morning, after giving the prisoner breakfast, Mrs Rika Ray marches him all the way into town, up the hill to the prison and delivers him to the front door. He's got about a hundred bites from the ankles to the knees and she's treated them with herbs so they won't get infected. Mr Sullivan thanks her and calls the doctor to give the prisoner a tetanus injection.

Remember, I also sit my matriculation exams that year. In fact, I'd just finished them the week before Sarah's graduation. Of course, I didn't do as well as she did, not even half as well, but I think I passed okay and Nancy wants me to go to university if I get the marks. The Victorian Forestry Commission are giving out a scholarship and Mr McDonald, the district officer, is keen for me to apply for it. But I don't know. It sounds attractive and Nancy is dead keen I should do it, but

I've seen Mr McDonald and he seldom gets out in the bush, mostly he's in his office pushing a pen and he doesn't even have a degree. I've noticed before that blokes with degrees always end up behind desks.

Besides, there's been something nagging me for months, ever since Tommy's death this idea has been knocking around in my head. I wake up suddenly in the middle of the night and it's there. It's there first thing in the morning when we get up for the garbage run. I know it's mad and it don't make sense, in fact, just the opposite, but I want to join the army. Yeah, I know, knowing what I know and what Tommy's been through it's a bloody stupid idea, but I can't help it, that's what I've set my heart on doing.

Nancy goes spare. When I finally summon up enough courage to tell her, she's in the kitchen rolling pastry for sausage rolls for little Colleen's birthday. I tell her right off, because if I don't I'll lose the courage.

'Mum, I've decided to join the army.'

She doesn't move for a moment, then she turns around and I think she's going to brain me on the spot. 'Join the what?'

'The army, I've made up my mind.'

'Over my dead body, Mole Maloney!' Only the way she's coming at me with the rolling pin, I reckon it's going to be over mine. Even for Nancy, you've never heard such a fuss, it's nearly as bad as when Sarah told her she was pregnant.

I've spoken to Bozo long before I went to see Nancy and he thought it was a ratshit idea and said I should go to university, or if I didn't want to, he'd like me to join him in the transport business. But after a while he could see it was no good, that I'd made up my mind.

'You're a bloke who thinks about everything first, Mole. I've got to give you that. Been the steady one. But I have to ask you one last time, are you *absolutely* sure that's what you want to do?'

I've always thought of Bozo as being the steady one, I've just been the person standing there listening, stickybeaking, so it's a nice compliment, I think. 'Yeah, that's what I want,' I tell him. 'Definitely.'

'Righto then, I'll support you with Nancy. Better speak to Sarah first though, you'll need her on your side as well.'

So the day after Sarah's graduation, I take her aside, tell her and ask her to help me with Nancy. I've got to admit, like Bozo she's not happy and tries her best to dissuade me. When she sees she can't, she says, 'Will you go to Duntroon? If you get a university entrance pass in your exams you could take a degree with them, they'll pay for you to study and you'll still be in the army and be an officer.'

I wonder what she's thinking when she says it. To my knowledge she's never seen Murray Templeton since he ran away. Now he's graduated as an officer. We've seen him around town a few times. Once when Bozo and me were at a footie game we saw him with his uniform on, the one pip on his shoulder. Naturally we didn't speak to him and he looked over and saw us, but he didn't come over or wave or anything. Bozo said he was a bloody coward. It was like he didn't know who we were. Now Sarah, like always, guesses what I'm thinking.

'No, Mole, I don't love Murray, that's all over long ago. I've got my daughter and that's the best thing that's ever happened to me. It wouldn't upset me in the least if you went to Duntroon and became an officer.'

'Nah, I want to join the proper army, I don't want to be an officer.' She has another go at me and points out how disappointed Nancy is going to be in me. But in the end Sarah gives me her blessing. Funny, she says the same thing as Bozo, that I've always thought things out and am the steady one in the family. I'm not so sure now that that's supposed to be a compliment, although they both said it like it was one. Sarah then smiles, gives me a big hug and a kiss, and says, 'Mole, I'll always love you whatever you do, you'll make a wonderful soldier.'

Morrie, when he hears, says the world's not a safe place and good soldiers are needed and Sophie bursts into tears, she can only remember one kind of soldier.

I don't want to go on about Nancy. She raves and sulks for a week and argues with Bozo and calls Sarah who's gone to Queensland with Morrie and Sophie for their first holiday in six years. Templeton's staying with us because little Colleen loves to have her and the other way round. The three of them, Morrie, Sophie and Sarah, are having a rest, Sarah needs one before she starts as a resident medical officer at the Royal Melbourne in January. Nancy calls Sarah at her hotel and speaks to her for an hour and I can hear her arguing. It must have cost a fortune and I'm feeling guilty. Then Nancy comes off the phone and sits down, while little Colleen makes her a cup of tea and gives her a Bex. Templeton climbs into her lap and Nancy strokes her flaming red hair that's just like her mother's. After a while, she calls me over and says, 'Yer a typical bloody Maloney, Mole. Two paths to take, one good, one bad, you'll choose the wrong one, every time!'

'What's that mean?' I ask.

'You can join the bloody army! Gawd help us all!'

I haven't talked about Mike in London, that's mostly because he doesn't write to us much, though we know he's okay because Sophie gets these sketches for kids' clothes in the mail and he writes at the bottom, *'Still surviving! Love to all, Mike.'*

I write to him every month and give him all the gossip but I don't expect he'll write back, Mike's the sort of person who's got a tongue sharp as an axe, he's good on his feet and he's got imagination. He'll see a picture of a dress and, quick as lightning, he'll redraw it, changing it, and suddenly it's a new dress that's much better than the old one. But he's not the sort to sit down and write. Though he does sometimes say at the bottom of the kids' sketches: *'Please tell Mole to keep writing to me.'*

Then out of the blue, just before I join the army in January 1962, I get this long letter from Mike. I can't believe it, it's taken him ages to write because the pen he's using isn't always the same colour, though it's all in ballpoint except when he writes in pencil. It's scrawled because even Mike's writing is impatient, more like drawing than writing. There are big sweeps in the letters and sometimes where a word ends in 's', the 's' is connected to a sweeping line that's nearly a quarter of an inch away from the letter behind it. When I point this out to Nancy, she says, 'That's his artistic nature.' But I reckon it's because he's impatient to finish the word and get on to the next one. The letter has no date on it so that's also a sign that it's been written over a long time. Besides, Mike probably didn't know the date anyway. He'd know the month all right, and maybe what day of the week it was, but he wouldn't know the date unless the next day was Christmas or New Year.

324 Earls Court Road
Earls Court,
London SW5
England.

Dear Mole & Family,

I haven't written before because as you know writing is not my strong point. But thanks, Mole, for writing and also Sarah, who's written four times. Tell Mum to write because I really love to get letters from you all.

Well, to tell you the truth I haven't written because things have been tough. I better start at the beginning because it's OK now because I've got a job and I'm learning heaps. But more about that later also.

The boat docked at Tilbury and we took the train up to London. One of the friends I made on the boat knew of a place in Earls Court which he said was cheap and I could come with him. It wasn't that cheap and we could only have a bath once a week. The room I've got, it's really a garret, isn't much bigger than a cupboard. In fact, I can't stand up straight without my head hitting the ceiling and the bed fits into a cupboard and you pull it down at night and it fills all the space there is in the room except for the gas ring. There's also an army fold-up table and chair you can use when the bed is locked in the cupboard and a set of shelves for your clothes on one wall. The other wall has a tiny window you can see the rooftops of other houses from.

When you want to use the bed, you fold the table and chair up, pull the bed down and store the table and chair in the cupboard. The gas ring is for cooking and it has its own meter. You cook on it by putting a shilling in. I can tell you now that spaghetti brought to the boil with a small tin of camp stew mixed in at the last minute costs a shilling. You can get four kettles boiled if you only put enough water in for one cup of tea or powdered soup.

That's enough about the sleeping and cooking arrangements. Boy, do I miss Sophie's cooking!

But the thing I miss the most is having a shower every day, even a cold one like at home in winter after garbage. The English only have baths and it costs two shillings to feed the meter in the bathroom to get about four inches of hot water in the tub. Even if you were rich, you're only allowed one bath a week in this first-class establishment. The landlady, Mrs Gibson, said I'd be destroying the natural oils in my skin if I bathed more than once a week and that 'it ain't natural in a healthy boy'!

But you can forget all that, because London is the capital of the world! No flamin' risk! I haven't had the money to go to the theatre yet but just the art galleries and the museums and other places you can go to practically for free leave you gobsmacked. Like the British Museum and the Victoria & Albert. I'll tell you all about them some other time.

When I first came here I froze my balls off. I wore every stitch of clothing I owned to bed at night and I still froze. Shit, it's cold here in the winter! It also rains quite a lot, but when it shines the parks are beautiful and green and there's flowers everywhere in the spring, daffodils and hyacinths and bluebells in the woods, they just grow out of the grass natural as anything. In the winter, when I first came, I saw a robin in Kensington Gardens, it was weird, like straight out of Peter Pan or something.

I like the English a lot, well some of them, they can be very snooty and sometimes bloody condescending, but when you get to know them they're not such a bad bunch. The ordinary people are great but there's a definite class structure here and everyone knows their place and, boy, don't you dare step out of line! It's how people speak that decides what class you're in and they're all experts at picking up on who's who. Workmen wear caps here and they touch the rim of their caps and stand to attention if somebody who looks posh comes up to them and asks them a question.

But the people in the fashion biz are, to put it mildly, bloody dishonest. They're very tactful but they don't tell the truth a lot of the time. I'm the boy from the bush and at first I believe everything they say but soon I learn the hard way what's said and what's done are two different things entirely.

Like, when I first got here, I schlepped my sketches around to all the London manufacturers. You'd go to the front office and say you were looking for a position and could you please see the chief designer. Generally some bloke would eventually come out and I soon learnt he probably was an assistant designer or something like that because the chief designers wouldn't stoop to coming out for an out-of-work kid. This is how the interview goes. It's generally in the foyer.

HIM: Good morning.

ME: Ahem, I'm looking for a job as an assistant designer.

HIM: I see, where else have you worked?

ME: In Australia, I did my apprenticeship in Flinders Lane, that's in Melbourne.

HIM (not meaning it): How interesting. Fascinating. Do you have any sketches? *(You soon learn that words like 'interesting' and 'fascinating' mean 'who's this little upstart from the colonies flogging shit?' or something like that.)*

ME: Yes, of course. *(I hand him my folio. He starts to look at the sketches turning them over, at first pretty fast, then a little slower, perhaps he likes what he sees, you'd never know from his expression.)*

HIM: Hmm! You'd better leave these with me, our chief designer has hopped over to Paris for a couple of days and I'd like him to see your work. Well done, Michael. Er, what did you say your surname was?

ME: Maloney, sir.

HIM (one eyebrow raised): Irish, are you?

Me: No, sir, I'm Australian.

If I'd told him I was from Yankalillee in north-eastern Victoria, later he'd have pissed his pants laughing. As it is, he most likely thinks Melbourne is pretty Hicksville. Which I suppose it is. Compared to London, everything is.

So you walk away on cloud nine, thinking, well at least he's liked your work, never know what can happen in the big city. He's asked you to come back in three days when the chief designer will be back from Paris. In the meantime the chief designer is eating a cheese and pickle sandwich in the company canteen, though, of course, you don't know this.

I come back three days later to collect my samples, all wide-eyed and bushy-tailed, and I'm waiting in the foyer when this model comes out to take a phone call. She's wearing a calico garment, that's a garment cut from a pattern made up from the original. All it is is pins and stitches to see how the garment will work on a live model. The calico the model's wearing is one of my patterns. Only difference is that the chalk marks where the buttons will go are in a slightly different configuration.

I'm excited as anything. I'm on my way, I think. Then the original bloke comes out and hands me back my folio and says he's shown them to the boss but they're not really interested, there's nothing they can offer me.

'What about the model?' I ask.

'What model?' he says.

'The model who came out to take a phone call, she was wearing my calico. You've ripped off my design, you bastard!'

'What? What are you saying? Are you saying I stole your design?' he shouts.

'Yes, bring back the model and I'll prove it!' I take out my folio and pull out the design. 'There you go, that one, you've ripped it off. Only thing you've marked differently are the button holes! Go on, bring that model back out, I'll prove it to you!'

Suddenly the designer jabs his finger into my chest. 'Look, sonny boy, if you don't get off these premises right now I'll call the police. You don't know what you're talking about! Now bugger off!'

I suppose it's a compliment, because it's happened three times, one winter suit and two summer outfits all at different manufacturers. So I guess I'm a slow learner. But what I don't understand is, if they're ripping off my designs why don't they give me a job? I'm not asking for a lot of bread, I just want to learn.

Then later, when I've got a job, I learn why. Most of the manufacturers have blokes designing who are well past it. There's a fashion revolution going on and they don't know what's hit them. They know how to cut a pattern but they've got no new ideas. So they rip off the young designers who come in, same as they did me. It wasn't just me they've done it to, it's standard procedure. They don't want the youngsters to show them up, see.

I have got to know some of the young designers. I met one in the foyer of a manufacturer's, a real nice bloke, and he introduced me to his friends, who are also designers and some even have jobs. They like my stuff so I'm invited into their group, most of whom are as broke as I am. My money is just about run out and I'm buying a packet of dried apples and eating eight apple rings in the morning and drinking a pint of water with it so the apples swell up in my stomach and I feel full for a good part of the day.

Then I land a job, one of the designers in our group wins a scholarship to go to America and he recommends me for his old job as a junior designer where he's been working. A place called **Exquizeet**. *It's middle-of-the-road and it's not much dough but I can pay the rent and eat once a day at Walls. That's a cheap restaurant you can get fish and chips and sausages and mash, pork pies, toad in the hole, food like that.*

The good thing is that they got a design room at **Exquizeet** *and turn out quite a wide range and some stuff for the young people that doesn't look like what their mums wear. But I soon learn that, as the new boy, it ain't going to be easy. I design my first garment which the boss likes and tells me to cut the pattern. The head designer isn't all that impressed when the boss tells him. 'The boy's good, see how he handles the pattern.'*

I cut the pattern and the chief designer can't find a fault with it, so I think I'm doing OK. The next thing is to do the calico on a model and choose the fabric and make up the garment. Well, they bring in a model and I make up the calico and it looks beaut. But the model says it doesn't feel right and she doesn't like it. 'It simply won't do, darling!' I don't know at that time that some of the models are real bitches or that this one has been put up to it by the chief designer and is a real bitch all on her own.

Anyway, the chief designer is in the process of telling me the design is ratshit and, while the sketch was promising and the pattern looked good, it simply doesn't translate into calico. All the other designers say nothing, they know it works great but they're too scared to speak up. But I get lucky again. The big boss walks in and sees the calico on the model. 'My dear, that's perfect!' he says, and he turns to me. 'What fabric do you have in mind, Mike?'

'Well, I don't like it,' the model sniffs, pushing her nose in the air.

'Darling, when I want your opinion I'll pull the lavatory chain,' he says. 'I've been in the rag trade thirty years and that calico is a perfect fit, don't try and tell me my job!' He turns to the chief designer, 'Don't you agree, Mr Charlton?'

The slimy bastard nods, too scared to speak up. 'Good then, let's proceed with choosing the fabric.' He pats me on the shoulder, 'Good work, my son.'

So now everyone hates me. But I don't care. I've got my first design through, which I learn later is unheard of. But the tsuris, *the troubles, aren't over yet. A couple of days later the floor manager comes into the design room with the head machinist and tells Mr Charlton that my garment can't be sewn. 'Mrs Roberts here says it can't be done,' he says, nodding his head to the machinist, who doesn't look too happy herself.*

'Oh dear,' says Mr Charlton, 'I thought this might happen.' He turns to me and says, 'Bad luck, Mike, we'll have to scrap it.'

I've come this far and I reckon I've got nothing to lose, they all hate me anyway. 'Bullshit!' I say.

'Hey, don't you go saying that, son,' says the foreman. 'If Mrs Roberts says it can't be done, it can't!'

'Bullshit,' I say again and Mr Charlton has gone so red in the face I think his head is going to burst like a party balloon.

'And how would you know?' he suddenly shouts at me, 'How dare you speak to Brothers like that!' Brothers is the name of the foreman, who in the pecking order doesn't rate as a Mister, because he's blue-collar.

'Take me to your machine, Mrs Roberts, show me why it can't be done.'

'Are you questioning my work, sir?' Mrs Roberts says.

'Yes, madam, I bloody am! Take me to your bloody sewing machine!' I reckon if I'm going to be fired, may as well go out with both barrels blazing.

In England most designers can't sew, or if they can, it's straight up and down hem stitch, they can't do the tricky work. So out we traipse on to the work floor. It's like old times in Flinders Lane, machines whirring. Mrs Roberts sits down and brings my garment up and starts to talk crap about the overlocking being impossible because of the way the garment is cut. She's trying to blind me with science. It's a deliberate con and I lose my temper. 'Move yer fat arse and I'll show you how it's done, and I push her out of the way with my bum. Then I do the overlocking and one or two other bits and pieces that might be thought hard by someone who wasn't a skilled machinist.

Someone's called the boss and he's come up and I don't know he's there but he's watching me and when I've finished, he puts his hand on my shoulder. 'You're a brash kid, Mike Maloney, but it seems to me you always put your money where your mouth is. I've never seen a junior designer who can cut a pattern, work up a calico and sew, much less sew like that. What do you earn?'

'Ten pounds a week, sir.'

'As of next pay day that will be twelve pounds and ten shillings. But we don't want the Garment Union to go on strike, so, if you don't mind, lad, stay off the floor!'

Next pay day he's true to his word, there's two pounds ten shillings extra. I take ten shillings out of my pay packet, go to the florist on the corner and buy a big bunch of red roses and have them wrapped up in cellophane, with a ribbon, the works. Then I give them to Mrs Roberts and say, 'No hard feelings, Mrs Roberts, but we've all got to survive and I'm the Australian here, so I'm the expendable one.' Well, for a moment she's a bit mooshy round the mouth, then she smiles and relaxes and says, 'Where'd you learn to sew like that, love?'

I laugh and say, 'That's nothing, you should see me embroider!' But I don't think she believes me and calls me a cheeky sod and we're friends for life. From that moment on there's never a problem sewing my stuff.

But, of course, now I'm public enemy number one in the design room and the models don't think all that much of me either. A few weeks later we're preparing to do a show for some buyers coming in from the Midlands. I've got two things in, a light summer suit like the one I made for Sarah at uni and a short reversible trench coat that's a raincoat on one side and a fashion garment that can be worn at night when you reverse it. The fashion side is lightly sequinned on the sleeves and the lapels and is in a gorgeous teal blue and very pretty. The daywear cum raincoat is a light beige gaberdine with a high turn-up collar with lapel and collar stitching showing as a feature. The same model who was wearing the calico when the boss walked in that day is wearing both my garments in the show. She's the head model and so it's supposed to be a compliment. But she's told Mr Charlton she doesn't like the garments, that 'they're too brash and flashy, very outré, *my dear.'*

Well, minutes before she has to show the first garment, which is the reversible coat, the dresser comes up to me and says the model has unfortunately caught a pocket of the coat on the dressing-room door handle and it's ripped right down the seam and has to be withdrawn from the show. Half an hour later when the model's about to wear the suit, same thing happens, this time she's caught her spike heel in the hem of the skirt when she's pulling it on and ripped out the silk lining.

Afterwards the model comes up to me, her name is Deborah Phipps-Gordon, she's all wide-eyed and says in her plummy accent, 'Oh, Michael, I'm so sorry, but there's such a fuss and to-do in there, accidents are simply bound to happen, darling!'

It's not too hard to see the writing is on the wall. But I'm learning heaps and the people on the factory floor like me and the boss thinks I'm just what the doctor ordered so there's not a lot the others can do about it, except try to make me feel unwanted, a job they do very successfully.

Meanwhile, at night I'm designing and sewing the costumes for a repertory company who are putting on a play called Back to the Future *and part of the plot is set in the present and part ten years from now. There's lots of garments to design. I don't get paid, of course, but it's great fun and I can indulge my imagination. The play opens in Bath, which is a town that's got a lot of posh English people living there.*

Next thing I know I get a call from Madame Jardine, who is a famous couturière to 'the establishment', that means the aristocrats and the very rich. She says she happened to pop in to see the play because one of her nieces had a small part in it, she likes some of the ideas she's seen in the garments and she offers me a job as a junior designer at twenty pounds a week.

It takes me about ten seconds to make up my mind. Couturière, that's where you really learn new stuff. Working at **Exquizeet** *has been good, but it's not all that different from Flinders Lane. What I want is to learn haute couture, that's where all the secrets are.*

I've been with Madame Jardine a month and she's a real old dragon, she calls me 'the boy' and pretends she's taking no notice of what I'm saying or doing. But nobody hates me here yet and I don't mind her being a dragon. After Flinders Lane and some of the hand-finishers there, I'm an expert on dragons and have practically got a bottoms-wiping certificate in dragon-taming.

I know this will sound very arrogant, but already I can see, as a fashion house, we're losing the plot. Fashion is a movable thing and Madame Jardine has stagnated. There's a designer in the Kings Road called Mary Quant who's killing them all. She's taken on Chanel and Dior in Paris and us and Hartnell in London and she's blitzing us all.

What she's done in London is what I always wanted to do in Melbourne, she's created styles at the working-girl level, same as Tullo. They're called the MODS and they're young people who want fashion, but want it outrageous! Or what the couturiers think is outrageous anyway. The rich and famous are also buying her stuff and she's broken down the couturier barrier. Skirts well above the knees, crazy new colours and prints, simple elegant lines, bold-as-brass colours. She's taken away high heels and brought back flat shoes and go-go boots and her skirts practically climb up a pretty girl's thighs all by themselves! The girls are all wearing her clothes with dark eyes, lots of black mascara and eye liner. They're going crazy about her work and she's turning the fashion industry upside down. I'm going to have to get to meet her even if it kills me.

Two nights ago I waited until everyone had gone home except the night watchman and I cut a pattern for a garment design I'd made. A little bit similar to one of the ones I'd done for Sarah but with an a la Andre Courreges/Quant pencil-line mini skirt and a few other little modifications I've thought up, interchangeable zip-on lapels in different colours and the same for the pocket patches. I finished it at 2 a.m. and left it displayed on the cutting table for when Madame came in next morning.

At lunchtime I'm just about to go out to get my main meal for the day at Walls when Madame's secretary calls to me and says that Madame Jardine wants to see me in the cutting room. I go in, I'm pretty nervous. She's got the pattern still laid out with the sketches I've made and left with them.

'Did you do this, boy?' she says, pointing. She's got fingernails practically long as your arm and her mouth is all red lipstick and she doesn't look that happy.

'Yes, Madame Jardine.'

'And what is it supposed to mean?'

'It's a summer suit for the working girl, personal secretaries and girls who want to be fashionable and a bit outrageous,' I say.

'Secretaries! Madame Jardine doesn't design for secretaries!'

'Yes, well, you see that's at one level.' I go over and pick up a sketch. 'This is the same suit, only a different fabric and heavily hand-embroidered. It would be a very expensive garment for the younger rich set or the slimmer figure.'

'Embroidered? Hand-embroidered! Are there still little people who do that? This is ridiculous!'

'Please, Madame Jardine, let me make up both versions so you can see what I mean.'

'Oh, I see, the boy will design them, cut the pattern and do the sewing? I suppose you'll do the embroidery as well,' she says, real sarcastic.

'Yes, Madame Jardine, I will.'

You should have seen her face! But she can't turn back now, she's been challenged, see. Except she says, 'Boy! A haute couturière doesn't cut patterns, a patternmaker does that. She, or in your case should you ever become one, he doesn't sew, a machinist does that. He doesn't hand-finish, an expert hand-finisher does that and he most definitely doesn't embroider! What on earth are you talking about?'

'Please, Madame Jardine, let me make up a sample of each, then you can fire me if you want. I'll do it in my own time if you'll let me have the fabrics.'

So that was yesterday, and tomorrow I start on the two suits. The old dragon is giving me a chance. But she's tough as nails and if I fail I'll be out on my ear. I can't believe it. It's been less than a year and I'm getting a go at something original of my own in London!!!!!!!!!!!!!!! Yippeee!!!!!!!!!

Mole, this is the longest letter I've ever written in my whole life and it brings you up to date. One more thing. I am bloody horrified that you want to go into the army!! But there you go, you were always the steady one in the family who thinks things out. But have you suddenly gone stark staring mad or something? Wasn't Tommy enough for you? OK, now I've said it.

Let everyone read this letter and tell them I love them. Tell Mum I'll take a photo of the suit with the embroidery and send it to her. Maybe we'll put it in the Royal Melbourne Show next year, eh? See if the Queen likes it enough to give it a blue ribbon or Best of Show! On twenty pounds a week I'm going to see my first opera at Covent Garden soon as I've done the suits. You can sit in a place called The Gods and it's not so expensive.

With lots of love to everyone, I miss you a lot.

Mike

Chapter Twenty-six

Well, here I am at Kapooka which is near Wagga Wagga in New South Wales and I've been going a month in the regular army. I've got two more months as a recruit and I'm not sure I'm going to make it.

Blokes from the bush aren't meant for this kind of stuff. Weapons training and such, yeah, I like that a lot, but the drill is total crap. We've spent two days learning to salute. I mean, how useful is that? I'm not going to spend my life saluting people, or if I am, then I'll be seeking an early retirement. *Bring the right arm by the longest way smartly to the salute position, keeping the hand in line with the arm and square to the front.* I do as the drill sergeant says, then it's 'Number three in the front rank, you are paying a compliment to an officer of the Australian Army, NOT BLOODY WAVING TO YOUR GIRLFRIEND!' That's me he's yelling at. So I do what he says, which is what I'm doing in the first place, it ain't too hard if you can see the sense of it in the first place.

Now, with him yelling at me, he's put two distractions into my mind. The first is: why would I want to pay a compliment to an officer? They were the ones that did bugger-all work at Sandakan and got transferred to Kuching, where their biggest problem was boredom. There was Matthews, of course, you'd pay a bloke like that a compliment, but there weren't too many like him around. Secondly, I ain't got a girlfriend, which makes me think of Anna Dombrowski and

I start wondering how she is and there's a bit of a longing in me. I've never forgotten her, though she's probably married to Crocodile Brown and having a baby by now. I can't bring myself to even imagine that.

'NUMBER THREE IN THE FRONT I SAID TURN RIGHT BY NUMBERS, THE OTHER "RIGHT" YOU IDIOT!' Suddenly I'm moving in a direction away from the platoon because I've been thinking these things. It's like being in Crocodile Brown's class after garbage collection all over again.

It's the endless drill, turning, saluting, marching, eyes right, eyes left, open order march, close order march that's bugging me. I can't believe Tommy and his lot had to do all this shit just to get themselves killed. Rifle drill goes on for bloody ever! I can use a rifle already, it comes naturally to me. We've been on the range and I'm ahead of everyone, even the other bushies. All the other stuff you've got to do with a rifle strikes me as pointless.

Then there's the inspections, your dress and your gear. I've spent my life doing the laundry in the copper back home. No, that's not true, but ever since Sarah went to uni I know how to keep clean and iron a shirt. Washing and ironing isn't a problem I have. Besides they've got washing machines here, just throw the stuff in and out it comes washed, so that's something you can't complain about.

But it's all the spit and polish, getting your boots so you can see your face in the bootcaps, starching your greens and getting the creases in the right places. You have to laugh at some of the blokes, those who've never seen an iron in their lives. I reckon I could become an ironing instructor in the army, be better than some of the stupid things you do to become a soldier.

Like, here's a 'for instance', the platoon sergeant inspects my rising-sun hat badge. 'This is the rising sun,' he says, pointing to my hat badge. 'It's bloody sinking from the weight of the shit all over it!' He rips my hat off and points to the badge, far as I can see it's polished so it practically blinds you. 'See that, you idiot. Brasso! Brasso fucking everywhere in the rays, haven't you ever heard of a toothbrush? You may think it's an implement for cleaning teeth. Well, it's fucking not! It's for removing fucking Brasso from your rising-sun badge you idiot!' Next thing I know I've had my Sunday afternoon cancelled and I'm gardening outside Company Headquarters, all because he's seen an imaginary spot of Brasso in the rays of the rising sun.

What I've just told you about was the first month. Things were pretty crook, but they get a bit better after a while. We learn how to strip and assemble the new SLRs. Even the instructors are a bit shaky on this, because the SLR has just taken over from the .303 Lee Enfield.

Cleaning your rifle barrel makes a bit of sense, but I already know how to do this. They give you this piece of cloth called a 'four-by-two'. It's tied to a piece of string with its other end tied to a small lead weight and you drop the weight down the barrel and then pull the string through with the four-by-two to clean it. The biggest crime in the army is to have a dirty barrel on your rifle. But, see what I mean, there's even a special drill for getting your rifle in position where the officer can look down the barrel and see if you've cleaned it right. It's called 'For inspection, port arms!'

Tommy once told me what his sergeant said about his rifle when he was training as a young bloke same age as me. Now the platoon sergeant says exactly the same thing to us. It goes like this:

> *'You blokes probably think your family is the most important thing in the world. The dirty minds amongst you probably think it's your girlfriend. But from now on, it's none of those. Righto, what is it, Private Maloney?'*
>
> *'My rifle, Sergeant.'*
>
> *'That's right. Now look after it like you love it and one day it might look after you.'*

I'll bet some sergeant with a handlebar moustache said that to Grandpa Baloney when he went to the Boer War.

But there's one thing I learn in the army that's bloody good. All my life there's been us and the Protestants, us and the wogs or reffos or Abos or whatever, people separating themselves from each other because of something or other, skin colour, religion, language, food. Now there's blokes from everywhere and every kind, Protestants, Catholics, a few dago blokes and one Abo. But it doesn't mean a thing.

First thing they do here is cut all your hair off. I never realised how hair has its own language and tells you who people are. But now that's all gone, we're wearing the same haircut, same uniform and we're under constant attack from the same enemy, the contrary and difficult bastards in charge of us.

Religion doesn't count, nationality don't, colour doesn't. When the Abo bloke's got his hand in yours helping you over a wooden fence in the obstacle course, you don't think about his family living, mostly as drunks, on the edge of town, like people say they do. You learn that there's good blokes and bad ones, even Japs, like Sergeant Major Gotunda who went down the river in a boat to get the POWs rice and a bag of vegies and who couldn't bring himself to shoot a prisoner. It doesn't matter what nationality a bloke's parents are, or what religion or colour he is, it's who he is that matters.

Of course the blokes have a go, they call you a 'rockchopper' if you're a Catholic, but it's all in good fun, not meant to hurt. They know you're their family now. There's this song one of the blokes made up in our platoon, it's funny that, Tommy talked of Nelson Short and his ukulele at Sandakan, how he cheered them up. Jimmy Stephenson in our platoon is the same, he plays the mouth organ and sings this song he made up. It's become our song and the idea is to sing it real sad.

I'm so sorry, Sergeant,
I can't come on parade,
I haven't had a shave,
I've lost me razor blade!
Me rifle's dirty,
I've got no four-by-two,
To pull me rifle through,
Oh, Sergeant, dear
Whatever shall I do?

So I think you can see that after a while I've settled down a bit and finished my training. I've got to admit by the end of the three months I'm a bit proud, on parade with the senior platoon ready to march out, and there's me and the Abo and a dago, the front three marching out, first to be seen in the whole battalion, giving the battalion commander the old 'eyes right', our necks stiff as a board and our line straight as an arrow.

I'm posted to the Royal Australian Infantry Corps and it's another three months' training, this time at Ingleburn, outside Sydney. There's a lot of bush work now and I really like this, I'm in my element. We're learning section tactics from the sergeant instructor and I enjoy the lectures. There's one lecture that made me understand how Tommy could have come through what he'd done. When Tommy talked about jungle training, I thought, you know, go into the jungle and rat-tat-tat-tat or out with the knife or fix bayonets and charge. That it's all like one-on-one, the Jap or you, which turns out not to be untrue, but what's always worried me is, what if you're scared and you freeze or run away, like I think I might do?

Then a lieutenant gives us an introductory lecture that I reckon I'll never forget. He talks about fear, how would it be if you came up to the enemy all of a sudden. I suppose every bloke asks himself this question at some time or another. Anyway, here is what he says, it's taken directly from my notes.

> *There are four natural reactions to fear. You either freeze, or faint, or run away or become irrationally aggressive. When the enemy fires on your section, you'll get a helluva shock. If we all reacted in one of these four ways, it would be a disaster. Even if you run away, besides that being cowardly, the action would put you in more danger than if you took more considered action. So, to overcome your instinct to react in one of these ways, we practise 'contact drills'. We practise them and practise them until they take over from our natural instincts, and replace them with a planned action. It's the contact drill that allows us to react in such a way that we are ready to take on the enemy and defeat him.*

The army is beginning to make more sense to me. It's bloody hard work, we practise every kind of contact drill imaginable, we have permanent gravel rash from falling to the ground again and again on to our knees and elbows. Then there are the drills for being ambushed. Now I understand what Tommy was talking about. If you're ambushed, there's just about nothing you can do except retaliate by charging the enemy. You are on *his* killing ground and he's waiting for you. The best thing you can do is hit back as fast and as hard as you can, because frankly there's bugger-all else you can do.

We spend a long time learning how to mount an ambush ourselves. Once you've prepared the ambush, it's the sentry who's the most important bloke. It's a huge responsibility because the lives of your mates are in your hands. 'You'll never have a bigger responsibility in your life, so DON'T FUCK IT UP!' is what our sergeant says over and over again. The army is constant repetition. So here's the next scare, what happens if you fall asleep? The trick is never to be comfortable and to sit in such a way that if you fall asleep, you drop your head and it hits something and you wake up with the shock.

I suppose because of me and Tommy in the bush, the job I liked the best was forward scouting. You're the leading man in your section. It is a matter of good bushcraft, of looking for signs of the enemy presence, hoping you see him before he sees you. I know I shouldn't big-note myself, but when the sergeant says to me one day, 'Never know, Private Maloney, might yet make a forward scout out of you', it was one of the bigger days of my life. They don't throw those sorts of compliments around in the army. But really, I should thank Tommy for that, acute observation of every tiny detail was at the centre of everything he taught me.

So my life now is route marches with weapons and full gear, nine-mile runs, map reading, which fortunately I knew from fighting fires, and constant contact drill. On the marches the blokes laugh when we're trudging along and I name all the trees and bushes. Half the time they think I'm bullshitting, like just making up the names. There's none of them knows Latin so they think it's just gibberish and the English names I've just made up. At first I'd tell them the history of the fires in an area by looking at the burnt-out stumps, after a while I stop because they think either I'm some sort of weirdo or the biggest liar in Australia. Most blokes can't tell a daisy from a petunia and, in the army, showing you're different is not a great idea. But I think the instructors cotton on that I'm a bloke who likes detail and takes it seriously.

Then there's grenade practice with live grenades, real scary stuff.

You think you're going to freeze and drop the grenade with the pin out at your feet but you've practised it so many times with dummy grenades, it doesn't happen.

The climax of this second lot of training is the two-week tactical exercises, simulated attacks, patrolling sometimes all night and into the next day so your feet end up just one big blister. The whole idea is to toughen you up, get you accustomed to acute discomfort. Finally the graduation parade comes about and now you think of yourself as Private Mole Maloney, Australian Infantry.

I'm posted to the 2nd Battalion, Royal Australian Regiment, as a reinforcement. The battalion's in Malaya and although the Malayan Emergency has come to an end some eighteen months ago, I'm still excited. I'm going to Malaya, it's the jungle and it's where Tommy began his fighting career. It all seems an amazing coincidence.

The battalion's stationed at Terendak, the new 28th Commonwealth Brigade Barracks near Malacca. We're there together with the 1st King's Own Yorkshire Infantry and the 1st Battalion, Royal New Zealand Regiment, all of us part of the Commonwealth Far East Strategic Reserve.

I get kitted out and in no time flat I'm in the middle of the Malayan jungle with my new platoon on a training exercise. They tell me it's to prepare the battalion for operations on the Thai border against the remnants of Ching Peng's once dangerous Communist army.

I think I'm a pretty good soldier until I strike Corporal Jake Tingle, who's my new section commander and has already been in Malaya on one tour when the Emergency was really on. 'Private Maloney, the skipper tells me you know your way around the bush, eh?'

'No, Corporal.'

'Well, that's the right reply, because you don't know your arse from your elbow about the jungle, so from now on you look, listen and keep yer bloody trap shut! Understand?'

'Yes, Corporal.'

And he proves to be right. What we've learned up to now is practically nothing. If this is what Tommy did when they put his battalion through jungle training then I can see why they were so much better than the British garrison troops who'd spurned such training.

The thing is silence. Everything is based on silence, getting somewhere by not being seen or heard. Everything is done by hand signals, then you learn to anticipate changes in section formation, how to look through bushes and not at them, how to recognise ground that might be the killing ground of an enemy ambush. And how to silently and quickly set our own ambush if the scout signals 'enemy approaching'.

There's squillions of things to learn, some of them seem small, but turn out to be critical. Like taking off your boots when things are safe to air and dry your feet. Also, your feet's worst enemy is socks that don't fit. If the socks bunch up, they'll wear the skin off your feet.

Towards the end of the exercise, Jake Tingle signals me to take over as forward scout. I'm exhilarated but also shitting meself. If I screw it up, I'll never be able to lift my head up again. So off we go through the bushes, careful as all get-out. Then I stop and see the underside of a leaf on a bush facing up the wrong way. I look more closely and see there's a couple of tiny twigs fresh broken, a bit of trodden-down grass and two small stones kicked out of their original positions. I signal for the corporal. He comes up and agrees a small group of 'exercise enemy' has taken a right-angle turn from where we were heading. He looks at his map and sees there's a little creek nearby and reasons they've made for the creek, maybe to fill their water bottles. So we lay an ambush and wait for them to return. They do and we've got them. We get a few brownie points for that. Corporal Jake Tingle now calls me Mole and expects me to call him Jake. It's the sign that he'd trust me in the jungle as a forward scout.

After what Tommy told me, I have a healthy respect for the tropical jungle, but also a fascination. What I know about the Australian bush, I now want to know about the jungle. Of course, that's impossible, it would take a lifetime, but there's a good few things you can learn if you keep your eyes peeled and ask questions, like I've always done since I was a little kid. Nancy used to say when she didn't want to answer, 'Curiosity killed the cat!' I've often wondered how that saying came about, but nobody has ever been able to give me an answer when I've asked. See what I mean?

I was always fascinated about the big tree at Sandakan and how Tommy, when he escaped and thought he was going to die, wanted to die safe in the buttress of a big tree he'd seen while carrying rice.

Thank God, he never found it or he may have given up. But the reason those big jungle trees have buttresses is because the soil is very poor and so jungle trees don't have deep roots and nature's developed these buttresses to hold them up.

There's lots that's new to find out about the big old blokes and how so much takes advantage of them. The vines in particular use them to grow up the trunks so they can reach the sunlight on the canopy. That's another thing, the canopy is so thick with vines and leaves that even in a fierce storm the wind doesn't get down to the ground, the rain will come down in buckets but the ground is otherwise quite calm. It's also reasonably easy to walk in the jungle because all the action is happening up top, everything stretching for the sun. Orchids, Tommy would always call them epiphytes, ferns and some other small plants simply grow on the tree, doing it no harm. But there's a group of villains as well, take the aerial herniparasite for instance, it's a leathery green-leafed vine with white berries, don't know why but it looks a bit evil too, well, it hooks its roots into the trunk or a branch of the tree and feeds from it. It can sometimes kill the tree outright. There's mistletoe, you know, the stuff they hang up at Christmas parties where, if you can catch a girl under it, you can kiss her, it's here in the jungle. I always thought it would be growing in the snow in England or something. I liked the rattan vine, because of what it does for mankind. I suppose you wouldn't strictly call it a vine because it's actually a sort of pine, only for jungles. Its trunk is long and very thin and has hooks in it that latch on to the tree trunk and up she goes all the way to the canopy to get its share of sunlight.

Rattan is the stuff they use to make wicker chairs and baskets and it's a generally useful sort of plant. Many's the time Bozo and me have rescued a wicker couch or chair and then got some rattan and mended it and sold it in Wang. Tommy, sometimes when he was hungry, would say, 'I'm that hungry I could eat a baby's bum through a wicker chair!'

There's lots to learn that isn't just jungle-fighting tactics and I reckon the more you know, the easier it is to survive. Just one more tiny thing. I'm standing next to this tree, my section's just returned from a patrol into the protection of the platoon harbour and we've having a bit of a smoko. I count, in one square yard, eight hundred or so ants belonging to fifty different species. One of the blokes asks me what I'm doing. 'Counting ants,' I tell him. He signals the others to come have a look, 'Hey, Mole's finally gone troppo, now he's counting the fucking ants in the jungle. He's already up to a hundred billion!' The point is that everywhere you go in the jungle there's ants.

You've got to have a bit of luck to progress quickly in the permanent army, it's like the public service, you've got to have done the hard yards and put in the time before promotion comes. It's different when there's a war on, of course. Well, I get lucky, and the skipper calls me in and says they like what they've seen of me and I'm going to Kota Tingui Jungle Warfare School. Later my platoon sergeant, who's on his second tour of duty, says he's never seen it happen before, I've been in the jungle less than six months and I'm going to learn from the legendary Blue Johnston. 'Private Maloney, if I'm still around when you come back, I want you back in my platoon, you understand?' I guess it's a compliment.

Blue Johnston, an Australian, is the chief instructor at the Tracking Wing. There was nobody like him in the army that was a white bloke anyway. He could look at and smell a disused campfire and tell you how long ago, up to five years or five minutes, it was used. He could tell to a startling degree of accuracy when a cut had been made in a tree or a twig snapped, or a branch used to construct a shelter had been broken off and so tell you when the camp site was active. He could follow a trail picking up clues that were invisible to all but the legendary Eban trackers from Sabah. In fact, it was rumoured he had learned his tracking from living with the Eban deep in the jungles of Borneo, although he never said.

Well, you don't get someone like that every day of your life, do you? And I'm asking him a heap of questions whenever it seems appropriate. He is surprised I know about the jungle plants and insects and have a bit of general knowledge and he doesn't put me down, but explains things. Sometimes the other blokes are looking up at the ceiling, impatiently rolling their eyes, even though, like me, they're handpicked for extra jungle training. But I can't help myself, like I said, I never grew out of asking questions.

Anyhow, I learn later that Blue Johnston gives me a commendation in my pass, which again is something he's never done before. But, of course, he doesn't say anything to me. Except when we leave the course, he comes up and shakes my hand, 'You done good, Private Maloney. Good luck, son,' is all he said.

When I got back to the battalion, maybe because of what Blue Johnston had said in my report, I'm sent to a Junior NCO course. Again it's a bit on the quick side, I should have had another year in the army before that happened. Next thing I know, I'm a lance corporal and because the corporal section commander on our platoon goes down with malaria and there are no senior soldiers in our platoon, one of whom would automatically have got the job, it's given to me.

After I get back from Blue Johnston's training camp, the battalion does the best part of a year on the Thai border chasing the die-hards in Ching Peng's army. I suppose all this training and endless tracking and setting ambushes for these few ever-elusive terrorists is a bit boring, but it's important, because it means I'll know what I'm doing when I eventually get to Vietnam.

The battalion is sent home from Malaya in August 1963 and when we get back I'm sent on the Senior NCO course. After that I'm promoted to sergeant and posted as an instructor to the Battle Wing of the Infantry Centre at Ingleburn again and now I'm one of those bastards who made my life a misery when I joined up, I'm a Corps Training Instructor.

I'm the first to admit, it's not me that's made such rapid progress in the army, it's what Tommy taught me. If it hadn't been for him teaching me everything as a kid, I reckon I'd just be your average army shit-kicker and would have stayed a private all my life.

At the end of 1964, they tell me to pack my kit, I'm off overseas again, going to Vietnam where I'm posted to the Australian Army Training Team Vietnam, shortened to AATT or just 'the Team'.

It's a Qantas flight to Singapore and overnight at Nec Soon barracks, then on a Pan Am flight to Saigon. All of this is done in civilian dress as our presence in Vietnam is hush-hush. It's impossible to pack an Australian slouch hat for fear it will get out of shape. (In fact, it is forbidden in this man's army.) I can't help wondering what the people at Singapore airport must have thought about a civilian carrying an army hat, sporting an army haircut and carrying a civilian suitcase, lining up to fly to Vietnam. It wouldn't have taken a master spy to figure it out.

Half an hour out of Saigon I do as required and go into the toilet to change into my uniform. I've left my run too late and I'm just about ready when I'm knocked arse over tit in the toilet as the Pan Am jet makes a steep spiralling descent over Tan Son Nhut airfield, so as to be less exposed to any enemy fire aimed at it from the nearby swamplands. Back in my seat, I see the sun reflecting off the rice paddies that seem to stretch out forever from the airfield.

As we taxi in, I get a whiff of what the Yanks mean by war and I can't help wondering, even in a guerilla war, how an enemy with almost no resources will be able to stand up to this lot. We pass planes parked seemingly everywhere, Phantom jets, Caribou and Hercules C130 Transports, helicopters, dozens and dozens in clusters and, in the distance, the huge, lumbering B52 bombers that carry racks of 1000-pound bombs. Then I see one of them trundling along a runway and I think of a pelican back home. Pelicans don't look like they can fly, they almost can't walk, each step in slow motion and they really seem to battle to get into the air, but once airborne they are one of the mightiest fliers of them all, graceful and beautiful to behold in flight. The B52 miraculously rises into the air, so slowly I think it must fall out of the sky any moment, but it doesn't, and like a pelican, once up, it appears to fly effortlessly.

I've seen a few airports since going to Malaya, but I've never seen one where there's almost only military, with US soldiers in combat greens filing in and out of Hercules C130s carrying their packs, weapons and other equipment. There seem to be a lot of black blokes among them.

An Australian warrant officer is there to meet me. 'John Dean, mate, 'ow yer goin'?' he says.

'Mole Maloney,' I reply, shaking his hand, 'pleased ter meetcha, John.'

'Mole, that a nickname?' he asks right off.

'Yeah, but I can hardly remember what my rightful christened name is, always been Mole.'

'Fair enough,' he says. 'Welcome to Vietnam, Mole.'

Oh, I forgot to say, LBJ wanted more Australian advisers in Vietnam so the Yanks wouldn't look as though they were going it alone as the big bully and it's put a bit of a strain on the Australian system. Instead of only officers and warrant officers being sent, quite a bunch of us sergeants are going too. But to better fit the US Army administration system we're all getting temporary promotion. So, say hello to temporary Warrant Officer Mole Maloney.

John Dean puts me in the front seat of a small bus with him and I notice the windows are covered with chicken wire as a defence against a lobbed grenade. I realise for the first time that the enemy is probably everywhere and that this one doesn't necessarily wear a uniform or hide in the jungle. It's Malaya and the terrorists all over again, but these cats aren't ending a guerilla war, they've been fighting one for years and if the defeat of the French is any indication, they're bloody good at it.

As we drive along the busy airport road and then into the city, it's as if we're driving in a sea of bicycles, two-stroke motorbikes and Vespa scooters. The French influence is still here on the road, in the wide boulevards and some of the beautiful colonial buildings. The noise of all the bicycle bells and the angry, *rippppping* sound of two-stroke exhausts and scooters is almost deafening. Busy is the word. Everyone is going someplace and anxious to get there.

What I notice most is the white. The men all wear white shirts and black pants. But the shirts are not just white, they're Persil-white and look crisp like they've just been ironed and put on. Already I'm sweating like a pig in the tropical heat and these buggers look cool as a cucumber. The women too are dressed in white *ao dais*, it's the national costume of long pants and a long fitted dress with a mandarin collar. We pass a bunch of young girls and I gasp at how beautiful they are, elegant too. I should take an *ao dais* home for Sarah, I reckon it would be a good thing for a doctor to wear. Even the cops wear white, white trousers, coats, caps, gloves and the warrant officer tells me they're called 'White Mice' and have a pretty bad reputation for shooting first and asking questions later.

I'm dropped off at a fleapit hotel to spend the night. I don't mind because I'll probably spend half the night looking around the town. The warrant officer apologises and says hotel accommodation in Saigon is at a premium and the Australian government is reluctant to put warrant officers up at the Inter-Continental.

Next morning I'm collected by John Dean and driven back to the airport and I board a Hercules for Da Nang. Next to Tan Son Nhut airbase in Saigon, it's the biggest US airbase in South Vietnam. It's also the headquarters of the US Special Forces, the mob I'll be working with.

In downtown Da Nang, as the Yanks refer to it, even though it is almost next door to the airbase perimeter, is Australia House, a modest white bungalow with an iron picket fence, shaped not unlike a barracks, with a tiled roof. I'm taken there in a jeep by the administrative warrant officer of the establishment, where I'm welcomed by the RSM, which stands for Regimental Sergeant Major.

'Welcome to Australia House, Warrant Officer Maloney.' The RSM extends his hand, which is pretty unusual. Must be a friendly mob, I think. So far so good.

'Thank you, RSM.'

'Good flight?' he asks, then adds, 'No, don't answer that.'

He's right, a Hercules flight is always uncomfortable, also bloody cold. You sit on webbing seats along the sides, facing mountains of cargo tied down in the centre of the plane. The noise is dreadful and you have to shout to be heard. If it wasn't compulsory, nobody would do it.

'You're right, but we got here,' I say, laughing. He seems a nice enough bloke.

'Come inside.' He steps inside to let me pass. 'I expect you'd like a beer?'

I'm not sure I should say yes, but it's hot and a beer would go down well, so I nod. It's wonderfully cool inside, tiled floor and louvres to allow cross ventilation. He leads me down a corridor to a room with a bar and explains it's where Australian advisers stationed in I Corps (pronounced 'eye') meet to have a beer when they come out of the field for a couple of days every month or two. The RSM goes to the fridge and hands me a can of Foster's. 'We've got plenty of American beer, a Bud or Coors, if you'd prefer?' he says.

I wouldn't prefer, a Foster's will do me great, and I get the impression that he wouldn't have liked me to have asked for a Yank beer. I pop the can, he does the same. I lift the can. 'Cheers!' I'm still hot and sticky from the short ride in from the airport and the first long, sharp swallow is nectar from the gods. I'm not a big drinker, but there are times nothing else but cold, foaming lager will fit the bill.

Then the RSM explains that he and his staff look after the Australian members of the Team in I Corps. This is where my personal gear will be stowed, my records kept and my mail collected.

On the wall behind the bar is this plaque, *Nuoc Mam Hall, Home of The Expendables, Da Nang, Vietnam*.

The RSM sees me looking at it and I can sense he's waiting for the question. I suppose he's explained it every time a newcomer arrives, so I don't ask him. For once in his life Mole doesn't ask a question, which for me must be a world record. But afterwards, I can't help wondering what's meant by 'Expendables'. It will probably drive me mad. If you ask me, it doesn't sound all that promising.

Just then the warrant officer who drove me over from the airbase comes in and excuses himself to the RSM and says to me, 'Your new C.O. wants to see you immediately, I'll take you over in the jeep.'

'Christ, I'll smell of beer!' I say.

'You're Australian, what could be more natural?' the RSM laughs. I reckon he's a bit cranky because I didn't ask him about the 'Expendable' plaque.

I've got a bit of gum in my pocket so I pop it into my mouth, hoping the spearmint will kill the grog on my breath. I've only had a couple of good sips, but it would be a crook way to start my Vietnam career if my new C.O. comes out and says, 'You smell of beer, Warrant Officer Maloney!'

We race across the airbase and I'm dropped at the door of a building, called 'C Detachment, 5th Special Forces Group (Airborne)'. Christ, what's the hurry, could have let me finish the beer, I think to myself as I take the gum out of my mouth and hurl it. But I know enough about the army and officers to know that their time ain't your time.

To my surprise this American lieutenant colonel meets me at the front door. I jump to attention and salute him. *Bring the right arm by the longest way smartly to the salute position, keeping the hand in line with the arm and square to the front*. I've got it so perfect I'm practically a parody.

He doesn't seem to notice and sort of touches the peak of his cap real lazy. 'Welcome, nice to have you with us,' he says and shakes my hand. Jesus, what's goin' on here? 'Follow me please, Mister Maloney,' he's even got my name right off without consulting a piece of paper or having it shouted out by the RSM!

Then he leads me into the command post. It's not hard to see there's something going on and that his staff are dealing with an emergency. Most command headquarters are about the same. It doesn't take long to figure it out, the shit's hit the fan and they're running around like chooks with their heads cut off. People always think command headquarters are quiet with everyone going about their business calm and dispassionate. Not true, they're in the war same as us all. They may not be frontline, but they're still fighting men. It's not like those Pommie movies where everyone's sucking on pipes and thinking before they speak. Those days are long over, that is if they ever existed in the first place.

The C.O. briefs me. A company patrol of Vietnamese CIDG (short for Civil Irregular Defence Group) from the Special Forces outpost of Tran Xa is in trouble. It seems they were expecting to find some local Viet Cong and, instead, have run into some North Vietnamese regulars, well-trained soldiers. The company is taking a hiding.

'My Nung reaction force is already deployed, along with most of my advisers, so I can't send them. I've got a Montagnard company just in from training camp at Hoa Cam. They don't have much experience,' he says, then not too convincingly adds, 'but they should be okay.' He pauses and looks straight at me, 'Warrant Officer Maloney, I want you to join them.'

Shit, haven't seen too much combat myself. Chasing a few CTs around in the Malayan jungle isn't exactly going into battle with weapons blazing. But, as Morrie would say, 'My boy, stay *stumm*, what you don't say, they don't know about you already.' Jesus, I haven't even had time to have proper jetlag. My stomach starts to churn and my mouth is dry.

'There'll be a senior adviser with you, Captain Jones, report to him at the airbase.'

'Sir, is the senior adviser an experienced jungle fighter?'

The C.O. looks at me. 'Warrant Officer Maloney, we've learned to respect the Australian jungle training, it's the best in the world. There's also an Australian adviser with the company that's in trouble.'

I sigh a sigh of relief, it must be a mostly Australian operation. 'My senior adviser is an Australian, sir?'

'No, Maloney, *you're* the Australian. The only other Australian in this operation is with the company you're going to reinforce. Your senior is Captain Jones, who flew in from Guam three days ago.' He grins but in a tired sort of a way. 'Before that he was stationed at 29 Palms in Northern California. I'd like you to get over to your company as soon as possible, the Montagnard troops are at this very moment being issued with ammunition and rations, and the choppers are standing by,' the CO says. 'I have no other advisers available to accompany them except you and Captain Jones, it's over to you two. Good luck, there's a car outside, sort yourself out, soldier.'

I salute him and he gives me another brief touch of his cap brim, losing a maximum of half a calorie from the effort.

'I can't even drive on the right side of the fucking road!' is what I immediately think.

Lucky, I'm a bit of a reader. I've read all my briefing notes and anything else I can lay my hands on about Vietnam. Which isn't a lot. Australia isn't exactly making a big fuss about our helping hand stretched out in friendship and mutual cooperation to the Yanks. The thing to understand is, the Americans, and that includes us Australians, are not officially at war with either the Viet Cong insurgents in South Vietnam or with the country of North Vietnam. We're only 'advisers' to the South Vietnam army. Sort of international peacekeepers who bring their own weapons along in case the enemy doesn't want to take our advice.

I've read about two paragraphs on the Montagnard people. I know they're a mountain people, ethnically different from the regular lowland Vietnamese, good trackers, reliable, but looked down upon by the Vietnamese people as primitives, so they've got a bit of a grudge. Whoever wins in Vietnam, they'll still be a minority with all the usual disadvantages. It seems smart to have them on our side, blokes fighting with a grudge are generally more willing to get stuck into a stoush.

Later I will learn it was a CIA initiative. The South Vietnamese government was very reluctant to arm and organise the Montagnard tribes because they had ideas about independence. But the CIA feared that unless the Montagnard were brought in on the South Vietnamese side, they may be lured by the Viet Cong. So the CIA recruited the Montagnard and raised the Civil Irregular Defence Group, which eventually included Vietnamese as well. What they developed were these outposts trying to prevent enemy infiltration across the Lao and Cambodian borders. This program was later taken over by the Special Forces, who established more of these isolated outposts.

I will come to know from bitter experience how unreliable these Vietnamese Civil Irregulars are. The Special Forces tried to recruit Catholics who had fled from the communist north, hoping they would be well motivated, but most of them, the Civil Irregulars, didn't really give a fuck who won as long as they survived. And worse, there were usually a few Viet Cong plants among them. With the Montagnard, you never knew you would turn up to go on an operation, but once there they usually fought pretty well.

But none of them got much formal training, it was mostly up to the Special Forces advisers to train the troops in the field, usually much too little much too late. While we were only advisers, in practice it was very different. When a battle started, the Vietnamese commanders of the Civil Irregular soldiers were often nowhere to be seen. It was usual for the advisers to have to take over command and, at great risk to themselves, try to get the troops going. Quite a few copped it in the process.

And it was not only the Civil Irregulars who were unreliable, it could be pretty hairy working with the Territorial units too. There's the story of how last year a Vietnamese Territorial battalion outpost was surrounded and taking a pounding. After a few days of this, the Viet Cong set up a loudspeaker to tell the territorial soldiers to desert, that they're not interested in them. Unless, of course, they're stupid enough to stay put. All they want are the Imperialist Americans and their running dogs, that is, the advisers. The soldiers are free to leave and walk the ten clicks to the city of Hue.

It doesn't take them long to decide. The bastards up and leave, and the advisers get down and man the machine guns, holding the Viet Cong off on their own, though they're now vastly outnumbered and it's only a matter of time, they think.

The Viet Cong allow the territorials to walk about three clicks down the road before they pounce and shoot the shit out of them. Those who survive hot-foot it back to the battalion, frightened and embarrassed, and soon they're manning the bunkers and going at it hell for leather. The next day the Viet Cong mount an all-out attack and after a pretty fierce battle they are sent packing.

I mentioned before how you never know who the enemy is. He can be right there amongst you, serving you a Coke or offering to polish your boots in the hotel foyer in Saigon. There is the true story of Bluey Stewart who runs the platoon commander's course for the Ranger battalions over at Duc My. It's called the Jungle, Swamp & Mountain School and he's very good at what he does.

Anyway, Bluey's got forty Ranger lieutenants there and he's putting them through their paces, each student acting out a turn as platoon commander and learning how to respond, with Bluey close behind, watching, correcting and getting them up to scratch. He's eating with them, sharing a hutchie (tent) and he knows the lingo so they're all great mates.

Finally it comes to graduation day when the soldiers parade and get their passing-out certificates. It's an occasion the young Ranger officers take very seriously and in which they take great pride. Bluey goes down to his letter box first thing in the morning and finds a note from one of the graduates, thanking him for the great course and apologising profusely that he can't attend the passing-out parade and ceremony but he's been urgently recalled to his Viet Cong unit.

There's another apparently true story of a Yank adviser at Hiep Khanh, only difference is that he received a letter from the whole company, thanking him for the course and regretting that they had to go under the wire as the Viet Cong needed them up north a bit to pass on their knowledge as instructors.

Of course, I don't know any of this at the time. What I do know is that I've been in the country five minutes and haven't even unpacked my suitcase and I'm off to war with a company of indigenous mountain people who've had little training or operational experience. That I'm under the command of a Yank captain who's from 29 Palms, a military base in Northern California that's so dry it's only got twenty-nine palm trees. I think about how I was after three months' basic training and the answer I tell myself is that there would have been no way I could have gone into the jungle as an effective soldier. These blokes haven't done anything like three months.

I get to the Da Nang airstrip and the whole place is buzzing. My company of Montagnard soldiers in various states of preparedness are being bundled into UH-1B helicopters. There's an American airforce sergeant supervising their loading and he's pushing them in like sardines in a can, yelling and cussing, and I'm positive he's overloading the chopper, pushing them in one side and they're falling out the other.

I find Captain Jones, who turns out to be a big black bloke, very white teeth, or maybe it's just because his face is very dark.

I salute him, and he responds properly, then says 'Combustible Jones', sticking out a hand big as a West Indian fast bowler's.

'Mole Maloney.' I'm relieved to see he's a US Special Forces officer. Whether he's jungle-trained or not, he'll be a damn good soldier.

He grins. 'Some day I'll tell you how I got my name if you'll tell me how you got yours, Warrant Officer. Meanwhile, let's get the show on the road, hey, brother Mole.'

He tells me the first three choppers are my responsibility, my platoon, he'll follow in one of the six others flying out. He's looking a bit harassed, but then I guess so am I. I'm wearing US combat greens and equipment and I'm equipped with an M16. I'm not too fussed, it's a good rifle and I've fired one before. I guess when you know how to shoot, it's only a question of adapting, making minor adjustments.

I'm jammed into a chopper so tight I can't get my arms loose from my sides and the whole place has got this smell of fish that's bloody overwhelming. Later I'll learn it's the fish sauce *nuoc mam*, which the Vietnamese use on everything they eat.

The chopper gains altitude and fortunately I can see out and there's a strip of beach bordering the blue ocean, then the rice paddy fields glistening in the sun, stretching inwards forever. We turn slightly and start to fly towards the backdrop of a great green mountain range. In flight, with the air coming in, the smell of fish sauce all but disappears. I think to myself, bloody good thing the Viet Cong also use the stuff or they'd be able to smell us a mile before they reach us. I also wonder if a white bloke might not smell an ambush before he's caught in one.

Soon the mountains loom larger as we approach. Now, with nothing much to do but wait for the landing, the true absurdity of my situation hits me, I'm in an overloaded helicopter with troops I haven't even met, much less trained, going in to fight a battle I know bugger-all about. No briefing, no knowledge of the country or terrain, can't speak to my troops as there's no interpreter, or if there is, he's in one of the other helicopters and I haven't met him yet.

A radio-set handpiece is thrust at me by a brown arm pushed between soldiers' bodies. 'Lancer, this is Knife Edge, do you hear me, over?' It is Combustible Jones speaking from one of the following helicopters. He's got a slow drawling voice like he's got all the time in the world, but I realise that's just how he talks because he was the same at Da Nang airstrip.

'Lancer, loud and clear, over.'

Jones tells me the situation on the ground has worsened. There are quite a few casualties, including one of the two US Special Forces advisers, which is the one they know about. The other Special Forces adviser with the company is missing and that's just about the ball game, there ain't no others and the troops appear to have damn all leadership among themselves. As I'm first to land, I'm in charge the moment I hit the ground until he gets there. I confirm: 'Lancer, Roger, out.' I tell myself I'd rather be in charge than taking directions from an officer who's never seen the jungle. Though, of course, I don't know this for sure. Weeks later, we're having a beer and he tells me how he got his name.

It seems Combustible Jones was born in Chicago, in New Town, it is a black part of town. His daddy's done the deed and left, and his pregnant mother is living in one room with a single-bar heater in the middle of a Chicago winter, which I gather is pretty awesome. When she's about eight months pregnant, she wakes up in the middle of the night to find the bedclothes alight. She's resourceful enough to get the fire under control, whereupon she goes down on her knees to thank the Lord for her deliverance. But the shock is a bit much and the baby starts coming and a neighbour calls the ambulance and she gets her true deliverance in the ambulance. Ever after, his mother insists, the Lord told her to name her son 'Elijah Combustible Jones'. The 'Elijah' is because of the burning bush in the Bible and the 'Combustible', because of her personal burning bed which God woke her up in time to save her life and her baby's. I've got to admit, it's a much better story than me being called Mole.

Now the door gunner sitting close to me with his machine gun sticking out of the helicopter hands me his earphones and shouts up that the pilot wants a word.

'Eight o'clock your side, two Vietnamese Air Force A-1 Skyraiders, looks like they're going in to attack the spurline, can you see them?'

I look down and see the aircraft swoop through an iridescent stream of green tracer bullets coming up from the jungle to meet them. Then, in front of my eyes, the jungle erupts in bright flashes and billowing smoke as bombs explode. I watch as the two aircraft pull up and turn slightly to line up for another run over the target. This time I can't quite believe what I see, a great fireball engulfs the jungle. I've never seen it in action but I know instantly it's napalm, a mixture of petrol and some sort of jellying agent. We've been briefed on napalm, it burns with the same heat as a Red Steer in a bushfire, over 3500 degrees F. It will instantly kill anyone exposed to it, even if they're in underground bunkers. If the bunkers are under the fireball, they'll be asphyxiated. I can't believe how much it looks like the fireball I saw rise out of the eucalyptus growth, the day John Crowe and Whacka Morrissey died.

The pilot then draws my attention to a helicopter taking off from a clearing about half a click from the enemy position, 'That's the dustoff taking out our wounded,' he explains. Then says, 'We're going in to land. Good luck.' I hand the earphones back to the door gunner, thinking this time, Mole Maloney, you're going to need all the luck you've ever had bundled up into one. I can't even take the spoon out of the sink before the tap is turned on because the tap's already running and the spoon's there and the shit is hitting the fan overtime, if that's not mixing my metaphors.

We arrive over the clearing, or LZ as it is known in army parlance, and quickly descend. The downdraft from the chopper blades flattens the grass and stirs up the dust. The noses of the choppers rise slightly as they no longer move forward although the skids barely touch the ground. It's standard practice for the pilots to keep the blades whirring at a speed so they can take off instantly should the need arise.

The troops secure their hats in their webbing or under their shirts. This is because otherwise the updraught would suck them off their heads into the rotors. With the dust blinding us, we jump and make for the edge of the clearing. There's a mighty explosion not too far off but I can't see anything because of the trees.

The Hueys totter for a moment as they build up power and then rise into the air to an even bigger cloud of dust. It's amazing how quickly a chopper can empty its load and be off, they're gone before you can scratch your bum, banking away against the trees, engines screaming for quick altitude.

Then the handset is thrust into my hands again. 'This is Knife Edge, over.'

'Lancer, over,' I reply.

'That explosion you no doubt heard, that's a mortar bomb landed four hundred yards to your south-east. It's coming from the valley and it looks like it's targeting the LZ. We'll watch for the primary and organise an air strike. Meanwhile the pilot says no more choppers to land. You're on your ownsome so don't be lonesome, over,' Combustible says.

'Lancer, Roger, out,' I reply, short and sweet, there ain't nothing clever I can think to say and I don't have time to shit my pants.

Another mortar round lands, but it's a little further away, which is a good sign. With the choppers gone, the enemy may have lost their line to the target. Maybe I'll have a few minutes to organise things. I look around me, there's bunches of Vietnamese Civil Irregulars huddled around the LZ with no sign of anyone in command. I speak almost no Vietnamese, only the very little we've learned in training back in Oz and I'm hoping someone speaks a bit of English.

'Who's in command?' I shout. 'Who's senior?' The faces stare blankly back at me. Then a soldier comes up to me. 'Me Hong, in-ter-plet–ta!' He grabs me by the shirt and I can see he's panicking. '*Trung si, trung si*! Uc Da Loi *dai uy* maybe dead,' he points down the ridge.

I get the 'maybe dead' bit and I reckon he's not going to be saying it for one of his own kind, he must mean the other US Special Forces adviser, the Australian.

He confirms this, 'Captain!' and he points again down the ridge.

Then I'm saved. One of the Montagnard soldiers from my own platoon comes up and he speaks a bit of English, maybe not a lot more than the overexcited Hong, but he's calmer and more importantly he's the platoon commander. I talk to him and he seems to understand, nodding his head. I tell him we're going in to reconnoitre the battle area and try to recover the 'maybe dead' Special Forces adviser.

He looks doubtful, but translates this and immediately there's a great deal of yapping going on. My platoon has been talking to the gaggle of dispirited Vietnamese Irregulars waiting around the clearing. Finally the platoon commander turns back to me.

'No go. Viet Minh, Viet Minh,' he points down the ridgeline. 'Velly bad! Helicopter bring more soldier, we go, Trung si.'

I know what he means by Viet Minh. It is their name for the regular troops of the North Vietnamese Army. These are not your local Viet Cong in their black pyjamas and light weapons who are down at the ridgeline, it is the Viet Minh, the legendary troops of Ho Chi Minh, who whipped the best the French could muster, including the Foreign Legion, at the Battle of Dien Bien Phu.

I shake my head and indicate that we're going, like it or not, to pick up their gear. The enemy have been driven back with the napalm and the bombing, but they'll be back to do their own reconnaissance, so we don't have a lot of time. I order them again and nobody moves. So much for my forceful leadership. There's no way they'll move till the rest of the company lands.

I can't think what else to do, but I feel like shooting the lot of them, do the job for the enemy. So I use a few choice words that would land me on my back if I said them to any Australian. Then I walk over to the medical orderly and take a first-aid kit. I move out alone and see the platoon commander is following, about twenty paces behind me. But he's on his own and his men haven't been persuaded to follow him.

I enter the jungle and almost immediately come up to a group of Vietnamese soldiers still manning a 30 cal machine gun that is pointing directly down the ridge. I indicate that I'm going in and I want them to watch for my return. They look at me blankly, and then the platoon commander, who must have understood, comes up and explains and they nod their heads, indicating, I hope, that they know what it is I want them to do. I walk on, then turn to see where my platoon commander is. He's still standing with the machine-gunners and drops his head, avoiding my eyes. I'm learning this game fast.

So there I am, heading down the ridgeline, my own forward scout. It doesn't take a genius to read the battlefield, the telltale signs are there for all to see. I think how different it would be with a jungle-ready Aussie company. Here's the track made by the company snaking along single file, then the broken stems and fallen leaves verifying the progress they've made. After that, on either side of the track, are all the signs of a hasty retreat; vegetation trampled by feet in a panic, foliage indicating the backwards direction of the retreat, though it's more like running away, there's no apparent design, these are soldiers moving out of order, every man for himself.

A while further on I see where one platoon has suddenly broken off and turned sharply to the left, that will be a left hook to attack the enemy's flank. Moments later, I see where the rear elements of the forward platoon have gone to ground. It will not be far to where the forward troops have engaged the enemy.

I sense that there's a clearing ahead, I don't know how I know, it's something to do with the light. So I prop and wait on a bit, there's no sound, that's unusual, then I pick up the scent of burning tyres. I've only read about it, but that's what napalm is supposed to smell like afterwards. The clearing, if there is one, would be well before where the napalm hit, or the smell would be stronger. I move forward, pausing with each step to listen, then I see the change in the intensity of the light, which must be the clearing. Now there's piles of spent cartridges everywhere though no sign of the enemy. The air strike and the napalm have driven the enemy back, caused them to withdraw from the immediate area, but I'd be very surprised, with us on the run, if they don't come back soon enough.

Then a sound. I'm down on one knee, my M16 to my shoulder, pointing in the direction of the sound, which I now recognise as human. My eyes are straining to see through the undergrowth, trying to adapt to the changing light conditions. Then I see it, the jungle greens are doing what they're supposed to do, concealing the wearer. It's the Australian, our bloke.

I move slowly up to him and kneel down beside him, his wounds are bad but the bleeding has been staunched by shell dressings. He has a broken arm roughly bandaged and wounds to both legs. He is also unconscious but breathing. I learn lesson number two, don't expect the Vietnamese Civil Irregular to carry out a wounded adviser. Even in withdrawal, there is no question that this man would have been taken along in an Australian outfit. Still and all, at least the medical orderly stopped long enough to staunch his blood and tie his arm. I'll find out who he is and get him a commendation.

My first aid is not a strong part of my army knowledge, we all learn it, of course, but you get to depend on the medical orderlies and get on with other things. I struggle to remember what it was about administering morphine, which this bloke is going to need when he comes to. Something to do with head wounds. That's it, never administer morphine unless you have to and *never* if the casualty has a head wound. It's got something to do with masking the condition and leading to a misdiagnosis when the man reaches a hospital. Too bad about the pain, eh? I think briefly of Tommy and how he must have felt when the butt of Kawakami's rifle smashed his face in.

The first priority seeing the blood is staunched is to splint the arm. I cast about for a stick. Breaking one off would make a noise, so it's a matter of searching. I find one and bandage it securely to the adviser's arm. Then I put the arm in a sling. So far I'm not doing too bad. I wrap more shell dressings around his leg wounds. If I have to move him, I don't want him to lose any more blood.

He half wakes up and tries to move his arm and gasps with the pain, but doesn't pass out again. 'Soldier, it's bloody good to see you,' he whispers. His face is crusted with dried blood and I have to check he hasn't got a bad head wound, I want to give the poor bastard morphine if I can. I take my scarf and wet it from my water bottle and start to clean the blood from his face, from his nose and his scalp where he's fallen. The blood is superficial. That's good, I can give him a shot of morph. I wipe his face as clean as I can and then, I can't believe what I'm looking at, I'm looking straight into Murray Templeton's face.

Jesus Christ, how could this happen? Why didn't I know before? But then how could I have? They wouldn't have told me in Australia and I've been in Vietnam less than twenty-four hours. The shock is too much for me, what with what's happened in the last few hours and suddenly I know I'm going to throw up. I get up and take a few paces and vomit. I can leave Murray Templeton where I found him, nobody will ever know. I'll simply return to my troops. Shrug my shoulders, I don't even have to explain anything to them.

I'm ashamed, dead ashamed the thought occurs to me. Of course, it's not on. Never was. Fate has presented me with the perfect murder, the perfect revenge for what he did to my sister, my precious Sarah. I tell myself the bastard's a coward, the way he wouldn't face up to things and ran away. I even try to tell myself I've got a right to walk away, let him die without me laying a hand on him. It's all bullshit that's going on in my mind because it can't happen. I'm bound in duty to the army brotherhood. I have no choice. I have to save him. Or I have to try, give it my best shot, even if I have to give my own life in the attempt.

Then I hear a stick breaking. Fuck, what was that? Just the tiny snap more than a hundred yards away brings me out of my shock. The sound came from the direction of the enemy. I was right, they've come back, it's their reconnaissance patrol returning. I've just about finished cleaning Murray Templeton's face and head when he regains consciousness. I clamp my hand over his mouth, he's in great pain and he could call out, give us away. He grimaces but remains silent as I remove my hand, poor bugger, but he's holding the pain in. My hand over his mouth alerted him that we're in danger.

I reach into the first-aid tin and take out what I've always thought looked like an artist's tube of paint, though I know what it is. The needle is protected by the plastic cap screwed into the top. I've done this only once in practice nearly a year ago and I'm trying to remember the procedure. Inserted down the needle's hollow stem is a piece of wire of the tiniest diameter. I'm supposed to pull that out, or do I press it? Press it, I think. If I get it wrong there isn't another one. I press down on the wire and the seal breaks on the lead tube. I pull the wire out and press gently on the tube and the needle fills with morphine, a tiny drop escaping from the end. 'Think, think,' I urge myself, 'where is the best vein?' Then I remember, if there's too much blood lost, the veins are hard to find, they've collapsed. Then another stick cracks, this time closer, maybe eighty yards. I tie a piece of bandage just above the elbow of Murray Templeton's good arm, making a tourniquet. He's too weak to make a fist to pump the blood into one of the bigger veins behind his wrist. Morphine can be injected into muscle but its effect is considerably delayed as it tries to get into the bloodstream. I can see a vein, still blue behind his wrist, the big veins I seem to remember are not always the certainties but I have to take a chance. My luck holds, the needle glides in at a shallow angle and instantly the morphine colours red as the blood pumps into the plastic needle. I squeeze the tube slow as I can and the liquid in the needle clears and the morphine enters Templeton's body.

I wait, anxious to see what happens. I've never seen this in real life. Suddenly a smile crosses Murray's face, not a smile really, just relief flooding his face. Thank Christ for that. Now he'll stay *stumm*.

I can hear legs brushing against the foliage and twigs breaking. Then a lowered human voice. Then two. The enemy have stopped twenty yards away.

I wonder if I can catch them by surprise and whether I can take them out. But a recce patrol will probably be of section strength and include a machine gun, so I can't really take them on. If I try to drag Murray Templeton, they'll hear us. If I pick him up, they'll see me and I'll be helpless to defend myself. My mind is in turmoil. There's no chance now of both of us getting out of this. Maybe on my own. I've done the best I can for him. Taken him out of his pain. What more can I do? I've got a right to try and escape. In fact, it's my duty. But in my mind's eye I see Tommy kissing The Gold-Toothed-Shin-Kicking-Bastard's boots, begging for the lives of his mates, knowing they'll kill him. I have to stay. Fuck! I've been in active combat three hours and I'm going to die. All that training, and I'm dead meat the moment I step into a jungle where there's a fair-dinkum stoush going on.

I look up, there's a big tree, not as big as the Maloney tree, but big, buttresses stretching fifteen feet, splayed out like toes gripping the earth, their walls four or five feet above the ground. I can't believe my eyes. It's a big buttress tree, just like the Mengarris, the big tree at Sandakan. It must be some sort of sign or am I just bullshitting myself, clutching at straws trying to make my own luck?

Then it happens. Just like Tommy said it happened that first day when they discovered they were going to build an airport at Sandakan. The heavens opened. That's the whole point about tropical rain, there's no warning, it's all or nothing, a deluge coming down in seconds. It buckets down so that you'd have to scream hard to be heard as the water crashes into the vegetation. If a shot went off, you wouldn't know where it was coming from and it's impossible to see more than ten yards. It's my chance to escape if I can carry Murray Templeton.

I get up and hoist him onto my shoulders, I can't believe my luck. I move forward about twenty paces when my foot goes into a hole and I crash down and I spill Murray Templeton. Christ, I hope the morphine's working, though luckily he falls fairly softly. But I realise I've done my ankle. I try to walk on it, but I collapse, I'm history. Somehow I manage to grab a hold of him and drag him along the ground to the big tree and shove him between two thick buttresses with walls on either side about five feet off the ground. Then I crawl in beside him and strap my ankle as tight as I can.

It rains for half an hour and stops as suddenly as it started, just like Tommy said it did that day at Sandakan when they were cutting a path to where the aerodrome was going to be. Suddenly there's silence, the odd drip, drip, drip of water splashing off the bigger leaves. I hear voices again. I take my rifle and limp around the buttress and take a look. It's the enemy, four of them, they're taking off their waterproof groundsheets and shaking themselves like dogs. They're in NVA uniform and carrying AK47s and are preparing to continue their reconnaissance. Four soldiers doesn't mean there ain't more, I'd expect a recce patrol to have a few more, including a machine-gunner.

I try to think, keep my wits about me. This is not a target to be taken out with a burst of automatic fire; automatic fire makes the rifle jump and it takes too much time to re-aim. I'm a good shot, I don't like to say it, but I'm close to the best in the battalion. The task now is to fire with complete finesse. Four beautifully aimed shots so fast that the enemy soldiers don't have time to react. I've done it hundreds of times with rabbits, four bunnies going like the clappers of hell for their burrows and *bang, bang, bang, bang*. Tommy would laugh and say, 'You done good, all four good shots.'

But these Nogs are not bunnies, they're elite fighting soldiers, trained to react quickly and fire back. They'll start moving any second now and then I'll lose my chance. I slip the catch on my M16 to single shot. I become calm, visualisation is everything when you're going for this kind of multiple shooting. The universe recedes, it's just me and the rifle and the four chests in front of me crossed diagonally with canvas magazine pouches.

One gone, he topples backwards, not even a sound. Two gone, he didn't even have time to move. Three looks surprised but his brain doesn't work fast enough as he's hit. The fourth is on his way down to take cover as I readjust my aim slightly and he spins as the bullets knock him off his feet.

There is silence for a moment then a machine gun opens up. There's two or three soldiers left, which is what I supposed, and they're moving to get a better shot at me. I return fire. There's tracer from the machine gun whizzing above my head, knocking chunks out of the tree and getting closer, more accurate.

I reckon with only three of them I can hold them off for a while, but it's a machine gun against a rifle and the odds don't stack up, three to one and the machine gun, it's only a matter of time.

Then I hear more rifles firing. Shit, that's it, there's more of the bastards coming. At least I've seen a bit of action before I die, I think. But it's not the enemy, it's the Montagnard. The rest of the choppers must have come in and, with the whole company together, the Montagnard have been persuaded to head down the ridge. Then I hear Combustible Jones calling out through the gunfire, 'If you is there, don't despair, I've come to save your soul, brother Mole!'

Almost at once the enemy machine gun goes silent, they've taken it out. I'm pretty whacked, and shaking like a leaf after the adrenalin is out of my system. But as they carry us out, I can't help thinking what Nancy's going to say when I tell her the story of Murray Templeton's rescue.

She won't say anything, of course, because she'll know in her heart that I've done the right thing. But they'll probably give me some sort of commendation. The army's pretty big on pieces of paper. Suddenly I know exactly what she'll do. She'll tear the bottoms-wiping certificate they give me down the centre and then into four pieces, stick them into an envelope and send it by registered letter to Mr & Mrs Philip Templeton. As Nancy says, 'If you wait long enough it all comes round, the good and the bad.'

EPILOGUE

1989–1999

I recall the day in 1989 when the phone rang for two reasons. I was marking my first set of mid-term papers at my new university. The writing standard of the first-year students wasn't exactly blistering and I recall wondering whether I had done the right thing leaving America. The second reason was that the weather outside was blowing a gale and had been doing so for three days.

I picked the phone up with some impatience, it hadn't stopped ringing all day. 'Hello?'

'Michael Proctor here, Professor Lessing. Come over right away, we've got a bit of a crisis on.' It was the deputy vice-chancellor being his usual abrupt self. No first name, no initial greeting, no polite request, nothing except a short, sharp instruction that just naturally sounded as though it contained a liberal dose of invective as a part of its hidden meaning. Without waiting for a reply from me, I heard the clatter of the receiver being replaced.

A visit to Mike Proctor was the last thing I needed on a day like this one. You sometimes wonder where some men learn their manners or what it is in their childhood that makes them so bloody rude as adults. I'd known him at Edinburgh, though not well enough to call him a friend, if indeed he had any friends. He'd been in part instrumental in recruiting me to my new position, so I suppose I was under some sort of obligation.

His office was an eight-minute walk across the campus, normally nothing to be concerned about except for the gale outside. So, cursing the man under my breath, I put on my raincoat. 'Must get a new raincoat,' I reminded myself. I'd been reminding myself to get a new raincoat every time it'd rained for the past ten years. My raincoat was never exactly smart or, for that matter, ever new. It had been bequeathed to me second-hand when I'd arrived in England from Australia twenty-eight years ago. Too big for me then and still was. I recall being embarrassed that I had to roll up the sleeves and that the hem came down almost to my ankles in a city where the miniskirt was becoming all the rage.

Still, in a country where the rainy days outnumber the ones that contain a modicum of sunlight, it was an essential item and after a while it didn't seem to matter. The raincoat was a discard back then and I dare say even a pervert would turn his nose up at it now. I'll go into the city to David Jones and get a new one, a posh one, maybe an Aquascutum, to make up for all the shabby years, but I knew I was kidding myself, and the next time I needed to wear a raincoat I'd be going through the same silly litany whilst pushing my arms through the broken lining of this one.

Though there aren't that many of them, I was discovering that a foul day in Sydney could be just as bad as a miserable one in London or Santa Monica, California, for that matter. Fighting the weather, I was annoyed with myself for not showing my independence with the deputy vice-chancellor by delaying my departure for at least fifteen or twenty minutes before venturing out into this windblown, rain-torn, miserable dog's day afternoon.

'You're weak, that's what you are, too willing to please everyone, time you stood up for yourself, you let people like Mike Proctor walk all over you.' I knew this wasn't true, but I was feeling sorry for myself. We're all allowed occasionally to indulge in that sort of specious analysis, particularly if one is a psychiatrist and so can dismiss it as a perfectly normal bout of self-castigation, positive proof that, unlike most of your profession, you are still perfectly normal.

Perhaps I should explain myself. I took my initial medical degree at Edinburgh and then my postgraduate training at the Maudsley in London, where I did my thesis on the effects of the concentration-camp experiences of victims of the Holocaust. Here I received tuition on desensitisation programs and relaxation therapy.

After that I spent eight years as a research fellow at Sepulveda Veterans Administration Hospital in West Los Angeles near Santa Monica. In conjunction with my work at the hospital, I was an assistant professor at UCLA, which has its campus practically next door and where I completed my doctorate. My patients at first were soldiers returning from Vietnam. Treatment, which included counselling, consisted mostly of group therapy and training in relaxation with some form of medication added, the most popular being Valium.

Then later, when Vietnam veterans started being admitted with unexpected complications, we realised that we needed to develop new forms of treatment and that a great deal of research was required in the trauma area. We simply did not understand much of what appeared to be happening with these post-war patients. Though I must say the US government was less than interested in our gaining any further knowledge into what would become known as PTSD or Post-traumatic Stress Disorder. The grants that enabled us to continue researching had essentially come from private sources and from the university itself.

The offer of a full professorship meant I could come home, back to Australia, after many years abroad. The States had seen my marriage come and go with all the bitter recriminations and acrimony not unusual in a man who had been badly spoilt by a doting and interfering mother and a family loath to part with a cent in a divorce settlement, even though Californian law allowed for me to receive half of our joint assets.

My desire was to continue to work in the same field, that is in the new area of Post-traumatic Stress Disorder and in particular with Vietnam War veterans. Australia had participated in the Vietnam War and so I was anxious to continue my research here amongst my own people. I quickly enough discovered that the Australian government's attitude to the problems experienced by Vietnam veterans, like that of the US, could best be described as one of white-hot apathy.

Even the RSL was rubbishing the symptoms we were increasingly beginning to see in outpatients. They called the vets 'a bunch of whingers who never fought in a proper war'. As well, the students in my lectures would constantly question me. Their attitude to Vietnam and its post-war effects, which they'd largely learned from the media and the movies, was that Vietnam veterans were baby-killers. The famous picture of the little girl torched by napalm running down the road had fixed this notion in their minds and they'd transferred it to every Vietnam veteran. Public sympathy hardly existed, the vets were seen as an embarrassment, almost un-Australian.

I tapped on Proctor's door, only to hear a single 'Come!'

'Your usual charming self, I see, Deputy Vice-chancellor.' I was determined to start with the advantage this time around. I hung my coat on the stand next to the door.

He didn't appear to hear the gibe, looked up and said again, 'We've got a crisis.'

'Yes, so you said on the phone.'

'One of my senior lecturers has walked out in the middle of a lecture and handed in his resignation. Sit down, Professor,' he pointed in the direction of a well-worn, comfortable-looking leather couch and its matching club chair, the leather rubbed dull at its arms from constant use. Both the couch and the chair contrasted strangely with the aluminium and glass office interior with its battleship-grey carpet and strong sense of indifferent government architecture. It was as if a couple of bushies from the country had happened into the city for a day wearing their working clothes. I chose to sit in the old chair, it seemed a less female thing to do.

'I imagine that's happened before, it's not unusual in academic institutions,' I replied.

'Of course, but not with this man. He's one of the most popular lecturers at the university. His lectures are always packed. You're right, some academics just wear out, but not this chap, he loves his job, he's popular with the faculty, students love him and he's active on a number of the university committees and his papers are widely respected.'

'I'm not sure I know what you expect me to do as a clinical psychiatrist.'

'Well, you're a specialist in trauma, aren't you? That's the fancy name they're giving to a bit of stress these days, isn't it?'

I don't bite. 'Depends on what caused it. Stress and Post-traumatic Stress Disorder are not the same thing. My clinical work is mostly in PTSD. Your lecturer may, as you've said, be under a great deal of stress and needs a break because it's all become rather too much for him. There are others on campus who might do a better job with him than me.'

'He's been working pretty hard. That's probably it.'

'Has he shown any previous incidents of erratic behaviour?'

'On the contrary, he's a pretty easygoing sort of chap. Relaxed. As I said, he's a charismatic teacher and a well-liked member of the faculty. Always seems to be in complete control.'

'Always?' I didn't like the sound of this affirmation. People who are always in control are, well, to put it simply, seldom in control.

'Yes, very together sort of chap. I've already told you that.'

'Married?'

'No, he's a bachelor.'

'Homosexual?'

'Not that I know, certainly doesn't give that impression.'

'Any past drinking problems?'

Proctor shrugged. 'Nothing unusual, he likes an occasional drink like most of us, though I've never seen him under the weather. Now I want you to have a word with him, get to the bottom of this incident. Get him to withdraw his resignation. A quiet chat is all I think will be necessary.'

'If, in your opinion, that's all he needs, why haven't you talked to him yourself?'

'I have, woman!' he roared, annoyed at my persistent questioning. 'He wasn't very responsive. I suggested he calm down and then come and see me again. But then I thought of you. You know, a softer touch.'

'You mean someone who doesn't go at things with a sledge hammer?'

He looked surprised but said nothing, it was one infinitely small blow for the female of the species. 'Has he always been an academic?'

'Interesting you should ask that. No, as a matter of fact he spent part of his working life in the army, permanent army that is. Quite a remarkable story, he rose from the ranks, all the way from private to lieutenant colonel in the Army Reserve. Everything about this fellow is fairly spectacular. He attended Macquarie University on a military scholarship after returning from Vietnam. Brilliant student, they had to get permission to let him submit for his doctorate in only three years, part-time.'

'Vietnam? Why didn't you say so?' I was suddenly interested.

'Oh, is it important? He doesn't talk about it much. It's well into his past by now, I should think.'

'Is he willing to accept help, treatment?'

Michael Proctor had pulled back in his chair, tilting his chin. 'Treatment? Oh, I'm not sure it's as bad as that! Help, yes, I'm sure he'd be willing to have a talk with you. That's why I called you in. I'm told you're good at your job. I'd be surprised if you don't get to the bottom of this fairly quickly, we certainly don't want to lose him.'

I ignored the subtle sexism of his remarks. What was the point? The Mike Proctors of this world have hides like a rhinoceros. 'He'll have to agree to see me and that might not prove to be as easy as you think.'

Mike Proctor raised one bushy eyebrow, his expression clearly indicating I was making much too much of the situation. 'I'm sure you'll manage it, Professor.' He had plainly completed what he had to say to me and wished me to leave. Picking up his fountain pen, he continued working at his desk.

'And how might I contact this man, whatever his name is?'

He looked up, impatient. 'Well, naturally I'll arrange that and give you a call.'

'And his name?'

'I'd rather call him first, reputations may be at stake. Loose lips sink ships.'

It was a stupid remark, the campus would have been full of the rumour of the lecturer's walk out and resignation. A university, even a new one, is simply an advanced high school. People don't basically change and the gossips would be having a field day. A couple of phone calls would have revealed his identity. It wasn't worth pursuing. The Vietnam veteran would either agree to an initial interview or stick to his macho image and refuse. If he was like most Vietnam vets, he'd be confused, ashamed and somewhat bitter, thinking himself weak if he asked for help.

However, in this instance, this was not the case. Or if it was, the veteran had overcome his neurosis and was desperate enough to want to talk to someone.

Two days later I met Dr Mole Maloney, a noted expert in environmental studies. What began that day between us was to continue for years, in fact, in some respects, it continues to this day.

It is not usual practice for a patient's notes to be made available but, as a fellow academic, Dr Maloney has agreed to allow me to publish them in a paper, on the basis that they represent a clear insight into the condition of Post-traumatic Stress Disorder as experienced by an individual.

For the purposes of this paper I have eliminated my own analysis. Dr Maloney's verbatim comments during the period of six years while under analysis were all recorded and transcribed. I believe they testify to his mind-set and need very little comment from his analyst. They stand as an epitome of the PTSD condition. They include, of course, not only the narrative yet to come in this final paper but all that has gone before, some 1160 pages of typed notes in his own voice with only some punctuation added to emphasise meaning.

The clinical reason for these copious background notes is easily explained. Dr Maloney's condition, though primarily a result of the time he served in Vietnam, is not its sole cause. Dr Maloney's father substitute, Tommy Maloney, was himself deeply traumatised as a result of being a POW in Borneo. We now know that suicide levels go up in veterans as they become older, so that Tommy's eventual suicide after showing Mole the big tree is entirely consistent with clinical experience.

We now begin to know the extent to which the children of PTSD sufferers are affected by all the complex issues that arise in the family. Tommy's condition would have had a profound effect on all his children, but in particular on the young Mole Maloney who spent the most time with him. Although not recognised until recently, PTSD has been clearly present after every war in which Australians have participated, often resulting in deep trauma in subsequent family life.

With the returned veteran unable or unwilling because of guilt and fear of rejection to seek help, or even having the ability to admit to his condition, he often resorts to self-medication, with the use of alcohol and, in earlier times, barbiturates and now drugs, legal or otherwise. The result often leads to disastrous consequences for the veteran's family and for the veteran himself. Wives end up living lives of quiet desperation. Unable to unburden themselves, their world becomes one of fear and a sense of deep obligation and is completely determined by the moods, needs and demands of the veteran. Their children suffer and continue to suffer from the results of their father's behaviour. Children often develop a love–hate relationship with him, deeply felt ambivalence. They also feel guilty for resenting, even hating him, a guilt that lasts throughout their lives because in spite of the pain and emotional abuse they continue to love him.

Putting it into lay terms, I believe that Dr Maloney has received a double dose of PTSD. In a great many respects, he could be said to be in an even worse predicament than that of his surrogate father. Although there seems to be some evidence that the notorious 'Mr Baloney', Tommy's father, a veteran of the Boer War, may have manifested many of the same symptoms.

PTSD, shell-shock, combat fatigue or whatever name it has been given in the past, has been going on for a long time. There is even some historical evidence that it was present in the male population after the Peloponnesian Wars in ancient Greece. However, the recent experience of veterans in Vietnam contains an extra ingredient not present in the return of most heroes. It is the first time in history that a population has physically spat on returning veterans as happened on numerous occasions to Vietnam vets. The concept of 'the war hero' always present in a returning army has been rejected by the general population for these returned Vietnam soldiers and, instead, replaced with vilification and a sense of disgust never experienced before by any Australian soldier returning to his homeland.

Returning veterans were psychologically tortured by their own people, who largely came to regard them in a deeply hostile manner. Their subsequent medical and psychiatric problems have been ignored or disparaged, and their rightful place in society as the men who believed they had defended freedom has been denied to them. This has had a deeply negative effect which has exacerbated their sense of alienation from the community at large.

As a matter of possible interest, you will note that as Mole delivers the commentary on his childhood years, 'the narrative voice', while always being delivered by an adult and often containing adult conceits, sometimes shifts in emphasis and syntax into a childlike way of observing the world around him.

Usually this behaviour comes from a greater degree of pathology than PTSD and occurs when a child has been sexually abused or suffered extensively at the hands of a parent or adult, such as being beaten or punished unfairly.

When I first questioned Dr Maloney, he denied any such abusive treatment in childhood. Finally he admitted to several occasions when, as a very small child, Tommy had locked him in the garden shed for several hours. Nancy, his mother, had eventually discovered this and the problem had ceased. However, these episodes, and the extreme fear associated with them, almost forgotten by Mole Maloney, could have triggered the episodes of age regression as seen in his therapy.

In psychiatric terms, this is known simply enough as regression and is an attempt by the subject to dissociate himself from the painful present and to retreat to a place of greater comfort. It is more likely to be the 'shed incidents', when taken in combination with his PTSD, that explain Dr Maloney's inconsistency of voice, both his naivety and sophistication, during some parts of his narrative. Put simply, there are two Maloneys speaking, Dr Maloney and the Mole Maloney still within him, the 'voice' of either can appear at any moment during the commentary.

I have also excluded the logical time sequences and day-by-day routines of Dr Maloney's second and third tour in Vietnam, initially as a warrant officer and later as a captain and company commander. This is because the primary concern to us is his post-Vietnam psychological and medical experience. Though, of course, some of his three Vietnam episodes, known in army vernacular as 'tours', inevitably appear in his own narrative as an explanation of one or another incident of importance to him.

Signed: Professor A. Lessing, MB BS(Edin) FRC Psych. FRANZCP

The continued transcript of Dr Mole Maloney's clinical notes

After my chaotic introduction to Vietnam, I was sent to Tran Xa outpost to join US Special Detachment A115. While I was in Tran Xa, the Yank build-up started. Now the US were sending fighting units as well as advisers, and Australia had contributed an infantry battalion and planned to follow. Towards the end of my year-long tour, I found myself relieving besieged outposts with the Montagnard Mobile Strike Force. By this time, Combustible Jones had been sent home in a body bag and I'd had about enough of the Viet Cong, the Vietnamese National Army, the South Vietnamese Irregulars and even my own Montagnard to last me a lifetime.

Then I was posted back to the Jungle Training Centre at Canungra in Queensland to help train the increasing flow of soldiers to the war. It was a tough course. Soldiers returning from Vietnam sometimes remarked only half jokingly that they didn't know if they feared most another tour in Vietnam or another course at Canungra. After almost a year there, I was posted back to Vietnam, this time replacing a 6RAR Company Sergeant Major, or CSM, who'd been evacuated home sick.

This was a different Vietnam to the one where I was always dependent on local troops with a varying sense of loyalty to the cause of peace in the free world. The Australians were a different kettle of fish altogether, better trained, well motivated, and quick to learn on the job and acquitted themselves with distinction in Vietnam. There is no question that they were the best-trained troops in Vietnam and the NVA, the highly professional North Vietnamese army, grew to fear and respect them to a very high degree.

I don't want to go into my second tour of Vietnam, suffice to say I felt okay most of the time but there were periods when I couldn't believe I wasn't coming home at the end of it in a black body bag. At times, life had become somewhat meaningless and I believed myself expendable, which was what was meant by the sign I'd read in the bar at Australia House in Da Nang when I'd first arrived. It was very difficult getting myself through those dark periods but I kept it to myself and did my job.

I returned home with 6RAR and walked into the terminal at Mascot with my carry bag and a bottle of duty-free scotch, a commodity which had increasingly become my constant sleeping companion and often enough my most cherished and dependable friend. I was drinking heavily and was secretly ashamed of it. You'd have thought Tommy would have taught me that particular lesson.

Even the Sydney terminal was like a new experience. I'd forgotten what peacetime looked and felt like, it was all so very different to Saigon with its heat and noise and smell of fish sauce and the constant importuning of the local population.

There were no MPs with rifles and pistols, no anti-rocket grenade screens on the windows, no tanks or concrete revetments containing armed F4 fighter bombers, only the bizarre experience of civilian aircraft, their tails painted in bright colours, big and small, bustling about the airport. Most of all, as we walked across the tarmac, there was no oblong stack of shiny aluminium caskets awaiting the arrival of the C5 Starlifter to freight the fresh killed, that is the grunts who'd died in the past seven days, to destinations where weeping mothers were waiting for them at some lonely small-town airport in the USA with the local Lions or Rotary Club members lined up to pay tribute to a son born and bred in Nowhereville.

We are directed by a corporal from 'the corps of trucks' through a door to a secure area, a large room behind Customs where a captain was waiting to address us.

'Men, you're back in civilisation. If you've brought any weapons with you, please leave them in the amnesty bin, the customs officers are waiting outside and I don't have to tell you what the penalty is for bringing in a concealed weapon.' Then he told us that if we became ill with malaria or venereal disease to go straight to the nearest base hospital. It was suggested that after the two days of R & R in Saigon, it wasn't a good idea to have sex with a waiting wife or girlfriend without using a condom for the first two weeks.

After this bit of a talk, we lined up in front of an army pay clerk to draw our money and receive our leave passes. I received a fistful of money, enough ten-dollar notes to choke a horse and 105 days' accrued leave, three and a half months sitting on my arse thinking about nothing in particular before I had to report back to the army. After Vietnam, it seemed like a lifetime of freedom.

A corporal, wearing Vietnam ribbons, yells at us, 'Okay, you heroes, put your ribbons on before yer go out to meet yer family and friends!'

It wasn't something at the forefront of my mind and it must have taken me a good five minutes to find the two of them at the bottom of my carry bag. The two ribbons were on a bar, the Vietnam Medal and the Vietnamese Campaign Medal. I pinned these clumsily to my breast. I must admit, I glanced down to see if the oak leaf was intact on the Vietnam Medal Ribbon. It indicated that I'd been Mentioned in Despatches, which I'd won on the first tour with the Training Team. I'd received it mainly for when I'd rescued Murray Templeton.

Nancy had been delighted when I told her the story but she wouldn't tear up the Mention in Despatches citation and send it to Mr and Mrs Philip Templeton like I suggested. But she did take the bus into Wangaratta and have a photographer make an exact-sized colour copy of this latest bottoms-wiping certificate, then did as I suggested, tearing the photo into four and mailing it to you know who. Though when Vera 'Big Mouth Saggy Tits' Forbes came around and asked if she could photograph the citation for the *Gazette*, Nancy told her to go to buggery among other things that shouldn't be repeated.

Now here's the lovely thing. I came out of Customs expecting to climb into the green army Bedford bus that the corporal of the 'corps of trucks' told us to look out for and which would take us to Central Station to catch the overnight train to Melbourne. Instead, standing in the arrival lounge, was Nancy, Sarah, Bozo, little Colleen, Templeton, Morrie, Sophie and Mrs Rika Ray. They had this ginormous hand-painted banner which said:

MOLE POWER!

We're soon hugging and kissing. Nancy and Sarah, Sophie and Mrs Rika Ray are having a big bawl, grabbing a hold of each other and Morrie is off on the side doing the same, bawling. Bozo is pumping my hand and little Colleen and Templeton are jumping up and down and pecking me on the cheeks and grabbing me around the waist, I can't believe how much they've both grown.

Then an RSM in full dress uniform comes up to us, 'Sorry about this, Mr Maloney, but you're to report immediately to Colonel Payne at the Education Centre just inside the gates of the Victoria Barracks.'

'Hey, wait on! What about my family?' I protest.

The RSM shakes his head. 'We only have one military vehicle, a Holden, it can take four of them, driver's waiting outside.'

'She'll be right,' Bozo says, 'We've hired a great big Merc, the rest of us will meet you there.' I notice he's put on a bit of weight. 'Oh, Big Jack Donovan sends his best, he'd have come but he's got a police conference on this weekend.'

We get to Victoria Barracks about four in the afternoon and there's a guard of honour standing at the gates.

'We'd better wait, something's happening,' I tell Nancy and Sophie, who take up the back seat, the rest of the mob are in the big black Mercedes following us.

A staff sergeant comes up to the driver. 'Mr Maloney?' he asks. I nod. He instructs the army driver, 'Take the car to the Education Centre and drop the visitors off.'

'There's others following, Staff,' I tell him, 'in a black Mercedes.'

'Righto,' he says, 'Would you mind coming with me, sir?'

Next thing I know I'm being escorted by a guard of honour to a flag pole within Victoria Barracks. The Colonel is waiting for me and he congratulates me in front of my whole family and tells me the Queen has approved the award of the Military Medal for bravery whilst serving in the Training Team in Vietnam.

It turns out that Colonel Murray Templeton has been the moving force behind the recommendation and that the US Army has also made a submission to the Australian Army from US Marine Captain Elijah Combustible Jones. It's dated two weeks before the US Airforce mistakenly dropped napalm on their own troops and Captain Jones was included. Born in flames, died in flames.

All I can say, it's a day of tears, though in the end Nancy says, 'It don't mean Murray Templeton is any less a coward and a little shit for not fronting up for what he done to Sarah!'

But Sarah says, 'Mum, it's the best thing that could have happened. We've got Templeton and we've showed them it's the Maloneys who have the real class in Yankalillee.'

We stayed the night in the Hilton in Sydney at the expense of Crowe Transport, drinking Great Western champagne half the night. Last thing I remember is Mrs Rika Ray saying, 'We are thanking the Lord Vishnu very, very much and we are burning the incense forty days and forty nights and putting some gold leaf on the God for safe deliverance. Only I am asking one thing, why is the Queen of England, Her Most Gracious Majesty with the handsome Prince Philip, not giving our Mole the Victoria Cross?'

I think I passed out on the plush carpet. It had been a bloody long day and I'd been sipping scotch since the 707 Qantas flight left Saigon, twenty-two hours earlier.

I woke up thinking I was back in Nui Dat with the usual hangover and with two days to recover from it before I was back on patrol. I was still in my uniform, lying on the softest bed I can ever remember with Templeton in pink rosebud pyjamas, asleep beside me, sucking her thumb. Later I would learn that the treasured pyjamas bore the **Suckfizzle** label.

The 105 days of freedom pass in a blur. Nothing much has changed in Yankalillee, people greet you in the street as though they'd seen you only yesterday, incurious and complacent. My whole life has been turned upside down, I've been killing people in black pyjamas who are equally determined to kill me and all they could talk about is the weather, the weekend footie results and the price of cattle at the Wodonga saleyards.

I must admit, there wasn't any of the recriminations the blokes who lived in the city copped from the assorted do-gooders and pot-smoking weekend hippies. The bush simply didn't care that much. You were back, safe and sound, have a beer, son.

The nights are beginning to be a difficult time for me, they hold black dreams, night sweats and startled awakenings. I tell myself I must be in control, same old Mole that people know. I've become a secret drinker, not daring to go into the pub but with a bottle of scotch tucked away where I can find it any time I need it. I'm popping Valium and Vietnam seems more real to me than the small town I've lived in all my life.

I return from leave and report to the Eastern Command Personnel Depot at Watsons Bay in Sydney where I'm given a medical and a new posting as Warrant Officer Instructor in the Tactics Wing at the Infantry Centre at Ingleburn. I take to the job like a duck to water and simply love the teaching involved. The one thing I know hasn't changed is that I need to know things. The old Mole, full of questions, is still alive within me.

In November 1967 I see an advertisement in the *Sydney Morning Herald*. It's for a third university that's only been going a year at North Ryde, Macquarie University, where they're offering positions to full or part-time students. I think about it for a while then I come to the conclusion it would be a good way to keep me out of the sergeants' mess where my own bottle of scotch resides under the bar counter. I've bought myself an almost new 1964 Toyota Crown from a sergeant who's been posted to Vietnam and the university is no more than an hour and a half from the barracks, so why not?

I take an accrued stand-down day and visit the university for an interview, my matriculation pass is accepted and the registrar directs me to Professor Alan Voisey, who's the head of the School of Earth Sciences. This is because in my application form I've written under 'Desired Degree': *Something to do with trees and the bush*. The professor is a real good bloke and discusses Geology, Physical Geography and Human Geography. I tell him some of that stuff sounds like just what the doctor ordered and I fill in the appropriate forms and, well, here's hoping.

In the meantime I'm enjoying my instructor's job, I'm training platoon after platoon of kids, half of them permanent army and the others nashos. Some are pretty bright and some pretty green and you hope like hell some of the really bright ones don't go to Vietnam. Which I know isn't the way I should be thinking, they've all got mothers who love them.

I go back home on my Christmas leave and find, like Tommy, I can't talk about my war, even to Nancy and Bozo or Big Jack Donovan, who really wants to know.

Bozo with his right-hand man, Mrs Rika Ray, are going gangbusters with the transport business. They're talking of opening a depot in Wangaratta. They've got four new second-hand trucks and they're flat out over the Christmas period. So I'm grateful when Bozo asks me if I'd like to drive one of them. It means I'm busy and on my own and don't have to talk to people much. I'm getting a bit short-fused too but managing to keep a lid on it most of the time.

On my return to my teaching job, there's a letter waiting for me from Macquarie University, I've been accepted to do a degree. 'Watch out, Sarah, here I come!' I shout out, pleased as punch. Sarah's working as a GP in Yankalillee. Morrie, who is a gynaecologist in Melbourne because Sophie's business has become so successful, visits Sarah once a month and runs a clinic in her practice for pregnant mothers and women with medical problems. Though she could probably afford to live in a better house, Sarah has extended the one in Bell Street and the family, including Bozo, still live together. Bozo reckons he's too busy to be married even though Sarah tells me every girl in town is after him as the big catch.

It's February 1968 and I'm sitting on my bed in the sergeants' quarters, having just returned from the orientation weekend at the university, where I bought some of the textbooks I'm going to require. I am surrounded by these books and my only reaction is a numb feeling. I pick up Stahler's *Introduction to Earth Sciences* and turn to the back page, it's page 1231, fuck, how can anyone learn all this stuff in one year and this is only one book! But the CI (Chief Instructor), who is a lieutenant colonel, likes the idea of one of his instructors doing a university degree and tells me I can have half a day off each week to attend lectures.

It's not all plain sailing though. I have bad insomnia and when I finally go to sleep, the nightmares take over. *It's always pissing down rain in the jungle with Nogs crawling about everywhere, sometimes it's Murray Templeton and sometimes it's me bleeding to death, then,* flash *and it's months later and the napalm hits the village again and again.* I think about seeing a doctor, but I worry that everyone will think me a sheila. Besides, what do I tell the quack? That I'm having bad dreams? Doesn't everyone? So it's carry on, grin and bear it, Dr Scotch will solve the problem. But I figure that if I can't sleep, I might as well use all those extra waking hours studying, so I take on a full-time student's load. I'm gunna try for a full twenty-two credit points. The only time I stop is occasionally to go into Sydney, to Kings Cross, to pick up a girl. Even this little necessity has its moments, there are long periods when even if I wanted to, I can't get it up. Anyway, all the study pays off and I not only get all the credit points but I score As and Bs.

In January 1969, the chief clerk at Ingleburn Barracks calls me to come down to the Admin Block. He tells me he has a posting order. All I can think is, please God, let it be in Sydney so I can finish my degree.

'Which battalion, Chief?' I ask, fearfully.

'You're to be posted to the Long-Term Students' Unallotted List.' He smiles. 'Clever bastard, aren't you, sir?'

I can't believe my ears, because then he adds that I am also to be a full-time student, paid for by the army with full pay, to do the last two years at Macquarie University. I don't even have to attend pay parade, they'll post it to me!

My farewell is held the following Friday at the Happy Hour in the Infantry Centre where the RSM holds court. 'Well, it's time for the hails and farewells,' he announces. 'Today we welcome a new sergeant, Sergeant David Eck. Will you please raise your glasses in a warm welcome to David.' We do as he says. 'Righto, now we have one to farewell, none other than the student, Mole Maloney. This illustrious warrant officer has been despatched from the duty of proper soldiering and as a gentleman of the infantry to have his mind fully bent by the pinkos and supporters of the Vietnam moratorium at Macquarie University. You will all know this is a highly subversive institution where said infantry gentleman will spend the next two years completing his degree.' He stops and looks around at the gathering. 'Now, gentlemen and madams, a full year I have watched this fine soldier work at his own destruction going to that unmentionable place in North Ryde. I wish to go on record now as saying that I did warn him that he was destroying a fine career. What was a possibility is even more than a probability, it is now, I think, an inevitability. The bastards will turn our Mole into a fucking officer!'

I cannot believe the joy of full-time university, though I still can't sleep. The scotch bottle remains my best friend. I need twenty-three credit points for each year but in fact I complete thirty for each of the years. As I've said, when you can't sleep or are afraid of what will happen when you do, you can get through a whole heap of studying, even when half-drunk.

I've always been a bit of a letter writer but now I'm compulsive. I write to Mike in London every week, gathering the news of the family by phone. I'm getting generally more anxious too, which is driving me mad but making me get things done.

Mike's staying in London. He's met a bloke he's living with and says he's really happy. We've all been waiting for it for a long time, his one-night stand with Sally Harris we all knew was a one-off. The bloke's from a posh family, what Mike calls 'County', Eton and Cambridge, and the parents are aristocracy and not one of the poor ones. Mike and his mate, who has a degree from the London School of Economics as well, are starting in business together, Mike the designer and haute couturière, and his partner doing the business side.

He sends me clippings from the fashion magazines every once in a while and it seems him and a young designer called Vivienne Westwood are the up and comers with a big, big future. Sophie is broken-hearted he isn't coming back because she loves Mike, and Nancy isn't too pleased either. The **Suckfizzle** label is now getting to be really big and, even though Mike continues to send the odd kid's design, Sophie has to employ other designers to keep up with demand. Templeton, who is pretty as a picture, goes down to stay with them during school holidays and Sophie uses her as a model when the buyers come in. The kid loves showing off and is a natural extrovert. Sophie has turned out to be a brilliant businesswoman and she and Morrie are going to be very rich, except that she says Mike always owned fifty per cent of the business and always will. She will finance his share of his London business until it starts to make money. She doesn't want Mike to go cap in hand to his partner's relatives.

Well, my course is finished by mid-October and with most of the marks being for essays throughout the year, I pretty much know I've graduated with two double majors and a major. One of the final year subjects taught by Dr Alan Rundle is Land Management, the role of bushfires in shaping and changing the Australian ecology. I don't have to tell you how well I did in that.

With my study finished, I'm told to report to Canungra in Queensland to do the Officer Qualifying Course. I don't have to but I'm sort of into studying and so I agree to do the 'Knife and Forker', which is the name other ranks use for one of their kind doing it. This is because they reckon the main purpose of the course is to teach you how to use a knife and fork properly.

I get my uni results during the course and they're pretty good. I do quite well on the Knife and Forker too and because I've got the Science degree, I'm commissioned as a captain. It seems to be going all right, except for what's happening inside my head. I'm given a posting to Vietnam, which worries me because of the stuff going on in my head. But the posting is adjutant of the Training Team, which I'm told is a desk job at Headquarters, Australian Force Vietnam, Saigon, and well out of the battle, so I reckon it will be all right.

Then Sarah phones, crying. Nancy's real crook and has kidney failure. Sarah explains that she's been taking three Bex powders a day for thirty years and the phenacetin has had an insidious effect which has been chronic for some time but has now reached end-stage kidney failure. Sarah, not sparing the details, says Nancy's had a minor urinary infection and, small as it seems, it's the last straw. 'I've organised a dialysis machine at Albury, but she won't hear of it.'

She tells me what Nancy said: 'I've had enough, darling. Ever since Tommy done himself in, it's not been the same. You're all grown up now and I've got the best family in the whole world. Every one of yiz has achieved something, crawled out from under the rock. The Maloneys are no longer on the bottom rung, we're damn near at the top. Can't ask for more than that, can yer. Now little Colleen's engaged to John Barrington-Stone, she'll be right as rain. It's all done and come out well enough.'

John Barrington-Stone is Mrs Barrington-Stone's nephew. His family also owns a big property near Bright, abutting the Mount Buffalo National Park.

'How long has she got?' I ask Sarah.

'She's going fast,' Sarah says tearfully. 'Can you come please, Mole, she's asked for you? She said you've stickybeaked everything up to now, may as well be there when she goes.'

I get compassionate leave and catch the plane that night to Melbourne. John Barrington-Stone meets me at the airport, he's a nice young fella and he's got a Piper Cherokee and we're in Yankalillee slightly more than an hour later.

We've always thought Nancy would go with a heart attack, because of her weight. Sarah's been trying to get her on a diet for years. When I arrive at Bell Street, Nancy's still conscious and there's a black Holden Special parked outside, a cross painted on its door with flames twisting around the cross. Nancy was right, Father bloody Crosby has got himself a limousine. I wonder if he's just come barging in as usual. If he has, I'll send him on his bike quick-smart, even if it is a car now.

When I walk in, the whole family is there except, of course, for Mike. There's also Morrie and Sophie, Mrs Rika Ray, Big Jack Donovan, Mrs Barrington-Stone and Father Crosby wearing his crook-looking, fire-appliquéd surplice.

Sarah sees me looking aggressively at Father Crosby. 'It's okay, Mole, Mum wanted all of us to be here, Father Crosby comes as a friend.'

'Aye, and that I've been all my life,' says Father Crosby promptly. 'We've had our differences, that I'll admit, but we're both Irish, that's how it should be, a good stoush and then all is forgiven. With Nancy now, I'm sending a warning up to heaven that she's on her way and the Lord will need to be on his toes!'

We all laugh, old enemies are friends at last. Though I wonder if Nancy will be willing to make her confession and take communion.

We're all crowded into the small bedroom. I fight my way through and kiss Nancy on paper-dry lips. She gives me a weak smile and squeezes my hand and I immediately burst into tears. Shit, it's not like me, I've seen scores of people dying, but I can't help it, she's my mum. All I think about is that I hope she's too far gone to notice Father Crosby's fucking appliquéd surplice. Nancy going to heaven with that being the last thing she sees is just not on.

I'm about to ask Father Crosby to take it off but then Nancy speaks. It's not her usual booming voice but it's Nancy, still clear-minded. 'You've all come except Mike and that's not his fault. All the people in this room are my whole life. My whole beautiful life.' She fixes a beady eye on Father Crosby. 'Even you, Father.' Despite ourselves, we grin. Then Nancy looks at me and points to the dresser. 'In the bottom drawer, Mole.' Her voice is fading, 'There's a parcel, bring it here.'

I go to the drawer and there's a brown-paper parcel like all the other ones we'd left dozens of times in people's garbage bins when they'd showed us kindness. It was usually a christening dress when someone in the street was having a baby. This parcel is tied in the traditional Nancy manner with a piece of butcher's twine.

I take it over to Nancy who says I should give it to Father Crosby. Inside is a cotton surplice, made from the finest sea-island cotton. We all gasp as Father Crosby unfolds it. The back has an embroidered gold cross set among a stand of green eucalyptus trees, the trees are on fire, the flames leaping up, high into the sky. It is the most beautiful piece of embroidery I have ever seen.

'Put it on,' Nancy whispers.

Father Crosby removes the surplice he's wearing and replaces it with Nancy's. The silk embroidery catches the light, it is a truly magnificent garment. Nancy closes her eyes, 'Silly old bugger, why didn't you come to me in the first place? Now you look decent, I'll make my confession, make my peace with my Maker.'

'Bless me, Father, for I have sinned,' she begins, then finally says, 'But there's nothing I'm ashamed of doing, nothing I wouldn't do again. I confess to being angry at the Holy Church, but never with you, God. Thanks for a lovely life.'

Her eyes are closed and her lips hardly move as Father Crosby places the wafer on her tongue, the drop of purple wine he offers her runs down the side of her mouth. Nancy, a soft sweet young Nancy, who let Tommy's bag of bones into her compliant, safe body when he came back from the war. The Nancy who was a fierce defender of her children. The Nancy who, single-handed, took on the Church. The Nancy of 'hell hath no fury'. The Nancy who always welcomed Tommy back home no matter what. The Nancy who made us Maloneys crawl out from under the rock. The Nancy who drove a garbage truck and then went home to embroider exquisite baby clothes so her children could grow up to be respectable. The Nancy who taught us to take the spoon out of the sink before turning on the tap. The fearless, uncompromising Nancy. All of them were our mother, and now our mum is dead. The best Maloney of them all is gone from us and we're howling, even Father Crosby.

I don't want to rabbit on, but after Nancy's death the insides of my head becomes even more unmanageable. At least my posting is a desk job.

On the twenty-second of December 1970 at 11 p.m. I catch the 707 back to Saigon. The government has all flights carrying reinforcement troops leave at this late hour to escape the possibility of picketing by the 'Save our Sons' mothers and the anti-war demonstrators. I guess they figured all the good and worthy citizens who make up the demonstrations are safely tucked into their little wooden beds.

Vietnam and Saigon are déjà vu, the heat, the smells, the jabbering, bustling world where sudden death is as common as the Mr Whippy truck outside an Australian school. I fly to Nui Dat, where after a two-week orientation course, I am to return to Saigon to take up my job.

However, arriving in Nui Dat on Christmas Eve, I have the distinction of being made duty officer for Christmas Day. I don't really mind, the other officers deserve a break and, as I don't know any of them, it's nice they can have a drink with their mates and celebrate Christmas Day.

Lunchtime, Christmas Day, I'm having a bite to eat, American turkey with cranberry sauce as well as good old Aussie brown gravy poured over everything, when I hear a burst of rifle fire. As duty officer, I have a look-see. Jumping into a jeep, I go towards where I heard the rifle fire. It's Christmas and there's a lot of grog about and I think some clown has fired his rifle into the air. Probably some grunt on his way home in a day or so. Still, that's not allowed on the base and I'm obliged to do something about it.

I arrive at the Task Force sergeants' mess and I am confronted with a scene of utter horror. A soldier, Private Faraday, has staggered down the road blind drunk and somehow entered the Task Force sergeant's mess and fired a full magazine from his SLR 7.62 mm rifle into the room. Two men are killed and four wounded, one will be a quadriplegic. Both the sergeants killed were due to fly home on Boxing Day, having completed their tour of duty.

I've been in Vietnam less than forty-eight hours. Somewhere, deep within me, I hear myself asking why I've returned, but there's no answer.

I take up my job in Saigon, which, as I've said, has the singular advantage of not being anywhere near a jungle patrol. There are captains doing the hard yards in the boondocks, but, thank bloody Christ, I'm not among them. I've got a cushy job by most standards, I travel throughout South Vietnam visiting our outlying bases, bringing a bit of news, checking they're okay, being a general dogsbody.

In May 1971 I visit a warrant officer who is responsible for a fire-support base at Dang Hoa in the Mekong Delta. I come in by helicopter arriving with a case of VB beer and a box of frozen steaks for a Saturday barbecue, a bit of a treat for the blokes. But as I jump out the helicopter and the box of goodies is handed out, I realise things are not right. In fact, the support base is standing to.

The weather clags in and I am unable to leave and, instead of a friendly visit with old friends, the Viet Cong and the NVA mount a major assault which lasts two days, including them breaching the wire and storming some of our forward weapon pits with bayonets before we can repulse them. Hundreds of them are killed in two days of barbaric fighting, with twelve of our guys also dead. I finally leave on Monday evening on one of the first relief helicopters. I haven't been injured and I've done pretty good with the SLR. Being a good shot has come in real handy, but my nerves are shot. I can't take much more.

As it turns out, there isn't a great deal more to take. The Americans are getting out. I now understand the utter futility of Australia's ten years in Vietnam. It's not a war I can support any longer. Troops are not being replaced, units are downscaled, equipment begins to be sent home and I'm drinking heavily, trying to avoid feeling anything and to keep my nerves under control.

It's late 1971 and I fly to Nui Dat on the final day we abandon the Australian base. The main gates are known by all Australian troops as 'The Pearly Gates' for the obvious reason. Now, stretching from The

Pearly Gates for several kilometres down the road to Baria, is every type of vehicle you can imagine, right down to people pushing wheelbarrows. As the last of the Australians fly out from Luscombe Field, I watch while the Vietnamese, like a swarm of locusts, strip Nui Dat down to the last nail and bolt. Thirty years of fighting have taught them how to survive.

Back home I am posted to the officer training unit at Scheyville. It's a paradox that, now that the bulk of Australia's forces are out of Vietnam, there's a huge increase in volunteer recruiting. Why is that? Buggered if I know. But we're overworked trying to cope, twelve-hour days, seven days a week. I'm sleeping less, drinking more (if that's possible), and I'm no longer known for my good humour.

Then, at the end of 1972, Gough Whitlam is elected the first Labor prime minister in twenty-three years, conscription is abolished and National Servicemen are sent home. The training centre is closed and we're all thinking about finding jobs in civilian life as there's suddenly a surplus of officers in what's become a shrinking army.

I hang on a bit, I reckon I'm in no shape to take on a new life dressed in civvies. I get posted to Randwick Barracks as the staff officer. This posting is best described as supervising ground maintenance, lawn mowing and soldiers' recreation. I know for sure that I am dying.

Well, the *Sydney Morning Herald* once again comes to my rescue. I see an advertisement for a lecturer at the Catholic College of Education. Nancy wouldn't have approved but I get the job. I resign my commission and join the Army Reserve and start a new life as a civilian. Living alone in a small flat is torture but I keep at it. I'm not worth a pinch of shit as a married man, that much I know for sure, so I stay single and occasionally, when the old fella will respond, I visit the girls at the Cross.

But I've already got one pattern I can rely on. I enrol as a part-time student at Sydney University to do my honours and, due to the fact I can also put in an extra working day studying most nights because I can't sleep, I graduate with first-class honours in 1975 as well as maintaining my position at the Catholic College.

What follows is ten years of hiding in the university and State Libraries. In 1977 I complete an MSc in Environmental Science and I'm now teaching part-time at Macquarie University. The hiding in libraries goes on, in 1978 and 1979, I do another MSc, this time it's a Master of Science and Society at the School of History and Philosophy of Science at the University of New South Wales, which is a huge joke. I have become the original misfit, a complete bluff merchant, nice guy on the surface, bag of worms underneath. I'm not living life, I'm acting it out day by day, trying to stay alive.

But I'm not through yet. In 1981 I enrol for a PhD as a part-time student and I complete this in 1984. As a part-time student, it is supposed to take six years and I have to receive special permission from the university senate to submit a thesis.

I am beginning to realise that 'The Wall' as it's becoming known among Vietnam vets is very close. I've also been putting a lot of time into the Army Reserve, anchoring myself with something I know. Anyway, I'm promoted to lieutenant colonel. I'm just about hanging in, but in a military sense I couldn't fight myself out of a wet paper bag. I'm popping Valium, slugging scotch, reading books and keeping to myself. The nightmares are sending me slowly crazy, bad dreams, waking up screaming, and flashbacks starting during the day.

In 1986 I apply for and am offered a position as a senior lecturer at the University of New South Wales. My so-called army career and obvious leadership skills count hugely in getting me the job. I can't really hide in libraries any more and I'm a fairly skilled army instructor, which translates easily enough into being a lecturer and I manage the big bluff fairly well.

Three years pass and then, one day, right in the middle of a lecture on the importance of fire to the Australian environment, I suddenly see the Red Steer rise in front of my eyes. It rises above the eucalyptus trees as I sit on Ann's little bicycle and I watch as it hits half a mile further on. My mind simply explodes and I walk off the stage, out of the lecture theatre and across the campus and into the office of Mike Proctor where I hand in my resignation. It's all over, red rover, Mole Maloney has had enough. No more. Finish. *Kaput*. Over and out.

Dr Mole Maloney was a patient of mine for nearly ten years during which he was accepted as TPI. To a psychiatrist, he presented a great many new problems. His obvious intelligence often made it more difficult rather than easier to work with him. He knew all the answers in theory but none of them in practice.

And there was something else. He is a man of enormous charisma and character, instantly likeable though capable of complete deceit. I don't mean deceit in a dishonest sense, there was nothing dishonest in him, but in his capacity to completely hide his every emotion. 'Protect', rather than 'hide' is perhaps a better word. He could protect himself against any reaction, whether good or bad. Mole Maloney was the human equivalent of an armadillo, completely armoured against any true emotional reaction. He would smile, laugh, be hail fellow well met until you learned to look into his eyes.

Quite frankly, my biggest professional task was not to be too fascinated with him. He was damaged and desperately in need of help, and part of it was trying to find him some sort of loving relationship. He writes constantly to his sister, a doctor at last, and also to his brother Michael, a hugely successful and world-famous London clothes designer and couturière. Most people aware of fashion know of him, though I confess, with my raincoat neurosis, I wasn't one of them. His brother Bozo Maloney is the biggest cartage contractor in Australia and owns the nation's largest bus line. It is difficult to go any distance on any highway without seeing a truck or a bus with the crow symbol on it.

Dr Maloney also sees his family as including three other people. These are Bozo Maloney's business partner, an Indian lady by the name of Mrs Rika Ray. She has stood for parliament and has recently won the local National Party seat in the state government. Then there's Morrie Suckfizzle, a famous gynaecologist, and his wife Sophie, a millionaire many times over. There cannot possibly be a child in Australia who hasn't at some time or another worn a **Suckfizzle** garment. These three people are as much a part of his family as his siblings.

By all counts, the Maloney family has made its mark and his extended family are totally supportive. Perhaps the brightest of them all is Mole. So very clever and so very damaged. By using Mole's family, we begin to work on his love for them and those people who have supported them all in his childhood. I also add Mrs Barrington-Stone and Big Jack Donovan to the mix.

However, the biggest breakthrough comes when one day he mentions the twin aunties, Dot and Gwen, who have languished in a mental institution for nearly fifty years. I suggest that he might like to see them and get to know them a little better. He visits them in Yankalillee and soon afterwards has them brought to an old-age home in Sydney where they all spend a great deal of time together. It is this simple arrangement that starts to turn things around and we begin very slowly to get to the real Mole Maloney, the man who wants to love more than anything else in his life.

In 1997, Mole felt sufficiently confident to take on a teaching job at a prominent private boys' school. He holds the position of senior Science master to this day and is regarded with great respect by his fellow staff members.

I'm not sure what the future holds for him, PTSD is such a very tricky thing and we still don't know enough.

But this I do know, Mole Maloney has a heart filled to capacity with love. I think it is about to explode and I want to be around when it does. Last night, at an Indonesian restaurant in Newtown, I was sucking on a chilli crab claw when he proposed. I nearly swallowed the claw, we've never even slept together.

'Anna,' he said quietly, 'I know I'm not much, but will you marry me?'

I looked at him, beautiful, beautiful Mole. 'Mole Maloney, I've loved you ever since I first saw you fast asleep in Crocodile Brown's class. But no, I won't.' I laugh, trying to cover any embarrassment he might feel. 'Mole, we haven't even slept together!'

He grins, 'Once that would have been a primary consideration, I guess it isn't any more.'

'It will be again, but I don't think either of us is quite ready for a permanent relationship. I've already been through one failed marriage and it wasn't all his fault.'

'Does that mean you're turning me down?'

'No, Mole, it means I love you and I'm prepared to wait.'

He is thoughtful for a while, then looks up at me and smiles. 'Okay, that's it then, how long?'

'We'll both know when the time comes.'

'You mean when I'm better? I am going to get better, ain't I?'

It's the question I have most feared he'd ask me. 'I think so, it will take time.'

He nods his head slowly. 'There's one other thing.'

'What's that?' I ask, grateful he isn't going to make a fuss.

'Would you consider changing your name?'

'Mole,' I said, 'not yet, we'll need to wait, see how things turn out.'

He laughs, 'No, Anna, not to Maloney! Change it back to your maiden name.'

'Dombrowski? Why?'

'Why? Because she's the girl I've always loved and always will. That's why, Anna Dumb-cow-ski.'

Author's Note

Tommy and his five mates are fictional characters, though many of the Australian soldiers in the book are not. I simply cannot begin to do justice to the tragic story of the POWs in Borneo and in particular to the three Death Marches which took place towards the end of the war. The horror and barbarity perpetrated by the Japanese on Australian soldiers is almost unimaginable.

I urge you to read *Sandakan – A Conspiracy of Silence* by the noted writer, researcher and historian of the Australian 8th Division Association, Lynette Ramsay Silver. Her historically accurate book reads like fiction, the tragedy is that it is fact so horrific that the Australian government has kept the story of Sandakan secret from the public for more than fifty years. Lynette Ramsay Silver spent five years clawing it out bit by bit from the government archives where it had been carefully and systematically concealed. It is a formidable work of scholarship by a very persistent woman.

When we know our history, we begin to understand who we are as a people. When the past is hidden from us, the future becomes confused. *Sandakan – A Conspiracy of Silence* ought to be compulsory reading for every Australian.

Two other invaluable books are *Sandakan: the last march*, by Don Wall, and *Borneo: Australia's proud but tragic heritage*, by Kevin Smith.

Acknowledgements

Of all the books I have written, none has used up so much of the kindness of friends and strangers. Authors in fact know very little, but if they're half smart, they know people who know a great deal. Or they know people who know people who are very intelligent. The people whose names follow all gave generously of their time, energy and intellect, and, as a result, your combined efforts will make me appear much smarter than I am.

To my two full-time researchers, Celia Jarvis and Christine Gee, you never faltered, never gave up, I thank you for your persistence and dedication from the bottom of my heart. *Four Fires* becomes as much your book as it does mine.

To John Arnold, Deputy Director, National Key Centre for Australian Studies, Monash University, for his expertise on Melbourne University and the history of the state of Victoria. To Graham Walker and Dr Barry Wright, both Vietnam veterans, for their counsel, guidance and help. With them were Alec Morris, Barry Rust and Rick Ryan. Lynette Ramsay Silver, official historian to the Australian 8th Division Association, for her time, information, expertise on the Malayan campaign, and insights into Sandakan. You were tough on me but wonderful. Don Wall, AM, MID, and Kevin Smith, for their guidance and help on POWs in Borneo.

Ann and Lindsay Jarvis, who taught me the nature of bushfire from the dry grass up to the blazing canopy. Anna Epstein, curator of 'Schmatte Business: Jews in the Garment Trade' at the Jewish Museum of Australia, and to everyone at that wonderful museum. Diana Kahn and Robert Salter, who brought the beginnings of the post-war rag trade to life and made me see Flinders Lane as a place where migrant history was made. Ros Marshall, who allowed me the use of her thesis on the Melbourne rag trade. Rex Tompkins, who told me about the fashion scene in London during the '50s. Elizabeth Stead, author, who generously allowed me to appropriate her delightful and so very wise 'spoon in the sink' homily. Dr Peter M. Snowdon, psychiatrist, and Diana B. Shipman, psychologist, for their insights into Post-traumatic Stress Disorder, and Dr Michael Gliksman, for more of the same, as well as for his general medical information and counsel.

Without your knowledge and intellectual input and energy this book could not have been written. You generously shared with me a lifetime of knowledge.

The people whose names follow all helped substantially to give my book its sense of authenticity. I believe that the history we read should be real, which largely depends not only on historians, but also on the recall and experiences of the people who lived through it and subsequently gave generously of their insight, knowledge and skill. People such as Benita Courtenay, Alan Jacobs of Consensus Research, designer Robbee Spadafora, Prue Acton, Ken Allen, David Austin, Guy Baillieau, Robin Barrett, DVA, Ed Baynes, George Bindley, Cheryl Bockman, Cheryl Bowman, Betty Burgess, Ed Campion, Robert Chalwell, Lorne Clark, the Country Fire Authority of Victoria, the Country Women's Association of Victoria, Jenny Crameri, Owen Denmeade, Reg Dixon, Peter Doherty, Bob Downey, Jean Downing, Bill Fogarty, Lindsay Fox, Bruce Furnell, Gerry Garreto, Catherine Herrick, DEAT, Alex Hamill, Bill Houston, Barbara Hunt, InfoZone (Museum of Victoria), Tracey Jarvis-Ball, Graham Jordan, Professor Gabriel Kune, Brian Lawrence, Alf Lazer, Dr Irwin Light, Terry Loftus, Rod McCloud, Tim McCombe, Neil McGavock, Michael McGirr, Ian McGuffie, Jack McLean, Lawrence Money, Harold Mundy, John Nicholson, AFSM, Murray Nicoll, Margaret O'Loughlan, Catherine O'Rourke, Aussie Ostara, Julius Patching, Nerida Piggin, Peter Rothwell, 'Snowy' Savill, Glenda Sluga, Allen Stephens, David Stevens, Roy Symes, Vietnam Veterans Federation of Australia – Granville Office, Moira Wallace, Vic Watts, Heather Wood, Nev Woodward and Dr Rena Zimmet.

Finally, I need to thank those people who are my mentors and helpers in the publishing and allied industries, who make a book possible in the first place. But first I thank the numerous authors whose work, whether in books or on the internet, has proved invaluable: the Australian Army Training Team Vietnam Association, *The Team in Pictures: a pictorial history of the Australian Army Training Team Vietnam 1962–1972*; Tim Bowden, *P.O.W. Australians Under Nippon*, ABC Radio; Michael J. Clarke,

Boxing, 1960–1970; the Country Women's Association of Victoria, *Years of Adventure*; Stan Krasnoff, *Where to? for valour: a true story of Keith Payne*; Ian McNeill, *The Team: Australian Army advisers in Vietnam 1962–1972*; Aussie Osborn, *As I Saw It*; Major General A. B. Stretton, *On Active Service in Malaya*; Joan Webster, *The Complete Bushfire Safety Book*. Those who go before beat the path for all of us to follow. Feel free to use my book as I have used yours.

Publishing is still one of the few professions that requires skill, love and enthusiasm in equal proportion. I have benefited hugely from all three virtues with the team put at my disposal by Penguin Books. Publishing Director Bob Sessions, Executive Publisher Julie Gibbs and Adult Publisher Clare Forster, the last my personal publisher, you make writing for you a pleasure. I cannot thank you enough for your patience, encouragement and good counsel.

Then there are those who labour unseen to bring a book to the reader. My proofreader and constant companion, Dorothy Gliksman, and at Penguin, Lyn McGaurr, Cathy Larsen, who designed the jacket, Tony Palmer, who designed the text, Carmen De La Rue, Mark Evans, Peter Field, Peter Blake, Gabrielle Coyne, Elizabeth Hardy, Louise O'Leary, Margaret Thompson, Leonie Stott and Beverley Waldron, all of whom have the consummate skill required to make the difficult task of publishing a novel seem simple.

But in the end, there is your editor, like your mum, she is indispensable. In Kay Ronai I have simply the best, she is my friend, my mentor and the hand I reach out to in the dark. She has never failed me.

I thank you all.

BRYCE COURTENAY

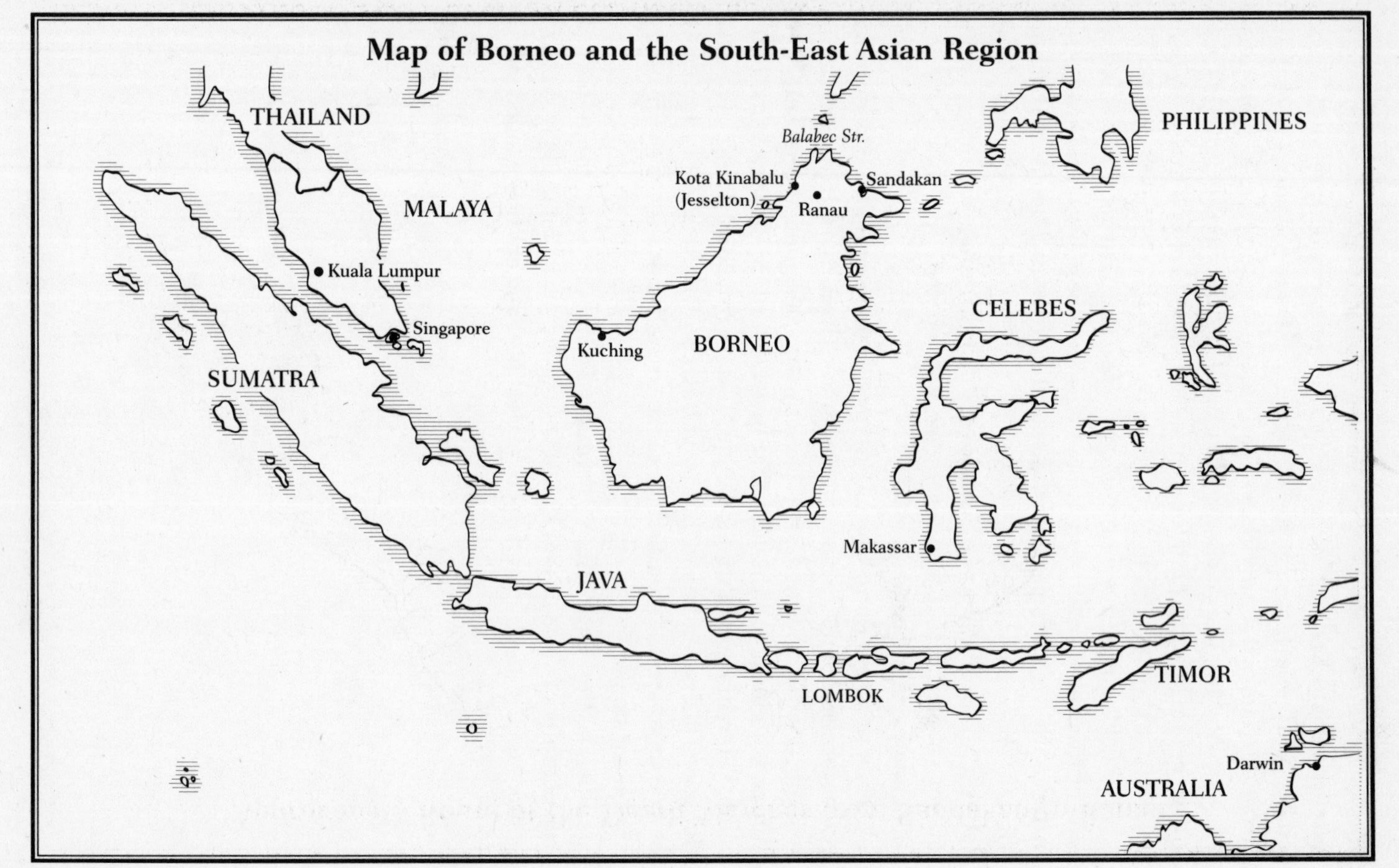
Map of Borneo and the South-East Asian Region
THAILAND
MALAYA
Kuala Lumpur
Singapore
SUMATRA
JAVA
Kuching
BORNEO
Kota Kinabalu
(Jesselton)
Ranau
Balabec Str.
Sandakan
PHILIPPINES
CELEBES
Makassar
LOMBOK
TIMOR
Darwin
AUSTRALIA

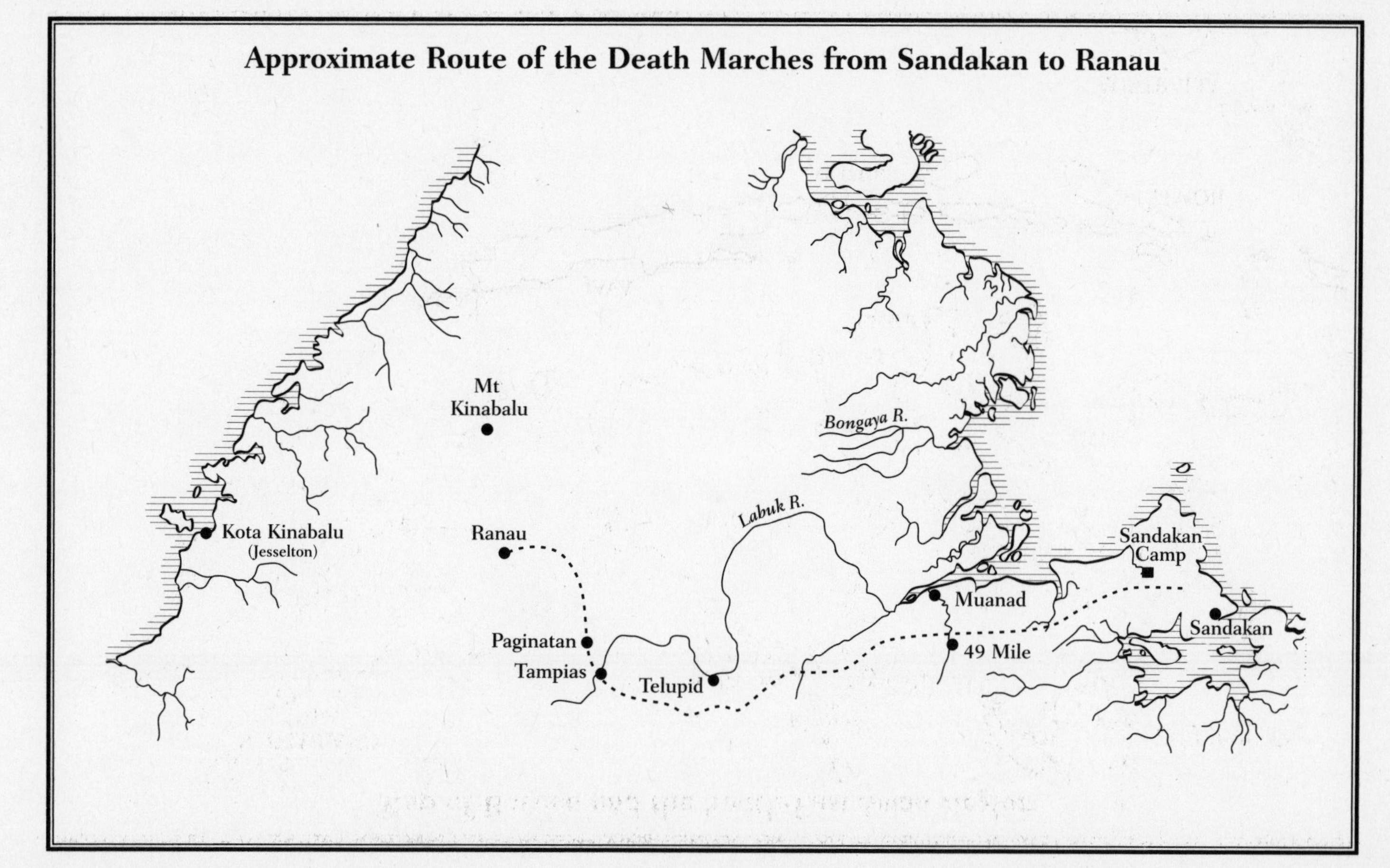
Approximate Route of the Death Marches from Sandakan to Ranau
Mt
Kinabalu
Bongaya R.
Labuk R.
Kota Kinabalu
(Jesselton)
Ranau
Paginatan
Tampias
Telupid
Muanad
49 Mile
Sandakan
Camp
Sandakan